PARADIGM SHIFT

PARADIGM SHIFT

RETURN OF THE ANGELS

A Novel

HARRY S. FRANKLIN

iUniverse, Inc.

New York Bloomington Shanghai

Paradigm Shift
Return of the Angels

Copyright © 2008 by Harry S. Franklin

iUniverse books may be ordered through booksellers or by contacting:

iUniverse
1663 Liberty Drive
Bloomington, IN 47403
www.iuniverse.com
1-800-Authors (1-800-288-4677)

Because of the dynamic nature of the Internet, any Web addresses or links contained in this book may have changed since publication and may no longer be valid.

This is a work of fiction. All of the characters, names, incidents, organizations, and dialogue in this novel are either the products of the author's imagination or are used fictitiously.

ISBN: 978-0-595-48258-0 (pbk)
ISBN: 978-0-595-71701-9 (cloth)
ISBN: 978-0-595-60345-9 (ebk)

Printed in the United States of America

Paradigm: A set of assumptions, concepts, and values that constitute a way of viewing reality for the community that shares them. The prevailing view of things.

The movement from an old to a new paradigm is called a *paradigm shift*. The shift may occur slowly over many years, or it might occur abruptly as the result of conscious analysis and evaluation of the current paradigm. Take, for example, the Copernican revolution. The old paradigm held that Earth was the center of God's perfect creation. The realization that Earth revolved around the sun and was not the center of the universe led to a revolution in thought, changing our view of the world and changing our view of humanity.

Several of the major paradigm shifts in human understanding can trace their roots to a handful of forward-thinking people, but the greatest paradigm shift of all owes its beginnings to one unlikely man.

Paradigm I
Chapter 1

The spasm began somewhere near his spine, pushing him from behind and sending him leaping into the open. Now fully committed, anticipating the fatal shock with a familiar dread, he lowered his head and charged headlong into the gap between walls of crushed brick. Seeing him exposed, the Somali mob exploded with crackling fits of flame. White-hot tracers skipped down the alleyway, whirring past his ears like vicious whispers. Jets of earth erupted all around him, enveloping him in a surreal, reddish haze.

Hank's eyes fixed on the black-faced soldier a few meters away. The world beyond the space between them ceased to exist. His eyes narrowed on the man's face, and he held his breath for the last desperate strides.

He knew leaving cover was a fatal mistake even before he made his first move. Helpless, he watched himself act on a will unknown to him. He felt like a man clinging to the neck of a bull that was making a suicidal charge toward a cliff. He tried to scream, but his voice was silent as the bullets zipped past and death surrounded him. His boots pounded the ground as if in slow motion; each step weighed with expectation. The tips of his fingers stretched out to grab the ominous figure—despite the knowledge that just a touch meant death.

With the blackened face only inches away, in the last possible instant before touching death's unremitting cruelty, Hank screamed aloud. The noise ripped him from sleep. His fingers clawed the air above him, and an echoing howl rang in his ears.

His eyes drifted reluctantly to the digits glowing green on the alarm clock. He knew exactly what time it was without looking: his body was still programmed to military time and couldn't reconcile with his mind's reluctance to get out of bed. A fine shower of sweat leaped from his scalp as he scrubbed his hands over his crew cut and stared at the clock.

Knowing that sleep—real sleep—was out of the question, Hank stretched a weary finger to the radio and began acting out his day. The familiar voice of Howard Stern emanated from the radio, but Hank didn't register a word he was saying. He remained stuck, his thoughts lingering over his dreams. The nightmares were so vivid and full of sensation, so unlike his real world. He felt almost sorry that the horrible dream was over; he even felt an odd comfort in knowing he would have it again and again.

He stared vacantly into the void until Howard Stern's words rang out with sudden clarity: it was October third. The date issued so casually by Howard struck home like a dart, causing Hank's eyes to shoot anxiously to the wall calendar still stuck on July. Dates and figures ran through his mind—the math was all too easy. The dark anniversary marked three years to the day, he knew he would be turning thirty this year, and nothing had changed.

A nauseous cramp gripped his stomach as he brooded over the date. He swung out of bed and hopped toward the bathroom. The pain began immediately. It crept up his thighs and set fire to his spine. He stood naked in the bathroom, feeling suddenly worn thin. The dull weight of depression and the mental erosion caused by lack of sleep numbed his thoughts. Goose bumps crawled over his flesh, and the muscles of his arms trembled. Insistent, consuming pain chewed at him with every step as he crossed the floor to his closet.

The first glow of sunlight invaded his room through the seams of the room's only window. The early warmth promised a beautiful autumn morning. A day like today was a treat for most people in the sometimes fog-infested Bay. Today, girls would be showing off their tans and guys would be wearing shorts, but the pleasures of a sunny day were lost on him. He didn't own any shorts.

He grabbed a pair of bulky sweatpants from a dresser and spun around to sit on the bed. After slipping into the sweatpants, he hopped onto his left foot, letting the pant-leg hang listlessly over the stump of his right leg. The empty leg swung whip-like, back and forth, as he hopped back to the dresser and climbed into a plain white T-shirt.

He returned to the bed with a sock, feeling more than seeing the roll of fat on his gut when he bent over. Alarmed, he straightened himself and ran a hand over his abdominal muscles. The roll of flesh was gone, but he still felt soft somehow.

His eyes jumped to the nightstand, where an empty bottle of Vodka stood surrounded by pill vials.

He stood for a moment, probing the firm grooves of his stomach, before grabbing his Walkman and shoving the earphones into place. He found his prosthetic lying on the kitchen floor. He caught his reflection in the bluish titanium shaft as he peered down to examine the running shoe. The heel looked disproportionately worn on one side, and he was sure it was partially responsible for the limp in his step, but he wasn't about to run out to Footlocker to replace it.

He strapped the leg to his thigh and began looking for his other shoe while his attention shifted to the banter coming from the radio in his ear.

He'd been hooked on Howard Stern's radio show since he was a teen growing up in Brooklyn. He'd even paid a guy to send him tapes while he was overseas. Now he listened to the entire four-hour broadcast. It was the only time he allowed himself to laugh at the messed-up world around him. Losing himself in the on-air reality show helped him climb the grueling city streets on his morning jogs. Eventually exertion overwhelmed the pain in his phantom shin, and for a brief time Hank could enjoy a respite in the feeling of normalcy.

Today, the comfort faded just as he took the last smoothly mechanical strides back to his doorstep. His fingers poked around his midsection as he stretched from side to side until he was convinced that he'd left the bulge of fat back on the Embarcadero somewhere. As he leaned over to stretch, he caught sight of some freshly painted gangland scribbling on the concrete steps leading to his front door. A sudden rage washed over him as the Walkman fell from his fists and shattered on the ground.

The earphones swung from his ears as Hank yelled, kicking the broken Walkman, sending batteries skittering down the steps. He wet his fingers in the fresh paint and glanced up to see an elderly neighbor staring at him. Hank felt quick hatred for the old man and all the other neighbors who tolerated the constant tagging. Their brightly painted row houses were covered with red and blue graffiti. Hank's intense, fury-filled stare made the old man cringe and quickly turn away.

Now irreversibly worked into a blistering rage, Hank fantasized about catching the punk gangbangers. His mind began plotting disproportionate revenge as he begrudgingly knelt to collect his broken radio. Anger and humiliation pounded his temples, and the phantom pain in his absent calf crept back with vengeance. Once again, it felt as if his missing calf muscle was engorged with blood and about to explode.

The inner debate began as soon as he mounted his front steps. He began list-ing all the reasons why he shouldn't extinguish the pain with a fistful of Vicodin and a stiff drink. He tried to reassure himself that the pain was all in his head, that is was all a cruel illusion, but the sensation eating him alive was all too real. Getting slapped in the face with more graffiti was the final straw.

Hank slid the bolt back and opened the door just enough to allow him to retrieve his keys from the lock. The hair on the back of his neck bristled. A famil-iar fluttering of endorphins tickled his guts and his long-dormant Delta instincts fired to life. His mind cleared and his breathing slowed as his ears strained for sound.

Holding the door open a crack, he turned subtly to scan the street behind him. Nothing was out of place; traffic rolled past, and nobody paid him any attention, but alarms still sounded in his senses. He had learned to trust his instincts, and these were now telling him that he was in real danger.

Turning back to his door, he paused for a moment and wondered if this feel-ing was what the doctors had meant when they'd cautioned him about hypervigi-lance. They had also said something about a psychosis. Hank's mind spun as he felt himself being taken back to a past life. He felt as if he were about to force entry into a hostile space with his Delta Team, but it was only his front door. He wondered if, like his phantom pain, he was being plagued by the ghostly feelings of a past life, or if he was simply succumbing to the insidious psychosis of sleep deprivation brought on by all the drugs.

Hank lifted his hands to his face as if to wash himself with ice-cold water, hop-ing to literally wipe the anxiety away, but he could not shake the feeling that something was amiss. As he pushed the door open and prepared to step inside, he caught the first tangible clue to his tension. There was a faint hint of perfume in the air. He opened the door further, pushing his face through the threshold to sniff the air. The scent was clear: a cheap perfume, the type a young girl would wear.

Now certain that there was an intruder in his home, Hank flushed with relief, oddly more grateful for his sanity than alarmed by the intrusion. Dozens of sce-narios formed in his mind as he contemplated who or what was waiting for him. The door had still been locked when he'd arrived, and there wasn't any reason to expect a lady visitor. He began to suspect that a drunken derelict had broken in through the rear window—and if she had, she probably wasn't alone. Blowing out his anxiety through pursed lips, Hank readied himself for the unknown and cautiously stepped in, closing the door behind him.

The narrow hallway was empty and appeared undisturbed. A faint stereophonic chatter came from the radio in his room. Hank fought the urge to call out; instead, he threw his keys onto the hall-tree and proceeded toward the kitchen. Wishing to seem oblivious to the intrusion, he made no effort to walk quietly. After a few paces the aroma of coffee permeated his olfactory senses, and he could no longer detect the flowery perfume. Ready to pounce at any movement, his fists balled up for a fight, Hank prepared to round the corner into the open space of his kitchen and living room.

As he stepped into the kitchen, the heel of his right shoe squealed on the linoleum floor. He cringed at the loud chirp and silently cursed his toy leg. From the corner of his eye he caught the amber glow from the light on the coffee maker. The pot was now more than half empty. He paused, cocking his head and scanning the kitchen as the shoot/don't shoot reflex in his mind told him to stand down. Hank forced open his clenched fists and let out a long breath. He turned from the kitchen and stepped evenly into the living room. As soon as he rounded the corner, he stopped short with astonishment, his chin dropping to his chest in a dumbfounded gape.

A stunning young woman sat on the desk opposite him. Her youthful, slender body was nearly naked. She sat with her legs crossed. Hank could barely make out the thin black line of her panties arcing over her hips. She smiled apprehensively, shrugging her bare shoulders slightly as she chewed her lower lip. Dark hair, cropped uneven and wild, hung over her face and obscured her eyes. Her flawless skin glowed in the dimness, making her appear shockingly young. She was trying hard to look sexy, but Hank could tell she was frightened.

Hank's shocked expression seemed to satisfy the young woman, and her smile warmed as she uncrossed her legs and slid smoothly from the desk. Her bare, white breasts swayed gently as she got to her feet. Hank froze, staring at her from across the room. The butterflies in his stomach morphed into a new sensation.

She stepped forward, her hands caressing the smooth lines of her belly. Her lips parted as if about to speak. Just then, a slight shift in her gaze and an almost imperceptible change in the air current behind him sent Hank's heart crashing into his bowels.

Before he could think to react, someone struck him from behind, crashing into his lower back with the force of an NFL linebacker. Two heavily tattooed arms locked together around his waist. Hank's feet were unable to check the speed of the tackle, and both men came crashing down at the feet of the now shrieking girl.

Hank grabbed at the man's hands as they fell. He managed to grip his assailant's pinky finger the instant the floor came up to greet him. The full weight of his attacker slammed down on him, and Hank fought to suppress the panic that follows having the wind knocked out of you. As both men bounced up, fighting to recover from the impact, Hank twisted his hips and ripped away at the man's pinky finger. The man yelped with pain and released his hold around Hank's waist.

With quickness and skill he'd not used in some time, Hank thrust his hips to one side and worked his body free. As soon as he had maneuvered to one side, Hank jerked his head backward and sent the back of his skull crashing into his opponent's face. A loud crack was followed by a high-pitched howl, and the man loosened his grip just long enough for Hank to escape. Hank spun violently, turning to face his assailant. He still clutched the intruder's angulated pinky finger in his fist and was leveraging it against the now-groaning man.

"Oooouuuwww!! Let go, man! Let Go! Come on, Tank!"

The two men now knelt on the floor facing each other. The would-be attacker's face was contorted with pain. Blood trickled from his nose, dripping over his bushy moustache and beard. A menacing smile gradually overcame the ferocious scowl on Hank's face as he continued to tweak the man's finger. The man's free hand moved to strike out, but Hank surged forward, ramming into his opponent's flank, rolling the captured arm behind his back.

"You wanna play with me, dumb-ass?" Hank growled in the man's ear, briefly tempted by the urge to bite it.

"Okay! Okay! I give! Get the fuck off me, man!" The defeated man cried out with an odd, laughing yelp.

"What in the hell are you thinking?" Hank bent forward, adding pressure to the arm-lock. "You want more, you overgrown sissy?"

"Way to go, Curt. Let me know when you're done teaching him a lesson," the young girl teased, trying to cover her breasts with her crossed arms.

Prompted by her teasing, the massive man bucked his hips in an attempt to throw Hank off his back. His face pushed against the floor, and he strained the muscles of his free arm in an effort to get to his knees. Hank clung to his back, momentarily riding him like a pony. Then, as soon as there was enough room, Hank sank his heels between the man's legs, pushing forward with all his weight, driving his heels backward down his thighs. The man collapsed with a groan. The straps holding Hank's prosthetic popped, and his right leg slackened, but he continued to press the attack.

"I give! I give!" Curt shouted.

"Why in the hell are you jumping out of my closet, dumb-ass?" Hank gave the pinned wrist another twist.

"I'm sorry. Okay?" Curt's voice was laden with humiliation. "Let me go, dammit!"

"And what's this?" Hank's eyes fixed on the girl. Still topless, she was busy squeezing into an undersized leather miniskirt. "You thought you could distract me and kick my ass, right?" Hank pressed against the arm again. "What do you think I woulda done to you if you *did* get one over on me? Huh? Did you think about that?"

"Ooouuwww! Come on, get off of me! You're gonna break my fucking arm!"

"I'm *so* sorry! Curt made me do it! I swear!" The girl seemed genuinely shaken by the sudden violence. Hank looked up and stared pointedly into her eyes. She quickly averted her face and began collecting her clothes.

"Dude! Get off of me! I mean it!" Curt lowered his voice in an attempt to convey his seriousness.

Hank slapped him hard across the back of his neck, forehand then backhand, clipping his ears with each stroke. "Or what, tough guy?"

Curt writhed spasmodically, renewed physical pain compounding his humiliation. "Oh, you're dead now!" The big man growled, but he was still helplessly pinned.

"No way. You're gonna learn a lesson. How many times am I gonna have to whip your ass? We're supposed to be buddies." Again he slapped Curt hard across the neck. Hank didn't feel enraged by Curt's semiplayful attack, but he knew that if the tables were turned, mercy would be out of the question. Curt was a dangerous man who wasn't accustomed to getting beat. He still ached to repay Hank for the all-too-public beating he'd received when they had first met.

For Hank, any fighting challenge was to be met with unequaled savagery. He knew no other way. At times, it seemed as if that quality was all he had left. "You've got to learn that I can't be fucked with!" Hank raised his hand to strike again. Curt's free hand reached back to cover his neck.

Hank froze and was suddenly struck by the thought of what he must look like in the eyes of the young girl. With a final grunt of triumph, he pushed the man's folded arm away and righted himself on Curt's back. "What are you doin' here Curt?" Hank began to untangle his legs from his victim, but his prosthetic snagged on something. "How did you get in here?"

"Your hide-a-key," Curt groaned in defeat.

"Key? What key?"

"I know about the dog shit."

"Hmm?" Hank's attention drifted back to the girl as he continued tugging on his leg.

"The fake dog shit in the bushes." Curt wiped the smeared blood from his face with the back of his hand. "You showed it to me, remember?"

"So you decided you'd let yourself in?"

"I thought I had you this time, man!" Curt rubbed the pain from his wrists. "I still owe you one!"

"Only one? How many times am I gonna to have to kick your ass?" Content in victory, Hank changed his tone and patted Curt's head good-naturedly. "Who's this? For a second there, I thought it was my lucky day."

"Hi. I'm Jenna. I'm so sorry. I didn't know what he was doing. He said he wanted to scare you … that's all." A reluctant smile animated her face for a moment but quickly melted under the intensity of Hank's eyes.

Hank attempted a tentative smile, but it was wasted as she turned away and looked everywhere but at him. Her face made it clear that she, like most people, was uncomfortable with the way he looked at them. Eye contact never held long. It was something he was getting used to, and now it allowed him to appraise her without challenge. Dark motives quickly formed in his imagination as he asked himself why a girl like her was with a monster like Curt.

"You still haven't said what you're doing here." Confident that his leg was disengaged, Hank tried to spring to his feet, but his right leg spun around and came to rest with its foot facing the opposite direction.

Jenna's eyes went wide with horror, and both men burst into laughter.

"Oh shit, call a doctor!" Hank laughed sarcastically, gesturing at the cartoonish disposition of his leg. "What's wrong? Never seen a one-legged man win an ass-kicking contest before?"

Curt rolled onto his side in childlike hysterics, relishing the baffled look on Jenna's face and coughing blood onto the floor.

After settling down and composing their respective body parts, all three moved to the kitchen. Hank passed the coffee pot and opened the refrigerator to retrieve two beers. "You want something to drink Jenna?"

"No thanks." He noticed that her hands still trembled as she fidgeted with her clothes.

"This is the girl I told you about the other night." Curt strode over and wrapped his arm around her. He looked rather like an Ogre standing next to her, dwarfing her in every way as he pulled her close. Curt was a huge man, towering over Hank's six feet. His features were rough and ugly. Coarse stubble covered his pockmarked face. Multiple scars accented his thick brow, and long greasy hair hung over his ears from under a dirty red bandana. He looked like the poster boy for biker-scum USA, and Hank felt odd to think that Curt was one of his only associates.

"The girl from the Internet?" Hank opened the bottles and passed one to Curt, keeping his eye on Jenna. She seemed oblivious to Curt's repulsiveness. She caressed his beer belly and gazed affectionately into his face as she wiped the bloody mucus from his lip with her thumb. Bewildered, Hank shook his head and turned away from the odd coupling.

"That's why we came over here. You're the only guy I know that knows computer stuff." Hank caught Curt rolling his eyes beyond Jenna's view.

"I just wanted to show him my portfolio on the Internet." Jenna pushed the hair from her face, showing off her perfect, youthful features.

"Oh yeah? You're a model, huh?" Hank said in between gulps of beer. "That makes sense."

"She's a stunner, ain't she Henry?" Curt was clearly gloating over his prize. "I told you, but you thought I was full of shit. Didn't ya?"

"I just thought you were trying to get me to join your nutty biker gang." Hank's lips curled into a mock-smile, and he flashed Curt a knowing wink before draining his beer.

"You don't need to join any gang … shit, I was just saying we need to get you a bike, that's all. I got a buddy who can modify one for your peg leg." Curt pushed away from Jenna and once again appealed to Hank with the same expression he had worn only a few nights before.

"I don't ride motorcycles. Too many idiots out there." Hank raised an eyebrow from over his beer.

"I'll take you for a spin—you'll change your mind." Curt pumped his fist with emotion, spilling beer across the floor and not giving it a second thought. "But seriously, Henry, we could use a smart guy like you. Lots of money to be made out there."

"I don't need the money. I'm not interested."

"Whatever, man. I don't get it." Curt downed the rest of his beer wearing a childish scowl.

"Can I use your computer? I'm gonna get one, but I don't know which one I want yet." Jenna slid past, soothing Curt with a gentle caress and a turn of her hips.

"Sure. Help yourself." Hank watched her cross the room for a moment and then returned to the fridge to retrieve two more beers.

"Do you have AOL?" Jenna bent over the chair looking for the computer's power button, but Hank's attention was caught by Curt's not-so-subtle hand waves and head jerks.

"Huh? Oh, the Internet." Hank caught sight of a small bundle of white powder coming from Curt's pocket, and he immediately turned to face Jenna. "Yeah, I've got the Internet."

"Hmmm. How do you make it work?"

"Here, let me get it going for you."

Jenna stood to let Hank sit, and after a few moments of obligatory hums and clicks the computer glowed to life and filled the dark corner with sky blue light. Hank's fingers flew over the keys, but his eyes were focused on Curt's reflection on the screen. Hank didn't even want to think about cocaine. All he wanted was sleep. Temptation had transformed into torture. His frustrations boiled beneath the surface as he found himself taking deep whiffs of Jenna's scent. The overpowering effect of her perfume had worn off, and she now smelled of sweet vanilla body lotion and sticky girlish lip gloss. Her breast brushed against him as she leaned in to point at the screen.

"Is this some kind of army thing?" Jenna spoke just above a whisper.

"Didn't I tell you?" Curt's voice boomed from the kitchen, where he was indulging in the fruits of his trade. "Yeah, I told you on the way over here, Tank was a Navy SEAL."

Hank wasn't navy, but he didn't bother to make the correction.

"Like Charlie Sheen, in that movie, what was it called?" Jenna tapped on Hank's shoulder, trying to jog her memory.

"Um … *Navy SEALs?*" Curt groaned sarcastically, then inhaled a line of cocaine.

"Oh shut up, Curt!" Hank could see her pouting at Curt in the screen's reflection, but then her eyes met his on the screen and he felt her attention on him. "But that was you? You did that?"

"Yeah, that was me, just like Charlie Sheen."

"Is that how you lost your …?"

"Yep." Hank cut her short. Heaviness gripped his chest, and his stomach began to flutter. His eyes locked onto a message along the bottom of the screen. The system was saying he had received e-mail, and that was a serious problem. His computer operated as part of a classified system, and he was no longer classified.

"So, do you work on computers or something? You can type pretty fast."

"No, not anymore." Hank stared at the blinking script. The U.S. Army was listed as the sender, and it was dated two days ago. With the stroke of a key, Hank switched screens to the system's search engine and pushed himself away from the desk to make room for Jenna.

Slowly, key by key, Jenna tapped in the Internet address of a San Francisco-based porn site. "My girlfriend started her own, um, Web site. She makes mad cash off it. See, that's her. The screen flashed with the stop motion action of an enormously large-breasted blonde, winking and squeezing her over-inflated tits. "They're not real."

"No kidding." Hank feigned interest in the poorly produced porn, and began to stare at Jenna's reflection on the monitor instead.

Curt passed by, completely uninterested in the computer. He gestured to the kitchen counter, where several thick lines of cocaine were drawn out. Hank tried to dismiss him with a hard stare and a quick wave of his hand, but he couldn't turn his attention back to the screen. He had seen it.

Curt's stupid grin and casual recklessness were once again boring a hole in Hank's guts. Hank's fists clenched as he thought once again that he didn't want any of this, hadn't asked for any of this. He wanted to be done with the drugs and the pills. He wanted to sleep again, but he felt unable to step off the path; each attempt felt futile. Tremendous self-loathing washed over him as he viewed himself through Curt's eyes. He knew Curt was thinking it was only a matter of time before Hank joined his underworld business. Hank hated the strange allure those temptations brought with them. They felt like whispers of a new life, base but at least interesting.

Hank tried to occupy himself with the vapid babble streaming from Jenna as they browsed through naked poses, but felt physical relief when she broke away to indulge in the cocaine. Hank followed, passing her to pull a bottle of Scotch from a cupboard. He poured two glasses, unceremoniously draining his in a single, sour gulp.

The next few hours were spent locked in meaningless conversation. The Scotch didn't last, but Curt's supply of cocaine seemed endless. Curt eventually suggested going to the strip club where Jenna worked, and Hank couldn't think of a better idea.

Once they arrived at the Lap Jockey Lounge, they were given the VIP treatment. Everyone knew Curt, and soon Jenna's girlfriends crowded their private booth. Hank was drunk with the idea that they actually thought his roughneck Brooklyn accent was cute. None of them seemed to notice his leg. The hours flew by in an alcoholic haze, and all too soon he found himself alone on his doorstep.

He bounced off the walls as he staggered into his bedroom. He found a bottle of Valium in his dresser and gulped them down. He collapsed onto his bed and watched the blank ceiling spin above him. Inwardly, saturated with toxins and on fire from lack of sleep, his mind began screaming for it all to stop. But nothing stopped—the room still spun, and after many heavy breaths dull sleep arrived at last.

Hank's eyes fluttered weakly against the unwelcome sunlight as great spasms of nausea tore him from sleep. Bile soured his throat, and the room spun beyond his blurred vision. He groggily gauged the distance to the toilet and weighed the odds. Careful to take only the shallowest of breaths, he swallowed hard against the saliva pouring into his mouth and groped for the sheets. His heavy, clumsy touch revealed that there weren't any sheets to pull away. This was the second time in recent memory that he'd passed out still fully clothed.

The raw flesh of his stump itched cruelly beneath his prosthetic, but at least he would have two legs beneath him when it came time to make to the inevitable dash for the toilet. Without thinking, he shook his head in disgust—and that was all it took for the dam of vomit to break. He scrambled out of bed, choking back the terrible surge from his core, and made one good stride before stumbling, then falling over his still-sleeping limbs to come crashing down on the floor. He bounced, crawling and pulling himself toward the toilet like a madman, until his arms wrapped around the bowl and he erupted.

Leaning heavily against the sink, drinking greedily and splashing the cold water over his face, Hank coughed and hacked to loosen the phlegm in his throat. There was no mirror over the sink, nor anywhere else in his home, so he examined his face in the reflection of a chrome fixture. Even this dim, distorted reflection revealed the effects the drugs were having on him. Mornings and moments like this reminded him without a doubt that it was time to change, but as he swiveled his head from side to side to stare at himself, it all seemed futile.

Shaking his head with self-loathing, Hank closed his eyes and began the systematic, methodical check of his bodily systems he had learned as an elite Delta warrior. The self-assessment had been taught to him by his Special Operations instructors and reinforced by a lifetime of training and hard-gained experience. The almost meditative ritual was designed to evaluate the effects of stress on highly trained soldier-athletes. Now he was obliged to use it to see if he would survive the terrible hangover long enough to perform his morning workout.

Once he was finally convinced that he was finished vomiting, Hank slowly shuffled into his bedroom and undressed. His stump felt raw, and his absent right leg throbbed invisibly beneath him. He threw his metal leg across the room as soon as it was unstrapped. He slid to the edge of his bed, grabbed the cane hidden behind the door, and used it to propel himself into the kitchen.

The illuminated blue screen of his computer cast a glow over the scattered beer bottles in the corner. Brow bent, staring into the blue gloom, he ran his eyes over the computer and pulled at memories from the day before. His chest tightened with a familiar twinge as he remembered the unexpected electronic mail. Curiosity pulled him from his path toward the coffee maker, and he sat himself in front of the computer.

A stream of fearful possibilities flowed through his thoughts as his fingers tapped the keyboard. After a long moment, he decided there were only two possibilities: either the army had somehow caught on to his unauthorized computer access, or there was something wrong with his father. He hadn't given the address to anyone else after deciding to disappear.

With the click of a mouse, the message was open. Hank sighed with relief. His eyes quickly focused on the sender's address: Captain William Kemp. He quickly scanned the single page and saw no mention of his father. Hank slumped back into his chair, his eyes fixed on Bill's formal name and rank.

"An officer? They made him an officer?"

It was a long moment before Hank could pull his eyes away from the name to read the brief note.

> Sergeant Hank Foster:
> Hank, I hope this finds you, and I hope you are doing well. I'm embarrassed that a couple years have passed since we've talked. As you've probably already noticed, they've promoted me to captain. I've spent the last couple of years in the academy, but that is a poor excuse. At the same time, I've had a hard time tracking you down. The only thing I know is that you left your assignment at JSOC and have quit the army for good. Did you really tell General Garrison that you'd found Jesus and didn't want to burn in hell with him and his minions? I wouldn't put it past you. Well, as far as the army is concerned, you've effectively dropped off the map—but I see that they're sending your pay to a PO Box in California. I bet the sunny weather has done wonders for your pleasant disposition. I'm hoping to catch up with you. In fact, there is an important matter I would like to discuss with you. I'm back home in California, and like you I have left the army for good. I know that doesn't make a lot of sense after going through the Academy; I'll explain later. Please give me a call as soon as you receive this.
> Your friend,
> Bill Kemp (650-849-8102)

Curiosity mixed with dread as Hank read the note a second time. He wondered if guilt or pity had finally overwhelmed the young Boy Scout playing soldier. Up until now he had respected Bill for his discretion and avoidance, but the date attached to the message couldn't have been a coincidence. October third would forever be an anniversary of sorts for Hank, and as his eyes blurred over the words on the screen, he imagined Bill celebrating the date with friends as if it were some bizarre birthday.

Hank shook away the revulsion he felt at the thought of a reunion with Bill and shut down the computer without sending a reply. He had no desire to share his pathetic state with anyone, especially Bill. He liked Bill and was disappointed to think his old friend might have been calling to ease his own suffering. Bill always seemed too smart, too sensitive to indulge in anything like that.

Hank closed his eyes and rubbed at the pain in his temples. His thoughts drifted back to that life-altering day in Mogadishu. Bill's face didn't appear to him right away, but the sounds and smells of combat came rushing back from memory, just as they had countless times before. His memories of the Bakara Market ghettos were marked by the ear-shattering explosions of rockets and grenades, and the constant wail of men screaming. The distinctive report from AK-47s counted time in his head as his mind's eye recalled the surreal details of that moment. The symphony of thought grew and the world outside faded as if he were stepping into a dream. The press of deadly violence surrounded him. He could virtually feel his legs carrying him across the razor's edge of survival once more.

Bill was there, his blackened, burnt face still unrecognizable as the man he later came to know. His back was pressed against the mud wall of a building, the butt of his rifle was pulled into his chin in the proper army firing position. He was pumping rounds down the alley into the mob of Somali militiamen. The young Ranger was oblivious to the danger he faced. Rounds smacked into the wall behind him, showering him with red dust. Glowing phosphorous tracers ricocheted along the walls. He seemed totally unaware that he was about to be killed by the withering fire. A fellow Ranger lay dying at his feet; the body jerked and exploded with crimson puffs as bullets tore into the flesh.

A crescendo of unintelligible screaming cascaded over Hank's thoughts. Men's voices were straining and breaking under the stress of combat. The violent, bloody images swirled in a montage of pain and confusion. Once again Hank could see the brilliant white orbs of Bill's eyes against his blackened and powder-burnt face as he grabbed him and flung him to safety.

It was his last act of heroism, a moment relived time and again, distorting reality and meaning each time it passed. Now more than ever, Hank wished he had died right there in the hellish Mogadishu dirt.

Hank moved away from the computer and stared at the empty bottle of vodka on the kitchen counter. Another day of last resorts stared back at him from the clear, rounded glass. Without thinking, Hank's hand passed over his desk and wrote Bill's phone number on an envelope. He tapped the number with the pen, pondering what young Billy Kemp really wanted. A few moments later, he was punching Bill's number into the phone.

"Kemp here."

The sound of Bill's voice clarified his face in Hank's memory, and he fought the urge to hang up. "Aye Billy. It's me."

"Hank? You got my message?"

"Yeah, I just found it. What's going on, Billy?"

"Hank, I'm glad you called. I've had a real bitch of a time tracking you down."

"Yeah, well."

"Where are you?"

"San Francisco."

"You're in the city? Right on, that's my home turf."

"Yeah. I remember."

"I'm in Oakland right now. I'm just driving back from the Capitol. I was going to see my mother, but I'd like to meet with you if you're free."

"What? Now?"

"Sure, why not? You're not busy, are you?"

"I guess not." Hank scanned the bleak dimness with a caustic grin. "What's it all about, Billy? Why are you looking for me?"

"Can't a guy look up an old friend?" Bill's tone sounded overly casual, reminding Hank of the smooth-talking kid he had grown to know in the German hospital.

"I guess. Your note mentioned something important."

"Well, there is something I want to discuss with you, but it can wait until we get together. How are you doing? What have you been up to?"

"Not much, really. What about you? Got yourself promoted, I see."

"Yeah, that might take a bit of explaining. Don't get the wrong idea—it's probably not the way you're imagining."

"Didn't bag yourself a dishonorable, did ya?"

"No, nothing like that, but I'm really digging civilian life again."

"Oh yeah, what are ya doin?"

"That might take even more explaining." Bill sounded suddenly exasperated, as if overwhelmed by something. "But I can tell you that I got a job working for a congressman."

"Politics, eh? Somehow that makes perfect sense."

"How you liking Frisco?" Bill was quick to change the subject. "It's no Brooklyn."

"No, it's definitely not Brooklyn. I'm still getting used to it."

"I'm sure it's good for you, mellow you out some. So can we get together?"

"I suppose. I don't know what you're hoping to find out. I know it's been three years since … but if you wanna talk about the Mog, I don't think that's such a great idea."

"No, Hank. That's not it at all. There is something else, something important. I don't want to do it over the phone."

"Business or pleasure?"

"Business, but I think it will be a pleasure for you."

"Oh yeah?"

"Can we meet?"

"Yeah, sure."

"Great, give me your number."

"Sure, one question first."

"Shoot."

"How'd ya find me?"

"I talked with your father." A short silence grew after Bill's reply. "He's doing good. He wants you to call him."

"All right Billy, let's get together."

"You want me to pick you up? We can talk over lunch."

"Yeah. Why not?"

Hank hung up the phone, convinced Bill wasn't interested in indulging in any psychodrama. He seemed anxious. The phrase *pleasure* held an ominous salience in its tone. He knew that what Bill considered a pleasure for Hank could be seen as repulsive to normal men. A flash of anger washed over him as he considered the possibility that Bill needed him for some callous dirty work. The feeling was an instinctive reflex after years of hard experience and countless recruitments into *pleasurable* acts, but the thoughts were quickly tossed aside. Hank knew Bill wasn't the type to get involved in any really shady business, and he was convinced that Bill knew he was more than the cold-blooded assassin he appeared to be.

Hank brought his hands to his face to rub at the weariness. His thoughts spun with possibilities and slowly clearing memories. He thought back to the time spent with Bill in Germany after getting wounded. He didn't know whether it was the intensity surrounding their acquaintance or simply the virtue of Bill's personality, but even then, in those terrible times, he found himself connecting with the young soldier. Bill possessed that rare charm, a certain charismatic power that enabled him to talk anybody into anything. Although not seriously wounded, Bill managed to convince his commanding officer to fudge documents allowing him to follow Hank and the other seriously wounded to the army hospital in Germany while all the other soldiers were treated aboard the naval ships. That intangible charm, along with his natural style and intelligence, continued to impress Hank over the next month as the two convalesced together.

Bill only suffered from minor powder burns and temporary hearing loss, but he feigned brain injury and amnesia to stay on the critical list. His performances in the hospital were nothing short of brilliant. His comical fits and mock seizures were responsible for Hank's first laughter after losing his leg. Bill was the only one Hank found worthy of sharing his time with in the days and weeks to follow. Bill was the only one ever to hear Hank's tragic life story from his own lips.

Hank looked around the Spartan emptiness of his home and wished he'd had the presence of mind to arrange to meet Bill elsewhere. He didn't like the idea of Bill seeing him like this. He didn't want to see the pity on his face. He didn't want to be caught living like this, but now the moment seemed inevitable. Bill was on his way. The toxic effects from the night before still pulled at him, and his eyes rolled closed like a doll's as soon as he lay horizontal on his couch.

His sleep was cut short by a knock at the door. He staggered up from the couch, ill-tempered and bleary-eyed, to find a man standing in his doorway looking more like a figure off a fashion billboard than the kid he remembered from Germany. At first Hank wasn't convinced it was Bill. He had to give the face beneath the sandy blond locks a second look.

"How ya doing, Hank?"

Hank squinted hard against the sunlight beaming from over Bill's shoulder before taking his outstretched hand.

"Hey Billy."

Bill stepped through the open door, still gripping Hank's hand, and then wrapped him in an embrace, patting him on the back with manly affection. "It's good to see you."

"Yeah, you too Billy." Hank waited uncomfortably for Bill to end his embrace. Bill finally pushed back to arm's length and smiled at him, and all Hank could think to say was; "Damn, I barely recognized you with all that hair."

Bill's smile didn't break for an instant. "Well, you haven't changed a bit." His eyes remained locked with Hank's until, after a long moment, he broke off to glance over his shoulder as if to invite himself inside.

Hank found himself suddenly struggling to keep from looking down to his foot. He ran his free hand over his crew cut and attempted a smile. "You've filled out."

"Ah, it's the civilian life." Bill smiled casually, as if it were only natural for him to be standing there after all this time. "Aren't you going to invite me in?"

"Yeah, sure." Hank gave Bill's hand a final squeeze before stepping back to let him in. Bill's presence was forcing Hank to see his home through the eyes of another, and what he saw disturbed him. He hadn't even picked up the empty bottles from the night before. There was an awkward silence as Hank limped into the kitchen and considered clearing the empty bottles and vials from the table, but he then turned to face Bill with his chin thrust forward. "So what's going on, Billy?"

"I see you took my advice. How do you like living in Frisco?" Bill made a half-hearted gesture to the bright, sunny day shut out beyond the door.

Hank continued to stare intently into his eyes. He wasn't interesting in making small talk; he was looking for any subtle tells during the awkward silence, but Bill's face was a mask of good cheer.

"My parents still live downtown." Bill unbuttoned his jacket and appeared to make himself at home as he glanced around the darkened room. "I still love it here."

"Grab a seat." Hank gestured to the only chair not covered in reading material. He stood stock still with his arms folded across his chest. "Can I get you a drink?"

"I'll have one of those cocktails, if you're offering." Undeterred by Hank's stance, Bill winked and his smile broadened. "It's never too early, I suppose." Bill slid onto the chair, careful not to disturb the piles of books surrounding him.

A sick feeling settled in Hank's guts as he strode past Bill into the kitchen. He could feel his eyes scanning the emptiness of his home behind his back. It felt as if Bill were evaluating the effects of his shattered life. "So tell me again, how'd ya find me Billy?"

"Like I said, it wasn't easy. You really dropped off the radar. No one from the army knew where to find you." Bill accepted a drink without meeting his eyes. "So I looked up your father. He gave me your e-mail address." Bill finally eyed him over the rim of his drink. "He wants you to call him. He says he hasn't heard from you since you moved west."

"What's this all about, Billy?" A hint of anger flashed across Hank's voice. "What are you doing here?"

"Well …"

"If you came here to make yourself feel better somehow, you've made a mistake."

As if he'd anticipated the hostility, Bill raised a hand to check him. "I didn't come here for any of that. I'm not here to check up on you."

"Then what for?" Hank's arms remained folded over his drink.

"I've been meaning to talk with you about something."

"And the fact that yesterday was October third has nothing to do with it?"

"No." Bill's face turned solemnly earnest. "I didn't even think of it. Like I said, I wasn't even expecting to find you until you called me. I've been trying to track you down for months. It just worked out this way."

"Then let's have it: what do you want to talk about?"

"Come on, Hank, you've got it all wrong. I don't want to open old wounds here." Bill paused, cupping his drink between his hands. "I know we're not good old buddies from way back, but we've got history together. Apart from the obvious"—Bill pointed to his heart, acknowledging he owed his life to Hank—"The short time we spent together made a profound impact on my life. The whole experience really made me think. I'm not the same person you last saw in Germany."

"So you're doing well for yourself, is that it? And maybe you thought you'd spread it around a little?"

"No, Hank. That's not it at all." Bill dipped his head a little lower, as if he'd known it would come to this. "But in a way, you might be right. Everything I have, I owe to you."

"You don't owe me a damn thing! I'm responsible for my own choices."

"I'm not talking about what you did to save my life. I'm talking about how you changed the way I look at the world, how *I've* changed my life. Because of you I decided to do something with my life. Something meaningful. I'm going to make things happen ... and I want you to help me."

"Me?" Hank purposefully looked around the room, then back to Bill and his thousand-dollar suit. "What can I do for you?"

"I want you to take me seriously. I didn't want to jump right into to things with you, but I don't want you thinking I'm here for pity's sake either. I know you better than that, and I had hoped you would have thought better of me too."

"All right, Billy." Hank unfolded his arms and lifted his glass. "I'm listening. Why are we having this sit-down together? As you can see ... I'm a very busy man."

The broad smile reappeared on Bill's face, and he raised his glass to match Hank in a toast. "Salud!"

"Uh-rah!"

"Uh-rah!"

"Down to business then. I don't really know where to begin—there's so much to cover. I was hoping to feel you out a bit first." Bill paused long enough to take a long drink.

"Let's be up-front. I'm not into playing games, Billy. What kinda things were you hoping to find out?" Hank's tone remained serious. This wasn't the first time he'd been approached in shady conversation, and he didn't feel like going through the motions.

"Well, for starters, I don't really know much about what you've been into since you left the army." Bill let slip his first puzzled expression as he took in the bleak surroundings. "What have you been doing with yourself? Are you working? How do you make ends meet? I know you can't be living off of what the army is paying you."

"You might say that I haven't found the right line of work yet."

"Have you looked into interior design?" Bill laughed, blowing waves off the top of his glass. "You might be missing your calling."

"Could probably use a lady's touch, eh?" Hank smiled, relaxing slightly.

"I've got to tell you …" Bill grimaced as he gulped down another mouthful of vodka. "I'm more than a little surprised. I thought a guy like you would be cleaning up in an area like this. There's big money out here."

"I didn't take well to working in an office. I've got what the doctors call an *attitude problem*."

"No shit. But how are you paying the bills?"

"Severance packages mostly … I'm getting by. What about you? You must have had a few strings pulled to secure an early discharge."

"As a matter of fact, I did." Bill drained his glass and pushed it toward Hank for more. "The same strings landed me a job working for Congressman Thomas. I'm his chief of staff."

"So that's how you're gonna change the world? Politics?" Hank huffed sarcastically and wiped his mouth with an arm. "I thought you were going to stay away from all of that—isn't that what your father always wanted for you? President Kemp, wasn't it?"

"Yeah, yeah it is, but my father had nothing to do with me getting this job. At least not directly."

"Is that right?" A single eyebrow formed a questioning arch on Hank's brow. "You really think so? Come on, Billy, let's get real."

"I'm serious. He had nothing to do with it. In fact, my Dad is pissed. Gilbert Thomas is a Democrat." Bill's eyes rolled behind his glass. "This is something bigger than party politics."

"So what's the deal? You're what, not even twenty-five? How'd ya land a suit job with a congressman? You didn't even go to college."

"I've spent the last three years in Officer Candidate School. I've been groomed for the position."

"It doesn't work that way, Billy." Once again, Hank was boring into Bill's eyes looking for answers. "I know, believe me."

"The reason I was pushed through the Academy and secured an early discharge is the same reason I found myself working with Thomas. It's the same reason that brings me here today."

"I don't get it, Billy."

"I'm part of something big, and I need your help. Despite what you may think of yourself, you are an asset. You are the best of the best." Bill turned to pull a pack of cigarettes from his coat pocket and slid one into his mouth.

"Because I was Delta?"

"Because you were Delta." Bill clicked open a Zippo lighter engraved with the Special Forces logo and brought the flame to his face. "And because you have the particular worldview we need. The skill set you would bring as a Delta operator is secondary."

"Worldview? What has that got to do with anything? What are you talking about? Who are *we*?"

"After meeting you, I became vocal about certain issues, and that's why I'm here now."

Hank remained silent, electing to allow Bill to continue.

"You were the one that taught me that there are two types of people in the world: those who believe, and those who don't." Bill rolled the Zippo over his knuckles as he toked heavily on his cigarette. "I can see that look on your face. I know what you're thinking, but let me lay it out for you. Meeting you made a profound impact on me. I probably didn't even realize it at the time, but you did. I began questioning things, and like I said I became vocal about certain things."

"What kind of things?"

"The prevailing state of the world … today's society is fundamentally flawed; our perceptions are flawed. You taught me to stand up and question what we believe, what is right and what is only natural. You showed me how dangerous our beliefs truly are."

"I taught you all that?" Hank smiled skeptically.

"In a way. You taught me to look at the big picture, with a more historical point of view. You showed me that our current worldview was clouded by untruth, that the truth was out there to be found, but people were too frightened to look for it."

"The truth?"

"If not the truth, the ability to point out what is false. You showed me how the religious worldview affects every aspect of our lives, not just politics and culture, but everything. You showed me that our beliefs must be founded on reason, or else any level of madness is possible."

"You're such a paladin, Billy. What makes you think you can change what people believe?"

"Paladin?"

"Yeah, a paladin. A real, old-fashioned, good guy. The cowboy in the white hat. The guy who's gonna save the girl and not get dirty … the kind of guy who shoots the gun out of the bad guy's hand but never kills him. That's you."

"Maybe I am. Maybe I'm just idealistic."

"Oh, you are, Billy. You're not the first guy to rage against the insanity of religion, but, historically speaking, most of those guys have ended up dead. It's not a black-and-white world out there. And politics isn't a place for the guy with the white hat. It's a dirty business. It's a competitive enterprise, like anything else. There's no place for morality. In fact, there is no morality—only convenience."

"I know how the system works, but I'm talking about something different. This goes well beyond American politics. I, and many others, believe we're at a critical juncture. The pendulum has swung away from the age of reason back to a resurgence of religious fundamentalism. The Christian right is consolidating its power here in the states, and radical fundamentalist groups are popping up all over the world. We believe that a major faith-based conflict is brewing. We want to stop it. Now is the time."

"You're probably right."

"You've said it yourself: the entire Muslim view of its conflict with the West is seen through the prism of the Israel-Palestine conflict. It's a nightmarish, religious time bomb, and it's ready to explode. And what's even more frightening to me is that there are Christian fundamentalist groups right here in the U.S. who secretly support war in Israel. They want the second coming. They want Armageddon!"

"Megiddo." Hank muttered the name absently.

"What?"

"Megiddo, the city. That's where the rapture is supposed to take place—Armageddon. Har-Megiddo. It means 'the hill above Megiddo' in Hebrew. You can take a tour bus there if you want."

"I know you understand these things, probably better than I do, but what you don't understand is that there is a movement out there that believes such a war can be avoided. They have a plan. They have a mission."

"Oh yeah, and what's the plan? How do they expect to diffuse the ticking time-bomb?"

"We can end the insanity by destroying their faith. Destroying faith itself. We can substitute belief in a higher power for a better understanding of who we truly are."

"But you might not like who we truly are. You get rid of God—and, consequently, evil—then guys like Hitler and Stalin were just men like us."

"But they were just men. It's wrong to think they were something else. I know you believe that."

"I do, but the sheep out there are too afraid to think of themselves in that light. Religion is still around, even becoming more prevalent, because it works. It allows them to carry on with their lives without really thinking about it. People are too stupid, too lazy to think for themselves. They'd rather be mastered by an almighty. *That* is human nature Billy."

"There are smart people out there, too. People who *do* think for themselves, and they're ready for change."

"And they think they have the answers?"

"They have a plan."

Hank stirred the drink in his hand. He didn't feel like debating the unsolvable with the young idealist. He was reluctant to play the cynic and point out the futility of Bill's apparent dreams. He no longer held any passion for the great debate. He'd already spent his life fighting for a cause.

"Many of us think there is hope for humanity to evolve. I know it must be hard for you, especially considering the history of your family, but you know better than anyone what pain religion adds to suffering, what unnatural guilt and inferiority it brings to weigh down men's spirits."

"You know, huh? Because my brothers were all killed, and my mother became a born-again nut, you think you know why I despise religion? You think you know why I hate humanity?" Hank's expression turned hard as he stared Bill down.

"You know better than most that there is no God."

"You don't know shit about me! I hate God! I listened to my mother plead with him for hours on end, as if he were right there in the room with us. That's who I hate, the one who talks people out of their lives."

"I know you better than you think, Hank. I know more than what you've told me. I met with your father. We talked."

"Oh yeah? So what? He's a drunk."

"He told me what your mother said before she died. He told me the whole story. He helped to fill in some of the blanks."

"What did he tell you?" Hank found himself suddenly curious to hear his father's take on things.

"He said that you and your brothers were pretty shaken up after Tommy's death. He said you were all pretty tight. You were only thirteen."

"It was my first year of high school," Hank said absently, not fully remembering how much of the story he had told Bill. "Tommy wrapped his car around a tree on prom night. Three other kids died in the car with him. Everybody blamed Tommy because he was drunk. We all were blamed."

"And Jack—Jack Jr.—was killed a year later. Some kind of freak accident?"

"Some son of a bitch jumping off a building ..."

"He was the same age as Tommy, right?"

"Eighteen."

"And Mike died of an overdose on his eighteenth birthday." Bill's head hung low as he looked up at Hank. "Jack told me what your mother said to you, and how you left for the army just before your eighteenth birthday. He says he hasn't seen you since."

"What did he say about Mike's death?"

"Some kind of overdose."

"Accidental or ...?" Hank looked away and couldn't finish.

"Accidental. He said he'd been messing around with heroin."

Hank remained silent for a long while, collecting himself. "And what did he tell you my mother said to me?"

"He said by this point she had gone totally mad. She was dying of cancer and her religious delusions wouldn't allow her to get treatment."

"She wanted to die a martyr."

"He said she became more delusional with each death. She believed that you were all paying for the sins he committed in Vietnam. She said you were all cursed by God and that none of you would grow to manhood because he refused to accept Jesus."

"By that time she was already talking to angels." Hank drank deeply from his glass. The vodka no longer stung his palate, and he felt the pain of his hangover giving way. "You wouldn't believe what these *angels* would tell her."

"Jack said he couldn't take it."

"He escaped into a bottle! I was the only one left to take care of her! I was the one who had to kneel down and pray with her for hours on end! I was the one who had to bathe her, feed her, everything! In the end, she thought I was him and let me have it constantly."

"I can't even imagine." Bill lowered his head solemnly. "You know, he feels really bad for not being there."

"I don't blame him. She wouldn't really accept him anyway, no matter what he did. She was too far gone. She needed someone to blame. She fell in love with Jesus and out of love with him. Jesus was everything. He didn't stand a chance."

"She died when you were still in high school?"

"Right before graduation. I was seventeen. She was sick for most of my senior year. But when she died, suddenly I was free." Hank closed his hands together, as if the whole story had been told. "That's when I enlisted."

"And you haven't been home since?"

"Home? You don't understand. You don't know what it's like to try and put something like that behind you. There's nothing for me back there."

"What about your father?"

"He's a broken man. The Irish curse. My mother said Vietnam did it to him, but I think she did it to him, her and Jesus."

"He's worried you might think you're cursed."

"Gotta love the Catholics for keeping curses alive." Hank drained the rest of his cocktail with a smirk. "You know I never bought any of that shit. Besides, I'm thirty frickin' years old."

"Jack wanted me to tell you that he never did any of those things your mother accused him of."

"I know. I've read his jacket. I had plenty of time to kill while I was working at the Pentagon. There was never any hint of any misconduct. It wouldn't matter to me if there were. I'm a soldier; I understand." Hank filled both glasses again.

"To the army." Bill raised the reddish cocktail in a toast.

"Uh-rah." Hank said half heartedly, but he was thinking, *Fuck the army.*

"Listen, why don't you get showered up? We can take this up over some grub."

"Yeah, all this getting-to-know-you-again crap is getting me loaded."

"All right, I know this place downtown where the waitresses are all tens."

"Oh yeah?"

"Come on, I'm buying."

Hank stumbled dizzily into the shower. The hot water soothed his aching body and helped to clear his thoughts. He searched his closets in vain for clothing to match Bill's finely tailored suit, but realized it was hopeless.

After another round of drinks, they staggered outside to hail a cab. As expected, Bill managed to keep the conversation light, and Hank waited patiently for him to bring up the important business he had alluded to. Hank tolerated the bullshit, knowing that Bill must surely be building up courage for something big, but as the afternoon turned to evening, the evening rolled into night, and the bars became crowded with women, Bill seemed to lose all interest in serious conversation.

Hank's growing impatience turned to anger when he caught Bill posing as a wealthy Internet millionaire, and he finally pulled him out of the club into a waiting cab. He directed the driver to a topless bar where he knew there were quiet places to continue their conversation.

Once inside, they found the club lined with beautiful women all in varied degrees of undress. Hank managed to usher Bill past the front row seats, affectionately called "sniffer's row" by the girls, to the back of the club where the lights were dim and the booming speakers were nearly out of range. They found an empty booth, which more closely resembled two couches separated by a low glass table. Hank quickly scanned the neon glow for a glimpse of Jenna, but she was nowhere to be seen.

"Nice place, Hank. Looks kinda dirty—know what I mean?" Bill's brows arched eagerly on his face as his head swiveled from beauty to beauty.

"Yeah, I like it because they have a full bar." Hank turned his gaze back to Bill but his attention was broken by the caress of a hand across his back.

"Can I get you guys something to drink?" A tired looking, middle-aged waitress stood behind him with a tray of drinks resting on her upturned hand. Twenty dollars later, they were sipping watered-down cocktails through comically bright straws.

Bill noticed Hank scanning the room for Jenna. "See anybody you know?"

"Nah, not yet."

"What a bunch of hotties—shouldn't we sit a little closer?"

"No. We can talk here."

"That reminds me: I forgot to ask you, did that writer dude ever get a hold of you? Damn, I forget his name. He's writing a book about the Battle of the Black

Sea. I told him all about you. I think he's calling it Black Hawk Down or something."

The phrase that had changed his life forever rang in Hank's memory and was immediately felt in his absent leg. "No."

"He probably couldn't find you either. It's supposed to be a minute-to-minute account of the Battle of the Black Sea."

"Ma, Alinti Rangers." Hank said somberly in Somali.

"The day of the Rangers." Bill repeated in English.

"I like the Day of the Rangers better than the Battle of the Black Sea." Hank flung the straw to the floor and began gulping down his drink. "Battles make history. That coward Aspin stole that distinction from us." Hank glared at Bill from over his neon cup. "That day was ours. A hundred and fifty Rangers against a whole city of fanatic primitives, with every kid in diapers and every bony-assed grandma armed with an AK-47. The Somalis claim we killed three and a half thousand, the army says five hundred bad guys dead and one thousand wounded. Whatever, we only lost eighteen guys." Hank's hand reached down and absently massaged the stump under his prosthetic.

"It's surprising to hear it remembered like that."

"That's what happened when the cowards back in Washington pulled us out: it looks like a total defeat! It looks like we got our ass kicked! We were engaged in the hottest firefight since Vietnam, and nothing ever came of it. Those mercurial bastards in Washington lost their stomach for battle and gave away our advantage. They gave back all of our prisoners! Aidid was left in power, and we took off with our tail between our legs!"

"Did you know that Aidid's son was one of the Rangers in the Mog?"

"Yeah, I heard that." Hank shook his head in disgust. "You Rangers will take anybody."

"I guess he took over where papa left off."

"Doesn't it drive you crazy? We did it all for nothing!"

"Did you hear what happened when Clinton awarded the posthumous Medal of Honor to Shughart?"

"Yeah, I read about it. Randy's dad told him he wasn't fit to be commander in chief."

"Yeah, I heard he told him where to stick it."

"Good! He betrayed us. Here's to Randy's dad!" The two men toasted their fallen comrade, banging their plastic cups on the table in time for the waitress to return with fresh drinks.

"Here's to Les Aspin getting the clap—for the way he fucked us!" Hank raised his voice and tossed the straw to the floor as Bill paid out another twenty bucks. "He's the same son of a bitch that boned me in Panama."

"That's right, you started off in Delta A-squadron. I forgot you were in Panama."

"That's right, the A-Team. We ran the psych-ops. That was a fun campaign."

"Didn't you guys dress up a goat in Noriega's underwear? Some kinda voodoo thing?"

"Not just any underwear, a bright red thong! His *lucky* underwear. He'd been coked up for days once we trapped him in the embassy."

"The Vatican embassy, right? I still can't believe they took him in, considering they knew he was into Voodoo and all the satanic stuff."

"You wouldn't believe the stuff we found in his houses; kid porn, pictures of mutilated bodies, all kinds of weird stuff. He had bucket loads of cocaine. Anyway, he was way into Voodoo, traveled with his own priest and everything. We knew about his lucky red panties, so once we had him cornered we slipped a pair on this nasty old Billy goat and tied it up outside the church. Goats are way-bad mojo in the voodoo world; they've got devil's eyes. It reportedly drove him nuts."

"How long did the standoff last?"

"About a week. We tried every trick in the book, but he wouldn't budge and the Catholics wouldn't give him up. But that wasn't the funniest thing that happened during the operation."

"Oh yeah?"

"Dude, listen to this—you can't make this kinda stuff up. There was this real bad guy, some local drug lord that had all the villagers scared shitless. He was a real Hollywood-style scumbag. He owned this massive villa ... anyway, we were rounding up Noriega's men, and we came a-knocking at this guy's front door, you know with a little C-4. He had these two huge double doors, solid wood, with solid gold doorknobs, and we were gonna blow them. Meanwhile, this guy sees us coming and he doesn't know whether to shit his pants or play the piano. He starts running around back and forth behind the door and he's got this, I dunno, maybe ten-thousand-gallon fish tank behind him. Anyway, he's running around when—Bang!—We blow the doors. Shrapnel shatters the aquarium, and one of the door knobs gets blown off and ricochets off the floor and jumps right up this guy's ass!"

"No way!"

"I'm telling you: you can't make this stuff up. We made entry and find this guy spinnin' circles on the floor. He was howling, I mean screaming bloody murder. There were exotic fish floppin' around all over the place. We didn't know why he was screaming at first, but then we saw it! He had this fist-sized knob crammed up his ass, pants and all. He didn't have another scratch on him."

"Dude!"

"We carried him out on a stretcher. The villagers loved it. It was priceless!"

"It was still stuck in his ass?"

"Like you wouldn't believe."

"You couldn't get it out?"

"Get it out? Are you kidding? It was the highlight of the whole operation!"

The two men were still laughing when the waitress returned with their next round.

"So how did you end up in Delta C-squadron?"

"That's another story." Hank tried to wave off the question, pretending to focus his attention on the girls.

"What did you do?" Bill smiled knowingly, eager to hear more of his exploits.

"I shot one of Noriega's men when I wasn't supposed to."

"You what?"

"Well, it's complicated, but the *Reader's Digest* version goes like this: we were about a week into the standoff, and I was on sniper detail. We'd nabbed most of his men by now, but there was this one bodyguard who was sticking around. Big ugly guy, always carried some heavy artillery. Noriega wouldn't budge as long as he was around. So this gorilla stepped out to do a blast of coke, and I took my shot. I recovered the body, and the Catholics didn't know I took him out, but I got hammered anyway. The next thing I knew, I was in the Middle East. I learned Spanish for nothing."

"You didn't have orders to shoot?"

"Not on embassy grounds."

"Man, you've got balls."

"Noriega gave up the next day. It was a good shoot."

"I admire that about you. You do what you think is right, and you stand by your actions. Not many people do anymore."

"So let's cut the bullshit, Billy: what do you want? What's this all about?"

"Okay, Hank, but I need you to be up front with me about something first."

"Me? I'm an open book! You're the one dodging all the questions. I've let it slide this long because I trust you, but I'm done playing games."

"All right, Hank." Bill took out a cigarette and seemed to ready himself. "Who is Henry Patrick?"

The question struck Hank like a blow. Bill had obviously dug deeper into his past then he was letting on. "You know about Henry, huh?"

"Is he you? I need to know before I can play my hand."

Two silky dark arms slid across Hank's shoulders from behind. A beautiful Latina wearing a low-cut gown bent over behind him and offered him a dance. Hank stopped her with a crisp wave of his hand. "Not now!" She was about to persist, but Hank told her to beat it without ever looking back. His eyes were fixed on Bill's. "Why do you need to know about Henry?"

"I need to know if Henry—or you—has any trouble following him. I can't make a move until I know you're clean." Bill's tone turned serious, and he struggled to maintain eye contact.

"And I want to know what in the hell you're not telling me before I answer any more fucking questions!"

"I trust you, Hank, and I hope you trust me too. Just let me know you're not caught up in any bullshit, and I can tell you what this is all about. Why have you been using an alias?"

"I'm clean, Billy." Hank settled back into his seat, with his arms folded across his chest. "What do you need to know, Congressman?"

"Why does Henry's name keep popping up when I look for you?"

"Popping up?"

"I was trying to track you down, but your file was a total dead end. I found out that you had a job lined up after you left the army, Tech Solutions or something, but I checked with the company and they said they'd never heard of you. So I pulled a few strings and had a friend from the CIA look into it for me."

"CIA?" Hank bolted out of his chair.

Bill nearly dropped his drink, then recovered, talking fast. "He was able to find some documents from Tech Solutions that had your DD-214 number and discharge information on them, but they were for a guy named Henry Patrick."

"You had the CIA looking for me?"

"We checked Henry's records, but they were classified. All we knew was that he was a Navy SEAL, with almost the same vital stats as you. We couldn't get any further. It was classified."

"You had the motherfuckin' CIA looking for me!" Hank's fists pounded the table, nearly clearing the drinks.

"He was just a friend helping a friend, completely informal."

Hank could see that Bill was shaken by his volatile response, and he could feel the prickly heat of anger creeping up his neck. He'd had a special hatred for the

CIA ever since he'd failed their psych exam. "Who do you think you are? Who's behind all of this?"

"That's not important right now—we have to clear this up first. I don't understand ..."

"Fuck you! You have those bastards at the CIA looking for me, but you won't tell me why! What the hell were you looking for?"

"It's like this, Hank: I need you, but I'm in a delicate situation. You're no good to me if you're involved in anything shady. I need to know you're clean, and I can't understand why you're using the name Henry Patrick."

"All right, Billy, I've got nothing to hide from you." Hank forcibly relaxed his posture and unclenched his fists. "I'm not into anything that can tarnish the good congressman's reputation, so you don't have to worry about being seen with me."

"It's not about the congressman," Bill began, but Hank cut him short.

"The alias is simple. I don't want to get into all the reasons why, but let's just say the new name was part of a new life. When I worked at the Pentagon, I met this guy—he was navy, pretty sharp, but real talkative. We helped each other now and then. Anyway this guy was getting ready to leave the navy, and he planned on taking some of his expertise to South America with him. He was planning on making a killing in some of the more lucrative markets down there."

"What, drugs?"

"This guy was total adrenalin junky. He washed out of the SEALs three times. He was a real sharp operator, especially with computer systems, but otherwise he was all messed up."

"What happened to him?"

"He's dead now. He always told me he was going to be some high-tech drug lord with a harem of Latin babes, but I always thought he was full of it—until one day he came to me with some sensitive security questions. In exchange for my help, he showed me how he planned on changing his identity."

"How'd he do it?"

"The SEALs keep a list. It's a list of ready-made false identities for its field operators. It was that simple."

Bill rolled a cigarette between his fingers with an expression on his face that suggested he was waiting for bad news to follow.

"It seemed like a good idea at the time."

"And you've been using the name ever since?"

"What good is having an alias if you don't use it?"

Bill stuck the cigarette between his lips and squinted at Hank through the smoke. "That's it?"

"That's it. Nothing shady. No FBI's most wanted list, just a half-assed attempt at a fresh start." Hank's eyes hardened on Bill's. "Now are you gonna tell me what this is all about?"

"Okay, Hank: simply put, I need you. In fact, I may need Henry even more."

Hank tried to wait patiently for Bill to continue, but it was too much to take. "Who in the hell are you involved with? What do you want with me?"

The hard scowl on Hank's face caused Bill to stumble over second thoughts. The most dangerous man he knew sat across from him, angrily demanding answers, and he had foolishly complicated matters by getting him drunk. Hank's dark gaze bore into him, forcing Bill's eyes to the floor. The moment had come, and now his thoughts swirled with paranoid uncertainty. His lips pulled the last of his cigarette to the butt, and he rallied his nerve.

The fragments of thought he'd rehearsed scattered, and Bill suddenly found himself not knowing where to start. He bent low to rest his elbows on his knees, and looked up into Hank's face. The unwavering penetrative glare was unnerving, reminding him of what Hank was capable of and why he'd gone through the trouble of finding him in the first place. In the end, he knew all he had to do was open the door. Hank was a born Iconoclast.

"This is not the way I intended this conversation to take place." Bill smiled weakly in the direction of the two nearly naked women on stage.

Hank didn't move.

"What I'd like to propose is … is complicated, but I think I can make it simple for you … for both of us." Bill crushed his cigarette butt into a tray and opened his hands toward Hank. "What do you want?" Bill tried not to show that he already knew the answer. "What do you want more than anything else?"

"I want to know what the hell you're talking about!" Hank's raised a fist. "Cut the bullshit, Kemp!"

"You see …" Bill shifted in his seat, drying his palms on his pant-legs. "I think I've got what you want, and you've got what I need."

"Spit it out, Billy! I hope this isn't some kind of gay thing." There was no humor in Hank's tone, and his expression cautioned against any further games.

"I need an Operator with your talents." Bill let the words hang for a moment as he tried to read Hank's face. Feeling a kind of dismissal in Hank's unchanged expression, Bill lowered his voice somberly. "I need someone I can trust with my life." A long silence followed as Bill dug for another smoke. He wedged the cigarette between his lips and flashed Hank a well-practiced half smile, as if to say, "There you have it—it's that simple."

"And you know what I want, huh?" Hank's upper lip curled into a snarl.

"You want back in." Bill answered flatly, briefly meeting Hank's eyes before checking himself. "You're pissing your life away. Your talents are going to waste. You're the sharpest guy I've ever met; you speak what, seven languages? You were

Black Ops! I know you can't be ready to throw away your life because you lost your leg."

"I lost more than leg back there! Don't tell me what I'm pissing away!"

"You think that part of your life is over? You can't just turn it off like a switch; it's part of who you are! Hear me out on this—listen to what I have to offer you."

"I don't need your charity! I don't need some bullshit bodyguard job!"

"It's not charity. My debt to you can never be fully paid—I know that." Bill changed tone and straightened in his seat. "I have a job for you. No bullshit." Bill raised his cup, wagging a cautionary finger. "But just like when you were recruited into the Delta Force, there are some things I can't tell you right now. Not until I get some degree of commitment."

Hank sat back in his chair and folded his arms over his chest. "Okay Billy, I'm listening."

"First of all, I need you to understand that all this has very little to do with the congressman's office. I can only speak in generalities for now, but I am part of a clandestine organization much more powerful than any political office. And I hope it goes without saying that they wouldn't appreciate me speaking openly about any of this. I need to trust you. And I need you to take me very seriously."

After a long moment of hawklike staring, Hank simply nodded his head and reached out to take his drink from the table.

"Now don't get the wrong idea: these are good people. They have reason to stay underground."

"I would expect nothing less from you, Billy."

"I was dying to tell you about this from the start, but I had to be careful. I had to know about Henry first."

"So now you know."

Bill motioned for more drinks before coming back on point. "Let's say the organization—a movement, really—is on the verge of making a political break-out ... among other things. They've been busy seeding every level of government for almost a decade. That's how I got my position. That's why I was pushed through to an early discharge. But right now, I'm small potatoes: there are others, names you know. Our strength comes from our connections, and the network has grown strong enough to make a move. A new moderate political party is going to break out, and it's gonna rock the bipartisan system.

"Politics?" Hank looked disappointed but amused. "This is about politics?"

"Yes, but this is bigger than mere politics. The political breakout is only one prong of the attack. We need the legislative power, and we can steal it back. The two-party system is weak. It's ready to crumble, and we're gonna split them right down the middle. But don't underestimate what I'm talking about; I'm part of something bigger than any political party. We're thinking globally."

"Globally?"

"But we start local. Like I said, we have people already seeded into office. Power, real power, is all about connections. And right now, I'm connected. I've been charged with managing a network of people—operatives." Bill let some of the pride show as he squared his shoulders with Hank's. "That is why I need a man like you."

Hank screwed his face into a question mark, but didn't speak.

"I was recruited because of my beliefs ... and, more importantly, because of my talents and connections."

"Connections like your father?"

"Yeah, but not quite the way you think. He is not an Iconoclast. He has no idea about the organization."

"Iconoclast?" Curiosity surfaced on Hank's face.

Bill grimaced. He had not intended to let the term slip just yet. "Well, yeah. Iconoclast."

"Like the religious nuts? The old-school Protestants who went around burning relics because they were idolatrous?" Puzzlement was clear in Hank's eyes.

"But the term *means* idol breaker. Someone who attacks settled beliefs and institutions because they're hollow. Think in more modern, Western terms. Take out the religious zealot and replace him with someone who is willing to attack the established beliefs of countless generations, someone who is willing to expose the truth, someone who wants change."

"Someone like me?" Hank's voice dripped with sarcasm as he rolled his eyes above his drink.

"Someone like us. There are more of us than you think. Good, smart people. People who are fed up, who are ready to spark the change that's been a long time in coming."

"And you think I'm perfect for your movement because of my feelings toward religion? I dunno ..."

"Once you see for yourself, you'll understand what I'm talking about. But for right now, all I'm saying is that you're perfect for the job I have for you. This stuff is right up your alley. I need a guy to manage operations from behind the scenes and to perform some of the more sensitive operations within my sphere of influence. I'm not looking for an executive officer. I need a partner. A silent partner."

"What kind of operations are you talking about?"

"To talk about that, I would need the certain degree of commitment I mentioned."

"Well, let me ask you this: how's the severance package?" Hank cracked a smile, and for a moment Bill thought that he was playing with him.

"It's great, just like in Black Ops. You want out, they kill you."

Hank burst out in laughter and raised his cup with a wink.

"You know I'm kidding, right?" Bill asked half laughing. "You look so serious."

"It wouldn't be the first time I made that deal."

"To fully explain what kinds of things I would need you to do, I should start from the beginning. It's all about the Icons. 'The Iconoclasts' isn't what the organization officially calls itself, but the name has kind of stuck."

"It's catchy."

"The initial core group started as a think tank back in the sixties. Their focus was global conflict resolution. The group was mostly made up of scientists and academics, with a few theologians and psychologists, but it was under military direction. Early on in their talks, they found that their debates usually ended in an impasse over religion and its cultural effects. It was argued that religious inclinations and religious establishments were responsible for most of the wars throughout history. Some argued that humanity was ready to move past its archaic beliefs, but the debate ended in a stalemate. They never came to an effective resolution, and the group was eventually abandoned.

But before they all went their separate ways, a splinter group emerged and formed some powerful alliances. The members who felt strongly that the issue of religion was a paramount threat and needed to be addressed as one met secretly. This group began expanding its membership and setting goals for itself. They've been secretive until now because of the negative stigma attached to atheism, but they're finally ready to move forward with their mission."

"And what exactly is the mission?"

"Evolution—the next step. Freedom. Freedom from religion. Destroy the idols of the faithful … and with destruction comes change."

"Sounds pretty ambitious, Billy."

"Forget about the mission for a minute." The condescending expression on Hank's face made Bill flush with embarrassment. "Let's talk business for a moment, maybe then you'll have an idea of the scope of our organization. This is the real deal." For Bill, the mission was everything—and he didn't like Hank shrugging it off as simple idealism. "I can start you off with a hundred and fifty thousand a year, plus expenses. Multiply that by thousands and you'll get some idea what our payroll looks like."

"That's big money, but your mission is impossible. Don't get me wrong, I'm all for changing the system, but you'll never get rid of religion."

"How can you of all people say that? The time is right! The age of reason stumbled somehow, but it's time to take the next step."

"You want to enlighten humanity to the fact that there is no God? Well, I've got news for you: there is a God. Man created God from some deep-seated need for him. God is an extension of humanity, and religion is simply its semantics. It's in our genes. It's a part of our biology. At best, you'll only supplant one religion with another."

Bill felt at a loss for words as Hank casually insulted the goals that had grown to consume his life. He could only stare into his drink and brood over his poor timing.

"Think about it this way: *Homo sapiens* have been walking around on two feet for nearly three million years. We began cultivating crops and forming civilizations three thousand years ago. We came into the age of science and the industrial revolution less than three hundred years ago. We landed on the moon only fifty years ago. My point is that the same brain that learned to use tools to crack open bones all those centuries ago still rattles around inside our skulls. The same brain that concluded that lightning was hurled to earth by sky gods still believes in cutting off the tips of their son's cocks. The same hands that fashioned stone tools eventually made tools to land us on the moon. Religion only seems archaic to us now because our technology has outpaced our biology."

"But we have evolved."

"We've learned, but our brains haven't changed. We adapt our environment to suit us; we no longer adapt to suit our environment. We've stopped evolving."

"We're not primitives. This is not the end. It can't be the end. You'll never convince me we've reached the pinnacle of our development."

"Who's to say? It could all end tomorrow. Mother Nature could have that one bad day, or some fool could get hold of the button. Call me a pessimist, but I don't hold out much hope for mankind. Besides, I think we've already peaked. We're too decadent, too permissive. We're a society in decline."

Bill huffed with exasperation. "Oh yeah? So when did we peak?"

"With the Greeks, probably." Hank shifted in his seat, relaxing his arms. "But you're right about one thing, Billy: there's a war brewing. And you know what else? There's not a doubt in my mind we'll see a nuclear detonation in our lifetime. That's the real nightmare."

"You're preaching to the choir, Hank. We know, and we want to stop it. You can't give up hope. I know you're not one to roll over and take it."

"Hope for hope's sake, Billy?"

"There's time to change, but we must act." Bill leaned closer, mirroring Hank's posture. "A journey of a thousand miles starts with a single step."

Hank laughed in his face, then brought his fingers to the corners of his eyes, pulling back the skin, giving his best Chinese impression. "Ah, but the path to enlightenment leads to nowhere, Grasshopper."

Again, Bill was at a loss for words. He felt as if Hank was toying with him.

"What do you know about the Easter Islands, Billy?" Hank's voice was casual, and he began to relax his posture—giving Bill the impression he had already dismissed his offer.

"The place with all the giant heads?"

"Yeah, the Moi. Let me tell you a little something about those giant heads. The islands are stuck out in the middle of the Pacific Ocean. They were settled by some migrating Polynesians so long ago that no one knows where they came from or how long they've been there. They remained isolated for nearly two thousand years, and over time they developed their own civilization and their own religion: hence the giant heads."

"Okay."

"Their religion was similar to others around the world at the time, complete with priests, altars, and sacrifices. At one point the civilization numbered in the tens of thousands, but when the islands were discovered, only a few dozen inhabitants remained. This was not due to the influence of the evil white man or the Spanish Conquistadors; the decimation was caused by attrition resulting from years of religious wars. The islands had been completely deforested in order to rebuild after attacks, make weapons, and to make and move their Moi idols. In fact, when the islands were discovered on Easter Sunday, there were one hundred Moi for every person left on the island."

"You're only strengthening my point. We need to move beyond that kind of thinking."

"My point is that religion doesn't kill people; people kill people."

"We can move past that. Let people kill each other without evoking the name of God. Let us expose the motivations that drive humanity for what they truly are."

"Like what? Egotism? We can't relate to these concepts without thinking we're part of something bigger, something infinitely more important."

"I can see you're going to make this difficult for me. I don't know why I'm surprised. Just give me some time to show you what the Icons are capable of. They'll win you over, even if I can't."

"I'm not trying to be difficult, Billy. I'm just trying to show you: I'm all done with fighting for a higher cause. I've had enough. I've already done my part."

"Your fighting days are far from over, Hank. This is a fight we can win. The Icons have amassed huge financial resources. Our people are ready to act all over the world. I'm only involved in the Activist Branch of the organization. We are going to be the soldiers of the movement."

"Soldiers? Forming your own army?"

"There's a virtual army of people out there who have had their power stolen away by pious zealots. We'll give them a voice, a platform. There are more of them than you think. Some studies show that nearly 20 percent of the population doesn't believe in any kind of God; look at what the gays have done in the political arena—with just a fraction of those numbers."

"The gays?"

"An outstanding lobbying group, big money, media coverage, celebrity endorsements … they're a great model for any political minority. If diabetics had mobilized like that, there wouldn't be any more diabetes. There are far fewer gays than diabetics, and more people die from diabetes than AIDS, but AIDS research gets a hundred times the funding."

"You've modeled your campaign on the gay movement?"

"Why not? It's effective. Lawsuits, protests, marches, mass media coverage, the works. We bring everyone together under one banner, incorporate groups already involved with our causes: separation of church and state people, pro-choice advocates, whatever. We go after churches' tax-exempt status; we're pushing legislation to get the word God off our currency, out of the pledge of allegiance, out of the courts. The law, the constitution, is on our side. Only the moral majority stands in our way."

"What are you planning on calling this new party?"

"The Humanist Party. We split the system right down the middle. Strong on constitutionalism, separation of church and state, human rights—especially women's rights—but all for a smaller government. We see a huge opportunity to grab the woman's vote. The demographics look good. Really good. But politics isn't even our strongest suit; the media is where we have our most influence. If we control the media, we control our destiny." Bill paused to light another cigarette. As he did, his eyes caught on two rough looking men working their way toward them at the back of the club.

"So what do you need a guy like me for? Spy shit?"

The unlit cigarette hung from Bill's lips. His attention was still on the two burly, leather-clad bikers pushing through the chairs near the stage. They were headed right for them. The man in the lead was huge, taking up the width of the aisle as he lumbered toward them. Tattoos covered his heavily muscled arms like two dark sleeves. Ink crept up his neck, highlighting his ferocious features. He pointed his giant fist to where Bill and Hank were sitting, then turned to say something to his friend.

The second man was shorter, but equally scary looking. His face was half-hidden beneath a bushy beard, and the black lights overhead made the whites of his eyes glow, giving him a crazed Charlie Manson look. When the massive biker turned again, Bill was looking directly into his pockmarked face.

Bill gestured to Hank with his eyebrows, arching them high on his forehead and tilting his head toward the approaching bikers. He didn't like the look of the big one, and for a second he doubted if even Hank could take him. Hank peered at Bill curiously for a moment and then slowly turned to see what had caught his attention.

By the time Hank had turned around to face the two bikers, they were already standing above them. Bill clenched his fists and waited for Hank. When Hank finally moved, it was with an open-handed high five, not a closed fist.

"Yo, Curt." Hank reached out and embraced the ugly biker, slapping him on the back before stepping away to make room for them on the couch. "What's goin' on, Antony?"

"What's up, H?" The smaller man spoke with a lisp. His front teeth were missing, and Bill could see the rotting flesh in his mouth through the scruffy beard.

"Ah, nothing." Hank turned to Bill, rolling his eyes. "This is my buddy Bill. Bill, this is Curt. The Muppet over here is Anthony. Anferny if you got no teeth."

"What's happenin' brother?" Curt's voice boomed over the club noise as he gripped Bill's hand.

"Just checking out the ladies." Bill gestured to the girls who had followed the bikers to the back of the club.

"All right! I like it!" A mischievous smile spread across the man's face, more clearly revealing the gaps where teeth had been. "See Spike, I told you we'd find some trouble tonight. Tank's on the loose. I didn't expect to find you out. Not after last night. You were so hammered."

"Bill is an old army buddy. He talked me out of the house. What are you two ladies up too?"

"Not much. Just getting' fucked up, ya know?" Anthony's head jerked compulsively as he stammered out the barely comprehendible phrase.

"What about you, Henry? How long you been here?" Curt made himself at home, pushing the glass table away to accommodate his bulk.

"Not long."

"Seen Jenna?" Curt scanned the room with a grin.

"Nah. Where's the rest of your buddies? Where are the Empty Skulls?"

"You mean the Bloody Skulls?" Curt groaned; it wasn't the first time he'd heard the jab. "Why you keep messing with them? You know we're down with the Hell's Angels."

"I'm sorry, I forgot. How's the nose?" Hank smirked.

"Fuck you, man!" Curt's lip curled into an angry snarl for an instant, but then he burst into a hearty laugh. "Who does a guy have to bang to get a couple of drinks around here?"

The waitress appeared from behind Curt, and—much to Bill's chagrin—the cocktails appeared to be on the house.

"So you were in the army with Tank?" Curt threw the neon straw to the floor and slurped his drink.

"Are you one of them commando-sniper guys too?" Anthony blurted out as he slid into the seat next to Bill.

"Shut up, Spike!" Curt flashed Anthony a hard look as if he was letting out some kind of secret. "Henry wasn't a sniper."

"No, I didn't serve with Han … Henry. I was Airborne." Bill raised his drink to salute Hank.

Hank took up his drink and issued a toast. "Rangers lead the way!"

"So what were you guys doin', swappin' army stories?"

"Just shooting the breeze." Hank eyed Bill from over his drink.

"Good! Here's to bullshit! I'm full of it!" Curt drained the rest of his drink, letting it spill out from the corners of his mouth before he slammed the empty cup to the table. Curt's boisterous shouting seemed to be the cue all the strippers were waiting for, and in no time at all they were swarmed by every kind of exotic beauty. Bill tore his eyes away from the half-naked women to make eye contact with Hank. Hank simply shrugged his shoulders with a drunken smile and turned away to whisper into the ear of the voluptuous woman in his lap.

Bill wasn't sure why nearly every girl in the club now seemed to be at their booth, but when he saw Curt laying lines of cocaine on the glass table it all made sense. He tried to make eyes with Hank but was blocked by the girls. A fluttering of panic welled in his guts, and his eyes quickly scanned the room. He couldn't believe the man was laying it out so openly. He wanted to excuse himself and get away from the table, but a girl was already lowering herself into his lap.

Bill slumped into the couch and buried himself under the smooth flesh. The swirl of alcohol and body lotion eased his anxieties while conversation turned to a mixture of shouts and whispers. Hours sped by in a blur of debauchery until the club closed its doors and the four men found themselves on the street.

Curt and Anthony disappeared into a cab, and Hank convinced Bill they were within walking distance of his home. After a few missed steps and near falls, Bill found himself under Hank's shoulder, half carrying him down the sidewalk. They made it to within a half block from Hank's front door, but Bill couldn't wait any longer. He complained to Hank for the last time and then broke away to urinate behind a phone booth.

From the corner of his eye he could see Hank trying to steady himself by resting all of his weight on his prosthetic. He shifted and hopped around, spinning stationary circles around his mechanical leg. He would have continued to spin, never fully catching his balance, but something across the street caught his attention. Hank's eyes focused on the object and his body followed, righting itself and stopping the drunken spiral.

"Those sons a bitches!" Hank stiffened with rage. His fists balled up and pumped the air as he began to march across the street. He threw himself into every step until he was running.

At first Bill was only idly curious why Hank had taken off. At the moment, he was more concerned with finishing his business undisturbed. As he peered through the fog, he noticed what Hank had seen. Two shadowy figures were crouched at the base of one of the row houses, spray-painting the walls in quick, fluid motions. Their backs were turned, and they didn't see Hank coming.

Bill was still in midstream. He would ordinarily have called out to stop Hank, but he was stuck by sudden modesty. He remained silent for a moment, feeling the guilty surge of pleasure that accompanied what was sure to be a one-sided spectacle.

One of the vandals finally heard the mechanical clanking of Hank's sprint and jumped to his feet. From where Bill stood, they appeared to be two black teenagers, identically dressed in dark, hooded sweatshirts. For an instant, Bill feared the worst and thought he might actually get shot while his pants were down, but Hank quickly closed the distance. Bill stood numb, pants undone, as the scene played out in front of him.

The first teenager slapped his friend on the back and bolted, but it was too late. As he tried to streak down the sidewalk, Hank closed in and shot the foot of his prosthetic leg in front of him. The frightened teen swerved to avoid being tripped, and Hank grabbed hold of the loose sweatshirt hood. Hank pivoted and jerked, swinging the hapless boy by his neck. The kid's feet left the ground, and Hank whipped him through the air. The second teen tried to slip past the melee at precisely the wrong moment; his now horizontal friend spun around and crashed into him, sending both of them to the pavement.

Before they were able to draw their first, shocked breaths, Hank was on them. The one he had thrown through the air now scrambled to get away. Hank's fist jabbed him in the stomach, and boy doubled over with a sickening grunt.

Bill forgot his modesty and began running across the street, awkwardly tugging on his zipper. "Hank! No!"

Hank never acknowledged him. He simply turned and made a grab for the second teen. The boy moved with lightening quickness, narrowly slipping past Hank's fists. Hank tried to stop him with a powerful side kick, but his prosthetic buckled beneath him. The kid took the opportunity to streak down the street, making it twenty yards before turning to look back. His partner was still doubled over in pain, attempting to stagger off and looking ready to vomit at any moment. Hank followed only inches behind, preparing to collar him again.

Bill locked eyes with the kid down the street. He'd stopped running, and bounced nervously for a second before launching himself back down the sidewalk to help his friend.

Hank's back was turned to the second kid as he spun the other boy around by the collar. The youth squirmed wildly, almost coming out of his hooded sweatshirt. Hank held him fast with one hand and reared back with the other to deliver a backhand blow. He was about to strike when the boy's friend leaped at Hank's back, sending everyone crashing to the pavement. The speed of the boy's attack was impressive. The kid had covered twice the distance in half the time it took Bill to cross the street.

Hank was the first back on his feet, although he seemed to struggle with his balance. Bill could see the fury in his face. Hank crouched low and leaped for the boy who had knocked him down. He landed near him like a wild animal, using one hand on the ground to steady himself as he swept the boy's legs out from under him with the other hand. The boy landed hard on his back, his head smacking the concrete with a thud. The second boy jumped to his feet and sprinted madly down the sidewalk. Hank didn't give him a second glance.

"Dude! What are you doing?" Bill slowed his approach, carefully maintaining a respectful distance from Hank.

"These little cocksuckers have been taggin' my building for months!" Hank's chest heaved, and muscles rippled on his arms. The veins on his neck protruded grotesquely as he raged and frothed. "I'm gonna teach this bastard a lesson!" Hank strode over to where the boys had been painting and grabbed an abandon paint can.

"Dude, what are you going to do with that? Come on, Hank, he's had enough."

"I've had enough! This stupid little punk is gonna pay!"

The boy lay motionless for a moment, and then feebly tried to get up. Hank was on him in a flash. He sat on the boy's chest, pinning his arms with his knees.

"You like to paint, huh? Well me too!" Hank growled into the boy's face and then let the paint fly from the can in thick, red streams. The boy bucked and kicked but was unable to escape.

"He's just a kid! Come on, Hank, stop!"

Paint pooled in the boy's eye sockets and streamed down his face. The shimmering paint made a gory contrast against his dark skin and was strangely highlighted when it ran down a white, powderlike patch of skin on his neck. Lights began popping on in the buildings around them. Hank jumped to his feet, shaking the can in his fist. The boy's hands immediately wiped at his eyes and he blew clouds of paint from his nostrils. Hank bent over him again, this time reaching down to grab the boy's wrists, and began painting the palms of his hands.

"There, caught you red-handed! If I ever see you around here again, I'll whip your sorry little ass!" Hank stepped away, booting the boy once more for good measure.

Sleep was coming; it weighed on Hank's eyelids and slowed his steps as he crossed the street to his block. After hours of insomnia, his hands still stained red with paint, he had forced himself from his bed and began walking the streets aimlessly. The fresh air did little to clear his thoughts, but the long walk readied his body for sleep.

The streets around him were empty. People and their cars seemed to be idling down for the evening. Noise from the neighborhood seemed to fade into the back of his mind until the quiet peace ended abruptly with sharp crack of gunfire.

A car's motor accelerated behind him as the loud blasts continued. With only a fleeting, cringing hesitation, Hank instinctively crouched low before turning to see a large, purple sedan charging toward him. Kneeling on the sidewalk to the right of the oncoming car, Hank could see the snub barrel of an automatic pistol spouting flame at him from the passenger window. A sawed-off shotgun was being pushed through the window behind it.

Hank could hear the whip of bullets tearing through the air over his head. Miniature explosions and ricochets leaped off the concrete. The empty sidewalk was void of any cover, and he found himself trapped in a deadly field of fire. In a matter of seconds, the car would be virtually on top of him and firing at point-blank range.

Hank's Delta instincts took charge, quickly calculating the risks and pushing his body into motion. He jumped from the curb and took two great strides onto the open street directly in front of the fast-approaching car. Bullets ripped up the walls and pavement where he had stood a half second before. A blast of shotgun spray whistled through the air. He could see the automatic pistol firing wildly from the passenger window, but now that he was directly in front of the car, it no longer had an angle on him. Hank readied himself for the oncoming pain, pinning his hopes on a last-second dive: his mind's eye could see no hope for an escape.

The car charged on, speeding up to run him down. His mind quickly counted the shadows of four heads through the windshield, and he saw another gun being thrust through the rear driver's-side window. His hopes for a last-second leap to safety evaporated as he realized that even if he was able to dodge the bullets and the speeding car, they could easily slow down and finish him off as he scrambled away. There was only one move left, and staring at the grill of the speeding car made him realize that the odds were hopelessly stacked against him.

The car quickly closed the distance as bullets flew by on both sides. Charged with the endorphins of impending death, Hank played his last and only gambit. He waved his arms at the gunmen, urging them to come on, pounding his chest in defiant bravado.

The car's engine roared with a sudden stomp of the accelerator, accepting his challenge.

His soldier's will urged him into his next steps, knowing that any hesitation meant death. The first step felt as if his feet were made of iron and totally unprepared for the suicidal sprint, but his body soon fell into the motion of his charge, and his feet gained speed beneath him. The car surged, shifting gears and aligning Hank dead center in its path.

Now just feet away, Hank could see white teeth standing out against the screaming black faces of the attackers. The timing of his next steps meant life or death. He knew he had to make the leap from his left leg, or he would end up in the grill. Hank planted his left foot firmly on the ground and leaped for all he was worth.

His prosthetic foot smashed into the hood, sliding along the smooth metal until it caught the base of the windshield. The jarring impact propelled Hank even further into the air, knocking his legs behind him in a pain-filled instant and spinning him violently out of control.

Hank narrowly avoided the blunt impact of the windshield and came crashing down on the roof, crumpling the metal and battering the air from his chest. The car sped out from under him as he bounced off the roof and rolled down the trunk, finally slamming onto the pavement. Tumbling violently, his sprawling limbs flung out of control, he rolled along the street several more times before unfolding to a stop. His entire body was griped by paralyzing pain, and his chest was unable to draw a breath, but he was conscious. He was alive. He looked up to see taillights disappearing around the corner, and then his face collapsed back onto the pavement.

A woman in the distance screamed for help. Hank began the conscious, methodical check of his body's vital systems. He was able to think, see, and hear, and was able to move his limbs. He was conscious of an all-over, biting pain, and he felt the dampness of urine soaking his pants, but the ache was nothing compared to the life-shattering pain of a bullet wound.

A clearly panic-stricken man came rushing to his side, shouting into his cell phone. Hank could see the man's house slippers as he shuffled up close to his face. "He's moving ... yes ... he's moving! He's hurt real bad! Send someone right away ... oh, man."

Hank slowly raised his head to stare into the man's horrified face.

"You're going to be okay ... don't move, buddy!" The man gestured for him to be still. "Yes, he's breathing! He's trying to get up! What do I do?" He continued to plead into his cell phone, too afraid to touch him. "Is he shot? I dunno ... I see blood, and his legs are ... oh man." Repulsed, the man looked away from Hank's bloodied body to stare into his eyes. "Hey, buddy, did you get shot?"

It took a moment before he was able to answer. Pain showered his body like a thousand knife wounds, but the exquisite shock that followed a bullet tearing through his body was not there. "No."

Moving his arms forward to push himself up, Hank saw that his elbows were torn open and grotesquely swollen. Great strips of flesh had been torn from his arms, and the white cartilage of his knuckles was exposed under the torn flaps of skin.

"Don't move, man! You're busted up pretty bad ... help's on the way! Hang on ... don't get up!" The man bent down and placed a hand on his shoulder to stop him.

"I'm all right." Hank swatted the man's hand away, almost falling back onto his face in the process. He pushed himself into a kneeling position and saw that the man's attention was focused behind him. He was staring with horror at his legs. Slowly, painfully, Hank turned to see what held the man in such spellbinding horror.

His prosthetic leg was bent away from his body at an excruciating angle. His plastic foot was missing.

Blinding anger suddenly coursed through his veins, momentarily pushing away the pain. The high-tech prosthetic was virtually irreplaceable, and he didn't like the idea of losing the same leg twice in one lifetime. "Did anyone ... see those ... motherfuckers?" Hank tried to shout, yelling to no one in particular as he pushed himself onto his left leg. As he stood erect, he felt the full measure of the pain in his chest, hips, and back. The gathering crowd simply gaped at him in amazement.

The man with the phone stepped in to steady him, but Hank quickly pushed him away. "Did anyone see them?" Hank pleaded with the drop-jawed crowd, but none of them said a word. Disgusted, Hank spat frothy blood onto the street and bent over to unstrap the shattered remnants of his prosthetic.

A groan came from the bystanders as Hank removed the rest of his mangled leg and tucked it under his arm. He scanned the street, saw his foot lying in the gutter down the block, and began hopping toward it. After collecting his severed foot, Hank eased himself down to the curb and inspected the damage. It was total.

Sirens echoed off the buildings. The people on the block kept their distance. Even the man with the phone retreated to his doorstep to await the squad cars. When the police came screeching up to the scene, Hank found himself staring down the barrel of their semi-automatics.

"Drop it! Put your hands in the air!" Two officers shouted at him from behind their weapons.

Hank lifted his foot to show them he wasn't armed but refused to put his hands in the air. Half an hour passed before he was able to convince the ambulance crew that he wasn't going to any hospital, then he spent another half hour answering questions for the police. They finally escorted him to his front door, and he hopped inside, battered and exhausted. He rummaged through the kitchen trashcan to find the half-empty pill bottles he'd thrown away that morning and swallowed a handful of pills without any water.

He caught only a glimpse of her, just the trail of her flowing white robes disappearing down the alleyway, but he was sure it was her. The flawless brilliance of her robes stood out in stark contrast to the reddish gray world around them. Feeling an equal measure of elation and dread at finding her, something deep inside him reassured him that he would kill the Witch this time.

All was silent in this surreal world. The communication earpiece was silent in his ear. His comrades' voices and the chaotic sounds of combat were gone. He knew they were all dead. It was just the two of them, and this time he was the hunter. The names of his brothers lingered in his mind, but he urged himself on, left foot, then right, knowing that each step put him that much closer to his prey.

Again, a flash of white robes passed in front of him. He brought his heavy rifle to bear, tracking the target as she stopped in the open. The deadly weapon in his hands felt unfamiliar. He couldn't find the sights on the strange rifle, but he saw the hideous black Witch pointing and laughing at him from the other end of the weapon. Squeezing the trigger sent an enormous volley of fire hurling toward her.

She disappeared behind the flame and smoke, emerging untouched, still screaming her curses at him. Her gigantic Afro quivered with laughter above her rutted face as she mocked and taunted him. She clutched her AK-47 in one hand while thrashing the air with the other.

Frustrated, Hank examined the weapon in his hands. Wisps of gray smoke eked from several of the redundant looking barrels. The weapon's design didn't make any sense. The Witch arched her head back with wild laughter at his frustration. Once again she screamed her curses, taunting: he could never kill her.

Hank thrust the rifle at her again and let loose another torrent of fire. Untouched by the explosions all around her, her brilliant white robes unmarred by the clouds of red dust, the Witch danced through the withering fire to the cover of a mud-brick building.

Furious, desperate to prove that he could bury her, Hank pursued her around the corner. The way ahead of him was clear, but an ear-shattering shriek pierced him from behind. He turned with a snap to see her standing behind him with her AK-47 aimed at his face. Up close, she was more hideous than ever. The black-lipped rim of her mouth was now a cavernous demonic laceration exposing horrible, jagged teeth. Her eyes were two enormous white orbs seated deep in her coal black skin.

Hank shouldered his rifle and took aim, peering down the myriad of redundant shafts, unable to find the sights. There was no need. He was so close.

The Witch continued her shrill curses without firing at him, and Hank realized that she had no fear of him or his weapon.

Hank slammed the heavy rifle to the ground, shattering it. The next instant, his .45 caliber pistol was leveled at her face.

Bam! Bam! Bam! Hank squeezed off three quick rounds.

The shots found their mark. The first punched a hole right between her eyes, snapping her foul head back; the next shot struck her in the chest, knocking her off her feet and sending her crashing to her back.

Hank covered her with his pistol as he moved in. She lay motionless, blood splattered across her pure white robes. As he stepped closer, he saw a bundle of cloth roll out from beneath her robes. The tattered linen bundle oozed crimson gore. The cloth and the Witch's own robes now appeared dingy and tattered, with none of the brilliance of before. Through the thin veil of cloth, Hank could make out the battered form of an infant's head. A bloody bullet hole was burned through the cloth.

An unbearable wave of nausea assaulted him as he counted off shots in his mind. He shifted his eyes from the dead infant to the cavernous hole in the Witch's forehead. Blood covered her face, obscuring her features. The wound had transformed her, making her appear more pathetic than terrifying, but the image of her corpse continued to change as he stared down at her.

The hideous and ancient Witch began to morph and change. Her dark skin softened with the appearance of youth. Her toothy, demonic grin shrank to a mouth of more human proportions, and the wild, bushy Afro atop her head receded to a normal height. She now looked like any other Somalian youth on the battlefield, not the weathered, black harpy he had hunted.

As blood flowed down her face, Hank's attention was caught by the contrast of the red blood against a white patch of skin on her neck. The mark was somehow familiar to him. Stepping back, Hank could see that the bundle next to the Witch was no longer the body of an infant, but a paint-stained bag of spray cans.

His eyes traveled back to the body. Nothing about it resembled the Witch anymore. It was a boy. A loud humming vibration shook the body. Then another buzzing vibration, this one shooting panic through Hank's body. He spotted a pager buzzing on the waistband of the boy's jeans. Its red light flashed between hums. Each successive vibration grew louder and louder, finally giving way to the sound of a ringing telephone.

Pain enveloped Hank as he jerked back to consciousness. The phone rang persistently on the nightstand. His elbow clung to the sheets as he reached for it, tearing away the scabs and sending fresh blood onto the floor.

"Hello?" Hank croaked.

"Hank?" Bill's voice sounded confused, as if he had dialed the wrong number.

"Yeah. What's up, Billy?" Each breath shot fire through Hank's chest.

"Dude, are you all right? You sound like shit."

"Yeah ..."

"What happened? You were supposed to call. Did you forget?" Bill sounded irritated.

"No. Something happened last night ... yesterday really." Hank cringed, suppressing a cough he was sure would tear him in two. "Hey, can you come over? I ... I need your help with something?"

"What's going on? Are you okay?"

"I'm fine ... can you come over or what?"

"Yeah ... Yeah, I can come over. What happened?"

"Some punk-ass gangbangers tried to punch my ticket last night." Hank said flatly.

"*What?*"

"Drive-by ... they missed me, though." Hank didn't feel like he'd been missed by anything.

"A drive-by?!"

"Just come over, would ya? I'll explain everything when you get here."

"All right, Hank—A drive-by? Really? Someone shot at you?"

"Yeah. See you when you get here." Hank hung up the phone, and a wave of anger enveloped him as he shot a sideways glance toward his shattered prosthetic and the crutches he'd dug out of his closet. He hated the crutches. He hated the idea of being footless. He damned himself for getting caught up in something so asinine.

A hot shower only seemed to fan his fury. He scrubbed at the black road rash where skin had been, and wild fantasies of retribution played out in his mind. The thought of being gunned down by lowlife hoodrats infuriated him to the point that it was all he could think of.

He was still seething when Bill arrived an hour later. Bill sat stunned as Hank recounted what had happened.

"Do you think it was those kids from the other night?"

"I know it was."

"Did you tell the cops?"

"No. It all happened so fast. I didn't really put it all together until this morning."

"Are you going to call them?"

"And what, tell them I think it was some kids I beat up for tagging my building?"

"Why not? It might help find them."

"I doubt it … and what if it did? They're probably too young to prosecute. And what if I have to testify against them? One of their buddies can still come after me. No way. There are better ways to handle trash like this."

Bill looked worried. "So what are you going to do?"

"I need your help." Hank absentmindedly picked at the abrasions on his elbow.

"I don't want to be part of anything crazy."

"Relax. Trust me. I'm not going to do anything foolish. I need you to help me remember some things, that's all. Maybe I can find a way to track these little bastards down."

"What do you mean, remember stuff? What don't you remember?" Bill looked puzzled.

"If I knew that, I wouldn't need your help, Billy." Hank smirked. "Like I said, it all happened so fast. There wasn't a lot of time to pick out details. I need you to assist me in a Rapid Sequence Induction."

"Rapid what?"

"Hypnotism. I need you to hypnotize me."

"You want me to hypnotize you?"

"Yeah. It's easy. But I can't do it myself."

"Easy?" Bill said warily.

"Yeah, I'm … preprogrammed. It's a technique we used in Delta." Hank stopped picking his elbow and directed his attention to Bill. "We were trained to perform all kinds of reconnaissance. We were taught to take mental snapshots, if you will. Scan an area just for an instant, and make a mental picture of the moment. In times of stress, endorphins kick in and trigger the same response. The technique allows you to take in information and store it without possessing it, which frees up your mind to focus on fighting for your ass or running for your life. I need you to help me read those snapshots. Maybe I saw something."

"But I don't know anything about hypnotism."

"Just do what I tell you, and read from this list. It'll be easy. This is a strobe light." Hank held up a pocket watch-sized, flip-up strobe light. The Special Forces emblem was engraved on the chrome lid. "It's all about rapid eye movements—you know, REM sleep. Set the right speed, and it's all ready to go. It takes a few minutes to get ready. You put me under, and then you can turn it off.

Just close it like this." Hank snapped the round box closed and the strobe mechanism folded into the case.

"And you're going to be under?"

"Only to a certain extent ... not too deep, I hope."

"What do mean, hope? I don't want to go poking around inside anybody's head—especially not yours."

"Relax." Hank placed a small tape recorder on the table and handed Bill a list of questions. "Give me a couple of minutes to get ready, and then read off the sheet. Just address me as Hank, no last names or anything, and say we are going to enter Zeta-One Sleep-State Debriefing. Just like that, no funny voices or anything. Then count backward from thirty, speaking softer and softer until you get to zero. I should be under by then. Ask me if I'm in Zeta-One Sleep State. I should say, 'yes sir'." Hank opened the strobe and set it on the table. White light flashed over him in rapid intervals, eerily animating the movements of his arms as he got into position.

"Yes, sir," Bill repeated.

"Then you can start reading off the list. When you're finished, just say, 'thank you very much, Hank, the debriefing is over. It's time to wake up.'"

"You'll be asleep?"

"No, just relaxed, highly suggestible—you know, *hypnotized.*"

"Will you remember?"

"Probably. We'll see. I've never tried this at home before. I was always debriefed by my commanders ... I suppose I only remembered what they wanted me to."

Bill picked up the list of questions, squinting his eyes in the darkness. Only the outline of his form was visible past the fading background. Hank felt the sedating affect of the sequence wash over him as it always had in the past. He felt good, sleepy; he wondered why he hadn't tried hypnotism to ease his insomnia before now.

"I got to admit—I'm skeptical." Bill said from the darkness.

"You've never seen anyone hypnotized before?" Hank asked dully.

"At shows and stuff, but I thought it took a long time to prep people. And the hypnotist always knew what he was doing. I don't know what I'm doing."

"I've been put under countless times. It's all programming ... that's what the people do before they come on stage. Programming." Hank said wearily. He wished Bill would shut up so he could get some sleep.

"What's stopping someone from putting you under any time?"

"You have to be willing; you're still conscious. You can't make me do anything I really don't want to do. Now shut up, will ya? I need to relax."

"All right, let's do it." Hank could see a smile broaden on Bill's face in between flashes. "All I have to do is say, 'thank you, and it's time to wake up'?"

"Thank you very much, Hank, the debriefing is over. It's time to wake up." Hank yawned. "The phrasing is important, for some reason. I wrote it all down."

Bill held the sheet of paper under the light to better read the questions, and Hank drifted easily into the silence. After a moment, Bill lit a cigarette. Smoke trailed in front of the pulsing light, further filling Hank's view and blocking out his surroundings. The scent of the smoke itself took him back to a time when his commanders would smoke during similar debriefings, then even further back to memories of his father and the smell of cheap scotch and Marlboros.

Bill watched Hank's eyes bang closed as his chin fell to his chest. He took another long pull from his cigarette and wondered what other secret protocols the elite Delta teams practiced. His imagination spun with wild stories of assassinations and subterfuge as he prepared to read from the list Hank had prepared for him. "Hank, we are going to enter a Zeta-One Sleep-State Debriefing."

"Yes sir." Hank's eyes remained closed as he spoke into his chest.

Bill began counting backward from thirty trying to sound serious and solemn, gradually softening his voice into silence as he reached zero. "Hank, are you in Zeta-One Sleep State?"

"Yes, sir." Hank's eyes snapped open, startling Bill for an instant. Hank's left foot remained planted on the floor while he brought the scarred white flesh of his bare stump up to cross over his knee. The gnarled flesh glowed grotesquely under the flashing white light.

Bill leaned forward, clicking the strobe closed and pitching the room into relative darkness. He couldn't believe he was actually sitting here, doing this, but if nothing else, it proved beyond a doubt that Hank truly trusted him. "Hank, today is Sunday. Yesterday you were attacked and struck by a car. Do you remember?"

"Yes, sir."

"Did you see the car that struck you?"

"Yes, sir."

"Can you describe it for me?"

"Sir, yes sir, it was an older model Chevy sedan. Faded purple, with black material on the roof. The occupants were armed with two automatic pistols and a sawed-off pump-action shotgun. The sedan was lowered, with an urban profile."

"Did you see a purple sedan as you walked down Becker Street before the attack?"

"No, sir. My head was down. I felt extremely fatigued, sir. There is something wrong with my foot. Walking is difficult. I was limping. Sir, I may have been injured, sir." Hank eyes stared right through Bill from across the table, never looking down toward his mangled stump.

Bill returned to the list. "Had you ever seen that car before?"

"No, sir."

"Did you recognize any of the men inside the car?"

"No, sir."

"Describe them."

"Four black youths, late teens or early twenties. The two men in front were wearing red bandanas over their heads. Sir, my view was obstructed by the windshield. They were firing at me. They closed in from twenty meters, at speed. There was no time, sir."

"Did you see the car's license plate?"

"There was no front plate, sir. They struck me head-on. I had to leap over the front end."

"Did you see the car as it fled?"

"Yes sir."

"You saw the rear end of the car?"

"Yes, sir. I saw it turn right onto Kelly Street."

"Was there a plate on the back?"

"Yes, sir. There was a chrome, linked-chain license plate frame."

"What were the numbers on the license plate?"

"2ZTL808. California plates, sir."

"Well, that answers that." Bill scanned the rest of the questions designed to identify the vehicle before putting the list down.

"Hank, did any of the youths in the car look at all familiar to you?" Bill followed his impulses and went off-script.

"No, sir."

"Do you remember a confrontation you had with two youths on the street outside your house?" Bill eyed the tape recorder and bit his lip.

"Yes, sir."

"Did any of the men in the car that attacked you look like the ones you fought with?"

"Sir, they were black, sir."

Bill dashed out his cigarette and continued. "Going back to the street fight—why did you attack them?"

"Sir?" Hank appeared puzzled, but eager to answer the question. "Why, sir?"

"Why did you engage them? Why did you spray paint in his face?" Bill shifted uncomfortably.

"Sir, I caught them vandalizing property. They're bad guys. They're parasites." Hank spoke flatly, the look on his face hardening.

"Did you want to punish them?"

"Yes, sir."

"Why is it up to you to punish them?"

"Because I am not afraid of them. I hate them."

"How would you punish the men who tried to kill you?"

The puzzled expression disappeared from Hank's face, as if the answer were easy. "Eliminate them, sir. Eliminate them, their gang, and their entire families. Eliminate the threat. Draw no quarter, sir."

The brutal statement rattled Bill. He looked at the recorder on the desk and contemplated stopping it, erasing his interjections and Hank's response, but he didn't want dig himself any deeper. He picked up the sheet and read the last line exactly. "All right, thank you very much Hank, the debriefing is over. It's time to wake up."

At those words, Hank's posture changed, and he wearily rubbed his eyes. Bill slid another cigarette into his mouth and collapsed back into his chair feeling the anxiety of guilt creep up on him. He knew that Hank coveted his privacy and wore his sacred, self-righteous credo like a badge of honor; he would not appreciate Bill's going off-script to probe the conviction behind those beliefs.

"How do you feel?" Bill clinched the cigarette in his teeth, lighting it as he spoke.

"Tired." Hank yawned. "I haven't been getting enough sleep."

"Do you remember anything?"

"Nah, not really, the last thing I remember is you lighting a cigarette."

"That was two smokes ago. I don't usually smoke so much …" Bill was cut short as Hank reached out and grabbed the recorder, pressing the stop button with his thumb. "I can tell you what you said." Bill continued, hoping Hank might disregard the tape.

"Anything useful?" Hank asked.

"You nailed the license plate number."

"Really?" Hank began rewinding the tape. "That'll do."

"Purple Chevy ragtop. License plate number"—Bill leaned over to read the number he had scribble on the sheet—"2ZTL808."

"Anything else?"

"What else do you need? Now you can hand it over to the cops."

"Are you crazy? I can handle this." The recorder clicked to a stop. Hank pressed play and set the recorder down on the table. "It's always weird to hear yourself on tape. Man, I sound really out of it."

"You were under, all right." Bill inhaled deeply, his mouth dry from chain-smoking.

"They never let us listen to the interviews back in Ops," Hank said as he listened to himself addressing Bill as "sir." "Don't get used to it, Billy." A strange smile appeared on Hank's face as he interlaced his fingers and listened to the recording.

"What?"

"Me calling you sir. If I'm gonna work for you, you oughtta call *me* sir. I don't care what bullshit rank they gave you—I'm still older than you." Hank winked as his smile broadened.

"So you've made a decision? I thought you were gonna give me a hard time." Bill suddenly cheered at the thought of Hank's enlistment.

"Two hundred K a year is nothing to turn your nose up at." Hank's eyes widened playfully.

"Two hundred? I thought I said one and a half." Bill scrambled to recall the drunken conversation from the previous night.

"With expenses."

"Dude, you're taking advantage of me because you could kick my ass." Bill laughed.

"Come on, Billy, I'm cheap at twice that price."

"Done." Bill reached out and took Hank's hand.

"Done."

"You're right—cheap at twice the price. I woulda gone up to three hundred if it came down to money. But I thought I could sell you on the mission."

"Shhh," Hank hissed under his breath, motioning for quiet. He was just about to identify the license plate number on the recording. "Amazing, just like looking at a snapshot. I musta rolled, I dunno, maybe ten times before I came to a stop." Hank closed his eyes, deep in thought. "I can't even picture it now … just tail lights, that's all I remember."

"I've never …" Bill hoped to cover the next question coming from the recorder, but Hank cut him short with a wave of his hand. His focus was trained on the recorder now. A scowl grew on his face, and Bill was glad he'd stopped prying when he did.

The recording ended with the words *no quarter* uttered coolly by Hank.

Hank reached forward and hit stop. "What's with the improvisation, Billy?"

"I'm sorry, Hank … I didn't mean … I didn't mean to get too personal. I didn't know it was so black-and-white for you."

"I would think twice before playing amateur psychologist with me, Billy." Hank looked up to engage Bill's eyes. "If you want to know something, just ask me. I'll always tell you the hard truth, no matter what." Bill knew that blunt honesty was Hank's most virtuous flaw. His biting piety kept most people at a distance, but Bill was fascinated by his capacity for raw honesty and his resolve to suffer its consequences. "For instance, don't fuck around like this again, or I will definitely fuck you up." There was dead seriousness beneath Hank's odd smile.

"Yes, sir," Bill said, deprecating himself before Hank.

"Good." Hank nodded his agreement. "I like the sound of that."

Hank's mood was clearly improving, now that a germ of a plan was cooking. "So, what now? What are you going to do?"

"I've got the plates; this should be easy." Hank stood up and grabbed a cane. He hopped across the room and sat at his desk, turning on the computer.

"You know the cops could pin these guys with attempted murder, assault with a deadly weapon. Serious charges."

"Screw the cops. I can't start fresh with this kinda crap hangin' over my head." The computer came to life, and Hank's hands started to dance over the keys.

"What are you planning?"

"Rule number one on a job like this; keep it simple. First, we gotta find these guys, find out who they are and what we're dealing with." Hank patted the computer affectionately. "That should be easy with this baby."

"Are you going to hack into the DMV or something?"

"No, not the DMV. That's a hard nut to crack, lots of security, very sophisticated. But pick some hick, backwater police department somewhere, let's say Placerville, for instance"—the screen now showed the Placerville Police dispatch terminal—"and you have them run the plates, like this." Hank clicked the digits into place.

"Here we go … a seventy-six Chevy El Dorado. Registered to … Wow, what a pig." The driver's license photo came up showing an extremely fat, black woman. "Yikes, Shawanda James, born September of seventy-five. Five foot two and 210 pounds. Definitely not our guy … Oakland address, but she doesn't seem like the low-rider type." Hank's fingers flew over the keys. "Let's see who else has been drivin' Shawanda's ride. Just cross-reference the plates with any moving violations … and here we go, this looks better. Shawn James, born in seventy-nine, which makes him seventeen. San Francisco address: 530009 Caver Ave, apartment 148. I bet that's not far from here."

"Hunter's point. I know that street, bad area." Bill said, still amazed at how quickly Hank worked.

"Look, here he is." The face of a young black kid appeared in the corner of the screen.

Bill read the screen. "No priors."

"That's not him." Hank said staring at the screen. "That's the kid who got away, not the one I painted."

"You're sure?"

"The one I'm after had a white birthmark on his neck. He's the leader. He's the one that came back for his friend. He's the one with enough balls to come after me. This is the kid that pissed his pants and ran away." Hank traced a finger over the screen. "Shawn James."

"So what now?"

"If I can find Shawn, I can find his buddy. I'll figure out what to do when I find a way to get a hold of him. But first I'll have to do a little shopping."

"Shopping? For what?"

"First thing I need is a new leg. Can't go hunting gangbangers on crutches." Hank smiled. "I'll make up the rest as I go along. Don't look so worried. Trust me—let me clean a little house, and I'll be ready to work for you and the Iconoclasts."

"You're no good to me if you get caught up in any bullshit. This isn't the army. You can go to prison for killing people around here."

"Pay attention, Billy. I know I can't go off and kill them—even if that *is* what I want to do. This is all about retribution. If I take them out, their buddies will come after me. I need to squash this. Trust me. I know what I'm doing."

Hank felt pathetic and small. Under normal circumstances, he wouldn't have been able to stand it. People looked down on him—if they bothered to look his way at all. Most avoided looking at him, as if he didn't exist, and tonight he was counting on going unnoticed. Tonight he was just some white kid in a wheel-chair trying to act black.

He thought the disguise made him look stupid—but to him, all wannabe rap stars looked stupid. He prepped himself by watching two tedious hours of MTV rap videos and tried to emulate the look the best he could. At thirty years old, he was playing the role of a teenaged "wigger": what the kids on the street called a "white nigger," a wannabe. He dressed himself in an oversized 49ers jersey with gold chains draped low over his neck. Fake tattoos covered his wrists, and he'd used magnetic jewelry to make it look as if he'd pierced his nose and lower lip. Shaving his head down to a coarse stubble and capping a tooth with gold completed the look, but he knew the wheelchair was the most critical element of his costume. No one ever challenges the guy in the chair.

Hank was satisfied with the job he'd done—considering that he'd only hatched his plan hours before, when he learned that Shawn and his brother Shug were planning on sneaking off to a club that night. Shug was the one he was after. He'd seen the powder white birthmark on his neck while he spied out their home, and he had been able to listen in while Shug talked with a girlfriend on the phone. From that one golden conversation, he was able to get Shug's cell phone number, and the germ of a plan blossomed.

Until that moment, he had struggled for a way to take down his target. The boys were never alone. They spent their days at school, and all four siblings shared a single bed at night. The project complex where they lived was crowded with eyes and ears; that meant they would have to be taken out in plain view, but doing that was never easy or simple. The difficulty he faced sank home with the realization that he was working completely alone for the first time, but at the same moment an excitement he'd almost forgotten caused his knees to tremble. The surge of feelings grew as he plotted and planned—but even as he shadowed his prey, his enthusiasm was tempered by the fact that he was only hunting teen-aged punks not even out of high school.

Hank turned the corner and let the rims of his wheelchair slide beneath his hands as the sidewalk sloped downhill. The lights of the club were visible down the block, and he paused long enough to tuck his left leg up under his butt—leaving two empty pant-legs to dangle in front of him. A heavy bass beat throbbed from behind the closed doors of the club. The front windows were painted black, and graffiti covered the walls. The sign which had once spelled out *Bombastic* was unlit, the neon tubes broken and hanging. Three men stood in the darkness at the front door. The glow from their cigarettes moved like fireflies as they talked.

Their conversation stopped as Hank rolled close. His eyes met theirs briefly and he thrust his chin upward in a show of youthful bravado. He wheeled to a stop, tilting and spinning his chair to face the clique of young black men.

"Waz up, Little Cuz?" The man nearest the door stepped aside, holding the door open with a smile.

"Juss chillin'." Hank nodded his thanks, surprised by the lack of hostility, and then pulled himself backward through the threshold.

The three men seemed impressed by how easily he maneuvered his chair and waited for him to clear the door before they resumed their conversation.

The decibel level quadrupled once Hank was through the doors. The beat throbbed in his ears, and a wave of humidity enveloped him as he turned his chair to face the club. The stale stench of body odor and malt liquor assaulted his nose. Cigarette smoke filled the air, hiding the ceiling from view. To his relief, the club was already packed with people. No one seemed to notice him wheeling in.

Hank flipped his ball cap forward to cover his face as he pushed his way toward a dark, empty corner of the room. Besides the multicolored lights spinning and flashing over the DJ's stand, the club only had two other working lights. One was over the front door, and another was at the opposite end of the club, presumably leading to the bathrooms. Hank faded easily into the darkness, scanning the crowd as he disappeared.

His was the only white face in the club, if it could be called at club at all. Most of the customers were teenagers, bobbing their heads to the beat. Some were older, rough-looking men, but all seemed focused on the music and grinding against each other. Everyone had a bottle in hand. The floor stuck to his wheels as he rolled across. The bar was abandoned, functioning as a bench for young women and empty, discarded bottles. A few people tried to mingle at the back of the club, shouting over the music, and others strutted about exchanging hard looks or high fives. Hank knew he needed to find a spot that led to the back door, so he began to push himself through the crowd toward the dimly lit hallway.

Most people failed to see him until he was practically bumping into their legs. When they did see him, they were quick to make way and allowed him to part the crowds on his way to the back of the club. His own head found the beat and began nodding in unison with the rest of the crowd. Keeping his head down, careful to not make any eye contact he eventually made his way through the throng of gyrating, overexposed flesh.

He wheeled up to the hallway leading to the restrooms, where he could see the dim glow of an exit light down the hall. Looking past the restroom doors, Hank caught sight of a third door and pushed down the hallway. The door was what he'd been looking for: an unlocked storage closet. Hank pushed the door open and rolled inside, closing the door behind him.

Once inside, he pulled his aching leg out from underneath him and climbed out of the chair. His hands found the switch on the wall and he clicked on the overhead lights. The narrow closet was packed with folding chairs and tables, but there was plenty of room; it was perfect. Hank checked his watch. Every piece of his plan was falling into place beautifully. It would be another hour before the boys were due to sneak out of their Grandma's place.

Hank pushed his chair aside and retrieved a small wooden wedge from the kitbag hidden beneath the wheelchair. He slipped the wedge under the door, jamming it closed. With that done, Hank pulled the rest of the bag from the chair and got himself ready. He transformed the empty closet into a virtual wolf spider's lair and began patiently waiting for the arrival of his prey.

A full hour passed in hiding before Hank kicked loose the wedge to open the door a crack. Although a perfect spot for an ambush, the closet had a poor view of the main floor. There was little chance of spotting either of the boys in the growing crowd. Hank contemplated changing his plans: putting the disguise back on, getting back into the wheelchair, and doing some quick reconnaissance to see if they had arrived, but in the end patience won out. He closed the door and waited.

Twenty more minutes passed, plenty of time to sneak out and walk the two blocks, before Hank pulled the phone from his pocket and punched in Shug's number.

Shug answered, shouting into the phone. "Waz up?" Hank could tell he was inside the club by the music echoing in the background.

"Good boy." Hank murmured under his breath.

"Hello ... Hello?" Shug's deep voice boomed into the phone.

"Yo! Where you at?" Hank spoke quietly into the phone.

"Yo, I can't hear ya man. Who dis?"

"Where you at, G?" Hank spoke a little louder, giving his best attempt at speaking Ebonics.

"Huh? I'm at da Bomb. Where you at?"

"Huuh?" Hank repeated.

"I'm at da club, nigga! Who dis?"

"Yo, dawg, it's me … Bin tryin' to find you, Shug. I got two hot bitches out here wit some chronic bud! Where you at?"

"Who is this?"

"Meet me out back, Shug. Come on, I got two chicks wit me and one wants to get with you!

"Back where? At da Bomb? Who …"

"Yeah man! I'm outside right now! I can't hear you, dawg … jus get out here … bitches got some weed …"

"I can't hear you good … you're at da Bomb, out in the back?"

"Meet me out back, nigga … and come by yourself, only got two chicks out here man … yo, yo, waz your name, shorty?" Hank pretended to chat with the imaginary girls.

"Hold on, hold on. I can't hear ya. I'll be right there!" Shug sounded like he was laughing on the other end of the line.

Hank slipped the phone into his pocket and readied himself at the door. He recognized Shug immediately as he rounded the corner and bounced down the hall. The white birthmark was clearly visible on the side of his neck. He appeared relaxed, unconcerned, maybe even a little excited as he headed into the trap. Most importantly, he was alone.

Shug's shadow passed over the crack of light, and Hank flung the door open, pulling the startled teen inside with ease. Hank's left hand grabbed Shug by the throat, thumb pressed against his larynx, stifling the scream. His right hand gripped Shug's wrist like a vice as he pulled him into the room and slammed him against the wall, kicking the door closed behind them. Once closed in darkness, Hank released Shug's throat and delivered a wicked blow to his stomach, pounding the vulnerable area just below the ribs. The punch knocked the wind out of the boy, keeping him from crying out. Hank's hand quickly returned to Shug's throat, now thrusting a silencer-capped pistol into his neck. "Don't fuckin' move! Don't make a sound!" Hank growled, pressing his weight against Shug and tightening the grip on his wrist.

A painful grimace froze on Shug's face. His eyes shut tight against the fear and pain. He tried to recover his breath in sharp, hesitant gasps, but Hank didn't give him time to recover. He swung him around, slamming him into the opposite wall, still pushing the deadly steel into his neck, and then pushed him backward until he fell into the waiting wheelchair.

While Shug was desperately trying to catch his breath and make some sense out of his situation, Hank secured his wrists to the arms of the wheelchair with thick plastic zip ties. Once his hands were tightly secure, Hank turned for an instant to slam the wooden wedge under the door. When he turned back around, Shug was about to speak. Hank stopped him short, jamming his pistol into his mouth and rattling the cruel steel against his teeth.

"Remember me, bitch?" Spittle flew from Hank's mouth as he snarled. His eyes burned into Shug's. He could tell by the astonished, panicked look in his eyes that the boy recognized him. "Now listen up, dumbshit! If you want to live, keep your mouth shut and do exactly what I say. If not, say something right now, and I'll open up your head right here and walk away. Okay?" Hank pulled the barrel from Shug's mouth, leveling it against his forehead. Shug stared up at him in horror without making a sound.

"Good." Hank slipped the elongated barrel of the pistol into his waistband and reached into his bag to retrieve more zip ties. "We've got some unfinished business to handle, Sugar." Hank knelt in front of the wheelchair, looking up into Shug's frightened face. He grabbed the metal leg supports beneath the wheelchair and extended the right side. He forcefully pulled Shug's leg into the metal support and secured it with zip ties.

"Nice shoes." Hank slipped the boy's shoe from his foot, examining it mockingly. "How does a broke-ass hoodrat afford such nice shoes? These gotta cost a hundred bucks." He pressed the sole of the sneaker against the sole of the black, steel-toed boot he wore, then threw it across the room. "You won't be needing this." He then secured Shug's left foot to the chair's footrest without extending the support.

With all four limbs tightly secured to the wheelchair Hank relieved Shug of his wallet and cell phone, then shifted his attention back to the open kit bag. Hank had already made his costume change and now wore the dark blue uniform of an ambulance driver, complete with polished, military-style boots. The golden tooth, tattoos, and jewelry were all gone. A blue ball cap with "Paramedic" written on the front was pulled low over his brow.

Hank stood towering over the boy strapped into the chair and flexed his muscles under the tight uniform shirt. He removed Shug's ID from his wallet and held it up to his face. "Now, Tyrell: I know you're wondering what the fuck is going on … so I'll spell it out for you." Hank leaned in close enough to smell Shug's breath. He tossed his ID and wallet into the kitbag and pulled out a small parcel wrapped in plastic. "Me and you got some shit to finish. If you want to make it out alive, you do exactly what I say. Got it?"

Shug slowly nodded his head as sweat trickled down his face.

"Good. You and I are going to roll out of here and take care of our business." Hank unwrapped the plastic package and slowly tore a small handful of the clay-like material from the bundle. He kneaded the material in his palms as he turned to face Shug, making sure the teenager could see every move.

"This is plastique, C-4 plastic explosive." He molded the C-4 into an oblong pancake and slapped it onto Shug's exposed ankle. "This Play-Doh here can blow a fist-sized hole in a car door. Just think what that would do to your scrawny little chicken leg." Hank then pulled two small wire leads from the bag and inserted them into the C-4 on Shug's ankle.

"And this is a wireless detonator." Hank held up a small black box resembling a small car alarm in his hand. "Once it's active, like this"—Hank unlocked the mechanism on the box—"All I have to do is let go of this right here." Hank demonstrated, holding the button firmly between his thumb and forefinger. "And bye-bye foot! No more basketball, no more fancy shoes, no more fuckin' leg. So if you want to gamble and not do what you're told, that's what you're betting with. Okay?"

With his free hand he tore off another smaller chunk of C-4, rolling it between his fingers. He mashed the small ball of clay onto the back of folding table leaning against the wall. With out any explanation, he pushed a miniature blackjack firecracker into the chewing gum-sized wad of material. "Just in case you're as dumb as you look, and you think I'm full of shit ..." Hank flicked open his Special Forces lighter and struck the flame to the fuse. There was a brief puff of smoke from the fuse and then a sudden crack as the C-4 exploded, sending the table crashing to the floor with a quarter-sized hole blown through the wood laminate. The loud crack echoed off the walls, and a light, acrid smoke filled the tiny room.

"Now, like I said, you and I are going to wheel right out of here. If anybody asks, you broke your ankle." Hank pulled an ice pack from the bag and placed it over the C-4 on his ankle. He then began to wrap an ace bandage around his foot to keep the explosive in place. "I'm taking you to the hospital." Hank slipped an emergency radio onto his belt and fixed an ID badge to his shirt. "Got it?"

"Now, you may be thinkin' 'this fuckin' nut is gonna kill me.' And you might be right, who knows? After all, you did try to kill me; it would only be fair. You might even think it's better to be alive and legless than tortured and killed by some nut job." Once again, Hank tore a piece of C-4 from the package, dramatically kneading it between his thumb and forefinger. "Well, let me make up your mind for you." Hank inserted another pair of wire detonators and calmly dropped the minibomb into Shug's lap. "Don't know about you, but I'd rather be dead than dickless."

Hank turned his attention away from Shug for an instant, leaving him to gape at the bomb in his lap. He collected his gear, stuffing it into the bag, and then set the bag in the young man's lap—covering the emasculating explosive. He handed the trigger device to Shug, thrusting it into his trembling fist, until Shug was holding the button. "Here. Hold this for a minute, would ya?"

"That's it, you're doing great ... just don't let go of that button—whatever you do!" Hank smiled, straightening his uniform. "All right, let's go." He kicked the wedge away and pulled the door open. The loud, pulsating rhythms of the dance floor broke the spellbinding psychodrama of the closet, and Hank pushed Shug down the hall into the club.

A few partygoers jeered the horrified kid as they quickly passed through the dance floor. Hank shrugged off their abuse with a smile. Everything was going according to plan, and a long-forgotten elation welled in his chest. The feeling grew as he pushed his captive out of the club and down the sidewalk to a waiting minibus. The most difficult phase of his plan was finished, and he'd done it all on his own.

Shug finally broke his silence as they approached the rented lift-assist van. "Yo, man, where you takin' me?"

"Aye! You've done a good job keeping your mouth shut so far, don't make me kill you!" Hank spun the chair around, trying hard to conceal his smile. He unlocked the door and lowered the hydraulic lift. Mustering a final hard look, he pulled the chair onto the ramp and raised Shug into the empty van.

The landmarks of the city Shug knew so well vanished as they crossed the bridge into the unknown. The simple task of holding down a button on a small plastic box was becoming excruciatingly difficult. The muscles of Shug's thumb began to cramp under the persistent strain. He knew a single slip could change his life forever. Time wore on inexorably slow under the stress. The maniac behind the wheel never said a word and only occasionally glared back at him through the rearview mirror.

He had somehow kept himself from breaking down into tears, but he felt them close to the surface behind his eyes. There was nothing he could say or do. He knew the crazed white man could kill him any time, and he realized that his survival depended on doing what he was told. Before long, the brightly lit freeway signs gave way to the darkness of open roads and rolling, tree-covered hills.

As he focused his effort on his grip, he couldn't help dwelling on the circumstances that had landed him here. Once again, Shawn's big mouth and stupid ideas had gotten him in trouble, possibly for the last time. He'd never known trouble like this before. He'd never even heard of someone being kidnapped and strapped with explosives. This was a threat on a different level all together, well beyond the savagery of his ordinary world. The specter of death had never been as frightening as the man behind the wheel.

Darkness fell over the van as it passed into a densely wooded area, renewing Shug's sense of dread. Wild, terrifying images assaulted his thoughts. He imagined himself chained to one of those trees, slowly tortured to death where no one could hear him scream. Shug choked back the tears and swallowed his fear, not wanting to show how frightened he was. He forced himself to stare straight ahead, hoping to see a road sign through the glow of the headlights ... something, anything.

He caught the man's eyes looking back in the rearview. He fought the urge to look away and stared back at him. He was hoping the man would break his silence, even if only to taunt him. He was desperate for some kind of dialogue, an explanation, anything, but the man's eyes returned to the road without a word.

After another twenty minutes of agonizing silence, the van turned off the road into the parking lot of a Super 8 motel. Parking around back, the man casually stepped out of the driver's seat and pulled off his ambulance uniform shirt. He strode unevenly around the front of the van, as if his legs were asleep after the long drive. By this time Shug's own legs were heavy with pain from being lashed in place. The plastic cords pinning him to the chair dug into his wrists. The small mound of clay sat heavily in his lap. The doors of the minibus swung open and the man stood smiling demonically at him.

"Go ahead, you can ask: 'are we there yet?'" The man's smile was cold and humorless. "Better not, you've done a good job keepin' you're mouth shut. Keep it up." The man leaned forward to lower the hydraulic lift. As Shug was lowered to the ground, the man reached out and carefully took the trigger box out of his clenched fist.

"I'll take that. Thanks for holding on to it … bet your hand is tired." He kept the button pressed under his thumb as he unlocked the chair and pulled him off the lift. Shug forced open his clenched hand. His fingers were unable to straighten. The man took up position behind him and began pushing him toward the rooms. They stopped in front of room number seven. Shug looked on in horror as the man unlocked the door and pushed it open.

The opening door slid over some plastic covering the floor with a distinctive hissing, chilling Shug to the core with the realization of what it meant. The man's hand quickly reached in and flicked on the lights, confirming Shug's fears. The motel room was covered floor to ceiling with thick plastic sheets. Duct tape lined the floor, sealing the seams together. Shug's hair stood on end. Repulsive shock kept him from screaming out. He looked away as he was pushed into the room. The wheels of the chair made a sickening crackle as they rolled over the plastic.

As the man turned to shut the door behind them, Shug suddenly leaped in his chair. His arms and legs were pinned, but he was able to thrust his hips forward, tipping the chair to one side and sending the clay bomb out of his lap onto the floor. The man quickly turned and caught the chair before it tumbled over.

"Where are you going?"

"What are you gonna do to me?"

"That's up to you, so stop screwing around." The man walked in front of him, bent over, and picked up the minibomb Shug had tossed from his lap. "Don't forget about your leg." The man pulled the wires from the clump of explosive, slipping them into his pocket and throwing the clay into an open bag on the floor. "I would think twice about sacrificing your leg for something stupid." The man lifted his leg, setting his boot down hard on Shug's knee. He rolled up the dark uniform pant-leg to reveal a pink plastic shaft entering his boot. "It's a real bitch."

Shug stared at the fake leg, amazed and confused. The potential reality of losing his leg sank home hard. He couldn't believe the man was still alive after they had run him down. Shug could see the bruising around his eyes and the scabs covering his knuckles.

"Think about this next time you feel like doing something stupid." The man slid his pant-leg down and stepped away. He turned, holding the trigger in one hand and Shug's ID in the other. "So tell me, Tyrell—you must think you're some kinda bad-ass, huh?" He stood tall and imposing, looking down at him from over his thick chest. He was frightening and intense; his eyes bore into Shug's. "Why do they call you Shug, anyway?"

Shug remained silent.

"Go on, spit it out!" The man barked.

"'Cuz of my birthmark. My G-ma always called me Sugar." Shug tried not to let his naturally deep voice crack with emotion, but the thought of never seeing his grandmother or his cousins again won over and his voice broke.

"That's real sweet, Sugar. That would be your grandma Shirley, right? And the rest of your family—little Trevor, Latisha, ... your brother Shawn—they all call you Shug, too?"

Shug's eyes widened at hearing the names of his family. Unable to answer, tears welling in his eyes, he turned away from the menacing figure.

"What about your parents? Where are they?" The crazed man continued, lowering his voice and speaking calmly.

"Mom's dead," Shug said flatly, looking up at the man once more.

"What about your father?"

"I dunno ... dead too. Why you askin' me all dis?"

"I need to impress something on you right away, so you have an understanding of your situation. Then we can figure out what to do with you. I need you to know that I know where your family lives, everyone you care about. I've seen where you live, and I can take them out anytime. I could have easily taken you out already. I could have popped you and your brother Shawn while you were on your way to school today. I want you to know that their lives hang on the decisions you make tonight." The man pulled the pistol from his waistband and set it on the table.

"You and I have some shit to work out, young man. Your life is in my hands now. It has been ever since you decided to put my life in your hands. You tried to kill me, and now that I have you, it's time for some justice. No one can help you. No one knows where you are. No one will be able to hear you scream. I've rented all of these rooms tonight, and the manager is drunk off his ass. It's just you and me ... and for you, it's life or death. You understand me?"

"Yes, sir." Shug said glumly, fearing that his life was already forfeit. The only possible reward was a promise of safety for his family.

"Good. You're a lot smarter than you look. It'll be a lot easier if you just answer my questions the first time I ask them. I don't want to wait, either. I want the truth right away. It'll save you a lot of pain." The man stepped closer, bending over him. "Were you driving the car when you decided to gun me down?"

"No, I wasn't drivin'. I was in da back."

"Behind the driver?"

"Yeah."

"Behind the driver? You had an automatic pistol. Where did you get it?"

A quiver shot through Shug's muscles. "One of the guys gave it to me."

"One of your gang?"

"Yeah."

"What gang?"

"Umm …"

"Tell me now!" The man pounded the table with a fist.

"South Point Crips … Bad-Siders."

"What's his name?"

"Huh?"

"The guy who gave you the gun."

"He's just a …"

"Name, motherfucker! I ain't playin' around here! I ain't no fuckin' cop! I'll chop off a finger for every fuckin' name you know! Got it?"

"Snapps … everyone calls him Snapps. I think his real name's Isaac."

"And where was Isaac sitting?"

"He was in the front."

"With the Tech-nine?"

Shug nodded his head. "Uh-huh."

"What about your brother Shawn? Where was he?"

"He's not my brother. He's my cousin."

"Did he have the shotgun?"

Shug hesitated, not wanting to implicate his cousin.

"He was driving!" The man shouted. "I knew I didn't like that little son of a bitch!" He pounded his fist against the arm of the chair. "He was with you the night I caught you tagging houses, right?"

"Yeah."

"Remember what I told you that night? After I tagged your face? What did I tell you?"

"You said if you saw me around you would kick my ass." Shug stumbled over the words.

"That's right. Now, if I was willing to kick your ass over a little spray paint, what do you think I'm gonna do to you for trying to kill me? You've got a big fuckin' problem. You fucked with the wrong guy!" The veins in the man's neck bulged as he yelled. "Tell me, what do you think I'm gonna do to you for that?"

"Kill me?" Shug cringed.

"That's not good enough. If I kill you, I'm gonna have to kill everyone: Shawn, Isaac … quick—who was the kid with the shotgun? What's his name?"

"Marcus."

"Marcus too. I won't take a chance on any more bullshit from you or your low-life crew. I'll kill the whole fucking South Point clique if I have to! You have no idea who you've pissed off! I'm a fuckin' pit bull off its leash!" The man was raging. His face was terrifying.

"Who are you?"

"That's the question, isn't it? Who am I, and what am I gonna do? You didn't stop to ask yourself that when you were out vandalizing my home, did you? Hell, you probably didn't ask yourself that when you borrowed Shawanda's car and got your punk-ass friends to gun me down. But now you're asking yourself, aren't you? 'Who *is* this guy who kicked my butt and painted my face as red as a baboon's ass? Who's this guy who bounces off cars and dodges bullets? Who is this nut who kidnaps me in front of all my friends … and what's he gonna *do* with me?'" The man looked as if he was going to lose it, but he slowly unclenched his fists and drew a deep breath. "Well, let me tell you something … it doesn't matter who I am. The only thing that matters is who you are. Your life depends on what kind of man you are."

"Can this thing still go off?" Shug glanced down to his extended right leg and the bomb on his ankle.

"You bet your ass, and it's stayin' on until we settle things. I've seen you move. You're fast. You knocked me off my feet that night. I haven't forgotten. I noticed that you came back for Shawn, too. You took a beating for him, I haven't forgotten that either."

"I just don't want it to go off by accident."

"I don't blame you. I'm glad that you know this is for real. I didn't want to have to pound that fact into you. You're a smart kid, so listen up." The man backed away and crossed his arms over his chest. "Tell me why you decided to escalate things between us. Why did you try to kill me? I want the truth, no bullshit." The man's tone was more curious than violent now.

"Honestly, man, it wasn't my idea," Shug pleaded truthfully.

"Now look, I've learned that when some jackass says 'honestly, man,' they're full of shit. Tell me the truth: I'm not buying 'it's not my fault.'"

"It's true. I didn't want to do it. I barely know Snapps and Marcus. They're older, hardcore. Shawn talked all the shit! He's the one that got me in trouble the other night when you painted my face, and he's the one who started sayin' shit about payin' you back. I jus wanted to forget about it."

"But you went along anyway. You shot at me. Tell me why you were willing to pull the trigger."

"I dunno … I was angry." Shug searched for something better to say, but the man's eyes made the long silence painful. Careful not to justify his actions with simple anger, Shug chose his next words carefully. "I had to defend my self-respect. The other guys would think I was pussy. I didn't think we would actually find you, you know what I mean? I thought it was all a bunch of talk. I never even shot a gun before."

"So you thought you'd be a man, do what you had to do? Is that it?"

"I didn't think it would happen …"

"You mean you didn't think I'd survive to come after you!"

"No man, even after I saw the guns … I didn't really think that we would go through with it!"

"But you were ready to take a man's life? What's stopping me from taking your life right now? What's your life mean to anyone? You're nothing, a parasite. Why are you worth sparing? You're probably just going to leech your way through life, knock up a couple of bitches, get yourself strung out on crack and end up in jail. Tell me why I shouldn't chop you up and flush you down the toilet."

"I'm not going out like that! I ain't no crackhead—I don't do that shit. I'm no leech!"

"You gotta job?"

"No … I'm still in school. But I'll get a job … I'll work."

"Selling crack ain't a job."

"You jus' think that I'm some hoodrat! I ain't like that. I got brains."

"Life is worthless to someone like you. You only have a future making others miserable. What are you going to do for humanity? Nothing!"

"You're just saying that because I'm black and live in the projects. You think you already know everything about me!" Shug raised his voice tentatively.

"I know you're a punk son of a bitch who's willing to take a life so he can look like a man. You'll never be a real man. You're doomed to be a punk forever."

"Jus because I ain't got shit doesn't mean I'm not worth anything! I'm a good person." Shug pleaded.

"You're a good person ... you just have enemies like anyone else, is that it?" The man raised his eyebrows.

"You have to fight when you live in the projects. It's more than just respect ... you can't show any weakness."

"Are you afraid to die?"

"Yeah. But I'm more afraid about that stuff you said about my family. I don't want them getting hurt because of me."

The man straightened, reflecting on what he had said. Shug sat in awkward silence while the man contemplated the ceiling. He appeared deep in thought, and Shug didn't know what to do or say next.

Finally the man looked down at him and broke the silent tension. "You believe in God?"

Shug hesitated, not sure how to answer.

"Tell the truth, do you believe there's a God? Yes or no? Do you believe in an afterlife?"

Shug had a feeling that his life hinged on his next answer. "Yeah. I believe in God."

"So where do you think you're headed, heaven or hell?"

"I dunno ... for me, hell's right here in the projects."

"You don't know what hell is. You don't know shit! You should be crying for your life, boy ... but you just sit there like this is some kinda movie. You don't know what pain is. If you truly knew pain, you'd be begging me to end it for you right now."

"I will beg ... beg you to let me go. I don't wanna fuck wit you, man. I can forget everything! That's what you want, right? I can forget about it all!"

"Forget? That's awfully big of you ... maybe you want me to forgive you, is that it? Good old Christian forgiveness? You think God will forgive you for wasting your life? You think this will all go away because you're sorry?"

"I am sorry, real sorry. If you forgive me, I promise I'll change ... I'll make up for it."

"You're begging the wrong guy. I don't believe in forgiveness or your God! I think they're both bullshit!"

"What? I thought ..."

"You thought I wasn't gonna kill you because I'm a good Christian? Big mistake. I'd be doing the world a favor by killing you."

"Then why did you ask me if I believed in God? Why do you care?"

"You wanna know what I think? I think you don't really know what you believe. I think you only know what you were told to believe. You don't really think about it … you probably don't think much, period. Your God is purely imaginary, a fantasy with nothing to do with the real world. A fantasy with a made-up God, made-up souls and made-up concepts like forgiveness, sin, and redemption. There is no Devil to blame for your actions. There is no eternal life … it's all a fantasy to soothe the fears of the weak-minded. I think you don't know shit and probably never will."

The man's rant left Shug speechless. Once again, the fear that he might actually kill him sank in hard.

"But I'll tell you something: you're a lot smarter than I guessed. You were right about one thing. I do want you to forget. You obviously understand that if I wanted to kill you, you'd be dead by now. I want to squash this thing between us. I need to end it, but I'm not about to settle so unevenly. So the question remains: what to do?"

"You can let me go … I swear … you'll never see me again!"

"Why? Why should I just let you go? What are you worth?"

"I'm only seventeen! I want to live!"

"What life could you possibly have? You know the truth … there's nothing out there for you. You're a hoodrat."

"I can get out of the projects! I can get a job."

"You're just a punk-ass gangbanger. How are you gonna get out of the hood?"

"I'm no gangbanger. I don't really hang out wit them. I jus go to school. I wanna learn. I want to get out of all that. I wanna get my G-ma out too."

"And when you're done with school, what then?"

"I dunno … find a job. Stay out of trouble. I'm not the way you think."

"You're just saying what you think I want to hear. You're the one misjudging me. I don't wanna hear your bullshit. I wanna hear the one good reason why I shouldn't do the world a favor. I wanna hear it from the kid who had the balls to run back and take an ass-whippin' for his loudmouthed cousin. I wanna hear it from the kid who's sittin' here facing death in the eyes and who is still somehow keepin' it together. I see quality in you. You have more potential than you realize. I wanna know if you have any idea what that quality is. Do you?" There was something entirely different in the man's tone now, something just as unsettling, as if his fate was about to be decided.

"I don't know …"

"What are you willing to do to save yourself?"

"I'll do whatever it takes."

"A job ain't going to get you out of the hood. How far are you willing to go? Or are you just tryin' to save your ass and feed me a line of crap?"

"I'm not bullshitting you … you were right. I don't really believe in God, but I want to live. I don't want to die."

"Why not? What have you got to live for?"

"I dunno … because life is good … because I want to do things with my life."

The man took in Shug's words in total silence and didn't speak for several agonizing seconds. He stood up and walked away as if debating with himself. When he turned to face Shug, his expression had changed and his voice was softer. He no longer flexed his muscles at him. "How far are you willing to go to make a life for yourself—a real life?"

"What can I do? I don't know what to say."

"Are you willing to commit yourself to something? Something long-term?"

"Like what, the army?"

"Yeah, let's say the army … somewhere totally removed from your life here. Would you do it?"

"Is that who you're with?"

"No. Just hypothetically. For the sake of argument, know what I mean? Would you cut your ties here for the chance at a better life?"

"Yeah. I would do it … hypothetically." Shug repeated the phrase carefully, hoping he'd gotten it right.

"Do you think you could stick with it? Do you think you could handle a white guy giving you orders?"

"Yeah. If it was worth it."

"Wouldn't it be worth it just to get out of here? Look around you." The man gestured to the ominous, plastic-covered room.

"Yeah. It would be worth it."

"Smart kid."

"So what do you want me to do, join the army or something?"

"It's not a bad idea, but I was thinking of something else." The man reached into his pocket and pulled out a cruel looking blade."

"Whatcha gonna do wit dat?"

"Relax, Sugar." The man bent over his legs and cut the cords holding them to the chair. He unwrapped the bandage from his ankle and pulled the wires from the clay bomb. "I have something else in mind for you." The man cut the rest of the plastic cords holding his limbs to the chair and put the knife back into his pocket. "I know you're not going to do anything stupid, right? I know that if I squash this beef between us right now, that will be the end of it, right?"

"Thank you, thank you … Yes it will. I don't wanna mess around wit you."

"In that case, let's end things properly." The man reached out with his right hand as if he wanted to shake on it. "I apologize for whipping your ass and painting your face. I shouldn't have done it."

Shocked, Shug didn't know what to do, but his hand reached out and took the man's hand.

"And … and I have a very interesting proposition for you."

Dumbfounded, Shug stared at him for several long seconds.

"This is the part where you say 'thank you very much, and I'm terribly sorry for painting your house, gunning you down in the street, and running you over with my car … what possible proposition could you have for an undeserving punk like me?'"

Shug was still unable to speak as he stared up at the man's odd, sarcastic smile.

"Well, I'm glad you asked. You see, you may live in a world of shit, and you may not see a future for yourself, but I see a blank slate. I intended to bring you here to scare the shit out of you, but I think you figured that out already. But now that I'm looking at you, I can sense other possibilities. I see potential. If you were willing to completely leave your life behind, I would be willing to put you to work for me."

For an instant, Shug was convinced that the man was completely insane, but he wasn't about to show it.

"I could train you. Give you an education … a real education. I could pay you enough to move your whole family out of the hood. I'm not crazy. This is the real deal. I could use a kid like you. Like I said, you're a blank slate and you've got no strings holding you down." The man released Shug's hand and crossed his arms over his chest. "If not … Hunter's point is waiting for you."

Paradigm I
Chapter 2

Bamian, Afghanistan. March 7, 2001

Blinding, late-afternoon sunlight beamed off the van's windows, causing the disheveled figure to block the glare with a raised arm. The dirt-stained van sat unattended between two abandoned mud-brick hovels. Waves of heat danced over the metal roof as the man paused to scan the empty buildings. He stooped low, using his rifle as a crutch as he bent down to look under the van itself. Convinced he was alone, the man moved again, now stepping with purpose, closing the remaining distance to the van.

He stopped at the rear doors, pulling the red and white-checkered turban away from his ears and cocking his head to probe the silence. He waited for several more seconds before slipping the key into the lock and opening the doors. Strips of cloth were wrapped around the charms and brass coins decorating his rifle, keeping the tiny bells quiet and the sun's rays off the polished coins. The broken, shabby-looking figure now moved with careful diligence as he slid his long-barreled Jezail rifle along the floor. He moved silently as he pulled himself inside the van. He could not afford to be seen entering the white man's vehicle.

Closing the doors felt like locking himself inside a furnace. The good air had been cooked away, making it difficult to catch his breath. He pulled the veil of his turban from him face and mopped at the sweat with the sleeve of his woolen cloak. There was no time to climb out of his heavy robe, and there would be no relief from the heat if he did; he would simply have to suffer as he always did. He propped himself up on his elbows, pulling his wooden peg of a leg beneath him before pushing himself up onto the seat.

He caught sight of his reflection in a dust-covered monitor and immediately stopped to wipe away the dust. He grinned at himself. He stroked and pulled at his long, scraggly beard, and a roguish smile curled on his lips. He turned to look at himself in profile, examining his features, and made faces one only makes when alone with a mirror. A black swath of cloth cut across his brow, serving as an eye patch. He leaned forward, lifting the patch from his eye and flipping it back onto his brow. He gave himself a final wink and turned his attention to the communication terminal.

He checked the time on a digital display. The window on the satellite connection was closing fast. He had taken too much time sneaking his way to the van, but caution was a must. He had already made three attempts at getting to the satellite phone this week, but each time he had been stymied by some loitering Afghani. His frustration was tempered by the knowledge that he was working in a region where most people would never make a single phone call in their entire lives.

After an interval of watching the green lights flicker—and some nail biting— Hank finally heard the tones that signaled a positive connection. He quickly scanned the windows and pressed the phone to his ear.

"Congressman Thomas's office. How may I direct your call?" The secretary's voice was distant and interrupted by static, but her pleasant, familiar tone still came through.

"Hi, Linda." Hank struggled to find his natural voice. "Is Willy in?"

"Is that you, Henry? I can barely hear you. Where …" Static silenced her for an instant.

"Yeah, it's me. I'm …" Hank funneled his voice into the phone with his hands in an attempt to keep quiet, but Linda cut him short.

"Sounds like you're in a tin can. Where are you?"

"I'm on satellite." The full-second delay began playing havoc with the conversation. "Can you hear me?"

"Yes. I can hear you. Mr. Kemp is on another line. I'll get him for you."

Hank covered the receiver and peered through the dust-covered windows.

"Hello, Hank … Hello, are you …" Bill shouted on the other end of the line as if he were on speakerphone.

"Yo, Billy, it's me. Can you hear me?" Hank fought his instinct to whisper and spoke loud and clear into the receiver.

"Yeah, buddy, I can hear you. Where are you?"

"Afghanistan."

"Good work. You made it. Can you talk?"

"Yeah. Listen, I've only got a few minutes. I've been trying to reach you for days."

"How are things going over there? What can I do for you?"

"Ahh … This whole scheme is a bunch of crap. I don't know what the Icons are doing out here. And that French fag is giving my asshole a headache!"

"Le Boux?"

"Yeah, he still thinks he's running the show."

"Well, the film crew is his … and the operation came through his people in the Islam Group. You were brought in as a ringer. Remember?"

"But I'm the one responsible for keeping the skin on our backs!"

"And you have the authority when it comes to any security issues."

"And Shug is with me! La Boux has got nothing on him."

"Shug will always do what you tell him."

"Ah, forget it."

"How is Shug's French coming along?" Bill casually changed the subject.

"Terrible. But who's gonna know out here?

"He's come a long way in five years. I can't believe what you've done with him."

"Yeah, he's a champ. Hey, listen up Billy, La Boux is not my problem. I can handle him. This whole thing is wrapping up. They were gonna blow the Buddhas yesterday, but there was too much snow on the ground."

"Snow?"

"Yeah, it's colder than a witch's tit."

"I thought it was hot as hell over there."

"Oh, it is. And I've got to hop around wearing these damn pajamas. I haven't bathed in weeks. This beard feels like a scab on my face, and it's starting to smell … which is just fine, because now I smell just like the locals." Hank checked his reflection in the window and examined his fake beard methodically. He didn't trust the ruse. He was sure it would be his undoing on this mission. He wished he'd had the time to grow his own. "What day is it in the real world, anyway? I've lost track."

"It's Tuesday, March second." Bill sounded as if he was stifling a yawn.

"That means I've been on this bullshit assignment for twenty-seven days now." Hank groaned and scratched his constantly itching scalp.

"I wish I could see you now."

"Careful what you wish for, Billy. This whole operation is crazy." Hank lowered his voice and peered through the windows. "Everyone knows the Taliban are screwed up, but nobody cares. Especially the Muslims. Do you think they care if every shrine from here to Yemen gets blown up?"

"It's not about the Muslims, Hank."

"Then what's it for? I don't get it."

"You've got to think about the bigger picture."

Hank had heard the big picture lecture before. The Icons thought big but moved slow. "I don't care. This will be over in a few days. And I can ditch this frickin' rat they glued to my face and come home." Hank fought to keep his voice low. "I wanna talk about operation Devil's Peak. How's it going?"

Bill was silent for a long moment, then he cleared his throat. "I'm afraid we're still working within Case Yellow."

"Did you even speak to them?"

"No. Not yet. I've sent out some feelers, and they tell me the Icon leadership doesn't want to get involved with anything so ... so radical." Bill let out a deep sigh while Hank fumed in silence. "Hank, you know they're strictly top-down when it comes to things like this."

"Are you getting cold feet on me, Billy? Dammit! I should've never agreed to come out here." Hank pounded the console. "There's gonna be hell to pay if I find out I was sent out here just to get me out of the way."

"Slow down, Hank. I'm still with you. Nobody is trying to get you out of the way. This is your *job*. This is why you get paid the big bucks."

Hank laughed, despite his bitterness.

"I'm still with you on Devil's Peak, too. In fact, I've pulled in a few of the players we've been looking for."

"Really? Who?"

"We can't really talk on satellite. I'll tell you when you get home."

"You're right. I'm sorry. I'm just a little wound up out here. There's a lot of risk and very little gain in this operation. And I'm the one taking all the risks."

"You'll be all right." Bill switched to his congressman's baby-kissing tone. "You're the best we've got."

"You don't get it. It's another world out here, Billy. It's worse than I expected. Half the country is starving, and the Taliban are killing people like it's going out of style."

"Is it really that bad?"

"They publicly gang-raped a girl because her brother made eyes at the wrong woman. That's their idea of Islamic justice."

"Are you kidding?"

"No, it happened. The court got away with it because the girl's family wasn't Pashtun. And that was ordered by the local Imams, their holy leaders ... you don't want to meet the real bad guys."

"And you don't know why you're over there? These guys are the reason the Iconoclasts exist."

"I know why I'm here. I just don't think documenting this kind of crap is going to do any good. Muslims don't care about Muslims killing other Muslims; they only care about infidels killing Muslims."

"Well, that remains to be seen. So what do I tell the higher-ups about the mission when they ask? Is everything on track?"

"Like I said, there have been a lot of delays. If these guys don't pull their heads out of their asses soon, I'm gonna lose my cool and blow the fucking things up myself!"

"Are they going to go through with it? I've heard there's a lot of pressure coming from Pakistan. They've threatened this stunt before, right?"

"Oh, it's gonna' happen all right. They've been working like crazy to take these things down before someone stops them. It's been a pretty amateur attempt so far, but a couple of days ago they brought in some demolitions experts from somewhere. Arabs. But before then, it was like fifty moneys fucking a football."

"Arabs, huh? You think they're al-Qaeda?"

"I wouldn't doubt it. They're thick as thieves with the Taliban. They flew in on helicopters a couple days back. They wired the statues up pretty good. They'll blow."

"You're sure?"

"Does the Pope wear funny hats? The head dude, a guy named Mullah Omar ordered the slaughter of a hundred cows today. He said it was to make up for the embarrassing delays. You should have seen them. They were shooting the Buddhas with tanks and artillery. They shot rockets, grenades, whatever they had. I kept hoping they would get fed up and launch a suicide attack. But they only chipped away at them."

"These Buddhas sound tough."

"Been around for almost two thousand years. They've managed to blow off the arms and legs of the big one, and they blew the tits off the small one, but the bodies are still intact."

"Buddha has tits? I know he's fat, but tits?"

"They're not like the big roly-poly Buddhas you see in a Chinese restaurant. These go back to the days of Alexander the Great. These Buddhas wear togas. The smaller one is female. She's called the King Mother."

"I can't believe they're going to destroy them."

"Yeah, everybody's all concerned about a couple of artifacts, but no one cares if the people are starving and killing each other wholesale. I don't give a rat's ass about the Buddhas! We're supposed to be Iconoclasts, right? Doesn't this whole operation seem a bit ironic?"

"It does." Bill sucked in air between his teeth. "But you can find the irony in anything. The Icons believe in this operation. When do you think you'll be back?"

"The charges are set. They'll finish the job tomorrow. It'll take a few days to get out of Bamian and probably another couple of weeks to get to France via Iran and Turkey."

"You've put in some overtime on this one."

"I'm not looking forward to two more weeks in the van with that smelly pig La Boux. The boys in the tower are gonna have to cut me a big fat check for this one."

"Are you getting the footage we need?"

"Yeah. Tomorrow will be the big show, but Shug and I have got some stuff that'll blow your mind."

"What kind of stuff?"

"I've been taking Shug out at night with a hidden camera. You'll die when you see what we bring back."

"Like what?"

"Let's just say that young boys are good for more than fetching water around here. Pretty soon they'll have to wear those frickin' burqas, too."

"You're kidding."

"Just wait till you see the tapes."

"Hank, none of that was on the agenda."

"Shut up, Billy, you're startin' to sound like that poof Le Boux."

"Just be careful. Remember, we're there for the Buddhas."

"They want footage of a religious state gone mad. They wanna see Muslims going nuts. That's what I'm doing. But I'm not putting my balls on the chopping block for footage CNN can get."

"I don't want you taking any unnecessary risks."

"I can handle it."

"Just be careful, Hank."

"Don't worry about me. Just keep an eye on Devil's Peak for me. I have a couple of ideas I want to bounce off of you."

"Like what?"

"Well, the key to this operation is going to be controlling the spin once this thing hits the press. How do you feel about bringing in some of the cable network players? The boys in the tower wouldn't have to know about it if we did it right."

"Who are you talking about?" Bill sounded suddenly tense.

"Well, I don't want to mention any names, but I was thinking of some of the executive types at the network."

"What? We've never talked about any of those people!"

"We're talking about them now, aren't we?

"Where are you getting this stuff?"

"Relax, Billy."

"Don't 'relax, Billy' me! We're already hanging out on a limb on this one. We agreed to keep this small. You can't just call up members you're not even supposed to know about! If anyone from the tower caught onto us, we could ..." The transmission cut out abruptly and red lights flashed over the board. The call was dropped: the satellite window had closed for the day.

"Fuck you!" Hank slammed the phone into its cradle. He pulled at his turban and cursed Bill and the Icons under his breath.

Time had run out, and he turned his thoughts to escaping the cruel heat inside the van. He forced himself to calm down, switching gears to play the part of the half-crazed Arab opium smuggler.

His mind ran through the mental checklist of things he needed to perform. Every gesture, every phrase and action, had to come from someone else. He had to let go of himself and become Ali Ali-Akkba. He checked his reflection for the last time and began to lose himself in character. What he saw disturbed him. He was beginning to loathe Afghanistan and its people. He was beginning to understand why they believed the earth was the devil's domain. Life here was a trial to be endured without pleasure.

The call to prayer had begun as he locked the van and scanned his reflection in the window. The melodic sura, sung in Arabic, fell into the courtyard and alleyways, echoing off the low-roofed buildings. Convinced that no one had seen him leave the van, Hank pulled the ancient Jezail rifle under his arm and used it as a crutch as he made his way to the courtyard. Looking into the darkening sky, he found the direction of Mecca and sank to his knees.

There was no water to perform the rites, but according to the regional interpretation of the Quran, washing the hands, feet, and face with the pure soil of an Islamic state was good enough for Allah. Hank behaved as if the sandy dirt was gold, reverently scrubbing it into his skin. He began to pray silently, mouthing each syllable and bowing rhythmically. He found the constant prayer to be a good way to consolidate Ali Ali-Akkba's character in his mind. Passing the scrutiny of the Taliban required the right look and feel.

His look was complete. His complexion was dark enough, and he spent most of his time hidden beneath layers of clothing. He had traded his prosthetic for a simple wooden peg and wore an eye patch to distract from his Western features. The wooden leg was uncomfortable, but nothing compared to the prosthetic beard. Any Afghani caught without a beard Muhammad himself could be proud of faced imprisonment until one grew long enough. Hank's beard was half glued, half woven onto his chin. The supposedly hypoallergenic glue burned—and when it didn't burn, it itched.

The other elements of his disguise were all inventions of necessity. His main job was interpreting for the French film crew, so he had invented Shaheed Ali Ali-Akkba, son of a Saudi Mujahideen who now trafficked opium into Europe. Ali had fought with the Mujahideen in Pakistan and lost his leg to a landmine— allowing him to adopt the title Shaheed, signifying that he was a veteran of Jihad. The Iconoclasts had used their CIA connections to buy a few names to drop, and Ali had been accepted as one of the Harakat-ul-Ansar, a sort of exchange program for Jihadists and terrorists who operated in Afghanistan. The Taliban had accepted him without too much suspicion, taking him for one of the countless foreigners occupied with moving half the world's supply of opium out of their borders.

Ali Ali-Akkba's life was just interesting enough to be believable, and Hank's skills as an operator carried the rest of the performance. It was the type of performance he'd trained for, but now he was doing it without any help from his Delta team. Now he was working with utter amateurs.

"Monsieur Ali," Xavier called out into the silence. Hank could see him approaching from the van but ignored him to continue his prayers. "Monsieur Ali. Have you seen Monsieur La Boux? I cannot find him anywhere."

Hank looked up to glare at him for a moment, then pushed his face to the ground in a bowing motion. Xavier stopped, shifting his eyes from side to side. A cigarette hung limply between his lips. He was a short, fat little man who stank of athlete's foot. The mere sight of him filled Hank with contempt.

"Monsieur Akkba?" After another awkward minute of waiting, the chubby, hairy man walked away, scratching his ass in confusion.

Hank remained prostrate in prayer until he was gone. "Ignorant son of a pig." Ali Ali-Akkba spat into the dirt as he cursed Xavier in guttural Pashto.

A harsh voice startled him from behind. "The Frenchmen lack true devotion, my Brother." Ali Ali-Akkba turned to face a militiaman leaning against his rifle. "They believe in the morning and reject truth in the evening."

"Asalaam aleikum. The Muslims in Europe have much to learn about the one true faith, my Brother." Ali grinned as best he could through his beard. "Allah be praised." Hank jerked his head and began swatting at the imaginary insects buzzing his ears.

"Asalaam aleikum. Peace be with you, old soldier." The man shouldered his AK-47 and adjusted his turban with a twisted smile at Ali Ali-Akkba's craziness.

"Allah-u-Akbar—God is Great, my brother. His retribution is terrible for the unbeliever. Al-Samee, Al Aleem, All Knowing, All Seeing, may Allah protect his children." Ali Ali-Akkba turned to excuse himself with a bow. He leaned heavily on his rifle and made a great show of limping out of the courtyard.

Hank's mind raced as rage fluttered in his guts. Once again, the French Iconoclasts had showed their ineptitude. At least Xavier had addressed him in French, but interrupting a man in prayer was unthinkable. Xavier hadn't even evoked the name of the almighty when he'd left, and it was that kind of laziness that infuriated him. It was that kind of stupidity that would get them all killed.

Ali hobbled along the narrow street. Wind started to whip up clouds of dust and pull at his robes. It was late in the day, and he knew that when the winds changed, the freezing temperatures came right behind them like a crashing wave. Not even the thick woolen trousers or cloaks that roasted him during the day would offer any protection against the bitter night air. The trek through Bamian to the Frenchman's billet wasn't long, but it robbed him of his remaining strength. By the time he reached their door, the sweat on his neck felt ready to freeze.

Ali Ali-Akkba rapped his knuckles on the door, using the code worked out between the Iconoclasts.

"Al-suamm rhieem. This place is closed to nonbelievers." A familiar voice sounded an answer from beyond the door.

"Al-Samee' Al-Aleem. I am a believer, my friend. Open the doors. I am freezing."

The heavy door swung open, and Ali stepped aside. The immense figure of Shug filled the door and greeted him with a brilliant smile. "Bon soir, ami." His French was comically awful, but Hank was glad to see him.

"Bon soir, Monsieur Muhammad Ali." Hank greeted him with a flourish of his arms before stepping inside and pushing the door closed behind him. His eyes scanned the room as he shook off the cold. "Have we any friends tonight, Monsieur Ali?" Hank mixed his French with a heavy Arabic accent.

Shug leaned close, whispering English into his ear. "No friends tonight—just these assholes."

Hank took the small room in at a glance. La Boux glared at him from under his spectacles, and Xavier busied himself with camera equipment in the corner. The room stank after endless days cramped together with all their gear. Both Frenchmen smoked constantly, and the air was stale with sweat, but they were well away from the ears of others and could speak freely.

"What's for supper, Sugar?"

"Ah, tonight we're having Big Macs, fries, and um ... chocolate shakes. No, vanilla. Yeah, that's the ticket." Shug looked at the ceiling, which was only inches from his head, and he wrung his hands together greedily. Hank could practically see the drool forming in his mouth "Man, I could eat about a dozen burgers right now."

"All right, Let's eat. I'm starving." Hank made his way to a small blanket on the floor, where some cold flatbread and dates were laid out for him.

"Where have you been?" La Boux stood to challenge him as he crossed the room. "You did not tell me where you were going."

"I went for a jog," Hank replied with a caustic snarl. "I didn't know I had to keep you up-to-date on these things, Ibrim. Did you miss me?" Hank pushed past Evan, almost knocking the spectacles from his hands.

"Like a dog misses the taste of his own ass," La Boux spat out in angry French. "I am supposed to know everything that goes on here. What were you doing?" La Boux stood his ground, not giving way to Hank.

"None of your business, garlic breath." Hank wanted to sit and dive into his meal, but La Boux's confrontational tone was too much to take. He squared his shoulders, facing down the much smaller man.

"Xavier said he saw you coming from the van. Isn't that right, Xavier?"

Xavier sat mutely in the corner like a fat, sullen dog. He refused to look up at the two men standing before him.

"Xavier?" Evan shrank away from Hank and turned on Xavier. "Didn't you, Xavier? You saw him?"

"I saw him ... near the van, Mr. La Boux." Xavier remained seated, with his face down. He fumbled with a film canister and refused to meet Hank's eyes.

"Did you go to the van, Mr. Foster?" Evan La Boux persisted in his headmasterly voice, "tell me."

"No."

"No, you didn't go, or no, you won't tell me?"

"What I do is my business. And my name is Ali Ali-Akkba." Hank raised his jaw to look down on La Boux from over his nose.

"Would you like to know what I think? I think you have been to the van again. I think you were trying to use the satellite phone again." La Boux began to pace in front of Hank. "Well, let me tell you, Mr. Ali-Akkba, I have put an encrypted code on the phone. You will never use it!"

"Listen up, you ferret-faced pansy. If I want any shit from you, I'll beat it out of you! Got that?" Hank let his rage explode. "You have no idea what I'm doing here, operationally speaking! You haven't got the slightest clue what *you're* doing here! The way you and your lap dog are behaving is going to get your throats slit."

"What are you talking about? I am in complete control here." La Boux said irately.

"First of all, if you two don't start at least acting like Muslims, the whole job is going to blow up in your face. These people are fanatics: they eat, drink, and sleep Islam. They are constantly questioning each others' faith. Do you think for one moment that because you were sent by Dr. Rashad and you wear a skullcap you are above their suspicions? They don't trust you. They truly believe the devil has sent his Jinn to undermine the faithful with those who merely pretend to submit to Allah. What do you think will happen to you if they suspect that you are one of these demons? Do you think you'll be able to talk your way out of trouble? You think that I'll be able to talk you out of it? How am I supposed to come to your defense when you don't even properly observe the Salat?" Hank checked La Boux's mounting protest with a raised hand. "Do you even know the words for the call to prayer? I've watched you two at prayer, and so have others. They can tell you're faking it. I've even seen you pray during sunrise and sunset."

"But we are supposed to pray at those times!" Xavier said, finally looking up from the film canister.

"No, dumbshit, you're not." Hank glared at him, flipping up his eye patch to fully reveal the intensity of his stare.

Shug laughed and nudged Xavier with his knee. "The prayer should be done before or after sunrise or sunset. Not during. Only sun-worshiping infidels pray when the sun goes up or down. Ain't that right?" Shug looked at Hank and winked.

"That's right, Grasshopper." Hank sat down and ripped off a piece of stale flatbread with his teeth. "I saw the both of you smoking after Friday prayers. You do know about the Saum, right? Do you not know about these prohibitions, or are you so stupid that you choose to ignore them?" Hank shoved the whole piece of bread into his mouth.

"That is absurd, coming from you! You think I don't know what you've been up to when you go out at night?"

"You said you didn't want anything to do with that, so mind your own business. I'm talking about your behavior in public."

"And you don't think smoking hash with the Hazaras will get you killed if the Taliban catch you?"

"We each have our own agendas out here," Hank laughed as he piled more bread into his gullet. "I'm a drug trafficker. Remember? I'm just staying in character. You want to show how evil the Taliban are; I want to show how hypocritical they are, not just the Taliban, but all Muslims. That's what we do, we expose. We destroy piety with truth. That's the mission."

"So you think footage of the local villagers getting high is more important than documenting the travesties committed by the Taliban?"

"They're not just villagers, they're Muslims. Like all other Muslims—and Christians, and Jews—all of them are hypocrites who hide behind their faith. I'm going to expose them for what they are. That's what the mission of the Iconoclasts is all about."

"By smoking hash?"

"By showing devout followers of God's word beating their women, fucking their children, lying, kidnapping, torturing—and yes, smoking dope. Yeah, that's right. Visual, brutally honest proof of all these things is what I intend to bring back. And I might as well get a little high along the way. I'm no Saint."

"You won't be using any of my equipment for this, this … merde! And I refuse to let you take either one of my men with you."

At that, Hank burst with laughter. "And who in the hell do you think you are? Or, rather, who do you think I am? You think you're the captain of this ship?"

"I'm in charge of this operation!" La Boux said sharply.

"You're a tripod. You're only good for one thing, holding a camera."

"I financed this operation. I …"

"I get paid by the Icons. Not you. I'm the expert here. I know the people, the culture, and the lingo. I'm the one with all the know-how here. I've been trained for this, trained by the best. I was running insurgency operations while you were filming gay porn and trying to get your master's degree. We are in very dangerous territory here, and that's my department."

"We are part of an organization, all of us. And you report to me."

"Okay, Frenchy." Hank pushed himself off the floor and stood on his foot, grabbing the last of the bread and a handful of dates. He stood tall and erect in front of La Boux and raised his right hand to his turban in a mock salute. "I have a report for you: tonight is the last night the Great Buddha will stand. My friends and I are going to go smoke some Hashish! So go pound sand up you ass—sir."

Shug couldn't contain himself any longer and bust out in hysterics. After a brief moment, so did Xavier and Hank.

"Yes. And a fine soldier you are, Mr. Foster. Maybe if you were a little better, you would still have both legs, eh!" La Boux spoke coolly, eyeing Hank from head to toe.

In a flash, Hank had grabbed La Boux by one of his shirtsleeves and smashed his fist into the man's face, knocking him unconscious.

La Boux fell sprawled on the floor, making odd sucking noises through his nose. His eyes rolled back in his head, and his body twitched. Hank stood over him, hopping on one foot, still clutching the torn shirtsleeve in his fist. "Man, I've wanted to do that for a long time." He looked to Shug, who was still trying to catch his breath after the shock of seeing La Boux turned off like a switch. "Shall we?"

The narrow trail was difficult for the weary, one-legged Ali Ali-Akkba. His limbs quaked as the endorphins brought to a boil by his confrontation with La Boux drained from his body. The altitude and fatigue kept him from catching his breath, no matter how many breaks he forced on Shug.

"Come and give me your shoulder, Monsieur Shug." Hank reinforced the rudimentary French with plenty of sign language as he motioned for Shug to carry him.

Shug bounced back down the trail with a smile that reflected the moonlight. "No problem, my friend. But I'll remind you; my name is Mohammad Ali. I do not know this Shug fellow." He slipped his arm under Hank's shoulder, lifting him off his feet. The move was effortless. Hank felt like a child on Shug's back as he carried him over the boulders.

"You see, Muhammad Ali, I told you all the weight-training would pay off." Hank was amazed how Shug continued to pack on size and muscle. He had grown a foot and added a hundred pounds of muscle since Hank had taken him in.

"Paid off for you!" Shug laughed.

"I don't hear any of your girlfriends complaining. Go on, put me down. I can climb. Just give me your arm when I need it." Hank slid off Shug's hip and balanced himself on one foot.

"Take your time, old soldier." Shug used the Pashtun name the locals had given Hank. The one-legged madman with the wild circling eye and scandalous stories had become famous in Bamian.

Hank blew warm air into his hands and shuddered under his cloak. Ali Ali-Akkba's costume was not as warm as Mohammad Ali's. Hank had dressed Shug like one of the local Hazaras, with a thick tunic and heavy robes. The look was complete except for the boots. He couldn't find a pair of boots to match Shug's giant feet.

"There. See that plateau? That's where we're headed." Hank pointed past the gigantic figure of Buddha hiding in the shadows of his high, arched frame. The cave they were looking for was one hundred feet above the plateau. Hank strained his eyes to stare at the cliff face next to the giant statue, but the vertical wall was pockmarked with dozens of caves.

"All right, you lead the way." Shug stopped for a moment and checked the camera concealed in the sleeve of his robe.

Hank passed by, pleased with Shug's talent for hiding the camera. He took another couple of paces, then stopped to make sure his own concealed package was in its proper place. Besides the bundle tucked into his sleeve, he carried an ancient Russian revolver. A largely ceremonial Khyber blade was proudly displayed in his belt.

Hank struggled up the trail until they crested the rim of the plateau. Shug breathed deeply and easily, but Hank needed to stop and catch his wind. He set his Jezail aside and lay against the rocks. His eyes rested on Shug and the huge bellows of steam he blew into the moonlight. He marveled at how far the kid had come and what a loyal friend he had become.

Shug craned his neck to see the top of the cliff. "How do you know where to go from here?" he whispered in English.

Hank leaned back, looking past the three hundred feet of vertical cliff until his eyes caught a thin trail of gray smoke twisting into the sky. "There. See the smoke?"

"No."

"Look harder. Look for the stars to blur."

"Okay. Yeah, I see it."

"We make our way along the cliff until the smoke is right above us."

Shug held out an arm. "You ready?"

"Calm down already. Can't a guy take in the scenery for moment?" Hank tried not to pant as he pinched the growing cramp in his side.

"You're just out of shape."

"Bite me. Come on." Hank used Shug's arm to pull himself to his feet. They walked along the plateau for another hundred yards until Hank stopped to listen. He cupped his hands over his mouth and blew into them, imitating the mournful call of a dove.

The call was repeated from somewhere above them. Hank returned it once more, and a thin rope ladder silently unfurled, bouncing down the cliff to land at their feet.

Hank took the rope in his hand and measured it against his wooden leg. He looked at Shug, rolling his one uncovered eye. "I'll climb first. I want you right behind me."

"Don't worry. I gotcha." Shug stepped forward and offered to help him onto the ladder, but Hank pushed him away to grip high on the rope.

"And remember, Mohammad, only French from now on. Oui?"

"Oui."

Hank pulled himself up the makeshift ladder, skipping every other rung with his good leg. He doubted the ladder had ever held such a load, but Shug's weight below him kept the ropes taught, making it easier to find a foothold. They passed several black cave openings in the limestone as they climbed. Hank's arms burned, and his hands were numb. As the wind shifted, the smell of burning pine and another enticing scent told them they were close.

As Hank's eyes focused on the top of the ledge above him, his nose placed the scent wafting down toward them. It was the unmistakable smell of beef cooking on an open fire. Hank's mouth began to water despite his panting breaths. The rope became hard to grab near the ledge, and several strong hands reached over the precipice to pull him over.

Ali Ali-Akkba collapsed on the cave floor, touching his head with his fingertips and praising Allah. The air seemed even thinner in the high cave.

Mohammad scaled the edge and bounded into the cave, almost tripping over Ali Ali-Akkba. "Al-Rahmaan, Salaam! A most gracious hello!" Shug made a quick bow, his eyes locked on the spit turning over the fire. A chorus of greetings followed as the men in the cave circled them with arms outstretched.

Ali Ali-Akkba sat up from the floor and blew out hard. "Hello, my friends. Bless you for your hospitality … but perhaps you blasphemous Hazaras could find a shorter climb next time."

Amused snickering echoed along the cave walls, and several hands lifted Ali to his feet.

"Our apologies, old soldier. Any lower, and the Taliban goats would join us."

"Come join us by the fire, brothers. Tonight is indeed a very special night."

"Can you smell the delight we are cooking?" The circle of men parted, leading them toward the fire.

Muhammad Ali tugged on Hank's sleeve as they greeted each man in turn. "Is that what I think it is, Ali-Akkba?"

"Looks like a heifer's leg if I've ever seen one, Monsieur Ali."

"Tonight we finally have reason to thank those Taliban dogs. Tonight we eat like our grandfathers' kings!" A man with a gravely voice and few teeth pointed to the beef dripping fat onto the fire.

The cave was much larger than the entrance suggested. At a glance, Ali counted twelve turbaned heads. A second fire was heating a kettle further back. "Al-Hamdu Lillah, praise be to Allah. How did you come by such treasure, my brothers?" Ali dusted himself off as he made his way into the fray. He rolled his eyes wildly in mock confusion. The comic effect of the one bright eye turning circles under his turban somehow appealed to the others, and they began to laugh in their distinctive Afghani way. "Whose throat was cut for this bounty?" Ali continued to roll his eye and began hopping toward the fire, staring into the eyes of each man as he passed. He relished playing the part of the crazy drug smuggler, and these local villagers were his favorite audience.

"The feast is a gift from those that have raped our land. Maa Shaa Allah. This is Allah's will." A Hazaras villager named Kamal Al-Rawi spoke over the others. Hank had met him several times before, and liked him. He was young, quick-witted, and serious.

"Courtesy of the Taliban and their Sipah-E-Sahaba pigs. They kill *our* wealth to atone for their incompetence."

"We will eat like kings today, and maybe tomorrow, but after that ... our families will starve," said another man solemnly.

"Thanks to that pig Mullah Omar," shouted another. At the mention of his name, several men spat into the fire.

"He ordered one hundred of our herd to be killed! One hundred head! That is more than any other time. Not even the eldest Shayka can remember such a sacrifice."

"It is not a *true* burnt offering." An elder Bamian local spoke, his eyes licking the beef turning over the fire. "Allah be praised."

"Allahu Akbar. Allah is Great," the others repeated.

"They do this to us because we are Hazaras!"

"Because we are Shiite, descendants of Muhammad!"

"They want to starve us!"

"He is right! There is nothing like it in the teachings of Muhammad. It is murder!"

"The Taliban are Sunni. The Taliban are Pashtun." Kamal Al-Rawi turned toward Hank and began making apologies with his hands. "No offence to my traveling brother; you are the salt of the earth to us Hazaras, and we will all meet in paradise, but the Taliban and all the Pashtun people want to kill the Hazaras people."

The other men fell silent as Kamal stepped closer to the fire. "And the Uzbek, and the Tajik, the Taliban will kill them all. They preach that submission to Allah also means submission to the Teachers. This is not Islam's way." He gripped at the shirt beneath his robe, looking ready to rip it from his chest, and then checked his emotions, pointing a finger to the sky above him. "Even so, we must keep our faith and trust that Allah's retribution will be severe for those who distort his message. Some day Mullah Omar will roast in agony. But tonight we will eat. There will be time for tears tomorrow."

"Well said, brother. Tomorrow will be a sad day indeed. The beautiful Buddhas of Bamian will be gone."

"And so will any chance of income for our village. It has been many years since the infidels filled the valley to take photos of our Buddhas, and now all hope for their return is gone."

"I remember as a small boy when a man paid me *One hundred dunar* to stand before the King Mother and let him take my photo. *One hundred dunar!* More than my father made all year!"

"I think that I would like a photograph of the Buddhas before they are destroyed."

"Ali, do you think that your European friend has taken many photos of the Buddhas?" The man took hold of Ali Ali-Akkba's wrist and pointed to where Shug stood mesmerized by the slowly turning spit.

"Yes, Ali, ask the Frenchman if he has taken photos," another man pressed, tugging the sleeve of Hank's cloak and nearly dislodging the package he concealed.

The others fell silent, and Hank could feel their eyes on him. "Muhammad Ali is a young man who wants to see life with his own eyes." Hank spoke slowly, displaying the mannerisms of the half-crazed Bedouin smuggler whose persona he had perfected. He opened his eye wide and stared back at each man in turn. "That is why he is here with me tonight. He does not care that they say I am a madman, he doesn't care that I leave my body parts behind like a bird leaves droppings. He loves his life and this world." Ali pointed to where Muhammad Ali sat. "He fears the Taliban as much as any man fears death. He would not risk his life in this world to make photos." Hank drew his finger across his throat in an exaggerated sawing motion.

"But we all know the Europeans are here to make photos of the Buddhas. The Taliban allow their cameras."

"I have heard they make photos when the Taliban are not looking." A man spoke from his place near the fire, and Ali Ali-Akkba snapped his head around to eye him.

"I have seen the big black man make photos of the Taliban when they do not see. I have seen him with cameras in his clothing." The man shrank from Ali Ali-Akkba's wild glare and pointed toward Shug. All eyes seemed to follow his finger—to find Muhammad Ali still blissfully unaware that he was the center of attention.

Hank stepped forward with a flourish. "The stinking Frenchmen pay me handsomely to speak Pashto for them ... and to watch over their sleep at night."

Crazy Ali flashed open his robes to reveal the ancient Khyber knife tucked into his waist. "I know nothing about cameras and photos. They are the devil's toys. But I will ask the big, ugly one if he has taken photos." Ali turned, sticking out his chest as he faced Muhammad Ali at the fire's edge. "Young Muhammad Ali, my brothers say they have seen you make photos, photos of the Buddha. Photos the Taliban do not know of. Have you made forbidden photos?" Ali spoke to him in French, picking his words carefully.

Muhammad's eyes opened wide, but he quickly checked his shocked expression. He scanned the crowd and found that all eyes were on him. An immense smile spread across his jaw. "I cannot lie to such a gracious host. I took some pictures." He paused long enough for Ali to interpret. "I think the Buddhas are amazing. When I return to France, no one will believe what I have seen. And I have no words to describe their beauty." Ali Ali-Akkba struggled to find the right translation as Shug turned to point to the Bamian valley behind them. "And when I am an old man, I want to show my children the land of Afghanistan."

The men murmured beyond Hank's ability to hear them as he tried to gauge their response.

"I know the Taliban have made a threat of death, but that is why I am here. I am a photographer." Shug's smile broadened as Hank interpreted.

"I would also like to show the Buddhas to my own children, but I would not risk death to show them." The speaker waggled his head in disbelief.

Ali Ali-Akkba did not translate his words for Shug. He changed the subject instead, turning to face the ring of men and pointing to Muhammad Ali, who stood smiling by the fire. "The French do not believe the Taliban will kill them." Ali stifled a maniacal giggle. "Their passage was bought in Pakistan, by a doctor there who is connected to Mullah Omar himself!" Ali shook his head in mock admiration for the hated, one-eyed Mullah Omar. "Mullah Omar says the photos are for the great Jihad! They will show the righteousness of the Taliban. The Frenchmen trust that their money will keep their heads on their shoulders … they do not understand the Taliban like we do, my brothers." A quiet murmur of laughter spread around the fire before Ali continued.

Successfully stealing the attention away from Shug, Ali Ali-Akkba skipped into the middle of the circle and began speaking to them in a singsong manner. "And they trust Ali Ali-Akkba to speak for them. Now who is the bigger fool? The madman or the man who hires him?" Ali Ali-Akkba danced a wide circle around the fire, giggling to himself.

Shug caught his eye and moved close when he passed. "What have they said, Ali? Am I in deep shit?"

"They think you're crazy. Do us both a favor: no filming tonight. Oui?"

"Oui."

The kettle was brought from the fire, and each man was given a small iron cup. The men sipped tea and shared dry fruits and some even dryer cakes as they eagerly awaited the leg of beef. One of the men emerged from the darkness with a skin filled with sweet liquor, and each man took turns pouring shots into his mouth.

The talk turned to remembering men who should have been present but weren't. The harshness of the land and the brutality of the Taliban had taken their toll on the local inhabitants. Many of the young men had disappeared, and there were many widows to provide for. The Sipah-e-Sahaba, the so-called Guardians of the Prophet, had moved into Bamian with the Taliban and were making life miserable for the Hazaras. The massive tyrant Ghazi was the worst of them. He led the Sipah-e-Sahaba and loved nothing more than grinding the locals under his heel.

"He broke his staff across my back," one man recounted angrily, "Look! There is a lump!"

"He is the spawn of the devil himself! Look at my hands! They are torn like paper!"

"You should see the rope burns on my thighs. He had them hang me upside down, and then he beat me for working too slowly. My hands would not stop shaking. The height was terrible."

"Look … look at this lump," the first man kept insisting, leaning his shoulder into the firelight.

"Nobody cares for your wounds. We all have our own gifts from Ghazi. If only we could give him one of our own …" another man grumbled over a steaming cup of tea.

"He is too fierce. I heard he cut a man to pieces and made him to eat his own flesh before he choked to death!"

"He is too large. His hands could strangle a donkey."

"He truly is the son of the devil! How else could a man grow so large?"

"If this is true, old soldier, then your European friend must also be spawn from Satan." One of the Hazaras poked Ali Ali-Akkba in the ribs with his elbow and snickered, showing the gaps between his teeth. "He is just as large as Ghazi."

"He is bigger! Look at the size of his arms." Another man joined in, flexing his bicep and comparing it to Shug's.

"But Ghazi is a demon! The Frenchman has the smile of a child."

"The giant Frenchman smiles for the same reason that he is huge. He would eat that whole cow if he were left alone with it!" Ali laughed in his eccentric way, sending spittle down his beard.

"If he could eat ninety-nine head of cattle, then none of the Taliban's blasphemous sacrifice would go to waste." Karim Khalili pointed to the beef being lifted from the spit. "It is the Taliban, and not the shameful Sipah-e-Sahaba, we should focus our hatred on. Ghazi and his men are simply vultures picking at our carcasses. It is the Taliban that have taken our Buddhas and killed Bamian."

"The Taliban kidnapped me to dig their foxholes. They kept me six months! And I have seen them kill more than the Sipah-e-Sahaba could ever dream of. They killed my brothers and all of their wives." An unfamiliar voice came from the back of the crowded circle. Hank had seen the man in the company of the Hazaras on some of the previous nights, but he had never heard him speak until now. He was a younger man and wore the customary dress of an Uzbek villager.

"Even worse for you Hazaras, the Taliban are not even true Afghani." Ali Ali-Akkba laughed at their misery, ending the talk as quickly as fingernails across a chalkboard. With all eyes on him, he continued to speak, slowly working into a singsong cadence. "They may have dropped from their mothers in Kabul or Kandahar, but their bellies and hearts belong to Pakistan! To curse the Taliban is not good enough. You must look to those who steal your birthright."

"What have we to steal?"

"Schools in Pakistan feed your children and teach them the Quran. They send them home to protect Pakistan and her secrets." Ali raised his pointed finger to his temple and spun around to glare at the man.

"What secrets do you speak of, madman?" Khalili looked insulted.

"There is a reason the Pakistanis buy your children with so much bread. If they did not, then the children of Afghanistan might learn that they are the true owners of most of Pakistan!"

"You speak madness. Opium has slowed your mind, Ali Ali-Akkba." Khalili shouted him down amid groans from the group.

"It is true! I am not from this land. I've traveled far from here. My father is a Jihadeen, myself a Jihadeen, I have made the great pilgrimage to Mecca and many lesser pilgrimages as well. I have taken my trade over many lands, and I know what you do not! The Taliban are for Pakistan! There is no Afghanistan!"

"He is right … there will never be one Afghanistan!" Another man shouted.

Ali Ali-Akkba appeared amused by the emotion he had stirred. "It should be the other way around, my brothers—there should be no Pakistan!" Ali giggled, stealing a long pour of sweet liquor and letting it pour down his cheeks.

"You are a crazy man, old soldier."

"Am I? Who is the crazy one here? Are we not all hiding like dogs from the Taliban? I will run from this place tomorrow … where will you go? Why not to Pakistan? Maybe you could become Taliban, too." Ali broke into a giggle.

"What are you saying to us? Stop playing games."

Ali stopped his laughter as quickly as it had begun. "Please do not be upset with me … I am your humble servant. I see that you suffer, and I simply wish you to know your enemy. Because of my … occupation, I am well versed in the matters of politics. Because of my travels, I have met many people, and they have told me many interesting things."

"Why would Pakistan want to control Afghanistan?"

"Why? Why does a young man want many wives? Why does an old man want many sons? There are many whys. Why is not important, only law is important … less important only than Allah's law. Allah be praised. Most Merciful. All Knowing." Ali acknowledged the prayer by looking up the roof of the cave. "Are you familiar with what the Inglisi call the Durand Line? No? Of course you are not. You know nothing outside Bamian. If you knew the history of this place you would know why almost half of Pakistan rightfully belongs to Afghanistan." Hank could feel the warmth of the liquor in his belly and the eyes of the others on him.

Ali Ali-Akkba pointed to the vastness of the valley beneath them. "All of Pakistan was once just a part of India, back in the days of the British. Well, before the Pakistanis broke away from India and formed Pakistan, the British made a treaty with India stating that after one hundred years, the Pashtunistan region would be annexed to its own rule. Today that land would be part of Afghanistan. The British drew a line on a map and called it the Durand line, naming it after one of their famous killing generals. But later, when Pakistan broke free from the Hindu infidels in India, they took the land of Pashtunistan with them. Now the hundred years have passed. According to international law, Pakistan is supposed to give Pashtunistan back to Afghanistan. It is law. That is why Pakistan needs the Taliban to oppress its neighbor."

Ali let them mutter a few words to each other before he continued. "Pakistan still fights for the Kashmir. Do you think they would give away Pashtunistan? No, it is better to oppress your neighbor and call him friend. It is better to keep him at war so he can breed soldiers for you. Even now they send your sons to die in the Hindu Kush!" Ali Ali-Akkba spat into the dirt for effect.

"They say that you fought for the Pakistani: is that true, old soldier?"

"Yes, yes, it is true. I had the glory of killing many Hindus for the Pakistani! And all it cost me was one leg!" Ali giggled as he gulped down another shot of the sticky liquor. "Now I can do nothing but move poppy for the Taliban and keep bread on my plate."

"I do not know if what you said is true ... but I am sure of one thing: there is no Afghanistan. There will never be an Afghanistan. Hazaras will never bow to Pashtuns, and Pashtuns will always fight the Uzbek. This is a land of tribes and their fathers." Khalili spoke somberly, and all heads turned to hear him.

"Now it is Pakistan's turn to occupy our lands," said another.

"We will chase them away! Like we chased away the British and the Russians and all the rest that trample on our lands." One of the men drained a shot of the liquor into his throat. "Allah be praised."

"We can't even fight off the soldiers who come to our own village! We are forced to run into the caves of the Monks and hide like children. We leave our families unprotected."

"Allah will watch over our families. Does he not see all? He knows how we suffer, and he will make all things righteous."

"Allah is Great," sighed the crowed in unison.

"Allah be praised indeed! Look at the blessing that he has sent to us." One of the men presented the hindquarter on a large stone slab. The men all circled around the beef, gathering their various wooden bowls. Shug crowded in alongside them, the intoxicating aroma holding him spellbound. All conversation was lost on him.

"Let us pray, my brothers. And let us remember that this was meant as a burnt offering to Allah, the one true All Knower, All Seer. May this gathering of starving men be forgiven."

"He would truly rather we live than not eat his sacrifice. Is it not so?"

"It is not a sin to eat when one is starving!"

"Yes, Allah knows that our faith is strong and that we lead righteous lives."

"Let us all honor his offerings and say words for the ones that cannot taste of the livestock raised on their own fields." Khalili lead the others. "Ashadu Allah illaha ilalallah, wa ashadu ana Muahammador rasulallah. I bear witness that there is no God except God, and Muhammad is his messenger."

The beef was sliced off the bone, and each man ate until his stomach could hold no more. Stories were told, and the liquor was passed from hand to hand, but the talk inevitably drifted back to the Buddhas and their eminent destruction.

Shug finished the last scrap of meat, to the astonishment of the others—all except for Hank, who took his cue and stood before the circle of men, motioning for their attention. "All of you know I am a smuggler. Not one of you good men has reproached me. You have forgiven my madness and shared your food with me. And I would thank you with some of the fruits of my labor." Hank reached into his sleeve and pulled the bundle from its pocket. "Good Afghani hashish is better than any other in the world!"

A small cheer bubbled from the men as Ali Ali-Akkba unfolded his parcel.

"You are a prince of fools, old soldier!"

Hank held the brick of hash under the light for all to see. "I thank you all for your hospitality. You do well to look after travelers. Tomorrow the Buddhas will fall and the Frenchman will make their movie, but tonight we smoke. We smoke, and we forget our troubles."

Some of the men looked hesitant at first, but each of them accepted a small share with great thanks. Taking turns, flattening the dough-like hashish into small cakes, they balanced the small cakes on pins from Ali's cloak and set them ablaze. A wooden bowl was placed over the burning hash, dampening the flame and trapping the smoke. Men sipped the smoke and stifled their coughs. The ritual of passing the bowl from man to man filled the remaining hours, and all the men in the cave became quite high before slipping into sleep where they sat.

Everything was in place: after two thousand years of standing sentry over the Bamian valley, the Great Buddha was about to be demolished. Excitement rippled through the Taliban ranks, but Ali Ali-Akkba couldn't care less. His head ached, and his throat was hash-burnt. He sat alone in the shade of a crumbling wall while the Iconoclast film crew set their tripod to face the Great Buddha.

Big men were flying in for the show, and the Taliban camp hummed with activity. The elderly cleric Mullah Abu Bakkar announced to his men that Mullah Omar himself was moments away from landing.

Hank watched apathetically as a group of militiamen, lead by a Taliban officer wearing the ceremonial black turban, corralled the last remaining villagers. Their orders must have been to get every last villager out of the village before Mullah Omar arrived, because they began to panic once they heard he was moments away. Angry shouts and harsh commands mixed with the wailing hysteria of women wrenched from their homes.

Ali Ali-Akkba peered through a cloud of flies and watched as an elderly Hazaras man was pulled from his home. Two armed militiamen wearing the marks of the Sipah-e-Sahaba pulled the man by his wrists. The old man's feet kicked and scratched at the ground. One of the Sipah-e-Sahaba thugs became impatient and pointed his rifle at the old man's face.

The half-blind elder simply raised his hands in protest and continued wailing. For an instant Hank was sure the Sipah-e-Sahaba thug was going to fire, then another cry broke from behind them. A village woman broke away and ran toward the old man. She made a few quick strides with her arms outstretched, screaming like a madwoman. In Hank's stupor, the woman looked like the Grim Reaper floating through the air. The black robes of her burqua flowed behind her like dark flame.

Her spectral image stopped brutally fast as a rifle butt smashed into her face. The woman disappeared like water poured into the desert sand. A motionless pile of black cloth at the soldier's feet was all that remained.

The old man stopped wailing and feebly grabbed at his nearest tormentor, flailing his fists against the man's shoulder. The second soldier stepped in and shot him in the face. The air filled with a red cloud as the man's body folded onto the dirt.

Hank watched all of this in a surreal haze. His head opened and shut with the dull pain of a Hashish hangover. The report from the single shot seemed unnecessarily loud. The blast echoed off the cliff face and seemed to pass right through his aching head. The gunshot also caught the attention of La Boux, Xavier, and Shug, who were manning their camera a few meters away.

Through the waves of heat between them, Hank could see Shug swing the camera away from the Buddha to capture the violence unfolding in the village. La Boux noticed too, and stepped in front of the camera, chastising Shug under his breath. Shug hesitated for a moment, then swung the camera around to face the Buddha once more.

Helicopter blades thumped in the distance, announcing the arrival of the Mullah Omar. The limp bodies were dragged away, and the villagers were hidden.

Ali Ali-Akkba decided it was time to hobble over toward the Icon cameramen, and he mustered the strength to move. The radiant fire of sunlight pressed down from above. Every shuffling hop on his wooden peg tore away at the tender flesh of his stump. Every step with his left foot felt like a pole-vaulter's leap. His lungs wheezed, and he couldn't expel the phlegm clinging to his throat. By the time he reached the crewmen, the helicopter was coming up from the valley.

Ali attempted a greeting, but only managed to hack up a mouthful of brownish green mucus. He hacked and spat into the dirt; La Boux instantly took offense and turned his back. Hank tried to speak, but he couldn't stop wheezing and hacking. Embarrassed, he tried to apologize with his hands, but soon they were gripping his throat as he fought for air.

Shug and Xavier began to laugh, not even slightly concerned, and La Boux assumed the joke was on him. "What is it? Spit it out already! This is no time for your games!"

Hank's eyes blurred. He couldn't draw a breath without his lungs rejecting it in painful spasms. No one moved to help him. Fury fused with frustration as he tried to force the bad air from his lungs. A prickly sweat enveloped him under his robes. His eyes bulged, and his head threatened to explode with every gagging cough. Helicopter blades thumped the air, filling his ears, and the inferno of the sun's rays spun wildly in front of him. The next instant, he was face down in the dirt.

Hank awoke to warm water being poured down his parched throat. Dirt crunched between his teeth as he swallowed. The last of three big helicopters was touching down in the foreground, kicking up huge amounts of dust in the downdraft.

Shug shielded him from the sun's rays as he held the flask over his mouth. "Don't say a word, my friend." Shug spoke in nervous, broken French. "You've had a spell." At first Hank didn't understand why Shug was trying to speak

French, but as his eyes settled on the ranks of Taliban falling into formation, his memory came flooding back.

He scanned the men around him and discovered that he had become the center of attention. Angry, turbaned faces stopped what they were doing to stare at him. He recognized the look in their eyes and realized the danger he was in. An accusation of drunkenness could be fatal. Once again, sweat blistered on his body as he rallied the strength to stand.

"Is he all right?" La Boux peered through his glasses with a genuinely concerned look on his face.

"Ali Ali-Akkba—can you hear me, my brother? It is me, Muhammad Ali." Shug forced a smile.

"What is going on here? What is wrong with this man?" The words came in an angry flood of Pashto. "Why aren't you making the movie of the helicopters?" Hank understood the words, but they weren't directed at him and somehow held little meaning.

"Our man is ill." La Boux turned to face the local leader of the Taliban militia. He struggled to sound the words out in Pashto.

Mullah Abu Bakkar curled his lip into a snarl and barked for one of his men to approach. He stopped La Boux with a wave of his hand and then bent down to examine Ali Ali-Akkba. His face was withered and bent with spite.

Hank shook away the haze and found his voice, the voice of crazy Ali Ali-Akkba. "Salamun 'Alaykum. Peace be upon you, my teacher." Hank took Shug's arm and pulled himself to his knees. "I am Ali Ali-Akkba, son of Abduallah Akkba Husayn. Forgive me, for I have been touched by the spirit of the Almighty Allah; glory to the Most High, I am prone to fits of his divine ecstasy." Hank spoke flawless Arabic and forced himself to stand tall as he dusted himself off.

"He speaks Arabic?" The man's weathered face looked puzzled as he turned to his aid.

"He is the Frenchmen's translator, my teacher." The Mullah's hawk-faced assistant spoke softly into his ear. "He is from Haralat-ul Ansar."

"You are Mujahideen?" The elderly Mullah's eyes softened.

"You honor me with the title, wise teacher." Ali Ali-Akkba made a great show of bowing and waggling his head.

"He is an opium smuggler, Mullah Bakkar. He is probably drunk from vice." The Mullah's assistant continued to hold Hank in contempt with his eyes.

"Drunk?" The old Mullah's eyes widened.

"Allah be merciful! I am not drunk! Never would I lie to such a man ... not in the presence of the Almighty himself! No, I am not drunk, only ... at times, I live in the ecstasy of the divine."

"He is a drug smuggler, my Master. Shall I have him removed from your sight?" The hard-looking assistant loomed threateningly.

"Forgive me, my teacher ... I am back in the land of the living for now, but beware, master Bakkar, we are both sharing the realm of evil Jinn." Ali's eye rolled wildly beneath his turban.

"Is this true? Are you an opium smuggler?" The old man's finger jabbed Ali Ali-Akkba in the chest.

"It is the only way for a one legged soldier to survive in these times. I have no family, no tribe, only Allah to guide my days. It is by virtue of his charity that I am able to make a living doing work no healthy man may touch."

"He is unclean, my teacher. Let us leave him."

"Do not be so harsh, Omar. This old soldier is Mujahideen. He has sacrificed for the glory of Allah. Let him earn his bread by whatever means he can. Allah teaches us to be compassionate toward the lame. As a holy fighter, this man deserves our respect." The elderly Mullah placed his arm around Hank, nearly knocking him off balance. "You say your fits are sent from Allah himself, most merciful, most wise? What have you learned from your gifts, old warrior?" The Mullah spoke Pashto so the others could hear him, Omar in particular.

"I've tasted Allah's painful retribution! I am blessed with a reminder of what pain awaits the Infidels at the end of days. Allah is God, there is no other God but him, and Mohammad is his messenger."

"Allah forgives those who are righteous in their submission. You are truly fortunate to have such insight. If only all of us had such a reminder from above." The Mullah worked his face into a mask of benevolence.

"Allah is everything." Hank tried to pull away, but the old man held him firm.

"You have learned well the lessons that have been sent to us. How did you suffer you wounds, brother?"

"I fought Jihad with the Mujahideen in Pakistan. Death to Hindus!" Ali spat into the dirt angrily, playing the part of the madman as much as he dared. No sane man would ever spit in front of the high cleric.

"And you, you are the speaker for these Europeans?" The Mullah pointed a gnarled finger at the others.

"They have paid me very handsomely, and in return I have made a sizable almsgiving this year. Allah be glorified."

"How is it that you come to speak the language of the European?"

"I am blessed with a tongue of many words." Ali shrugged, as if the skill were something beyond him.

"And you know the language of the Prophet?" The Mullah asked in Arabic.

"I speak the Prophet's language because I was born in land of the Prophet himself! I can read the holiest of the scriptures and understand the message of the Profits," Ali replied in a flourish of Arabic.

"Ask these men if they made the movie of the helicopters." The Mullah gestured to the nervous-looking camera crew.

"Did you guys shoot the copters or what?" Hank asked La Boux and the others in curtly spoken French.

"Oui, we did." La Boux nodded enthusiastically toward the Mullah.

"Yes, they made the movie of helicopters, my teacher." Hank bowed deeply as he replied in Pashto.

"Tell them we want … tell them … they can make the movie of the helicopters, but they must not make the movie of the men who come out. Tell them not to make the movie on any of the chosen men who have come to witness the holy event. This is Allah's will. Tell them this." Another man from the Mullah's entourage stepped forward and spoke into his ear, pointing to the landing site. Noise from the chopper blades kept Hank from hearing what was said, and Mullah Bakkar hurried him for a translation with a wave of his hand.

As Ali told La Boux and the others what the Mullah had said, the other black-turbaned Talibs gathered around the Mullah. The huddle ended abruptly, before Hank could finish, and the elderly Mullah reached out to grab his shoulder. "Tell them to stop the movie. I will tell them when to continue. Only make a movie of the Infidel's statue, nothing else." The Mullah waved his finger ominously at the others for effect. "You will come with me," he added, grabbing Hank by the sleeve.

At first Hank was stunned. He turned to face the Mullah, but he didn't know what to say. All he wanted was to find a cool place to sit down. The sun on his back made him feel as if he were going to pass out, and he didn't want to go anywhere with the sharp-eyed Mullah. "By your word, my teacher. I will do as you say, only … please allow me time, because I am so lame." Ali turned wearily to translate the Mullah's orders.

"You and I are equally lame, young warrior. I am bent from a lifetime of fighting for righteousness, and you have been crippled by an instant of it. We will walk together. Let the young men among us run ahead to wish good greetings to our friends. We lame ones will follow behind." With a nod and a wave from the Mullah, four of the Taliban bowed hurriedly and ran full-tilt toward the gathering group disembarking the helicopters. Only one man remained behind with the Taliban chief.

Now standing vigilantly behind the elderly Mullah, the sharp-featured assistant looked more like a personal bodyguard to Hank. He was tall and lean, with a large, beakish nose that added to his raptorlike demeanor. He wore the traditional black turban of a Taliban scholar, but—unlike all of the other religious soldiers—he appeared to be unarmed. Mullah Bakkar pushed Ali Ali-Akkba aside to grab his Bedouin rifle from Shug's hands.

The Mullah graciously handed the symbolic weapon back to Ali and gestured for them to move ahead. Unable to refuse any request from the headman, Ali slung the barrel under his armpit and used the butt to help propel himself over the rocky ground.

"That black man is very large, isn't he?" The Mullah turned back to Shug as he shuffled along.

"He is enormous." Hank kept his eyes to the ground.

"He looks like an American black." The Mullah turned to walk up the path, and Hank nearly stumbled over his crutch. "I understand that the Americans bred them for their size, as slaves." The Mullah continued on, speaking casual Pashto. Fear seized Hank's guts, and the early spasms of diarrhea threatened to cut short his next step.

"If that is true, then I think that they must have bred that one's mother to a gorilla!" Hank wished he could have stopped the words from coming out as soon as he said them. He was desperate to change the subject, but this type of humor was unknown to men like the Mullah. It took all the control he had to stifle the nervous laughter about to erupt, and he began to giggle like a little girl. It was important to giggle just right, as Arabs did not laugh like Westerners. To cover his mistake, Ali giggled like the madman he was—complete with snot shooting from his nose. Luckily the Mullah must have felt the image was equally funny, and the two of them laughed together like old women. The only one not laughing was the stone-faced bodyguard.

"See, Omar, see the truths I have taught you. Even the blind and crippled among us can see humor in life. Allah loves the happy ones; do not be afraid to let him see you smile, my boy."

"Yes, my teacher." The man shot Ali an angry glance behind the Mullah's back.

"I believe this man has truly been blessed as he describes. For his service in Jihad, and because he believes in the last days, I am sure he will find grace in the eyes of Allah."

"Allah most merciful, most wise." Ali Ali-Akkba spoke in Arabic as he looked to the sky. He bit his lip in an effort to keep a straight face.

"Your speech is good. My Arabic is unfortunately limited to my knowledge of the Quran. Would you be you so gracious as to stand by me in case there are no others to relay my words? There are very important men over there, and I'm sure they have good speakers, but just in case I would like to have you standing by me, as an Arab."

"They are Arab?" Ali pretended to stare off to where the men had gathered.

"Some are Arab. The head-man is Arab and speaks no Pashto."

"Of course it would be my honor, but I am unworthy."

"Come along, we are all Mujahideen."

By the time they had reached the others, the copters were winding down and the noise was less severe. All of the dignitaries in the Taliban's entourage had left the landing site and massed in the courtyard of a building near by.

Hank didn't need introductions to some of the men; he had seen the supreme Taliban leader Mullah Omar and his crowd before. Ali Ali-Akkba faded into the mix when Mullah Bakkar greeted the others and ceremonially passed authority to Mullah Omar. Hank was glad to finally be off the hot seat, and was about to breath a sigh of relief, when he spotted the Mullah's assistant eyeing him from his blind side. There was something unsettling in the look; the man had an intelligent, suspicious quality about him that always made Hank nervous.

There was always one person bright enough or perceptive enough to see through any disguise, and the character Hank had created for himself was designed to handle him. Ali Ali-Akkba's ultimate defense was the fact that he was certifiably insane. Hank worked hard to establish this fact whenever he could. Playing the fool was a risky gambit, but it was Hank's favorite.

The hawk-faced Omar remained at Hank's side—his blind side. They were standing on the periphery of a large circle of men, most everybody's attention focused on the two Mullahs standing in the middle. Hank felt Omar's eyes on him, and—without alerting him to the fact that he knew he was being watched—Ali did something no sane man would do: he shifted his weight, leaning heavily against his crutch, and then farted loudly. Without any hesitation, and to the utter revulsion of the men standing nearest him, Ali groped at his ass, scratching deep into the foulest of areas and then brought his hand to his nose to sniff his fingers.

Men standing near him stepped away, waving their hands in front of their faces, but Ali pretended not to notice. Hank kept from looking in Omar's direction. Convinced that the man was still scrutinizing him across the group, he decided to take it a little further.

Mullah Bakkar turned and pointed, drawing attention to the massive cliff face where the Buddha still sat. He seemed to be addressing one particularly tall Arab man among the group. The group's attention was firmly fixed on him as he condemned the Buddhist statues as blasphemous idols. Hank took the moment to catch Omar staring at him from the corner of his eye.

Ali Ali-Akkba began to swat at invisible insects swarming around him, muttering curses at them under his breath. He appeared suddenly furious with them, and then stopped abruptly, freezing every muscle and staring off into space. Then he burst into a renewed flurry of swings at the phantom bugs. The men around him took yet another step back.

Ali stopped his wild slicing of the air, bringing his hands together and muttering to himself. After a moment, he slowly turned to face Omar. Hank's eye blazed into Omar's as he raised his eyebrows in a bizarre manner. Omar simply gazed back in amazement until Ali stuck out his tongue, mimicking the ferocious taunt of the Maori warrior. The expression was fearsome and ridiculous at the same time. It quickly broke the stare down between them, causing Omar to look around at the others in disbelief. None of the other men seemed to notice, and by the time Omar looked back to Hank, Ali Ali-Akkba was already walking away behind the crowd, picking his nose and eating his boogers.

The walk to the Plateau of the Buddha was accompanied by evangelical sermons by both Mullahs. "Surely, those who disbelieve in our revelations will be condemned to hell's fire. Whenever their skins are burnt away from them, we will give them new skins! And they will burn again. Thus, they will suffer continuously. Allah is Almighty, Most Wise."

"Allah does not forgive idolatry. It is the worst offense! Anyone who sets up idols beside Allah has committed a horrendous offense!" The two men took turns preaching to the crowd of obediently nodding heads. Ali Ali-Akkba was having trouble keeping the pace the elderly Mullah Bakkar was setting now.

Ali fell in behind a group of men who seemed to surround one leader. He stood out due to his height but was plainly dressed. He wore a dingy gray skullcap and a graying Wahabbi beard. His AK-47 was slung casually over one shoulder.

When they finally reached the base of the cliff where the larger Buddha was situated, Mullah Omar presented it as if they were seeing it for the first time, even though the enormous statue could be seen for miles. There was an odd hint of pride in the Mullah's voice as he explained that the Buddha was nearly two thousand years old.

The party of men craned their necks to take in the entire 175-foot statue, which was set back into a high arched cave. The Buddha's face had been sheared off a thousand years before when a Muslim army captured Bamian, his long, slender arms were blown off past the elbows, and his legs were gone below the knees.

Mullah Omar pointed to a quote from the Quran painted on the cliff wall next to the Buddha: "The just replaces the unjust." The intricate symbols were painted in bright red. "Many pious Muslims have tried to rid the world of idols and unbelievers. Great men like Yaquub ebn Leys as-Saffar have tried in vain to destroy these terrible monsters. With all of his power, his empire, not even he could do more than make the idols faceless. Not even the mighty 'Idol Breaker' himself, Sultan Mahmood Ghaznani, could destroy what we will bring crashing down today." Murmurs of approval rippled through the crowd of men.

"How the nonbelievers wish to stop us! But not even the American missiles could come in time to stop us now; the bombs are already in place!" Mullah Omar began to usher one of the Arab men forward. "This is the man who is responsible for placing the explosives. I will let him tell you men what you have been patiently waiting to hear. Thank you. Praise be to Allah." The elder Mullahs huddled together for a moment while the young Arab began talking rapidly about the type and amount of explosives used.

The interest among the men in the group had picked up dramatically when the talk turned from theology to technology. Ali Ali-Akkba smacked his parched lips and was listening intently to the young man when he was snapped back to reality by a tap on his shoulder. He turned to face the withered Mullah Bakkar and the hawkish Omar. "Do you deal in explosives as well as opium, brother Ali-Akkba? You seem to have an interest in many things." Mullah Bakkar pointed to the clique of Arabs.

"Salaam, my teacher, I am only interested in water at the moment." Ali was barely able to choke the words out over his roughened tongue.

"I will have my student assist you to the well. Omar, assist this infirm man back to the movie men. Advise the movie men to begin once all of the soldiers are out of view. Not before. Swear on Allah that you understand."

Omar forcefully took up a position under Ali's arm. "I swear before the Almighty, Most Wise, they will not begin before every man has gone from view, my teacher."

Omar waited near the camera crew until all of the Taliban and Arab guests had either retired to safe locations in the village or foxholes dug in the desert floor. Hank was beyond caring what the man was thinking by now; he truly did need water in the worst way. He sat in the shade pouring water into himself, wetting his face and neck until he was convinced he was sweating again. Omar, finally satisfied that they had not filmed any of the guests, left without a word.

Hank wanted to join the camera crew, but once he'd sat down, he couldn't get up. He curled himself into the shadow of a wall and buried his fingers in his ears. Moments later, he was startled awake by a massive blast tearing through the valley. A torrential downpour of dirt and debris rained down on him, and a massive cloud of dust enveloped the valley for the next few hours. The dust refused to yield, and the destruction of the second Buddha was postponed until later in the day.

Hank had once promised Shug that a time would come when the job grabbed him and never let go, and it seemed that the moment was right now. Shug's first real mission was winding down, and pride filled the empty pit of his stomach as he stowed the last of his camera equipment. One after another, all of Hank's promises had come true. The last five years had changed him into a man he couldn't have imagined before. He saw himself as a legitimate, real life spy, with money in the bank and a future waiting for him when they got home. A grin spread across his face and he laughed aloud.

"What is it this time, Muhammad Ali? Thinking about cheeseburgers again?" Xavier looked at him, the usual cigarette hanging from his lips. He sat cross-legged on the floor, surrounded by film canisters.

"No." Shug laughed again, and his smile widened. "Not this time, my chubby little friend. It's time to go home. I'm thinking about eating something even tastier."

"Oh? There is something you enjoy more than cheeseburgers?"

"Yeah—pussy!" Shug reverted back to English as he danced an obscene pantomime for Xavier and La Boux.

"You better not let your friend Ali Ali-Akkba hear you speaking English." Xavier arched his brows and sealed another canister. "He'll be on you like a pit bull."

"Monsieur Akkba is sound asleep." Shug motioned to the small courtyard outside their cramped billet.

"He's been sleeping most of the day." Xavier smiled knowingly.

"He'll be okay. He said something about wanting to post guard tonight." Shug scanned the room for more gear to be packed.

La Boux looked up from his work and sucked air over his teeth. "Your friend is simply making excuses for his drunkenness." He slammed the viewfinder closed on the reel of film he was editing. "There is no reason to post a lookout tonight."

"I don't care if you know it or not, but he's been on watch most of these nights. It's no wonder he's exhausted."

"You are making excuses too! You can't see that he was stoned out of his mind? His foolishness almost cost him his head today."

"He knows what he's doing."

"He is full of shit! He thinks he is so great, but he is nothing more than a washed up drug addict!"

"Stoned or not, he's done things you could have never done. We couldn't have gotten this footage without him."

"You Americans are all a bunch of cowboys!"

"Watch your mouth, La Boux." Shug rose to Hank's defense, picking his French phrases carefully. "Don't forget where we are."

"I have not forgotten." La Boux was about to stand up from behind the small wooden table, but a harsh banging on the door interrupted him. The glasses nearly fell from his face as his head whipped toward the door.

Another determined round of pounding followed, and Shug threw a blanket over the exposed gear. La Boux stood and moved cautiously toward the doorway.

"Ba'asem az darwaaza!" A loud Pashto voice boomed from behind the door.

La Boux's hands trembled on the bolt while Shug and Xavier scrambled to hide what they could. "Ba'asem az darwaaza!" The door shook on its iron hinges and dust fell from the cracks in the wood.

La Boux lifted the bolt and hesitantly swung the door open. Shug recognized Ghazi's bearded face as he filled the door and pushed La Boux aside with the point of his rifle. Ghazi was one of the few people here he knew by name as well as by reputation. He led the Sipah-e-Sahaba and was the most feared man in Bamian. He had a Russian-made AKS-74 assault rifle clenched in his meaty fists and a full band of ammunition slung around his chest.

"Khaberi kawem faranigay." Ghazi pushed his pockmarked face into La Boux's. "Zzbaarra khaberi kawem!" Two more black-turbaned Taliban soldiers poured through the door as Ghazi raged commands to La Boux.

"Mu'aafi!" La Boux shrank away from a threatening, upturned hand. "Mu'aafi, ze ya zheba Pashto. I do not speak Pashto. I don't understand what you are saying!"

"Raakawem muzz sineema asbaab!" Ghazi snarled and pointed a gnarled fist to the camera equipment.

"Sineema asbaab?" La Boux repeated. "My camera? You want the movie camera? I do not understand. Let me fetch my interpreter." La Boux walked his fingers along the palm of his hand and gestured to the door with his head. "Our interpreter is outside. I will get him for you."

Ghazi stopped him with the working end of his rifle. A demonic smile appeared beneath his beard. "Give ... me ... movie." He spoke in slow, rehearsed French. "Give me movie Faranigay." He pushed La Boux toward the table loaded with film.

"But our movie is not finished yet! We need more time!" La Boux smiled and pointed to his wristwatch. "I need more time to make the movie for you."

Ghazi barked an order and the Taliban men crossed the room with their weapons pointed at Shug and Xavier. One of the men stopped to stuff film canisters into a sack.

"No! Please, you must stop!" La Boux lunged for the man with the sack and Ghazi hammered him in the guts with his rifle. La Boux fell to his knees but sprang back to his feet with surprising vigor. He turned to face Ghazi and pleaded with him. "Please, there must be some misunderstanding!" He struggled with broken phrases in Pashto and then babbled curses in French. "Not the film. Oh shit, God help us!"

Ghazi didn't understand, but Shug realized why La Boux was risking his neck to keep the film out of their hands. La Boux must have taken the opportunity to view the secret footage while Hank was out of the billet, and now the film sat dangerously exposed on the viewing table. A sickening feeling settled in Shug's stomach as he stared at the weapons pointed at his face. He knew the film would be just as deadly if viewed by the wrong person, and the absolute worst person he could think of was about to help himself to it.

A soldier shouted at him, and Shug tried to remember what Hank had told him about moments like this. He asked himself what Hank would do, but things moved too quickly. He found himself being ordered to the ground. There was no room to move. Six men now packed the room, which was built for no more than four. He contemplated making a grab for one of the grenades the Taliban soldier had strapped to his chest, but the idea was sure suicide. He slowly raised his hands and looked to La Boux for help.

"Stop! Please!" La Boux grabbed at Ghazi's tunic and was slapped into silence.

Shug could think of nothing else to do—he broke his silence to call for Hank. "Yo, brother! Where you at?" His shouts in English startled the Taliban, and everybody began shouting at once.

La Boux took advantage of the disorder and made a dive for the table, but Ghazi collared him and flung him across the room. Ghazi shouted another set of orders in Pashto and then pulled a long curved Khyber blade from his belt.

Xavier buried himself behind Shug's mass, and La Boux shrank before the massive man and his cruel blade. Ghazi Al-Kazim grabbed La Boux by the sparse hair atop his head and dragged him to the center of the room. A trickle of blood ran down La Boux's neck as the knife was pulled tight under his chin. Ghazi rummaged through La Boux's pockets and threw a fistful of cash onto the table.

Shug turned his head toward the door and shouted. "Hank, we got problems here!" He half hoped Hank would burst into the room but feared he would have his head blown off as soon as he did. Ghazi stopped pulling at La Boux's pockets and shouted to the man covering Shug.

The assault rifle was pushed higher into his face, and the other soldier began searching his pockets. Ghazi turned his attention to the viewfinder set up on the table and eyed it curiously. He contemplated pushing the machine into the sack, then noticed the film trailing from the side. "Al sineema blalee." He lifted the small machine, turning it in his hands and running a finger along the rubber face piece. His thumb pressed down on the play button, and light poured from the small screen.

Ghazi pushed his face into the box and didn't move for several long seconds. His hands shook, and his knife tumbled to the floor. He pulled the viewfinder from his face and screamed at the top of his lungs. "Sharmawem ghayem hale-kina!" Spittle flew from his lips as he raged at La Boux. "Ksseebaasem teer-wezem!" His own men seemed startled by his outburst and turned to stare at him.

Almost without thinking, Shug capitalized on the confusion and grabbed the barrel of the nearest weapon. He pushed the point away from his face as the soldier fought to angle it toward him. The second soldier bashed the butt of his weapon into Shug's ribs and Shug spun around to push both men into the corner. He was stunned by their sinewy strength. He wanted to kick them, but Xavier blubbered at his feet.

Ghazi bellowed a final command, then stepped forward with his assault rifle. La Boux, sprawled at his feet, grabbed the fallen knife as Ghazi turned. Shug pushed and pulled with all his strength, but now two rifles jockeyed for a shot at his face. La Boux charged Ghazi's back, letting out a murderous yell. Ghazi turned with a snarl and fired point-blank into La Boux's stomach. La Boux pitched over and fell to the floor.

All heads turned to follow Evan La Boux's body to the floor. In the same instant, Hank burst through the room's only door. Ali Ali-Akkba's patch was pulled from his eyes and a pistol was held out in front of him. He fired a single shot into Ghazi's face, snapping his head back and spattering his brains against the wall.

Shug fell to the floor, pulling a man on top of him. Hank fired two more shots into the chest of the Taliban soldier standing against the wall, and Shug rolled to pin the second soldier beneath him. Xavier wailed and screamed as he scrambled from the corner. Blood and gore covered his face.

Hank covered the rest of the room with his revolver as Shug struggled to hold the man under him. Both of them refused to release the assault rifle between them. "Hold him, Shug!" Hank stepped forward and pressed the muzzle of his pistol against the man's forehead. He pulled the trigger, and the shot nearly deafened Shug as the man's head leaped from the floor and erupted with blood.

Men's voices sounded at the door as the echo of the last shot rang out. Hank stole a quick, confused glance around the room and then threw his revolver toward La Boux's lifeless body. Hank unshouldered his ancient Jezail rifle and began to load a round into its muzzle, the tiny charms jingling on the painted butt of the weapon as he worked. Hank shot Shug a questioning look but didn't speak; Shug wondered what he was planning. The next instant, a rush of Taliban soldiers charged into the room. Once again, automatic weapons were pointed in Shug's face.

The Taliban men gaped, horrified, at their comrades' dead bodies. A torrent of babble flowed from the bewildered fighters, and Hank threw his hands into the air. Xavier collapsed to his knees and sobbed uncontrollably.

A wave of nausea crashed down on Shug. He'd never seen death up close. Blood and brain matter covered the room. He looked to Hank and then toward La Boux. He couldn't speak. He nearly vomited. More men pushed into the room, tripping over the bodies and slipping in the gore. A rifle butt cracked him across the back of his neck, and many hands began to pull him to his feet.

Hank was being pressed against the wall, a gun jammed into his chest. The Taliban soldier was screaming at him, but Hank didn't have the answers he was looking for. Shug fought against the pulling arms and stopped before they threw him through the door. "They came for the film! La Boux tried to stop them." A flurry of punches flew at his face, and he was pulled through the door.

Hank was pushed through the door behind him, and his wooden leg was kicked out from under him. Boots kicked at him from all directions, and the screaming intensified. Shug was knocked to the ground, where he could see Hank curled up in a ball, surrounded by a circle of men. Xavier blubbered, covered in blood and crying like a child as he was thrown to the dirt.

Hank pleaded in Pashto as the men continued to pound him. A Taliban soldier stepped out of the billet with Ali Ali-Akkba's Jezail in his hands. He sniffed the barrel suspiciously and shouted to the others. The beating stopped for an instant while a man shouted questions at Hank. An argument broke out between the Taliban soldiers and some of Ghazi's men. The men pushed each other and shouted furious curses, but Hank didn't speak.

Two of the Sipah-e-Sahaba hauled La Boux's body from the room and dumped him in the dirt. Shug could see thin puffs of air stirring the dust under his face. Another man came charging out of the room with tears streaming down his cheeks. He thrust the pistol Hank had used to kill the men into the hands of the Taliban leader and pointed to La Boux.

The crying Taliban soldier took a long stride and kicked La Boux in the face, finally closing his dull eyes. A second man grabbed him by the hair, lifting his head from the dirt, and screamed into his face. Blood drained from La Boux's mouth like a faucet.

The Taliban leader shouted to his men, and they pulled Hank along the ground to drop him next to La Boux. He shouted an order to Hank and pointed to La Boux. Hank simply looked back, face battered and swollen. The Taliban officer spat at him in disgust.

Ali Ali-Akkba pleaded with the soldier, recoiling from a threat made by the blunt end of a rifle. The man repeated his demand, and Ali appeased him by crawling toward La Boux's face. All shouting stopped as Ali bent low to speak into La Boux's ear.

The soldier standing over them lost patience and kicked Hank in the ribs, sending him sprawling. Hank began answering their questions in Pashto. Shug recognized one phrase repeated by Hank—ghlaa: *robbery*.

The angry soldier refused to believe what Hank was telling him and turned to La Boux, but the life had clearly drained from his body. Another soldier stepped forward and presented the commander with the pile of cash Ghazi had lifted from La Boux. Incensed, the leader stomped his boot down on Hank's face and encouraged his men to do the same.

Hank wrung his hands together and beat his brow as the men pounded him with fists and rifle butts. He didn't dodge the blows or fight back as they beat him. The lead man shouted an order, and two men lifted Hank by his arms, head hanging low on his chest. The leader stepped close and jammed the butt of his rifle across Hank's jaw. Hank's head spun and flopped back to his chest.

The enraged Afghanis dropped Hank back to the ground and continued to beat him. Shug buried his face in his arms and shielded himself from the blows and kicks leveled at him. The pain they delivered was nothing compared to the fear he felt for Hank.

Pain ushered in Hank's return to consciousness. At first there was only one sensation, one thought, but then a barrage of panicked impulses bombarded his brain. He couldn't move. He couldn't feel his hands or feet. A hellish heat enveloped and suffocated him. Slowly, piece by piece, odd fragments of memory colored his consciousness, and he pried an eye open.

The ground cooked beneath him even though the sun was low on the horizon. He lay on his side and stared at the cruel waves of heat dancing above the reddish earth. His swollen eye was crusted with sand and slow to focus, but the reddish haze spoke one name into his memory: Afghanistan. The metaphorical hell was now real, complete with the unbearable pain described by Dante.

His arms burned. His wrists and shoulders felt horribly lacerated. A molar was loose, keeping his jaw from closing, and his mouth was caked with dry blood. His swollen cheek throbbed against the ground with the beating of his heart, and for a moment he thought he had lost an eye to the melee. A beam of sunlight filtered through his eye patch, and memories of Ali Ali-Akkba flashed in his mind.

Breathing was difficult. His nose was broken and packed with dirt. If he breathed too deeply, a vice clamped around his chest and blinded him with pain. After trying to shift his weight off his chest, he realized that his arms were pinned behind him. He didn't remember being bound, but fragments of his ordeal began replaying themselves in his thoughts. He felt every blow all over again. Images of kicking boots and clawing hands assailed him. He remembered being awoken by shouts and Shug's calls for help. Shug's blood-covered face stared into his mind's eye.

He forced the image from his mind and stopped to look at his surroundings. He lay in an open courtyard. A colony of flies hovered over him, crawling in and out of his mouth, obliterating all other sound. His joints were aflame from the binding ropes. The rough fibrous wire wrapped his throat, chest, and legs. Something sticky and wet oiled his fingers as he pumped his fists and pulled at the knots behind his back. The putrid smell of cooked blood and excrement surrounded him.

Though his view was limited, he couldn't see any guards, only a low, blank wall a few meters away. Empty, featureless sand stretched twenty feet in front of him. He tried to turn his head to better his view, but he was blinded by the sun, and the coarse rope dug into his throat. He coughed as he sought a neutral, painless position. There was nothing to be seen, just pain to be felt. The first quiver of panic rippled through him. He was sure he had been left to die by inches in the desert. He tried to listen past the buzzing flies and focused on the provincial background noise of Bamian. Bells from a merchant's cart jingled in the distance.

As his strength crept back and his mind continued to clear, he started to struggle in earnest against his restraints. He pulled and jerked methodically in every direction. To his surprise, his wooden leg was still connected to his stump. The ropes around his waist gave a little as he pulled his stump free. Blood streamed into his hands as he pulled at the knots, and the cold rush of a thousand needles washed over his hands.

Hank heard the crunch of boots, and an angry voice cracked behind him. The sunlight above him dimmed, and Hank lifted his head to see a black-turbaned Taliban soldier standing over him. His name was Abrihim, and memories of the beating he and others had given him flashed in his head.

"What have you to say for yourself, son of pig excrement?" The soldier kicked him in the stomach before sitting on his haunches and peering into his face.

"Allah most merciful." Hank's croaking words were barely audible. "What have I done to deserve such suffering?

"You have allied yourself with the unclean. Now you will suffer and die with them. Soon you will be as foul as your friend."

"I do not understand! How have I offended the faithful? I have not sinned against the keepers of the faith. I did not kill …"

"You let a European kill your brothers while your rifle remained silent! You do not deserve to die like a man. The sun will vanish soon, and … the clean will become the unclean. You will break from Allah and suffer wretched retribution in hellfire." The man spat in Hank's face and stood to boot him again.

Hank coughed and choked on the bile surging from his guts. The Taliban soldier stepped away, but his shadow still covered him. All at once, he began cursing like a man possessed. "You filthy son of a dog! Your mother sleeps with donkeys, and your father was born a pig. You foul the earth with your filth." Hank readied himself for more blows, but none fell.

"Allah's judgment will be most severe on you. French pig! Allah doesn't look kindly on those who kill his faithful soldiers or his angels. Tonight we will break your pitiful covenant with Allah. Your rotting corpse will foul the air along with this smuggler trash! Your soul will be sent to the hottest level of hell!" The Afghani man's hard voice quaked with emotion.

"You should not have died so quickly! Weak, vomiting pig! Your dollars will do you little good now. You better pray your friends are worth money to someone—or they will join you, pig! Your body will be defiled by vermin … your soul will rot! We will dump you in the desert ... we will never bury you! Let the dogs have you both!"

Abrihim's ranting tirade added a horrible clarity to Hank's situation. The bulky weight holding him in place was La Boux's dead body. The viscous wetness covering his hands was La Boux's blood. The Taliban tortured even in death and aimed to deny Ali the Muslim burial rites. He had been sentenced to death by defilement. They planned to cast him into the desert, defiling his body with the touch of the unclean dead.

As Hank listened to the man curse, a thin ember of hope glowed to life. He was familiar with the Afghani custom of death by defilement. The condemned was confronted with the knowledge of his mortal end and his eternal damnation. It was a withering, loathsome death, full of humiliation and pain, but it was designed to torture a man's soul. Such an unclean death was unconscionable to a true believer, but their attempt at brutality gave Hank time. In the eyes of the Taliban, he was already a dead man.

Abrihim's angry speech had also made Hank aware that Shug was still alive and that his captors were planning to ransom him. He listened to Abrihim's boots scrape the ground and wild fantasies of ripping him apart spun in his mind. Hank knew he was in no position to make his tormentors suffer, but now there was hope. Soon it would be dark, and he could work the knots tying him to death. Until then, his task was to endure the pain and ready his battered body for an escape.

Hank controlled his rapid breathing and steeled himself against the brutal elements already assailing him. Soon the heat would turn to extreme cold. His body would be numb and frozen when it came time to work the knots. He recalled his lessons on combating hypothermia. There were ways. Muscle can be conditioned, fingers can be forced to move. There was hope. He knew he could endure the psychological torture. His forte was psychological warfare, and there were ways to cheat the terror. The fear of eternal damnation held no menace for him—only survival mattered.

Time was his enemy now. Minutes of agony seemed like hours. La Boux's slowly bloating corpse made for poor company, constantly filling him with guilt and self-doubt. He knew he had to occupy his thoughts if he was going to last. He could not allow himself to descend into madness. He searched his memory for ways to detach from the pain. His instructors at escape and evasion school had taught him the thoughts to stay away from, but now those thoughts were the only ones that came to mind.

Horrible images of torture played in his mind. The stories of cruelty were painted more vibrantly now that he could relate to the shock of it all. He knew that things could be worse. Death by defilement was almost commonplace, now that the Taliban ruled. The real barb in this otherwise passive form of punishment, of course, was that—by definition—it culminated in death. A merciful death was one that came after a single day. The more common and sadistic version saw the victim succumb more slowly.

After a single day in the blistering heat, the corpse and its companion would bake under a cloud of flies. If the victim were strong and not too used up, he might survive four or five days. Three and a half days would be long enough for the Ungaowa corpse fly to complete the larval stage of its accelerated life cycle and for a maggot swarm to begin its feast on the rotting flesh. Maggots and other insects would blanket the victims. The wiggling mass would invite the crows and jays to dine, and the pecking would begin. No man is known to have lasted more than five days. It was said that the crows pick away the last of the condemned man's soul and fly it straight to hell.

For the moment, these thoughts were only a remote curiosity to Hank, not a concern: he wasn't going that way. He could take their pain, and he could master their fear. As the flies buzzed and crawled over his face, his thoughts inevitably drifted back to La Boux. Images and questions flashed in his mind while the heaviness of guilt weighed in his heart. He still couldn't believe La Boux had stood up to Ghazi. Hank pictured the cluttered hovel in his mind, and the echo of Shug's words suddenly added a new thought. There was only one reason La Boux would risk his life for the film—it was the wrong film.

With that one horrible realization, Hank's ace in the hole evaporated. The threat of sudden death now loomed over him in earnest. The film La Boux had died for waited to expose him, and he couldn't do anything about it. Now he was forced to suffer his defilement in as much terror as all the others before him.

He could feel the fear draining his vital energy, and he reminded himself that his primary challenge was keeping his sanity. He swallowed the fear and racked his brain for topics that would distract from the pain, but nothing came. He remembered stories of men reciting whole books when confronted with the torture of time, but he could hardly recall a single book he'd read—let alone its first line. His life suddenly seemed cavernously empty, void of any real substance. Life as an Iconoclast had consumed his passion and his thoughts. Slowly, unconsciously at first, his thoughts once again turned to his work for that organization.

He knew that with the right touch, operation Devil's Peak could make a huge impact and prove everybody wrong. No one seemed to grasp its potential the way he did. No one else seemed to ask "what if?" What if we were suddenly confronted with life from another world? How would it affect our thinking? It wouldn't matter that it was a hoax. People would stop and think, some for the first time. There would be public debate and hard questions. People would have more on their minds than pop culture. Hollow beliefs would crumble. The Iconoclasts would have what they had always wanted, and they wouldn't have to wait a lifetime to see it happen.

Hank felt his body begin to relax somewhat as his mind strived for a meditative state. He critically analyzed every element of the operation, reciting names and their contacts until he could virtually see where they fit into his scheme. He rehearsed his plans as if they were to take place the next day—and as time wore on, and an angry mob didn't appear to cut him to pieces, he felt more confident that he would live to see another day.

The last trace of reddish sunlight disappeared, and the temperature fell with the light. Hank pumped his fists and worked his aching muscles. He knew the call to prayer was coming soon. Once the muezzin called out the Adham from his minaret, every man in Bamian would be face-down in prayer and the clock would begin ticking. Hank worked his fingers around the rope securing his legs. He arched his back against La Boux and pulled at the line until his fingertips could feel the cloth binding his wooden leg to his stump. He held his breath and dug his fingers into the cloth until it pulled away. The wooden leg fell away and a ripple of slack softened the ropes.

The relief was immediate, but it was quickly followed by immense pain as the fiery pins and needles of sensation flooded back to his limbs. He pulled with all the strength he could muster until it felt like the pressure on his lower back would break his vertebrae. He rested as much of his weight as he could on La Boux, then used the slack in the rope to untie La Boux's wrists. His fingers were numb and the knots were thick, but he finally loosened the ropes around La Boux's wrists enough to begin work on his own knots. La Boux's dried blood made the work difficult, but after several excruciating minutes he was finally able to release his legs and free his hands.

A loudspeaker crackled to life somewhere high above him, and the first utterances of the Muezzin cut through the silence. The high-pitched wail sounded alarmingly close, and Hank realized he must be near the mosque. He still couldn't move to improve his limited view, and a sudden fear that he was in plain view of the minaret soaked him with instant sweat. The thought of detection now—after so much pain and waiting—was maddening, but Hank pushed himself into action and began vigorously working the rest of his knots.

His joints and vertebrae popped and clicked with fresh movement. He freed his stump and leveraged it against the ground to push himself on top of La Boux. La Boux sagged and groaned beneath him as Hank crushed the stale air from his lungs. Millimeter by millimeter, he separated the ropes that bound him to La Boux. He lay with his back tottering over Evan's body and was finally able to move his head.

He recognized the buildings the Taliban had taken over as their own and saw that he sat in the middle of a small courtyard in the center of their compound. There were no guards in sight, only the haunting call of the Muezzin filling the air. As he thrashed his legs and kicked away the rest of the ropes, he scanned the buildings and wondered where the Taliban were keeping Shug. Some of the pre-historic buildings glowed with electric light, while others were ominously blacked out. The high stone wall surrounding the compound was taller than a man, and he doubted he had the strength to scale it. From his view atop La Boux, he could see that the two gateways were open to allow the Taliban men to attend evening prayer at the mosque.

Hank pulled his hands free from behind his back and rolled off of La Boux. He snatched his wooden leg, slipping it under an arm, and began rummaging through La Boux's pockets, but they had already been picked clean. He scanned the empty courtyard and dismissed any notion of simply bolting through one of the open gateways. A row of fuel drums were stacked against the outer wall, and he began crawling, crablike, toward them. He stopped, crammed himself between barrels, and took stock of his situation.

La Boux lay in the dirt, his dead eyes appearing to watch Hank's every move. Hank pushed against a barrel and heard the fuel slosh inside. He guessed he could scale the wall using the drum beneath him and pulled himself up. Every sound was magnified by terror. The barrel creaked and rattled under him as he fought to balance on its rim. He crouched with his hands pressed against the stone and slowly poked his head over the wall.

The lay of the land came back to him as he surveyed the village beyond the compound. The hovel he'd spent the last month in was a few hundred meters away. The main road lay to the right and the market spread out in front of him. Hank kicked his stump to the top of the wall and silently pulled himself up and over. He landed on one foot and rolled into the shadows.

He fought the urge to skirt the wall and make a hell-bent break for the open wilderness and turned his thoughts to rescuing Shug. His eyes narrowed on the darkness of a shadow of a nearby building and he summoned the energy to crawl toward it. He huddled in a pile of debris and blew warm air into his trembling hands. The Muezzin ended the call to prayer, and muffled voices sounded in the distance. He half expected to hear the call of alarm sound from the Taliban compound, but none came.

An overpowering thirst gripped him as he rubbed life back into his limbs. He began to rummage through the pile of refuse. He was desperate for a discarded melon rind or anything else he could eek some moisture from, but all he could find was leftover tea grindings. He looked at the building once more and recognized it as one of the three teahouses in Bamian. He had been here before and sipped tea with the Hazaras just days ago. The shop was small, and most of the seating was set outside. He remembered the ornate, hand-cranked ceiling fan above the serving table, and he knew there would be plenty of water inside.

The family that operated the humble business resided upstairs. He could see their laundry hanging on a line outside the window over his head. Hank crawled along the wall like an injured crab until he came to the front of the shop. After countless generations of civil war, banditry, and lawlessness, the homes in Afghanistan were all build like small fortresses. The walls were made from thick mud and straw, designed to be cool in the blazing sun and warm in the frigid night; the windows were no bigger than the width of a child and covered by heavy wooden shudders. The tea shop was unique; the open storefront meant there might be a way in.

A large canvas tapestry hung over the opening of the shop. It was secured with little knots every few inches along the fabric curtain. Hank didn't hesitate: motivated by fear and bitter cold, his frozen fingers went to work on the tiny knots. Once he had pulled a few of the knots apart, he pulled the flap open slightly. Tables and chairs were pushed up against the curtain, blocking the entrance. He lifted a chair out of the way and placed it behind him before pulling himself inside.

The inside was a featureless black void. He stopped for a moment, holding his breath and letting his eyes adjust to the darkness. The outline of the ceiling fan formed ahead of him, and the features of the room cleared in his mind. The rickety chair creaked beneath him as he struggled to pull himself inside. He stopped moving and silently cursed the noise he was making. His pulse pounding in his ears, he waited for the creaking to stop—and heard an aborted, shocked little gasp close to his ears.

Hank froze in place as a loud shriek of alarm shattered the silence. Hank jerked his head up to see the silhouette of a little girl standing over him. He leaped and made a lightning-fast grab for the child, but he became entangled in the chair and came crashing down to the floor. He lunged at her from the floor, grabbing her nightdress as chairs spilled down on him. He pulled her down and groped for her mouth, but she wouldn't stop screaming. Another child piped in with even more screaming, and Hank realized that the floor of the shop was covered with bodies.

Concerned voices blustered from the floor above him, and he became hopelessly entangled in the girl's bedding as he tried to stand. He tried to quell the screaming with gentle assurances, but he couldn't tell if they understood him. A large form suddenly sprang at him from the center of the room. A flash of light glinted from a cruel-looking blade. Hank threw the girl to one side and tried to untangle himself before the attacker closed the distance.

The dark figure lunged at him with the blade held high over his head. The knife came down, slashing at his face, but the man faltered in the darkness and fell, crashing into him. Pain ripped down Hank's arm as the blade cut his wrist and slid down his forearm.

Hank screamed with the madness of close combat as his hand grabbed for his attacker's neck. He pulled the man to the floor and hammered him in the face with his fists. The man crumbled under the rapid-fire strikes, and Hank pulled himself on top of him. The knife clattered to the floor, and the screaming redoubled in volume. Candlelight bounced down the steps across the room and was followed by a flow of curses. The children in the room answered the male voice and let it be known that a man was fighting with grandpa.

The pathetic light from the candle gave way to the illumination of an oil lantern, and Hank saw what he was up against. A semi-clad woman held the lantern for her husband, who was rushing down the steps wielding a long club. Four children screamed and pointed at Hank and the battered old man flailing beneath him.

Hank grabbed for the fallen blade and took a defensive position atop the elderly man. The knife was heavy and dull, probably as old as the man who wielded it, and would do little against the man and his long club. Hank backed off the old man and was about to snatch the girl to use as a shield when he remembered a lesson taught to him years ago by an ancient Mujahideen. Hank knew how the family hierarchy worked in Afghanistan: children were as beloved as anywhere else in the world, but as an asset they ranked far lower than the family's elder.

Hank pulled the old man from the floor, positioning him between himself and the man with the club. He slid the serpentine blade under the elder's beard and roared a harsh command: "Stop! Or I will cut him from ear to ear!" Hank pulled back the man's head to show he'd already drawn a line of blood. "This is a terrible mistake! Put away your stick and I will explain my intrusion!"

The man stopped and his jaw dropped. His children squealed past him and huddled around their mother on the steps.

"I wish no harm to your family—but if you take one more step, I will surely cut off this man's head and carry it off to hell with me!" Hank shouted above the hysterical cries.

"What do you want? Why are you in my home?" The father shouted back at him, raising the club in the air.

"Quiet yourself! And hush your family! Let me explain myself, and I will leave you unharmed!" Hank fought to sound controlled, yet menacing. "Hush those children, or I will!"

The mother pulled her children into her bosom and merciful silence filled the air. Hank strained his ears to hear past the shop for sounds of alarm, but the street outside was silent.

"We have nothing for you here! What do you want with us?" The father wore a nightdress and mopped at the sweat running down his face with its sleeve.

"You have a wealth of many children and a fine old shaykh to head your household, and I want none of it!" Hank backed the knife away from the old man's throat. "All I want from you is some water."

"Why are you here?"

"Fetch me some water." Hank lowered his tone and pointed to the bar with the tip of the knife. "Dryness is robbing my speech."

The father barked a command and the eldest daughter scurried to the bar to collect a pitcher of water. Hank tried to slow his breathing and collect his thoughts as the girl hesitantly placed the jug near his feet.

"Is there anyone else in your home, my brother?" Hank eyed the man as he lifted the jug to his lips.

"This is my whole family. There is no one else." The man was thin and frail looking, with a sparse, graying beard. He did not appear to be a man capable of much violence.

Hank drank greedily, letting the water run down his cheeks. "What is your name, shopkeeper?"

"Hasan Al-Din Fulayyih."

"You are Hazaras?"

"As is my father-in-law." The man pointed to the shaykh in Hank's arms.

"I am of the Hezb-I-Wahdat. I am from the land of the Prophet. I do not belong to these lands—but we are brothers, you and I." Hank wiped the water from his face and smeared blood from his wrist across his mouth. "Do as I ask of you, and I will leave you with nothing more than my humble apologies. If you refuse me, I will kill you and we will both spend our eternity in the hottest depths of hell! Do you understand me, my brother?"

"What do you ask of me? I have nothing!"

"My brother, there is a terrible evil in Bamian. I have just escaped them." Hank shot a worried glance to the opening behind him. "You must alert the Taliban soldiers! I cannot, for I am lame." Hank lifted his bare stump in the air. "You, you must run to the camp of the Taliban and tell them of the approaching evil!" Hank paused to compose his next thoughts as he drained more water into his mouth. "American soldiers and their helicopters are coming to kill the people of Bamian! Yes, they are coming. You must warn the Taliban so they can shoot them down for the glory of Allah!"

"Americans?" Hasan gaped at him in disbelief.

"It is true! I have escaped them but can go no further. You, you must go and alert the Taliban fighters!" Hank's mind spun with inspiration. "Go, run to the infidel's giant bell near the mosque. Bang the gong with all your strength. It is a signal to them! Do this, and I will hand over your father."

"I do not understand—Americans here?"

"Helicopters! Great big helicopters! They come to shoot fire and death! There is no time for talk: you must go now! Give me your club and run to the mosque. Ring the great bell, and then run to the Taliban camp and warn them. Do exactly as I say, and if Allah is willing there still may be time!"

"I do not understand."

"Do as I say or I will have his head! There is no time to argue! Go now and give me your staff. I will need it if I am to stand and fight the Americans!"

"I have your oath? You will not harm my wife's father?" The man lowered his club, looking torn with indecision.

"Allah as my witness. Now go! Before it is too late." Hank withdrew the knife and waved Hasan out of the shop.

Hasan shot his wife a worried look. She embraced her children and finally told him to leave for the sake of her father. He dropped the club and ducked through the opening, biting his lip.

As soon as he had disappeared through the flap, Hank pushed the old man away and picked up the abandoned club. He commanded the family to remain silent and then slipped out to follow Hasan into the darkness. He sat in the dirt and feverishly attached his wooden leg. He knew that if Hasan did exactly as he was told, the Buddhist gong would sound in a matter of minutes—which didn't leave him long to take advantage of the diversion. Using the long club as a crutch, Hank hobbled his way back toward the Taliban compound.

He reached the circular wall of the compound just as the warning gong sounded from the mosque behind him. Hank quickened his pace and found a guard standing at the gate. The black-turbaned guard held his weapon at the ready and cocked his head to listen to the strange sound of the Buddhist's bell. Hank slowed his pace and limped toward the soldier. "What is the cause for such noise?"

"I do not know. I have never heard such a ringing before." The Taliban soldier gave him a quick glance, then turned back to peer into the darkened village.

"Maybe there is a fire. Is that smoke over there?" Hank pointed toward the village with his nonbloodied hand.

As the soldier turned to follow his finger, Hank stepped close and smashed him across the bridge of his nose with the club. Blood spurted from his face, and he fell to the ground. His eyes rolled back, and he twitched spasmodically in the dirt. Hank pulled the assault rifle from his hands and turned to cover the entrance. Hank pulled a clip of ammunition from the fallen man's pockets. He could hear Hasan screaming in the distance.

Hank cautiously pushed the large metal door open and peered inside. Lights flickered in some of the buildings, but there were no soldiers in sight. Hank limped toward the barracks as quickly as he could, knowing that at any moment soldiers would come pouring out. Dim lamplight shone through the barracks' single, narrow window, and he heard men talking inside. Hasan arrived at the gate behind him and began pounding on the metal door.

Hank took up position in front of the barracks and held his breath. Boots stomped across the floor, and the heavy wooden door was thrown open. Half-dressed soldiers spilled out of the door, some still tugging at their boots, and Hank opened fire. A torrent of lead and flame tore the first three men into pieces. Other men fell back behind the exploding bodies. Hank stepped into the doorway and emptied his clip into the darkness. Once the last round was fired, he dropped the rifle and shoved the door closed.

Shouts of agony and confusion sounded from inside. Hank pulled a lifeless body from the ground and blocked the door from the outside. He grabbed an AK-47 from a dead man and noticed a strand of Russian-made grenades fixed to his belt. He grabbed three grenades and lobbed them through the small window, one at a time.

A huge cloud of dust and debris erupted from the window. The door was blown from its hinges with the second blast, and bright orange flame shot through the air. Dust enveloped the barracks as the last jolting concussion rocked the earth beneath him. Hank's ears rang, and he choked on the acrid smoke.

Hank knew that nothing could have survived the blasts, and instinct told him he was vulnerable in the open. There was more dust than smoke pouring from the doorway, but Hank hoped the room wasn't ablaze inside. He crawled back toward the door, staying low and pushing his weapon in front of him as he climbed over the bodies blocking the entrance. He clenched his eyes tight against the burning smoke as he felt his way through the barracks. Bodies and parts of bodies littered the floor. Beds lined either side of the narrow room.

The dust began to settle, and the orange glow from several small fires illuminated the haze. He crawled down the center of the room, between the rows of beds. His hands slipped and slid in piles of viscous gore. He wretched and choked, fighting to take in gulps of air as he scrambled over smoldering piles of debris, until finally he could make out the outline of another door at the back of the room.

He could hear men shouting outside as he pulled himself close to the door and tried to catch his breath. He knew someone might try to charge into the room to rescue their comrades, and he only had whatever ammunition was left in the single clip in his weapon. He scanned the room through the haze and saw a stack of RPG rounds against the wall. A shoulder-mounted launcher was partially buried near the pile of rocket-propelled grenades. Hank pulled it free and loaded the grenades into a blanket before dragging the load back to the rear door.

He loaded a grenade and overturned a desk near the door. Once he was sheltered under the desk, he pointed the weapon to the ceiling and fired. A huge explosion shook the room and showered him with smoking rubble. He still hoped to fool the Taliban into thinking they were under attack by American helicopters; he knew he didn't stand a chance as a lone gunman. As soon as he was able, he loaded another grenade and blasted the ceiling again. The second blast ripped the building apart from the inside. His ears rang, and all other sound was lost, but with any luck none of the soldiers would follow him into the barracks— all eyes would be trained on the sky looking for the helicopters.

Hank loaded the launcher again, this time setting it aside to grab the AK-47. He positioned himself beside the door and prepared to go through. He was ready to face a room full of bad guys, but he knew that if the door led to a closet, he was a dead man. He grabbed the levered handle and quickly pulled the door open. Fresh air washed over his face and into his lungs. A clear corridor opened in front of him. He stood and covered every angle with his weapon. He strained his ears for sounds of trouble, but all he could hear was a high-pitched ringing.

Hank paused for a moment to sling the rocket launcher over his shoulder, then pulled the blanket full of grenades into the hallway behind him. After a few feet, the hallway opened to another small room. Gray flashes of movement caught his eyes. Two turbaned men stood in front of him. Their backs were turned, and they were anxiously peering through a window. Neither of them noticed him as he crouched low and took aim.

Hank blasted the nearest man in the back, flattening him against the wall. The muzzle flashes illuminated other figures in the room as Hank took aim on the second man at the window. The man turned to face him, his eyes wild with fear, and Hank pumped three rounds into his chest. He spun around to take aim on the other men. His eyes went to their hands, looking for weapons. One of the men across the room held an AK. He stood his ground, bringing his rifle to a firing position, but Hank dropped him with a burst shot from the hip.

Another man dove across the room, and Hank followed him with a spray of automatic fire. The man fell or leaped behind a cot as Hank's rifle ran out of ammunition. Hank dropped the weapon where he stood and lunged for the dead man's AK. Another man flashed across Hank's peripheral vision; he turned, prepared to dive for cover, and recognized the ancient form of Mullah Bakkar. He was unarmed and wore a pitiful, frightened look on his face. The Mullah saw Hank's weapon lying on the floor and made a break for a door at the far end of the room. Hank could see more figures beyond the door before Mullah Bakkar disappeared inside.

Hank picked up the abandoned weapon and checked the ammunition clip. He counted rounds and limped his way back to the RPG. He shouldered the launcher and pulled the grenades toward the door. Hank stood to one side of the door and lifted his wooden leg to push the handle. The handle gave, and he pushed the door open with the business end of his weapon.

Shots burst from behind the door, filling the darkened room with flashes of light. Hank could feel the tiny sonic distortions as the bullets flew by him. He dropped to his belly and fired back at the muzzle flashes. A man folded over in front of him and fell to the floor, pinning Mullah Bakkar beneath him.

The room was small, not much bigger than a closet, and had no other doors or windows. Shug and Xavier sat on the floor, tied back to back. Hank pivoted to cover the area behind the door, but the space was empty.

"Hank!" Shug's eyes were wide, and his face was badly beaten.

Hank checked his emotions and spun around to grab the rocket launcher and slam the door closed behind him.

"Oh my God! It *is* you! Cut us loose!" Tears streamed down Xavier's cheeks as he pulled against the ropes holding him to Shug.

"What's happening, Hank?" Shug's voice was at its breaking point.

Hank couldn't speak. He could barely breathe. All sound was muffled beneath a painful ringing. He dropped his weapons and fumbled for the knife in his belt. He pulled out the long, serpentine blade and began sawing at the ropes.

"Quickly! Please!" Xavier wailed at him as he hacked at the ropes. "I don't want to die here! I want to go home!"

"What's going on? Are you alone?" Shug pulled against the ropes as the first cord was cut.

"No, fuckin' Rambo is right behind me." Hank croaked in between gasps.

"What is all that noise?" Shug stared at him wide-eyed.

"Jail break." Hank let his relief envelop him, and a half smile broke on his face.

"Please hurry! What is wrong with you?" Xavier screamed. "I smell smoke!"

The old knife refused to cut through the ropes, and the strength had left Hank's hands. "Shut up! I need a better knife." Hank slipped the knife into his belt and rushed over to the fallen soldier. His hands groped around the man's belt until he found his knife. A bullet had snapped the blade in two, but enough cutting edge remained.

The shattered knife easily cut through the ropes, and Shug sprang to his feet.

"Is there a fire? I smell smoke." Xavier sat and rubbed his wrists, sniffing the air.

Hank turned his attention back to the fallen Taliban man and dug through his vest to find more ammunition.

"What do we do now?" Shug asked as he stood over Mullah Bakkar and the dead soldier.

"Grab his weapon!" Hank jerked his head toward the AK lying on the ground. "Can you hear anything outside?"

"There are people out there." Shug pressed his ear close to the door. "Sounds like the place is on fire!" Shug bent down and picked up the blood-soaked rifle.

"Grab a weapon, Frenchy!" Hank barked at Xavier, who was still fretting over his injured wrists.

Xavier jumped into action, turning over chairs and piles of blankets as if he were going to find a bazooka under one of them.

"The bodies! Search the bodies!"

"What do we do now, Hank?" Shug chambered a round and wiped the blood from his hands.

"Time to get the hell out of here. What did they do with the van?"

"I dunno—I don't think they did anything with it yet. I don't think they knew what to do with us."

"They wanted to kill us!" Xavier stopped his dithering and looked pleadingly at Hank.

"Where's the van?" Hank repeated.

"I don't know. I don't speak any Pashto! I don't even have the keys. They took everything from us! La Boux had the keys, and La Boux ... he is dead!"

"Fuck La Boux—and fuck the keys! We'll make our way to the van. If it's not there, we'll make a new plan, but we're getting the hell out of Bamian!" Hank rechecked his weapon and readied himself near the door. "Shug, I don't know how much farther I can go. I'm spent. I need your help."

"I'll carry you all the way home if I have to. Just tell me what to do."

"He's alive! This one is still alive!" Xavier shrieked and leaped away from the men on the floor.

Hank looked down to see the Mullah under the dead soldier. His face was covered in blood, and his eyes were shut tight, feigning death. "Has he got any weapons on him?"

"I can't find any guns." Xavier backed into the wall.

"Kill him, Shug." Hank readied the rocket launcher and moved to the door.

"Me?"

"You've got a weapon, don't you?"

"But he's an old man!"

"We don't have time to mess around. Kill him so we can get out of here."

"Yes, let's go. I want to get out of here!" Xavier wiped at his tears as he paced the rear wall.

Hank pointed through the door with his weapon. "We go through here. It should be clear, but we may have to come out shooting, okay? Our billet is only a few hundred meters away. If the van is there, we take it."

"Okay, let's do it." Shug readied the rifle in his hands.

"What about him?" Hank jerked his head toward the Mullah.

"I'm not shooting some old fool!" Shug shook his head and refused to look at the frightened old man.

"Okay, whatever." Hank braced himself and nodded for Shug to open the door. Dark smoke poured into the tiny room, and a wave of heat knocked them to the floor. The opposite end of the room burned fiercely. Hank crawled through the door and covered the empty room with his AK. Shadows flashed across the window as men ran past outside.

Hank guided the others across the room and screamed above the roar of the fire. "Get down!"

"We must get out of here! We will burn to death!" Xavier grabbed at Hank's trousers and tried to push past him.

"Get back!" Hank pushed him aside and aimed the rocket launcher at the back wall. He pulled the trigger, sending a grenade zipping into the wall. A jet of flame filled the room as the wall exploded in a torrent of shrapnel and fiery debris.

Hank coughed and choked, pushing the launcher ahead of him as he crawled over the broken wall. Everything was black, except for the gray form of a hole punched through the wall. Seconds later, all three men fell through the gaping hole and lay on the ground coughing and sputtering.

Hank rubbed the soot from his eyes and focused on the road outside the Taliban compound. "That way. Past those buildings." Hank pulled Shug to his feet and pointed along the wall. "Do you know where you are?"

"I think so." Shug gagged and wiped the tears from his eyes.

"Good. Then carry me." Hank grabbed Shug by the collar and started to pull himself onto his back.

"But we've got to run."

"Yeah, and I'm spent. I can't do it."

Shug sagged under Hank's weight. "I don't think I can. My arms … my legs. I've been tied up for hours. I can't …"

"Cry me a river. Now run!" Hank dropped the rocket launcher and grabbed for Shug's rifle. He tried to keep the weapon pointed up, but he was physically tapped. The weapon bounced against Shug's chest as he chugged down the alley and across the road.

Shug stopped in the intersection and pointed to a man running toward them. "Shoot him!"

Hank squeezed the trigger, but he couldn't control the weapon. The figure disappeared behind a wall and didn't return fire. "Go … go … *go!*"

They crossed a narrow dirt road approaching one of the larger family compounds. Their billet lay on the other side. They rounded the corner, Shug breathing in great bellows. A high wall with towers on every corner surrounded the compound. Hank strained his arms to cover them. The thought of failure at this point was maddening. He had no strength left for fighting.

They finally rounded the last corner, and Hank's heart nearly burst with joy. The van sat where they had left it. The impossible now seemed possible.

"It's here!" Shug puffed.

Xavier boldly ran past them and began pulling on the door handles. "It's locked! I told you! It's locked! I don't have the keys! La Boux …"

"Put me down." Hank slid off Shug's back and covered them with his AK. "Shug, you drive."

"Right." Shug quickly strode over to the drivers' door and smashed the window. He swung the door open and began working the wires under the steering column. In a matter of seconds, the van belched smoke from the exhaust. "I still got it." Shug shot Hank a triumphant smile and motioned for him to climb in.

"You're in the back, Frenchy." Hank opened the door and Xavier scrambled inside. Sweat and tears poured down his chubby face. Hank pulled himself into the seat and rolled down the window to angle his weapon behind them. "Let's get the hell out of here."

"Laa Elaaha Ellaa Allah. There is no God except Allah." Omar Khalifa muttered the prayer absently. After days of pursuit without end, exhaustion had finally overwhelmed him, allowing all reason to escape. There was no way to make sense of what they were asking of him.

"Mullah Bakkar speaks well of you. Do you deserve his praise, pilgrim?" The fat-faced Arab smiled as if he were toying with a child. "Have you learned your lessons well enough to join in Allah's test?"

"If master Bakkar thinks it so." Omar chewed his lip and eyed the others waiting near the helicopter. "I am a poor judge of my own worthiness. I know nothing of Americans and their war against Islam."

Mustafa grinned, wrapping an arm around Omar's shoulder and pulling him close. "But you know of the devil and the righteousness of Allah." Omar could smell the cigarettes on the man's breath. "You have been blessed with a fine ear and a sharp mind. You speak American English. You have seen the demon himself! Surely you can see this is Allah's will."

"If Mullah Bakkar says it is providence, then I will not question him. But surely there are better men." Omar had never seen himself in the same light as the murderers from al-Qaeda, and he couldn't understand why was being pressured into joining them now.

"Nonsense. You have already proven yourself, pilgrim. I can think of few men as capable as you. If it was not for blind luck, we would be putting our blades to the man right now. You were so very close, Omar. Do not lose heart: this too is part of Allah's plan. By this time tomorrow, you will see that you have been blessed. This is your chance at paradise. Do not let the fatigue of your body hinder your peace in the afterlife."

"I do not hesitate because of lack of sleep. I too wish retribution on the man who attacked my teacher and killed my brothers. But I know little outside this land. If this man is as dangerous as you say, how am I to kill him?"

"What do you know of this man?"

"Only what Mullah Bakkar and you have told me."

"We have learned many things while you chased this man from Bamian. We've found his papers. He is a spy against Islam. He planned on making a very unhappy movie about your Taliban."

"Is it true he killed all those men?"

"Yes, my brother. He is a demon."

Omar closed his eyes, recalling the dead and burnt back in Bamian. He had never seen his beloved Mullah so shaken.

Mustafa lowered his tone and walked him further away from the others. "What else do you remember about this man?"

"I knew him as an Arab. A pathetic charity case who smuggled opium and had a gift for languages. He was disgusting and smelly. I thought he was mad or drunk, or both."

"Yes, but would you recognize his face? Which leg was missing, right or left?"

Omar silently lifted his right leg, showing Mustafa where Ali Ali-Akkba was missing his foot.

"Good—your mind is as sharp as your teachers said it was. Do you remember, was this man present when our men came to Bamian? Was he there? Did he talk with them?"

"He was there. He heard their talk about the Buddhas, but he did not speak with them."

Mustafa stopped walking, folding his arms over his chest. "This is good news." He let a long pause hang in the air while he chose his next words. "Do you think you will recognize him when he is not playing the part of actor?"

"I know his face."

"Good. We know his name. We have eyes watching the roads to Iran; if he passes that way, we will catch him. But if he does not, we must be prepared to follow him to the ends of the earth. He is a danger to our faith, brother. Are you willing to do Allah's bidding, pilgrim?"

"I will obey my teacher and my God."

"Are you willing to shave your chin and travel to America?"

"Me? Why me?"

"You know this man! You speak good English. Allah has chosen you."

"But I know nothing of these things. I am only a student."

"Al-Qaeda will help you, brother. Do not worry. We can help you find him. We can help you kill him."

Paradigm I
Chapter 3

Shug watched Hank hop across the hotel room to sit at the edge of the bed. The sight of Hank's stump kicking the air was still revolting, even though he'd spent the last four months staring at it. The adjoining hotel rooms felt more like prison cells, and Shug watched Hank's cell phone on the nightstand as if it were a ticking time bomb. Stress grew like mold in the cramped space. Personal flaws were magnified by boredom and over-familiarity—and to make matters worse, Hank insisted on listening to the Howard Stern show every morning.

Shug held his head in his hands as he stared at the oil painting on the wall. "Do you think today will be the day?"

"Bill says the Icons are having their big meeting today. All the bigwigs will be there."

"You really think they'll be talking about what happened in Afghanistan?"

"They've got to make a decision sooner or later. They can't suspend us indefinitely."

Shug pulled a chair from the desk and sat between the beds. "You think they'll dump us?"

"I doubt it. We're too dangerous to turn loose. They'll probably just separate us from Billy."

"I still don't get it. You're the one who saved us out there. La Boux's death wasn't your fault. How can they blame you?"

"I'm on their shit list." Hank turned away with a shrug of his shoulders. "People are talking about Iconoclasts, and they don't like it." His attention drifted back to the radio.

"What do you think they know about Devil's Peak?" Shug gritted his teeth, watching Hank for a reaction.

Hank's face worked into an annoyed sneer as he stared into his coffee. "That all depends on Bill."

"Don't worry about Bill; he's solid."

"We'll see."

Shug could see that conversation would be difficult while Howard was talking, so he turned his attention to the hotel menu by the phone. "You want anything from room service? I'm starving."

"No, go ahead, get whatever you want. Get crazy."

Shug ran his finger down the list and picked up the phone. "I just wish I could see their faces when Devil's Peak takes off."

"Who? The Icons?"

"No, the Taliban. It would almost be worth going back."

"Forget it. They'll never see it." Hank crossed his stump over his knee and peered at the television as if it were on. Howard Stern and his crew laughed in the background. "Most of the world will never see it."

"But they're gonna hear about it. I mean, come on, they have some televisions. Someone will see it."

"They don't trust their televisions the way we do. Most of us were raised on Star Trek. No one outside the Western world will buy our crap."

"Crap? You really think it's crap?" Shug had been steadily probing Hank for his real thoughts about the UFOs, but he never seemed to get a straight answer. "After everything we've pulled together?"

"It's dangerous to believe your own propaganda, Shug."

"It's not all propaganda. Don't you ever wonder about some of this stuff?"

"I haven't put much thought into it. It doesn't really matter what I believe. What's *believable* is what matters. I just want something convincing enough to get people talking."

Shug scratched his head while the operator answered the line. "Yeah, hi. I'd like an order of pancakes, three eggs over easy, bacon, sausage, and a side of toast, please." Shug covered the phone with his hand. "You sure you don't want anything?"

"Nah, just coffee."

"Can I please get some fruit, too?" Shug ran his eyes over the menu a second time. "That'll do it. Thanks." He hung up the line and stared at Hank. "Are you trying to tell me you haven't thought about it? After everything we've seen? Don't you think it's possible?"

"You're asking me what I think?" Hank raised an eyebrow with a smirk.

"Yeah, the truth. What do you really think?"

"I think it's likely that there's other life out there somewhere. It's a big universe. But I think it's unlikely that we'll ever come in contact with it. There's just too much space out there. We're just a tiny speck, occupying a tiny slice of time. The odds are against it."

"But what about all the pictures, all the videos? It can't all be a bunch of crap. Some of the stuff you've had me look up has really freaked me out. Don't you think that some of it could be real?"

"I don't care what's real. I just care about what's going to work and what's not. We've both met tons of people who believe in this stuff, but where does it get them?"

"So what—you just want to prove people wrong about their beliefs?"

"It's not about proving anything. People need to be shocked into thinking for themselves. Life scares people; they hide behind their beliefs so they don't have to think about the tough questions."

"But what about you? I've seen the look in your eye when you're talking to some of those people. What about all those old paintings you bought? You wouldn't have spent all that money if there wasn't something to it."

"The artwork is just another part of the plan." Hank dismissed his questions with a wave of his hand, signaling that he wanted to listen to the show. Howard Stern's tone shifted abruptly as he read an announcement over the air:

"I don't mean to interrupt the fun, but uh, there is a breaking news story … a serious news story … a plane has crashed into the World Trade Center."

"You're kidding!"

"The World Trade Center is on fire," Howard continued. "There's a huge fire at the World Trade Center."

Hank turned to face Shug. His eyes were wide, and his mouth hung open.

"He's got to be kidding." Shug waited for the punch line, but none came. "He's joking, right?"

"The whole thing is on fire! I mean not a little fire! It's huge! Oh my God!" A caller on the phone confirmed what Howard was saying.

"How does this happen? I mean, this is not the first time. A plane crashed into the Empire State Building in the forties." Gary, Howard's on-air producer, spoke into the silence. "It flew right into it."

"But what kind of plane was this," asked Robin, Howard's co host, "was it a private plane?"

"I hope this wasn't one of those crazy Kamikaze attacks." Gary continued.

"This is serious business. I'm still … trying to make sense of it." Howard's voice trailed off as a chorus of horrified gasps filled the studio.

"Good Lord! It looks like a portion of the plane is sticking out of the building," Robin shouted over the others.

"Can you see that?" Howard exclaimed in disbelief.

"Man, it's really smoking!"

"It's just like Towering Inferno." Gary shouted in the background.

"It's a huge fire."

Shug stopped searching for the remote control and leaped for the buttons on the television. The massive tower burned on the screen. A thick plume of smoke enveloped the upper third of the building, and the television announcer was confirming that a plane had struck the north tower. Shug stepped away from the screen and couldn't speak.

"Holy … Shug, look at that!" Hank pointed to the screen while the image of a plane exploded into the second building. "Did you see that?"

A huge fireball filled the screen, and Shug's eyes bounced back to the second tower and the giant column of smoke stretching into the sky. "What happened? Was that another plane?"

"Look! Both towers are burning!"

"Listen … they're saying it was another plane!" Both men fell silent as they listened to the anchorman confirm that a second plane had just impacted the World Trade Center. Shug couldn't believe what he was seeing and could barely comprehend what he was hearing. Hank didn't move, except to push his face closer to the screen. The voice on the television was saying that the two planes struck eighteen minutes apart.

Hank slowly turned to face Shug. There was a look in his eyes that Shug had never seen before. "We're at war."

"Howard, you've got to watch your monitor." Tom, Howard's station manager broke into the on-air conversation. "They are going to play it back. There's been another explosion."

"Oh my God!" The expression was repeated throughout the studio as the image of a plane crashing into the tower was broadcast over the monitor.

"Tom, what's happening? What do you know?" Howard shouted over the growing tumult of voices. "Was it a terrorist attack?"

"Look at that hole ... It's huge." Robin gasped.

"Look, the second tower is burning!"

"Wait a second. Let me see that thing again," Howard demanded, not believing his eyes.

"That ... That's the second building!"

"Oh my God!"

"No, no. That's a reflection," said Robin emphatically.

"Yes it is! The second building is on fire!" said one crewmember, then another.

"Howard, CNN is reporting that the other tower has been hit by a second plane." An intern burst into the studio. "It's got to be!"

"Stop it!" exclaimed Robin in disbelief.

"No, wait, the second building is burning!"

"So it's a terrorist attack, isn't it?" Howard was fighting to be heard above the others.

"Why do they always go after the World Trade Center?"

"It's the biggest landmark in New York," replied Howard.

"It's the financial center of the world," said Robin.

"And it's a place where people will get killed. You can't take down the statue of liberty and kill a whole bunch of people," Howard yelled into the microphone.

"Does this scare you?"

"Yes ... it scares me! Yes, it does scare me! We're totally too lax in this country."

"Do ya think they'll fall?" Shug was captivated by the footage repeated on the news. "What if they topple over?"

"I don't know ... look at them burn." Hank shook his head as he chewed his thumbnail. "I don't think anything can survive that fire."

"We're under attack! We're under attack!" Howard's voice quaked with emotion. "Its war! Come on!"

"It's just like the Japanese." Gary shouted.

"Come on! This is Pearl Harbor all over again!" Howard raged.

"We've got to go bomb everything over there," Robin said angrily.

"We've got to bomb the hell out of them! You know who it is, ... I can't say ... but you know who it is," Howard shouted. "They're doing it over here, now!"

"It's a suicide mission," said Gary.

"We're at war," Howard said flatly.

"Who did this?" A wave of nausea gripped Shug as he watched what appeared to be bodies falling from the towers.

The question seemed to break Hank's fixation on the screen, and he quickly stood to grab his prosthetic. He gathered his clothes and started to dress. "Looks like a hijacking. Probably al-Qaeda."

"So it's already started ... we're at war, just like you said."

Hank flopped onto the bed and pulled on his pants. "Shug, do you realize what this means?"

"We're at war, right? We're gonna go after them with everything we've got."

"It's war ... but we can't go dropping nukes on them. If we do, it will be all over. We'd just be inviting them to do the same here. They want us to drop the big ones."

Shug felt like putting his fist through something. "Well then, let's give them what they want!"

"It's no good, Shug. It can't go that way." Hank slipped his watch around his wrist and grabbed his cell phone. "But there's something else ..." Hank paused, pointing toward the television. President Bush was about to address the county.

The president was visibly shaken and faltered over what, for Shug, was the key statement. He vowed to hunt down and find the *folks* who had committed this terrible act.

Howard wasted no time in condemning the president's soft statement. "Folks ... folks! This was no act! I don't want to hear about hunting down people! I want to hear about bombing the hell out of these terrorists and the countries that support them!"

Howard let loose another bitter tirade as the president called for a moment of prayer. "Enough with the moment of silence already! Let's get those bastards! I don't want the president praying for me ... I want action. Bomb them back to the Stone Age! That's what they want, anyway!

Listen ... The only way to defend against these terrorists is to be a very strong parent ... We're the leaders in the world, we have the technology to spank these douche bags once and for all! We're too lenient … too liberal. When parents are too liberal, the kids get spoiled and they act out."

"Shug, listen to Howard—not because he's right, but because he's like every other guy out there. He's screaming for blood. Guys like Bin Laden are aching for us to start throwing our weight around. It's a military nightmare." Hank excused himself to use the bathroom, leaving Shug to digest the news coming from the television.

On the radio, Howard was taking a commercial break, reading a live commercial and hating it. The loathing in his voice was clear as he sarcastically pitched mattresses for Sleep Train. He stopped his pitch when Stuttering John broke into the studio. "The P-P-Pentag-g-gon!"

"The Pentagon? What?!"

"Howard, there ha … hux….. hu … has been another e-e-explosion at the P-P-Pentagon!" John choked out the words breathlessly.

"Another explosion?" Hank repeated from the bathroom.

"Get out here and listen to this!" Shug shouted toward the door.

Hank bolted from the bathroom and stepped out onto the balcony. "Check it out." He pointed to a rising cloud of black smoke barely visible on the horizon. Sirens began to echo off the downtown buildings. Shug began flipping channels on the television. All of the channels still showed the footage of a plane disappearing into a wall of glass.

Hank's cell phone started to ring on his bed—Bill's personalized ringtone. Hank grabbed the phone and stepped outside.

As Shug flipped through the news channels, the image of the Towers changed inexplicably before his eyes. He could not believe what he was seeing until it was verbalized by the voices on the radio.

"The whole World Trade Center just collapsed!"

"The whole thing just completely dropped!"

"Oh my God!!!" The sentiment volleyed back and forth between the radio and television.

"Hank! Get in here!"

Hank stepped into the room, covering the mouthpiece of the phone.

"Look—it's gone!" Shug pointed to the screen. "It's like a nuke hit the city!" The whole of Manhattan was shrouded in thick dust.

"Are you seeing this, Billy?" Hank spoke into the phone. "Which tower was that?"

"Are you sure?" Hank sat on the edge of his bed plugging one of his ears.

"Where are you?"

"What are they gonna do with Congressman Thomas?"

"Okay. We'll stay here. Call back as soon as you can get confirmation."

Hank flipped his phone closed and stared at the screen. "Shug, do you have any idea who was in that tower?"

"What do you mean? You know somebody …"

"The Iconoclasts' headquarters are on the top floor of Tower One." Hank let out a defeated sigh.

"*The boys in the tower …*" Shug groaned.

"The entire organizational branch of the Iconoclasts has just been … decapitated," Hank said flatly. "They were having a big meeting up there this morning. All of the bigwigs from around the world were supposed to be there. All of the records, everything was in that tower."

"Oh my God." Shug had managed not to utter that phrase so far this morning. He knew how it bothered Hank, but there was nothing else left to say—it was automatic.

"What can I say now? I don't think that there is any reason to stay on the air right now … right Tom?" Howard sounded lost.

"It's a place for people to call in … like a big encounter session." Tom encouraged Howard to stay on as a public service. "A lot of the other stations have been knocked off the air."

"All right. I'll stay on the air for a little while …"

"What did we do that was so wrong?" Gary asked angrily.

"We did nothing!"

"Ya know they're gon … gon … gonna say that we h-h-h-have participated in terrorism …" stuttering John was quickly cut short by Howard.

"Who cares! Now is the time to stop their rhetoric!" Howard screamed. "This is the first time we've really had an excuse to wipe out these animals!"

Bill was late. Ordinarily he wouldn't care, but he didn't need Hank thinking this was some form of passive-aggressive power play on his part. Not now. Not today. Hank always insisted on meeting in out-of-the-way motels like this, and he hated it. The tires on his Benz squealed to a stop as he nearly passed the Motel 6 for a second time. Bill gunned the engine and backed into a spot between two dusty wrecks. He checked the time on his Rolex and dug through his pockets until he found a pack of smokes.

Hank answered the door before he had finished knocking. He was fully dressed, but his prosthetic leg lay on the bed with his bags. He hopped across the room without a word and sat at a small desk where a laptop computer occupied the only phone line. "So how bad is it? How big was the meeting?"

"I'm fine, thanks for asking." Bill slid a cigarette between his lips and closed the door behind him.

"Sorry, Billy." Hank ventured an apologetic smile before offering him a seat. "I still can't believe this is happening."

"I know. This is crazy." Bill sat down shaking his head. The television was on, but the volume was turned down. No matter where he went, Bill couldn't escape the horrific images.

"Thanks for coming. I know it wasn't easy to get away." Hank checked the time on his watch.

"Forget it. I needed to get out of there before I went nuts."

"How's Congressman Thomas? Did you get him squared away?"

"Finally. It took me two days, but Gilbert is settled in. It's a madhouse over there."

"We're at war." Hank said dismissively.

"Yeah, I guess we are."

"So what can you tell me that I wouldn't already know from watching the news?"

Bill took a deep breath and eyed Hank through the smoke. "All business as usual, eh?"

"We don't have much time. If what you've told me is true, we're two days behind."

"It's true. Bush signed the War Powers Act: he can bypass congress."

"What about the Iconoclasts? Have you got a list of casualties yet?"

"Not yet."

"How big was the meeting?"

"Big." Bill took a pull from his smoke and let the emotion drain. "Most of the Icon bigwigs were there."

"How are you planning on getting your confirmation?"

"It's impossible. We may never know. I only know a few of the players myself. For all I know, the entire organizational branch has been wiped out."

"We've been decapitated," Hank said flatly.

The phrase hung in the air, and Bill remembered what a disaster like this meant to men like Hank. For anyone else, it would have been a catastrophic deathblow, but for the never-say-die men in Delta Force, it was just another setback. If only one man survived, a new head would grow from nothing more than pure determination.

Hank crossed his stump over his knee and folded his arms across his chest. "What floor were they on? Did any of them get out before the collapse?"

"They were on the top. If any of them got out, I haven't heard about it."

"What about the records?"

"I'm not sure, but I think all the data banks were there too."

"All of them?" Hank screwed his brow into a doubtful scowl. "What about off-site backups?"

"I don't know. Nobody knows."

"You're telling me all that stuff is gone." A flash of anger colored Hank's voice for the first time. "Billy, we've got to find where else this data is kept."

"Listen: I've talked with my boss, and he says we've got to sit tight until we get a handle on this. We're all over the place right now, and nobody knows who's in charge."

"Listen to *me,* Billy: we've got to pull the organization together right now, or the whole thing will crumble. The only way to survive decapitation is establish leadership right away." Bill was about to interrupt, but Hank checked him with a raised finger. "I'm talking about you, Billy. You can keep this thing alive."

"Me? I'm not even in the organizational branch. What am I going to do?"

"All of those people are gone, Billy. And what's left of them are disconnected. We need to find out who's left and reconnect them."

"But it's impossible! You're grossly overestimating my place in all this."

"It's a whole new ball game. We have to open things up if we're going to survive."

"Yeah, but …"

"Bill, every person in that meeting is going to be missed."

"I know." Bill slumped in his chair at the thought of so much loss. His dreams and aspirations now seemed hollow and easily crushed.

"No, Bill, I mean every Iconoclast in the tower will be missing!" Hank grabbed his wrist. His grip was hard as stone, and a light gleamed in his eyes. "Find out who was killed in that building, and you know all the names of the Icon leadership." Hank sat back and pointed toward his computer. "I've got Shug working on a filter program right now."

"But we're talking about thousands of people."

"I know. We've got our work cut out for us."

Bill shook his head, trying to take it all in. "It's all screwed up. There's no way we could pull things together from the bottom."

"Everything has changed. We're at war now. The Iconoclasts can't hide behind their anonymity anymore. We have to open up the books. We have to come face to face with the other Iconoclasts, or that's it—it's all over."

"But we don't even know how much of the organizational branch is left. We've got to assume someone is left. We're still small fish, Hank. We don't have that kind of power."

"What about Congressman Thomas? He's not a small fish."

"He's got his hands full with congress. He leaves the Icon stuff to me."

"But he understands where he fits in?"

"He does. Do you?" Bill wished he could have taken the words back as soon as they left his mouth, but Hank simply smiled back at him.

"I know my place too, Billy. I'm here to help you. And right now, I'm telling you what you need to do. You're a bigger player in this than you realize. This is the war the Icons have been trying to prevent. We have a part in this war."

Bill closed his eyes and let Hank's words replay in his mind. On the television, a single bugle played taps—a memorial for the eight hundred victims of the Pentagon attack. He opened his eyes to stare at the montage of images playing on the screen. "I don't ever think I'll get used to hearing that song."

"What, taps?"

"Yeah, I can't seem to get away from it."

"Do you know where it came from?"

"What, the song?"

"Yeah, taps."

Bill knew it was a standard at every military funeral, but he couldn't remember its history. "I don't remember."

"Come on, Billy. An enlisted man shouldn't have to tell an officer the story of taps."

"Yeah, well, I've got a lot on my mind right about now." Bill wasn't in the mood for one of Hank's lectures on military history, but Hank sat back in his chair and dove in.

"During the Civil War there was this Union army captain, Captain Ellicombe. He was with his men near Harrison's Landing, Virginia. They were squared off against the Confederate army across a narrow field. During the night, Captain Ellicombe heard the moans of a wounded soldier lying in the field. He didn't know if it was a Union or Confederate soldier, but something compelled him to risk his life and crawl out on his belly through the gunfire to pull the man back to his encampment.

When the captain finally reached his own lines, he discovered he was dragging a Confederate soldier. By now the man was dead. He caught sight of the young soldier's face—and realized that it was his own son."

"Really?" Bill stared absently at the graves of Arlington as Hank continued.

"His boy had been studying music in the South when the war broke out. He'd enlisted with the Confederate army without telling his father. The following morning, the father asked permission to give his son a full military burial despite his enemy status. His request was only partially granted. They let him pick a single musician to play at the funeral. Ellicombe chose a bugler and asked him to play a series of musical notes he'd found on a scrap of paper in his son's uniform. The bugler belted out taps for the first time. It's been played that way at U.S. military funerals ever since."

"I think I did hear that story once. I must have forgotten it somehow." Bill tore his eyes from the screen, dashing out his cigarette.

"It was a terrible war. People like to forget about things that don't sit right with them. They forget because they don't understand. We fought that war because we were something special. We represented the new world and the new ideal, and we went to war to keep that dream alive. We are still the new world. What happened September 11 was an attack on the new world, too. Every great nation is attacked by lesser powers. That's just the way it is. This is also a theological war. This is about belief and power. This is a war the Iconoclasts can play a major part in."

"There might not be any more Iconoclasts! What am I supposed to do about it? I don't have the power you think I have."

"Bill, if any of the Icon leadership somehow escaped and watched the towers fall, they would be saying the same thing. Everything has changed. Things are going to move fast. The military is on the move, our enemies are on the move, and people are going to want answers. They want action. The focus of the whole world has narrowed, and it's time for the Icons to make a move."

"I don't know, Hank. I know what you're saying, but ..." Bill shook his head. "But I don't see how we can do anything about it now."

"You have a choice. Sometimes there aren't any good choices, but the choice—such as it is—is yours. Do nothing, and the Iconoclasts die."

"You're overestimating me. I can't do what you're talking about."

Hank shrugged. "Why not?"

"We can't fill in the blanks and connect the dots. The organization is too big, too secretive."

"We have a few of the names already. We can find the rest. Once we do, we can piece things back together. But we can't operate in total secrecy anymore. That time is over."

"I guess I could make a few calls." Bill thought to himself that he might as well placate Hank until he came up with of a way to disengage himself from his plans.

"Good." Hank slapped a pad of paper onto the table. "Let's start with all the names you know off the top of your head."

"What?" Bill straightened in his seat and locked eyes with Hank. To know a name gave you power, and now Hank was asking for a share.

"We need the list, Billy."

Los Angeles; September 15, 2001

Alarm bells rang out from across the street. Hank checked his watch; it was eleven thirty-five on the button. "Right on time. I don't believe it."

A relieved smile grew under the shadow of Shug's helmet. "I told you he could do it."

They hid in the darkness of an underground parking lot and peered over the cars at the building twinkling with the strobes of a fire alarm. "Just make sure he keeps his mouth shut." Hank hadn't wanted to use Shug's cousin for something so important, but he couldn't afford to enlist any professional help. All Shawn had to do was crack open the sprinkler valve, release some water, and disappear before the fire engines arrived, but Hank couldn't stand him. He was nothing like Shug. "You ready for this?"

"I've always wanted to be a fireman." Shug clicked his chinstrap under his jaw. He looked bigger than ever in the bulky gear.

"Got all the tools?"

"Check." Shug hoisted his bag for Hank to see.

"And what do you do if another fireman approaches you before we get to the building?"

"Shine my light in his face." Shug playfully shined the flashlight strapped to his chest into Hank's face. The reflectors on his fire helmet and turnout coat momentarily glowed bright yellow.

"Smart ass." Hank covered the light with his hand and mockingly threatened to knock him in the head. "And what company are you with?"

"Firefighter Winter, engine company fifteen, sir."

"Good. What floor is our target?"

"You really want to go over this again?" Shug rolled his eyes in mock annoyance.

"Why not? We've got a couple minutes before the trucks arrive."

"Do you think any cops will show up?" Shug peered down the street between buildings.

"I doubt it. LA is a big city. There are probably a hundred false alarms a night." Hank rechecked the flaps on his coat and adjusted his helmet. "Besides, it doesn't matter. We're firemen. We're supposed to be here. There are over two thousand guys in this department; no one will think twice about never seeing us before."

A siren sounded in the distance, barely audible above the persistent clatter of alarm bells. The wail grew and bounced off the glass towers lining the downtown streets until the red flashing lights of a fire engine lit the intersection.

"Okay, we wait for the second fire engine to pull up to the front." Hank ducked out of the light as the first engine rolled to a stop near the building's sprinkler pipes. The crew casually climbed off the truck and walked to the front of the building.

Moments later, a second engine turned the corner and silenced their siren. They parked in front of the building, and the crew joined the others at its entrance. The men shuffled their heavy boots and looked as if they had been rudely awoken. Some were still pulling their coats on as they walked. Most of them left the metal clasps of their coats undone to let their jacket hang open.

Hank unfastened the clasps of his jacket and ripped open the Velcro flaps. He motioned for Shug to do the same, then turned his attention back to the firemen looking for the magnetic keys that opened the front doors. Another fire engine parked down the street, shutting off its lights and waiting with its crew inside.

Hank tapped Shug's shoulder and pointed toward the idling fire engine. "Okay, brother, that's our target. You ready?"

Shug nodded his head, and both men stepped out from the shadows to cross the parking lot. Most of the fireman congregated near the doors didn't notice their approach. Two other men bent over a fistful of keys under the beam of a flashlight.

Hank quickened his pace once he was behind the fire engine and out of view. He strode up to the passenger side door, Shug falling in behind him. Hank checked front and back before reaching for the handle and pulling open the heavy door. The cab lights clicked on, and his eyes scanned for the ring of keys that opened the building's fire access. He found them plugged into the dashboard on a metal pin. As he pulled himself in to grab the keys, a man's head popped up from the driver's seat to stare at him over the box of maps and radios. His eyes were half-closed, and his hair stuck out in all directions from under his earphones.

Hank tried not to look startled; he tilted his helmet down to block his face. "Captain needs the keys." He grabbed the ring of keys and sheered them from their metal pin with a sharp twist. He climbed backward out of the cab, and the driver disappeared to resume his catnap behind the wheel.

Hank closed the door and shot Shug a painful grimace. They walked back along the engine, away from the men at the entrance. The firemen had already opened the large glass doors and gone inside to silence the alarm. Hank and Shug skirted the building and disappeared around the corner. Once they had made their way to the rear of the building, they were completely alone and out of sight of the others.

Hank shone his flashlight along the wall until he found the nondescript black box mounted to the side of the building. He worked the keys one at a time while Shug pulled two radios from his bag and placed one in his pocket. The lock turned, and the metal box fell open in his hands. He found a magnetic keycard and a set of keys.

He passed the card through the sensor, and the door opened with a click. "You know what to do." Hank gave Shug a confident nod and offered his hand for a high five.

Shug slapped his hand, gripping it tightly, and flashed his biggest smile. Hank opened the door and stepped inside. Now the alarm was deafening. Flashes of light pulsed through the building. Hank pointed down a corridor, motioning Shug away. He turned, leaving Shug to find the security console, and made his way toward the stairs.

The doors to the stairwells were unlocked. He noticed cameras watching him from the ceiling and turned his helmet into them, shielding his face. He climbed to the second floor and pushed open the door. He was on his way to the twenty-second floor, but he wanted to fool the electronic surveillance into thinking he was just a fireman checking floors, so he made sure to open every door he passed.

By the tenth floor, Hank had to stop and catch his breath. He knew that opening every door was a good idea, but it was quickly becoming tedious. He wanted to sprint his way to the twenty-second floor, but forced himself to be patient and methodical.

He was sweating profusely under the heavy coat. He hadn't anticipated the heat his gear trapped. His calf muscles, both real and imaginary, burned with fatigue. Suddenly the ear-piercing alarm stopped, and the metal stairs banged eerily beneath him.

"The Alarm is reset." Shug whispered into his ear through the radio. "I'm in the security office."

"Copy that … I'm on my way to the … thirteenth."

"Yeah … I see you. You gonna make it all the way to the top … or do you want me to come up there and carry your lazy white ass?"

"I don't know how these guys get around in all this stuff." Hank flapped air into his jacket. "I'm dying."

"Looks like the firemen are wrapping it up down there. There's only one fire engine left."

"What about the alarm?"

"Everything looks good. I've got all green lights down here."

"Okay. Keep your eyes open. I'll let you know when I'm at the terminal." Hank turned the steps without opening the door. He seemed to get heavier with sweat at every step.

Hank stopped for breath once he reached the twenty-second floor. He set his helmet on the floor and mopped his brow. "All right, I'm going in." Hank had memorized every foot of the floor plan and knew exactly where he was going. He followed the beam of his flashlight between offices, stopping at a watercooler and greedily draining several miniature cups of water. The placard on the next door read *Synergistic Services*. Hank passed his key over the sensor and pushed open the door.

"Synergistic Services" was the front office for a man named Dr. Nicolas Blair. Dr. Blair administered the finances of the West Coast Icons—and he was one of the thousands reported missing after the September 11 attacks. Hank found his office, but the doors were locked tight and there was no place for his passkey.

"I've found the office. Let me know if I set off any alarms."

"Looks good down here."

Hank pulled two hockey-puck-sized magnets from his pockets and slapped them onto the door. He positioned them where the magnetic triggers would be and then dug his hands back into his pockets. He shook a small aerosol can in his fist and then sprayed the keyhole with cryogenic gas, instantly freezing the inner workings of the lock. He then inserted a metal spike and rammed it home with the butt of a metal wrench. The frozen metal fractured, and the lock fell apart. Hank pulled back the bolt, and the door swung open.

"You see anything down there?"

"Nope. Looking good."

"Okay, I'm inside."

Hank passed the reception desk and headed toward the polished wood door. Doctor Blair's name was engraved in gold on the door. He tried the handle, but it was locked. There was no place for a key, only a small touch pad on the wall near the handle. Hank pulled a screwdriver from his pocket and worked on the screws of the faceplate. The long screws finally pulled away, and Hank exposed the electronic guts controlling the door.

He carefully plucked out two wires, cutting them and exposing the metal. He plugged the loose ends into a calculator-sized computer and tightened the screws.

The screen glowed his palm and he punched in the commands that would break the code.

After a few moments of chewing his thumbnail and watching symbols scrolling across the screen, the correct sequence flashed and the door buzzed open.

"I've got the doctor's door. How do I look?"

"Good. You're moving fast."

Hank half expected to hear alarms as pushed the door open, but none came. He scanned the darkened room with his flashlight. "Nice office." The room seemed to have been carved from a single tree. The walls gleamed of polished wood.

"Oh yeah?"

"These Icons sure like to throw their money around." Hank pushed aside the leather chair and took up position in front the desktop computer. "All right, I'm at the doctor's terminal."

"What does he use?"

"A Mac."

"Should be no sweat for you."

Hank tapped the keys, illuminating the screen. "All I have to do is hack into a totally unknown private system, find a list of names that could be hidden anywhere, and somehow keep the system from crashing." Hank blew out a long breath as he browsed through the user settings, getting a feel for the system.

"You're looking good on time."

Hank slipped a disk into the drive and downloaded an infiltration program onto the desktop. He rummaged through scraps of paper and personal notes hoping to find a password while the program was loading, but nothing jumped out at him. His program went to work cracking the encrypted passcode, and after a few moments the system's new back door opened wide. "I'm in."

"Really?"

"Looks like it." Hank's eyes scanned over hundreds of vaguely named files.

"Do you see anything that looks promising?"

"Like what, secret Iconoclast directory? There are thousands of files here. This is gonna take some time." Hank scrolled through the files, looking for the proverbial needle in the electronic haystack. "Hey Shug, did you ever want a Swiss bank account?"

"You got one for me?"

"Hundreds."

"I'll settle for the list. Can you run a search on one of the names we know already?"

"I'm working on it."

"Just use Bill's name."

"Give me a minute, will ya?" Hank's all-access pass was drowning him with data. He scanned file after file, flipping spreadsheets and turning pivot tables. Minutes flew by, but he wasn't getting anywhere. "This may take longer than I thought."

"What about his e-mail?"

"What about it?" Hank was growing annoyed.

"Maybe he's got an address book."

"Yeah, right." Hank bit his thumbnail and tapped the mouse feverishly. "Leave the hacking to me, okay?"

"Just trying to help."

Hank knew the file he was looking for was huge, but all the files were crammed with data. None of the names meant anything to him, and he feared he would never find what he was looking for. Frustrated, he switched screens to the electronic mail server. "Son of a bitch!"

"What's wrong?"

"Once again, you're a lot smarter than you look, brother. I might have to give you a raise."

"Was it in the e-mail? Did you find it?"

Hank read over the list of names in the massive directory. A few names and titles jumped out at him right away—celebrities, actors, and politicians, all listed alphabetically. "I think I might be onto something." Each name was backed up with files of data. "I'm in an e-mail directory, but not all the names have an e-mail address. This has got to be it!"

"Are you sure?"

Hank scrolled to the letter 'K' and found what he was looking for: Kemp, William. "I think I've got it." He scrolled down a little farther, but his own name was nowhere to be found. He plugged a memory card into the hard drive and began copying the data. "Whoa. You're never gonna believe this." Hank's eyes widened as they bounced from name to name. "Bill is never going to believe this."

"Is it that good?"

"Amazing," Hank muttered under his breath. A thought he'd pushed out of his mind several times reasserted itself with a vengeance, causing his hands to tremble. He was one click away from erasing the list and stealing the power of the Iconoclasts for himself.

Omar stared up at the sign and mouthed the words *Bisbee, Arizona*. Without caring who saw him, he found the eastern sky and prostrated himself in prayer. He could feel the eyes of Allah watching over him. He had been lost and bewildered, but the All Knowing, Most Merciful had delivered him against all odds. He was beginning to feel the power guiding his destiny and was more certain then ever that his fate was linked to the American's.

The streets of Bisbee were dark except for the pale yellow glow of street lamps overhead. Omar moved into the shadows of a vacant lot behind a brightly lit market. Homeless men lay in a ragged line against the adjacent building. The night air was oddly warm, even warmer than the Mexican desert. He had already made the telephone call and spoken the special words. There was nothing left to do but wait. The men from al-Qaeda were on their way to get him.

Omar dug through the bag of food he had bought from the market. The Coca-Cola burned his guts, making him belch and leaving his stomach feeling empty. He was hoping to find more chocolates at the bottom of the bag, but he had already eaten the last of them. He pulled a brightly colored pack of chewing gum from the sack. The sweet smell of fruit filled his nose as he unwrapped a piece, dropping the paper to the ground. A comically shocked expression transformed his face as he began to chew. A rush of saliva flooded his mouth, and he nearly vomited as the gum stuck to his palate. Omar threw the gum to the ground, spitting pink foam and cursing American food.

He watched cars pass, waiting for one to stop at the phone in front of the market. Mustafa had said that the man named Jamal would signal him at the phone. Many cars passed. It seemed that every American man, woman, and child owned a car. There were cars of every color. Some were beautifully painted, thumping with music. There were many different colors of people as well. There were nearly as many brown men as there had been in Mexico—it was not at all what he had expected.

A steady stream of people came and went from the market. Omar couldn't take his eyes from the women as they climbed in and out of their cars. They were of every shape and size, but all were nearly naked. He could clearly see their bare legs. Their breasts were shamefully exposed under their clothing. None of them noticed him; in fact, no one paid him any attention. He felt grossly out of place.

Another hour passed before a small van parked near the phone. An Arab-looking man emerged from the passenger seat. He stepped out and walked directly toward the phone, scowling intensely. He tossed an unfinished cigarette to the ground and scanned the empty lot where Omar was hiding. Omar tried to avert his eyes, covering his face with his hands. Looking through his fingers, he could tell that the man was staring at him. He didn't like the angry look on his face.

The man looked away and walked to the phone. He picked up the receiver and pretended to punch in some numbers. When he was finished, he raised his foot and removed a shoe. He shook it, as if clearing it of stones: the signal Omar had been waiting for.

Omar stood from his position against the wall and approached the man. "Excuse me ..." Omar struggled with his English; he had been instructed to approach the man and ask him if there was a bus traveling to the Painted Desert. He had no idea what the words meant, but was told that his contact would be expecting it. "I am looking for bus to a painted desert?"

The man replaced his shoe and stared at Omar. His expression changed from an angry glare to a look of disbelief as he tilted his head to scrutinize him. "Yes! I will take you there if you wish." He grabbed Omar by the shoulders with both hands, nearly embracing him. He reeked of cigarettes and perspiration. Dark hair covered his body and crept out from beneath his clothing. He smiled; his teeth were yellow and stained. "You have obviously traveled very far. Come with me."

Omar followed him to the small van, where he could see another man waiting in the back seat. "I am Jamal. Let's go, eh?" He swung the sliding door open and immediately resumed his pained, angry expression. "Where is Sayyid?"

"I sent him in for cigarettes," said the man in the back seat. He spoke perfectly clear English as he extended his hand to greet Omar.

"What? What the fuck do you think we are doing?" Jamal peered into the store with a look that could have shattered the doors. "We did not come here for shopping, you idiot."

"Relax. We came to the store, and we are buying shit. What is wrong with that? He'll be out in a minute." The man's hand lingered for a moment waiting for Omar's, then he gestured for him to climb inside the van. "Don't worry. My name is Thomas Rashad. I'm pleased to see that you have made it all this way. It is a miracle, is it not?" He looked to Jamal, reminding him that some courtesy should be extended to their guest.

Omar did not know how to respond. He simply looked from one man to the other.

"He is here, and we should go! I should leave Sayyid in there with your fuck-ing smokes," Jamal spat angrily.

"Look, here he comes. I told you it would only take a minute."

"A life can end in a minute, you fool," Jamal said bitterly before opening the passenger's door, finding his seat, and slamming the door behind him.

"Come on, get in my friend," said the man named Thomas.

The stocky figure of Sayyid approached the driver's door and climbed in. He carried a small brown sack and had dollar bills stuffed between his fingers.

"Sayyid, what the fuck do you think you are doing? I told you to wait for me here! What if something went wrong, eh?" Jamal reared up his hand as if he were going to backhand the man.

Sayyid recoiled from the threatened blow. "But Thomas told me ..."

"I don't care what Thomas told you, stupid dog! Get in. Let's go." Jamal turned in his seat, crossing his hairy arms over his chest.

"Here is your change, Thomas ... they didn't have menthols." The man looked to Thomas as if he were ready to go back and correct his mistake.

"Get your stinkin' ass in the van. Let's go!" Jamal barked.

"He's here!" Sayyid grinned wide at Omar. "He has come!"

"We go now. Talk later. They could be watching us," Jamal hissed under his breath, looking over his shoulder.

The van sped through the streets, and the al-Qaeda men pressed him with questions about Afghanistan without listening to his answers. He had never heard such bickering from grown men, but he was happy to tell them of his odyssey crossing the border. To him it was nothing short of a miracle, and after some time they all agreed. Between insults and curses, they informed him that they were part of the great American Jihad. They seemed eager to take part in the war against the Americans but were upset by the chaos following the attack in New York.

Jamal was their leader. He had come from Saudi Arabia, leaving his wealthy family behind to work as a janitor at a child's school and wait for the day he could do Allah's will. Sayyid had arrived most recently, and his English was only slightly better than Omar's. He was a stocky, muscle-bound man whose breath could be smelt in the rear of the van. The man calling himself Thomas was far different from the others. He looked American. He spoke perfect English and reeked of cologne. He explained to Omar that he had come to America as a child and that it was his destiny to strike a blow for Islam.

"I have a good job, not like these two. I sell cars. That is why they are jealous of me."

Jamal shouted over his shoulder, "He is a whore. Do not listen to him. He will corrupt you, my friend."

"See. He is jealous. He would love to have just one of my girlfriends, but he is too ugly. American girls like handsome men, with fine cars and good clothes." Thomas stroked the collar of his shirt proudly.

"Where are you taking me?" Omar asked.

"We go to our house. We will call our man from there."

"And you men live together?" Omar could not believe the way the men attacked each other or the names they called one another. It was beyond blasphemy.

"No way—they live in a pigsty," Thomas said harshly.

"Sayyid and I live together. You will stay with us until we know what to do with you. Don't listen to him; all he cares about is girls."

Omar was relieved when the van stopped and the men climbed out. Inside Jamal's apartment, Omar prayed alone while Sayyid cooked and Jamal and Thomas argued. He had not seen any of these men pray or exalt the greatness of Allah in the hours they had spent together. He was beginning to loathe these men. All they talked about was what they were going to do to the Jew-loving infidels.

It wasn't until after they had eaten their meal of American hamburgers that Jamal made the phone call to his al-Qaeda contact. They all gathered around the phone as Jamal listened intently to his superior. Thomas quietly explained to Omar that this was the first time they had spoken to their contact since the attacks on the World Trade Center: this was the moment they had all been waiting for.

The call was a quick one, leaving Jamal staring at the phone.

"What did he say, Jamal?" pressed Sayyid.

"Omar is to expect a phone call," Jamal said despondently.

"What about us? Do we finally have a mission?" asked Thomas.

"We wait," Jamal said, looking away.

"Wait still? After all this time we wait?" Thomas raged, dashing his cigarette into a tray. "With all that is happening—we wait?"

"They want to hear our ideas." Jamal turned, scratching his head in confusion.

"You mean they do not know what to do with us?" Thomas scoffed bitterly.

The room quickly deteriorated into argument. Omar couldn't stomach it any longer and left to pray. The shouting didn't stop until the phone rang once more. Jamal answered the phone, but the call was for Omar. It was Mustafa calling from Afghanistan.

"This is Omar," he said hesitantly.

"You have done well, pilgrim. Very well." Hearing his native tongue was like music to Omar's ears.

"I thank the Almighty." Omar spoke Pashto and covered the phone with his hand.

"As you should. Allah Most Merciful is watching over you. Are you well, my friend?"

"I am here." He didn't know how else to explain his condition.

"I have news for you. It is indeed Allah's will that you were sent on this mission. We have found out many things about this man, this demon.

"He is a part of an organization bent on destroying Islam. Listen and I will explain why it is more important than ever for you to kill this man. The man you hunt, his true name is Henry Patrick; he was the real leader of the Frenchmen. They were on a mission to slander our faith, my brother, and maybe worse."

"Henry Patrick ..." Omar mumbled the name, trying to commit it to memory.

"After they fled, we found the fat man in France. Once we laid our hands on him, he cried like a coward. He told us everything we needed to know. He and the rest of them are part of a secret clan; he called them Iconoclasts. Blasphemers! And this man, the man you hunt, is one of their leaders. They planned to make great lies against us. They want war with Islam.

"This man, he has seen things. He may know things. He was there when our men came to see the idols destroyed. They are very important men, and what he knows may be very dangerous to us. He had many hidden cameras with him.

"Now we know where to find this man. We have men in place that can help you. You must kill this man! Your success thus far is proof that Allah wills this. You must leave for the city of San Francisco."

Omar listened intently, trying desperately to take it all in. Killing the man was shockingly real now. The importance of his mission felt like a weight crushing him once more. "Can I speak with Mullah Bakkar? I have much I wish to ask him."

Paradigm I
Chapter 4

San Francisco. January 17, 2002

"Go ahead, cupcake, Debbie is expecting you." Hank dismissed Shawn from the conversation once more, but as usual he lingered aimlessly. "Remember, we're calling her "White-Three," and she's running the show for Paul. Okay?" Hank practically pushed him out of the room like a child.

"I got it, man! And stop callin' me cupcake!" Shug's cousin and closest childhood friend grumbled sourly. "We's supposta be undercova."

"All right, Rob." Hank laughed.

"What was the name again?" Shug snickered, pinching tears between his eyes. Rob Whitey, wasn't it?"

"Dat's right ... you two assholes laugh it up." Shawn began a strut toward the door. "You're real funny."

"Go. Start filming." Hank's eyes pleaded for him to not screw up. "And listen to Debbie. But don't talk to her or anything. Just film the people. I don't want to see sixty minutes of Debbie's ass, either. Got it?"

"Don't get yourself hypnotized." Shug finally let go, bursting into laughter as he teased his cousin.

Shawn walked away. He swung the camera in one hand while he flipped them the middle finger with the other.

Hank turned his attention back to auditorium beyond the one-way glass window. Paul McKnight energetically paced the stage while he spoke to the audience. "How many heads we got down there?" Hank scanned the crowd and calculated a quick estimate.

Shug placed his clipboard on the console and squinted into the dim light. "This is session number three ... Group One. There should be fifty-two people down there."

"I only see forty-nine."

"Maybe some last minute dropouts." Shug double-checked his figures.

"Is this the last group?"

"Yep." Shug smiled back at him with his trademark tremendous grin.

"Before we go, I want you to get a final roll call from Debbie, along with all the release forms." Hank was repeating himself again. He trusted Shug. Shug had done an outstanding job as his number one, but he couldn't help himself. This was his turn to wield total control, and he was going to be on top of every detail.

"You got it."

"Sounds like Paul is wrapping it up down there. He'll be putting them back under soon." Hank nodded toward the auditorium.

On stage, "the amazing Paul McKnight" was busily engaging his audience. Paul had made a name for himself as a hypnotherapist, but he had become famous as a comedian. His outrageous group hypnosis shows had grabbed national attention and catapulted him from little comedy clubs to doing his own HBO specials. Outside of the entertainment world, he was known as a particularly bright and educated young philanthropist, with a reputation for being a ladies' man. But, more importantly to Hank, he was also an Iconoclast.

"It's getting close to *that* time, everybody. This will be our last session together. And I know we have really come together in all of these sessions. We can all feel it ... we are all going to be a part of something really wonderful, something so enormous ... and it has brought us all so close together. I can feel it. Can't you?" Paul paced back and forth, a wireless microphone hanging in front of his mouth. Everyone in the crowd looked to the people seated near them and nodded enthusiastically.

"We have come from all over: I know we have a couple here who flew in all the way from England. Bert and Flo, where are you guys? Stand up." Paul waved to the crowd, encouraging them to step forward.

"There they are. Say hi, everybody." Paul applauded the couple as they stood before the group. The crowd cheered them on, and Hank could practically see the old woman blush from his spot high in the back of the theater.

"This is going to be some vacation for you two!" Paul placed his hands on his hips and smiled at the couple.

Bert and his white-haired wife stood in front of their newfound friends and soaked up the good cheer. Paul had done a great job keeping everybody laughing since the sessions began. His tireless good mood was contagious among his subjects.

"It beats goin' to bloody France!" Bert yelled, to torrents of laughter from the crowd and one embarrassed slap on his shoulder from Flo.

"I'd say so," Paul laughed. "Bert and Flo here are going to see the flying saucer fly by from their vantage point on the Coit Tower." Paul let the crowd continue to applaud. He clapped his hands louder, and the group responded as if Bert and Flo had just won grand prize on *The Price is Right*.

"Aye. That's what it says on the wee dog collar ye have me wearin' round me neck." Bert held the color-coded card around his neck. The card designated where the witness would be, what their vantage point was, and any other information specific to their individual experience.

"Well, I want you two to be very careful … Coit Tower is a very, um, romantic place. I don't want you and Flo missing the show because of any Benny Hill type nonsense." Paul mimicked the Benny Hill soundtrack and did a suggestive little dance. Once again, the crowd erupted with laughter.

After a moment of pacing Paul continued, instantly gripping the audience's attention. "Others of you are going to have a different vantage point, but you are all going to share in a similar experience. You all have different motivations for being here. You come from all walks of life." The crowd followed his every move and drank up every word.

"This is going to be tougher for some than for others, but all of our lives are going to be turned upside down for the next six months. When this is all over, you'll all be a little richer"—once again, Paul alluded to the large sum of money each witness would receive after the six months under suggestion—"and I hope a little wiser, too. But one thing is for certain … we are all going to be a part of history. Part of a great social experiment that is going to spark a revolution of thought in our time!" Paul dramatically raised his hands to the ceiling.

"All of us have come together under that one great hope! Can you feel it? I feel it. I can see it all around me, and that's really cool. I didn't expect that when I came here." Paul started to pace, but stopped abruptly, facing the audience.

"You people have one thing in common in your hearts. And that's hope for our future and the courage to take part in it." Paul's tone softened, sounding like he was speaking to one person alone.

"And I want to say that it's been a real pleasure working with each and every one of you. And there are hundreds of you! You are all part of something very big, and I hope it meets all of your expectations."

"I want everyone to take a moment after we break into our groups to say good-bye to all of the people that you've been working with. You may very well be running into them later on today, but you will not remember them. You can find out what group you're in by the color on your 'dog collar,' as Bert so aptly put it. I'll put you back under once everyone is in the right group." Paul clapped his hands, refocusing everyone's attention. "And then comes the fun part"— Paul's voice was booming and jovial once again—"we'll be getting a good look at our UFO."

He waited a moment for the crowd to finish murmuring. "That's right. You've all heard so much about it, so why not have a look? You guys are part of our close encounter group. You'll be seeing it close up. You'll see it fly! I promise you, it will be the most amazing thing that you will ever see! After all, that's why we're here." Paul clapped his hands, then waved them as if breaking a spell. The crowd responded with a standing ovation while the stage lights dimmed and Paul disappeared.

The auditorium lights were switched on and Hank watched the people hug each other and chat excitedly. "Can you believe this man?" Hank had caught the contagious smile as he watched the group of total strangers share in a special display of intimacy.

"Yeah, man, we really did it, brother." Shug was smiling too, but Shug was always smiling. "Just the number of witnesses alone could make this thing fly."

"Almost." Hank checked the time on his watch, something he would be doing a lot of today. Timing was everything. "Have you heard anything from Mouse-Two?" Shug was acting as the voice of the control center today. He would be the point of contact for all of the various teams in the operation.

"They're at the airport gettin' ready." Shug checked his Rolex.

"Let me know when they are ready to fly."

"Forget about it. I've got all that handled." Shug beamed with confidence. He didn't choose to hide his excitement about the operation like Hank did.

The door to the studio booth cracked open and Paul McKnight and his assistant Debbie slipped into the room. As Paul's eyes adjusted to the dim light of the small studio and was confronted with the huge bulk of Shug standing in front of him, his smile faded momentarily.

"Wow … Hey, I didn't know you were bringing security with you!" Paul raised his hands over his head, jokingly preparing to be frisked.

Debbie slapped him in the ribs as she pushed past. "He's harmless. Believe me," she said with a friendly smile toward Shug.

"Oh that's not fair ... I can be a very dangerous man, you know." Paul turned to Debbie, continuing his flirtation for a moment before offering his hand to Shug. "Hello sir. Name's Paul."

"Right on. It's cool to meet you. I'm Shug." Paul's hand disappeared into Shug's palm. "I'm a big fan."

"Yes, very big. And this, of course, is the lovely Debbie." Paul gestured to Debbie, who fought to keep her armload of papers from sliding away from her.

"Shug?" She asked as she let his hand envelope hers. "Like sugar?"

"Yes Ma'am." Shug's already huge smile widened.

"How sweet."

"Looks like things are going nicely down there, eh Paul?" Hank stood up and shook Paul's hand. "Nice to see you again, Debbie."

"Really fantastic, Henry! What a great group." Paul mopped the scant sweat on his brow and began attending to his immaculately kept hair. "I've never done such a prolonged state of suggestion before, but I think this has been the right group of people to try it with."

"How many have dropped since yesterday?" Hank's tone was all business.

"Yes, well ... three this morning." Paul said, looking embarrassed.

"Five total since we talked yesterday, Mr. Patrick." Debbie efficiently handed Hank folders containing profiles of the absentees.

"Henry, please," Hank said casually. Shug's presence seemed to be adding a bit of tension, somehow.

"Like you said, if there were any reservations, drop them. There were a couple I didn't feel good about, and two that asked to go this morning."

"And they're safe?" Hank shot him a questioning glare.

"Oh certainly! They won't remember a thing about—what do we like to call it again?—Devil's Peak."

"That's right," Hank said, relaxing his posture slightly.

"Very clever. I must say, from my end I think things are going to work out spectacularly! The other groups really took to seeing *Little Betty*. And I'm sure this group will eat it up too."

"Are they under hypnosis right now?" Shug asked as he looked out over the audience.

"Yeah, they've been under all morning." Debbie joined Shug at the window, watching the group from behind the mirrored glass. "But right now they're behaving consciously, like they normally would. Paul will take them deeper in a little while, and then we're going to show them the UFO."

"Little Debbie?" Shug said absently as he watched crowd.

"Little Betty!" Debbie corrected him while Hank and Paul laughed.

"My bad." Shug cringed with embarrassment.

"I'm sure they will," Hank continued, turning back to Paul. "And I promise not to disappoint, either. Of course this is only part of Devil's Peak, but I think it will be the most convincing."

"Can you imagine, nearly two hundred eye witnesses reporting the same thing, simultaneously." Debbie stared out over the audience. "Their testimony will hold up against any lie-detector test. It will be sensational."

"It's certainly gonna stir things up a bit." Hank smiled as he pushed himself off the console.

The walkie-talkie on Shug's hip chirped to life. "Control One, Mouse-Two."

"Mouse-Two, this is Control. Go ahead." Shug's voice transformed into the controlled monotone of a dispatcher.

"Control One, Mouse-Two is RFA."

"Mouse-Two, Control, copy. Stand by." Shug nodded to Hank.

"Looks like things are happening." Paul clapped his hands, drawing their attention. "I can't wait see it all play out. Of course I'll be doing it from a coffee bar in Amsterdam." Paul winked at Hank with a gleam in his eyes.

"So you're that smooth voice on the walkie-talkie?" Debbie smiled at Shug.

"Smooth? You really think so?" Shug pretended to look shy. "I thought I sounded kinda dorky."

"No, not at all." Debbie smiled.

"You're White-Three; it's nice to put a face with the name." Shug returned her smile.

"Pleased to meet you, Control." Debbie slipped her hand into his once more.

"*La plaisir est mienne, belles dame.*" Shug attempted his best seductive French as he held her hand. Her eyes brightened, and he boldly pressed on. "I would do anything for such a beauty," he continued in French, smiling for all he was worth.

Her embarrassed laughter and the guffawing from the Hank and Paul signaled to Shug that everyone in the room spoke French, and that his cheesy French come-on had been clearly understood by all. Shug closed his eyes, mortified. His smile disappeared as Debbie recovered her composure.

"*Mercy boo-coo?*" Debbie asked sweetly, apparently loving Shug's sudden blush of embarrassment.

"Mercy is right! Oh brother." Hank rolled his eyes at Shug. "Anyway, Amsterdam huh? Nice choice. So that's where you decided to ride it out, eh?"

"You asked me to find some place remote, and believe me: I can waste six months in a place like that no problem. Especially with what you're paying me." Paul's smile widened.

"Well, I really want to thank you. I know you understand what you've entered into, and I appreciate it. The Iconoclasts appreciate it." Hank took his hand once more, holding it as he spoke.

"Say no more, my friend. We've talked many times, and you know how I feel. Thank you for finally doing something like this. Thanks for letting me be a part of it." Paul squeezed back, returning Hank's grip.

"Are you guys going to stick around to see them with Little Betty?" Paul said as he broke away from the handshake. "It's really quite amazing to see their reactions. It's like watching people see the real thing. Some of them break down in tears, some of them are too shocked to speak … it's marvelous."

"No, we gotta go. It's gonna be a little crazy today." Hank turned to face Debbie. "I'm leavin' a guy behind to shoot footage, for … prosperity's sake, ya know? Don't let him get in your way. He's a little bit retarded, so don't take any bullshit from him. Let him shoot the groups, then turn him loose when you're all finished. His name is Rob."

"He's all right. Just don't let him waste all the film on the pretty girls out there," Shug joked. "The only filmin' he's ever done was for *Girls Gone Wild*."

"No problem. Mr.… Henry. Here are all 180 personnel files—minus the five absentees, signed release forms, and statements." Debbie thrust the stack of forms at him.

"I'll grab that. Thank you, Debbie." Shug bent over to retrieve the files from her arms. "I'm the real brains behind this outfit anyway," Shug muttered under his breath into Debbie's ear, just loud enough for everyone to hear.

Paul bowed, preparing to leave. "Then that's it for now. I like what I see here Henry. Very Orson Welles." He shook is hands in the air as if he were shaking the entire world between them. "It'll be another couple hours before I'm finished here."

"All right, Paul. I can't thank you enough. And Debbie: you've been the greatest. You made this whole thing happen for me. We won't forget it. There is room in our organization for people like you. We're really looking for young blood right now." Hank turned to face Debbie.

"Well, you just tell whoever you have to that I'm ready. I hope I've proved I'm ready."

"You'll be getting a call. Always nice to see you." Hank took her hand and peered into her eyes. He wanted to tell her, to shout at the top of his lungs: "I'm the man! I *am* the Iconoclasts!" But like most people, she avoided the intensity of his stare altogether. He bit his lip, stifling his secret.

"Nice to meet you guys." Shug flashed the peace sign to Paul and took Debbie's hand gently as he passed.

"*Bon soir,* Monsieur Shug," Debbie said in perfect, sultry French.

San Francisco; January 17, 2002

Molly Porter buttoned up her knee-length winter coat, something she rarely did. The coat bulged in the middle, making her feel fat, but it was warm. A chill wind whipped her hair into streamers of blonde curls. She shivered under her winter coat and dreaded the thought of crossing the Bay on the ferry.

She didn't mind the hassle that came along with working in the city. She only worked a few days a week and was lucky to be working at all. There were just too many Chiropractors and not enough spines to crack between them all. She still enjoyed being called Dr. Porter, but in her heart she was better known as Mom.

She checked her watch compulsively and wondered how Rick was doing with the kids. Rick dreaded the days when she worked, and Molly prepared herself for the carnage awaiting her at home. He was no match for their two young boys. They walked all over him, and by the time she got home he would be a wreck. Molly smiled as she braced herself against the cold. She pictured her family greeting her with excited eyes and half-cooked, half-eaten meals all over the kids and all over the house. She was glad Rick was getting so much time with the kids. To her, he was far sexier covered in fingerpaint than he ever had been in an Armani business suit.

Molly's high heels clicked along the pavement as she pushed against the wind toward Fisherman's Wharf. The cold bit her cheeks and fingertips. She was beginning to look forward to the shelter of the ferry. Molly caught herself compulsively checking her watch. It was nearly six, and she wasn't running late, but she couldn't shake the feeling that she was forgetting something. She checked the time again as if it had changed.

Molly stopped in her tracks and contemplated rushing back to the office. She suddenly wanted to check her calendar, call Rick—do something, anything that would explain the feeling that she was forgetting something important.

Molly looked around to find that others in the street had stopped, as if the feeling was contagious. The streets were crowded with people returning home from a long day of work. The traffic was at its thickest, the city was at its noisiest, nothing was out of place, but there were other people checking their watches and scratching their heads while they blocked the flow on the sidewalk.

Molly's eyes stopped on an attractive black man wearing a finely tailored business suit. People pushed by him, but he seemed oblivious to them. He suddenly ran his hands down his pockets as if he'd lost something, but found nothing. He took another long look at his Rolex, and then absently raised his eyes to the sky. Molly's eyes followed his and stared up into the gray evening sky. The pink and orange of the sunset glowed over the ocean. A strange flash of motion caught her eye and instantly took her breath away. The silver streak in the sky lasted a full second before disappearing behind some buildings. It was the most amazing thing she had ever seen. There was no doubt in her mind what it was. She had seen it with her own two eyes. Nothing man-made could have traveled as fast as the silver disk that had just streaked through the air.

Still breathless, Molly scanned the sky again. The people near her reacted immediately. Molly's eyes fell back to earth and landed on the handsome black man. His eyes were wide with shock. He pointed to the sky and smiled. He tried to speak but couldn't.

"Oh my God! Did you see that?" A man in front of Molly grabbed another man by the shoulders and shook him.

A huge smile spread across the second man's face. "Yeah! Yeah, I think I did!"

Molly took a step toward them but quickly stopped as others around her pointed toward the sky and gushed emotion. Some were frozen, heads cranked back and eyes roaming. One woman burst into tears and fled into a building, but others pushed by, seemingly annoyed and not the least bit curious about the spontaneous outbreak of confusion.

"It flew right by us!"

"I saw it too!"

"What did you see?" A curious elderly woman stopped between the two strangers. "Did something happen?"

"We just saw a fucking UFO!" An astonished-looking man joined them and pointed his cup of Starbucks to the sky.

"Right there! It flew by right there!" One of the young women grabbed the elderly lady by the elbow and turned her toward the bay.

"It almost flew right over our heads! I swear to God! We saw it!"

"It was huge! As big as a house!"

Molly felt herself drawn into the group blocking traffic on the sidewalk. "I saw it too!"

Almost at once, people began pulling cell phones from the pockets and purses. Molly locked eyes with another young woman, and amazed smiles grew on their faces.

"Hello, mom? This is Charlie. Mom you won't believe this ... I just saw a flying saucer! No, really! Mom ... I swear." He was laughing as he shouted into his cell phone.

"It's really true, Mom. I saw it too!" A well-dressed woman shouted above the crowd noise for the benefit of Charlie's mom on the phone. The two strangers stared at each other for a moment, then burst into laughter.

More and more people gathered on the corner, and other groups dotted Beach Street. Traffic began to slow at the sight of so many people gathered on the sidewalk, and horns started blaring.

"Oh my God! I've got to call Rick!" Molly began to dig through her purse.

"It was big and silver, kinda shiny and metallic!"

"It just zipped by! I can't believe this!"

"No man, I'm telling you … it didn't make a sound—no lights, no nothing. It was just like a flying … disk. But it was amazing! It was the most amazing thing I've ever seen."

"It was there one second and gone the next."

"It was headed toward Oakland! It just zipped from here to there!"

"Has anybody called 9-1-1?"

"I can't believe this … do you think we should?"

"I'm on the phone with 9-1-1 right now!" A man in the crowd excitedly held out his phone for the crowd to see. The energy on the street was palpable. Distinguishing between the people who'd seen the UFO and those who hadn't was made easy by the disproportionate smiles on their faces. "The dispatcher just said they've had sightings all over the city."

"Shut up!" said a young woman who had just walked out of a store and into the fray. She immediately flipped open her phone, jamming a finger into her ear. "Monica … You'll never guess what happened. I'm downtown shopping, and all of the sudden people in the street start going crazy! They're saying a UFO just zoomed by in broad daylight! No really, everybody's acting nuts."

"There's a guy in there who said that a whole bunch of people saw it from the building." A bike messenger shouted to the crowd as he pushed his bike from the lobby of a skyscraper. Molly could see a large crowd forming in the lobby behind him. Everyone was staring into the sky.

"This is crazy!" The man holding the cup of coffee shook his head in disbelief.

"Of course they saw it! It flew right by the building."

"Do you think this will be on the news?"

Molly tore her eyes away from the sky and pressed her phone to her cheek. "Hey baby, it's me. Are you sitting down? Well, sit down. No, this is serious. No, I'm okay, I think. You know all those nights we've spent staring up at the stars and wondering *what if?* Well, I think I know!" Molly excitedly whispered into her phone, talking to her husband as if in a dream.

Oakland Hills; January 17, 2002

"Okay, Shug." Hank's eyes followed the seconds on his watch as he pointed a finger at Shug. "Take it away."

"Control to all units: let little Debbie—Betty!—loose." Shug cringed as he spoke into the radio. "Seventeen fifty-seven and zero seconds ... mark!"

Hank marked time on his stopwatch and turned to smile at Shug.

Shug buried the microphone between his hands and cursed himself for the silly slip of the tongue. "First words out of my mouth, and I screwed them up."

"Forget about it." Hank gave Shug a wink and slid down the bench. "Just nerves ... Why do ya think I had you run the radio tonight?" He pressed his face against the van's rear window and peered into the darkness. "I'm nervous as hell! I didn't wanna be the one responsible for blowing this thing."

"Control, Little Betty is away, on your mark." Young Brice chimed in over the radio from his rooftop location.

"Control, Radar Hit-One is up." A female voice followed Brice's almost immediately.

Hank turned to catch Shug staring at the microphone as he marked time on the charts. "Everything looks good outside."

The female voice returned over the radio, now sounding shrill with excitement. "Control, Radar Hit-One. RH-1 is down ... Now!"

Shug marked the time signifying the complete deployment of the first blimp.

"Control, Radar Hit-Two is up." A new, male voice took his turn on the air. A huge pop followed by a long hiss tore through the air outside the communications van.

Hank jumped in his seat. The force of the sound had surprised him. But he was forced to laugh when he saw how Shug had practically fallen from his seat.

"No shit it's up!" Shug muttered under his breath as he checked his watch and collected himself. "Nineteen forty-seven and twenty-two seconds, mark."

"Look!" Hank opened the rear door, causing the cab lights to turn on inside the van. "Come on ... you've got forty ... one seconds." Hank waved for Shug to look out into the sky.

Shug craned his neck to peer out of his window but didn't leave his seat. Hank slid out of the back door and stood at the back of the van arching his head back to peer high into the sky. Two men in the background struggled with long ropes that lifted them vertically, pulling them across the dirt. A third man stood by, not moving to help as he stared into the sky and worked the remote control in his hands.

High in the air, on the end of the rope pulling the men across the field, a large, gray blimp turned in the wind. Two other men fought with ropes another fifty feet away. The round white balloon, which measured twenty-five feet in diameter, was silhouetted against the darkening sky. An identical balloon had already been launched, inflated, and deflated fifteen miles away in the high hills. It had only been in the air for fifteen seconds, but that's all that was needed.

Hank's idea from the start had been to flood a brief period of time with as many different kinds of reports as possible. He had wanted to cover every angle and shift the burden of proof onto the cynics. It was imperative to show something, anything, on radar, and the balloons fit the bill nicely. Not only would they show up on almost every kind of radar, but they could be launched vertically and maintain a specific altitude. The Icon engineers had devised an ingenious method of launching the blimps and leaving them uninflated until they hit their target altitude. From Hank's vantage point, they were working beautifully. Once the blimps made a radar signature, they could be blown apart, deflated instantly, and hauled in.

The purpose of having two radar signature sites wasn't only to increase the number of sightings: it also made Betty appear to travel at unfathomable speeds. Radar only saw Betty when she was hovering. The first launch site was a ridge overlooking the Oakland Hills. Thirty seconds later, the second blimp was launched at site two: Darborow's farm, in the rolling hills above the City.

A positive radar sighting was crucial if the government was going to comment on his prank—and Hank knew any comment made by the government would legitimize Devil's Peak. Once the radar signatures were made public, it was only a matter of time before the other critical piece of the triad of proof would be discovered. As soon as someone connected the dots between sites, they would find the molten magnesium.

Hank felt childlike exhilaration as he stared up at the blimp. All of this was his doing. This was his baby. The seed for the idea had been planted in his mind five years ago, when he had first joined the Icons and dreamed of how he was going to shake up the world. His plan had blossomed into something he had never expected. Devil's Peak had taken on a life of its own, wrestling with his subconscious mind for attention until it was nearly all he thought about. He had convinced himself this was the opening salvo in the Iconoclasts' war against faith.

Hank stood in an open cow pasture overlooking one of the most beautiful vistas in the entire world. The fruition of his tireless effort was proudly flying above him for the entire world to see. His closest friend and protégée waited anxiously behind him in anticipation of what promised to be a truly historic moment, and competent, capable men were busily attending to his orders. He felt supremely satisfied. He knew that somewhere down there he had just convinced several people that they had seen a UFO, that there was life beyond ours, and that all they'd thought they knew about life was wrong.

"RH-2, Control: seventeen forty-eight and fifteen seconds." Hank heard Shug's controlled and measured voice in stereo, from behind him and from the radio on his belt.

A flameless explosion ripped the blimp in two, sending it falling to earth with material and rope raining down behind it. The men on the ground ran for cover, laughing and shouting to each other as they abandoned the tethers and covered their heads.

"Control, RH-2; RH-2 is down." The RH-2 leader shouted into the radio above the whoops and hollers of the guys behind him.

"Control copies. Control is terminated." Shug's voice finally carried some emotion over the radio with the termination of this phase of the operation. He scrambled out of the van to join Hank and the men outside.

"All right you guys! Nice job. Let's get that thing wrapped up," Hank yelled to the men now busily gathering up the spent balloon. He turned to Shug, embracing him. "Good job, man!"

"Yeah. We ain't finished yet."

"I know. Come on." Hank led the way past the van to where an old barn sat in ruins. A group of men in dull gray protective gear stood at the back of a large bread van.

Old man Darborow stood near a backhoe opposite them. He leaned against a shovel and nodded to Hank as he passed.

"That was a mighty fancy balloon, Henry." Mr. Darborow appeared to be unimpressed by the brief air show. "Was that what all this fuss is over?"

"Not quite ... now for the hard part." Hank smiled apologetically. "We're gonna shoot this radioactive magnesium all over your beautiful grazing land here. Are you guys all set?"

"Yes sir, Mr. Patrick." The leader of the radioactive team stepped forward and waved to the rest of the men wearing the protective suits.

"Shug, go ahead and move the van, would ya?" Hank pointed to the communications van sitting in the line of fire. "I'm sorry we gotta do it this way, but the stuff has to be radioactive, I'm afraid."

"Ah hell, that ain't no problem ... maybe I'll raise some kind of super beef." The pot-bellied old rancher beamed at Hank from over his shovel. "I'm just tickled pink to see you boys doing something like this before I die. I think this is just great! Makes me proud to be an Iconoclast."

"We couldn't have done it without you." Hank returned his smile.

"Are you only spraying that stuff right here?"

"Well, between you and me Mr. Darborow, we had some guys hit the treetops about ten miles from here ... but they should find this stuff first."

"You sprayed it on trees?"

"Yeah, from a plane."

"Won't that cause a fire?"

"Not in January. Okay, everyone's out of the way. Marty, it's all you ... go ahead." Hank pointed to the group leader, giving him the thumbs-up.

The three men near the rear of the van pulled a canvas tarp from a trash-can-sized contraption sitting in the dirt. With the coordination of an army mortar team, the three men went about their tasks and loaded a chrome cylinder into the opening. On Marty's command, all three men turned their heads and jammed their fingers into their ears.

With a huge blast of compressed air, the makeshift cannon hurled the hardened dry-ice mortar into the air where the blimp had been deployed. A chemical reaction liquefied the magnesium at one hundred feet, instantly melting the dry ice and exploding molten magnesium over the field. Glowing globules of molten metal rained down over the pasture in a shower of sparks. The fiery sparks fell to the earth, flitting out moments before hitting the ground.

Hank was pleased to see the expression on the old man's face as he gaped at the light show. "Okay, Mr. Darborow. That's it for us. We're gonna break down and get out of here." Hank extended his hand to the aging rancher. "You know what to do?"

"You boys take off. I'll cover up your tracks with my backhoe. If anybody, asks I moved the dirt earlier today, and I didn't see anything whacko." He smiled warmly and nodded good-bye to the men packing up their gear.

Hank took his hand and pumped his arm. "Don't forget to turn on the news. I don't want you missin' the show of a lifetime." Hank broke away to join Shug in the van. "You can expect company anytime ... don't be surprised if you see someone up here tonight."

"Not to worry. I imagine we've covered this enough times. I'm not that old. I know what to do."

"Thanks," Hank said as he slammed the door.

"You too, Henry. And good luck."

Shug had just parked the communications van and jumped into his Land Rover when the first reports of a UFO sighting came over the radio. A surge of adrenaline pumped through his chest while the disk jockey made the impromptu announcement between songs. He looked at his watch; the operation had wrapped up less than twenty minutes ago.

"Hey everyone, this is Cute Kate … and boy do I have a strange one for you tonight. I guess there's been a UFO sighting here in the city. Yep, that's right, a flying saucer. Reports are coming in from all over, 911 lines are jammed with calls—people are saying a flying saucer flew over the city! So keep your eyes peeled, maybe you'll see one too. Lord knows I didn't see anything. They keep me locked up in this box all night. Anyway, if any of you nut jobs out there see one, call me here at 976-KROK. Okay, anyway … here's Limp Biscuit. Spaceships—hfff …"

Shug looked at Hank as he leaned over to turn down Limp Biscuit. Hank sat next to him, anxiously chewing his thumbnail. He had never seen Hank so excited before. His fists were clenched and his knee jumped nervously in the seat. "It's only been twenty minutes," Shug said, arching his eyebrows for effect.

"We did it, brother. I mean the timing was perfect. Boom, one right after the other!"

"I know. I can't wait to get home and get in front of the big screen." Shug had spent the previous night setting up a home theater system and preparing for the after-party.

"How many phone lines have you got?" Hank asked for the third time.

"I've got our secure line, my home phone, and two cell phones. Why?"

"I think I'm gonna stay the night. We've got a lot of calls to make in the morning."

"I can't wait to see it." Shug's smile was beginning to ache on his face.

"I can't wait to party!" Hank slapped his hand with a high five.

Shug slowed the SUV as he rounded the corner into his driveway. He was surprised to find that they were the first ones there. He'd figured that at least Shawn would be waiting for them.

"Good, we're alone." Hank jumped from the seat and made a beeline for the front door.

Hank was already blindly pushing buttons on the remote by the time Shug entered the room. "How do you make this thing work? Put on the news!"

Shug kick-started his home theater system and scrolled the channels. "Which station?"

"Local—no, national!"

The doorbell chimed and Shug slapped the remote into Hank's hand.

He opened the door and Matt Healy stepped in to embrace him. "What's up, big man?" He was still in the flight suit he'd worn for his run dropping molten magnesium over the Oakland foothills.

"Hey, Darrel!" Shug reached past Matt and took Darrel's hand. "I'm glad to see your hands aren't glowing. Come on in. The party is just getting started."

"Hey Shug." The kid from the university took hold of Shug's hand and struggled with the correct cool-guy handshake.

"What's happening, Dennis? Your boys did a great job tonight." Shug held the door as the three men passed inside.

"Come on in. It's freezing out here." Shug scanned the streets hoping to see Shawn.

"Get in here, boys!" Hank shouted from in front of the big screen. Headline news was commenting on a developing story coming out of San Francisco. "Shug, how do you turn this thing up?"

"Our affiliates in San Francisco are reporting, now get this: UFO sightings in San Francisco and Oakland." The attractive female broadcaster raised her eyebrows skeptically as she read the report.

"In fact, so many calls have flooded the emergency 911 lines that they were temporarily jammed. The 911 system is up and running now, but they say the calls keep streaming in. Our affiliates in the Bay area have been flooded with calls reporting that a large, saucer-shaped disk flew over the bay and parts of San Francisco before disappearing into the Oakland foothills. Again, this is a late breaking story ... we don't know if this is a joke or what. But we will keep you informed ... right here on *Headline News*." The network broke for commercials, and the three newcomers stripped out of their coats and crowed into seats around the televisions.

On one of the smaller screens, the local channel was broadcasting an episode of *The Simpsons* when it broke for commercial. The anchorman for Channel Two News was at his desk peering into the camera. "Ladies and Gentlemen, I am Daniel Richman here in the Channel Two News studio, with a special announcement." The men in the room fell silent while Shug raised the volume.

"We here at Channel Two News have received numerous reports from eyewitnesses claiming that an unidentified flying object was sighted just moments ago. It reportedly flew over the North Shore area of downtown San Francisco and parts of Oakland." Shug silently pumped his fists.

"Now, none of these reports have been validated yet, and this could all be part of some kind of hoax, but we here at Eyewitness News are now reporting that several people, maybe even several hundred people, are calling in claiming to have seen something in the sky sometime around five fifty this evening.

The anchorman's face appeared skeptical as he read the hurriedly prepared notes on the Teleprompter. "Once again, an unidentified flying object has been reportedly sighted in the Bay area. We don't know if this is some kind of joke, but we will keep you informed as we learn more. Please tune in for all the late breaking events on the ten o'clock news."

Commercials came on once more, and the room erupted in cheers. The five men all jumped to their feet and began exchanging high fives and hearty embraces. Shug cradled a man beneath each arm. Hank was in front of the big-screen, silhouetted by the blur of color and celebrating like he had just scored the winning touchdown. He had never seen Hank so happy; his whole look changed on those rare occasions when he smiled, and right now he was beaming.

The moment was magic for Shug. The two of them had worked long and hard on this operation. When they downloaded the list, it was like finding the Holy Grail. Devil's Peak had exploded from that moment on. Hank was tapped into the organization like no other, anonymously pulling the strings of the biggest players among the Icon ranks. And he was a part of it too. Hank shared everything with him. He knew all the connections. He had seen the list; he knew about all of the plans to manipulate the media after the hoax. They were partners, and the two of them were poised to be pivotal characters in the movement that was destined to change the world.

"Yo, Healey. Come on, give me a hand." Shug called out across the room to his good friend. Matt Healey was one of the first men Hank had recruited into their primary cell. He was a former marine pilot with a crew-cut, leatherneck look backed up with a surly jarhead demeanor. Shug walked Matt into the kitchen, exchanging congratulations along the way, and returned to the living room with armfuls of champagne. "Let's get this party started!"

"Uh-rah!" Matt popped the cork on a bottle and sent foaming champagne all over the floor.

"Uh-rah!" Hank turned to greet them, accepting his own bottle. He immediately shook the bottle, covered the tip with his thumb and sprayed champagne all over Matt and Shug. Dennis and Darrel watched in amazement as a full-blown champagne war broke out between the three men. Eventually more bottles were opened and the guys began chugging it straight from the bottle, sending torrents of foam shooting from the corners of their mouths and at one point right out of Shug's nose.

The doorbell rang, and Darrel skirted the foaming mêlée to answer it. Shug followed him, grabbing another bottle along the way. Darrel opened the door to find the six Icon crewmembers who had worked at the site with Hank and Shug.

"Oh, yeah. It's a party now! We got ladies in the house." Shug pushed past Darrel and his good buddy Mike to extend his hand to Tanya.

"Only one girl, I'm afraid," Tanya said as she allowed Shug to usher her past the others. "And I'm not quite dressed for a party." She was slight, even tiny standing next to Shug, and was wearing jeans and a heavy sweatshirt. She was one of the "nerd team," as he and Hank called them privately, one of the university scientists pulled from the Iconoclast ranks to fill a technical position for the operation. Tanya was the one who had devised the method of containing the radioactive magnesium, and like half of the guys at the after-party she was a nerd, but Shug didn't care: after a couple of months working with her, he knew what was going on beneath that sweatshirt.

"That's my boy—leaves me hangin' when there's a girl around." Mike took off his heavy jacket and made his way inside.

"It's not like that, brother." Shug embraced his friend, patting him on the back as he passed. Mike was a longtime member of their inner cadre, too. He was an Iconoclast Hank had stolen from another cell long ago, and he too now worked full time for Hank's fictitious private investigation firm. "It's already been on the news!" Shug burst out, unable to contain himself.

"On TV? We heard something on the radio. But we figured you had people calling the radio stations." Mike checked his watch with a surprised smile.

The other guys began filing into the room, ditching their coats, grabbing glasses and finding chairs in front of the televisions. Hank entered the room pushing a small wet bar filled with bottles of every description. "All right! Let's show these nerds how to party! Screw the champagne!"

"Uh-rah!" Matt yelled, lifting his champagne bottle in salute.

"Uh-rah!"

"A toast! A toast!" Shug shouted above the others. "To Devil's Peak!"

Everyone raised their drinks and chanted. "To Devil's Peak!"

The attention shifted to Hank, who was greedily guzzling a vodka cocktail and hadn't noticed that the focus of the room was now on him. Shug laughed at the bemused look on the faces of the others—the nerds, at least. They had never seen Hank like this. To most of them he was a shadowy figure who constantly hounded them for results and was always all business.

After gulping nearly half his drink, letting some spill down his face, Hank finally noticed that the crowd was waiting for him to speak. He took a moment to wipe his face and then looked around almost shyly. "Well ... uh ... not everybody is here yet, and I know they've already mentioned it on the news ... but there is still a lot to come. So I want to save my best words for when we've heard enough and everybody's here." Hank leered at the group. "But I will say this. So far, it's perfect! And the credit belongs to all of you. The timing on this operation was paramount, and you people pulled it off like soldiers. That's not an easy thing to do, and it's a credit to all of you. So let's drink one for the Mission!" Everybody raised their drinks again.

"And let's drink one for Dennis! He shaped you college kids up like a proper drill Sergeant!" Hank pointed toward the couch where Dennis was sitting. "Thanks, Dennis." Hank threw back his drink to a round of applause.

"And let's drink one to the engineering skills of Eric, Tanya, Kevin, Gabe— oh, and you too, Mike." Hank raised his drink again. "Now, our boys from the other Radar Team aren't here yet, so we'll save those toasts for later." Hank pulled Shug toward him, patting his chest. "And I can't begin to tell ya how valuable this ugly fella right here has been. Many of you know him as the sexy, seductive voice of Control-One, but he did more behind the scenes than anyone else. Without him, this wouldn't have come together like it did. So we drink to him ... my little Sugar." With that, Hank pulled Shug's head down and kissed his temple.

"Uh-rah!" In the background, behind the sound of clanking glasses and high fives, news of the UFO sightings could be heard coming from the television. Hank was the first one planted in front of the screen. It was *Headline News* again, but now a new anchorwoman sat stone-faced behind the desk.

"It has been nearly half an hour since the first reports came flooding into various media outlets and local emergency services systems by people claiming to have seen an unidentified flying object flying through the skies of San Francisco and Oakland. At least one hundred people have called one San Francisco television station claiming to have seen the disklike object shoot thought the skies into the Oakland Hills. As of yet there has been no official statement concerning the sightings from any government officials.

"Most of the sightings took place here, in the North Beach section of downtown San Francisco, directly over Fisherman's Wharf." The anchorwoman was replaced by the image of a large map of the Bay area. She circled the areas on the map and drew a clear line across the bay, starting at the Golden Gate Bridge and ending in the hills behind the bay.

"These reports have not been substantiated in any way, and there are rumors circulating among some of the media that this may be some type of phone prank. In any event, this is poised to be one of the largest UFO sightings in modern history—and we here at *Headline News* promise you we will continue to follow this story as it develops."

"Phone prank!" Mike yelled at the screen. "Bullshit!"

"Just wait. This thing will happen fast." Hank's knee rattled his drink.

"When do ya suppose they'll air the video and pictures?" Mike's attention was fixed on Hank.

"It's still the first hour. It will be a while before anyone gets their hands on the good stuff," Hank replied with a smile half-hidden behind his drink. "That guy Wess—Bob Wess, the one with the video—is going to want to sell the footage to the highest bidder. I picked him because he was such a tightwad. It will seem more believable for a guy who thinks he has just shot the footage of the Millennium to want to make a big score. So that may take a while, maybe even tomorrow."

"And the photos?"

"There will be at least one picture of little Betty ready for the ten o'clock news." Hank smiled.

The conversations behind Hank stopped at the mention of video and pictures. Most of the different teams were only aware of their phases of the operation, so anything about pictures and video was news to them. Only the men in Hank's Icon crew knew the specific details about the other operations, and not all of them.

"There's really going to be pictures?" Tonya asked, her eyes wide.

"Little Betty flew over two cities during commute hours! There'd better be some kind of photographic evidence, or this thing won't sell." With a mischievous smile, Hank turned to face the group behind him. "With any luck, we've created the holy trinity of UFO sightings: reliable eyewitness testimony, physical evidence—thanks to you all—and convincing photographic proof. Without seeing it on TV, John Q. Public will never believe it."

The doorbell interrupted the conversations and attention shifted to the door.

Shug answered with a bucket filled with beer under his arm. It was the guys from the first Radar-Hit Team. "Waz up, fellas?"

Trevor Mc Bains was the first one through the door, sneaking a beer from Shug as he came in. BJ Callahan was right behind him, smoking a cigar though clenched teeth as he doffed his coat and embraced Shug. They were both part of Hank's Icon crew and were the real party animals within the cadre of friends. Shug was glad to see his good friends, but he was really hoping to see his cousin Shawn.

The third man to make his way out of the cold was Joe. He was older than the rest of the scientists plucked from the universities. Middle aged, heavyset, and balding, Joe shuffled through the door, nodding to Shug and declining a beer. He seemed tired and not at all in a partying mood.

"How'd it go up there Joe?" Shug stepped aside to allow him in.

"I froze my ass off." Joe grumbled.

"Come in and warm up. There's already been some talk on the news."

"I know. We heard it on the radio." Joe's head tilted back to stare up at Shug. "Where's the restroom?"

Shug pointed the way, then rejoined the party. Hank, Matt, and Mike were all on their feet getting ready to drink a toast to Trevor and BJ. Shug quickly joined in, and they began talking about their parts of the operation. After a minute, Shug made sure that everyone was introduced and made an effort to single Tanya out for special attention.

"Hey Shug, where's cupcake?" Hank called over to Shug across the room.

Shug shrugged his shoulders and pretended not to be concerned.

"He hasn't checked in?" Hank checked his watch.

"No. I thought he would be here when we got home."

"Hey, turn that up!" Darrel pointed to the television, shouting above the party.

A special announcement flashed across the screen as Shug jumped for the remote.

"… Interrupt your program for this special announcement. At approximately five fifty this evening, an unidentified flying object was reportedly seen streaking across the sky over downtown San Francisco, across the bay and over the city of Oakland. A representative from the Center for reporting UFO sightings has also informed us that his office has taken at least two hundred calls this past hour. As of yet, there has been no other official comment from any government agencies.

"But we here at Channel Two News do have an exclusive report for you. Our very own chief meteorologist, Brian Newman, found something very interesting on our weather radar. Take a look at this." The screen showed the radar signature over the Bay area, with multicolored lights scrolling in slow motion over view.

"This is what our Doppler weather radar showed at five forty-eight this evening over the Bay area. Take a close look at this part of your screen here." The screen highlighted a spot over the hills of Oakland. As the radar scrolled, a white dot flashed on the screen east of the bay. The round blip was almost too small to see, but it was there. It disappeared after a few seconds, and another small white dot appeared inches away. This new white dot lingered on the screen for nearly a full minute before flitting out.

A loud cheer erupted from the technicians in the room.

"You can see an object right here, the little white dot. It only lasts a few seconds ... and then another one appears right here. We've experienced record low temps this week, which yields an unusually clear view of the ... of the area." The meteorologist stood to one side, watching the eerie dot in silence for a moment.

Once again, people were on their feet in Shug's living room. They slapped each other on the back and tried to celebrate without screaming.

"We can only assume that if we are picking up this phenomenon on our radar, others have caught it too. The naval Air base at Alameda is less than ten miles from where these radar sighting took place, and both San Francisco and Oakland international airports are also close by. As of yet neither airport has made any public comment, and naval representatives have been unavailable."

On the screen, Daniel Richman was in front of the camera once more, addressing the audience with a stern look on his face. "Again, this is still a breaking story, and not all of the details are clear. But from what we have gathered here, from what witnesses have reported and what we have seen on radar, it seems that an unidentified object flew through the evening sky at incredible speeds and disappeared over the Oakland hills.

"We have what are now being called credible reports of sightings from the Golden Gate Bridge, Coit Tower, and Fishermen's Wharf; the Bay Bridge and several vessels in the Bay itself; and the city of Oakland and the Oakland Hills." A new map of the Bay area was brought up on screen with a straight yellow line drawn from the Golden Gate Bridge to the Cabot National Forest.

"Now we here at Channel Two news would like to caution our audience at home and say that there are unsubstantiated rumors that these sightings may be a part of some kind of media hoax. In fact, there are several different rumors coming across the wire now. And there are even some reports that photos taken of the UFO are coming forward.

"As of this moment, we have not seen any pictures and can only report that many people, maybe as many as two hundred, have reported these sightings. This story has already gained national attention and is said to be one of the largest UFO sightings in American history. This is an amazing story, and our producers are working hard to bring you the eyewitness accounts. We will bring you those interviews as soon as we can, and we promise to keep you informed of all the events of tonight's leading story. Stay tuned to this station for the ten o'clock news with Denise King and myself. We now return to our regularly scheduled program."

"There you have it, folks. We're the lead story!" Hank turned to address the jubilant crowd.

"Look, there's more." The other televisions were now similarly breaking in with special announcements. The room was becoming chaotic with the noise from the excited partygoers and the different television sets. Shug's cell phone chimed in, and seconds later so did Hank's.

Shug knew who was calling Hank by the distinctive ring on Hank's private cell. He and Bill had been having heated conversations all day; apparently Congressman Thomas hadn't liked what Hank and Bill had prepared for him. Shug had overheard Hank getting brutally tough with Bill during their talks throughout the day.

Shug flipped open his phone and walked into his empty kitchen. He was anxious to hear why Shawn was so late. He was slightly disappointed to find that it was only Morgan on the line.

"Waz up, Shug?"

"Yo Mo, waz up? Where you at?"

"Traffic was crazy comin' out of the city. We heard on the radio already!"

"Yo, man, it's all over da news!"

"All right man, we'll be by in a few. Dude, Brice told me to tell you that him and Nate are going to be late. Brice is going to drop off some stuff at Henry's place."

"Didn't hear much from you guys tonight. Everything go okay?" Shug eyed his door, hoping to see Shawn's head in the window.

"There weren't any goof-ups, so we were quiet."

"Right on. Good job."

"No sweat, baby. I can't wait to catch the news."

"See ya when you get here." Shug flipped his phone closed and returned to the living room to find people thoroughly enjoying themselves—except for Joe, who stood in front of the big screen with his hands in his pockets.

Harold Bains, known to everyone simply as BJ, had most every body else started on a kind of drinking game: every time the words UFO were said on the TV, everyone had to take a drink. Shug counted the heads in the room and included Morgan and Jeff from the cleanup crew and Brice and Nate from the remote camera team. Including himself, Shawn, and Hank, there were going to be sixteen mouths to feed. The takeout numbers were on speed dial, and within a few minutes Shug had ordered dinner from three different continents.

The only one missing from the room was Hank, and right at that moment CNN was broadcasting a story about Little Betty. BJ and the group of university guys cheered, throwing back another sloppy shot at the word UFO.

The story began as usual, but after Shug watched for a moment, a familiar voice played on the air. The newsroom was playing a taped phone conversation with a man claiming to have seen the UFO from his boat in the Bay. Shug recognized the old tugboat captain's voice right away; he remembered the nasal tone and high-pitched, nervous laugh. Robert Olson was laughing now as he described the impossible. He said there was no explaining it; the mere sight of it had changed something inside him.

Shug left the room to find Hank.

He found him sitting on the bed with a finger in his ear. He was clearly pissed about something—the veins bulging in his neck were a dead giveaway.

"What *exactly* doesn't he like?" Hank growled into the phone.

"But it's still early! He doesn't get that?

He knows about the video doesn't he?

Well, what's his problem? What about the goddamn radar?" Hank balled his fist around the phone.

"Well, tell him to turn on his TV!

Tell him to sit tight and stop fuckin' thinking! By tomorrow morning, this will be story of the century!

Listen to me, Billy, Gilbert has one part to play in this, and he's going to play it exactly how we wrote it! You got that?

I don't care ... I'll jam my hand up his ass and work him like a puppet if I have to! Just do it." Hank slapped the phone closed and glared at Shug.

"Waz up, our congressman getting cold feet?" Shug placed his drink on the nightstand.

"Son of a bitch thinks this will blow up in his face! He doesn't want to attach his name to anything that sounds like a hoax."

"But he knew from the start that this whole thing was going to turn out to be a hoax." Shug's mouth bent into a sneer.

"Yeah, in six months! He's afraid that it will be seen as a hoax from the start. Dumb-ass! Of course people are going to scream hoax. It's all part of the plan. When the hoax is revealed, people will scream cover-up. I just need him to do his part."

"We need him in that congressional committee." Shug said, almost to himself.

"That's the key. He's forgetting where he comes from and who he works for."

"Bill will get him in line by tomorrow. By tomorrow, everyone will have seen it." Shug smiled reassuringly.

"If Congressman Thomas isn't on some podium by ten o'clock tomorrow reading my speech, me and you are going to fly out to Washington to drag him in front of the press. He's got to be the first one going public, it's his district."

"Ah well, forget about them, tonight is for celebrating. Captain Bobby was just on CNN."

"Oh yeah?"

"Come on man, let's check it out."

"Yeah. All right." Hank unclenched his fists and blew out an exasperated breath. "You heard from cupcake yet?"

"No, not yet. The other guys have called." Shug quickly switched subjects. "They're on their way."

"He better not be screwing around."

"You can trust him. He'll be okay."

"Shug, I trust you—and that's it." Hank stood and looked earnestly into Shug's eyes. "You and I are in a unique position now. Me and you. We only trust each other."

"You got it, brother. Come on, we got some eats coming." Shug's smile broadened at the thought of food. "Should be here in time for the ten o'clock news."

Cries of *drink up* carried over the ruckus as Shug followed Hank into the room. Hank was briefed on all the news and handed a fresh drink. Eventually, Shug noticed, he seemed to forget about his troubles with the congressman. The talk in the room turned to the technical aspects of the radar findings and what the military radar would show. Hank was assaulted with questions concerning the photos he had promised, which he dismissed with a wait-and-see attitude, and everybody continued to drink with abandon.

"Well, unlike some of my colleagues, I've got to work in the morning." Joe stepped forward to interrupt the group. "I want to congratulate you on a job well done, Henry. And thank you. It's about time we got off our duffs and did something."

"This is only the beginning, Joe. This is going to kick start all of our plans."

"I certainly hope so. By the looks of it, you all have a lot to celebrate."

Hank stood and took the senior engineer's hand. "I can't thank you enough. Those balloons really did the trick."

"I don't need any thanks. I've wanted to be a part of something like this ever since I learned about the Iconoclasts. Action! That's what the Icons needed. We've finally weighed in on this ridiculous war."

"I know I can count on you. If you need anything, you know how to find me." Hank continued to press his hand.

"Don't worry about me. I can keep my mouth shut. The last thing I want is to have you and this big fellow looking me up." Joe patted Shug on the back as he and Hank walked to the door.

"Hey, if I'm looking' for you, it's because I'll be needing you to run for office in the Humanist party." Hank showed his respect for the long-established Iconoclast with a nod of his head.

"That's fine by me. You young people be careful. Remember, drunken lips sink ships." Joe faked a quick smile, then turned to leave. As he opened the door to let himself out, Shawn shot frantically into the room. Joe stepped out of his way, eyeing him suspiciously. Shawn had a wild look in his eyes and was breathing hard. Hank stopped him in the entryway with a stiff-arm to his chest.

"Good night, Joe." Hank bid farewell to Joe before addressing Shawn. "Where've you been hiding, cupcake?"

"Where's Shug at?" Shawn tried to push by Hank. "Yo man, where you at?" Shawn called out with panic in his eyes. "Yo, get this gorilla out my way, nigger," Shawn yelled over Hank's shoulder. The party suddenly stopped as the attention shifted to the door. Shawn squirmed like a madman until Hank let him pass into the room.

Shug met him in the hall. "Waz up, cuz? Why you trippin'?" Shawn didn't seem to notice the room full of people staring at him. There were tears welling up in his eyes.

"I dunno ... I dunno what you guys ..." Shawn's voice was strained. "I seen it! I was at da hotel ... then ..." Shawn shot Hank a confused, horrified look and then broke down into tears.

Shug put his arm around him and led him into the kitchen. "Come on." Hank began to follow them, but then thought better of it.

"What's the dilly, bro? What happened?" Shug lowered his voice and spoke into his ear.

"I don't know, man ... I did everything I was supposed to. I'm all fucked up, I dunno." Shawn continued to bawl into his shoulder.

"Why you trippin', you all right?"

"I don't know what's real anymore. I'm sorry, man, I'm sorry."

"Is everyone okay?" Shug felt suddenly concerned for their grandmother.

"I dunno, man. I seen it! I fuckin' seen it with my own eyes."

"What are you talkin' bout?"

"I was drivin' ... and then ... and then I saw it!"

"What, little Betty?" Shug cracked a smile.

"No, man! I mean ... I know what Betty is. Dis was ... Dis was real."

"What was real?"

"I saw it! I'm not crazy! I ain't all cracked out or nothin'! I seen it for real!"

"Chill out, man, chill. What did you see, what exactly?"

"I jus looked up ... I looked up and Bam! Jus like dat, an' it was real! I'm not crazy. I'm not crazy! I really saw it."

"What?"

"A spaceship! They really did come ... aliens!"

"Shawn, listen to me. You were at the hotel shootin' the video. Right?"

"Yeah, I remember all that shit!"

"You got the video?"

"It's in the car. What's happening to me?"

"Shug, what's going on in here?" Hank strode into the room with a beer in his hand. "Is he all messed up or something?"

"No, man." Shug laughed. "He's all right."

"What's up, cupcake?"

"Don't call me that!" Shawn bawled.

"Chill out. He's cool. Chill." Shug restrained his smaller cousin.

"What's he screaming' about?" Hank laughed.

"He just got his dumb ass hypnotized." Shug burst with laughter.

"Say what, nigger?" Shawn looked up at him indignantly.

"You didn't see shit, Cuz!" Shug could barely speak. "He musta got ... hypnotized ... when, when he was filming!"

"You see our flyin' saucer, tough guy?" Hank grabbed the top of Shawn's head and ruffled his hair.

"Fuck you guys! I know what I saw!"

"Gimme a break."

Shug's phone began ringing in his pocket. He pulled it out and flipped it open. "Hold up a minute." He gestured for some quiet.

"I can't believe you, man … You're fuckin' priceless." Hank laughed at Shawn from over his beer.

"Shug, it's Nate. Dude, Brice is dead."

"Say what?"

"He's dead! I'm at that guy's house. The private investigator's office. There are cops all over the place." Nate's voice was strained and cracking.

"What happened?"

"I was waiting for him in the car, and the whole side of the building blew up!"

"What blew up?"

"The whole thing, man! Brice, oh man, he's dead. The cops say it was a bomb!"

Shug gaped at Hank, mouth open.

"I don't know what to do … the cops are asking all kinds of questions. I didn't know what to tell them … Brice is … all over the place. It's really bad."

"Are you all right?" Shug didn't know what else to say.

"I don't know … I'm okay, I guess. I don't know anything about this kind of shit … I was just supposed to throw the fucking Frisbee! What should I do?"

"Fuck! I dunno … Hank … Hey, Henry, something's happened."

"What?"

"It's Nate: he says Brice is dead. He says there was a bomb at your house!"

"Brice?" Hank did a quick double take. "What!"

"A bomb!" Shug still couldn't believe what Nate was telling him. "He says there was an explosion—and Brice is dead! There are cops all over the place."

"My place?" Hank stared at him in utter disbelief.

"Yeah, at the office."

"What the …?"

"I don't know! Here." Shug handed Hank the phone.

"Nate. This is Henry. Tell me what happened.

You're sure?

Do they know it's Brice?

Can you get out of there?

Okay … okay, hang tight. Fuck!

What did you tell the police?

Good. You don't know me. Got it?

Just tell them he was dropping off a camera at the office … and nothing about tonight. I'll handle the rest."

The party in the other room began shouting that the ten o'clock news was coming on, but Hank stayed glued to the phone.

"I'll handle this. You call this number if you find out anything more."

Matt appeared around the corner. He recognized the concerned look on Shug's face. "What's going on, Shug?"

"It's Brice."

"What, on the phone?" Matt pointed to the room full of people. "The news is coming on."

"He's dead," Shug said, feeling the shock in own his voice.

"What!"

Hank flipped the phone closed, handing it to Shug. He ran his hands over his face and walked back to the television. Instead of news of the UFO, the anchorman was reporting on another local story.

"A huge explosion rocked the mission district downtown tonight, reportedly killing one man. It took place just moments ago at a local investigation firm. Detectives at the scene are calling it a homicide. The explosion was apparently the result of a large bomb that completely leveled one side of the three story building." The screen showed the shattered skeleton of Hank's home office. Red and blue police lights flashed over the demolished, smoldering building.

"This has certainly not been a slow news day here in the Bay area; we will try and bring you the events as they happen. Now back to today's top story. The first photos of the object spotted over the bay have come into the studio. Take a look at this …"

Paradigm I
Chapter 5

Washington DC. January 18, 2002

Bill couldn't believe how quickly Hank's hoax had dominated the news. Operation Devil's Peak now colored the front page of every newspaper in the country. Every conceivable media outlet was consumed with the story. Talk of flying saucers was on everybody's lips. Downtown San Francisco had become swamped with press. The streets were packed with satellite vans and crawled with people wanting to be part of the media circus. Bill had failed to grasp the enormity of Hank's plans until this morning.

The hour was approaching nine; he and Congressman Thomas had been up since six, taking in the news. They watched in amazement as Devil's Peak took on a life of its own. Late last night, the first picture of the spaceship had been shown to an alien-hungry public, instantly obliterating any rumors of a hoax. By midnight, a second picture surfaced. It clearly showed a silver disk streaking past the Golden Gate Bridge. At first, Bill couldn't believe his eyes. The image was shockingly real.

The networks aired the first video footage of the UFO a few hours later. Devil's Peak dominated the airwaves from that moment on. The short clip showing the disk streaking over the downtown skyscrapers was aired over and over. It was played backward and forward, broken down frame-by-frame, and fought over publicly. The footage was nothing short of fantastic, a real bombshell.

Gilbert could hardly keep up with rapidly unfolding events and pestered Bill with constant questions. For the moment, Bill was too preoccupied with the television to repeat the plans for Congressman Thomas. An intern at one of the San

Francisco news studios had discovered footage of the flying saucer caught on a remote weather camera. The view was from the top of one of the tallest buildings downtown and clearly showed a silver disk shooting across the skyline. Analyzed frame by frame, there were twelve shots of the flying saucer before it disappeared.

Bill marveled at the thoroughness and simplicity of Hank's plan. The Frisbee-sized disk looked massive contrasted against the buildings. Hank had made sure every conceivable angle had been covered. Each view of the spaceship looked realistic and uniform in appearance. The eyewitness testimony and radar sightings took a backseat to the graphic images of a flying saucer over the city.

Gilbert was practically drooling over the potential media coverage, but he tried hard to appear reluctant. He still insisted on having his way. They were waiting for his car to arrive and take them to their ten o'clock press conference at the Congressional Press Room. Gilbert still refused to read Hank's speech.

"How many more surprises can we expect, William?" Gilbert used his condescending, fatherly tone.

Bill couldn't stand it. Gilbert was being pigheaded and had no clue what he was jeopardizing. "You shouldn't be surprised. We've gone over all of this." Bill tried to appear as if he had expected the media frenzy. "We still haven't seen any of the physical evidence yet."

"Physical evidence?"

"The metal stuff." Now Bill used his own best condescending tone.

"Yeah, right ... the metal stuff."

Bill couldn't tell if Gilbert remembered the molten magnesium or not. He didn't care. He wasn't going to explain it again. There was too much going on, and he still had a job to do. Gilbert had to read the script exactly the way they wrote it, or there was going to be hell to pay. "The air force will find it soon."

Gilbert scratched his head. "Magnesium, right? Tell me again, why magnesium? I know it was important somehow, but I forgot why."

"The UFO nuts have claimed to find that kind of stuff at sites before. They claim it's some kind of UFO by-product. It's a common metal, so the assertion has been easily refuted—until now."

"What do you mean? Why now?"

"First of all, it's a link in a larger chain of evidence." Bill reached for a cigarette. He knew Gilbert didn't like him to smoke inside his apartment, but Bill didn't care. "And secondly, we've used nearly 100 percent pure magnesium."

"What will that prove?"

"Nobody manufactures pure magnesium. It's usually an alloy. There's no reason to make it that quality." Bill blew a cloud of smoke at Gilbert and stared him in the eyes. "But we made it."

"What about the stuff they supposedly found at Roswell? Was that magnesium too?"

Bill groaned. "I don't know. It doesn't matter! Listen, if things go according to plan, the air force will confiscate the magnesium at the first site, but the second site will be harder to find. The material from the second site will be made public. Remember, it's not a normal metal. It's radioactive."

Gilbert waved the smoke from his face. "What makes you so sure the government will confiscate it?"

"Of course they'll confiscate it! This is a national security issue. They'll launch an investigation. We want them to confiscate it. We want an investigation. It's all part of the plan. You've got to look at the big picture."

"You want to show a cover-up." Gilbert stared at the ceiling and slowly pulled the pieces together. "That's entrapment!"

"It would only be entrapment if we were the police, Gilbert. You're thinking way too small. If we're lucky, the Black Watch will expose themselves."

"The Black Watch doesn't exist."

"You don't know that!" Bill squared his shoulders to the congressman. "A lot of Iconoclast resources have gone into this operation. We need you to do your part. We need you to call for a special congressional committee. We need you to secure a seat on that committee, and we need you to read from the script the Iconoclasts have provided you."

"I still don't see how this has anything to do with the Humanist Party."

"The Humanist Party is just another piece of a much larger puzzle. Don't forget your place in all of this."

"I'm not reading that speech. Mine will do just fine." Gilbert shot Bill his best hardball congressman look.

Bill somehow managed to control the surge of anger and frustration. "You're making a big mistake, Gilbert." He blew a cloud of smoke across the room. "It's not smart to underestimate the people you work for."

"That sounds awfully threatening, William." Gilbert looked insulted.

"They're very unhappy to hear you're going off-script." Bill tried to look hard. He knew Gilbert would fold if Hank were sitting here instead of him. "Things could get ugly."

"I'm not going to tarnish my reputation! I was placed in this position for a reason. I'm not about to commit political suicide for some foolish hoax!"

"So you're disobeying a direct order?"

"It's my name. I'll do it my way!"

"You're making a mistake."

"You work for me, not the other way around!"

"Not if you continue going your own way. I'm an Iconoclast above all else."

Gilbert was about to respond, but Bill's cell phone interrupted him. Bill snatched up the phone and left Gilbert fuming. "Morning, Hank." Bill tried to sound as if it were just another day.

"Hey, Billy." Hank's voice was strangely subdued.

"Congratulations. Things are looking pretty good."

"Not really, Billy. We've got problems. Can you talk?"

"I can talk. What kind of problems?"

"Someone tried to kill me last night." Hank said it so calmly that Bill thought he had misheard—but then again, this was Hank. Anything was possible.

"What?"

"A bomb was set off at my place. It killed one of our guys, but I'm sure it was meant for me. It was placed in my private entrance."

"Oh my God. Who was killed?"

"A kid named Brice. The bomb went off in the middle of the operation. Someone was trying to stop me."

"Oh, man. Was anybody else hurt?"

"Billy, I've got to assume the Icons did it." Hank's voice was beginning to color with anger. "Who else would want to stop me?"

"No! No way! It couldn't have been the Icons. They don't work like that."

"Who else knows about Devil's Peak? Billy, I want names."

"Hank, this is crazy! It can't be the Icons."

"You don't know that! Who else knows about the list?"

"Hank, I swear. I haven't said a word."

"What about Thomas?"

"No, nothing."

"Billy, if it was just the three of us, that means it was you."

Bill's mouth hung open. "What in the hell are you talking about?"

"Relax. I'm not accusing you of anything. But if you haven't said anything about the list, then we've been breached."

"What about the people you used in Devil's Peak?"

"Anything is possible, but if any of them wanted me dead, they would have known exactly how to find me. This was a bomb! This was a hit!"

"Where are you now?"

"Me and Shug have gone underground. The FBI is crawling all over what's left of my place. My identity has been compromised."

"What can they find at your house?"

"Don't worry. The list is secure. They won't be able to tie me to the Iconoclasts. Not right away. I'll let them think I'm dead for as long as possible."

"What are you going to do?"

"I'll handle it. What I want to know is what you're going to do. Is the congressman ready?"

"We're about to drive over right now."

"Is he going to cooperate?"

"Fifty-fifty. He's doing the press conference, but he's reading his own speech."

"Son of a bitch!"

"I'm still working on him."

"What's his problem?"

"He's worried. He doesn't want to blow his shot at the presidency. He's just being full of himself as usual. I might be able to scare him into line."

"What does it look like?"

"What, his speech?"

"Is it even close?"

"Well, he wrote it himself ..."

"Is he asking for a congressional committee?"

"Yes, but he's distanced himself somewhat. He doesn't want to appear as if he bought this thing hook, line, and sinker."

"Billy, I don't have time for this. Do what you can. I've got to work the phones."

"Can I help you with anything?"

"No, just get his head screwed on straight." Hank paused for a moment. "Does he know about me?"

"He's never heard of you. He knows nothing about the list, I swear."

"Good, keep him in the dark about all of this."

"Okay. Was Brice married?"

"Two kids." Hank groaned.

"What happened?"

"He went back to my place to drop off some cameras. My door was booby-trapped. That's it. The kid he was working with saw the whole thing."

"Who's the kid?"

"A guy named Nate. They were working on the rooftop."

"I don't know Nate—is he one of yours?"

"No, he's not even an Iconoclast. He's a professional Frisbee golfer."

"A what?"

"He threw the model of Little Betty in front of the remote weather camera for us."

"I had no idea there were professional Frisbee throwers."

"Well, it worked. The shot came off beautifully."

"I can't believe how this thing is shaping up. You did an incredible job."

"I've been trying to tell you. Hey, I gotta go. They're looking for me, so don't try to contact me. I'll get ahold of you."

"Okay."

"And, Billy—when I find out who's responsible for this, they're dead. Do you understand?"

"I hear you."

"Good. I'm looking forward to Thomas's speech." Hank slammed down the phone, and the line went silent.

Gilbert could read the concern on Bill's face as he walked back into the room. "Everything okay?"

"No. No, they're not okay. Like I said … they're very disappointed to hear you're going off-script."

"Come on—what are they going to do?"

"Your words have been carefully chosen. This thing was planned down to the gnat's ass. They're talking about pulling your support."

"They would never do that! I would turn this whole thing over on them. I could expose everything."

"You would be dead before you dialed your first number."

The congressman was stunned. It was the first time Bill had ever talked to him like that. "You're serious?" Gilbert's tone changed.

"This is serious business."

That was the end of casual conversation between the congressman and his chief aid. Gilbert's Town Car arrived to take them to the Capitol. Bill was lost in thought, and Gilbert stared out of the window as the car made its way through DC. A small television played news of the UFO sightings in the back of the car, but neither man paid any attention.

"Look out!" Gilbert screamed, jarring Bill from his thoughts.

Bill turned to the window in time to see the grill of a huge cement truck barreling through the intersection toward them. The truck smacked into the side of the elongated Town Car with a deafening crunch. Glass exploded into Bill's face. Pain gripped the right side of his body and the air was crushed from his chest.

He opened his eyes to great pain. A warm, sticky mess covered his face—Gilbert's blood and brain matter had painted the crushed compartment. Gilbert's body was pressed in between the chrome bumper of the semi and the mangled frame of the Town Car. Steam blasted from the mangled grill of the huge truck. Blood was draining from Gilbert's mouth and nose; a gapping hole was punched into his head. Bill could see into the empty cavity that had once held the congressman's brain.

Gilbert's face was a frozen in a sour expression, his body badly contorted. The car's horn blared as Bill tried to free himself from the seatbelt that had saved his life. He couldn't think, but he could move—and he was getting as far away from Gilbert's body as possible.

Las Vegas, January 18, 2002

"What in the hell is keeping them?" Hank brooded over a cup of coffee in front of the television. News of Devil's Peak was airing without commercial interruptions, but he hadn't heard a word about Congressman Thomas.

Shug was lying flat on the hotel bed. His arm sluggishly lifted to check the time. "Maybe Thomas already gave his speech. What if it took a backseat to the other UFO stuff?" Shug's arm flopped back to the bed. "Maybe they taped it or something."

"Maybe, but I don't know; you'd think a congressional press conference would get some attention at a time like this." Hank shifted in his seat.

"People are going nuts over the videos." He could almost hear Shug smiling. "This is crazy."

"I know." Hank allowed himself to smile for a moment. "Now that we've got their attention, I hope we can still do something with it."

"Don't worry." Shug sounded as if he were ready to drop off. The electric buzz of Las Vegas hummed outside their window as if nothing had happened. Hank contemplated stretching out on the bed but the name Gilbert Thomas caught his attention.

"At nine fifteen this morning, while the Democratic congressman was on his way to the Capitol for a scheduled speech regarding the UFO sightings, his car was struck by a truck. We have confirmation at this hour that Congressman Gilbert Thomas was pronounced dead at the scene of the accident.

Two other people, including the driver of the cement truck, were rushed to a local trauma center. The driver of the truck reportedly ran a red light."

Shug bolted from the bed. Hank's coffee fell from his lap.

"One of the injured was Congressman Thomas's chief aid, William Kemp. We are taking you to St. Andrew's Hospital, where Mr. Kemp is making a statement."

Bill was propped up with a crutch and stood behind a podium full of microphones. A man wearing surgical scrubs stood at his side. They were outside the hospital's emergency entrance. Ambulances were parked behind them while their crews busily wheeled patients in and out. Bill was battered and disheveled, but he looked like a movie star on the screen. His arm was slung across his chest, and there were small white bandages on his chin. His shirt was splattered with streaks of dried black blood, but he looked calm and composed.

"Good morning. I am William Kemp, Congressman Thomas's chief of staff, and I'm afraid I have some very tragic news. Gilbert R. Thomas is dead.

"I have already spoken with his wife Marsha and his three children, and now it is my sad duty to inform the American public that one of their own, one of their best, has passed on." Bill paused for a moment, turning his head to scan the reporters as if he were addressing a much larger audience.

"I also feel it is my duty to convey Gilbert's last thoughts to all of you, especially to those of you in his district in California. I will not attempt to memorialize him here. It is far too early, and there are too many good things to say about my friend Gilbert. But something has happened that has changed everything ... and I think it's important to tell you what Congressman Thomas planned to do today.

"We were on our way to a press conference when Congressman Thomas was taken from us. Our phones were ringing off the hook this morning. Hundreds of our constituents called us, many of them with stories of their own. The excitement this event has sparked is palpable. I can see it in everyone here." Bill motioned to the crowd with his bandaged arm and winced with pain.

"I was with Congressman Thomas when the story broke. We, like everyone else glued to the television, were stunned by what we saw." Bill pointed a thumb over his shoulder at the paramedics behind him. "I even overheard these guys listening to the radio during my ride here."

Bill let his shoulders drop, and he sighed deeply before straightening himself. "Nobody was more excited than Congressman Thomas.

"In fact, in all the years that I've worked for him, I'd never seen him so enthusiastic. Anybody who knew Gilbert knew that he was driven and serious, but when he was truly excited, he was almost childlike." Bill's voice choked with just the right touch of grief.

"When he called last night, that childlike spirit was alive in him like I had never heard before. We spent the night watching the news. He grasped the enormity of what was happening right away, and he knew he wanted to be a part of it.

"As the hours passed and no other government official stepped forward to comment, his sense of duty compelled him to stand up and speak for the people of his district. Representing the people of California was an honor and responsibility Gilbert took very seriously.

"Sadly, Congressman Thomas will no longer represent the good people of California. His flame is extinguished, but I feel it is my duty to see that the message he had for the people does not die with him. He will be missed, and we should all grieve his passing, but I for one do not feel sorry for Congressman Thomas." Bill paused and drew a deep, painful breath. "I saw how happy he was. He died instantly and did not suffer. Moments before we were hit, Gilbert looked to me and said, 'Think of all the people throughout history who lived their entire lives and didn't know about this. This changes everything.' The congressman's life may have been cut tragically short, but at least he lived to see this, and he was happy about that.

"As Congressman Thomas's chief aid, I am compelled to carry out his last directive. And as Gilbert's friend, I feel I must put aside my grief and give you his final thoughts. Congressman Thomas wasn't merely going to comment about the UFO: as the representative of the thirteenth district of California, he was going to call for a Congressional Investigative Committee. He envisioned an open committee, accountable to the people. One with enough power to access any information the government might have. It is time we know the truth." Bill breathed deep while cameras flashed over him and the stone-faced doctor.

"When Gilbert and I talked last night, we were both amazed to learn that last night was not the largest UFO sighting in modern history. Over three thousand people reported seeing a UFO over Brussels and Germany one decade ago. And there are others. In 1948, then Senator Gerald Ford raised a public inquiry into the sudden flood of sightings across the U.S. It was quickly squashed, and the senator's career was saved.

"The lead scientist charged with debunking the sightings during the fifties now heads the world's largest organization dedicated to the search for extraterrestrial life. But the government still refuses to address the topic. They even go as far as hiding the truth from us.

"Well, what we saw over San Francisco was no swamp gas. And it's time our government steps forward to comment on the phenomena. The American people deserve answers. We deserve the truth. And I will do everything humanly possible to ensure that Congressman Thomas's last wish is carried out." Bill shook behind the microphones. "A commission answerable to the American public must be formed. The truth must be told.

"Gilbert was keenly aware of the potential harm these images, these newfound understandings might bring. People will be scared. We always fear what we don't understand, but only the truth can diminish the specter of the unknown.

"As I talked with Gilbert this morning, I began to understand why he seemed so happy. He was thinking of the future … and of the past. He understood how an event like this could bring the whole world together. The possibility of extra-terrestrial life adds a new perspective to all our lives. Our singular humanity can be realized. And I hope Gilbert's happiness can be realized by all of us."

Hank gazed at the screen, amazed by Bill's brilliant performance. Camera flashes bombarded him as he slowly nodded to the reporters and stepped away from the podium.

"Mr. Ellis has arrived, Mr. President." Donna Johnson, the president's private secretary, announced the arrival over the Oval Office intercom.

"Thank you, Donna. Please show him in." President George Walker Bush crossed the Oval Office floor to sit behind his desk. "Now we'll get to the bottom of all of this." He laid his hand on the desk and anxiously tapped his fingertips on the polished wood.

"I certainly hope so, Mr. President." Andrew Card stood off to the side and checked his watch.

"Where is that report on this Kemp character?" George felt his anger escaping.

"Our people are still working on it, Mr. President." Card shrugged his shoulders apologetically.

"He's sure stuck a stick into the hornets nest."

"Kemp is on his way to becoming a real media darling."

"This is the last thing we need. I want to put a lid on this as soon as possible."

"Yes, sir."

The double doors were pushed open, and a secret serviceman ushered in a short figure bent with age. He was not at all what George had anticipated. The plainly dressed elderly man looked like he'd been plucked from a bingo hall, not the head of the Black Watch. Until this morning, even the president wasn't sure if the group really existed, but now he was meeting the lead man face to face.

"Good afternoon, Mr. President." The man's face was a mask of old age, showing no emotion as he greeted the president.

"Hello, Mr. Ellis. Thank you for coming. Please have a seat. You know Mr. Card, of course."

"I was under the impression that this would be a private meeting." Ellis remained stone-faced, refusing to take a seat.

"Mr. Card is my chief of staff." The president was already taking his seat but stopped halfway, suddenly offended by the old man's impudence.

"At this point, Mr. President, I'm afraid that I have to ask that all recording devices in the room be turned off." Mr. Ellis stood stock-still, resting on his cane as he issued his demands.

"This is the Oval Office, Mr. Ellis." George forced a smile. "You can speak freely here." Once again, he gestured to the seat waiting for him.

"I'm afraid I cannot say another word until all the recording devices are turned off and you and I are alone, Mr. President." Mr. Ellis returned the forced grin, and the wrinkles of his weathered face moved for the first time.

A long, awkward silence passed as the men locked eyes and stared each other down.

"Andrew, please wait for me in the situation room." The president spun in his chair to face his assistant.

"Yes sir, Mr. President."

George W. pressed the button on his intercom as he glared at the mysterious figure standing defiantly before him. "Donna, send in Mr. Owens."

Mr. Ellis accepted the seat, guiding himself into the leather chair with care.

"Recording the conversations in this room for posterity has been a tradition of my office since Truman." The president reclined in his chair, folding his arms across his chest. "And frankly, I found the difficulty in arranging this meeting distasteful. I am the president of the United States." George scowled for all he was worth.

Mr. Ellis continued to stare mutely back at him until Mr. Owens, the secret service chief, entered the room through a concealed door.

"Mr. President?"

"Tom, I want you to turn off all of the audio equipment in the Oval Office."

"Sir? Yes sir. It will take a moment." The always serious man looked puzzled at the unusual request.

"Have Donna buzz me when it's off," George said, dismissing him grumpily.

"Yes sir." Agent Owens disappeared behind the concealed door, and once again the two men were left to stare at each other.

"I am willing to extend you this courtesy, Mr. Ellis, but I feel compelled to remind you: you work for me." Mr. Ellis simply nodded his agreement without saying a word. "I am deeply troubled by the fact that I haven't had any direct contact with your office until now," George said, feeling frustrated by the one-sided conversation. "We are in a state of war, Mr. Ellis. As president, I should have complete access to all matters concerning national security."

Mr. Ellis remained silent.

George felt himself heating up. They sat, silently regarding each other, until Donna's voice buzzed in over the intercom.

"The recorders have been turned off, Mr. President."

"Mr. President, I apologize for any offense, but secrecy has been a tradition in our office since well before the Truman era. I myself have sat in this very chair before and made the same request of your predecessors." Ellis remained expressionless.

"I understand." George had never heard of such a protocol, but he was not willing to admit that yet.

"In fact, the only reason that I have agreed to meet with you today is because we are faced with a very unique situation. Not every president has been privy to the activity of my office. However, I do not know how much your father has told you about our organization."

"My father?" George was taken aback.

"I cannot pretend to know what secrets are kept between fathers and sons, let alone between presidents." Mr. Ellis smiled knowingly over the table.

"My father has never mentioned anything about you or the Black Watch."

"Then I apologize. I have underestimated your father. He is a good man, and I think I may have made a mistake in coming here." Mr. Ellis stood, slowly getting to his feet. "Mr. President, I feel we would both be better served if I left now."

"Now wait a goddamn minute! I am the one who called you in here. I want answers from you, Mr. Ellis, and you are not going anywhere until I get them. Sit down." The president angrily pointed his finger to the chair.

"Mr. President, there are things that you do not want to know. That is why my organization works outside the auspices of your authority." Mr. Ellis eased calmly back into the seat.

"We are at war! My authority is total."

"It is a matter of your own protection, Mr. President."

"My interest lies with the protection of this country, not my office."

"The country is in no more danger than it was one week ago. Go fight your war against the terrorists, and leave these matters to us."

"The American public is demanding answers. Did you hear this guy, Kemp, yesterday? There will be an investigational commission breathing down my neck. I want to be fully aware of what is going on with this UFO stuff. I demand to know what is going on!"

"Mr. Kemp was tragically premature with his remarks." Ellis adjusted the spectacles on his nose.

"What are you saying? What do you know about the sightings in California?"

"Mr. President, what you're asking of me would put you in very exclusive company. There is a level of security that I'm sure even you are unaccustomed to. This is evidenced by the fact that even your father has declined to mention its very existence to you. It may be the best-kept secret in all of human history. If I am to share any of it with you, you must be aware of the magnitude of its implications."

"Are you saying there's something to these reports about aliens? This thing flew over one of our naval air bases, and I had to hear about it on CNN!"

"You are a religious man, are you not, Mr. President?" Mr. Ellis leaned forward in his seat.

"Yes I am. What has that got to do with it?"

"Knowing what I'm forced to tell you may change what you think you know about life."

"My faith is solid, Mr. Ellis. I want to know what you know about the UFO in California. Was it real or not?"

Mr. Ellis removed his glasses, wiping the lenses casually before he spoke. "It was not *our* boys."

"What do you mean by that? Our boys?"

"It's still early, but I think this is something new. It is all very similar to other events, but it's also distinctly different. The radar signature is different. The metallic debris is different. The eyewitness accounts are unusual. But the craft itself is familiar."

"I don't understand. Who are *our* boys?"

"The Grays. That is what we call them. They have been here before. They are *our* boys." Mr. Ellis smiled earnestly for the first time as he took in the shock on the president's face.

Paradigm II
Chapter 6

London, England. June 10, 2002

Naked beneath the flimsy paper gown, balancing on one foot and trying to appear casual, Hank was sure there had been a mistake. He tried talking to the nurse, but she insisted he undress to his underwear and put on a gown. He was cut short before he could explain that he never wore underwear, and now he felt dangerously overexposed as he thumbed through a British tabloid and waited for the doctor. This was his first visit with Dr. Ramachandran. He was sure the gown wasn't necessary; she was a neurologist, not a proctologist.

A quick tap on the door was followed by Dr. Meenakshi Ramachandran striding into the room with her head bent over her charts. Hank turned to greet her and was struck by an uncharacteristic self-consciousness. She didn't look like the woman on the back of her books; she was strikingly attractive for a woman in her fifties. Jet-black hair lay draped over her shoulder in a neat, intricately woven braid. The end of the braid rested in her cinnamon hued cleavage. She wore a brilliant red sari under a white lab coat. The low-cut dress danced with intricate white patterns, and her face was carefully painted.

"Good morning, Mr. Dunn." Her eyebrows arched slightly at seeing him naked under the gown, but her tone was even and professional. Her proper English accent, which sounded a bit odd coming from such an ethnic-looking woman, felt a touch cold as their eyes met.

"Please, call me Allen." Hank extended his hand and did his best to pretend he wasn't naked. "How do you do?"

"Very well, thank you. Please have a seat." She ignored his outstretched hand and gestured to the paper-covered bench behind him. She seemed unconcerned by his modest discomfort, or by his apologetic gestures for the lack of clothing, so he didn't protest. He simply turned to sit, letting everything show as he hopped onto the bench.

"I know we haven't had much time to speak directly, Allen, but I want to confess something right away. I am *not* a doctor who regularly treats patients, you see. I am a researcher. I usually treat patients only as part of some sort of clinical study. I have colleagues who do this sort of thing." Her eyes bore right into Hank's. "I agreed to this as a favor—because apparently you are a very important person." She raised one eyebrow in an exaggerated, silent question mark.

"It's an important favor, and I am extremely grateful. It has nothing to do with my status, however." The doctor's sudden directness surprised him. She continued to stare into his eyes as if waiting for him to break. "My success in getting an appointment with you was the result of a lot of arm-twisting on my part, I'm afraid. I've probably been a little over-persistent, and I'm sorry." Hank grimaced slightly, shrugging his shoulders.

Silence, and a persistent penetrating stare, was all he got from Dr. Ramachandran as she waited for him to explain himself further.

Hank shifted uncomfortably, then broke. "I guess I have something to confess as well. I do have ulterior motives for wanting to meet you. It's not simply because of my pain." Hank glanced to his stump. "I hope I wasn't being too selfish." He steadied himself, preparing to jump ahead of his planned material. "The truth is, I'm a, well I guess you could say I'm a big fan of your work. I've read *Phantoms in the Brain* and *God in the Limbic system*—and, well, I really wanted to meet you." Hank attempted to give his bottom line, "here's the truth" touch, but the look on her face filled him with doubt.

"If it makes things easier, I can take part in a study," Hank pleaded jokingly, but the tension held.

"Very well, Allen: if you were a subject in my study, and you truly wanted to get rid of your pain, I would have to know a great many things about you. Very personal things. I will have to know these things for … scientific reasons, and because *pain* is quite personal, you see. Do you understand?"

"Of course."

"Very well … Allen, why is it that I haven't ever heard of you before? Apparently we have friends in common." Her directness didn't let up, but her demeanor softened slightly. She finally broke the stare-down between them and looked down at her notes.

"Although we share the same friends, I'm afraid we run in different circles."

Dr. Ramachandran read her notes in silence for an awkward moment, a faint, knowing smile on her face. "All right, Allen, I understand." She placed her notes on the counter and strode within arm's length of him. She smelled of sweet, fragrant blossoms, not perfume. "Let's talk about your pain, if you please. I see you are an amputee. You lost your leg as a soldier. Is that right?" She lifted the flimsy gown that covered his knees and examined his mangled stump casually.

"It was nine years ago." Hank recoiled at the touch of her cold hands. "I was shot."

"And you have pain in your absent leg and foot." She peered into his face once again, but now she wore the look of a concerned healer.

"Mostly my foot, but sometimes I get a cramping sensation in my ... calf muscle." Hank stroked the empty air beneath his knee as if he were massaging his absent leg.

"Is it constant, or does it go away?" Her painted eyebrows danced on her forehead with each question.

"No. It gets better and worse." Hank pretended not to care that she had thrown the gown aside and now peered at both his legs. He knew without looking that his privates were now almost fully exposed. "It can get real bad." Hank coughed into his fist with modest discomfort as he stared at the blankness of the wall opposite him.

"Stand, please." She stepped back to watch clinically as Hank inched off the bench onto one foot. "Very good." She cocked her head to one side, apparently impressed with his balance. "Do you have any other major injuries or deformities?"

"No. No deformities," Hank smirked.

"Arms out, if you please." Doctor Ramachandran gracefully circled around him, her fingers gently prodding the bones of his pelvis. She flung open his gown once more, and this time it seemed that she was simply appraising his physique. "How old are you, Allen?" She squinted her eyes at the records on the table.

"Thirty-six."

"You are in very good condition. Do you train with weights?"

"Well ... I work out a lot. I run a lot, too. I've gotten pretty good with that thing over there." Hank pointed to his prosthesis against the wall.

"I run too. But I can never seem to lose this." She stepped to the side, smiling as she delicately tapped her own slightly padded midsection. "What I want to know is how to get one of these." She slipped her hand inside his gown and innocently ran her hand over his abdominal muscles. Hank was stunned for a moment, feeling as if the gown wasn't there at all. "Ah genetics, what can you do?" She turned to face him with a mock sigh.

"I don't think pretty women need six packs, Doc." Hank flushed with embarrassment as he caught himself flirting with the doctor.

"Doc? I like this *Doc*. It's very American, you know." Her voice held a hint of condescension, but her expression didn't change. "So you like to work out, and you were a soldier. Go ahead and sit down. What else do you do? Do you work?"

"I run a business … I'm very busy." Hank hopped back onto the bench, trying not to show too much.

"Are you married?" She bent forward to examine the tissue of his mangled stump.

"No."

"Ever been?" A single, probing eyebrow arched at him from her immaculately painted face.

"Nope."

"No children?"

"No Ma' am."

"Thirty-six, never married, no kids, and six-pack abs … My mother would want to know what's wrong with you, Mr. Dunn." She smiled at him quizzically, and Hank wondered for a moment if she were implying that he was gay.

"Like I said, our friends keep me pretty busy. You can reassure your mother that I'm just waiting for the right girl to come along." Hank smiled with mock defensiveness.

"My mother does not care to hear *that* excuse any more, thank you very much." She laughed to herself as she turned to her notes. "And how do you manage your pain? It doesn't look like you are a drinker."

"I guess I don't manage it that well." Hank implied with his hands that that was why he had gone to see her.

"Do you drink?" She held her notes in her hands and looked at him over the chart.

"Only when I want to get drunk." Hank attempted another smile, to no effect.

"We have to be honest with each other if I am going to help you. This will remain between you and I, so I want you to speak freely with me. It is very important for you to understand. I work with people that have the same pain as you, and I know what they will do to alleviate their symptoms." She was staring at him again, but all of the harshness had left her face. "Do you drink every day?"

Her hand moved toward his. As he opened his hand to take hers, she nimbly grabbed him by the wrist and began counting his pulse rate.

"No. But I do drink." He was suddenly conscious of his bounding pulse.

"Any history of alcoholism in your family?" She was counting off seconds on her watch, tracking his pulse. Her hands were soft and warm now as she gently clasped his wrist.

"Yeah, my father is a terrible alcoholic."

"And the rest of your family?" The doctor looked up from her watch, eyeing his change in posture suspiciously.

"They're all dead."

"Oh my. I am sorry, Mr. Dunn." She looked into his eyes apologetically. "This is going to get very personal, you know." She finished checking his pulse and continued to hold his hand, squeezing it sympathetically.

"I can handle it." Hank didn't know if he should return the affectionate grip.

"How did they die?" Her dark, almond shaped eyes shimmered compassionately.

"Who, my family?" Hank tried to hold her gaze, but his eyes strayed to the dark flesh of her breasts.

"I need your family history." She tapped Hank's medical chart with her pen, graciously pretending not to notice his distraction.

"Well ... my mother died from cancer, but the rest were all killed in accidents. I don't think that really counts as medical history."

"If you don't mind, I must know as much as I can about you. Pain is relative. It's not just about trauma. Physically or mentally, it can manifest itself all the same." The doctor took a half step forward, her hip pressing slightly into Hank's thigh. Hank's eyes drifted uncontrollably back to her chest.

"I understand."

"Good. If we are going to work together, there should be nothing between us." Hank felt her words were ironic, considering that only a few millimeters of paper stood between her and all of him.

"Well, like I said, my mom died of breast cancer." Hank struggled over the word breast, and once again he forced his face to transform into the brooding mask that protected him from having to retell his life story. He wasn't expecting to go through all of this again.

"How old?" She persisted, undeterred by his scowl.

"She was forty-one."

"No. I'm sorry, Mr. Dunn ... how old were *you*?" She pulled a small rubber mallet from her smock and began testing his reflexes.

"Oh. Seventeen. Right before I joined the army." Hank's stump jumped reflexively as she thumped his knee.

"And did you have siblings? You said they."

"Brothers."

"And they have all passed too?" She stopped thumping and regarded him quizzically.

"Yes."

"How did they die? Were they soldiers as well?"

"No. Accidents." He was trying to fend off her questions with the hard looks and quick answers that had worked in the past, but she persisted.

"All of them?" The doctor pulled up a swivel stool and sat in front of him.

"You really want to know about this stuff?"

"We can move on if it's too personal." The doctor smiled warmly at him. She was clearly inviting him to continue.

"It's all right, I guess. It's just that I really haven't talked about this stuff in a long time."

"But you have been to doctors before?"

"I hate psychiatrists. No offense. It just seems that I end up hearing more of their problems than anything else," Hank grumbled.

She smiled knowingly, rolling her eyes. "Tell me, how did they die? Were you close to your brothers?"

"Yeah, we were real close. I was the youngest." Hank looked away, letting the forgotten thoughts collect themselves. "My oldest brother Jack—he was the coolest—he died in a drunk-driving accident when I was twelve. That was the first time I had someone close to me die." Hank paused to tighten his lips against the swelling of emotion.

"Was your father already drinking by that time?"

"He's an Irishman through and through. He's also a Vietnam vet. He drank ever since I can remember."

"And your mother?"

"Did she drink? No, she was one of those ultra religious types."

"Catholic?"

"At first. Then born-again."

"I see." Her eyebrows arched sympathetically as she continued to grip his hand. "And you had other brothers?"

"Tommy and Mike. Tommy was killed by some idiot jumping out a high-rise window." Tommy's face flashed in his memory as he closed his eyes.

The irony of the tragedy didn't take long to show on her face. "Oh my! That is terrible."

"Things were a little crazy back then. Mikey died of a drug overdose not long after Tommy's wake."

"How awful ... did he commit suicide?"

Hank's eyes opened wide, meeting hers. There was a long pause before he could answer. "Yeah. I think he did. It was pretty nutty around the house back then. My mother was going crazy."

"That would certainly explain some things." Dr. Ramachandran spoke under her breath as she momentarily turned away.

"About my leg?" Hank asked, somewhat confused. "I though my phantom pain was because my brain's body image was starved for input."

"I'm sorry ... I simply meant it explains some things about our mutual friends." She released his hand to scribble some notes.

"Oh, I guess so." Hank had never thought of his involvement with the Icons in such simple terms before.

"What about you, have you ever done drugs?" She was peering at her checklist again.

"Yes."

"What kinds of drugs?"

"If you must know, I think that I've done just about all of them. But I gotta tell ya, mostly for fun, not for pain."

"What about analgesics, painkillers? Things of that sort?"

His brief spark of a smile disappeared as he prepared to level with her. "I've been addicted to one painkiller or another since my accident." It was the first time Hank had ever said those words aloud.

"What kind of painkillers?"

"Pills. I only take them once in a while now. As a matter fact, I've been so busy the last few months that I haven't been taking them at all. They never really worked on the pain anyway."

"Of course they didn't. How can painkillers work on a leg that is not there? Drugs simply ... distract the brain, pacify it if you will. Your pain emanates from your brain. It is all an illusion of sorts, because of course your brain does not actually feel any pain itself—there are no nerves inside your head. That is the problem you are facing; drugs cannot help you. When was the last time you took any painkillers?"

"Before I came to London, about three weeks ago." Hank scrolled through the calendar inside his head.

"And why are you here in London?"

"To see you."

"That's it? You have no other connections here in the UK?"

"I was telling the truth when I said I'm a fan of your work. They say that you know more about the brain than anyone. I wanted to meet the one they call *Dr. Brain*. That's what they call you, right? Dr. Brain?"

"That's what they call me, yes. But I don't call myself that." A frown appeared on her face for the first time.

"You have been credited for mapping out more of the brain than anyone else. Some say that you're well on your way to mapping out all of the different brain functions."

"It's not that simple. It's not really like making a road map. But yes, that is what I have been doing, looking at the brain. Why, does neurology interest you, Mr. Dunn?"

"To me, it's the most fascinating field there is. For years I've been plagued by the distinct sensation that my foot is still there." Hank lifted his stump into the air as if he were watching the toes wiggle on his absent foot. "I can wiggle my toes. There's no describing it. I first became acquainted with you when I saw a BBC special featuring your work with amputees and phantom limb syndrome." Dr. Ramachandran rolled her eyes contemptuously at the mention of the television broadcast, but Hank continued. "Michael Stafford produced the piece. He and I worked in television production back in the States, and he's a friend." Hank let the word "friend" hang in the air for a moment. "He turned me on to your work. I've read most of your books, at least the ones directed to the layman."

"Mr. Stafford? Really? I did not like the exposé he produced about my work. He jumped to too many conclusions. I did not approve the show before it aired, you know."

"But it was incredible. I couldn't believe what you were able to do with those amputees. The more familiar I became with your research, the more interested I became. It was like learning the brain all over again."

"Have you studied the brain, then?" She regarded him skeptically.

"Well no, I never went to university or anything, but in the army I did a lot of work in psychological warfare. We mostly studied psychology, not neurology."

"In the army?"

"I was in a special unit. We were trained to get into people's heads, under their skins, that sort of thing. I had never given any thought to the neurological element of our consciousness before."

"I'm glad to see that there is more than academic interest in my work. I had no idea that I have a fan base among young commandos." The doctor smiled brightly again.

"Like I said, I think it's the most fascinating—maybe the most *important*—field of study, at least for guys like me. I can grasp that the mind has power over the body. I can get that. I understand that pain, my body image, even my self is all an illusion generated in the brain. I really buy into it, but I can't seem to master it. I can't talk myself down from the pain." Hank rubbed his stump, attempting to soothe the throbbing kindled by his thoughts.

"It comes with understanding. It doesn't happen overnight, like you saw on that dreadful BBC promotion. It is not as easy as holding up a mirror against the good leg and telling your mind 'look, it is better now!' That is rubbish!" She flicked her hand over to the corner of the room, where Hank noticed an assortment of mirrors lining the wall. "That's what Mr. Stafford showed me doing on that awful program.

I believe that your brain's body image can rewrite itself, given time and the right stimuli, but it is never automatic—like you saw on the telly. And you, Mr. Dunn, carry a lot of pain around with you. It is plain as day on your face." She smiled at him and resumed her examination, feeling around his head and throat. "You have undoubtedly heard that we humans only use 10 percent of our brains. Well, it's my belief that we only know what 10 percent of our brain *does*. We *use* all of it—at least some of us do."

"And you have figured out what the other areas are for?" Hank tried to speak as she peered into his mouth and down his throat, her tiny hand clasped under his chin.

"I'd say we're up to 11 percent." She smirked.

"I think you're being modest. You're credited with finding the *G-spot*," Hank said as she released his chin.

"That is another unfortunate name my colleagues have hung on me. I do not care for it, either. They simply do not understand." She stopped her examination and glared at him with her hands on her hips.

"But you have found it? It's for real? The journals have called it the G-spot, too."

"Sensationalism. You know how the media works, Mr. Dunn. I have never called it that."

"Allan, please." Hank pleaded.

"If you must." Dr. Ramachandran spoke curtly, and with an expression on her face that showed she doubted his name was Allan. "They called it the God-spot for ratings. I had nothing to do with it." She rolled her eyes at the mere mention of the term.

"I really would love to hear more about it. If it's not too personal, that is." Hank's eyes were locked with hers again, this time more playfully.

"I thought we would be discussing your leg. Are you trying to change the subject—Allan?"

"I suppose I am, a little. But I've got to admit, it's the G-spot that really fascinates me."

"Well, first off, the G-spot or God Module is a misnomer. It has very little to do with God. If you have seen the BBC documentary, you probably saw how I first began looking at that part of the brain."

"The epileptics."

"Yes, I was confronted with a group of epileptics who were afflicted with an atypical seizure disorder, seizures originating from the temporal lobe. These types of disorders are nothing new; in fact, these patients have been referred to as Temporal Lobe Personalities for many years now. These particular seizures were fascinating because when those abnormal cells in the brain began firing off, the patient would go through a singular, particular type of … delusion."

"They would think they were God."

"Not exactly. Each case is unique, of course. They all had different experiences, but there were distinct similarities as well. Many would have intense spiritual experiences during the seizures and would become preoccupied with religious and moral issues during the seizure-free periods.

"But they all experienced a form of divine ecstasy, a totality of *self*. Call it whatever you like. They were flooded with thoughts and archetypal images that they could only describe in religious terms. They would say there was a divine light that illuminates all things. There are no other words to describe what omnipotence and divinity these people were trying to describe. But yes, for all intents and purposes, these people all felt as if they were God—or at least had direct communication with him. Please follow my pen with your eyes." She began moving her pen back and forth in front of his face, testing his ocular nerves.

"We began mapping them, as you would say, finding anomalies in the brain's limbic system, near the hypothalamus. The hypothalamus is responsible for what we neurologists call the four Fs. Are you familiar with the acronym?" There was a mischievous look on her face.

"The hypothalamus is the survival center, right? Fight or flight," Hank responded, confident he knew the functions of the hypothalamus.

"Very good. And the four Fs of course stand for fighting, fleeing, feeding—and fucking." There was no hint of shame in her delivery. "Using a device called a transcranial magnetic stimulator, we were eventually able to induce these episodes without harming our subjects, and then we began to interview them when they were in these altered states."

"So have you been able to duplicate the … sensation in healthy people?"

"You could use one of these machines to stimulate any area of the brain you wished. It is highly accurate and not very difficult to make. For instance, we know there is a cluster of cells near the septum, within the thalamus in the middle of the brain, which is responsible for feeling pleasure." Dr. Ramachandran pulled Hank's face to her chest so she could trace a fingernail over his scalp to where the septum lay. "There have been neurologists who have stimulated this part of their brains and described the sensation as a thousand orgasms rolled into one." She gently pushed his lingering head from her chest before continuing. "We were the first to experiment with the limbic system and the temporal lobes."

"So you've talked with these people when they thought they were God?"

"Yes. And each of them was speaking well beyond their personal consciousness, let me assure you. They had, it seemed, tapped into the unconscious collective of their communities, and they knew things the subject would have never known. Everything around them was imbued with cosmic significance. Some believed themselves to be omnipotent, removed from time entirely, and they each described what it felt like to be God." She beamed a tiny penlight into Hank's eyes.

"Keep in mind that these patients were people from all over the world. Very sick people, mostly; when the seizures would strike them, they were usually prone to violent convulsions and fits of delirium. For the most part, they had been cast out of the social world, but when in their unconscious states they were completely tapped into the social unconscious of their region. They knew the history of their people better than one knows one's own family. In their mind's delusion, they were central to all myth, and they knew all manner of things. Tremendously fascinating, I must tell you.

I remember one patient from America; he was only a young boy, maybe thirteen. He had never read the Bible or spent any significant time in church, but when he was under his delusion he would recite verse and tell me in his feeble, pubescent voice that he was God."

"So you're saying these things are imprinted in all of our brains."

"We have been able to reproduce our findings, but the research is in its infancy. We have simply identified the geography of the anomaly and the fact that it's different. It's too early to speculate on what we think its function is. That is where Mr. Stafford overstepped his knowledge."

"What do you mean, different?"

"Well, that part of the brain itself is entirely different. The chemistry is different. It seems to function differently than the rest of the cerebrum surrounding it. Its impulses have unwarranted priority in the brain, subordinating more important impulses that pertain to, let's say, survival functions."

"But you can recreate it? You could stimulate a part of my brain, and I would have the same delusion?"

"We all share the same basic cerebral structure, and like it or not, you do have a G-spot." She grinned lightheartedly at the double entendre. "Now that we've located it, it sticks out like a sore thumb. It is different."

"Don't you think the public should know about your research? Especially in light of what's going on in the world right now?"

"Like I said, my research is in its infancy. I have no desire to join in all of that nonsense." Her expression turned scornful as she dismissed the events causing a maelstrom of controversy with a wave of her hand.

"The existence of God has never been as hotly debated as right now. Your work can shed light on that argument. You could make the case that men like Mohammed and Moses were epileptics, not prophets. Evidence like this would rock the foundations of religious belief."

"What I have learned will not help you in your cause, Mr. Dunn."

"My cause? Isn't it our cause, doctor?"

"I am a researcher. I seek understanding, not proof for any cause."

"Our cause is ending the conflict that results from misunderstanding. You can show people that God is artificial, that it comes from our own heads. You can prove it's an instinct, not a real, supernatural presence controlling everything."

"Nothing in nature is artificial; everything has purpose."

"As an Iconoclast, I must admit I'm surprised. Do you believe in God?"

The doctor appeared amused as she once again smiled at Hank. "My family are Hindu. They have never believed in God as you know him, so the concept of a monotheistic godhead is altogether foreign to me. But if you must, you could say that I am a Deist. I believe there is purposeful direction in life. The world is too complex—the *brain* is too complex—for there not to be."

"But you believe that Mother Nature has shaped our brains through evolution, trial and error … isn't that just as good as saying there isn't a God?"

"You are still young and passionate, and I can appreciate your enthusiasm—and you are very handsome, too. I like you, so listen to me. It is almost cliché these days to say the human brain is the most complexly organized form of matter in the universe. But it is true: a piece of your brain the size of a grain of sand contains one hundred thousand neurons, two million axons, and one billion synapses, all talking to each other. Given these figures, it has been calculated that the number of possible brain states, the number of permutations and combinations of activity theoretically possible, exceeds the number of elementary particles in the universe! Something like this does not develop by chance alone."

"But we've evolved and adapted just like every other creature on the planet. We all come from the same primordial soup."

"Yet at the same time, humans have stepped beyond the bonds of evolution and adaptation. We no longer need to grow more hair when it gets cold; we put on clothing. It is the uniqueness of our brains that has allowed us to circumvent nature. We are special, and I believe there is a purpose for that. If it is all random, why have we attained this state we call consciousness? Why do we laugh, or cry, or dream? Why is there a cluster of neurons smaller than a grain of sand tucked into our heads that gives us spirituality? Why do we express ourselves with art or music?"

"Isn't it because society influences evolution? Can't it be explained rationally?"

"Insects have been around a lot longer, and have established vast, highly complicated societies, yet they have not developed any of these things."

"True, but imagine what would happen if insects did evolve a God of their own. Look at how much destruction and misery it's caused for us. Ant colonies work, bee colonies work—human colonies are dysfunctional and dangerous. And at the center of them is this thing we call God."

"I became an Iconoclast to end the madness caused by misunderstanding, not to destroy God." She was speaking more quietly now, but her tone didn't change.

"But God as we know him can't possibly exist. People are saying that life on other planets confirms it."

"You mean all of that UFO nonsense? I don't believe any of it."

"You don't think it's possible?"

"That is not what I said. I think anything is possible. In fact I have little doubt there is life outside of what we know." The doctor turned away from him and walked to the other side of the small room. "I think it has been very clever, don't get me wrong." Once again, her eyes locked with his as she turned to face him. "It's true; many people truly believe that it did happen. And yes, many people are very excited. That's all there is on the telly these days. People are talking about God, and UFOs. Some people are getting ready for the rapture; it has caused a great stir. But I don't believe it."

"You think it was a hoax?"

"I'll keep what I *think* to myself for the moment—because I like you, Mr. Dunn. And I will continue to help you with your pain, if that's what you really want. But let me tell you what I *know* for certain." She folded her arms across her chest, never breaking eye contact for an instant.

"I know the Iconoclasts have been implicated in the hoax. It may only be one of many rumors, but it is the first time the Iconoclasts have been mentioned publicly. And now the Humanist Party in America has stepped forward, without the direction of the Icon leadership, and prematurely released the Humanist Manifesto. Junior men like this Kemp fellow are taking the reins of leadership, and we are forced to support him because he is popular.

Is it a coincidence that the Humanist Party debuted on the heels of the sighting in California?" A spark gleamed in her eyes. "I doubt it.

I also *know* the authorities are looking for a man in connection with a bombing, a man who disappeared that same night under … mysterious circumstances. A man in his mid thirties, a man with only one leg. A man described as most likely ex-military."

An uncontrollable chill ran down Hank's spine, causing his whole body to shiver.

"What I *don't* know is why the Iconoclasts would have anything to do with a scheme like this."

Hank felt drained after climbing the three stories to his rented downtown London flat. The aroma of good, old-fashioned American cooking greeted him when he opened the door. He found Shug improvising a barbeque over the gas range. Dirty dishes cluttered the minuscule kitchen, and two thick steaks sizzled over the makeshift grill.

"Hi Honey, I'm home." Hank felt relieved to be back, but he had to force the levity as he hung his coat on its peg. "Smells good—what's for supper?"

"Do you have any idea how expensive real meat is over here?" Shug gestured to the steaks on the grill. "Had to go to three different shops before I found these bad boys."

"Good job. I'm getting tired of all the fried food." Hank squeezed past Shug to the miniature refrigerator and grabbed himself a beer. He stared at the bottle of Guinness in his hand for a moment, and then popped the top with a shrug of his shoulders. Dr. Ramachandran's questions about his drinking habits echoed in his head, but he was beyond caring; the thick ale was a treat.

"Did you get to see her?" Shug carefully flipped one of the steaks, using two forks as tongs.

"Oh yeah, I saw her."

"How'd it go?"

"Very interesting." Hank took a seat across the stove from Shug. "I think we're going to have to make another move."

"What do you mean?"

"Well, things have gotten a lot more complicated all of a sudden." Hank paused to chug a good portion of the Guinness. "As it turns out, she is exactly who we thought. And she, as well as the rest of the surviving organizational head, knows more than we expected."

"Knows more about what?" The steaks flamed over the grill as Shug gave him a puzzled look.

"They seem to know it was a hoax, and they think one of their own masterminded it. She said the authorities are looking for a guy with one leg." Hank paused to belch under his fist. "She knew it was me from the time she walked into the room."

"They know it's you?—I mean, you personally?" Shug's teeth ground together with a painful expression as the realization sank in.

"The six months is almost up anyway. It was only a matter of time before things would come back to me." Hank casually dismissed getting fingered for the hoax—that was expected—but Dr. Ramachandran had confirmed his worst fears about the Icons. "Today answered a lot of questions for me. More than I expected. If the organizational head knew about our plans from the beginning, it only confirms my suspicions about them."

"You talking about Brice?" Shug looked away to juggle the steaks.

"That bomb was meant for me. I'm sure of it."

"But that doesn't make any sense. The operation had already begun. And if they wanted to assassinate you, there are better ways to kill a guy."

"Come on, Shug, you've got to look at the bigger picture. There are a lot of names on that list, some real hard cases, too. Nothing would surprise me anymore. Anyway, now it's decision time. We've been made, and when you've been made, you're usually the last one to know about it."

Shug looked back at him pensively. "What are we gonna do?"

"That depends: what do we know? We know our cover is blown. We know that the FBI is looking for a one-legged man and that in a little over a week, our witnesses are going to end their suggestive state and come forward with the announcement that it was all a hoax. And we know that I've been fingered as its mastermind." Hank woefully shook his head.

"And the Iconoclasts will be implicated too," Shug said, putting together the bottom line.

"That's the clincher. I anticipated a backlash. It was part of the plan. At six months, the story would be losing momentum; I was planning on the witnesses stirring up more controversy, more coverage. I never imagined that the Humanist Party would take off like it did. If I'm connected to the hoax, and in turn connected to the Iconoclasts, the Humanist Party could be exposed, too."

"Bill."

"It could be very bad for Billy. I never imagined he would be thrust into the limelight like this." Hank bit into his thumbnail.

"Can you two be connected?" Shug passed him another beer from the miniature refrigerator.

"Easily."

"But we were so careful." Shug searched for the obvious connection between them, looking puzzled.

"Billy and I share history. We were in the Mog together. We were hospitalized together. There are connections to be found if someone digs deep enough."

Shug braced his arms against the stove. "We need to find a way to keep Billy clean."

"We can do it, but we've got to change plans before the witnesses come forward. And that won't be easy if people are looking for me."

"You want to scrap the plan now?"

"We have to change it up a bit. I hadn't counted on the Humanist Movement breaking out and gaining momentum like it has. I don't want to do anything to jeopardize that. If I'm already in the spotlight, and the Icons are being implicated, the public will be less likely to think the witnesses coming forward are part of a cover-up. But if I can steal the spotlight entirely, maybe the Icons won't be found guilty of fooling the public. The hoax would be the action of a single lunatic. We need to go back home."

"What are you talking about? Are you saying you want to step forward and take credit for this? You'll be arrested for sure." Shug stared at him in disbelief. "You want to give yourself up?"

"I don't plan on getting caught, just admitting to the crime. It's the only way to deflect attention away from the Iconoclasts, and Billy."

"Why do you want to go back to the States to do it? Can't you just claim responsibility from Sweden or something?" Shug clearly didn't like the sound of this new plan.

"We've got to cover our tracks first. Then I can confess from wherever I want. Screw Sweden: we'll do it from somewhere tropical. I can't stand this weather anymore."

The flow of conversation was interrupted by the unfamiliar sound of the doorbell. Its tone was naturally unfamiliar to Americans, but it seemed even more odd because they had never heard it before. With a sickening rumble of his guts, Hank realized that his situation had changed drastically; their cover was gone.

As Shug stared at the front door, Hank left his seat and strode over to his coat on the peg. He pulled the 9-millimeter pistol from its pocket, cocked the hammer, and then slipped into the darkness of the bedroom. He motioned for Shug to answer the door and made a gesture to get rid of whoever it was.

The doorbell rang again. Shug straightened himself, preparing to answer the unknown. A moment or two passed, seeming like an eternity, and all Hank could hear was the deep baritone of Shug's voice and the pounding pulse in his ears. Then he heard the door close. Hank uncocked his pistol and blew out a tense breath of air.

"Hank." Shug's voice was calm, almost whimsical, but the way he said "Hank" made him ripple with tension again. Shug seldom called him by his real name, especially during the last five months on the run. "Oh, Hank—there's a visitor here for you."

Hank quickly slipped the pistol into the waistband at the small of his back and stepped out into the entryway. A young woman stood near the door, partially hidden behind Shug. She was strikingly beautiful. She wore a short, pleated mini-skirt, reminiscent of a school uniform, and a low-cut blouse that clung to her figure. Her hair was long, flawlessly blonde, and pulled back into a ponytail. Hank knew before she said a word that she was an American.

"This is Cindy Laguellen. And she asked for you directly, Hank." Shug's eyebrows arched. "She wants to talk about your painting."

"*The Virgin and Saint Giovannino.* Hi, I'm Cindy. It's nice to finally meet you." She bounced into the room, beaming at Hank.

"Likewise. I'm, um … Hank." Hank felt a sudden flush of anger as he looked past Shug to the young woman pushing forward to greet him.

"Of course you are. You're a hard man to get ahold of." The young girl smiled innocently, stepping closer to take Hank's unoffered hand.

"What can I do for you, Cindy?" Hank wearily took her hand, which lingered in his until he pulled away.

"I'd like to talk with you about the Virgin. Can I come in?" She gestured to the living room, at the same time motioning for Shug to take her coat. A large art portfolio was slung under her arm.

"Well, we weren't expecting visitors, and to tell you the truth …" Hank was about to show her the door but was cut short.

"I'll only take a moment. And then I'll go, I promise." She was already handing her coat to Shug.

"I'm actually a very private person, you understand, and I'm not interested in …"

"Oh please, Mr. Foster, I've come a long way, and I don't have a lot of money. Just hear me out. Please?" she pleaded with him, clutching her portfolio to her chest. She couldn't have looked more innocent, more alluring; she was beautiful, and Hank knew she was counting on that fact.

"Well, I am curious, Cindy. Who are you, and how did you find me?" Hank followed her into the main room while he and Shug exchanged curious looks.

"I'm a student, an art student. An art history student really. And I want to talk with you about your painting of the Virgin. You still have it, don't you? Is it here?"

"The painting? You want to talk about the painting? How did you find me?" Hank's tone was controlled and even, but now he took his intimidator's stance, his muscled arms folded and flexed across his chest.

"Mr. Cramer. I don't want to get anybody in any trouble; I told him I wouldn't ever tell anyone he helped me."

"The art dealer?" Hank couldn't help but show his surprise.

"I've been trying to find the Virgin for a long time, and I found out it was sold through him. He wasn't going to tell me at first, but when he found out why I wanted it so bad, well, he helped me. He gave me your name, but he said I'd probably never find you. Except he gave me the name Henry Patrick. He said he didn't think that was your real name, so I figured you were some millionaire recluse or something." She glanced around the sparse apartment shared by the two men on the run and apparently thought differently. "But when I searched that name on the Internet, it led me to Hank Foster and his new name, Allen Dunn." She smiled up at him innocently, as if it were only a slight intrusion compared to the importance of her homework. "It took a little bit of digging, but I did it. Please don't be mad at me. It's very important."

"You found me on the Internet?" Hank felt horrified and skeptical all at once.

"Pretty much. I had some of the guys at school help me." She continued to smile at him, pitifully unaware of his growing anger.

"Guys like helping you, don't they?" Hank said without smiling.

"It's not like that. I'm just very passionate about my research, and I don't take no for an answer. And those guys are so good on the computers and stuff; it was no sweat for them." She tried to look defiant while still maintaining her innocent facade, but Hank could see that she was beginning to break under the intensity of his stare.

Hank let her sweat it out during a long silence before he unfolded his arms and spoke. "What do you want with my painting?"

"So you do have it! It's not here, is it?" She practically clapped her hands with excitement.

"No, it's not here." Hank shot back tersely. "And it looks like I'm gonna have to find a new art dealer to help me take care of it." Hank broke his gaze to look over at Shug.

"I could help you. I could take care of it. That's why I'm here. I want to study it. I mean really study it, with the right scientific equipment, the right tests."

"Why my painting?"

"It's the best example of the UFO phenomena artwork surviving the Renaissance era. *The Virgin and Saint Giovannino* is the cornerstone of my research, and now we have the technology to prove its authenticity."

"What are you trying to prove?"

"Your painting should be one of the most famous pieces in the entire world! Not because the imagery is so astounding, or because the artist was so famous, but because she has a history. She is one of the few paintings that avoided condemnation and burning. The Catholic Church is the reason she has been displaced from the public eye. I want to prove her authenticity and restore her place in history."

"My painting?" Hank was beginning to think the young student had been misinformed. His Virgin's history was cloudy at best.

"We can prove she's authentic. We can also prove the Catholic Church lied. The Virgin is not a forgery. They want to destroy it like they destroyed the others. They can't accept reality: the image is too clear, the implications are too enormous, and it's the best example of the alien conception theory in the world! Fra Fillippo Lippi is the most famous of all the known artists who included UFOs in their art. He worked with Da Vinci and Michelangelo, and his Virgin is one of the most important pieces of contact testimony to survive the Renaissance."

"And to authenticate it proves what, exactly?"

"Proven to be real evidence, she can be shown alongside all of the other surviving historical artwork depicting alien contact. We have documents that prove the Catholic Church has destroyed similar artifacts. We can prove there were others depicting the same images and that they were destroyed by the Church." The young girl thrust her portfolio toward him as if she were ready to show him the documents. "I know you can help me. I know who you are, Mr. Foster. I know you can publicize my work. Nobody else will even look at my research. They say I'm crazy. I know you're one of those Iconoclasts. And I know if you just take a minute to look at my work, you'll help me share it with the public—get it on the Discovery Channel or something." The young girl chewed her lower lip as she laid out her ambitions.

"I know you've probably traveled a long way on your looks, and are no doubt used to getting your way, but do you really think I'm gonna hand over that priceless piece of art because you're cute?"

"I don't have any money, I know. But you must believe in it. They say you're the man to talk to if you want to publish material like mine. And when I heard you owned the Virgin, I knew you had to believe, too!"

"Believe in what?"

"The Biblical alien connection. I know you've heard of it, you must have."

"You believe Jesus was an alien?"

She looked hurt. "That's not it at all. It's just … proof that aliens have been with us all along. There's *something* to it: why else would the church fight so hard to cover it up? The Bible is full of alien encounters: Genesis, Moses, Ezekiel, Isaiah … Sodom and Gomorrah, the star leading the Magi, the great column of smoke that led Moses and the Israelites out of Egypt … Looked at with an open mind and a modern understanding, many of the stories from our past depict alien encounters." Her arms crossed over the portfolio clutched to her chest, and she begged him with her eyes.

Hank shook his head and once again gestured toward the door.

"Please listen, the ancient Hebrew word for angel is Nephelium. Nephelium, literally translated, means "the ones who came down." The word "holy" means "other" … as in otherworldly. The angel, the Nephelium, Gabriel was responsible for putting the holy, otherworldly, Quran into Muhammad's head … It's an alien encounter. Moses received the Ten Commandments from the Mount in a UFO! The UFO phenomenon wasn't born in the forties. Look! This is a nearly four-thousand-year-old petroglyph found in a cave in France. It's clearly a flying saucer." She pulled the print from her portfolio, thrusting it at Hank. "These are Egyptian hieroglyphs showing the same craft. Three thousand years old! And this one is from India. There's more, a lot more. It's no coincidence that religions like Buddhism in the East and Judaism in the West emerged at the time when these alien interventions were appearing in the artwork. The painting of the Virgin is the best depiction of such an event. And she's one of only a few the Church hasn't destroyed. But there are others that have survived antiquity, and I want to bring them forward." The young woman breathlessly folded her arms over her chest and refused to budge.

"I don't care about any of that. Whoever told you that I was an Iconoclast and that I could pull strings for something like this was wrong. I'm an art lover, that's all. I bought the painting because I liked it. Nobody else wanted it. It was a steal. It was labeled a forgery."

"You must be wealthier than I thought, if you call a quarter million dollars a steal."

"Did Carter tell you that?"

"Information is always there if you know how to look for it. I'm a smart girl, even if I am cute. And my research can stand on its own. Please. Just have a look."

"I can't help you. I'm not in that kind of business, despite what you may have heard."

"Just look at it first! Only a few minutes, please!"

"It doesn't matter what I think. If your work is as compelling as you say, then you can get it produced. The climate is right; there's a market out there. But you want a television producer. Go seduce one of those guys. You're right; I do know some of those guys—and believe me, it will be easy for a girl like you."

"I'm not like that! I'm fighting for the truth. I can prove it. I just need a chance."

"The survival of the Virgin is proof enough. I don't want it touched. It's priceless to me."

"Then you won't let me see it?"

"It's not here. And soon, neither are we. Thank you for stopping by. Good luck with your schoolwork. I really hope you get the publicity you want." Hank pointed to the door and tentatively placed his hand on the small of her back to push her out of the room.

"But you didn't even look at my work." Tears began welling up in her eyes. "If I could only get people to stop and look, they would change their minds. That is how I got this far: not because I'm cute, because I'm right! I'm on to something. When they see it all put together they believe, too … they want to help me. I thought you of all people would believe." She was sobbing now, not even trying to hold back the tears.

Hank couldn't take the crushed look on her face any longer. Shug was staring at him as if he was being cruel, and the young girl didn't budge, despite his gentle pushing. "Okay, I'll look. Just stop cryin' will ya?"

Cindy followed his eyes with hers as the portfolio was opened. Now his attention was where she wanted it; firmly fixed on the astounding collection of images falling from their binding. His intimidating expression refused to soften as he flipped past the first prints showing his Madonna. The stern look held as he passed the pages showing the blown-up view of the UFO over the Virgin Mary's shoulder, but when his eyes fell on the next print, his brow furrowed and his face took on the look she was hoping for. He pulled the print aside, then held it juxtaposed next to his own painting. His eyes bounced from right to left in amazement. Bingo!—Cindy knew she had him.

"Who painted this?" The man's authoritative voice had softened somewhat. "When was it done?" The astonished look on his face told all. She had seen the look countless times before, but she had never relished it more than now. This was the man who could make it all happen, and his epiphany was taking place right before her eyes.

"Amazing, isn't it? It's almost an exact copy of Fra Lippi's *Virgin and Saint Giovannino*." Cindy reached over to point at some of less obvious similarities between the two paintings. "But this one, also from Italy, is much older. Its origins are somewhat dubious. It's called *de Tondo*. Its history isn't well known. We think it was painted by Mainardi Sommariva, but it serves as dramatic proof supporting my theory that there was an underground movement dedicated to keeping these images alive and out of the hands of the Church." Cindy paused, anticipating the doubtful scowl that always seemed to follow that statement, but his attention held fast to the prints in his hands.

"Look here." Cindy guided her finger along the brightly colored Renaissance piece to the upper right corner. "I'm sure you're familiar with this." Her pink-painted fingernail rested below a man and his dog painted unobtrusively into the background. The man's figure was small, consisting of only a few carefully placed brush strokes, yet his purpose was strikingly clear. With one arm raised, his hand flattened over his eyes, he was peering into the opaque sky behind the Madonna. The man's dog stood by him. The dog's head was also tilted back to gaze into the sky. The two diminutively painted figures gazed up at a silver, saucer-shaped disk angled against the horizon. Streaks of light, painted in brilliant gold, emanated from the small disk. "This is the man and his dog. Everybody can see what he's doing. Even his dog is looking at it." She leaned over his shoulder, letting one of her ponytails dangle over him.

"The man and his dog are a common device used to portray this scene. You can see it again in this earlier version." Cindy traced her finger back to the older, darker image. "Again, we see a man and his dog. Almost the identical composition … and they, too, are staring at a UFO." Her finger glided up to a similar disk hidden in the background. "Now, the man and his dog in this scene go way back to Biblical times. He is thought to be a shepherd, the same shepherd that heralded the coming of Christ, and he's been found hidden in many works, usually pointing to something easily overlooked in the background."

Hank didn't speak or move. He scrutinized the works silently, like a man who truly knew art and its subtleties. "The shepherd and his dog are seen over and over again, in countless other pieces." Cindy bent over to pull more prints from her portfolio.

"What's this?" He held a print to his face, peering into the background.

"That. *That* is another cornerstone of my work. She's Crivelli's *Madonna*. Can you see what she's hiding on either side?" Cindy slid another print of Crivelli's *Madonna* in front of him. This print showed the magnified background to either side of the Virgin Mary as she bent harmoniously over baby Jesus and Saint Paul. "You see here, these are clearly rockets launching. There are thirteen on this side, and seven over here. Complete with flames shooting out the bottom—and here, these small crosses … tell me those aren't airplanes."

"Shug, come have a look at this." He handed his giant bodyguard the print.

"Remember, these have been blown up ten times. You might not notice them with the naked eye. Paintings like this were designed that way. They had to be discrete; the Church destroyed anything overtly scandalous. Hardly any documents survived. You've got to remember, the Church was responsible for commissioning most of the artwork at the time."

"What does this say?" The muscle-bound black guy passed the print back to his boss.

Holding onto the print briefly, Hank focused his eyes on the words written in Latin across the bottom of the print. "*libertas ecclesiastica*," he read aloud. "Freedom from the Church."

Cindy was surprised by the quickness and ease of his translation. "You're an educated man, Mr. Foster." Cindy bit her lip and hoped she hadn't come across as a smart-ass.

"How old are these?" Shug asked as he joined in rummaging through the assortment of prints.

"Anywhere from a few hundred to three thousand years. I've collected samples from all over the world. Here, let me show you." She tried to turn to the next print in her portfolio, but Mr. Foster's hand lingered, keeping Crivelli's print face up. "You hold that, and I'll just move these to over here. Smells good in here. What's burning?"

"Oh shit!" The bodyguard lunged from the table and dashed into the kitchen.

"Here, here's something interesting. You can see an apple and a pickle growing out of the same tree behind yet another Madonna painted by Alananno. The symbols of the apple and pickle are repeated in many other works. I don't know what they represent, but I'm fairly certain this is the tree of life." Cindy pointed from one pair of curious vegetation to the next; each scene depicted a similar-looking tree behind the main subject.

"The tree of knowledge ... knowledge of good and evil." Hank said absently, as if to himself.

Once again, he surprised her by properly identifying the symbol. "That's right. It's in your painting too."

He looked at her for an instant, then turned to his man in the kitchen. "How are them steaks coming, brother?"

"Mostly all right ... I guess." The voice from the kitchen sounded doubtful.

"These prints are just the ones depicting the Virgin Mary. There are nearly enough to make up their own genre. I've collected samples from every time period, from all over the globe. I have pictures of cave paintings depicting flying saucers that date back nearly three thousand years. These types of images are all over the place in the East. The Indian Vedas speak of them. Some of them are quite famous. See this one? It's DeGelder's *Baptism on the Mount.* It survived because the Church proclaimed that the UFO in the sky beaming light down on Jesus is really a hole opening in the heavens and divine light pouring down. And look, see this one, the Church says this red flying saucer streaking through the sky is really a Cardinal's red hat being thrown through the air. No way! That's the same flying saucer being described by people today."

"Looks like Little Betty." The man appeared over his shoulder with two black steaks on a plate.

"Shut up, will ya?" Mr. Foster's focus broke momentarily as he shot his bodyguard an angry look.

Cindy pulled his attention back with a tap of her finger. "These two are the most famous in my collection. You can still find them hanging in galleries—like your Virgin should be. There was no way for the Church to say the UFO in your painting was a Cardinal's hat. So they discredited her as a forgery. I can prove it isn't."

"You'll have to forgive me. This is all very interesting, but what are you trying to prove?" He turned to face her; his deep amber eyes bore into hers. This was the moment she had been hoping for, the moment all of her hard work would pay off. If she could just win over this one last person, her mission would be complete. Her mother would be vindicated. The truth could be told. It all came down to this man and whether he was willing to help her or not.

Washington DC. June 14, 2002

"The French journalists have arrived, Mr. Kemp." Carla's voice crackled from the speaker on Bill's desk.

"Thanks, Carla. Send them in." Bill was exhausted. "That will be all for today. I really appreciate your staying late … again." He was annoyed by the hastily scheduled interview. Now they were almost an hour late. The last thing Bill wanted to do was run through the same song and dance he'd been trotting out all week.

"No problem, Mr. Kemp. Don't work too hard. You've got to look sharp for the cameras tomorrow."

"Thank you, Carla." Bill ran his hands through his hair before pressing the button on the intercom once more. "Remind me again, are these guys print or television?"

"Television, I think. You'd better put on your tie."

"All right. Good night, Carla." Bill buttoned his silk shirt and scanned the notes on his desk. There was something familiar about the name scribbled into his calendar: Enlightenment Press. He read the name aloud and tried to remember if he had spoken with them before. He knew they represented the French version of the Humanist movement somehow, but his head swam with the names of countless press outlets and publishers.

There was a quick set of taps at his door, and Bill stood to greet the last of today's visitors. The door swung open, and a giant black man filled its frame. Bill stopped in his tracks and his eyes shot to the man's face with a sudden flash of recognition. A second man stepped out from behind the young black man.

"Hank!"

A devilish grin was plastered across Hank's face as he raised a finger to his lips. "Shhh." Hank closed the door behind him.

"'Ello, Monsieur Kemp. Good day to you. I am very pleased to make your acquaintance." Shug stepped forward, offering his hand and affecting a ridiculous French accent. "My name is François Dillion."

Bill absently reached out to take his hand, but Shug clamped onto his shoulders and quickly kissed him on both cheeks.

"'Ello, Billy. Surprised to see us, no?" Hank stepped forward, smiling as if he didn't have a care in the world.

"Where have you been?" Bill flushed with relief but refused to smile. "Have you forgotten how to use the phone?"

"Ah, we have been away on holiday, Mr. Congressman." Hank pressed Bill's hand. "I thought we should talk in person." His smile disappeared as he cleared a seat for himself on the desk.

"What's going on? Why haven't I heard from you? This goddamn six-month deadline has been hanging over my head, and you just disappeared!"

"Yeah, well. That's the thing, Billy: we need to talk."

"It's about time!"

"We need to rethink our exit strategy for Devil's Peak. We've been found out."

"What?"

"The Iconoclasts are on to us. They know it was me."

"Oh, shit."

"Relax, Billy. I've got a plan."

"A plan? What are you talking about? In less than a week, your people will be coming forward to scream hoax! I can't get caught up in any of this bullshit!"

"I know, Billy. I've got it handled. We've just got a few loose ends to tie up first."

"Loose ends! Hank, the Icons can't get fingered for this, not now!"

"I know, Billy. I won't let that happen. Even if they did try to kill me."

"Jesus, Hank! For the last time, the Icons didn't try to kill you!"

"Bill, the Icons knew about Devil's Peak from the beginning. Somehow they knew all about me. Now I'm sure of it."

Bill was done with Hank's paranoia. "You don't know that. You're letting yourself get all crazy over this thing. There are more important …"

Hank cut him short. "I know more than you think. I've met with one of the surviving organizational leaders. She knew about Devil's Peak. And she knew about me."

Bill pulled at the mop of hair on his forehead. "That doesn't mean they tried to kill you!"

"Regardless, my identity has been compromised. It's only a matter of time before certain connections are made. When the witnesses come forward, it could get hairy for you."

"Dammit, Hank. Can't you keep them from coming forward or something?"

"No. That's what they signed up for, and that's what's going to happen. Besides, there's going to be a paper trail. Bank accounts are suddenly going to swell. This whole thing was designed to look like the witnesses were paid off. The press is going to scream cover-up.

"I know."

"All of the witnesses are Iconoclasts. Once they come out of their hypnotic states, they're going to point fingers. None of them know much about the Icons, but they all know me. So this is what we're gonna do: I'm going to come forward and admit everything."

"That's crazy! How is that supposed to help?"

"It'll create some distance between Devil's Peak and the Icons. If we can keep the Icons from being fingered, the Humanist party will keep its good name."

"You lost me—how is it going to help separate the Icons from Devil's Peak if one of their own steps forward and claims responsibility?"

"Simple, Billy: I cop to all of it! I take credit for the hoax. I admit to subverting the Iconoclasts for my own evil purposes. I admit to stealing the identities on the list, everything. I come clean on *everything*!" Hank smiled with a gleam in his eyes. "Let the hoax be blamed on a single lunatic mastermind … Me!"

"But why? I don't get it?"

"It's perfect because, in the end, you'll be the one to catch me." Hank jabbed a finger at him. "It will be your investigation that ferrets me out. You traced it back to one of your own men. And armed with proof of your findings—proof easily obtained from me, of course—you confront me and uncover my attempts to usurp the power of the Iconoclasts!" Hank raised his voice triumphantly for a moment, then he added, "Only, I escape—of course." Hank winked at Bill with a sly smile. "You'll be the hero of the day and the savior of the Iconoclasts' good name!"

"You'd do that?"

"Shug and I will watch the events unfold at our leisure somewhere. You'd become the Icon hero, identifying its cancer. And you will point to me as the confirmed mastermind before the witnesses even come forward. The Iconoclasts will be cleared, and the Humanist Party won't be tainted by scandal. You, young Billy Kemp, celebrity congressman, will be the voice of truth yet again. You can control the spin firsthand. It's the only viable solution. But we've got to get our ducks lined up in a hurry; there's not much time.

"I don't know, Hank. I don't like the sound of this. There's too much at stake now."

"The connection between me and you will be uncovered at some point. You're just too high profile now."

Bill stared at Hank and couldn't understand why he was willing to fall on the sword. He was about to ask why when a rapid knock on the door stopped him. "What is it?"

Carla poked her head inside the door. "Sorry, Mr. Kemp, but I thought you might want to see this. There's some kind of meteor shower on the news!" Her voice was high-pitched with excitement. "I know you asked not to be disturbed, but it's really quite spectacular. I've never seen anything like it."

Bill tried to conceal his annoyance. "Thank you, Carla, but I've seen meteor showers before."

"Not like this one, William. Not in broad daylight. You've got to see this." She stepped into his office and addressed Hank and Shug in flawless French: "*Pardon moi Messieurs, mais c' est très excitant!*"

Bill strode to the other side of his office to open a polished oak cabinet concealing a large television. When the screen came to life, the image of a white-hot fireball filled the screen. The words scrolling along the bottom said the view was from a telescopic camera somewhere in South America. The shot slowly panned back, showing the enormity of the fireball streaking across the blue sky. A tail of smoke boiled in its wake.

"And let me state once again, there was no advance notice of this spectacle ... all reports indicate that it is expected to burn up entirely in our atmosphere. Indeed, as you can see from this magnificent vantage point, it seems to be breaking up right before our very eyes. Our science editor tells me a display of this kind is very rare. The meteor seemingly came out of nowhere ... he says they estimate its diameter at roughly the same size as the Super Dome. But even so, they fully expect it to break up entirely in our atmosphere, so nobody knows for sure how long this wonderful display will last."

Bill broke away from the television to pull open the drapes. "Do you think we can see it from here?"

Paradigm II
Chapter 7

The early morning sun hung low over the horizon, reflecting its radiance over the vast unbroken expanse of the Philippine Sea. The deep greens and dark blues of the ocean were placid this morning and were coupled with a helpful, friendly breeze that pushed Anastacio and his small skiff out to sea. He was grateful for the calm waters today. Today he fished alone and had the work of two ahead of him.

Anastacio had woken early this morning, leaving the rest of the fishermen from his village to rise with the sun while he set out alone to fish the deep waters far from his coastal home on the island of Tinian. Two days ago his son-in-law had taken his daughter away to live with his family in the Philippines, and with him gone, the boat seemed pitiful and empty. He dreaded the thought of looking for a new fishing partner; there weren't any other men in the village he cared to spend the timeless hours at sea with. He would rather fish in solitude.

The waters near his home yielded too few fish during week so Anastacio hoped to change his luck by following the bigger boats into deeper seas. He took down and gathered up the sail as he surveyed the empty horizon. He would spend the rest of the day drifting back to his tiny island which lay somewhere behind the rolling swells. There wasn't another sail or ship visible anywhere in the water around him; there was only the lapping of the water against his boat and the persistent calls from the birds following him. He secured the sail and prepared to cast the deep nets he hoped would bring in some good fish, maybe even some stripers or some tasty game fish. Blocking the sun with his hand, he peered at its location on the horizon to gauge the time. His hand obscured the sunlight, but another light caught his eye. It was much smaller, but nearly as bright. It hovered just above the sun, a bright point in the sky looking like the sun itself had given birth to a small star.

Anastacio blinked, squinting and straining his eyes to make out its form. He thought his eyes might be playing tricks on him. He turned away to rub and rest his eyes before taking off his wide-brimmed hat to block the sun once more. With the rays of the sun blocked, he could clearly see that the light in the sky wasn't a figment of his imagination. There was a second, miniature sun in the sky over the horizon.

Although only a fraction of the size, the glowing fireball was almost as bright. It appeared to move through the sky like a falling star, but it was unlike any falling star he had ever seen. He'd seen countless shooting stars flitting through the night skies, but they had all been fleeting apparitions disappearing in the darkness. This star seemed to roll through the air at a casual pace.

He gaped at it for several moments, tracking the glowing ball with his finger as it moved through the sky. He wished Marco, his son-in-law, were here to see it. His boat pitched in a swell, and the sun's rays stung his eyes, reminding him there was work to do.

He replaced his hat and began working the nets, preparing to cast them over into the deep, placid waters. The work was not difficult, not in a boat his size, but every task was his alone. There was no one to share a smoke with, no one to talk to but the birds, and they made poor company—often shitting on him if given the chance. He busied himself by tying the lines of his two deep-sea poles and collecting a bucket of salt water to store the day's catch, and after a while he had nearly forgotten about the strange ball of light.

He kept his eyes on the lines angled into the water. As the swells lifted his skiff, he could see the far-off mound of green that was his home, as well as the slightly taller volcanic mountains of Saipan in the distance. His thoughts turned homeward, to his family. As he stared off into the reflective depths of the sea, a sparkling light suddenly danced over the rippling water all around him. The brilliance of the light on the water startled him out of his daze, then a horrendous crash filled the air. The enormous sound crushed his senses, causing the hairs to bristle on his body. He turned to face the warmth of the sun at his back, and his eyes caught the brilliant radiance of the fireball in the sky. It was not where he had left it in the sky—it was now almost directly over his head.

The second sun exploded with fire above him. It was not miniature anymore; it had quadrupled in size and burned with a tremendous ferocity. Sparks of light shot from its body in every direction. White-hot streaks of light flowed like jets of water from its fiery center. Its magnificent tail streaked for miles behind it. Anastacio recoiled from the intensity of the brightness and cowered in the well of his skiff.

The ever-present birds disappeared with the enormous sonic boom. The only remaining sound was the growing thunderous growl of the fireball as it tore through the sky. The sound caused his heart to race; it grew with intensity with each half second, many thousand times greater than the military jets that liked to fly low over his home to rattle the windows with their sonic blasts. He looked around in desperation, his heart threatening to explode with terror. The terrible noise shook his body, reverberating in his chest and rippling shock through his spine. He clasped his hands over his ears, but it was no use.

He screamed out in terror, but his voice was lost in the roar. He fell, slouching into the bottom of the boat, his back immersed in the brackish water. Urine escaped him in a panicked burst. Looking up to the sky from the bottom of his boat, he could see the fireball overhead. Its pace seemed inexorably fast now. He could feel its destructive power in his shaking limbs. He knew this was the end, the end of everything.

He closed his eyes, covering them with his hands. Blazing white spots danced in his vision. Another massive blast boomed overhead, momentarily obliterating the deafening roar. He felt the heat from the blast wash over him instantly. His skin seemed to curl with fire. He looked to see if he were actually on fire, but his skin was not burnt, just covered in goose-pimpled sweat. The scant clouds in the sky evaporated before the approaching inferno, leaving only the ball of fire in the air above him. It looked like the ball itself had exploded with the last blast, sending millions on millions of new fireballs cascading to the sea, but the main body of the fireball rolled on through the plume of its own smoke. The surface of the sea quaked in a vibrating mass under him.

The immense thundering never let up as the fireball passed high over him; it simply continued to grow. Anastacio could feel the radiant heat on his face and arms. He felt as though he would be cooked to death before the inevitable impact obliterated him. There were several more seconds of paralyzing fear and intolerable sound, and then he felt more than heard the insidious pop in his head as his eardrums ruptured. Then there was only ringing.

He opened his eyes, mainly to confirm that he wasn't dead. The fireball had passed. Only the brilliant trail of phosphorous sparks was visible overhead. He writhed in agony at the bottom of the boat, pushing his hands against his throbbing ears, and managed to turn his head to follow the path of the fireball. It had grown to unbelievable proportions as it made its final descent to the waiting ocean. It had missed him by miles, hundreds of miles, finding its mark in the ocean to the west of him.

Anastacio peered over the keel of his boat in awestruck terror. The giant ball of fire exploded into the ocean with a light so intense that it surely would have blinded him if he had not covered his face with his forearm. The initial shock wave of compressed air fell on him almost immediately, pitching his small boat sideways and shearing the mast in half. The air was forced from his lungs. An intense wave of heat washed over his skin, instantly singing the hair on his arms.

As the blast wave passed over him, he was left reeling in pain at the bottom of his boat. The boat spun in the water and was now facing the gigantic mushroom cloud above the ocean. He could feel its heat on his face. A boiling curtain of steam leaped from the sea near the impact.

The scene appeared to be a horrible dream. The mountain of fire raged into the sky hundreds of miles away. Pain alone confirmed its reality. Anastacio couldn't take his eyes from the deadly spectacle. He watched as the conflagration grew and threatened to devour the earth.

After a lifetime at sea, he watched as the impossible manifested itself in the water before him. A wave of unfathomable size and speed raced toward him. The ocean itself rushed to greet the monstrous wave, which was more like a sheer wall of water than any wave he had every seen. His boat was helplessly pulled along as the sea dipped and bowed to the oncoming wall. Anastacio's eyes were barely able to focus on the mighty wave as it raced toward him like the rolling back of a gigantic cracking whip.

His stomach, his body, and his boat pitched downward in the lea of the great wave, only to be propelled skyward as flotsam to the top of its gigantic face. The sensation of rocketing skyward, hundreds of meters into the air, robbed Anastacio's brain of blood, and he lost consciousness.

Once his body and mind were reunited at the summit of the monster Tsunami, Anastacio was once again able to see the horror and feel the fear in the pit of his stomach. The wave rolled beneath him as fast as it had come on him, never fully cresting, then hurled Anastacio and his boat down the treacherously steep slope of the wave's back. His tiny skiff clung to the water and raced down the churning swell like a boat on a fast-flowing river. He was blinded by bursts of spray, but his skiff didn't flip. He was alive; beyond all reason, he was still alive.

The horrible wave rolled out in all directions behind him. He knew the monster was headed for his home. Anastacio could see nothing beyond the enormous tsunami's back, but in a matter of seconds he watched the retreating swell raise slightly, foaming white on its crest, then expel the volcanic peaks of his home in its wake.

Alameda, California. June 14, 2002

Molly was ripped from sleep for the second time that night. "This has got to stop." Her head was pounding as she stomped down the hall to the boys' room. "I need to get some sleep."

As she approached the end of the hall, she could hear both boys crying. Once again, she loathed the fact that they'd had to settle for this little house and wished they could afford a place with separate bedrooms for her boys. They weren't used to sleeping in the same room. Mathew was having more and more nightmares, and Marshal woke at the drop of a pin. No one in the family was getting any sleep nowadays. She hated Alameda; she wanted to go back to the city.

Molly flung open the door and quickly gathered up Mathew. He was still asleep but sobbed as if he'd skinned his knee. "You're okay, baby. Wake up, honey."

"Mom, make him stop." Marshal covered his ears with his hands. The blue Power Ranger light was on over his bed.

"He's all right, honey. He's just having a bad dream."

"He keeps waking me up."

"I know, baby. I'll be there in a minute. Okay?"

"Okay, Mom."

"You're okay, sweetheart. Come on, close your eyes. Mommy loves you." She kissed little Mathew on the forehead as he drifted off in her arms. After tucking him into his blankets, she crossed the room to her older son Marshal. "Good night, sweetheart. Mommy loves you."

There was a truly frightened glimmer in her oldest son's eyes. The pale blue light from his nightlight shimmered on developing tears. "Mom, what's all that noise outside?"

"I don't know, sweetie. Good night." Molly bent low, tucking in his blankets. She hadn't noticed any noise; the response to her seven-year-old's question was automatic, but as she turned to leave, the sound of commotion outside caught her attention. It was midnight, but it sounded like rush hour outside. Muffled horns rang in the distance, and Molly thought she could hear shouting.

Suddenly some asshole blasted his air horn outside their window. The boys jumped in their beds, and Molly's heart skipped a beat. Sirens sounded in the distance as the ear-piercing air horn sounded again. The fine hairs on the back of her neck bristled.

Molly chewed her lip and eyed the phone in the hall. She didn't want to disturb Rick, but something was going on. She closed the door behind her and punched Rick's number into the phone. "Come on, baby … pick up."

After the first few rings, she realized he might not answer. He had taken a job as a security guard, working the nightshift at the same building where he had once traded stock when times were better. He still traded from home during the day, and he was exhausted by the time he got to work in the city. She knew he was probably stealing a quick nap and didn't want to wake him, but she was scared.

Ten rings. Molly hung up and clutched the phone to her chest. She sat there for a moment, wondering if she should try again, then turned and headed for the television. She took two steps and was stopped short by a loud pounding on the door. Her chest tightened and she froze in her tracks.

Bang! Bang! Bang! "Fire Department! Wake Up!" Bang! Bang! Bang! "Fire Department! Open the door!"

Her hands trembling, Molly moved to the door and peered through the peephole. The reflective coat of a fireman filled the view, and Molly pulled the door open. "What's going on?"

"This is an immediate evacuation! Who else is home with you?"

"My two sons …" Molly looked past the fireman to the throng of people streaming past her lawn.

"Is that it?" The fireman began writing something on a piece of thick, white tape he had stuck to his arm. Hastily scribbled addresses and numbers were scrawled over several pieces of tape.

"Yes, that's it"

"Good, listen to me. Grab your sons and get out of here right now. Don't take anything else, just your sons. You need to find higher ground right now!"

"What's happening?"

"Miss, just do as I say. Go, get your boys. We think this area may get hit by a giant tidal wave."

"What?" Molly was already headed to the boy's room.

"A giant asteroid hit the Pacific today. We were told to expect tidal waves up to five hundred feet tall. We're evacuating everyone! Get to higher ground—go anywhere, just go!" The fireman's voice was fading into the distance as he moved on to the next house. Molly felt the surge of panic grip her throat. The fear on the fireman's face was shocking.

Her boys were standing in the darkness when she flung open the door. The three of them stared at each other for an instant, all of them on the verge of tears.

"Mathew, Marshal, we need to get in the car right away!" She scooped up Mathew, pulling his face into her bosom. She looked around for the boy's shoes while hurrying Marshal along. *Forget the shoes, five hundred foot waves!*

"To the car. Go! Mommy will explain later! Go!"

Molly pressed the garage door opener with her elbow on the way to the car. She threw Mathew into his seat without securing the child seat. "Get in, quick!"

She stomped her foot on the accelerator, launching the Ford Explorer onto the driveway and nearly taking the garage door along with it. The street in front of her was clear, but there were headlights everywhere on the roads ahead.

"Where are we going, Mom?"

"We have to leave our house very quickly, honey. There might be a big wave coming, and we live too close to the water." Molly pressed the Explorer to move faster. She could see her neighbors loading their cars as she flew by.

"But where are we going?"

"Up, honey! We have to go up … find someplace high up." Molly struggled to think of someplace close, but there was really only one way to go: east, away from the Bay, through densely populated neighborhoods to the hills behind the Bay.

"What about Daddy?"

"Rick!" Molly gasped his name aloud. Her thought was cut short by a stream of slow-moving cars. She slammed the breaks hard, sending Mathew tumbling to the floor.

"Shit! Are you all right, honey? Get back in your seat and do your belt, baby. Help your brother, Marshal." She forced the Explorer into the traffic.

"What about Daddy, Mom?"

"Your Daddy will be okay, Sweetie. He's in a really tall building."

"But those people were in a really tall building too, Mommy."

"What people?—Shit! Damn! Move your ass, dumbshit!"

"The people in the Trade Center."

"Daddy will be okay, sweetheart! Right now I've got to move through all this traffic." Cars began passing in the opposite lanes. Molly worked her SUV over to the left and jumped the double yellow lines. Another car screeched to a stop behind her, blaring its horn, but she pressed ahead. Soon even these lanes were clogged with traffic. Cars in the left lane had blocked in a large fire truck, jamming all lanes.

Molly pounded the steering wheel in despair. People on foot began streaming past her on the sidewalks. They carried nothing, only their children, and they were passing all of the people sitting in their cars.

Molly knew where she was; in daylight, you could see the Bay from this inter-section. Her maternal survival instincts took over and did the majority of the driving from then on. She rammed the car in front of her and charged her SUV onto the sidewalk. People quickly scampered out of her way as the Explorer jumped along the curbs and driveways.

Her SUV barreled over lawns and through shrubs. A mailbox was sheared from its post as she smashed into it. The box flew up and cracked the windshield, making a gigantic spiderweb of shattered glass. The children screamed.

Molly deftly maneuvered the hulking SUV through the blocked traffic, but an intersection clogged with cars lay ahead. As she approached, she could see the ter-rain begin to slope into the foothills beyond. She also realized that there was no way she could bully her way through the mass of gridlocked cars in front of her.

She drove as far as she could, then slammed the brakes, leaving the car run-ning. "Come on kids, we have to hurry!"

In a flash, she was pulling them out of the car. "Run! Come on guys, this way." She pulled them by their wrists across the clogged intersection. They soon joined a mass exodus of people fleeing toward higher ground. They all traveled the same direction; there was only one way to go. People were throwing their children over fences—or crashing through them.

Soon Molly was completely breathless, but she was headed uphill. A young man slowed to help her get the boys over a tall fence. The slope picked up dra-matically beyond this yard. Her legs kicked furiously as she pulled herself up the fence. Once on top, she paused out of pure fatigue; that's when she heard the low rumble of an approaching tidal wave.

"Come on, lady!"

"I can hear it! It's coming!"

More screams echoed the same sentiment from all around.

"Come on, let's go!" The young man pulled Molly to the ground. She landed with a thud, jarring her shoulder.

"Fuck!" She cried out in pain, pulling her arm against her chest.

"Let's go! Come on, move!"

Molly began scrambling up the steep hillside, favoring her left arm and using her right to pull herself up the slope. The young man pushed and pulled the boys up the hill ahead of her.

The roar of the approaching tidal wave sounded like hundreds of freight trains echoing through the bay. The earth trembled beneath her. Then explosions boomed in the distance as the wave presumably made landfall. Molly continued to scramble higher and higher into the hills. She did not dare stop and look. The torrential noise grew with new ferocity. Now she could hear the telltale sound of water crashing behind her.

"Look. Look! The lights have gone out in the city," a man's voice bellowed from somewhere in the darkened hills.

"It's okay. We're okay! We're far enough. Look!"

Molly had no idea how far she had come, but the sounds of the crashing waves were far behind her. From this vantage, she could see moonlight glistening on the Bay; beyond lay only darkness. Where normally the lights of San Francisco shone bright, now there was only darkness.

Washington DC. June 15, 2002

"Man, I've got to take another leak. Gimme a shout if they say anything about home." Shug slowly pulled himself from the entirely too small Travelodge chair. The imitation leather had conformed to his back during the several uninter-rupted hours he had spent in front of the television, and it gasped for air as he pulled away.

After hours of sitting, Hank's back felt cast in cement, but he couldn't pull himself away from the television. The magnitude of the catastrophe seemed to swell with every new report. The network had forgone commercials since the impact, and the onslaught of coverage assailed them without a break.

"Get this," Hank called out to Shug, who was still in midstream of relief. "According to this guy, we got lucky."

"Lucky?"

"He says it coulda been worse." Hank bobbed his head toward the television.

"Here with us again is Doctor Timothy Wingaurd. Dr Wingaurd is a NASA astronomer and a member of project NEAT. Project NEAT, Near Earth Asteroid Tracking, is an organization that uses telescopes to probe outer space for objects that could potentially threaten Earth. Is that right, Doctor?" The camera switched views from the young female anchor to a disheveled but exuberant-look-ing middle-aged scientist.

"Yes. Project NEAT is a joint venture between NASA and the U.S. Air Force, and we do use our telescopes for that express purpose, yes."

"Yet there was no warning with this asteroid?"

"That is true. We became aware of '2002XF-13' at three thirty-seven standard time, when it became visible to the naked eye. But there is one thing that I must make perfectly clear. From what limited information we have, and that is very limited, you must understand"—the Doctor suppressed his tendency to ramble by nervously batting at the air with his pudgy fists—"we cannot say with any degree of certainty that 2002XF-13 was even an asteroid at all."

"What do you mean, not an asteroid?"

"2002XF-13 is radically different from any asteroid or meteor we have pro-jected. It has some very unusual characteristics. It may be something more like a comet, what we call a dead comet. But even so, it poses a lot of new questions for us."

"But we were told a comet of this size would break up in our atmosphere."

"A mistake, obviously. A dead comet only refers to a comet without any noticeable tail. A comet whose tail of ice and gas has all burnt up and therefore travels almost invisibly through space. A comet can be made of virtually anything, solid or not. Not to mention variables of size."

"So besides being practically invisible, what other unusual characteristics did 2002XF-13 exhibit? And why do you claim we were lucky?" After countless hours of reporting on the devastation, the idea was clearly repugnant to the anchorwoman.

"Well, that's just the thing; it could have been much, much worse. Because 2002XF-13 was traveling so slowly, it had less effect on impact. It entered our atmosphere at approximately one-third of the speed we would normally have expected. If it had impacted at the same velocity as a normal collision, the results would have been ten times as bad in the Pacific Rim. It might have been catastrophic for all of humanity."

"Why do you believe this collision was different?"

"In the field of astronomy, to us astronomers, this is something completely new! And it is far too early to speculate on the all the implications, but 2002XF-13 was visible to the naked eye for over thirteen minutes before impact! That's unprecedented! We are, of course, still collecting all of the data, and I don't want to further jeopardize our good name by making premature statements. But the fact that this celestial body approached us so slowly is remarkable."

"How do you account for this?"

"Right now, the best explanation that I've heard is that 2002XF-13 was traveling in a nearly perfect parallel-grade orbit with Earth."

"What does that mean, exactly?"

"There is no way to prove it yet, but we think this celestial body was traveling in line with Earth's orbit around the sun. Earth slowly caught up with it and collided with it. The mathematical likelihood of something like this happening is almost nil. But it's the best explanation I've heard."

"How does something like this—a meteor or a dead comet, whatever—suddenly just appear out of nowhere? Are there any early warning mechanisms in place?"

"I will remind you that our very own NEAT headquarters are based in Maui." The astronomer smiled defensively. "They didn't see it until it burned through the skies above them. And we haven't heard from any of them since."

"Hawaii suffered unbelievable damage from the tidal waves resulting from the impact. Our hearts go out to everyone over there. We wish the best for your people there too, Doctor Wingaurd."

"Well I'm sure the telescopes are undamaged; they're on top of mount Mauna Kea. But I'm sure that all of the people that live on that side of the island have perished. I have been there. My only hope is that some of my colleagues made it up to the observatory to watch 2002XF-13."

"I truly hope that is the case, Doctor. I want to thank you for joining us, and I want to invite you to stay longer. We certainly have more questions for you, but we need to break for other developments."

"Of course. It would be a pleasure."

"At this point, there still isn't any official word from Hawaii. Satellite disruptions are being held partly to blame." The anchorwoman read from the teleprompter, Dr. Wingaurd fidgeting next to her. "All power has been knocked out. One top-ranking admiral back here at home has been quoted as saying: 'we have no idea what is happening over there,' although he added that rescue operations are on the way."

The NEAT scientist spoke into his microphone from off camera. "Drinking water will be a huge problem. All of those flooded areas will undoubtedly be littered with corpses. That will lead to disease of epidemic proportions."

Embarrassment flashed across the face of the young anchorwoman. "Yes, but that should not detour people from going to help. We have seen great coastal cities like San Diego and Portland ravaged. The broken image of the Golden Gate Bridge is burnt into my memory. But of course that doesn't tell the whole story. There are thousands of smaller communities all along the coast, millions of tragic stories we will never hear. These devastated and now isolated areas need your help as well. Many of us have friends and family in these areas."

"You make a good point: in a sense, the entire West Coast is now very isolated." Once again Dr. Wingaurd offered his comment, and the cameraman shifted to catch him absentmindedly polishing his glasses. "It is likely that every Pacific port has been destroyed."

"I don't care what Chubby says. I don't feel very lucky." Shug stared at the screen. "What do you think about us going back to Frisco? Nobody will be looking for us now. Maybe we could get on a Red Cross flight or something."

Hank was wondering when Shug would ask, and he'd been searching in vain for a reason to deny him. Shug was desperate to see is family. "You wouldn't want to drive?"

"You mean you'd go?"

"I know you need to see your family. And you're right: I doubt that anybody gives a flying fuck about *us* anymore." Hank downed the rest of his beer.

"How long would it take to drive?"

"Three days if we hit it hard. I'd rather drive."

Shug's face brightened.

"We're back now with Doctor Timothy Wingaurd, a NASA astronomer and member of Project NEAT. Doctor, I would like to take a moment to talk about the comet itself, namely its brilliant tail. Undoubtedly this was the most spectacular display ever recorded. Why do you think this asteroid's tail was so brilliant? Or is it that any asteroid this size would have such a brilliant display on entering Earth's atmosphere?"

"Having never seen an impact of this scale before—no one has, not in recorded history at least—I can only speculate based on what we've seen through our lenses on other planets. We often see great flares of light as other bodies enter the influence of planets like Jupiter: take Shoemaker-Levee, for instance. But it is difficult to speculate about the magnitude or the brilliance of such a body." The doctor nervously shifted in his seat. "2002XF-13 was exceptionally brilliant once it entered our atmosphere. That is what led us to believe that the body would burn up entirely. It burnt so fiercely, so rapidly." The doctor's thick jowls jiggled with excitement.

"So I'll ask you again, Doctor, was there something special about 2002XF-13 which resulted in such brilliance? And how do you explain the variety of colors shown in the asteroid's wake?"

"It is far too early to tell. We have very little information to work off at the moment; we simply don't know much about 2002XF-13 yet. But yes, we think that 2002XF-13 was indeed something unique to our experience, which makes it very, very exciting! As for the variety of colors, that could have several explanations, from elements such as phosphorous trapped under the surface of the body to the fact that we simply see some colors faster than others. It's difficult to say when we're talking about these kinds of speeds, you see. Either way, we are sure that a good portion of the body did burn up on entry, reducing the mass substantially. Another reason I feel that we were quite lucky."

"It's hard to feel lucky at a time like this. Do you think we would have fared any better if 2002XF-13 had struck land? It seems that most of the damage has been caused by the giant tsunamis."

"Well, as we well know by now, 80 percent of the world's population resides on or near the coast of one great body of water or another. And 75 percent of Earth's surface is covered in water. Therefore we have asked ourselves that very question many times." The doctor appeared pensive to Hank, heavily qualifying his remarks with exaggerated, nervous hand gestures.

"The general consensus is that an ocean impact would be far more devastating to the public than a land impact." The doctor put his hands up to stop a possible interruption and to qualify the remark. "An impact on land would bring with it an entirely different set of horrors, you understand. Not only would there be waves of molten material hurled for hundreds of miles, with temperatures hot enough to turn sand to glass, there would be incredible flash fires surrounding the impact zone—fires so massive and intense that they would create their own weather, sending clouds of smoke into the atmosphere to join the ash and debris already lingering in the skies. This of course would have devastating effects on our climate and global ecosystem. There would be acid rain and darkness for years."

"So the ocean impact had less of an environmental impact than a land one?"

"They are as different as fire and water. It is going to be the impact on lives, property, and things like shipping and the economy that makes 2002XF-13 more destructive than a land impact. We have yet to know what effect the shock wave had on the ocean as an ecosystem; it could have killed every fish for hundreds of miles. So you see, it's hard to predict what we're in for."

"The effects of 2002Xf 13 are indeed being felt globally. Does the damage so far reflect what you have projected?"

"All of the data is not in of course, but I can say that we expected much worse from a solid body this size. We estimate that 2002XF-13 was .8 kilometers in diameter on entry. In the past, anything over one kilometer was believed to be of extinction magnitude. But again, 2002XF-13 collided with us at one-third of the projected speed!" The doctor shook his head, overwhelmed by the importance his work had now taken on.

"The mega shock tsunamis that Dr. Yamagotto so brilliantly described earlier—those thousand foot waves traveling faster than the speed of sound—those waves were much larger in our projections and dissipated far more slowly. A wave the size of our projections could retain a lot more energy, keeping its mass over a greater distance. Thus far, most of the damage has been caused by the far smaller and much slower Tidal Tsunamis. They are the residual effects of the shock wave and all the secondary effects of impact: oceanic landslides, earthquakes, things of that nature."

"So the estimates you projected were worse?"

"Once again, in the range of speeds that we felt were probable at the time, an asteroid eight-tenths of a kilometer was just short of extinction caliber."

"And you've said earlier that an event of that magnitude was likely to occur once every ten million years. How long has it been since Earth's last deadly encounter with an asteroid of this size?"

"Even though this has been a catastrophic event, 2002XF-13 is still relatively small. The one that probably killed the dinosaurs was over ten times its size. More recently, a large body exploded over Russian Siberia. But for the most part, the age of large impacts in this solar system is long past. The great galaxy-shaping collisions following the big bang have moved on. Our very own moon is a result of that era."

"The moon?" The camera switched to the anchorwoman just in time to catch the confused look on her face.

"Over three and a half billion years ago, an asteroid nearly the size of Mars struck our planet. The debris were hurled into space and then trapped by Earth's gravitational pull. They formed a stratified layer, similar to the planet Saturn. Eventually, the debris coalesced and cooled into a giant ball which we now call our moon."

"An asteroid the size of Mars?"

"Again, Ms. Bowden, I believe that we really were relatively lucky."

"Well, our conversation has been enlightening, Dr. Wingaurd. I hope that you'll stay with us while we break to follow some other stories. There are a lot more questions that our audience and our producers would like to ask you."

"It would be my pleasure. What's better than watching the news from the news studio?"

The blonde anchorwoman covered her ear with a hand. "My producers are telling me that we have our first confirmed contact from Hawaii!" A smile appeared on her face. "In fact, we have someone from Hawaii on the phone with us right now. Dr. Wingaurd, you may not believe this, but it's someone from project NEAT. He says he's calling from the observatory on mount Mauna Kea."

"Incredible. Who is it?"

"Hello, Dr. Russell. Can you hear me? This is Cynthia Bowden live in Washington."

"Yes, I can hear you." The line crackled with static, but the doctor's voice was clear enough.

"Doctor Russell, we can hear you too. You're calling from mount Mauna Kea, is that right?"

"Yes, from our observatory."

"This is wonderful, Doctor Russell. This is our first word from Hawaii since the impact. Can you tell us any thing about the conditions in Maui?"

"I'm afraid not. Our observatory is two thousand feet above sea level. We were spared by the giant tsunamis, but we remain somewhat cut off from the outside world. All we know is that it is very bad down there. We have been desperately trying to get word out …"

"So you don't know the extent of the damage in Hawaii?"

"No. But there's something …"

"Doctor Russell, we are lucky enough to have one of your collogues with us, Dr. Wingaurd."

Dr. Wingaurd smiled into the camera but was cut short before he could speak.

"I don't care who you have with you! Listen to me, for Christ's sake! There's another one coming! We've been trying to warn you!"

"Another what?" Cynthia Bowden asked from off camera.

"Another meteor the size of the last one!"

"Impossible!" Dr. Wingaurd leaped in his seat.

"It's true, Tim! Soon it will be visible to the naked eye!"

"Oh my God!" Cynthia's voice sounded nearly hysterical. "I'm getting word from my producer … there has indeed been another object seen in the skies. It's being reported over South America. We are apparently getting video of the meteor fed into the studio!"

"Phil, how, how can this be? It's impossible!" Dr. Wingaurd pleaded into the camera.

"I don't know, Tim."

"Any idea where it's headed?"

"It looks like it's the same size as the last one. If it does the same thing, we think it will smack into the Pacific somewhere."

"Ladies and Gentlemen, we do have that footage for you. Once again, this is breaking news. A second meteor is headed for Earth! Emergency broadcasts are being made as I speak to you. All indications are that it is similar in size to the one that struck seventeen hours ago. Here is the footage. Oh my God, look at that!"

Hank's face was pulled toward the screen as he stared at the white-hot meteor. His mind quickly flashed back to the brilliant fireball he had seen in Bill's office. It was nearly the same incredible image, but yesterday it was a mere spectacle, a diversion. Now it was an unbelievably menacing threat.

The cameraman in the studio was too transfixed by the image to switch screens; Dr. Wingaurd's face shared the split screen with the fireball. *"It's impossible ..."*

Mbake', Senegal. June 16, 2002

Twice over the past two days, Manadou Dou and his family had gathered to watch the brilliant trail of sparks behind the falling star. Last night's shooting star had caused a big stir among the clan elders, but it was only a passing curiosity then. Yesterday children had laughed at the wondrous lights, but not today; the third star to fall from the heavens was much different. Now Manadou understood. This was the End of Days.

As he looked past the vast expanse of his homeland to the west, he knew without a doubt this was the end. Where once he could see the glimmer of the Atlantic, now there was a horrific fire erupting from the sea. A dark, seething pyroclastic cloud boiled skyward, forming the demonic specter of a Godly citadel on the horizon. The fiery orange dome reached into the high heavens, the highest skies, casting its death shadow over the whole earth. Manadou's mind stumbled to recall what his Islamic studies had taught him about the approaching End of Days, but there were no words in the Quran to describe the fury he saw now.

The clouds in the sky vanished. Waves of heat distorted his view. His robes shielded him against most of the bright heat, but his arms bristled with pain. Manadou had thrown himself to the ground, prostrating himself in prayer as the slow-rolling fireball approached. This unconscious act of submission saved his eyes from the blinding light, allowing him to witness the unfolding doom. He stared dumbfounded at the gigantic mushroom cloud consuming the horizon.

He didn't care that his herd of cattle had bolted. The lifeblood of his family had fled, but it didn't matter. This was the End. At first the cattle were startled by the great noise, standing paralyzed in fear. But when the blast of all blasts came, the truly tremendous sound that shook the earth, they all panicked and ran off. His cattle were galloping away from the sea, away from Allah's death castle, but to Manadou it no longer mattered.

Now that the deafening blast had left his ears, all was eerily silent. The bells of his ever-present herd were gone, and so were the buzzing flies that seemed to have followed him since birth. There were no insects, no birds, nothing. He was utterly alone.

He had imagined that the end would come much differently, somehow, but then again—man was not supposed to know the ways of Allah. He began to wonder what he truly knew at the end of his life. Was Paradise waiting for him? Would his family already be there? Was he indeed a righteous man? In the end, he knew it was meaningless. His death was coming, and what he was seeing now was far beyond the Allah he knew.

Manadou could see the entire coast, spreading across the horizon over the flat-lands; all of it seemed to be burning. A gray, fulminating stream boiled over the coastal hills and swirled into the valleys. Streaming wisps of white smoke shot skyward from the cities of Dakar, Mbour, and Joal Fadiout like terrified spirits fleeing the death-shadow of the great fiery citadel.

The natural clouds had melted away, leaving only the brilliant tail of sparks in the sky. He and his family had marveled at a similar shower of lights only hours ago, but now the falling stars sparkled directly over his head. Manadou craned his neck to stare up at sky. The shaft of twinkling, falling sparks was thrust through the heavens like a spear piercing the belly of the demonic tower over the ocean. He swayed dizzily as he stared into the heavens, until he finally surrendered to the ground and sat in the dirt with his arms propping him up from behind.

He thought it strange that he wasn't compelled to run the short distance back to his home and family. "The end is now," he thought, "and I am alone in it." He didn't want to take his eyes away from the shooting stars; they were beautiful, while the demonic fire above the sea was fearsome and cruel. He knew it would soon grow to consume him too. He wondered how so many stars could be born and then die out so quickly, again and again, as they seemed to be doing in the sky above him. There were millions on millions of sparks coming to life, then flit-ting out. He kept his eyes on the falling stars high overhead and didn't notice the dark cloud beginning to obscure his view.

It was faint at first, almost as if his eyes were playing tricks on him. The daz-zling sparks blurred as the individual black pinpricks formed a thickening cloud. The darkness grew; he felt as if the sky itself were falling. A clattering, buzzing hiss fell with the weight of the sky. It was the first sound to revisit his ears since the blast, and with it came a horror renewed.

The black cloud fell to earth as quickly as it had materialized in the sky. All around him, as far as he could see, black specks fell to the earth like sheets of dark rain. Clouds of dust erupted as the dark, fallen stars smacked into the ground.

Manadou sprang to his feet. The clicking hiss surrounded him like the clatter-ing of a million seashells. He could hear the rip of the air as one of the charcoal black stars fell to the ground close by. They tore though the air all around him, shooting diagonally across his view in every direction.

Guided solely by instinct, Manadou ran to the only tree nearby. He covered his face with his hands and ran as fast as he could. The falling stars peppered the ground in front of him, sending eruptions of red dust into the air. He felt the whoosh of air as one shot past his face. It landed in the dirt right in front of him. The black clump was the size of a small water gourd and was lodged firmly in the ground where it had fallen. He nearly stepped on it and stumbled, but he recovered without falling to the ground. He stood a full pace away and bent over at the hip to stare into the small pit. He had never seen a star before.

The fallen star looked to be the shape of a thick, symmetrical cross. It rested in its crater at an odd angle. One arm of the cross was buried in the dirt. He began to see thin black barbs protruding from behind the flattened cross. The points of the barbs looked like tiny folded spear tips. He leaned over to examine it more closely, and suddenly one of the pointed barbs began to move. Manadou froze.

Another rip in the air near his ear reminded him to seek refuge under the tree. He covered his face with his hands once again and sprinted for the tree in total confusion. Without warning, a blow struck him from behind with such force that it sent him tumbling and rolling on the ground. Unbelievable pain gripped his arm. The side of his face felt as if it were on fire.

He tried to right himself by kneeling on all fours, but his right arm would not respond to support him. Blood drained from the right side of his face into dirt. He looked at his right arm in terror: the pain was indescribable, and what he saw was unbelievable. A hideous black cross was impaled in his arm. Both bones in his lower arm were broken and badly angulated, a blade from the cross wedged between them. The black material felt hot as worked iron, and wisps of smoke rose from his burning flesh.

Manadou screamed, unable to stand. In desperation he grabbed at the edge of the cross imbedded in his arm. It was incalculably hard and singed his free hand as soon as he grabbed it. He recoiled in pain. He attempted to maneuver his broken arm to a natural position, but the flat, hard cross remained fixed in place. As he turned to straighten his broken arm, the cross flopped over with his mangled limb and he saw a sight that nearly stopped his heart.

A hideous beetle clung to the black iron in his arm. It was unlike anything he had ever seen, but it was unmistakably a giant insect of some sort. Its dark shell was as black as the cross. The lack of contrast blurred its form, but he could see its spearlike legs clawing the air.

Manadou recoiled from his arm, wishing he could leave it behind. He shook his mangled limb, oblivious to the pain. Two long thin legs unfolded from the body of the beetle and stabbed the air. They were sharp and cruel looking, with hooked triangular claws at the tips. The beetle's legs probed the air frantically, finally extending over its body to sink their barbs into the flesh of Manadou's arm.

Manadou grabbed at the blade impaling his forearm. Its razor-sharp edges cut into his hand as he pulled away at it, but the crosslike blade did not budge. He looked around in desperation. Crosses zipped through the air all around him.

He staggered toward the tree. He continued to pull at the thing as he ran, trying to rip it free from his arm, until a sudden pain caused him to pull his hand away. The first two fingers on his hand had been torn away by the beetle. He could see his fingers in the gripping pincers on the beetle's belly, and for the first time he saw that his ear was caught between the flesh of his arm and the crosslike shell embedded between bones.

Fear was the only thing that kept him running for the shelter of the tree. There were beetles scattered on the ground before him. Some had seemingly abandoned the square crosses. He looked to his arm for a way to separate the hideous insect from it, but he didn't want to risk any more fingers by getting his hand anywhere near its hideous claws. There was another rip of air, and the smack of something against his chest, and Manadou was knocked flat on his back.

Another fallen beetle had crashed into his chest, stunning his senses and knocking the air from his lungs. The cross struck him flat without impaling him. Paralyzed with fear, gasping for air, Manadou raised his chin to his chest to see a horrible black insect on his stomach.

The giant insect busily worked itself free of its exoskeleton with its long, jointed legs. All pain was subordinate to fear. Manadou couldn't move.

The bug on his chest performed the necessary acrobatics and freed itself. After disengaging itself from the cross, it quickly crawled up over Manadou's chest and began probing his face with its long, sharp pincers. Manadou held what breath he could, closed his eyes, and prepared for the worst. He felt the sickening weight and the iron grip of the insect as it crawled over his face and then leaped to the ground near his head.

Manadou willed himself to his feet. The giant insects were everywhere. Some appeared to burrow into the dirt, while others set off crawling along the ground or leaped into the air so fast that they disappeared. He began clawing at the insect impaled in his arm again. His angulated, broken appendage was keeping the bug from escaping its shell. He picked up a stone and began bashing the insect, each time sending pain coursing through his arm.

Manadou staggered for the tree once more, hoping to find a branch to pry the beast loose. The insect's many legs battled against the blows from the stone until it was able to rip it out of Manadou's mangled hand. It clutched the rock in its pointed arms and vibrated itself violently in his arm. He stopped his lurching run for the tree and knelt in the dirt; the pain was too great to continue.

He began to bash his arm, and the insect, into the ground. He smashed it, harder and harder, regardless of the pain. He didn't know he had such strength in him. A rancid, chemical smell began to emanate from insect. Its spasmodic vibrating doubled. The pounding had almost separated the cross from his twisted, bloodied bone ends.

Another beetle appeared in the dirt in front of him, then another. He looked up to see that they were surrounding him. Dozens of them either crawled toward him or dropped in after huge, unseen leaps. Their spiny legs moved too fast to be seen.

The creature imbedded in his arm convulsed with one more furious flurry of shudders, and then Manadou was completely enveloped by the insects. They leaped on him from all directions, striking his chest like sharpened darts. Manadou screamed from the biting pain of their pincers, until one of them landed on his open jaw. Its cruelly powerful claws sliced through his flesh and ripped the jawbone from his face, tongue and all. Manadou was only able to imagine himself screaming as they tore away at the rest of his flesh, piece by piece.

Paradigm II
Chapter 8

Washington DC. June 17, 2002

Secret Serviceman Jackson somberly closed the doors to the Oval Office, and he was finally alone. It was the first time in two days that President Bush had had a moment to himself. He no longer had to maintain his composure in front of others. He didn't have to hide the anxious tightening in his chest behind a mask of stern-faced resolve and deep contemplation. He was alone at last, and he nearly burst with agonized relief, pulling the tie loose from his throat and letting out a stifled moan. The responsibility of his office had never seemed as heavy; things had never been so hopelessly out of control.

None of his staff seemed to think that it was unusual for the commander in chief to seek solitude in his chambers while a deadly asteroid half a mile wide was minutes away from impacting Earth and killing untold millions. Now the darkest moment in his life was the only opportunity he had to break away from his staff—and his country—and take a few moments of refuge in his office. Just moments before, his science advisor had informed him that the latest asteroid was probably going to impact somewhere in Central Asia. The United States would dodge another bullet, but now there seemed to be even worse news.

There were too many horrible tidings to digest, and not a moment of peace to take it all in. An hour ago, the scientists had said that the meteor would impact in the Pacific. Before then, it had been the Indian Ocean. Now they expected it to hit land. Eleven hours ago, no one had known where it would strike, just that it was coming—and that it promised to be deadly.

Since the unexpected arrival of the first asteroid, almost forty-eight hours ago, the lives of countless millions had been cut short, and his whole world had turned upside down. The scientists estimated that the first impacts had each landed with three hundred thousand megatons of force. The resulting tidal waves had killed millions, but those impacts had occurred in the ocean, not a densely populated landmass like Asia. That thought, and the fact that the U.S. had survived four near misses in the past two days, were enough to rattle any man, but what they were telling him now was unbelievable.

The shock of it terrified him to his core. The tightness in his chest increased as he clutched at his shirt and sucked in air. A wave of nausea sickened him, and uncontrollable tears began to well in his eyes. Once again, George fought the craving for a stiff drink.

Frozen in his tracks, just inside the historic office, he struggled to right himself from his crumpled posture and fought the urge to vomit on the presidential seal emblazoned on the floor. His legs trembled as he guided himself to the opposite side of the office and opened the cabinet containing a large television. He clicked on the set and laughed at himself in despair. Only moments ago, he had bravely told his staff that he wanted to watch the events like the American people at home. Now he was wiping away his tears and dreading what he would inevitably witness on the screen.

He stepped away from the wall and sat, slouching, on the desk. The anxiety he had been suppressing for so long now assaulted him with reckless abandon. He gasped and held his breath, trying to regain some semblance of composure, but his breathing was beyond control. He didn't dare call for help. Not in his condition. He didn't want anybody seeing the president of the United States whimpering like a baby, but he would have risked it all for a tumbler of bourbon. His hands shook as they fumbled with the remote control. He stopped on the first news channel he came across.

The asteroid was there, clear as day, taking up the entire screen with its colossal fireball. A litany of destruction scrolled across the bottom of the screen. A clock counted down in the corner. Two minutes, five seconds to impact!

He read that the video feed was coming from a ship in the Bay of Bengal, off the coast of Sri Lanka in the Indian Ocean. The anchorman was saying that the camera crew was so close that they were most likely filming the implement of their doom. According to the newsman, all experts were now fairly certain that the giant meteor would make landfall somewhere in India.

George had heard it all before: the blast radius, flash fires, the balls of molten glass and debris—not to mention the inevitable damage to the environment. The magnitude of the disaster was so great that it was impossible to comprehend, but it was happening. He was relieved not to hear any mention of giant bugs from outer space. His military cabinet continued to back the reports that the asteroids carried some form of alien life with them. This latest impact promised to bring confirmation, one way or another.

His thoughts raced back to the day almost six months ago when he had confronted his father about the Black Watch. Until a few minutes ago, he had still been exceedingly skeptical of his father's assertion that there really were extraterrestrial beings making fleeting contact with Earth, but now his father's words took on new meaning:

"As the executive leader of this country, you must keep your head here on Earth and not devote any energy to matters that are beyond your control. Let the Black Watch deal with those ... problems. That's what they're for. You have a country to run and a world to lead. That will keep you busy enough without worrying about ET and little green men."

He wished his father were with him right now. He would point his finger to the screen and tell him he was wrong. Everything he had once thought about the world was wrong. What was once so important had now been rendered totally meaningless.

The image on the screen suddenly changed; the atmospheric interference was too great, so another view of the plummeting asteroid was broadcast from farther away. The scrolling countdown continued: one minute and forty-five seconds to impact.

It was daytime in India, and the skies were tinted with a grayish pink haze, but the fireball was clearly visible as it blasted its way through the clouds. The newsman prepared the audience to hear from an Indian field reporter. He cautioned that the footage was raw, and that he himself did not know how close the reporter was to the inevitable impact. He assured the people at home that they would stay with the feed as long as possible.

"We take you now to Jasani Frambi, reporting from Hyberabad, central India."

President Bush's heart ached on seeing the lovely young reporter pushing the tousled hair from her face. Her dark, frightened eyes put a face to the multitudes facing their end. She was standing on a rooftop in the midst of a sprawling city, and the camera narrowed on her face as she rushed out her words.

The streets below her were a mass of panicked, fleeing people. She said that the public had only been notified a few minutes ago. The warning had come too late. The city was mad with terror. The roads leaving the city were clogged with traffic, and people on foot fled in every direction. The sounds of chaos filled the air.

The camera panned upward to show the fireball. The approaching roar drowned out the young reporter's words. People all around her were covering their ears against its deafening roar. The camera shook on the cameraman's shoulder. The image blurred and the young woman began to weep.

The noise from the asteroid obliterated all other sound. The reported yelled inaudibly into the camera.

Thirty seconds to impact.

The president's television screen was awash with white light. A further sonic blast rattled the cameraman and startled the president. The camera spun away from the light and was dropped to the ground. The picture was lost.

The horrible sound ended abruptly, and the screen once again featured the horrified face of the anchorman in the studio. He opened his mouth to speak, but he was unable to talk. He straightened in his chair and tried again, but no words came. The studio producers quickly brought up an overlay map of India. A large red circle indicated the projected impact zone. The countdown in the corner of the screen counted down the last ten seconds without commentary.

President Bush wept inconsolably, his face buried in his hands. The final seconds ticked down noiselessly on the television. Pain pulsed through the president's chest with every beat of his heart.

Assuming the worst, the newsman asked for a moment of silent prayer. For the first time since adolescence, the thought of prayer seemed absurd to George. He brushed at the tears running down his cheeks and clicked off the television set. He attempted to straighten himself and gain some form of composure. He knew that they would come for him soon. Emotion welled up in his throat as he once again fought the urge to vomit.

He stood alone in the middle of the Oval Office and wiped away any hint of moisture around his eyes. He turned to walk toward the double doors, but then quickly turned away. He stepped back to his desk and picked up the phone, then put it down. He paced back to the door and paused, trying to compose his next thoughts, his next words. He waited, trembling just inches from the closed door. A knock on the door stirred him into action, and he opened it before the secret serviceman had finished knocking.

"Mr. President, your cabinet is assembled and waiting for you in the Situation Room."

President Bush wordlessly allowed himself to be ushered into the Situation Room. He wasn't sure how his voice would respond if he were forced to speak; once again, he could feel tears glistening in the corners of his eyes. The marine guards opened the doors to reveal a packed house. The cabinet seats were occupied by their various ministers, and a great number of people pressed in behind them. He had never seen such confusion in the White House.

The large oval desk was piled high with papers and held several laptop computers. A large projection screen had been pulled down. The few secret servicemen present looked anxious and concerned, overwhelmed by the sheer number of people. As the president entered the room, everyone who had enough room to move stood to attention. The torrent of anxious voices was quickly suppressed by the sudden action and scraping of chairs.

"Mr. President." Mr. Carr ushered him to his seat at the head of the table.

The president's face remained grim as he took his seat and waited for others to do the same. Once those who could sit were seated, the president addressed his first question directly to the secretary of defense. "When will we hear from those pilots?"

"It's difficult to say, Mr. President. They're on their way to the impact zone as we speak, but it will take several minute before they're anywhere close."

"How long?"

"Ten minutes. At the very least, ten minutes."

"Why so long?"

"We had to keep all of our aircraft grounded until after the impact, Mr. President. Because of the shock wave. We're not sure if there was any kind of EMP generated by the impact."

"Electromagnetic pulse?"

"Yes, Mr. President. If there were, it would knock out a lot of our equipment."

"Was there an EMP?"

"I don't know yet. But I have confirmation that our planes are up and flying to the site."

"Let me know the moment we have any word from them."

"Yes sir."

"Until we hear back from them, I don't want to hear any more about … about what we discussed earlier." George tried his best to look stern in the face of all the questioning looks.

"Yes sir, Mr. President."

"What can you tell me about these asteroids? When are they going to stop?" He directed his next question to the room in general and was met by silent, anxious looks around the table.

It was a long moment before anyone ventured a response. "Well, Mr. President," ventured Doctor Sacks, the chief science advisor, "we are fairly certain that they're not asteroids. They're not comets or meteorites either. We don't know what they are. They are something entirely new." The crowd in the room listened anxiously to the man who should know more about these events than anybody else. Dr. Sacks worked for NASA and was a leading member of Project NEAT.

"At first we thought they were dead comets. That would explain the lack of a vapor tail and any visible warning."

"I understand all of that, Doctor. When can we expect this all to stop?"

"If I may, to answer that I must let you know what I think we are dealing with. The first astral body, Adam ..."

"Adam?"

"Well yes, sir, Adam. With the arrival of consecutive, um ... astral bodies, we began naming them, sort of like with hurricanes. 'A' for Adam, 'B' for Bertha, and 'C' for Cape Verde—named after the islands destroyed by the third, um ... body. This latest one we call David.

"David?"

"Adam hit the Earth with so much force that we don't think it burnt up much at all, it must have been a completely solid body, probably very, very dense. Most comets are a conglomeration of debris loosely held together or are composed of softer types of material, like asteroids. But asteroids are entirely different from these phenomena. They may be solid, even dense like these, but they move through space differently. Our bodies appear to be perfectly round, suggesting that that they have been subjected to gravity to a certain extent. And what is more fascinating, if you will—more frightening for certain—is that they are traveling with us, in our very own orbit!"

The doctor paused for a brief moment to let the room quiet down before he continued. "The mathematical probability of a single asteroid traveling with us in our orbit at this stage of the solar systems development is extremely remote. Most asteroids were cleared from our orbit millions, if not billions, of years ago. The prospect of more than one of these astral bodies is near impossible! Incalculable! It simply cannot happen, not naturally."

"So we are dealing with the impossible?"

"I would say that the mathematical likelihood of such a phenomenon borders on the impossible, yes. We estimate that these astral bodies are traveling in

Earth's elliptical orbit around the sun at 12 percent of the Earth's velocity. That in itself we have never seen before. If the object had been simply stationary in our orbit, we believe that the effects from the impact could have been much worse.

"Worse?"

"And if they had been traveling retrograde to Earth's orbit, just one of these objects would have been catastrophic. The very fact that there is more than one of these bodies in our path implies a purposeful intent."

"Purposeful intent?" The president and all of his advisors echoed the phrase.

"Purposeful celestial bombardment, Mr. President."

"It's true, Mr. President! It's an invasion!" shouted one of the military adjuncts, frustrated by the president's refusal to take into account his reports coming out of North Africa.

"Celestial bombardment? Invasion? Impos ... can't there be another explanation?" The secretary of defense was incredulous.

"We don't know, sir," Dr. Sacks continued over the noise in the room, "it's all new to us; it changes everything we know about astral physics."

The president quieted the room with a raised hand. "Are there any more of these 'astral bodies' headed our way?"

"It's very difficult to say ... but yes, we believe there are."

"It's true; we spotted Bertha on a fluke," Dr. Sacks' blue-eyed assistant blurted out excitedly. "It passed between us and the moon. That's when we learned that we were in for more than one of these encounters. Astrologically speaking, it was the discovery of lifetime."

"The impact at Cape Verde snuck up on us; we didn't actually see it coming, but it confirmed our greatest fears: purposeful celestial bombardment!" Dr. Sacks continued.

The cabinet members erupted in an uproar. Dr. Sacks was forced to shout over the tumult as the president sat stone-faced in his chair. "We've plotted them out. They have semiregular intervals. The last two were seventeen hours apart. They've all struck along our equatorial axis, near-direct hits—bull's eye! Mr. President, the mathematical calculations needed to pull that off are staggering ... beyond our comprehension. We've estimated that they're all the same size, just under a kilometer in diameter. It's amazing uniformity!"

Once again, the room exploded into disorder. The president's top aid was forced to scream to quiet them down.

"So we used this apparent regularity and looked seventeen hours into our future, into the darkness of space, and we think we've found something."

"You think?"

"It's extremely difficult to spot an object in space. We are confined to looking only during the night hours, and for all intents and purposes, these things don't give off any light until they rub up against our atmosphere. And then, of course, there's dark matter out there; we don't know what it is, but we know that we can't see through it. Not to mention that our most powerful observatory was wiped out by tsunamis in Hawaii."

"All of our resources are trained on space, searching the emptiness. Every filter, every computer bank is being used, but it's like looking for a shadow in the dark. We think we spotted something, but it was only a fleeting glimpse before it disappeared. We're working backward to plot its course and make confirmation. It was twelve hours behind David."

"Twelve hours!"

"Right now we can't see it. But we're fairly certain it's there."

All of the attention was quietly trained on the president.

"And what's worse, Mr. President, we think we see another one fifty-six hours behind David.

The phrase "Oh my God" quietly rippled through the room.

"That's two and a half days from now," Dr. Sacks continued. "At the rate of one every twelve hours, that would mean that we can expect at least nine impacts, Mr. President."

"Quiet down, everybody! Is there any way to predict where they'll hit? Can we blast them out of the sky?" asked the defense secretary bitterly.

"We can't even begin to calculate impact position until we can see it, not until it enters the atmosphere. And even then there are a lot of variables, a lot of guesswork. They pick up speed as they are influenced by Earth's gravity. They are very hard to pin down at any given time, so plotting their trajectory is extremely difficult. We guess that we have twenty minutes once we've spotted one in the upper atmosphere.

"That's not enough time, Mr. President," one of the chief military aids burst out.

"Can the planet take nine of these ... bombardments?" asked another of the presidential advisors.

"The earth has survived serious impacts in the past. The asteroid that was responsible for wiping out the dinosaurs was ten times the size of our one kilometer bodies."

"We'll be facing a nuclear winter," muttered one the aids taking notes behind the secretary of state.

"All the smoke and debris are going to have a huge impact on our environ-ment, but it's too early to predict anything specific. We are dealing with some-thing completely new. We've only had two days to work on it."

"As for the planet … it will be around for a long time to come. As long as the sun keeps us in its orbit, the planet itself will survive. We just won't be around to appreciate it," one of scientific advisors proclaimed gloomily from his place behind the secretary of the interior's chair.

"What about the bugs? Is it possible? Can anything survive on one of those things? Out in space?" An enormous tension was released in the room by the young military aid's questions. Finally, someone had asked what everyone wanted to know. The president had been waiting for it.

"We don't know anything about that, yet! We will not discuss that until I hear back from those planes! Do you understand me?" The president pounded his fists on the table. "Where are my fucking satellite photos? If there were aliens on these asteroids, I want to see one! If you can show me pictures of Saddam Hussein's balls while he lounges by the pool, why can't you produce a photo of these giant beetles crawling around in the millions?" The crowded room filled with talk after the first mention of aliens by the president.

"They're too small."

"Our satellites have been disrupted by the impacts." Excuses came in from every corner of the room. All decorum was lost.

"We've got contact reports coming out of North Africa, Mr. President."

"U.S. Air Force personnel claim to have one, sir."

"We're waiting to hear back from our planes, and that's final!" George shouted above the others. "I cannot continue like this. There needs to be order. I have to know what is going on. I need facts. And I can't have *you* going on about the end of the world, okay?" The president angrily pointed to the pessimistic young science advisor.

"I'm very sorry, Mr. President," the young advisor apologized solemnly.

"Has anyone got any solutions for me?" implored the president.

"Can't we shift our satellites to get a better look into space? Get a lock on these sons a bitches and blow them off course or something?" exclaimed a junior military aid.

"Not in fifty-six hours," admonished his superior.

"Mr. President, we have to evacuate you to a safe location within the next twelve hours," said the secretary of defense.

"He's right, Mr. President. We calculate that the tidal surge from any Atlantic impact could swamp most of the East Coast. DC is extremely vulnerable." Once again, Dr. Sacks talked above the others.

"Where am I supposed to go?"

"I doubt that even NORAD would survive a direct impact."

"We all appreciate your pessimism, Dr. Sacks, but so far I haven't heard any solutions from you."

"If you want to know what I think, Mr. President, I think we can weather nine impacts—supposing for the moment that there *are* only nine impacts. Our climate will change drastically, but I feel we will adapt. We have always adapted. We may even retain a society similar to what we have now, but I doubt it. We are facing a catastrophe we could never have dreamed of. The X-factor in the equation is this: what have these vessels brought with them?"

"We have planes in the air right now! We will wait for confirmation! I cannot work with what-ifs! I have to act! Where do we stand now?"

"Sir, we are getting information from the region now. No word from our planes, sir."

"Have you completed a damage assessment from the previous impacts?"

"Yes sir, we have a report, but it is far from complete. We have suffered massive damage to our Pacific fleet. The numbers are still coming in, but in effect we've lost two entire battle groups. We lost at least five hundred ships lost and thirty thousand servicemen. Over twenty naval ports have been severely damaged, including Pearl Harbor, which I've been informed is a total loss. The surviving ships in the area are overwhelmed. All coastal regions near any of the three previous impacts have been wiped clean. Our allies are all screaming for help. There is a desperate need for search and rescue, but officially all operations are on hold, and we've started to move assets to deeper waters and protected shores."

"If we pull out our transports, we leave a lot of personnel landlocked," another naval aid added.

"Then there's the issue of fuel. Most of our fuel depots were lost with the various naval bases."

"That alone poses a huge ecological disaster," interjected one of the presidential environmental advisors.

"There have been over three hundred reported oil tanker sinkings, and reports keep coming in. Not to mention non-ally oil depots and their coastal facilities. Or offshore oil rigs. The environmental damage is one thing, but our ships need that fuel!"

"I want our resources back home," the president said firmly. "We are going to need them right here."

"We need our forces to secure our interests abroad, Mr. President—the oil."

"What about all our troops abroad? We need those ships to bring them back," a junior naval aid broke in.

"I agree that we need them back, and as soon as possible. But we surely can't put them on ships with those things still crashing to Earth!"

"We have to keep our assets in their strategic locations!" the secretary of defense screamed, momentarily silencing the others. "We're under attack! It's an invasion! Can't anybody see that? If there are little green monsters landing in India right now, we need to be there to stop them!"

"We are facing social collapse right here at home. If we don't act decisively there will be anarchy!"

"Mr. President, you must enact martial law," urged the secretary of state. "When people learn that there will be more impacts, there will be chaos. If they learn that we're under alien invasion, who knows what they might do?"

"Mr. President, you can't overlook the fact that we need to rescue the dollar! We are facing complete global economic collapse!" The president's chief economic advisor practically pushed himself across the table and pleaded with him. "It can happen overnight! People will stop going to work. The market will crash across the globe. The dollar will be worthless. There will be hording and looting. Complete panic! We need martial law not only to put down the looters and keep the peace; we need it to save the economy! We can't have people walk away from vital jobs because they're panicked. We must support the infrastructure by any means necessary." The chief economist was almost seated in the lap of the man next to him as he demanded the president's attention. A secret serviceman closed the distance and glared at him suspiciously, but the economist was determined to make his point.

"You can count on other governments succumbing to this disaster. We have to take care of ourselves!"

"It's happening already. People are already fleeing the coastal areas here at home. They're leaving everything behind. Coastal cities are ghost towns." Others in the room began shouting the economist down, shaming him for thinking of the dollar value at a time like this, but he continued on. "If society collapses, many people will die very quickly."

"There will surely be widespread famine." Another advisor showed his support for the economist's request for martial law. "We could be looking at years without adequate sunlight."

"Mr. President! Mr. President! We've had word from our pilots over India!" An excited air force colonel burst into the room carrying the report in his hands. "Flight Command tells us they have lost three of the planes sent to the area." A hush fell over the excited crowd. "Three C-150 J-hawks loaded with equipment were dispatched to the site. They all reported a thick cloud of debris dispersed behind the comet before they were disabled and downed." A chilling hush fell over the room.

"We have more planes in route to the area now, sir."

"There is no word as of yet to the nature of the debris, sir, but we are fairly certain that we are looking at a wide area of dispersal, much wider than we anticipated. We weren't counting on getting that close. Those planes were one hundred miles away from the comet's path before they went down."

Washington DC. June 17, 2002

"Hey, brother, it's me. Open up." Shug strained to holler over the armload of goods, but they were stacked to his chin. He tried the doorbell with a free finger, but he couldn't hear anything. The button was dark. He was about to pound on the door with his foot when he heard the sound of a deadbolt being pulled back. Hank opened the door, shooting a quick look over his shoulder.

"Any luck?" Hank relieved him of some of his load. "What did you get?"

"I did okay. It's like another world out there. Is the power out?"

"Yeah, went out just after you left. Did any of the stores have power?"

"Who knows? Never went inside one—they're all closed."

"What did you get?" Hank peered into the plastic sack as they walked toward the doctor's expansive kitchen.

"Not much. I did get a few pounds of frozen hamburger meat. Fifty bucks! I bought all the guy had."

"What else?"

"Crap mostly, but I did manage to buy ten cartons of cigarettes."

"Plan on taking up smoking now that the Apocalypse is on us?"

"No, but you said buy anything that could be valuable. In a couple of days these things may become a real hot item. I found a guy selling these out of a semi trailer. There was a line all the way around the block. Guess how much per carton."

"I dunno. Fifty bucks?"

"Hundred bucks a carton!"

"Good job. What else we got?" Hank began placing the contents of the bag on the counter.

"Let's see. I got the burgers, no buns. Some guy was selling them out of a McDonald's truck. I got some canned pineapple, some soup—not very much, though. Hey, are we gonna be able to keep this meat cold without power?"

"For a little while. We'll go out later and see if we can't hunt down a generator."

"What about gas?"

"The gas still works ... I think. The doctor's got a gas grill out back we can use." Hank pointed to the patio outside the window.

"Not that kind of gas. People are screaming for it out there. Everybody's trying to get out of town. The gas stations are all empty, and all the cars left in the street have had their gas caps pried off."

"We'll worry about that when we get a generator. Right now, the Range Rover is full, and the Benz is half empty."

"Everyone I've run into says that we'll be swamped if one of those things hits anywhere near the coast. Do you think we should try and find higher ground?"

"How far are we gonna get with a tank and a half of fuel? Where we gonna go anyway?" Hank stacked cartons of cigarettes on the counter, taking a pack and rolling it up beneath the sleeve of his T-shirt.

"I heard the president made his speech from his jet this morning. You think he's gonna to stay up there?" Shug looked to the sky.

"Who knows? I don't know if it's any safer up there. I figure he'll probably go underground, some place like NORAD or something."

"But he's left the White House ..."

"The eastern seaboard is pretty flat. If one of those shock tsunamis hits, we'll all be swimmin' for sure. We can't worry about what-ifs anymore. If our number is up, it's up. There's no NORAD for us."

"What about makin' a run for the hills? I'm not a very good swimmer, ya know."

"We don't want to go out there blindly. It's only been three days, and people are already going crazy. Who knows what it's like right now in those mountains?"

"We've got guns. We can take care of ourselves."

"And they all have hardware, too. I don't want to get killed for a Land Rover or a half tank of gas. This isn't over yet. We have ... just under four hours before the next big one." Hank checked his watch.

"Any word on where it'll be?"

"Nope. The TV crapped out right after you left."

"Right, no power."

"But we've got a radio." Hank smiled. "And guess what?"

"Don't tell me: Howard is on."

"You bet. I guess he's been holed up in his building for the last couple of days. He's afraid to leave, but he's still on the air. Only a couple of stations are still broadcasting. Everyone else has taken their families and run for the hills."

"Has he got any news?" Shug could imagine Howard Stern barricaded in his studio, afraid to come down, his fanatical fans rallying to his aid.

"Not really, but he says he's still tapped into the news wire. Apparently nobody really knows for sure if there will even be another impact."

"But the president said there would be more. Why would he say it if he wasn't sure? That's got to panic people, right? Why would he say there were aliens if he wasn't sure? It's got to be true, right?"

"After you left this morning, they showed one." Hank stared at the television as if it were on.

"An alien?"

"Yeah. From Africa."

"What did it look like?"

"Like a huge bug. Like a flea, or a beetle. It was probably the size of your hand ... well, not *your* hand, I mean a normal-sized hand. It was dark black. The features were hard to make out, but it looked just like a bug. Maybe even kinda crablike, ya know, lots of spiny legs."

"Holy shit ..."

"This one was dead. They say that it was alive when some Moroccan policeman picked it up. He just picked it up off of the ground and threw it in a bucket."

"But we have one? We can study it?"

"By now I bet we have a lot more than one. They don't appear to be all that concerned with people."

"You can just pick one up?"

"If you've got enough balls to grab a one-pound flea from outer space, you can." Hank smiled at the thought, knowing Shug hated bugs.

"So it's for sure—we're being invaded by aliens!"

"Nothing is for sure. Not anymore." Hank was trying to make light of the situation, wiggling his fingers like giant bug legs and making his eyes roll crazy circles in his head, but Shug was not amused.

"I hope we get power again. I want to see it."

"I really wouldn't count on getting power back anytime soon. It's not like a tree knocked down some lines. There isn't anybody at the switch. Everyone is looking after themselves. Who can blame 'em? We've got to do the same."

"I've got to get back home." Shug had been telling himself that he was still bound for home, but now, as he heard the words leave his mouth, he knew they were unrealistic. "I guess all flights are down."

"Cupcake is there. He can take care of your grandma."

"I know, I just can't stand the thought of ... you know. Are the phones working?"

"My cell is working, but I haven't been able to get a hold of anybody on it. Hey, peanut butter cups! Man, I love these things."

"Twenty bucks for a box of twelve. Toss me one, would ya?"

"Mmm ... two great tastes that taste great together," Hank said through a mouthful of candy.

"I couldn't find any batteries."

"That's one thing the Doctor does have in stock: batteries, flashlights, first aid, and enough booze to kill a Kennedy."

"Good. If the place starts crawlin' with giant bugs, I want to be good and loaded." Shug laughed, his mouth full of chocolate.

"Can you imagine? It still blows my mind. A few days ago, I was worried about coming forward about Devil's Peak. Now, none of that matters. The planet is getting blasted apart and aliens are falling from the sky. All of a sudden, it's like I ain't got no more problems." Chocolate stained Hank's smile as he spoke.

"Where do you think the next one will be?" Shug asked, almost rhetorically.

"What, are you kidding? The question is how many of them there are. A few more like the last one, and that's it for everybody. We'll go the way of the dinosaurs. All that will be left will be cockroaches and space bugs making colonies in our empty cities. They should be very happy together."

"You think the smoke will block out the sun?"

"Look how dark it is."

"Did you see how pink the sky was this morning? Eerie!"

"And that was from impacts on the other side of the planet. Look how bad it is out there, the looting and hording, it's crazy already. What happens when one hits home? What happens when the food is gone and there's no sunlight to grow any more? Those are the questions we're dealing with. It doesn't matter where the next one hits. It's like a nuclear war; I'd rather get killed by a direct impact than survive and eventually starve to death—or get turned into some space bug's bitch."

"I wonder how many people have died already." Shug stared off into space.

"Stop wondering. All we can do is think about us. Right now it's just you and me. We're not so bad off. Come on, let's go tune into the radio. We can get a couple of these burgers fired up."

A small portable radio sat by a window overlooking the approach to the doctor's house. A shotgun was leaning against the wall at the ready. Howard Stern's voice emanated from the room.

"You have to go back to work! Done! It's that simple. Bush was right. If you're at home cowering with your family, it's like you've already given up. You might as well roll over and die." Howard charged on through his rant.

"Well, there are a lot of people doing just that, Howard. There are people out there killing themselves and taking their whole families with them. They think it's the end of the world," interjected Robin.

"Fine, let 'em die! But the rest of us, the ones that aren't religious freaks, have got to carry on! This isn't Armageddon! This is *Aliens*: part four! We've got to keep it together so we can kill these monsters!" Howard's voice strained with exhaustion.

"Well, p-p-people say it's Armageddon," Stuttering John interrupted him.

"Fine, let them die in rapture. I want to live. I have a family too, dammit, and I'm here! I'm working! Where all those pussies from the networks? I don't see them on TV!" Howard continued showering abuse on everybody not locked in the studio with him.

"That's because there's no power, Howard." Robin countered him in a condescending tone.

"I guarantee the news studios are empty, Robin. They're just as bad as everybody else. They could pull together a broadcast!"

"You're right; I suppose they could if they really tried." Robin said, acquiescing to Howard's anger.

"We're still on the air!"

"That's because you're too afraid to go home," a voice blurted out from deep within the studio.

"Listen: I'm no great fan of the president, but he's right, dammit! We need martial law! It's fucking crazy out there!"

"Did you just swear, Howard?" Robin asked, clearly shocked.

"You bet I did. You know those cocksuckers from the FCC aren't coming to work! Pussies. That's right!

Go ahead, fine me! Take me off the air now, pussies. I'm the only one doing my job!"

"There are some people still working, just not enough." Robin stopped him mid rant.

"I'm no dummy, Robin. I know how bad it is out there. I didn't want to leave the building, so we took it over. Yeah that's right, Robin. It's my building now! What do you say about that? It's now the Howard Stern Building."

"You're crazy."

"I know it sounds crazy, but this is a crazy time, baby. A few of the employees here at the station volunteered to stay and keep us running, and I agreed to stay on the air as long as I could. Some people are bringing their entire families here. We have a little community in this building now, and it's keeping us on the air.

Gary, make sure that someone out there is painting the new name on the building!"

"Howard, we have a call." Gary's voice broke in over the air.

"Jimmy, you're on the air."

"Hi Howard. I want to let you know that there are still people sucking it up and doing their jobs. I'm with Fire Truck Company Five, and we're fully staffed—in fact, we got guys comin' in pullin' extra shifts."

"You're a fireman?"

"That's right, Howard. And let me tell you, your city's cops are out there in force too, buddy!"

"You guys are better than heroes. These guys know what it's all about. If you panic, we're all done for. We've got to be brave like these guys." Howard's voice was full of admiration.

"I know there are a lot of you that think your jobs aren't important, but that doesn't matter. There's important work to do out there. It's a whole new ball game. If you can drive a truck, we need you." The fireman's voice was charged with emotion.

"We need everybody! Especially the ones with the technical expertise. We've got to get our power plants running." Howard echoed the sentiment.

"If you work at a water pumping station, we need you." Jimmy jumped in once again. "We've been coming up short of water, and there are fires everywhere. These idiots want to loot, then burn the fucking places down!" Jimmy shouted his frustration. "Sorry, Howard."

"Don't worry about it. You can say whatever you want. You're a hero in my book."

"You're a hero too, buddy. Maybe you can talk sense into some of these people."

"And we in New York are not the only ones. Cities are shutting down all over the country."

"All over the world, Howard," Robin countered.

"If any country can keep it together, it's us. We're the strongest for a reason. Our people are brave, and they are industrious.

Don't roll over and die. Go out there and help."

"Howard, there's a man downstairs who says he works for the electric company," another voice broke in over the phone line.

"Good, let's get him over to the power plant. We've got people who can get him there …"

"He's here with his family. He says that he's willing to leave them here and go to the plant if you promise to keep them safe."

"I promise. Bring him up here. That goes for everyone out there: if you bring your family here—and we have tons of families here already—we can keep them safe. Whatever it takes to get you back to work. As long as you can hear the sound of my voice on the air, you'll know that your families are safe.

This is a forty-eight-story building, and it's totally deserted. We have enough to get by for a while. And we have guys with guns securing the lobby."

"That's right, Howard. I want to tell you that there are a lot of cops out there, and they have orders to shoot all looters." Jimmy's voice broke in over the others.

"And they should be shot! Scum! Shame on you! Good, good—I hope that the cops *do* crack down. We've got to restore order."

"It's martial law, Howard; there will be army guys here soon."

"We can't count on the army saving us right now. They've got their own problems. This is like a war; we've got to keep it together to keep the army going, not the other way around."

"We don't need the army. We need people to keep their heads!" Jimmy shouted over the phone.

"I mean the army is going to go after the bugs! You know those guys aren't deserting. We've got to support them!" Howard shouted.

"We can wipe them out, Howard."

"Blast them with nukes!"

"They s-s-say that there are m-m-millions of them … and they are spread out all over the place. We can't carpet Africa and India with n-n-nukes."

"What if they're harmless? I heard they aren't aggressive." Gary added his voice to the mix.

"It doesn't matter, we have to kill them!" Howard shouted his producer down.

"I'm just saying they may not be all that dangerous. People shouldn't panic. I understand people panicking about the asteroids … but the bugs are still an unknown. I mean … people have picked them up with their bare hands."

"I've heard they burrow underground."

"Somehow that doesn't make me feel any better." Howard's voice was weak with fatigue. "It doesn't matter. We have to be concerned with the situation right here at home. I know we are less than four hours away from being struck by another asteroid. I know that people are scared, but to panic now is deadly. You have to have faith in our government. Just like Jimmy and all the other firemen and policemen. A single person's efforts can make the difference. Together we can keep the city alive. If we don't, there will be killing and starvation and all kinds of brutality: nobody will be safe. This is the scariest time in all of history. If humans are going to survive, we have to do it together."

Freemont, California. June 17, 2002

The Mosque was beautiful. This was the first time Omar had entered with his head held high. He no longer worried that one of these men would turn him in for the money Americans paid for terrorists. He no longer felt alone. Fear had become the great equalizer among men. It was the End of Days.

The muezzin sang the call to prayer, and the crowd of men tightened around him. They carried him through the doors, moving like a river, until he stopped in a pool of men looking for space on the floor. Hundreds of men already lined the space beneath the dome. Many of them were beginning their prayers, ignoring the trampling feet as they bowed and mouthed the words of the Quran. Omar scanned the space for a white patch of marble. He had never seen a Mosque so full.

A disgruntled rumble grew in the men's voices behind him as he was pushed deeper into the mass of prostrate men. Men were getting angry because there was no more room. They began shouting. The Mosque elders quickly shouted them down from their positions lining the entrance. A few enraged elders began attacking the crowd with rolled up paper, slapping the men's ears and shoulders, as was the custom. They made a good show of looking angry, but Omar could see that it was really fear that twisted their faces.

Omar dodged a swat from one of the elderly men and pushed past him to find a slice of floor between two thin men. He apologized as he knelt, then began performing the ritual ablutions. He joined the bowing rhythm of the men near him and tried to block out the angry rumble. The peace his prayers normally brought was elusive. His mind ran wild, and he couldn't focus on the greatness of Allah. The men around him had come to talk, not pray.

"Allah be praised!" The head Imam stood beneath the mark indicating the direction of Mecca. "Most Wise. Most Merciful." His ancient voice turned shrill as he shouted to be heard. "All Knowing and All Seeing!"

He waited for the noise to die down before he drew himself up and pointed a twisted finger at the crowd. "We await new heavens and a new earth—where, according to his promise, the justice of Allah will reside!" He raised his finger to the sky and spoke as if he had answered some unspoken question.

"Is it truly so? Is it really the End of Days?"

"It wasn't prophesied this way!" Men shouted from the throng of people crowding the entrance. Their heavily accented English was Omar's language, now. He even dreamed in English. He caught himself behaving like the American

Muslims more and more. They had no patience and showed their disrespect by shouting.

The elderly Imam became enraged and yelled at the men. "Do not great balls of fire fall from the heavens to consume us?" Others shouted the men down, but the Imam cast his voice across the entire mosque. "Do these not come from heaven up high, from his own hands? This is the End of Days! But if you have led a righteous life, do not fear! Today Allah smiteth all your enemies!"

"How do we know this is the will of Allah?"

A man close to Omar leaped to his feet and shouted to the Imam. "Does Allah really send insects to kill us?"

"*Basmalah!* In the name of Allah! Have you not seen the signs with your own eyes? *Maa Shaa Allah*. This is God's will. Have none of you read our Quran? Sura eighty-one, Al-Takweer; when the sun is rolled. The stars are crashed into each other. The mountains are wiped out. The reproduction is halted. The beasts are summoned! The oceans are set aflame!"

"Are those giant beetles the beasts?"

The headman shook, his lips turning purple. "Hell is ignited! Paradise is presented! The Quran is proof!"

"Do we let our families succumb to these … these things?"

"Do we protect our families from Allah?"

"Some of my family are dead already! Their bodies are lost to the floods! What happens to them? They were never buried according to the laws of Allah. Their bodies are still out there!"

"How clean will our deaths be? What do we do?"

"We have no food … do we starve?"

"What do I tell my family?"

The Imam reached out his gnarled hands as if he were grabbing and shaking the crowd. "Allah will take *all* of us! He knows who is unclean! Unclean in thought and unclean of body. If your family led the righteous life of a believer, their souls will remain clean. Have nothing to fear … Losers indeed are those who disbelieve in meeting Allah until the hour comes to them, then suddenly say, 'We deeply regret wasting our lives in this world.' They will carry loads of their sins on their backs: what a miserable load!" The Imam quoted the Quran aloud. "I see you with your sins loaded onto your backs. Your entire lives are loaded into your cars, and you want to flee. Ask yourselves: where can you go to escape Allah?" Most of the men fell silent as the Imam took a long breath.

"The day will come when this earth will be substituted with a new earth, and also the heavens and everyone will be brought before Allah, the One, the

Supreme." Omar had heard these words recited countless times, but now they held new meaning. Any doubt he had ever felt suddenly weighed on him doubly. "It is the inevitable! Al-Waaqe'ah. When the inevitable comes to pass, nothing can stop it from happening. It will lower some, and raise others."

The Imam lowered his voice and began quoting in Arabic. "The earth will be shaken up! The mountains will be wiped out as if they never existed!

You will be stratified into three kinds. Those who deserved bliss will be in bliss. Those who deserved misery will be in misery. Then there is the elite of the elite. They are those who will be closest to Allah, in the gardens of bliss. Many fr...."

"English, please. We cannot follow your Arabic." A voice shouted from near the door. "We do not understand, Imam."

"You must tell us what to do!"

"Do we slaughter our families to save them from this horrible death?"

"No! You mustn't do that!" The Imam shouted angrily. "Oh you who believe, you shall not kill yourselves. Allah is merciful toward you." The Imam broke out into fiery Arabic again. "Anyone who commits these transgressions, maliciously and deliberately, we will condemn him to hell. This is easy for Allah to do!" The seventy-year-old Imam gasped. White froth formed in the corners of his mouth. "It is clearly written. Only he can take life righteously!"

"Only Allah ..." Another Mullah attempted to relieve his teacher but was cut short by more questions from the agitated men.

"They say these are creatures from another planet. How can this be?" A Western-sounding man broke through the crowd noise. "They are saying it's an alien invasion. That the balls of fire are really spaceships! What if they are not sent from Allah?" He continued, regardless of the harsh looks from the men around him.

"Not from Allah?" gasped the Imam.

"Disbeliever! Blasphemer!" Men from the crowd began to shout the young man down.

"But even Allah says there are other planets!" cried another young man.

"Allah creates all things ... *Subhanahu Wa Ta'aala*, Glory be to the Most High," The elder Mullah scolded him. "*Maa Shaa Allah*. This is Allah's will."

"But the prophecy says there would be other signs."

"The signs are here! Listen to your proof. Hear it with your heart. The End of Days will be marked by these signs; the splitting of the moon! Like many messages in the Final Testament, this was meant metaphorically. And the moon was indeed *split* in June of 1969, when astronauts brought pieces of it back to Earth.

Secondly, there is the proof that verifies the validity of the very Quran itself! This scientific proof came in 1974, when the mathematical code within the Quran was revealed." The Imam counted off the proofs on his fingers.

"Thirdly, there is the *creature*." The Imam once again broke into dramatic Arabic prose. "At the right time, we will produce for them a creature made of earthly materials. It will alert the people that they have been oblivious to their Creator. And indeed there are many in the world who still do not believe what their own creature has told them. They would still deny the truth. This creature of whom Allah speaks of is the computer! Made from earthly materials, this creature was instrumental in unveiling the mathematical miracle that proves the Quran's divinity. No human mind alone could have devised the Quran's numerical code!

And of course we cannot overlook the *smoke*. Therefore watch for the day when the sky brings a profound smoke," the Imam quoted. "It will envelop the people; this is a painful retribution!" He pointed to the sky beyond the dome. "Look at the skies! Look, and then tell me the signs have not come! It is truth!"

"The prophecy said nothing about giant insects!" A man clinging to one of the massive pillars shouted back at the Imam.

"Allah caused a plague of insects in Egypt!" The elderly Imam looked exasperated.

"Fool! Don't you hear what your Imam is saying to you?"

"Do I let insects take my family? No!" The man countered bitterly.

"No!" Many others found their voices and echoed the man's words.

"Will there be nothing left?"

Another Mullah stepped forward. "This life will end to make way for another."

"We must fight for our families!"

"You cannot fight Allah's will! You must give in to peace."

"I will not let my family die!"

"Nor I."

"Fire will consume you from the sky! It will come for all of us. Let the righteous among you have no fear!"

"Until that time, I will fight to feed my family!"

The word *fight* echoed in Omar's warrior heart. Although he had no family to protect, there was a girl he desired and a life he wanted to realize. He wanted no quarrel with Allah, but he felt the need to fight, to survive no matter what.

"Do what you must, but the End of Days is here! There will be no mercy for those who deny him. Paradise awaits those of you who are true to him!"

Off the coast of Brazil. June 18, 2002

Kincaid slumped wearily against his rucksack. He'd been on the move for fifty hours straight. He was exhausted, but any thought of sleep was out of the question; he had gotten *the call*. He'd survived the nights of despair where he'd believed the call would never come—or even worse, that it would come too late, passing him by after a life spent waiting. And now it was official. The Black Watch network buzzed with activity, eventually landing him here in the loading bay of a U.S. aircraft carrier off the coast of Buenos Aires.

It was a familiar scene. Kincaid had been packed into just about every kind of flying machine imaginable, and he had started countless missions from aircraft carriers just like this one. In fact, he had once been just like the young, hard-nosed Navy SEALs sitting opposite him in the loading area. But that was a lifetime ago.

He was introduced to the SEAL team as Kincaid, *OSA*—Special Operations lingo for *Other Special Agency*. They had been told that he was running the show. Naturally there were some hard, questioning looks from the young commandos. These guys didn't appreciate being kept in the dark, but there wasn't enough liberty to speak, and he didn't feel like playing games with these kids.

Kincaid was glad to be with men like the SEALs right now. They were all awaiting word from CIN-PAC before they could go ahead with the mission. They were doing what soldiers did before going into combat; they checked their gear and acted nonchalant. He was relieved to be far removed from all of the hysteria out there in the real world.

The *Go* order would come from Command once the latest asteroid, George, hit its mark. Until then, all aircraft were grounded and all operations were on hold. It was the seventh time the people of Earth had held their breath and hoped for the best. There would be little warning for the doomed, only blinding light and thirteen minutes of terror. Apparently no one really knew where George was going to hit. Kincaid was tapped into the highest levels of the Black Watch, and even they couldn't make a confident guess, but ten minutes ago George had been spotted in the skies over the Eastern Hemisphere.

"The brass figures it'll probably hit China." The SEAL captain gave his guys the thumbs up, which was answered back with a quick "whoop, whoop!" from his men.

None of these guys were talking about lost loved ones or the massive calamity taking place. It was all gung-ho professionalism and military bravado. The young men reminded Kincaid that his own totalitarian lifestyle might now actually be rewarded. He, like the young men around him, was unencumbered by thoughts of his family. He didn't have a family. He couldn't afford one. That was what it really meant to be in the Black Watch. He had lived his entire life for this moment. And like these men, he was ready.

The bright-eyed captain appeared at the door once again. "All right guys, we got a green light … you know what to do. Let's get it on!"

Men all along the wall got to their feet and high-fived each other. They all knew the word could have been much different if the guesswork had been wrong and George slammed into the ocean somewhere. Even the enormous aircraft carrier wasn't a sure thing in the face of eight-hundred-foot shock tsunamis. Despite the good news and the green light order, there was still very little celebrating; it was just a momentary break in the tension of waiting. Now they had to load onto the helicopters and endure another three hours of waiting. There were still six hours before sunrise. The name of the game was hurry up and wait, and these guys knew it.

"Looks like our friend George plopped down right in the middle of Manchuria, China. Good fuckin' shot, I'd say!" The young captain made his way down the column of men.

"Whoop, whoop!"

"Our scientists predict there is at least one more of these sons a bitches up there, and it's about thirty-six hours out. They've seen this one! We got lucky this time, so let's make the most of it. If George was anything like Eddie, you can expect to have a blast radius of 250 kilometers. That's what we'll be looking at in Brazil." The captain grinned at his men. "Yeah, Eddie. They're calling our asteroid Edward. I like Eddie better."

Kincaid didn't really enjoy these little pep talks, so he busied himself with his gear and tried to make eye contact with his Black Watch partner in the adjacent loading bay. He couldn't see much past the pacing captain, so he pulled the radio microphone down from behind his ear.

"Bravo, Charlie, this is Alpha." Kincaid pulled a laminated map out of its cylinder as he spoke into the microphone.

"Go ahead for Charlie."

"Go for Bravo."

"Okay guys, George is in China. We've got a green light. I'll inform the captain of the change in plans once all the teams are on board the choppers."

"Copy that."

"See you out there, Kincaid."

"Make sure you've brought lots of shotguns. And remember, we split up for a reason. You guys command your own teams out there, okay?" Kincaid lowered his voice and turned his back to the SEALs.

"You got it, boss."

The captain raised his voice to shout to the men at the far end of the loading bay. "Our satellite imagery has been pretty shaky over this area; that's why we've loaded the imaging equipment. For you guys operating the on-boards and the remotes, that's going to be priority one. This will be the first pass over this area. We don't know what to expect. So keep your eyes open and your equipment running.

As for the alien factor in today's mission, I can only tell you this: if we are indeed under the threat of alien invasion, you men right here, all of us, are going to be the first ones into battle!" The young captain glared into his men's eyes with prideful intensity.

"Whoop, whoop!"

"We're going in armed to the teeth, with the most powerful military machine at our backs, and no fucking bug is going to stop us!"

"Yeah!" The men roared together.

"Even though we will be flying low," the captain continued, "we might not see any bugs today." Kincaid looked up from his gear and tried to hide his sly smile.

"Reports out of Africa are saying these things are still relatively small. I've got a picture of one. You can see that its body is just over a foot long." The captain held up an eight-by-eleven photo of a dead alien lying next to a ruler. The long, crosslike arms lay flat behind the beetle's body, extending well past the one-foot mark on the ruler. The sharp, spindly legs lay folded along the body like the legs on a dead shrimp's belly. Its only other distinguishable feature was its tremendous hind legs, which lay extended outward from the body.

"It's possible that we may not see any of them as we make our pass. There are reports that they tend to burrow underground once they make landfall. So we'll need to keep our eyes open."

"Are we gonna hunt any bugs?"

"We have our mission parameters. But Kincaid here will be calling all the shots when it comes to any potential, um, aliens." The captain motioned to Kincaid, who was shouldering his pack, and then turned to face his men once more. "Remember this: there are still rules for engagement out there, boys! You're on tape, every last one of you. Don't be thinking that just because these fucking bugs won't be crying on CNN, that you can go hog wild out there! We have no idea what we're dealing with yet. I want professionalism from you guys. I don't want to be responsible for making one really big fuckup, okay?"

The SEAL who had ventured the comment about bug hunting, straightened against the wall. "Yes, sir."

"Kincaid will let you know what he needs from you as the situation develops. And yes, one of today's objectives involves capturing an alien specimen. You've all trained with the equipment, or at least you've put your hands on it. I know that you haven't had much time with it—but hell, it's not *rocket surgery*, is it?"

"Sir, how shall we address you, sir?" There was no rank adorning Kincaid's black commando fatigues, and except for his advanced years and the extra equipment he carried, he looked just like all the other SEALs in their combat gear.

"It's just Kincaid, fellas." Kincaid smiled wearily from under his helmet. "The captain here is still going to run the show; I probably won't remember all of your names, so I'll let him call the shots with you guys. All I care about is getting as many specimens into those crates over there as we can. Where's my collection team?"

"Right here, sir." Six men led by a junior officer raised their hands.

"Good. You guys sit next to me on the bird.

As for the rules of engagement: I don't give a fuck how many of those things we kill, as long as I get mine! We protect each other. Understand?"

"Whoop, whoop!"

"Whoop, whoop," repeated Kincaid. "There will three teams of choppers, three Team leaders. We all want the same thing. We want footage, we want intel, and we want prisoners. Let's be the team that gets all three! I don't need to tell you how important it is. Now come on, lads, looks like the other two birds are already loaded."

"You heard him, boys, find your seats." The captain stood next to the open door of the Black Hawk as the team of eleven men filed in. Elevators were already lifting the other helicopters to the flight deck.

"All right, Captain, looks good." Kincaid wrapped his arm around the captain's shoulder and pulled him close. When the captain's ear was within whispering distance, Kincaid let him know he'd been keeping a surprise from him. "There's been a change of plans. Teams one and two are taking a new heading. Three is carrying on with the original mission."

"A change, now? But we're ..."

"We and the choppers from team two are headed here"—Kincaid pressed the laminated map against the wall of the Black Hawk—"over a place called Sao Carlos, where we'll refuel and then proceed to the epicenter of the impact, here." He traced a line to where the impact crater was traced in red over the map.

"Refuel? It's too late …"

"It's all set into motion: refueling planes will rendezvous with us at 2300 hours. We'll be at the target for sunrise."

"Why weren't we notified? How long have you known about this?" The captain angled his helmet away from his face, clearly angry about the last minute changes.

"It all depended on George." Kincaid shrugged his shoulders and tapped the center of the map with a finger.

"So we're going all the way to the crater?" The young captain chewed his lower lip. "I was told the bugs couldn't survive so close to the point of impact. Are you gonna find your specimens there?"

"They want us to fly over the crater. They think they're seeing something strange in the satellite pics. They want us to take a closer look."

"Why don't they send in planes? This is a job for spy planes, not helicopters."

"Too much smoke, too much airborne crap … I don't know. But if they think there's alien activity in that crater, that's where we're going. That's where I'm getting my specimen."

"Okay. I'll inform the men that we've got a longer flight coming up."

"I'll be back with you once we take off. I'll be up front until then." Kincaid rolled up the map, slipping it into its tube.

"Yes sir."

The sortie of six helicopters left the aircraft carrier USS *Regan* and headed for the dark skies over Rio de Janeiro. At high altitude, Rio was a dim, smoldering ruin below them. No electric lights illuminated the city; only the scattered points of light from burning buildings dotted the deck.

Once over the city, the formation of copters split up. Team three broke off to recon the blast perimeter to the south. The remaining two Black Hawks and the two smaller gunship escorts continued on, leaving the coast of Brazil behind.

After a half hour of flight, a brilliant orange wall of flame lit up the horizon in front of them. Above the orange flame rose a wall of black smoke that stretched into the sky without end. The tremendous heat generated by the impact had ignited the rainforest, which now burned in an unstoppable ring of fire.

"Will you be able to make it over that header?" Kincaid eyed the wall of fire as he leaned over the pilot's shoulder.

"I don't see why not," the pilot said casually, to the amusement of the copilot. "It's just a five-hundred-foot flame, with firestorm winds and smoke you can't see through. No problem."

"I'll be back. See if you can't find some kind of break in all of that."

"You know it, sir. We're gonna drop down low for a while so we can climb at speed when the time comes."

As Kincaid made his way to the back of the Black Hawk, he could feel the machine dip down and head for the deck. The chopper was crammed full of SEALs craning their necks to peer into the darkness below them.

"We're good and low now—has anybody seen anything yet?" the gunner manning the heavy machine gun called out from his perch in the open door.

"If you're looking for survivors, you're wasting your time." The captain surveyed the destruction stretching out below them. "Nothing survived down there."

"Ain't looking for survivors, sir. Looking for targets!" replied the gunner, full of bravado.

"You'd be doing pretty good to hit something the size of a football from up here, hotshot." Kincaid brushed past the kid manning the gun and found a spot on the bench where his capture team was assembled.

The gunner patted his weapon affectionately. "Just give me a target … this bitch will do the rest."

Kincaid slumped onto the bench. "Well, you've got to love his enthusiasm." He rummaged through the pockets of his fatigues and pulled out a tin of chewing tobacco. He smacked the tin against his leg, compacting the tobacco, then opened the lid to smell the bittersweet aroma.

One of the young SEALs leaned over from his seat. "So what, are you CIA or something?"

"No, I'm no spy." Kincaid packed his lower lip full of tobacco.

"You're one of those Black Watch guys, aren't you?" asked another young SEAL.

"There ain't no such thing as the Black Watch." His friend pounded him in the shoulder. "You watch too many fucking movies, Sanchez."

"You look a little old to be doin' Special Ops." The largest member of the SEAL team bent forward and flexed his pumped-up biceps for Kincaid's benefit. "If you're not CIA … who are you?"

"Yeah, why are they sending *you* to collect aliens?" All eyes were trained on Kincaid now.

"He's OSA; that's all you guys have to know! Don't forget yourself, Jamison."

"No, Captain, it's okay." Kincaid spat into an empty water bottle. "I mean, since these guys have just *got to know* ... and since they're so big and scary"—he smiled with his lower lip packed with chew—"and because I'm far too old to defend myself, I might as well tell you everything." Kincaid paused; he loved nothing more than sparring with an alpha male, and he'd busted the heads of guys much tougher than young Sergeant Jamison. "If you must know—and you might as well, seeing as we may not come back alive—I'm with a super-secret organization that exists to defend Earth against intergalactic threats."

"I knew it! You're Black Watch! I told you, Brenner!"

"How long have you known? How long has this been going on?"

"I'm sorry, guys ..." Kincaid leaned back against his gear and smiled. "It's my first day on the job. Our organization has sworn to fight this intergalactic scum for just over ... seventy-six hours now."

"Ah, he's fucking joking!"

"Son of a bitch—he had you, Sanchez!"

"He still hasn't explained why they sent *him*," sergeant Jamison continued, curling his lip into a snarl. "What do you know about these fucking bugs?"

Kincaid locked eyes with the square-jawed soldier. "I'll tell you all I know, because it's not much, and because by the end of today, you men will know more about these creatures than anyone in the world. Right here in Brazil is where we're going to get our best look at them. In Africa, the meteorite impacted in the ocean, just off the island of Cape Verde. It didn't strike land, and it didn't make an accessible impact crater. A lot of the bugs fell into the sea. Adam and Bertha also landed in the ocean. That leaves us here with Edward, and the boys over in India with David, as the only two impact sites where the impact crater is accessible.

Intel reports a lot of alien activity around these craters. What's going on? They don't know. That's where we come in. Now the boys over in India have a nineteen-hour head start on us. That is, the activity there has had nineteen more hours to develop. From what we've seen in India, we're expecting to find a large exodus of aliens converging on the crater. But we've got the upper hand on the guys in India. They haven't got any ships in the area, and they're heading to the impact site over land. They'll have a tougher time than we will. The terrain is pretty rough over there. We can beat 'em in." Kincaid paused to spit into his bottle.

"Our mission is to fly directly over the crater and gather intel. Once that's complete, our team will find a site and begin collecting samples. I need live bugs. I can't tell you what to expect down there. I can only describe these things the way they were described to me. But let me say this: these aren't bugs! They're from another planet. They may resemble insects, but don't be fooled: they are completely alien. Our ignorance of them makes them very dangerous. They will be nothing like the monsters you have seen in the movies. This is not *Starship Troopers*! This is real. And it is completely unknown. Do not assume anything about this enemy."

Kincaid let a ripple of talk buzz through the belly of the Black Hawk before he continued. "I can say that the bugs themselves are relatively small—when compared to a man, not a real bug, of course. They are probably the size of your boot. They're also incredibly rugged. Their exoskeleton is made from a very dense material. It's supposedly heat resistant to incredible temperatures. We haven't seen any other material like it. That exoskeleton acts as its heat shield on entering Earth's atmosphere. So for all intents and purposes, we can't burn them."

"Do they fly?"

"You remember that picture your captain held up? There were large black wings underneath that bug. Looks sort of like one of the old German flying crosses. The blades on that cross are thin and tapered slightly, like the blades on a helicopter. When the bugs hit land, they break away from these crosses and go on their way. We figure the bugs use them like parachutes. They all pile out at the right altitude, and they fall to Earth. We think the crosses on their backs act like rotor blades, slowing them down and spreading them as far a possible." Kincaid demonstrated with his hands how fast they could disperse after leaving the falling meteorite.

"They use parachutes?"

"Like I said, these aren't bugs."

"What are they calling them? Officially, I mean."

"Extraterrestrials, I suppose. It doesn't matter; some smart-ass will come up with a name for 'em. I'm just interested in getting ahold of some. You guys have worked with the nets?"

"Yes sir. We especially like the sticky foam."

"I'd like to avoid using the foam if we can. I don't like the idea of being stationary for that long. It all depends on how fast these suckers move. If it's anything like trying to catch a fly back home, we're in big trouble. If they're slow enough, I want to use the nets. We wear gloves, biological-level protection, eyewear—the whole bit. We work in two teams. As soon a one team has a specimen, they lock it up."

"Hey guys, we're coming up on a city."

"The pilot says that's Campo Grande."

"Oh my God!"

The city of Campo Grande was razed to the ground. It had been knocked flat by the mighty shock wave and scorched over by fire. No trees stood for endless miles in all directions. The landscape was covered in a dreary gray ash. There was no color anywhere, no signs of life, only gray below and gray above.

"We're climbing!"

"The pilot has to build some momentum to climb over that fire."

"Look at that!"

"Those are our rainforests burning!"

"We can't make it over that! Hey Captain, is he going to fly over that?"

"No one said anything about flying into a fucking fire!"

"Those flames have got to be three hundred feet high!"

"Five hundred," Kincaid said casually.

"We can't make that!"

"It looks a lot bigger when you're this close up, doesn't it?" Kincaid turned in his seat and yawned. "It'll look a little better when we get over it, lads."

The chopper began to shudder violently as it was buffeted by the fierce winds generated by the firestorm. They continued at full speed, upward toward the wall of fire. The Black Hawk's engines screamed with the strain of the rapid ascent.

"We'll get over those flames, boys. Don't worry!" The captain was shouting over the roar from the copter. The horrified expression on his face was hardly reassuring.

"We're gonna burn up!"

The copter climbed higher and higher in the face of the fire and smoke, until it was filled with the scent of burnt green wood. Then, as quickly as turning off a switch, it went completely dark. Smoke filled the copter as the rotors pumped in swirls of dense black smoke.

Cries of alarm could be heard above the roar from the copter. The blinding smoke choked everyone inside. Currents of heat flowed over Kincaid as he held his breath and closed his eyes tight. Some of the men began to scream, taking in huge lungfuls of the acrid smoke. After a few seconds the smoke began to clear, leaving men wrenching in their harnesses.

Fires still burned below them, but nothing like the huge flame front they had passed over. For miles in every direction, the forests lay scorched and smoldering. The four naval helicopters were inside a great ring of fire, one hundred and fifty miles from the point of Edward's impact. Its front spread out behind them in gigantic crescent arching as far as they could see. Before them, on the ground and in the sky, was total blackness.

The copter dipped, making its decent. "Okay, guys, let's get that equipment up and running. We are going back down to the deck. Keep your eyes peeled."

"You heard the man, let's get those cameras rolling. You know what to do. Peters, stop vomiting and get busy."

One of the smaller gunships roared past the diving Black Hawk and made an impressive banking move before skimming over the blackened hills. The Black Hawk followed the maneuver, leaving everyone's guts in their chests with the sudden drop in g-forces. The copilot let out a loud celebratory whoop, and the heavy Black Hawk leveled off fifty feet over the burnt landscape. Kincaid unstrapped his belt and had begun inventorying his equipment when one of the soldiers yelled out.

"I saw one! bug at two o'clock!" The young sergeant pointed the barrel of his rifle from the right flank of the ship.

"Where is it?"

"It's gone. We passed it!"

"I see one!" another voice called out from the other side of the chopper.

"I saw one too! Again, two o'clock!"

"Kincaid! The pilot says you should come up front."

That was all the invitation he needed: Kincaid was halfway past the captain before he could finish his sentence.

"Look at this! They're like fleas jumpin' off a dog's back! Look at all of 'em!" The pilot pointed to the blackened landscape below them. The ground was alive with tiny black dots jumping away from the approaching helicopters. "I don't think they like the noise we're making. Look how many there are."

"I bet the fire burnt right over them … no way our satellites could have picked this up. Are we rolling back there?" Kincaid shouted over his shoulder.

"Yes sir."

"You're right: they look like fleas. Millions of giant fleas." Kincaid glanced back to the excited men filming the bugs and watching their monitors.

"They make a signature on infrared, but they don't give off much heat!"

"They're just about invisible on my camera!"

"Look at how fast they jump. Look, they disappear."

"Charlie can you track one once it's jumped?"

"I dunno, man. Let me see … fuck, look at that, gone! There's another one."

"Keep it running, guys; we don't want to screw this up." The captain steadied himself against the frame and yelled to his men.

Kincaid turned back to the pilot. "How far are we from the crater?"

"Take a look … that's it over there. She's still smokin'. About another ten minutes, I guess."

The copilot whipped around to question him. "You want us to fly over that thing?" It looks like a fucking volcano!"

"Flying over forest fires is one thing—I don't know if I like the idea flying over that. Who knows what the wind is doing over something like that?"

"If conditions permit, and I see what we need, you'll be landing in that son of a bitch if I say so." Kincaid clicked his helmet into place.

"Yes sir."

"Keep me informed if you see anything interesting." Kincaid turned to leave, but his eyes remained locked on the scattering alien life forms. It was his first real live sighting of an extraterrestrial. It was something he had waited thirty years to see, and it couldn't have been more different than what he'd imagined. "Can you guys hit the deck a little lower? I wanna get a closer look at these things."

"You bet. Let's take it down to the treetops, Stokeman—as if there were any trees left, that is."

"You got it, boss."

"I'm going to take a picture of this." The pilot unbelted himself as the copilot took over. He pulled his personal camera out of his flight suit and prepared to snap a couple of shots.

Kincaid's immediate reaction was to snatch the camera away behind the barrel of his pistol, but he somehow restrained himself in time. Normally, every last bit of his energy and effort went into preventing such acts by anyone other than Black Watch operatives. Now, he realized, it was a whole new ball game. Earth was under the imminent threat of alien invasion; there would be no more hiding the truth from the public. He let the pilot take his snapshots.

The darting shapes of the alien beetles grew larger as the helicopter descended. They leaped away even more furiously as the copter got lower. Their individual features were impossible to make out; they disappeared too quickly. Kincaid soon realized that he would have his hands full trying to capture one of these bugs alive.

"Hey, Kincaid … Alpha, this is Bravo." The voice of Kincaid's Black Watch partner sounded in his earpiece.

"Bravo, go ahead for Alpha. What's up, Pete?"

"Looks like you guys are stirring em up pretty good down there, but from up here they look like they're all going the same direction. Looks like they're headed the same way we are."

"Take us up to three hundred feet." Kincaid tapped the copilot's shoulder and pointed up. "Copy that, Bravo: we're coming up to take a look." At that moment, a loud metallic bang sounded in the cockpit. It sounded as if the copter had been shot by small arms fire.

"What was that, skipper?"

"Sounds like something hit the prop!"

"All systems normal. What the fuck was that?"

"It was a bug … one of them must have been sucked into the prop," Kincaid said in amazement.

"Must be hard sons a bitches! That sounded like a round from an AK. Let's climb out of here, Stokeman."

"Yes sir, climbing to three hundred feet."

From the copter's new altitude, the bugs had all but disappeared. Their pitch-black forms were camouflaged against the black-scorched earth, but from this altitude he had a much clearer view of their overall movement. They were indeed all following the same course. They were also headed for the crater.

Individual bugs were funneling together in the valleys of the low-lying hills. They flowed together into ever-growing streams running toward the center of the crater. The light was turning; the pale grays of night were giving way to morning sunlight. In an instant, as the men all gazed at the surreal spectacle below them, the sky gave birth to a fiery flood. The bright morning sunlight turned the smoke and ash in the skies into a swirling red. Kincaid didn't know whether it was the smoke from the Brazilian rain forests or from the previous impacts around the globe, but the sight stunned him. He had never seen sky like it and wondered if he would ever see another normal sunrise again. The thought occurred to him that humanity could not possibly live under skies so ominous and alien.

"Look at that sunrise—have you ever seen anything so red?" the pilot gasped.

"It's got to be all the smoke and stuff, huh Skipper?"

"What's the ETA to that crater?"

"Um, we can do it in five. We've got the fuel."

"Go ahead: the sooner the better, I guess." Kincaid pulled his microphone to his mouth. "Alpha to Bravo. Five minutes to the crater. Have your capture teams ready."

"Bravo, Alpha. Copy that. Do ya see how they're falling in? Look like ants on a pheromone trail."

"Yeah, I see that. What are you planning on using for cover fire down there?"

"Large caliber from the ship, with grenades. Most of the guys have automatics."

"Have the cover teams use the shotguns. They should have some kind of riot gun with them. Use it. I'm gonna carry a twelve gauge."

"Fast little buggers, aren't they?"

"And powerful, too. One of them jumped up and hit us in the prop before we pulled up. Sounded like a brick hit us."

"You're kidding! Did you get a good look?"

"Not really … they all look uniform, though. Like giant, oval-shaped beetles. No crosses. None of them had the crosses."

"Bugs smart enough to use tools …"

"Smart enough to travel through space!"

"Yeah, right. Can't wait to get to that crater." Pete sounded doubtful.

"We get our look in, shoot plenty of film, then we're in and out. Don't worry."

"Hey, I'm not worried. I just hope you're right about those shotguns. Bravo out."

"Copy that, Alpha out." Kincaid gripped the pilot by the shoulder. "Gimme a minute's heads-up when we get to the crater."

"Yes sir."

Kincaid worked his way back to where the capture team was getting ready. "Break out the riot sweeper. And you guys on the cover team, I want you all carrying shotguns. We'll leave a perimeter team with the ship; they'll have the heavy artillery."

"Shotguns, sir?"

"These things are small and fast. They can jump like crazy. If the shit hits the fan, we can expect them to close the distance in short order. I want you to be able to hit them if they get in close."

"Yes sir. Whoop, whoop."

"I want the street sweeper up front. Carry as much ammo as you can. I don't need to remind you that there are potentially millions of those things down there."

"When should we open up, sir?" The ship's gunner manning the .30 caliber minigun smiled eagerly at him.

"Only if the shit hits the fan. Not until I give word or until it becomes grossly obvious. Do you understand, Corporal?" The kid on the thirty-cal wasn't Special Ops. He was just another naval crewmen and had probably never fired his weapon in anger before. Kincaid hoped he wouldn't open up at the wrong time out there. The minigun could wipe out his team in seconds if this kid got out of control.

"Yes sir. I'll look for word from you, sir. I don't want to start some kinda intergalactic shit!" The young kid joked as he turned to face the open door and the thousands of alien invaders.

"The rest of you can shoot if you don't like what you're seeing. You guys are our best; if I can't trust you to make the right call, who can I trust?"

"Whoop, whoop!"

"Who's got my nets?"

"Right here, sir."

"Oh my God! Look at them. Rivers of them!"

The dark red morning light revealed streams of aliens that had massed into wide columns headed straight for the impact crater. The scene below them was otherworldly. The blasted, pockmarked earth was unrecognizable. Sunlight reflected off the streaks of molten glass that emanated from the impact point. Everything below them was covered in a pinkish dust. The choppers were soon flying directly over a wide river of aliens flowing up the piled earth of the crater's face. Walls of rock grew high above the crater's rim, and once again individual bugs could be seen on its lip.

From this height, the perimeter of the crater was clearly defined. Kincaid estimated that it was at least ten kilometers wide and slightly oval in shape. Its fresh, sharp features reminded Kincaid of the craters made in the soft soil of Vietnam by artillery rounds, only on a whole new scale. This crater was made by a shell a kilometer wide, not a few mere millimeters.

Kincaid worked his way back to the cockpit for a better look at the terrain. "Take us high around the perimeter, then give me half a lap around. I want you to look for a gap in that smoke."

"Yes sir. It doesn't look too bad from here. Wind speeds are workable."

The giant beetles could be seen cresting the lip of the crater, massing by the thousands in a black swarming ring of movement before descending into the gapping hole left by the impact.

"Sir, can you see that? It looks like they're carrying something."

"Yeah, look at that ..."

"Look, they're pushing them over the lip of the crater."

"You sure that's not just more bugs?" asked the pilot.

"It's the crosses ... they're carrying the crosses," Kincaid exclaimed in disbelief. "Bravo, this is Alpha."

"Go ahead, Alpha."

"Can you see them down there? Looks like every fifth bug or so is carrying a mass of crosses. Why would they be taking them into the crater?"

"You got me, Kincaid."

"Follow us for a hot lap. Then we'll go into the crater and see if we can't get some footage through all this smoke."

"Roger. Hey Kincaid, look at that! Are those crosses, too?"

Kincaid looked below him to his right, into the crater itself. Sticklike crosses were piled like logs just inside the crater's lip. Bugs clambered over the black, pointed mounds, stacking more crosses on top of the already huge piles. "Yeah, looks like it. Look, just below the piles! What are those?"

"Wow, Stokeman, look at that!"

"What are those, skipper?"

"Looks like black grass …"

"Whatever it is, it's covered in bugs."

"Bravo … it looks like we're looking at an egg field, you see that?"

"Copy that, Alpha. I can see them all around the inner perimeter."

"Egg field?" The pilot was looking through his binoculars at the mass of tightly packed black tubes. "Shit, you can see 'em. They're laying eggs."

"Alpha, Bravo. What do you want to do?"

"We get our intel, and we get out. This is not a fire mission. We'll set down near the egg fields if we have too."

The pilot craned his neck to look back at Kincaid. "There aren't any places on that ridge, sir. There's nowhere to set down."

"Let's finish the perimeter sweep and split the center, then we'll worry about where to land."

"Yes sir."

"Give me those binoculars, would ya? I want to have a look for the Meteorite."

"There's a trail of smoke coming from dead center, sir. But I can't see Eddie."

"We've just about completed our circle; do you want to go in?"

"Yeah, dip down low. I wanna have a good look."

The copter made a hard right and descended into the crater. The pilot weaved through the columns of smoke rising from the crater's floor. There were fewer bugs crawling around the funneled shape of the crater's basin, but Kincaid could make out a thin trail of them making their way to the epicenter. None of them carried the crosses now.

The copilot squinted into the darkness. "I can't see anything in the middle, sir. Looks like Eddie either went subterranean on us or exploded on impact."

"Why are they converging on the site?" Kincaid wondered aloud as he gazed at the barren epicenter. "I was told to expect something at the epicenter. They said the alien vessel was extremely dense."

"Alien vessel? I guess I never thought of it like that. I figured it was more like a meteor than a spaceship." The copilot rubbed his eyes and checked his controls.

"Maybe it was covered up by all the falling debris," said the Pilot.

"That's a good guess."

"We're just about over the center of it now," said the copilot. The center of the crater was covered in a smooth layer of ash.

"Either of you see any bugs down there?"

"No sir."

"None."

"But we saw bugs coming down the slope, right? Where did they all go?"

"Alpha, Bravo. No sign of Eddie. Must be covered over."

"Bravo, any sign of ETs near the epicenter?"

"No. Not from where I'm sitting."

"You think they're going underground?"

"Could be. I saw a trail of bugs coming down to the center on our way down."

"All right, good enough for me. Follow us back to the crest: we'll find an egg field and get our samples there. Let's see if we can't get our hands on some of those eggs, Pete."

"Copy that. We'll follow your lead. Bravo out."

"Locate a spot on the interior side of the crater where we can land. Make it as close as possible to one of those egg fields."

"I'll have a look, but it's pretty steep on this side."

"I want to be below the fields, if we can. I want to use the blades from your ship like an umbrella if any of those things start jumping at us. We'll take cover positions right below the ship. Position the minigun facing downhill to cover our rear."

"I'll try, sir."

"Have the Little Birds fly close cover with the miniguns. I want them on a close circle over the egg field we choose."

"Yes sir. Champ-Two, this is Ringo. We're headed to the summit. We want to find an LZ on the interior, repeat, interior. You and Champ-One are flying close cover on a target of our choosing. Stand by for location."

Kincaid left the pilot to rejoin his team in the back. "Captain, we're done with the recon, get your men ready for phase two."

"Yes sir. Okay guys, let's switch gears. Cover team with me. Capture team on Kincaid. Load your weapons if you haven't already."

"We're going to land near a site which I believe is an egg field. We will land down slope, as close as possible. Captain, have your cover team set up fire support from right below the ship. The blades of the helicopter will provide air cover for you if these things start jumping at us. All close support units will carry shotguns. I want you right behind the guys collecting specimens.

Collection teams, you'll be split into two teams. Team one will be led by me. We'll go after bugs. Team two will be led by you, Mr. Jamison. I want you to go after the eggs."

"Yes sir! You mean the wavy black tubes, sir?"

"Yeah, they're packed close together and crawling with bugs. I don't imagine they'll be very happy to have you screwing with them, so be careful. Cut them at the base if you can. Get as many as you can. Do you have a machete or something?"

"Yes sir."

"Put them in the bug crates. Have the foam with you, lay down a blanket over the eggs if you have to, but leave some to collect."

"Yes sir. Thank you, sir."

"Team one, we'll be working on Sergeant Jamison's flank. We'll interlock our cover fire with theirs and collect bugs from the egg field."

"Kincaid, the pilot is calling you up front."

"All right, guys, get your shit together—we're about to stir up a real hornet's nest down there." Kincaid made his way up front; the helicopter was hovering inside the rim of the giant crater.

"I've got a possible LZ down there below that big egg field. It's a little dodgy, but it's flat. We'll only be able to fit one bird down there."

"Good job. We're good and close. Have Whiskey-One find their own LZ." Kincaid pulled the radio to his face. "Bravo, Alpha. We've found our spot, but it's not big enough for the two of us. Take your cover ship and find your own LZ."

"Copy that, Alpha. I think I can see a good LZ to your left."

"We're heading in."

"Good hunting!"

"Alpha out." Kincaid pulled the tobacco from his lip and threw it out the open door behind him. "Have Champ One fly close cover over that field. Once they're in place, take us in."

"Yes sir."

All fatigue left Kincaid's body as his heart began pumping with enthusiasm and fear. He was about to confront an alien life-form for the first time. After years of waiting, it was his time—but instead of being an alien ambassador, he would be locked in combat with this unknown foe. Whatever the case, he was ready.

"Okay, guys, we're going in. Cover teams out first. Collection team after me." Kincaid strode over and gripped the shoulder of the gunner manning the thirty-cal. "Watch our backs. Most of the bugs will be on the other side of the ship, but I want your eyes down that slope. Do ya hear me?"

"Yes sir!"

The copter made its descent to the landing zone while the Little Bird circled in front of them. Kincaid made his way to the open door, his eyes narrowed on the sprawling egg field lining the crater's lip. The black tubes clung to the slope and rippled with movement as the alien beetles crawled through them. Kincaid's eyes drifted to the perimeter, where a massive beetle stood tall on its hind legs and aimed its rear into the air. As the tube began to emerge, the beetle thrust its back into the slope, pinning the beginnings of the tube to the rock.

The alien bugs and their egg tubes were barely contrasted against the complete blackness of the crater, making them difficult to hold in focus. There were countless swarms of them cresting the crater's lip every second. Some fought the rotor wash and clung to the rocky slope, while others leaped away, disappearing in an instant. Kincaid noticed that the bugs near the egg fields didn't flee. He picked his spot, knowing that his odds were better among the eggs.

"Down in three, two, one ..." The captain called time from the door. "We're down! Move ... Move ... Move!"

"Collection teams follow me." Kincaid leaped from the Black Hawk, his knees and back reminding him of his age as he hit the ground.

Most of the men were out in seconds. The cover team took up positions under the canopy created by the spinning rotors overhead, and Kincaid and the collection teams shot past them toward the egg field ten meters up the slope. The ground was loose, rocky dirt, and Kincaid slipped as he scrambled up the slope. None of the bugs had taken any notice of their approach, and only a few seemed bothered by the winds generated from the rotor wash.

Kincaid scanned for targets as he and the others hurried up the slope. All the bugs seemed to be concentrated on the egg field and the two raised mounds behind it. A massive pile of black crosses filled the space above the nest. Bugs streamed over the pile and disappeared into the mound of earth. None of them moved to defend themselves.

Sergeant Jamison and his men were the first to reach the outskirts of egg field. He glanced back at Kincaid, who was still struggling up the slope, and then turned to shout an order to his team. Kincaid saw the eruption of sticky foam shoot from a nozzle held by one of the SEALs to Jamison's left. The soldier laid a blanket of foam over a cluster of black tubes. As Kincaid drew closer, he could see bugs trapped in the foam only meters from Jamison and his men. For an instant he imagined that their task might be easier than he had thought.

Jamison drew his machete and bent low, tentatively grabbing the closest stock of an egg tube and beginning to hack away at its base. As soon as his first strike was delivered, a shotgun blast rang out from behind him, followed quickly by another. Jamison glanced up with fright.

Kincaid's Team was already taking up positions on Jamison's right flank. The cover men immediately opened up with their shotguns. Kincaid was only a meter from the nest when he spotted a bug frozen in the act of laying an egg and trapped by a sticky thread of foam: he had found his first specimen.

Shotgun blasts popped off at increasing intervals as Kincaid scrambled up to his men at the edge of the nest. He took a second to catch his breath, scanning the area. The cover men were doing their job, blasting away at anything that moved in the egg field. Jamison had his back to Kincaid and was still stooped over a tube—Kincaid couldn't tell if he was having much success or not. His collection team was proceeding into the egg field with their nets, and the men seemed to move with confidence.

Kincaid readied the net in his hand and circled toward his trapped egg layer. Hundreds of bugs moved in the background, but none of them made a move toward him or his men. As he extended the telescoping net, the movement of a beetle caught his eye. Kincaid pulled his shotgun into his shoulder, aimed, and pulled the trigger. The shot rang in his ears, and the bug disappeared with a clump of earth. His shot had lacerated some of the tubes, and in the next instant three more beetles appeared from their base. They darted out with incredible speed. Their legs were invisible beneath them as they moved. Kincaid couldn't track them with his weapon, and he nearly dropped the net.

He fired three times and chambered another round, not sure if he had hit anything. More bugs moved among the tubes near him, but they didn't close on him. He shouldered his weapon and readied both hands on the net. He extended the Kevlar net over the trapped bug. The beetle shifted to face him and struck out with its long, pointed arms. Kincaid was about to bring down the net when the bug began a tremendous shuddering, clicking its miniature armored plates with the speed of an engine. He paused, taking in the strange display, when shouts rang out from behind him.

"Spiders! Fuck, get them off of me!"

"Spiders! They're everywhere!"

Kincaid looked up to see some of the men backing away from the perimeter. The cover men had shifted their fire to the ground at their feet. Jamison was frantically brushing off his fatigues with both hands; his weapon and machete were abandoned on the ground at his feet. "Get them off of me!" Kincaid could see him pulling at something on his face. It was too small to be one of the bugs.

"Spiders!"

Now he saw what they were shouting about. The nest and the slope behind the men was alive with ash gray spiders. They scurried out from the egg field all around them. They moved lightning fast, far faster than any Earth spider, but they were the size of the largest tarantulas. Their perfectly round bodies were about four inches across. Suddenly they were everywhere. Kincaid froze with surprise; he hadn't heard anything about spiders.

Gunfire jolted him back into action, and he slammed the net down on his bug. He pulled at the net, trying to rip it from the trail of foam, but the bug seemed to pull against him. Men screamed behind him. Blood streaked across Jamison's face. Men were trying to swat the spiders from his back.

"I've got one! I got one!" One of Kincaid's team waved wildly at him. "I got it in the net!"

Kincaid dug his boots into the soil and jerked back on his pole. "Get it back to the ship!" The bug held fast. "Someone get one of those tubes in a box!"

A flurry of shots rang out from the helicopter below them. Kincaid's eyes followed the SEAL retreating with a captured bug. The ground behind him was erupting with shot. The heavy-caliber weapons were blasting away at the slope. Kincaid realized with horror that the rest of the bugs were now keenly aware of their presence. They were flowing down the slope toward the copter. They crawled over the egg field from all directions. Cover fire increased behind him, and the men were falling back.

"I got one!" It was one of Jamison's team. "It just landed on my chest! Help me get it into the net!"

"Grenades! Fire in the hole!" Everybody crouched as two grenades exploded on the far side of the nest.

Men began screaming all around him. Big black bugs and hundreds of grayish spiders swarmed in front of him. He knew they were moments away from being overrun. Kincaid pulled his knife from his boot and began slicing away at the foam stuck to his bug. Claws tore at him through the net but were held at bay by the Kevlar. He pulled at the foam, sawing with his blade, and a gray blur ran over his hand. It stopped at his elbow before he could move and was immediately followed by another. Kincaid pulled away, jerking the net free.

Pain bit into him as the creatures ripped away at the flesh on his arms. He frantically brushed at the spiders, but they remained locked onto his fatigues.

One of the men was screaming behind him. "Sanchez is down! Get over there!"

Kincaid slid away from the nest, pulling his net behind him as he grabbed at the spiders with his free hand. Sergeant Sanchez rolled in the dirt next to him. He was writhing in agony. A beetle had clamped onto him behind his knee while he tore away at another on his neck. Other bugs were closing in on him fast. Shotgun blasts erupted all around him.

"Grab him! Get back to the choppers!" Kincaid yelled to the men still working the perimeter of the nest. A black sea of bugs swirled behind the men.

Two men rushed to Sanchez's side and began pulling him by his gear. One of the men grabbed at a bug on his back only to have it clamp down on his hand. The man screamed and tried in vain to shake the creature loose. Another bug leaped onto his neck, and bright blood streaked across his face. More beetles appeared from thin air and attacked the soldiers scrambling down the slope to the copter.

"Back to the Bird!" Men fell back as fast as they could, pumping rounds into the swarming mass as they retreated. The slope behind them was alive with bugs. A soldier with a semiautomatic shotgun cleared a path for the men bolting back to the ship.

Sergeant Jamison lay prone in the dirt, not moving. Spiders crawled all over him. The black domes of the larger bugs enveloped him. Kincaid watched in horror as Sergeant Sanchez's leg was ripped away at the knee by one of the giant beetles. The man dragging him was knocked away by a leaping bug. Kincaid counted three men down near the nest. It was too late for them. They were nearly overrun. His team had stopped firing and was now making a hell-bent run for the copter.

Kincaid turned to run down the slope, folding the captured bug under his arm. His shotgun flopped uselessly across his back. He sprinted the distance back to the copter as fast as he could. His chest burned and his ears rang with the sound of fire erupting from the ship. Every weapon spat fire toward the slope. Intense pain gripped his arm and blood ran down his hands.

Sparks bounced from the props of the helicopter as he approached. Black streaks filled the air like thousands of angry darts. Another man fell on his way to the chopper; he slid face-first down the slope, with two bugs digging at his back and another gripping his leg as he slid. A man from the copter rushed out to assist him, and the men shifted their fire to cover him. A bug flew past Kincaid's face, slicing him across the cheek.

"Have you got your sample, sir?" The captain waved him into the belly of the ship.

Kincaid grunted and motioned to the net under his arm.

"We've got two more inside!"

"Let's go! Quick!"

"What about the others?" The captain shouted, pointing to the men beyond the cover of the ship.

"You've got three down … they're dead. We've gotta go!"

The young captain blinked and nodded. "Okay." He turned to his men. "Fall back! We're bugging out! Right now! Everybody!"

The last of the cover men waited outside for the last of the wounded collection team to be pulled to safety. A vibrating and shuddering bug still clung to the man's boot.

Three men lay beyond the protection of the guns. The beetles swarmed them. The Little Bird helicopter hovered over the body of Jamison, who had fallen near the perimeter of egg nest and had not gotten up. The Little Bird's twin miniguns poured a torrent of lead onto the egg field. Glowing brass shell casings rained down on Jamison's lifeless body.

The last man was pulled into the copter as it was lifting into the air. Men still fired from the ship, and bugs continued to bounce off the walls of the Black Hawk. Loud smacks could be heard overhead as they were torn apart by the rotor blades. The thirty-cal opened up behind them as the Black Hawk headed for the open sky.

"Who's missing?" shouted the captain.

"Jamison, Sanchez, and Douglass, sir."

"Chemo's got one on his leg—get it off him!"

"Gimme a crate over here!"

"Grab it! Grab it! It's gonna rip off my foot!"

"Get those fucking spiders! Stomp 'em!"

Kincaid was shoving his captive into a crate, trying to ignore the spider crawling up his elbow toward his face. He slammed the door of the crate closed and grabbed at the spider with the Kevlar net. "Catch 'em if you can! Put them in the nets!" He yelled to the others. "Did anybody get any of the tubes?" Kincaid assessed the situation in the belly of the Black Hawk. Two men were down; three others were on top of them snatching at a couple of loose bugs. The other men were firing their weapons at the ground with vengeance.

"Jamison …" The captain pointed to where Jamison lay near the nest. His body was being dragged away by a mass of bugs.

"Kincaid! Look!" The captain pointed through the open door. The second helicopter was rocking unsteadily over its landing zone, hovering just feet above the ground where Bravo's team had landed. Men were retreating to it as fast as they could, fire support was pouring from the open door, and sparks of light were leaping from the spinning rotors. Swarms of black dots enveloped the slope.

A handful of men had gone down just in front of the hovering chopper; their bodies were covered in hideous wounds. The chopper rocked sideways and spun around slightly. Smoke and flame shot out of the cockpit, and the copter dipped down on one side. The rotors slapped against the slope, and in an instant the top the air ship disintegrated, propelling the broken body of the craft down the slope with bodies flying out the open doors.

"Holy shit! They're down!"

"Champ Two is down!"

The second Little Bird support ship fired a volley of missiles into the swarm of bugs while the Black Hawk tumbled helplessly underneath it.

"Kincaid! Pilot needs you up front! Wants to know if we're going for a rescue!" The captain screamed over the volley of exploding missiles.

Kincaid knew no one could have survived in the still-tumbling body of the Black Hawk, and his surviving crew was in no condition to effect a rescue. Most of them were still wrestling with bugs on the deck. Shock was clear on every one of their faces. "Call in Whiskey. We're getting out of here!"

Paradigm II
Chapter 9

Boca Raton, Florida. June 19, 2002

A blood-curdling scream tore Nathan from sleep. A woman was wailing outside his bedroom window. She sounded like the siren on a fire truck, stopping and starting again. His room was completely dark. Nathan began sobbing into his pillow, too afraid to cry out. His blue Power Ranger nightlight didn't work anymore, and the space between the door and his bed was dark. His light didn't work anymore because his house had lost its power days ago. Nathan couldn't understand how or why his house could lose anything, but he was afraid of the dark, and the woman outside was screaming her head off.

Nathan clutched his sheets. Something really bad was happening out there. He could hear all kinds of noise now. A very angry man was shouting. Nathan cried out for his mother. He couldn't see Zachary. He couldn't see anything. His room was too dark. Nathan yelled for his mother again. Tears were making his face wet. He wondered why he couldn't hear his mother's footsteps stomping down the hall. His six-year-old mind raced with terrible thoughts, and his cries remained unanswered. "Mommy!"

"Shut up, Nathan! You're scaring me!" Nathan's older brother Zachary shined his tiny flashlight in his face from across the dark room. "Mom! *Mom*! Nathan's crying!"

Nathan gagged on his tears and rubbed his eyes. "Where did you get that? Dad said he needed all the flashlights." Zachary moved his light to the door but there were no footsteps charging down the hall.

"It's mine! Why are you crying? Where's Mom?"

"Mommy!" Nathan called out again as loud as he could. Even more people seemed to be yelling outside.

"Dad!" Zachary yelled. Nathan could tell he was crying, too, and that scared him even more.

Dogs were barking and car horns blared outside. Both boys screamed for their parents, but Nathan couldn't hear them. Finally, their door opened, letting in the dim light from a candle. Their mother silently slipped into the bedroom.

"Its okay, sweethearts … don't be afraid of all the noise. Everything is going to be okay." His mother moved slowly, balancing the candle's flame in front of her. He could barely see her face. She hadn't rushed into the room like he'd expected. She didn't seem to hear the woman screaming outside.

"What's happening, Mom?" Zachary shrieked at her, beaming his light into her face. Her eyes were red, as if she'd been crying.

Nathan's jaw shook, and he started to really cry. "I can hear screaming … and you … and you didn't come … and it's dark … and Zachary has a flashlight, and I don't!"

"Come here, boys, sit down with me. We don't have to be loud." Nathan's mother lowered herself slowly to the floor. She looked graceful in the candlelight, like a fairy from one of his stories. She spoke softly. Her voice was sad. "It's okay. Stop crying, honey. Come sit with Mommy."

Nathan threw back his covers and took quick little steps to sit in his mother's lap.

Zachary shined his light out the window. "What's going on, Mom? Was there another meteorite?"

"Come here, honey, I've got room for both of you."

"I'm scared, Mommy!" Nathan hid his face in her chest.

"I know, sweetheart. It's okay. Let's read a book together. Come here, Zachary, sit down with me, baby." She opened her arms to her older son and waved him closer. "Look, I brought a book for us to read. It's your Bible stories. Come on, Nathan, you pick one. What's your favorite?"

Nathan looked at the book in her hands. It wasn't *his* Bible stories. It was his Mommy's and Daddy's Bible with the fancy cover. "Ummm … I like Noah's ark."

"Mom, I don't like that one." Zachary rushed into his mother's arms. Zachary's knees knocked into his as he pushed his way into her lap. "I want the picture one."

She wrapped her arms around them both and squeezed tight. "It's the same, honey ... the stories are the same. Come on, you like this one." She turned to the beginning of the book, where the story of Noah began.

"I'm scared, Mommy." Zachary curled into a ball in her lap. "What's going on out there?"

"It'll be okay. We're gonna be okay."

Nathan could tell she was trying not to be scared, but her legs shook beneath him. "Where's Daddy?"

"He's coming." She almost cried. "He's coming." She peered back at the door behind her and looked worried. "Okay guys, settle down ... I'm going to start ..." She used Zachary's light to read the small words in her Bible.

"'Then the Lord saw that the wickedness of man was great in the earth, and that every intent of the thoughts of his heart was only evil continually. And the Lord was sorry that he had made man on the earth, and he was grieved in his heart.

"'So the Lord said: *I will destroy man whom I have created from the face of the earth, both man and beast, creeping things and birds of the air, for I am sorry that I have made them.*'"

"Mom, I don't think I want this one."

She squeezed him tight and continued in a rush of words. "'But Noah found grace in the eyes of the Lord.

"'Noah was a just man, perfect in his generations. Noah walked with God. And God said to Noah: *The end of all flesh has come before me, for the earth is filled with violence through them; and behold, I will destroy them with the earth.*'

"Don't be frightened; you know how it goes."

"'*Make yourself an ark of gopherwood; make rooms in the ark and cover it inside and outside with pitch.*'"

"What's gopherwood?" Nathan looked into her eyes, and Zachary laughed nervously.

"Sounds funny, huh? Listen up, my babies." She looked nervously to the door before she continued. "'*And behold, I myself am bringing floodwaters on the earth, to destroy from under heaven all flesh in which is the breath of life; everything that is on the earth shall die.*

"'*But I will establish my covenant with you; and you shall go into the ark, you, your sons, your wives, and your son's wives with you. And every living thing of all flesh you shall bring two of every sort into the ark, to keep them alive with you; they shall be male and female.*

"'Thus Noah did; according to all that God commanded him, so he did.'"

"What about the dinosaurs, Mom? Did he bring them, too?" Zachary was crazy about dinosaurs.

"I don't think so, honey. *'You shall take with you seven each of every clean animal, a male and his female; two each of animals that are unclean, a male and his female'*"

"What's a clean animal?"

"I don't know, honey … *'For after seven more days I will cause it to rain on the earth forty days and forty nights, and I will destroy from the face of the earth all living things that I have made.*

"'Noah was six hundred years old when the floodwaters were on the earth.'" She looked as if she were reading the words for the first time. "'And the waters prevailed exceedingly on the earth, and all the high hills under the whole heaven were covered.'" A rumble grew outside, and Nathan's mother covered his ears.

"'And all flesh died that moved on the earth; birds and cattle and beasts and every creeping thing that creeps on the earth, and every man. All in whose nostrils was the breath of the spirit of life, all that was on the dry land, died. And the waters prevailed on the earth one hundred and fifty days.

"'Then God remembered Noah, and every living thing, and all the animals that were with him in the ark. And God made a wind to pass over the earth, and the waters subsided.'"

"Are we gonna die, Mommy?" Nathan could feel the sound getting bigger in his stomach.

"Shut up, Nathan!" Zachary shouted.

"Don't worry, honey …" She looked to the door behind her; there was no sign of his father. More shouting erupted outside. Nathan heard screams, then gunshots, one after the other like in the movies—Bang … Bang … Bang! Bang! Bang!

"What was that?" Zachary screamed, and both boys dug deep into her lap.

"It's okay." She rocked them in her arms, her voice choked with tears. "It's okay, I'll just keep reading … don't worry about that." She held the Bible close to her face. "'So God blessed Noah and his sons, and said to them: *Be fruitful and multiply, and fill the earth.*

"'*And the fear of you and the dread of you shall be on every beast of the earth, on every bird of the air, an all that move on the earth, and on all the fish of the sea. They are given into your hand.*'"

Zachary began sobbing, too. "What's that sound? Mommy, what's that sound?"

She ignored him and kept on reading, saying the words faster and faster. "*Every moving thing that lives shall be food for you. I have given you all things, even the green herbs.*"

"What's that noise?"

Nathan thought he could hear a train outside, but there weren't any trains near his house.

"'*Thus I establish my covenant with you; never again shall all flesh be cut off by the waters of the flood; never again shall there be a flood to destroy the earth.*'" She burst into tears; her whole body began shaking. The rumbling noise grew and grew, rattling the windows.

"Mommy ... what's happening?"

"Is the power back on? I can see light."

"'And God said: *This is the sign of the covenant which I make between me and you, and every living creature that is with you, for perpetual generations. I set my rainbow in the cloud, and it shall be the sign of the covenant between me and the earth.*'" She folded the book closed and squeezed them. Nathan listened to the roar of the train. It grew and grew. His whole room shook.

"Is that a meteorite, Mommy?" Zachary questioned his mother frantically. "Mommy ..."

Sobbing, she reopened the Bible and continued to read. "'And Noah began to be a farmer, and he planted a vineyard. Then he drank of the wine and was drunk, and became uncovered in his tent ... 'Oh, I can't ...'"

"Mommy! I'm scared!"

"What's that noise? Are we going to die?"

"'And Noah lived after the flood three hundred and fifty years ...'" She could barely read because she was crying. "'So all the days of Noah were nine hundred and fifty years, and he died.'" She slammed the Bible closed with a groan.

Just then their father entered the room. He dropped his flashlight and slumped to his knees behind their mother. There was a gun in his hands and he was crying, too. Nathan had never seen him cry before.

"I can't do it!"

His mother turned with a shriek, hiding Nathan's face in her bosom.

"I can't do it ... I'm sorry! I love you, baby ... but I can't!" He sobbed real loud. The gun hung from a finger in his lap.

"Come here, Lover ... I love you, too ..." She reached for him, almost spilling Nathan from her lap.

The gun hitting the floor barely made a sound over the growing roar outside. A loud noise exploded over them with a terrible boom. His father jumped up, taking them in his arms.

Zachary screamed, and his mother pulled his face to hers and began kissing him, kissing him all over his face. "I love you ... I love you so much!"

Nathan's father pulled him into his lap and began kissing his face the same way. His face was wet with tears; his mustache tickled, and his breath smelled like booze. They were all crying. Even his Daddy was crying.

The noise hurt his ears. He couldn't hear anything else now. It looked like it was daytime outside. Bright light came through the window. The room was wasn't dark anymore, but he had never been more frightened than he was right now. His heart thumped in his chest. He cried so hard that it hurt him inside. His mother and father were squeezing the breath out of him.

The room shook as if it were going to fall apart. Then, all at once, the noise knocked them back. The window shattered, and everything in the room fell. Air rushed in, slamming the door behind them. His breath was sucked from his chest, and he couldn't hear anymore. Pain stabbed him everywhere.

They were all knocked flat by the house as it fell in on them. There was only blackness and pain. Nathan couldn't feel the arms of his parents around him anymore, only the crushing weight of his bedroom walls.

As quickly as at it had collapsed on him, the wall was lifted away by a ripping gust of wind. Nathan was carried into the air with his bedroom wall. He spun through the air, sharp whips lashing his body. He couldn't even scream. His arms and legs twisted and pulled. He flew through the air like a living piece of his house. Dark shapes swirled around him and then, in a blinding flash of searing light ... nothing.

Washington DC. June 20, 2002

A full hour passed, and still no one from his office showed. No one from the building had come to work this morning except for two confused-looking security officers. Bill tried the phone lines repeatedly without ever getting a dial tone. He knew there were people working at the White House, which was acting as a central hub for the different federal organizations, but he didn't have a car. After half a pack of smokes, he decided to walk the four miles to the Grand Mall.

His driver and most of his staff had disappeared into underground bunkers with Mrs. Thomas. She was the real congresswoman; he was really only her chief of staff. She and her family were safely tucked away, even though she knew nothing of the office. Bill refused to go underground. It didn't seem right. He didn't have a family, and there was so much work to do. If he was going to get anything done, he knew he had to get to the Capitol Building or the White House—and to do that, he realized that he was going to have to walk.

The streets were deserted, littered with abandoned cars. Washington was a ghost town. Everyone feared that an Atlantic impact would swamp the eastern seaboard, DC included. The immediate frenzy of looting had passed, and everybody waited for the next blow from whatever shelter they could find. It suddenly looked like a lonely and potentially dangerous four-mile walk.

Bill paused, about to ask the lone marine guarding the entrance if there was any possibility of finding a ride, when two men ran across the street toward him. One man carried a video camera over his shoulder and lagged behind the other man as they sprinted across the street.

"Hey—you're William Kemp! Congressman Kemp, can we talk for a moment?"

"Yeah, of course … but I'm not actually a congressman. I'm Congressman Thomas's chief of staff."

"But you're the guy … that Humanist guy, right?"

"Yeah, I'm that guy. What can I do for you?"

"You're the first recognizable face we've seen. Can we ask you a few questions?" The reporter readied his microphone and waited for his cameraman to take position.

"I'd be more than happy to talk to you guys. Do you have a broadcast signal?"

"We've got a signal going into some cities."

"What about power?"

"I don't know. Some places have got it, I suppose. I'm not really a reporter. I'm just an intern. I'm just trying to get any kind of story I can. Everyone is focused on Florida. The Capitol is empty."

"Is that your van over there?"

"Yeah."

"Does it have any gas?"

"Yeah, we've got plenty."

"I'll tell you what; you give me a ride down to the Capitol Building, and I'll give you an exclusive."

"You got it! Larry, get the van."

Bill surveyed the emptiness around him before climbing into the front seat of the van. It had been ten hours since Ida had struck Florida. If there was going to be another impact, it could happen at any moment. Nine asteroids had crashed into Earth in the last week. No one knew if there was going to be a tenth. He thought he might have made a big mistake staying in Washington, but he was going to do what the president and everybody else had screamed for him to do: he was going to work.

"So why are you here? Where is everybody else?"

"Most of the congressional staff has been sequestered in bunkers. Congress operates from there now, but communication is difficult."

"Where?"

"Can't say."

"Can't?"

"Can't ... won't ... whatever." Bill lit a smoke and stared out the window.

"And you say you're not a congressman; you're chief of staff for Gilbert Thomas's widow?"

"That's right.

"But you're the one we see on TV."

"I have been trying to carry on where Gilbert left off. He was instrumental in founding the Humanist Party."

"What can you tell us about the aliens? Do you have any insight into what the Feds are saying?"

"I can only tell you what's been reported already ... what the president has told us. The asteroids are carrying some kind of life form with them. I can only imagine that they're in Florida now."

"What about further impacts? Do you have any idea if they've spotted any more out there?"

"I'm not tapped into that kind of information, but if you ask me ... I think we've seen the last of them." Bill blew out a stream of smoke and gave the reporter his most practiced smile.

"What? How can you say that? They might never stop!"

"What's your name, kid?" Bill took a long, reflective pull on his cigarette.

"Cal. My real name is Pascal."

"Pascal, really?" Bill huffed. "Do you know who you're named after?"

"My grandmother told me he was some kind of saint or something. But I'm not religious. I'm like you. I don't believe in God. Especially now."

"Well Pascal was famous for more than his sainthood. He was famous for making a wager." Bill inhaled deeply and leaned back to stare at Pascal sitting in the back.

"He was a real smart fella. He spent most of his life asking himself if God really existed. His faith was shaken, and he ultimately he decided it was impossible to say for sure one way or the other. But he figured that it was best to place your faith in God—just in case. What have you got to lose when your immortal soul hangs in the balance?" Bill could read the confusion on the young intern's face.

"That's why I'm betting we've seen the last of the asteroids. If I'm wrong, we're dead anyway. But if I'm right, we still have a chance. If we do nothing but cower in fear, we're all dead. I'm putting my money on humanity. We can survive if we stick together."

The young man smiled over his notepad. "Can I quote you on that?"

"Sure." Bill caustically blew a mouthful of smoke through the window. "You can call it Kemp's wager."

"Look, I'm just not convinced! This could be any number of things … dark matter … debris … bad exposure! It's nothing! I can't go to the president with this!" Dr. Wingaurd was beyond agitation; he was feeling belligerent with fatigue and stress. His eyes blurred as he stared at the blown-up photograph. He needed a candy bar.

"It's the only thing we've got!" Dillon, his junior partner, pleaded with him, pushing the photograph back at him.

"My point exactly! That's all you have! Nothing! A missing star so remote you can't always see it anyway. Never mind that the atmosphere is so saturated with debris that we can barely see the stars in our own system! I can't raise the alarm because of this!" Dr. Wingaurd tossed the photograph to his desk and rose from his chair. He jammed his pudgy hands into his pockets and rummaged around for change.

"But you can see the stars around it clear as day! Some are even farther from OR247. Look, OR247 is right there in this shot, and again in that one. It's only missing on this single frame. How much proof do you need?" Tim recognized the desperation on his friend's face. They both know how important spotting one of these things could be.

"Dillon, I see what you mean. It's good deductive reasoning, and I personally find it very compelling evidence, but it doesn't stand alone. If there were more time, we could run the necessary computations to confirm it, but we don't have that kind of time. You're asking me to run to the president and tell him that I believe there's another asteroid—*vessel* on the way. Me! His top astronomical advisor! I can't go to him and say, 'I think,' or 'there is a very remote possibility that …'"

"Why not? If there's even the slightest chance, don't you think he should know about it?"

"No! What's he going to do about it anyway? He's got his hands full already. We're under an alien invasion, Dillon! The whole world is going to shit. The president should stay focused on things within his control! Do you have any change for a candy bar or something? I need some sugar."

"I'm sure the food is free here, Tim. It's the central command for the entire government now."

"Oh, yeah. It's easy to forget where you are down here. Looks like every other office I've ever worked in."

"Not to me. This place gives me the creeps. It's weird to think that the military can build a place like this, and nobody knows about it. I mean, this place must have cost billions."

"I know. They dump billions into underground bunkers, and yet they can't spare a few hundred million on the technology that could have spared us all of this."

"How have they been able to keep it secret? Not just the money, but building a place like this."

"We're in the middle of nowhere. Not many people live in this part of the Blue Ridge Mountains, and they built it right under a huge granite quarry. It's the perfect cover; trucks can come in with building material and leave with the excavation leftovers. There's nothing unusual about trucks going in and out of a quarry. Let's go get a bite to eat. Come on, I'm buying."

"Tim, stop. This is serious. We *are* under alien invasion, so you have to think like one of these military guys for a moment, not like a scientist. If I were one of those generals out there, I would want every bit of information possible. No matter how … ambiguous. Let *them* make the decision on what to do with it. That's their job. Our job is to look for incoming alien space vessels. We're not asteroid hunters anymore. We're lookouts, and we've seen something."

"But even if we *have* found something, we can't say where it was, or which way it was headed. We can't tell them anything, and they're going to ask questions."

"You can only tell them what the guys in Arizona have shown us. So what if you don't have the answers? If this *is* another vessel, we've answered the big question: 'is there another one coming?' That's all we can do, but we have to do that."

"But …"

"But, if we're wrong, and Ida was the last one, who cares? Everyone will be happy that is *was* the last one."

"But we've looked ahead into Earth's trajectory, and we can't see anything. OR247 is almost in another grid …"

"Arizona's cameras took the shots at 0245 hours. It's possible … well, that whatever blocked our view of OR247 was moving into our trajectory from this way." Dillon traced his finger along the photo.

"Moving in an entirely different direction before it entered our path?"

"Why not? It's a spaceship, not an asteroid—right?"

"Let me see that." Dr. Wingaurd placed a grid over the photo and squinted at the measurements.

"We need to tell the president," Dillon said.

"We need to tell the president," Tim repeated somberly. "Okay, call Operational Command. Tell them I'm coming down with a priority one briefing. Get ahold of that adjutant general ... What's his name ...?"

"Parker."

"Right, tell General Parker that I need to brief the president."

"Better get one of those marines to guide you down there."

"Good idea. Do me another favor, will ya? Meet me down there with some food. And some coffee. Doughnuts too, if you can find them." Dr. Wingaurd smoothed his receding hair back over his head and hastily tucked his shirt into his pants.

"What about the photos ... don't you want to take the charts?"

"The charts don't show anything. I'm going to him with a hunch—that's all we have."

"All right, Tim. I'll try and catch you down there. Good luck."

"Don't forget the doughnuts; my stomach is doing summersaults."

Dr. Wingaurd met with the marine captain stationed outside his office and informed him that he needed an immediate escort to Central Command. The young captain struggled to keep quiet as he guided the doctor through the maze of offices. It was plain on his face that he was dying to ask the big question, and he wasn't the only one. As they marched past the countless other military personnel and civilian advisors, all heads turned to watch them. Tim could hear them questioning each other as they passed. *More, were there going to be more?* He felt like the Grim Reaper floating down the corridor.

As they made their way down the elevator, Dr. Wingaurd fought off the fatigue and hunger and tried to collect his thoughts. This could be the biggest meeting in his life, and he felt woefully unprepared. He was about to address the president during the biggest crisis in the history of humanity, and all he had to go on was a hunch.

The elevator doors opened, and he was met by an air force colonel wearing a communications headset. "Dr. Wingaurd, General Parker has been informed that you're coming down; he will be here soon. I have orders to take you to the Situation Staging room."

"Very good. I need to meet with the president as soon as possible."

"Yes sir. As you can see, there's a lot going on right now." The air force colonel led him through the crowded passageway leading into the central bunker. Soldiers armed with automatic weapons were station at every doorway and every corner. "Right now the president is in the War Room with his cabinet. I'm not sure when he will be free. General Parker would like to know what you want to brief the president about."

"I'm not quite sure of what kind of protocol we're dealing with, Colonel. I was told to confer with the general's staff or the president himself."

"Everyone down here has priority one security clearance. Maybe if you just tell me the subject matter, I can inform General Parker and he can determine the order in which you are seen."

"I'm afraid I must be seen right away ... time is critical."

The colonel opened a door marked SIT/STA and ushered him in. The room was packed with military advisors and command staff, all wearing full military dress. Every chair in the large conference room was taken, and there were several men standing around quietly clutching attaché cases.

"As you can see, there are several departments cued up to brief Command. If you could give me an idea what you need to speak with the president about, we can establish an order of importance for you.

"We think there is a possibility—a probability—that more impacts are likely."

"Another asteroid?"

"Another alien vessel, Colonel."

"Do you have a projected timeline?"

"No."

"You have a visual confirmation?"

"No."

"But you think there is a likelihood of another impact?"

"No, but there is a potential."

"But you can't say when this may happen?"

"No, no I can't. But all of the other impacts have occurred between eight and nineteen hours apart. Ida stuck Florida over twelve hours ago ... all things considered, if there were going to be another impact, it would happen sometime within the next eight hours."

"I see. Is it your intention to suggest that we will be hit again today?"

"My intention is to inform the president that there is a possibility of more impacts. Unfortunately, we lack the time and physical evidence to make definitive projections."

"Other than the history of the previous impacts, what leads you to believe that another impact is immanent?"

"One of our telescopes in Arizona has discovered an anomaly that *may* be one of these vessels moving through space. It isn't much to go on, but I feel it's important enough to alert the president. What he chooses to do with the information is up to him. Unfortunately it's all I have to work with right now. Any kind of computer projection of this sort would take hours of supercomputer time. Of course, we don't have anywhere near that kind of time." Dr. Wingaurd fought the urge to use the phrase "guesswork."

"Was this anomaly seen in Earth's orbit, in its immediate trajectory?"

"No. We've scanned Earth's path the best we can and haven't seen anything. But that doesn't mean much, I'm afraid. These vessels are virtually invisible until they enter our stratosphere. But ... again, we are dealing with a complete unknown. It's possible that these vessels are moving in a different vector before entering our path. They have to come from somewhere, and it's possible that we've spotted one on its way to our orbit around the sun."

"I see. Okay, Dr. Wingaurd, I will report to General Parker. He may want to speak with you while the president is conferring with his cabinet. For now, you can wait here."

"Can't you interrupt the meeting? This information may affect their planning."

"I can't interrupt them now, but General Parker is in direct communication with the command staff. He will act as your liaison. If he feels that your report needs to be heard right away, he can make it happen."

"Very well, I'll wait to hear from him. Is there any food in here?"

"You can requisition some food through the Captain Vandemberg over there. There's a kitchen close by."

"I just need a candy bar and a soda."

"Are you a diabetic, sir?"

"No, just a chocoholic, I'm afraid." Tim patted his protruding belly with a forced smile."

"Captain Vandemberg will take care of you, sir. I'll return with General Parker in a few minutes."

"Thank you." As the air force colonel left the conference room, Dr. Wingaurd approached the young marine captain and quietly asked for a Snickers bar and a Coke.

"Excuse me, sir, but do you really think that there will be another impact?"

Tim turned to face an army general in full dress uniform; four gold stars adorned his lapel. He was one of a handful of men who didn't have a seat to wait in. He was a bright-eyed older man who stood tall with his ribbon-covered chest thrust outward. There was a briefcase chained to his wrist.

"I'm sorry: I couldn't help but overhear your conversation with the intel officer back there. You are one of the aerospace advisors?"

"No, I'm an astronomer."

"You have evidence of another alien vessel?" There was no hesitation on the part of the general. His bushy gray eyebrows arched, highlighting the intensity of his ice-blue eyes.

"Well ..."

"You'll have to excuse my bluntness, Dr ..." The general extended his unchained hand to him.

"Wingaurd, Tim Wingaurd."

"General Simon, North American Aerospace Command." The general pointed to a crimson and blue ribbon on his chest, which meant absolutely nothing to Tim. "Doctor, if you have discovered anything, anything at all, the sooner we know about it the better. You can speak freely here, I assure you. Do you have *any* evidence of an incoming vessel?

"You work for NORAD." Tim suddenly remembered what the North American Aerospace Command was responsible for. Tim looked down at the briefcase chained to the general's wrist and realized that it probably contained the launching codes for the country's nuclear arsenal.

"Excuse me, but did you say that you have actually seen something?" an air force general wearing immaculate dress blues asked from his seat against the wall. Tim realized that all eyes were on him.

His stomached growled and turned over on itself in a disquieting fashion. "Not really ... it's more correct to say that we didn't see something; a distant star, OR247, *disappeared.* That is to say, we think that something was blocking our view of it for a brief moment."

"Like an eclipse?" asked yet another finely dressed military man standing close by.

"Yes, just like an eclipse, but of a star hundreds of light-years away. OR247 is a mere pinprick of light in the Milky Way, but for an instant something passed between it and us ... we think."

"But it's your intention to brief the president that we can expect another impact?" The NORAD general issued his question, silencing all other chatter behind him.

"I only want to inform him that it's possible. And in light of the pattern of events thus far, I would even say that it is probable."

"Just how many of these things were we able to spot before they hit us?" asked General Simon.

"If you remember, we spotted the second one in a similar fashion—when it passed between us and the moon. We were able to get a good look at that one, but there was no time to raise an alarm. We didn't really know what we were looking at until after it struck the Pacific. The sixth one, Frank, arrived at night. We were able to see it telescopically a couple of hours before impact. And, of course, we spotted Ida very early on; it was visible for a moment as it passed in front of Mars."

"But they come in so slowly … if we employ counter measures beforehand, we might have a shot at knocking them off course, right?" A younger, less decorated military aid stood from his seat.

"From what I gather, they haven't seen anything in our trajectory. Is that right, Dr. Wingaurd?"

"That's correct … but if you're talking about intercepting one of these ships or vessels—whatever you want to call them—and blowing it off course with nukes, it will never work. Not with the present timeline. You have to understand that once we've seen one of these things in our upper stratosphere, for all intents and purposes it has already hit us. You won't be able to knock anything out of Earth's gravitational pull once it gets that close."

"We still have our eyes up there, Doctor. Not all of the satellites have been disrupted. We have a few high-powered telescopes of our own, many of which I'm sure you guys at NEAT have never heard about. And I can assure you that they're all directed ahead of us, for now. If there is a possibility for more impacts, we need to keep them focused ahead." The steely-eyed general addressed the entire room as he spoke. "There are some who think it's time to point them back to Earth. They're getting nervous because they can't see what's going on. What we need is a way to find these things before they get too close. If we need to shift our attention to another part of space, we can do it. Lord knows we haven't seen anything where we've been looking."

"Well, that's just it really. If there is even a possibility that our minuscule information proves to be correct, it's because they're doing something entirely unexpected. If the shadow we saw over OR247 does in fact enter our celestial orbit, it would have had to make a radical change in direction. It defies everything we know about astral physics, but knowing what we know now … anything is possible."

"We can't turn to defend ourselves on the ground when we're still vulnerable from above. There may be hundreds of them lining up to bombard us. We need to knock as many out of the sky as we can."

"You heard the doctor; it's impossible." A green-clad army general stood to debate the air force general.

"It will certainly be impossible if we turn our cameras around and stop looking!" General Simon shot back angrily.

"Think about it tactically. After studying the dispersal pattern in Africa, we calculated that each ship can disperse over a billion troops—um, I mean, bugs." All of the general staff and their aids joined the debate.

"A billion? That's a guess! I've got dispersal reports of one hundred bugs per ten meters squared."

"Over how long?"

"Most of them landed in the Indian Ocean, so the main body of that invasion drowned."

"Excuse me: we don't know that they drown."

"They drown, all right! I've seen the tests."

"They all die in captivity! You can't say they drown; we don't know how they breathe, or if they breathe at all."

"Well Doctor, you've started a pretty lively debate. They were all pretty quiet before you came along."

"Me! You were the one ..."

"Come here, I still have a few questions." The general pulled him into the corner by his elbow. "Do you need more computer time?"

"Do you have a supercomputer available?"

"I can make some time. I'll have my man take you upstairs when you're done with the president."

"The computer is here?"

"Three of them. All Strategic Operations are run through here now."

"Even NORAD?"

"Yes, even NORAD. This is a Specialized Central Command Station, it was designed for ... well, the worst case scenario."

"I figured the president would've bunkered somewhere safer, like NORAD's facility in the Cheyenne Mountains. It was designed for impacts the size we are experiencing. It was designed to take a direct strike; this place is nowhere near that deep."

"This facility is more secure than you think. But you're right; it was never intended to defend against nuclear weapons—or alien asteroids. It's primary objective is command continuity during an event. Its focus has always been secrecy. Trucks have been rolling out of that quarry above us for over fifty years, yet this base remains a secret known only at the highest levels. It was built during a time that necessitated great secrecy, but that time is over. As you can tell by the conversations going on around us, people are realizing that secrecy is no longer the priority: information is key now. That's why someone like you has been brought into the fold. We need what you know—and in turn, you'll learn what we know."

The general leaned close and lowered his voice. "This facility was not made to protect our command and control in the event of a preemptive nuclear strike; it exists to ensure the continuous leadership after a socially destabilizing event. The truth is that this complex was designed to weather the aftermath of anarchy that some predicted would follow alien contact or invasion."

"You mean it's true—the government knew?"

"Nobody ever predicted anything like this. We were preparing to deal with something completely different. Asteroids loaded with alien bugs are a completely new threat."

The main double doors of the conference room opened up, and a cadre of military officers entered. The one man not in military uniform stepped forward and announced that the president had finished conferring with his cabinet and had time to meet with a few of his advisors.

The presidential aid read a list of names from his clipboard. "General Higgs, General Simon, and Admiral Houser, the president will see you first."

As the other two men rose from their seats, General Simon broke away from Dr. Wingaurd and addressed the aid. "Dr. Wingaurd is coming with us."

"But sir, Dr. Wingaurd hasn't got ..."

"I don't care. He's coming in." The general hurried him along with a quick wave of his hand. "I'm not going to tell the president what I have to say until after you've had your say first."

The dead quiet of outer space was broken by something striking the outer hull of the space station. Several sharp claps followed, sending vibrations rippling through the ship like miniature earthquakes. The unexpected noise was unlike anything ever heard aboard the International Space Station. Metal strained and squealed as the battering continued. Finally, the ship itself gasped with defeat, and a hissing rush of air tore through the main corridor. Moments later, the sound of metal on metal returned—but this time the noise came from within the space station itself.

The interior airlock portal rolled open. An eerie greenish light followed the opening seam, quickly flooding the inner chamber as the portal opened. Two silhouetted forms darkened the opening. One held a box of light in front of it.

The two figures appeared to glide across the threshold. They paused to examine a portal door. The green light reflected off the walls and danced over the metallic material covering their strangely frail-looking bodies. Three slender, elongated fingers reached out to probe the mechanism controlling the inner airlock.

The last protective door rolled open, and the two figures floated into the main body of the space station. They headed straight for the living quarters. The sleeping module glowed green as they entered. One of the figures pushed past an empty space suit and a decapitated helmet floating in its path. They beamed their light onto the command module at the other end of the corridor. The door was open.

They moved to the opening and panned their light across the cramped command chamber. The skeletal remains of the station's crew floated above the seats. The stark white skulls and disjointed bones mingled together in the zero-gravity atmosphere. A thin alien hand reached out and grabbed the nearest body by the sleeve of its flight suit. The long fingered fist grabbed just below the American flag sewn into the shoulder and pulled it away from the entrance. The suit and body pulled away, but the skull remained where it had been, now slowly spinning in zero gravity. A ghastly smile remained frozen on its face.

Colonel Sharp woke with a start. Thick beads of sweat covered his face, pooling on his brow and upper lip. The absence of gravity kept the sweat from running off his face. Pearls of perspiration covered his goose-pimpled skin. His body shuddered, as if the space station's door had been left open and the ice-cold vacuum of space had enveloped him. He imagined he could see his breath crystallizing before him. Tiny rivulets of sweat leaped from his upper lip and danced around his breath. He gasped for air, almost expecting none to be there.

"Winston ... Winston ... Are you all right, friend?" Yuri Masmanoff, Colonel Winston Sharp's Russian counterpart, floated toward him from across the sleeping quarters. He pushed a weightless terrycloth towel through the space between them. "You have a bad dream ... take this. No sweating on instruments."

"Yuri!" Winston buried his face in the towel. "Oh man, thank you. I just had a terrible dream." He could feel the warmth returning to him as he wiped the sweat away. He peered out the small porthole window next him. Earth was clearly visible hundreds of miles below them. Everything looked normal; Earth looked beautiful and peaceful. He would have had to look more closely to see the gray streams of smoke that wrapped around the globe.

"Must have been a frightening dream—you look like shit."

"It was so real. I though we were dead."

"Bad dreams I too am having. Many bad dreams."

"But this was so real. I've never had a dream like it. What time is it?"

"It is 5:30 in Houston, 11:30 back home in Moscow. I think it is Thursday. I lost count of the days."

"Any news from home?"

"No, nothing. We still await a briefing from Houston—a few more hours, I think."

"Where is Smith?"

"Manning the telescope monitor." Yuri checked the instruments and pushed himself through the air. "Tell me about your dream. What frightens you American flyers?"

"It was ... so vivid." Winston shut his eyes tightly, pinching the bridge of his nose between his thumb and forefinger. "Aliens came aboard the station through airlock number one ... we were all dead." The surreal details of the dream were already evaporating from his memory.

"Ah. You have been dreaming about bugs, too."

"No, not that kind of aliens ... they were more like the little green men you hear about. You know, big heads and dark, almond-shaped eyes. They came on board through the airlock and made their way through here to the command module." Winston pointed to the entrance behind Yuri and traced a path back to the entrance to the command module. "We were all dead. We were just bones, like we'd been dead for a hundred years."

"There you have it. Not to worry, my friend, it was just a dream. If it were a premonition, our bodies would not have decomposed. If you were having a true premonition, our bodies would be as pretty as they are now." Yuri smiled like only he could, considering the circumstances. "That is how I expect we will be found someday. Looking just the way we do now, forever."

"But you think somebody will find us?"

"Knowing what we know now, I'm sure of it. We are not alone in this grand universe, that much has been proven. Why not little green men? There are many stories of them within the Russian Astronomical community. I never believed any of them before, but now ..." Yuri shrugged his shoulders as he hovered above him.

"To be honest, neither did I. I don't know why it seemed so impossible before."

"I find it strange that you dream of these types of extraterrestrials instead of the monster insects. I have dreamt about those horrible creatures picking my bones clean many times since we saw those pictures from home."

"I'm sorry. I don't want to dwell on the negative. We can't rule out a retrieval mission yet. It was just a bad dream, that's all." The three crewmen aboard the space station avoided talking about their future prospects or the threat that loomed over their home. Instead, the conversations had turned philosophical. No one wished to talk about being stranded in outer space.

"Of course not. Space missions will be a greater priority than ever before. But if things get much worse down there, I'm afraid bringing us home will be of very little concern." Yuri grabbed another towel and began to swipe at the beads of Winston's sweat being pushed around by the two men's breath. "Maybe it will be our own people that find us some day. Who knows, we may even be brought home as heroes."

"Oh yes, the great TV repairmen from of outer space." Winston forced himself to smile.

"Our mission is different now." Yuri's smile faded. "We are no longer satellite repairmen; we are soldiers once more. Our shifts on the telescope have much meaning now, and if we do find something, we will be heroes. You can bet your bottom."

"How long has it been since 2002XF-21?"

"Ida? Almost seventeen hours."

"Seventeen? Maybe that was the last one."

"Soon we will know for sure. They have averaged about seventeen hour intervals. The most has been eighteen hours. So far we haven't seen anything through Big Red."

"It looks so peaceful down there, like nothing ever happened."

"You missed it earlier; the impact crater in India looked like a bullet hole." Yuri swam through the air until they were both peering through the same small porthole window. Most of India was covered by smoke and cloud cover. The space station orbited over the Southeastern Hemisphere, flying over the Middle East at over ten thousand miles an hour.

"You could actually see the impact crater?"

"Through the telescope, yes. And still nothing is visible over the Pacific. We passed over the extreme Western Hemisphere while you were sleeping, and the entire globe was white with precipitation. The whole Pacific Ocean looks like a giant fog bank."

"Have you seen anything over Manchuria?"

"Some smoke ... Smith took some photos of Florida. You should have a look at them."

"What did it ... Wow, Yuri! Look at that!" A small flash of light fired up between their view from the space station and the Earth. A tiny black dot was visible in the center of the point of light as it broke through the upper most layer of Earth's atmosphere.

Spittle flew from Yuri's lips as he spat out an unintelligible Russian expletive.

Winston stared at the point of light. "No wonder we can't see them. Look how small they are!"

"It has just entered our stratosphere ... it will get much bigger!" As Yuri spoke, the small point of light exploded in fiery brilliance over the blue contrast of the planet below. An infant bolide of fire grew around the black speck. There was no fiery trail behind the fledgling falling star, just a small ball of rolling fire traversing the sky above the planet.

"How close are we?"

"Too close! This is the closest yet!"

"Close enough to feel the energy pulse?"

"I don't know! Too late to contact Control!"

"They would have seen this by now!"

"Captain Smith!" Yuri scrambled for the communications headset. "Bob ... we have got another meteor! Brace for possible energy wave impact! Another meteor has hit the atmosphere!"

Colonel Sharp remained glued to the view from his porthole window while Yuri scrambled to strap himself into his command seat. The fireball grew below them, giving the illusion that it was coming up from Earth and not the other way around. The ball of fire boiled and pulsed as it transversed the planet, exploding with brilliant colors and growing in diameter as it passed from one layer of the atmosphere to another.

"Winston, get to your seat! Brace yourself!"

Winston didn't move from the porthole; he was not going to miss this, no matter what happened. His knuckles turned white as he gripped the round frame of the porthole. He squinted his eyes to lessen the intensity of the miniature falling star. The black speck of the alien vessel was invisible inside the growing ball of fire now. The fireball took on an oval shape as it grew and descended.

After a few seconds of rolling across the sky, the fireball struck the denser air below the ozone layer and exploded with a fury of friction. Brilliant sparks shot from the falling fireball, and the telltale trail of light began to form behind it.

"Winston!"

"Look, you can see the aliens spinning off! Look at that!"

"You are crazy! The shock wave!"

"Yuri, look! Look at this ... it's amazing ..."

"You will be blinded! Come, take your seat!"

"It's headed right for Africa. This baby is going to hit land!"

Paradigm II
Chapter 10

St. Augustine, Florida. June 19, 2002

"Hello ... anybody ... anybody out there?" Her voice was almost gone now. The back of her throat felt like scorched wood. It stung with every sob. "Anybody? Please ..." Her teeth crunched the ashy grit in her mouth. Her body could no longer produce enough saliva to expel the dust that collected in her mouth with every breath.

She stopped on Main Boulevard, where hundreds of students had once traveled back and forth between classes. Now the campus was empty and virtually unrecognizable. No one answered her calls. No one came to her aid as she stood bent over and retching. She had waited too long: nobody was left. She had never felt so frightened, so utterly alone.

After a minute of dry heaves and choking coughs, she felt her breath coming back, but the tightness in her chest wouldn't subside. The sound of falling debris caught her ears from somewhere behind her, and she quickly looked around in every direction. Panic drove her into the open. The tall buildings on either side of her were blasted and crumbling, smoke trailing from the uppermost floors, but all was still. Her eyes darted from building to building, frantically searching for the cause of the noise. She tried to reassure herself that it was only the sound of bricks crumbling under the weight of slumping buildings, but every piece of falling glass and every crack or pop from some hidden fire caused her heart to thump wildly.

She forced herself to continue down the street toward the main entrance of the campus and the city of St. Augustine beyond. Every step was difficult. The streets were piled with broken glass and rubble. It was clear that the blast wave had come from left to right. The buildings to her right were covered with piles of debris, as if some catastrophic snowdrift had settled against them. The buildings themselves were blackened and scorched. The buildings to her left were better off. Even so, every last window had been blown out, and now the shattered glass covered her escape route like a field of razor blades.

A sharp pain in her foot stopped her once again. When she examined her foot, she found that her sneakers had been completely chewed through by the serrated ground. There was a cut on the sole of her foot, but it wasn't bad. A shard of glass was lodged in her shoe. She picked up some loose papers and lined the bottom of her shoe before continuing on.

"Hello ... is there anybody out there?" Her voice croaked as she limped along, but there was no answer. She wiped the dust from her wristwatch and peered through the broken crystal. It was almost six in the evening, but it was already as dark as night. She looked up to the opaque orb of the sun, dimmed by the smoke-filled sky. She knew she only had an hour or two before total darkness. The thought of being alone in the dark with those things out there threatened to drive her mad.

Cindy ignored the pain in her feet, but she couldn't ignore her thirst anymore. She hadn't eaten anything since the impact twenty hours ago. She looked to the building on her left, contemplating the odds of finding some water, but the fear of being trapped inside one of those buildings again kept her in the middle of the street.

She passed several cars piled amongst the debris, some of which looked drivable, but she kept walking. She knew there was no way to drive a car through the wreckage, even if the keys were left in the ignition. Seeing people's cars and all their possessions strewn indiscriminately over the boulevard made her think of all the things she was leaving behind. As a young, struggling student she didn't have much to call her own, but even so, it was shocking to realize that now she had nothing. The worn art portfolio under her arm was now her only possession, and so it took on more importance than ever before. Right now she would gladly have traded her beloved Cabriolet for a pair of sturdy hiking boots in a size six.

She began hopping from one large piece of concrete to another; like jumping stones to cross a stream, until she turned her ankle and fell onto her hands and knees. Her ankle throbbing, she looked up from the street to see that a large dorm building had collapsed, blocking her way off campus. Once again she felt utterly defeated and began to weep dry tears. Only the fear of what she had left behind got her on her feet again.

Scaling the pile of rubble looked dangerous, if not impossible, and the thought of backtracking through the broken street seemed absurd. "Hello … anybody?" Again, no response came. She looked around for other options. The dorm building to her left was still standing, although she could see huge cracks spiderwebbing through the concrete. All the widows were blown out, and bits of bedding and clothing hung from the jagged openings. Wisps of smoke trailed into the air from the upper floors.

"Help me! Hello … I need help." She got to her feet and tested her weight on her ankle. "Shit!" Pain bit at her lower leg, but she could stand. She gingerly limped her way over to the dorm building's double doors and tried to pull them open. They were unlocked but wouldn't budge. The building had been had shifted off its foundation and the doors were jammed shut. Again she felt helpless and defeated.

The open windows on the ground floor were too high for her to reach, so she looked around for something to help her climb inside. She found a bus bench that had broken loose and slowly made her way to it. She would only have to drag it a few feet, lean it against the wall, and climb into the open window, but as she began to pull on the tubular metal frame, the jagged metal cut her hands. Again she was stymied. Once again on the verge of tears, she sat down on the bench and buried her face in her hands.

After a few moments of pulling herself together, she looked up to see an over-turned electrician's van across the street. The butt end of a ladder poked out of the back doors. She left the bench and crossed the street. As she got closer, she saw that a black boulder had crushed the front of the van. It was like nothing she had ever seen before—like a giant marble, burnt black and split down the middle. As she looked closer, she began to notice that the ground was covered with smaller obsidian rivulets. She knew from her geology lectures that this was proba-bly the molten silica that had rained down after the impact, but there was no time to reflect on the oddity; she pulled at the small ladder, and it slid out easily.

She carried the ladder to the nearest open widow and scaled it, leaving bloody palm prints on the rungs. She straddled the glassless window, careful not to get caught on the jagged metal edge, and slipped inside. She was in a small dorm room, like the one she had spent a few weeks in when she first came to St. Augus-tine's School of Fine Art. It was obviously a boy's dorm; she couldn't tell if it had been devastated by the blast or whether it had always looked like this. Clothing covered the floor and personal belongings were strewn everywhere.

It was dark inside, and she fought the urge to call out. She didn't like being surrounded by the walls. Images of the last building she had been trapped in began to flash in her mind. She could feel the crushing weight of them. She could see her friend's face again. Panic welled inside her throat. She didn't want to revisit the horrible image of her friend again. The not-so-distant memories were too painful, too frightening, but she was helpless to stop them.

She gave no thought to sheltering inside the dorm for the night, deciding to get what she could from this room and get out as quickly as she could. She found a half-empty bottle of water and greedily gulped it down. Then she rummaged around the floor until she found a pair of leather football cleats. They were far too big, but they looked very rugged and had a hard plastic sole with plastic studs. She found several pairs of almost-clean socks, and she put on layer after layer until her feet fit snugly inside. She also found a heavy high school letterman's jacket with the name "Wallace" embroidered across the chest and climbed into it. As she rummaged through the personal effects in the room, the utter silence became disconcerting. She was sure that all the noise she was making was attracting unwanted attention, so she moved even faster.

She flung open desk drawers, hoping to find a flashlight, until she came upon Wallace's stash of weed and porno magazines. She was half tempted to take the weed—maybe even roll a joint—but she left it behind, taking only the lighter. She used the lighter to illuminate the room as she looked for more necessities, finding another half-empty bottle of water under the bed. Next to the bottle of water was a butterfly knife, like the ones she had seen other guys playing with when she was a young girl. It had a long, sharp blade in between two flat handles that could be flicked open and twirled about. She slipped the blade into her coat pocket and continued to feel her way around the floor.

She came across a small radio plugged into the wall and jerked it out of the socket. She fiddled with the power button, but nothing happened. She flipped it over in her hands and found the batteries missing. "Fuck!" She paused for a moment and considered searching the other rooms for some batteries, maybe even some food or water or a flashlight, but she was too frightened. Her hands trembled at the thought of leaving this room and heading into the unknown of the next.

She grabbed the water bottle, tucked her portfolio under her arm, and made her way to the dim light of the open window. Before she straddled the window frame, she stopped to grab another pair of sneakers she saw poking out from behind a closet door. She tied the laces together and slung the shoes around her neck. There were so many other things she could have grabbed, so many things that she could have used, but her nerves had left her. She clambered down the ladder as fast as she could, the plastic soles of her new shoes sliding along the rungs as she hurried down.

The large, flat shoes made it almost easy to backtrack the distance along the dorm building; it only took a minute to cover the same distance that had seemed to take hours before. She moved away from the dead end and worked her way around the building. A building across the street was on fire. She could feel the radiant heat on her face. The red glow from the upper windows lit her way somewhat, but the dancing shadows from the fire spooked her. She saw bugs in every moving shadow. Every glint of light reflecting off broken glass seemed to be tiny eyes staring back at her. She quickened her pace, oblivious to the pain in her ankle.

She stumbled along in a panicked daze, the plastic soles clacking against the broken pavement, her friend's face flashing across her mind's eye. The persistent questions rolled through her mind. Why had she stayed with her? She couldn't help her. Why did she stay? Why did she have to witness her horrible death? She kicked herself for not leaving with the others—but then she remembered what had happened to the others.

She was the only one who had been willing to stay with Tiffany when the wall came down to trap her. Others had said they would send help, but none ever came. After an eternity of hearing her friend's cries, she had gone outside to find help. That's when she had seen them; bodies, bodies everywhere, blood covering the ground, blood covering the bodies. People were being torn apart, torn apart right in front of her eyes. The bugs, the bugs were everywhere. They were only the size of a hand, but just one of them could tug on a limb until it came off. Some dragged bodies or parts of bodies with them. The giant beetles feasted on the dead or simply tore them apart.

Cindy knew it was all her fault. The beetles had followed her back to Tiffany. They moved so fast … they attacked Tiffany, not her. They had torn her apart while she hid in a cupboard and watched through a crack in the door. Tiffany had screamed for her but she couldn't move. Finally Tiff's screams had gurgled to a stop, and the bugs left.

She couldn't believe that it was really happening, that everything had changed so quickly—that she was alone, and those things were out there, and they were real. Her breathing was getting out of control, but she couldn't stop moving. She just wanted to get away from here, to find some help and get away. She wondered how many of her classmates had gotten away, where they had gone, if there was anywhere to escape to.

She forced these thoughts out of her mind and pressed on numbly. She looked up, away from the obstacles in front of her and past the burning building, and her heart leaped with joy. There was a break in the collapsed buildings, and she could see the open streets beyond the campus that led to the city. Her pace quickened to a jog; the plastic cleats clicked along the ground beneath her. She passed into the open boulevard and took in the scene outside the campus.

She had lived in Florida her entire life, but now the landscape was unrecognizable. Fires raged in the distance, and the ground was covered in molten debris. Not a single tree stood in her view. They had all been knocked flat by the blast and now all pointed the same direction—the same way she was headed now, into town.

"Hello, is there anybody out there?" Her parched throat was barely able to get the words out. She drained the last of the water and threw the empty bottle on the ground. She knew there would be no answer—there was only flattened openness and devastation before her—but the sound of her own voice was oddly reassuring.

She began the long walk into the city, which only took a minute or two in her sporty Cabriolet but now looked like an insurmountable distance. The agonizing march was made worse by the shocking images she couldn't escape. The sun was sinking, and she knew she had to find someone soon, or else find a place to hide out for the night. Cars lined the street in the distance. She clutched her portfolio under her arm and picked up her pace. There were buildings beyond the intersection. Smoke trailed into the sky above them, but they were standing.

As she got closer, she could see that the cars had been rocked by the blast. They had all been shifted to the right side of the street; slammed together by the shock wave. They were crushed and tangled among fallen telephone poles. The metal was pockmarked and chewed. The intersection was clogged with gridlocked cars, cars for as far as she could see.

As she approached the first car, she could see the shadows of bodies inside through the fractured glass. She passed it quickly, not wanting a closer view. Every car was filled with bodies. A growing stench filled her nose. It was the stench of rotting flesh. Her nose had grown accustomed to the acrid smell of burning material, but this new smell was overpowering, nauseating. Thin clouds of flies hovered over the line of cars. She covered her mouth and swallowed hard against the upcoming vomit.

She realized that these were the people who had attempted to escape in those final moments before impact. Every car was filled with dead. Some hung out of the windows or lay in the streets. Mothers still clutched their children. All the bodies were horribly disfigured. She sprinted away from the gory scene and collapsed on the sidewalk next to a building. She couldn't stop the tears and broke down completely.

She wept uncontrollably, pulling at her hair with clenched fists, until an abrupt sound ripped her back to her surroundings. Her ears trained on the distinctive clattering sound. She looked up and thought she saw some movement near the line of cars. She looked harder, peering through her tears, but couldn't see anything. The sound continued, like hundreds of fingernails on metal. In her mind's eye she pictured a swarm of bugs clamoring up the street behind her, but the streets were empty; nothing moved.

Again, a flash of movement caught her eyes; she whipped her head around to follow the blur, but nothing was there. The sound grew louder. She couldn't hold it in any longer and yelled out. "Who's there? Hello?" To her astonishment, the noise died immediately, but only for a moment. The clattering redoubled, becoming even louder, closer, as if hundreds more fingernails now plied themselves against the metal hoods down the line of cars. Another flash of movement zipped into the shadows. This time her eyes caught sight of dark shape before it disappeared.

"Shit!" She tried to stand, but her body wouldn't respond. The sound grew closer. She pressed herself against the wall and stifled a scream by holding her breath. Then she saw it again: a small, black object landed with a thud on the hood of a nearby car. For an instant, it looked like a massive, charcoal black cricket—much different than the beetles she had seen back at campus. This creature was bigger, leaner, with long, thin appendages. Its body was oval-shaped and as black as the burnt buildings around her.

Before she could even think to react, another bug appeared from beneath the car. Then another appeared next to it, as if it had fallen from the sky. Her eyes darted around frantically; they were appearing everywhere. The bug on the car's hood disappeared with a click, but others soon took its place. They banged against the metal like some kind of horrible black rain.

She could hear their hard, spiky legs scraping along the twisted metal. They didn't seem to notice her, but she was sure it was only a matter of time before they heard her panicked breathing. Cindy was sure they were hunting her. One of the bugs sat atop the car and looked like it was sniffing the air. Its front legs began swiping at the air. It seemed to be swatting at the cloud of flies that hovered above the cars. She watched, paralyzed with fear, as they grew in numbers and got ever closer.

One of the bugs scurried along the ground next to the row of cars. Its many legs were invisible as it sped along the street. The car door was open, hanging from its hinges, and the horribly burnt body of a man hung half out of the car. The bug stopped short before the lifeless body, then reached up with a slender, spiked arm and probed the soft tissue at the back of the man's neck. The bug then leaped onto the base of the man's head and bit into the shirt around his neck. It pulled at the collar, leveraging its legs along the car's frame, and the body came tumbling out of the door to land on top of the bug.

The other bugs immediately converged on the fallen body and began tearing it into bloody bits. Cindy's legs found their feet and she sprinted blindly back down street.

Still running, she looked behind to see that they had seen her. "No! No! No!!"

She could hear the clattering of many feet behind her, and black blurs flew past her face. They had already closed the distance. They moved too fast, and there was nowhere to run. She opened the closest car door and slingshot her way inside, plowing headlong onto the lap of the putrefying body of the driver. She slammed the door closed behind her and slipped over the mess beneath her. Black bugs smacked into the door and onto the windshield. The stench inside the car was awful; her body was pressed against the rotting flesh. She screamed in revulsion, pushing the body away from hers. Bugs continued to pelt the car from above.

They climbed all over the car, trying to get in, trying to get her, raking their spiked legs over the glass and metal. She screamed at them and cried. She shut her eyes to block them out, but there was no escaping the sound or the smell. She slammed the horn with her hand, hoping to scare them away, but they were undeterred. She blasted the horn again and again, continuously now, but they wouldn't leave.

She stopped pressing the horn, about to give up and let the bugs swarm the car. There was nothing she could do but let them rip her apart like they had ripped apart Tiff and the others. She stopped struggling and listened in resignation to the echo of the car's horn—until, suddenly, she understood in amazement what she was hearing. The second horn continued, and Cindy realized that another car was answering her horn.

She blasted away on the horn and tried to see past the growing number of bugs covering the windows, but there was no sign of help. Bugs were smashing their bodies against the glass with dull thuds. She didn't think that something so small could break through the windows, but she had seen what the little bugs could do and was sure it was only a matter of time before one of them got in. She blasted the horn again, stopping to hear it reply, and then whipped around to follow the sound. To her dismay, she saw that the back window had been shattered by the blast and was wide open.

In the distance, behind her car, two headlights lit up the road. The car was approaching fast, blaring its horn and bouncing over the rubble-covered road. It was about to pass her.

With dozens of bugs covering the outside of the car, she flung open the door and bounded onto the road, madly waving her arms and running toward the fast approaching headlights.

An old, battered four-wheel drive screeched to a stop just feet from where she was running. Smoke billowed from the tires. Without hesitation she grabbed the handle and flung open the door. A strong set of hands pulled her in and the truck surged forward, laying rubber along the road as it sped off.

She lay face down on the bench, her face pressed against the denim jeans of a man's lap. She was utterly spent, utterly relieved, unable to catch her breath or make a sound. She looked up at the man behind the wheel; he was older, and like herself incredibly frightened. He looked down at her, taking his eyes off the road for an instant, then began screaming at her.

His eyes were wild, and he wouldn't stop screaming at her. She couldn't tell what he was saying. She felt as if she were about to pass out. She didn't know what was going on; nothing made sense anymore. He slammed the brakes, almost sending her to the floor. He grabbed her by the hair and pulled hard. Pain shot across her head. She looked up imploringly, confused and scared. He had a thick pipe in his hand; he was about to hit her with it. She closed her eyes and screamed, feebly trying to fend off the blow by scratching at him with her flailing hands.

"Hold still, goddammit!" He shouted.

The man hacked at her back with the metal pipe, glancing off her back without hurting her.

"Don't move!" She felt another hack on her shoulder. She buried her face in the leather sleeve of her jacket and wept.

"Get up! Get up! Move!" He shouted madly.

She sprung onto her hands and knees atop the bench and saw what he was shouting about. He had knocked a bug off her back, and it had rolled onto the floorboards. He reached over with his leg and brought his heavy boot down on the stunned bug, stomping it repeatedly with his heel. She heard an awful crunch as he smashed it into the floor.

"Got it! I got it. You're okay. You're gonna be okay."

She looked up at him; his expression had softened, and a broad smile appeared beneath his bushy mustache.

"My name's Jim."

"Can you speak?" Jim took his hand off of the wheel just long enough to gently shake her shoulder. "Come on, you're all right ... aren't you?" His eyes jumped between her and the road. She lay face down across the bench. Her legs were bent at the knees, her feet bounced against the window, and her head was nearly in his lap. Her back heaved beneath the shredded jacket as she sobbed. "Look ... look, they're gone. We're okay." The truck bounced hard, jarred by a crater in the road, and Jim fought to keep from sideswiping the line of crushed cars.

"Can you sit up?" Ash-covered hair lay in a tangled mess over her face and clung to the corners of her mouth as she looked up at him. Coils of hair danced in and out of her mouth with every breath. Another big bump in the road grabbed at the steering wheel, and Jim had to fight for control of the truck with both hands. The sun was getting low in the sky. He was having a hard time seeing the road ahead of him. His headlights, like his windshield, were coated in a thick layer of ash and dust.

"Come on, let's sit up and have a look at you." Jim coaxed her up, keeping a lookout for a clearing ahead. "Atta girl ... you don't look so bad. You can wipe your face on this." Jim grabbed a T-shirt from behind the seat. "That's it." He gently helped to push her upright but she kept her eyes on the floor.

"You don't look injured. Are you hurting anywhere?" Jim leaned forward to see past the mess of hair that covered her face, but she said nothing. She held the shirt in her lap but didn't try to clean the grime from her face.

"It's okay. Take your time, honey. You're safe now. I'll get you out of here." Jim turned his attention to the road, struggling to find a landmark that might lead him home.

He swerved back and forth avoiding wrecked cars, piles of debris, and the ever-present globules of molten glass that covered the road. The V-8 motor roared in front of them as the truck bounced over obstacles. "I've got some water ... you want water, don't ya?" The girl didn't respond.

"You must be from the college. I thought everyone had been evacuated from there already."

Finally she turned to face him and brushed the hair from her face. "Evacuated? They got out?" Her face was covered with ash and grime, her eyes were red and swollen, and blood oozed from small abrasions on her cheeks, but Jim was stuck by how pretty she was. She was only a kid, maybe still only a teenager like his daughter.

"So you can talk." Jim smiled back at her.

"Where did they go? I didn't think ... I thought they were all ..." Once again she buried her face in her hands and began to cry.

"I don't really know. All I know is that everyone headed north, away from the blast."

"Where?"

"I dunno ... I didn't stick around to watch 'em go." Jim cleared the ash from the windshield with the wipers.

"No, no ... where did the asteroid hit?"

"That weren't no asteroid! They say it was a spaceship! It's a full-scale alien invasion!" Jim still couldn't believe he was saying it. A few days ago, he hadn't even believed in aliens. Now he had seen more of them than he cared to remember.

Jim glanced to the floor, arching his brows at the splattered alien corpse. "But I haven't seen bugs like this one before. The ones that fell from the sky were different. These are bigger. Meaner too!"

"I saw them ... They killed my ... my ..." The young girl lifted her face from her hands.

"But you're alive. That's what counts. Hold on, kid ... here comes a big bump."

"They tore her to pieces!" She pulled at her hair and shook her head before the jolt tossed her from the seat.

"I'm sorry." Jim knew what she had witnessed. "The spaceship hit smack-dab in the middle of the peninsula. Right into the marsh. They say the blast wave stretches all the way up to Jacksonville. The whole state is on fire. Another one hit somewhere in Africa a few hours ago. Kenya, I think."

"Another one?"

"Yeah ... they haven't stopped. They've hit us all over the globe."

"But people got away? Where are we going? We have to get out of here!"

"Everybody that could drove off yesterday. There was a big convoy. Didn't anyone come to the school?"

"I was trapped. My friend was pinned under a wall ... we couldn't ... I couldn't leave her. I saw ... I saw people getting eaten by those ... those bugs." The girl finally noticed the shirt in her lap and began to wipe the filth from her face.

"I don't think they eat people."

"But I saw them! It was horrible."

"I know. I seen it, too. But they don't eat people, they just ... well, they just leave them there after they kill them. But I haven't seen bugs like those back there until I found you." Jim pushed away the images of disemboweled and dismembered bodies that had littered the streets after the deluge of alien bugs had disappeared. "Hold on, big bump!" The truck leaped over a pile of rubble, and Jim struck his head on the ceiling. "Fuck! Better put on your seat belt; the road's a little rough." Jim scanned the road ahead, looking for a familiar street.

"Where are we going?"

"I'm trying to find a way back to the delta."

"You mean you're lost!" The girl looked horrified.

"No, not lost. But a lot of these roads are blocked. Keep your eyes open for me, would ya? We need to head over in that direction. My eyes don't see so good in the dark."

"We need to go north … with the others. We need to get out of here! I can't …"

"I know where to go … you'll be safe with me."

"That way … what about that way? It looks pretty clear." She pointed to the left, where a freeway bridge still stood. The buildings behind it seemed intact.

"We should stay out of the city. It's pretty bad in there. Lots of buildings came down. The streets are no good. We should try and make our way around the outside, but watch out for trees … one of those could stop us good."

"What's that light over there? Is there power over there?"

"That's just the glow from the fire. Every thing's burning."

"Why didn't you leave with the others when you had the chance?" The young girl indiscreetly picked the crust from her nose and wiped it on the shirt.

"Not me. I'm stayin'. You're looking at a millionaire. I'm gonna stay and protect what's mine!"

"What good is money now?"

"Not money … you're right, money ain't no good anymore. I've got land!" Jim pumped his fist in triumph. "When everyone was in a panic to get away from the coast, I kept my head. I mortgaged everything I had, took on loans that I could never have paid back, and I bought it up cheap! Beachfront properties, every last one. I own a good part of the St. Augustine coast, and I'm gonna do what it takes to keep it!"

"That's crazy. We've to get out of here."

"What's crazy is everyone selling off and going inland! Lots of good that did them, the fucking spaceship landed right in the middle. Life's a gamble, and I'm gonna be a big winner!"

"You're insane …"

"Life goes on, honey; you do what you can. What's your name anyway? I'm sure you don't want some old man calling you 'Honey.' You young girls don't like that. I have a daughter about your age, you know."

"Cindy. My name's Cindy."

"Cindy. Good. Like I said, my name's Jim. 'Lucky Jim O'Donnell.' How old are you, Cindy?"

"Twenty three. Look out for that rock!"

"Hold on!" Jim swerved to avoid the trashcan-sized boulder of glass.

"How many people got away?"

"I dunno, thousands probably. Everything that still had wheels lined up and headed north. Like I said, St. Augustine was relatively lucky. People got out of the city pretty quick after the bugs took off."

"Where did they go?"

"Most people say that they burrowed underground. But I've seen them walking around—hopping, really: man, do they jump! Some of them hung around for a few hours after the blast, but most of them disappeared." Jim hit the brakes hard, avoiding a large mound of earth in the road. "The bugs didn't seem too concerned about cars. We're safe inside. I don't think they can get in. Only people who got out were attacked. And after a while, all the bugs disappeared."

"No, where did all of the *people* go?"

"Like I said, I don't know. And I don't care, either! Right now who's to say that things are any better up in Jacksonville or any place else? Those places were madhouses before we were hit. It's not safe around so many people when they're scared out of their minds. There were riots ... people were getting killed."

"People are getting killed here! I was almost killed! They're monsters! We have to get away from here! You saw them ... I can't believe you want to stay!"

"My family is here! My wife. My daughter, too. I've got them and a neighbor family on my houseboat in the delta. We'll be safe there. We have food and fuel, and I don't think the bugs will find us out on the water."

"But what if another asteroid hits the Atlantic?"

"Ah, what if? ... life's a gamble, and you can't go on what-ifs anymore. You do what you can and pray to God." The wheel ripped away from Jim's hands, sending severe pain down both his wrists and sending the truck pitching to the left, up onto the sidewalk. The left front tire had blown out. Jim fought to regain control as the truck barreled over the rubble-covered sidewalk.

The truck came to a stop with a hideous crunch; the motor sputtered on the brink of stalling.

"What happened?"

"Tire blew. Fuck! I was afraid of this!"

"Don't you have a spare?"

"Spare's already on. There's just too much glass on the road ... it's ripping the tires to shreds."

"What can we do?"

"I don't like the idea of driving around on my rims ... maybe we can pull some tires off those cars over there."

"No! I don't want to get out! I don't want you to get out! We're safe in here ... let's just go!"

"Settle down ... you don't have to get out. I'm gonna back up a little and pull over some place where there's enough room." Jim put the truck in reverse and slowly backed out of the pile of broken concrete.

He pulled the tuck to a stop in the middle of the street. An overturned pickup closely flanked the passenger side, allowing him just enough room to change the tire. "I'll just take a quick look. Hang tight."

"Don't ..."

Jim fended off her pleading arms and opened the door. He reached under the seat and grabbed a flashlight. Jim stood on the street and stretched his aching back, testing the flashlight on the ground. He quickly saw that the tire was hopelessly shredded, and was about to turn to examine the rear tire, when a faint clattering sound caught his attention. He spun around to look back down the street, beaming his flashlight into the dusty gloom. His eyes perceived a far-off movement, and his ears immediately recognized the sound of hard alien legs clamoring on concrete. He leaped back into the seat, locking the door behind him.

"What is it?" Cindy shrieked.

"We have to go now!" Jim thrust the truck into drive and slammed his foot down on the accelerator. The powerful motor propelled them down the broken street, and Jim struggled to keep from pitching off to the left.

"What's wrong? What did you see?"

"Nothing ... I didn't *see* anything. I heard them! A lot of them!"

Cindy leaned over and peered out of the back window. All Jim could see in his mirror was a cloud of dust as they tore down the road.

"I can't see anything ..."

"Help me find some place to turn."

"Did they follow us? Are these the same ones?"

"It doesn't matter! We need to find another direction!" The remaining tire flew off at that moment, once again ripping the wheel out of Jim's hands and sending a stream of brilliant sparks flying from the wheel. He regained control without crashing into the buildings. He slammed his foot down on the accelerator once again, and the truck charged down the street.

"There, that way looks open!" Cindy shouted above the noise of the screeching metal.

"Hold on!" Jim slammed on the brakes and wheeled frantically to the right. The truck skittered around the corner; the bare metal wheel smacking the curb with a sickening crunch and throwing the truck onto the sidewalk. Another tire blew with a noise like a gun. Cindy screamed, and the truck was pulled back onto the road, narrowly missing the trunk of a telephone pole.

Propelled by the image of all those stabbing claws and biting pinchers, Jim urged the truck forward with all of its power. The truck fishtailed under the torque but eventually straightened out, making good speed down street.

"How long can we go on like this?" Cindy asked, staring at the fiery trail of sparks flying up from the wheels.

"As long as the wheels keep spinnin' … or until we catch fire."

A loud smack above his head rang in Jim's ears. It wasn't just a piece of rubble flying up and striking the undercarriage; something had hit the roof.

"Did you hear that? What was it?" Cindy gasped.

Another loud smack raked the metal and was followed by the image of a crab-like bug sliding up the hood toward the windshield. Its long spikes were thrust out in all directions; its thin oval body was black as coal. It slid along the hood until one of its long pinchers found a purchase point along the seam of the hood. Its spiky appendages clawed along the hood, slicing at the windshield.

Another bug appeared on the rearview mirror, clinging like a giant spider in the lee of the truck's wind. Cindy screamed again, and Jim noticed a bug clinging to her window.

"They're attacking us!" She yelled hysterically.

Jim figured they were safe as long as he kept the truck on the road, so he focused all his attention on what lay beyond the hideous creature. Obstacles came up far too quickly, and the truck turned sluggishly: he was forced to barrel straight ahead or risk spinning out of control. He prayed that the street continued unobstructed and pressed on.

"They can't get in, can they?"

Jim remained focused on the road, wincing as a dark shadow sped out in front of them. He noticed a road sign alerting them to a stoplight ahead, and his heart sank. They were going to have to make a turn. Jim let off of the accelerator slightly, careful not to kill their momentum or give away precious traction, and prepared to make the split second decision: left or right. The shadow looming in front of them evolved into a towering building. The smaller buildings on either side were burning. Black smoke rolled out the windows, and the red glow lit the intersection.

With the deceleration came more frightening smacks as more bugs leaped onto the truck. He could see three bugs attacking the back window through his rear view. He swiveled his head left to right, hoping to catch a glimpse of open road on one side or the other, but both directions looked equally daunting.

Time was up. He tapped the brakes. The bug on the windshield shifted but held firm. Jim spun the wheel to the right. The truck skittered along, slow to respond, but eventually veered to the right.

"Come on, baby ... you can do it!" Slowly, the truck aligned itself to the right, and Jim hit the gas. The powerful truck surged forward, overriding the traction-less wheels, and lurched over a curb into the already-shattered front window of a store. They came to a sudden jolting stop. Cindy rolled to the floor. The truck's motor died.

Jim's face smacked the steering wheel, and bright spots danced in his vision. He felt himself slipping away. Falling bits of the shattered storefront fell on the hood in front of him, but none of it made any sound. Cindy was clawing her way up from the floor, pulling on his pant legs, but he didn't feel a thing. His mind went dark, but his vision was filled with bright dancing lights.

"Wake up, dammit!" Jim's face stung. He opened his eyes to see Cindy rearing back to take another swipe at him.

"I'm up ... I'm up ... don't hit me, dammit. Ow! My jaw ..."

"They're out there! Quiet! Look!"

Jim turned to look out the cracked rear window; a swarm of bugs were frantically attacking a demolished Coke machine. Bugs leaped from every direction and wrestled with the cans of soda rolling on the sidewalk.

"What are they doing?"

"They think we're the cans." The smashed-open machine was swamped with black shapes tearing into it.

"We must have hit a Coke machine. They went wild attacking it. Some of the cans were spinning around and hissing, that set them off."

Jim noticed that the ground was covered in Coke cans ripped in half.

"They think they've got us." Cindy pressed a finger to her lips.

"Are you hurt?"

"No. We should be quiet."

"Is the truck okay?" Jim glanced around for holes in the truck's fractured windows.

"I think so. Look, some of them are leaving."

The mass of swarming bugs on the Coke machine began to turn away. Some disappeared with a click of their rear legs. A few seconds later, nearly all of the bugs were gone and the ground was covered in shredded Coke cans. A few of the bugs lingered around the machine, crawling in and out of sight. As far as Jim could tell, none of them were on the truck anymore.

"Let's give them a minute; maybe they'll all leave," Jim whispered.

The two of them peered over the back seat, crouched down, breathing in whispers. The Coke machine was forgotten while the remaining bugs scouted around the intersection or rummaged through the demolished convenience store.

"I only see two now," Cindy whispered.

"There's at least one in the store … I can hear him."

"Why aren't they leaving?"

"Do you want me to see if the truck will start?"

"No!"

"Shhh! We might be able to get out of here."

"No, don't do it … please … we'll just wait."

"I don't know if this thing will even start up." Jim tested the battery by turning the key in the ignition.

"Stop! What are you doing?"

"Just checking to see if we have any juice."

"Do we?"

"Yeah, think so. Still don't have any front tires, though. And we're not going anywhere if the back ones go."

"Look, one is coming out of the store."

"How can you see that?"

"You can't see that? Look, those two are coming over to it." Cindy jabbed her finger in the direction of the bugs. "There's three of them, right there in the street."

"Okay, I see 'em. Quiet down will ya?"

"What are they doing? They're just sitting there. Go … go … go away. Go away, you stupid bugs."

"Look, they started moving again. Go, do it!" Jim urged them on under his breath, but the three bugs remained where they were. They huddled in a tight circle, gesticulating their narrow bodies up and down, slicing at the air in unison. Their arms moved so fast he couldn't see them until they stopped—and then, as if a storm cloud had burst overhead, dark clumps fell to the earth, landing en masse where the three bugs had clustered. In an instant, there were hundreds of bugs swarming the intersection. The ash gray ground turned a boiling black with alien creatures.

Cindy crouched low in the seat, hiding her face in her hands and stifling a scream. Jim continued to watch, wide-eyed, as the countless multitudes of aliens crowded the street. It became impossible to focus on a single bug; they were a blur of seething black. Every bug was on the move, pausing for only an instant before rejoining the throng of movement. The now-familiar clicking sound was almost deafening. The fine hairs on his neck stood on end.

The swarm on the street grew into an impenetrable black cloud, alive with the sound of countless clicking legs. Jim glanced down to see Cindy cowering in the seat with her fingers jammed in her ears. He looked around at the windows protecting them; each one was broken to some degree. He began to doubt that anything could stop the boiling mass of bugs in the intersection. Dread washed over him. His thoughts raced back to his family; he was going to leave them unprotected against all of this. Greed had made him leave them. He should have stayed home. There were plenty of supplies on the boat. What good were all of the diamonds and jewels now? He was never going to see his family again.

"Listen, we have to get out of here. I'm gonna start the truck, and we can make a break for it." Consumed with panic, Jim turned in his seat and prepared to turn the key.

"No! No! You can't! Let them go away. Please." Cindy lunged for the ignition and caught him by the wrist.

"There are hundreds of them. We can't stay here!"

"If we move, or they hear us, we're dead! Use your head. Listen, shhh. Listen, can you hear? They're not as loud anymore."

The insidious clicking drone had lessened, and once again Jim could hear the pounding of his own heart. He turned in his seat and peered through the cracked rear window. The mass of writhing black was still there, but smaller, the movement seemed to slow. With every second, more bugs disappeared, leaping away by the dozens.

"See, they *are* leaving, aren't they? I can hear them." Cindy remained slumped in the seat, too afraid to look.

"I think so." Their numbers were shrinking so fast that Jim thought that they would all be gone in a matter of seconds. He was able to distinguish individual bugs now, although his eyes were drawn to a single dark mass of bugs in the center. "They're almost all gone. Come on, have a look. Your eyes are better than mine."

"I don't want to."

"Come o n … what is that?"

"What?"

"I can't tell." It looked as if several of the bugs were moving some dark object. "Come on, look."

Cindy slowly worked her way to her knees until see could see over the seat. "What?"

"Look right there … what are those bugs carrying?"

"Shit! It's a bug! A big one!"

"No!"

"Look! You can't see that? It's the size of damn dog!"

"That's a bug?"

"It's coming this way. Be quiet." Cindy hissed.

"Oh my God … I can see it." The giant beetle didn't move like the others; its legs were short, and it moved low to the ground, pulling its two thick hind legs behind it. It was ten times the size of the others. Two smaller bugs flanked its sides.

As Jim peered over the seat, his face nearly pressed against the glass, a bug leaped from out of nowhere and landed on the piles of duffle bags in the bed of his truck. Jim jerked back in horror, almost sounding the truck's horn as his back slammed against the steering wheel. He could see through the cracks in the rear window that the bug hadn't noticed him. Instead, the bug began probing the bags with its front claws and then ripping the tough canvas with its other appendages, scattering Jim's loot.

"What is it?" Cindy whispered.

Jim was unable to speak. A second bug leaped into the truck's bed, and still the larger bug glided along the ground only a few feet from the truck.

The first bug left the duffle bags alone and began exploring the perimeter of the truck's bed. It circled the bed, prodding the duffle bags with its long spikes. It quickly made its way to the rear window, only a foot from Jim's face. Its long front probes ran over the fractured glass, finding the cracks and tracing the hard point of its claws along the grooves.

"What's that sound? What are they doing?"

"Don't move … there's one on the window." Jim didn't move a muscle, and Cindy remained dead still, but the truck heaved and lurched. Jim looked past the bug on the window and saw the looming shadow of the giant bug clawing its way over the tailgate.

"What was that?"

"The big one." Jim whispered.

Cindy buried her face in her arms. The bug on the window clambered up and over the roof; its hard spikes tapped along the metal over their heads. The second smaller bug gave way before the giant, standing sentry on the rails of the truck bed as the larger bug passed.

Up close Jim could see the beetle as more than a dark blur. Its narrow, humped back was covered in two oval shields. Two front arms waved before it like antennae, periodically sweeping back to the featureless face which poked out from beneath the crest of an armored helm. The rest of the legs effortlessly carried the hulking insect over the shredded duffle bags directly toward the rear window.

Jim was sure this was the end; he expected the giant alien to launch himself through the window and devour him at any moment. Then, while stopped at the base of the window, the giant bug reached out with its multiple arms and grabbed the rim around the truck's bed in all directions. With its arms gripping the expanse of the bed, the creature spun around, rotating its many legs like a massive spider. The helmeted front end faced the tailgate as its dark black rear lifted high in the air, level with the window. The rear legs smoothly guided the rear end down to the level of the bed like a wasp injecting its stinger.

The oval tip of the bug's abdomen came thrusting down past the window. Jim was sure it was coming straight through to get them, but it stopped short at the base of the window. Suddenly, a light gray circle was contrasted against the creature's black, armored hide. The circle grew into a long, slender gray tube, which extended a couple of feet into the air. The tube swayed slightly with its release, but stood erect.

The process was repeated twice in a matter of seconds, leaving three gray tubes jutting out of the truck's bed below the window.

"What' happening?" Cindy chewed her clenched fists.

"Eggs. I think it's laying eggs."

"Oh God."

"Shhhh! Hear that?" Jim could feel the vibrations in his guts more than he heard the growing droning in his ears. The sickening sound of thousands of hard alien legs clicking together was approaching fast.

"Oh God … they're coming back!" Cindy pressed herself to the bottom of the floor.

The dim light illuminating the storefront was blotted out as a dark cloud of aliens descended on the truck. They hit every surface. The windshield erupted, showering them with fine shards of glass, then sagged under the mass of landing bugs.

Desperate to see if any bugs had made it into the truck, Jim sat up in the seat, his eyes darting to the windows in all directions. Almost every surface was coved in bugs. Now, only inches away, they looked much bigger. The sound was overpowering, terrifying.

Suddenly the smacking of falling aliens stopped, and the humming drone took on a new pitch. The orientation of the bugs on the window seemed to flip in an instant, and they began leaping away. The truck lurched, and within a second almost all of the bugs were gone. The clicking hum was moving into the distance as quickly as it had overcome them.

"It's okay … Shhhh … come on, now. We're okay. They're gone." Jim reached out and tried to pry Cindy's clenched fists away from her face. "Listen … they just took off … they didn't see us."

"Where are they?"

"I don't care. They're gone." Jim tried to peer out of the driver's window but couldn't see past the shattered glass.

Cindy pushed herself off of the floor and crawled onto the seat. "Look!" She thrust her finger to the bed and pulled his collar.

Jim looked to see a bug flattened in the truck's bed.

"Is it dead? It's not moving."

"I don't know."

"What are those?"

"I think those are eggs."

"Look over there … there's another one!" Cindy bit her lip.

Jim looked to the street; there was another bug, and this one was moving. The boot-sized bug was carrying a twisted piece of metal twice its size along the street. With a quick snap of its legs, the bug and metal leaped into the bed. Shielded behind the scrap metal, the bug approached the rear window and then placed the metal at the base of the gray tubes. Once the piece was in place, the bug disappeared with a snap of its legs.

"What's it doing?"

"Another one!" Jim exclaimed, pointing to a bug that had been out of view from the window until it crawled over to the gray tubes. It too was dragging material to place around the tubes.

"What is that?" Cindy sat forward to peer at the bug and the glittering material it clenched in its front pinchers.

"Those are diamonds … be quiet, will ya?" Jim whispered.

"Where did they get those?" The bug outside wrapped the strand of diamonds around the tubes and quickly turned away. The second bug reappeared, laden with a heavy chunk of concrete.

"Those are mine." Jim could see his loot scattered over the truck bed. Sacks of jewelry had been torn open, and bank notes were strewn everywhere.

As the bug pushed the concrete into place, the second bug appeared again, dragging a gold wristwatch behind it.

"What is all that stuff?"

"Salvage," Jim said flatly. He didn't think the term "looting" was applicable anymore, considering the circumstances. "Look, it doesn't look like these things are going anywhere any time soon. I say we make a break for it while we still can."

"No. They'll come back. They'll see us."

"We can make a run for that building over there."

"No! We can't."

"Then let's see if we can drive out of here."

"They'll hear us."

"We have to get out of here. I don't want to stick around to see what comes out of those eggs!"

Cindy stopped and glared at the gray tubes. The bugs continued to pile debris around them, completely oblivious to their presence. "Do you think it'll start?"

"I think so ... but I don't know about driving it."

"Where are we going to go?"

"We go as far as we can, or until we find something better. We can handle two of these things."

"Three." Cindy pointed to the frozen sentry sitting at the end of the truck's bed.

"We can't stay here like this." Jim positioned himself in the seat and gripped the key with a trembling hand. He turned the keys and feathered the throttle. The truck sputtered briefly, causing his heart to sink, and then fired to life. He gunned the motor and slammed into reverse. The rear tires gripped hard and pulled them free of the broken storefront with a horrendous crunch. The rear wheels smoked, and the truck crashed backward onto the street, bouncing Jim hard in his seat. The tireless front rims squealed along the ground without traction.

"Hold on." The truck slammed into an abandoned car with a jarring smash. Jim pushed it into drive and stomped the accelerator.

The street in front of them was mercifully clear of big obstacles, and Jim was able to keep the truck pointed straight ahead. He made his way down the broad avenue toward a break in the dark gray foreground, a gap between two tall buildings.

"They're still there!" Cindy looked back frantically.

"We're doing okay … I can see a break in the buildings." The truck picked up speed.

"Look out!" Cindy screamed, but it was too late. Jim hadn't seen the big pile of earth. The truck hit with a lurch, but its momentum carried it over, battering Jim and Cindy as it slammed back to the street.

When Jim managed to right himself in his seat, he saw what the empty space before them was: a tall sound wall had been knocked flat and lay in the street. The gap opened up to a steep decline leading to the freeway below. With no traction in the front tires, there wasn't enough control to turn left or right. There was no time to stop.

"Hold on!" The bare front rims stuck the fallen brick wall, launching them skyward before plummeting down the embankment toward the freeway. The truck bounced down the slope, nearly pitching over, finally slamming into the flattened empty lanes of the freeway. The front end spun; the wheel had been ripped from Jim's hands, and his feet were unable to find the brake peddle.

They came to a jarring stop against a guardrail in the median. The truck's motor bumped and hissed.

"You okay?" Jim gasped; his chest ached from the battering it had taken from the steering wheel.

"Are they gone?" Cindy croaked as she raised her head up to peer at him.

Jim slowly turned to look out the back window. The truck's bed was completely empty, except for the three gray tubes.

"I don't see any. Come on, get up." Jim took Cindy's arm and pulled her to the seat.

"Shhh. Listen … Oh my God … Can you hear it?" Cindy gripped his arm and pulled him close. Jim pulled himself away and cocked his ear to the world outside. A sound was growing, but it was different from the drone that had chased them.

Jim grabbed for the gearshift and pulled the truck into reverse. He revved the motor to pull away from the guardrail, but the truck sputtered and died. With the engine noise gone, the sound outside grew.

"Start the truck!" Cindy yelled.

Jim tried to ignore her screams, focusing his attention on getting the battered truck running again, but the engine just clicked over and wouldn't start. The inside of the truck began to reverberate with vibrations. Rhythmic booms caused glass to dance across the dashboard.

"Listen, hear that?"

"I know, ... I know!"

"No. Stop. Listen ... music! It's music! I know that song!" Cindy came alive and propped herself up on the seat. "Metallica!"

"Music?" Jim stopped turning the keys and strained his ears to hear past the drone of clicking bugs.

"It's getting closer. Can you hear it?"

"I hear something. That's not music."

"From over there ... it's music!" Cindy flung the door open and leaped to the ground.

"Get in here!"

"Over there! Look!" Cindy pointed down the freeway and began waving her arms. Jim leaned over the seat and peered out the open door. He could hear the music clearly through the opening. It was fast, booming heavy metal. He could see the fast-moving shape of a vehicle charging down the freeway toward them.

"Over here!" Cindy jumped up and down, waving her arms.

Jim tugged at the door handle, but it wouldn't open. He rammed his shoulder into the door and spilled out onto the road. A massive four-wheel drive pickup sped toward them. Heavy metal blared from two enormous speakers mounted to the top of the cab. The music overwhelmed all other sound.

A dark cloud seethed in front of the pickup and suddenly materialized into thousands of black shapes. Jim was about to shout over the noise but Cindy had already seen them. "Shit!" Cindy dove into the cab and slammed the door behind her.

Jim followed, but his door wouldn't close. He held it tight as the thick cloud quickly flashed past them. The monster truck passed by, and gunshots rang out. The music faded as the truck sped past. The swarming mass of bugs seemed to be driven forward by the truck.

Cindy screamed. "Stop! Don't go!" She clung to the door and peered through the shattered glass. "Where are they going?"

Jim could see a Confederate flag streaming from the back of the truck as it continued down the freeway. A second set of headlights followed from behind. Jim squinted into the darkness and saw the profile of a military Humvee closing the distance. Still another pair of headlights—a larger truck—followed behind. "Cindy! Behind you, look!"

Jim could see the outline of a man poking through the top of the Humvee. The long barrel of a machine gun jutted out in front of him. The Humvee passed with a rush of air but didn't slow. The black man behind the wheel stared at him as they passed, then rolled the heavy jeep to the shoulder of the road. Clouds of dust shot from the tires as the jeep skidded to a stop.

The second larger truck rumbled by and screeched to a stop, angling sideways across the freeway. The loud music redoubled in volume, and Jim caught sight of the monster truck turning around in the distance. The truck with the speakers worked its way back, veering from side to side. He could see that they still drove a cloud of bugs in front of them.

Men spilled out of the canvas-covered diesel, and seconds later the canvas was pulled away to reveal a huge anti-aircraft gun. The monster truck stopped, and the ball of insects hovered over the open road. Men armed with shotguns took cover around the massive diesel.

An ear-shattering blast ripped through the air, and flame shot from the multi-barreled weapon mounted on the truck. Brass shell casings rained down and danced over the road. Others took aim on the swarm and fired their shotguns. The withering fire pulverized the dark cloud of bugs. Sparks and clouds of concrete tore through the air where the bugs hovered. The enormous gun spit flame at an unbelievable rate, vaporizing the sound wall behind the bugs.

Moments later, the mighty gun stopped. The road was littered with shards of black, and the massive cloud was gone. Men closed in with their shotguns and blasted anything that moved. The heavy metal music stopped, and the monster truck slowly rolled back to the scene.

A loud cheer went up from the men around the big diesel. The Humvee drove toward the truck, and the cheering increased. Some of the men ran out into the street and began stomping the wounded insects. Jim noticed that none of the men wore military uniforms. Some were older than he was.

Jim pried his fingers from the door handle and crawled out of his truck. He turned his attention to the men getting out of the Hummer, expecting to see a military officer taking charge. The turret gunner remained in place, covering the freeway with his machine gun, while a man awkwardly worked his way out of the front seat. Slowly, the barrel of a sawed-off shotgun poked out of the door and was followed by a cautious first step. The man's hands seemed to guide his leg out of the seat, placing his first step onto the road. Jim was stunned to realize that man was wearing sneakers, not army boots.

Most of the men around them were hell-bent on smashing the greasy alien corpses littering the freeway. No one seemed to take notice of the rescued survivors. Cindy slammed the door and sprinted over to the large diesel.

The first to take notice of her was a frail-looking man who was stooped over scooping up spent shells. The army helmet on his head almost blocked out his eyes completely. He lifted it off his brow as he looked up at Cindy rushing toward him. "That's right. Come over here, girl."

"You've to get me out of here!" Cindy nearly leaped into the open truck bed where three men attended to the big anti aircraft gun.

"Wait right there! Arthur … Arthur, go get the sergeant." A man from atop the truck was shouting to the elderly man standing next to Cindy. "Arthur, go tell the Sergeant we have the survivors over here."

"What?" The old man shouted back at him and raised his hand to his ear.

The man in the truck waved him to the front, and the old man shuffled off. "Poor guy, the guns made him totally deaf."

"Thank you … you have to get me out of here, please!"

"You'll be all right with us. Hey, buddy, over here." The man waved Jim over with his hand.

Jim's legs were slow to respond and shook with every step as he crossed the road. He couldn't believe his luck had held out again.

"You guys run off the road or something? You're headed the wrong way."

Cindy looked utterly frustrated by the lack of attention she was getting. "We were being attacked by those things! You came just in time! They were about to kill us!"

"These bugs here?" Another man questioned her as he loaded shells into his shotgun. "Couldn't have been these ones. We've chased these ones from back there." The man pointed down the barren freeway.

"They swarmed us! They chased us off the road!"

"There were hundreds of them! A big one laid eggs in the back of my truck." Jim jerked a thumb over his shoulder and wiped the sweat from his brow.

"What did you say, Mister?" Another man stuck his head out from the cab of the big diesel and eyed him skeptically.

"You saw one of the big ones?" Asked another man standing near the big gun. Suddenly the two survivors were not lacking for attention.

"The goddamn thing laid eggs in the back of my truck." Jim motioned to where his demolished truck rested against the guardrail. "Don't believe me?"

"Trent, we've got eggs over here! Tell Sarge!" One of the men leaped from the truck and chambered a round in his shotgun. "What did the eggs look like?"

"Long tubes." Jim estimated the length with his hands.

"Shit! Spiders!"

"Someone get the sergeant over here. Tom, where's the dynamite?"

"I'll get some."

Cindy's mouth hung open. "Spiders?"

"When were they laid?"

"I dunno—only a few minutes ago."

"Good, we've got time." Men clustered around Jim and stared over at his truck. "How many? Three?"

"Yeah, three."

"And you saw the egg layer?"

"Yeah, it was bigger. What are in those tubes?"

"Probably spiders. Those ones that we just blew away were scouts. They travel with the egg layers who leave those egg tubes everywhere. Spiders come out the tubes. Nasty little fuckers too. Bite everything." The man turned from Jim at the sound of approaching footsteps. "Over here, Sarge. He says there are some egg tubes in his truck."

Jim looked up to see the immense figure of the black man he had seen driving the Hummer rounding the corner of the diesel. Another man walked beside him. They were both wearing civilian clothes, but the smaller, white man had a hardened military look. He was the one they were calling sergeant.

"You've got egg tubes over there?" The man they called sergeant pointed the barrel of his gun over to Jim's truck.

Jim was about to answer when he was cut short by Cindy. "Hank? Hank, is that you?" She pushed her way past the curtain of men and stood in front of the Sergeant. "It's me. I can't believe ... Mr. Foster, you've got to help me!"

"Cindy?" The steely-eyed Sergeant raised an eyebrow in disbelief.

"Holy shit! It *is* her. Look at that!" The big black man's eyes went white with astonishment.

Cindy leaped forward and stopped short of throwing her arms around the man with the crew cut. "How did you get here? Oh, I don't care ... you're the only people I know in the whole world right now! You've got to get me out of here!"

"You know this girl, Sarge?"

"I just met her couple of weeks ago ... in England." The man eyed Cindy as if he wasn't sure.

"What should we do with the egg tubes, Sarge?"

"Do you want us to try and keep 'em? Or blow them up?"

"It's dark. Blow 'em up." He waved nonchalantly to where Jim's truck sat pressed against the guardrail. "Are you two all right?"

"Yeah, think so. My name's Jim. Thanks for finding us when you did."

"Name's Hank. Are you okay, Cindy?"

"I can't believe it … yes, I'm okay. I just want to get out of here."

"We'll get you to somewhere safe. But first we have to blow up your truck, Jim."

"Go ahead."

The man unlocked Cindy's hands from his waist and turned to the others. "Where's my guy with the TNT?"

"Ready when you are, Sarge."

"Let's do it."

"Wait! You can't blow it up! My work!" Cindy came alive with panic and moved to stop the man with a fistful of dynamite.

"What is she talking about?"

"She has some kind of art portfolio in there." Jim explained. "Don't worry about that now, kid. I don't like the sound of those spiders."

"Let me get it." Cindy broke free.

"Come back here, girl!" Jim yelled after her as if she were his own teenager.

"It's important!" She yelled without looking back.

"Trent, bring the explosives and follow me." Sarge chambered a round in his shotgun and gave the big black man a strange look. "Come on, Shug, let's help her get that portfolio of hers."

The jeep's door opened with a clank and a long creak. Hank reached inside to cover the cab light with his hand. Cindy didn't move. She was curled into a ball with her hands tucked under her chin. Hair covered her face. Shug snored in the back, his feet stretched into the driver's seat. Everyone was exhausted, but Hank couldn't settle. His mind was on fire.

The dust-covered portfolio lay on the floor under Cindy's feet. Hank reached in and grabbed it, keeping his eyes on the mop of hair covering her face. Her breathing was deep and rhythmic and didn't change as Hank snuck away with his curious prize.

He couldn't account for his desire to look at the paintings again, but seeing the way she had protected them planted the seed in his mind. Once again he found himself questioning the nature of coincidence. This girl, here … she had no idea that the original painting of the Madonna was the only possession he had taken with him to Florida, and the cheap photocopies of the Virgin tucked into her portfolio were her only possession. His painting was safe, too delicate to remove from her protective tube, but he somehow thought staring at the familiar image might clear his mind.

Brady, one of the younger kids, stood watch by the fire and jokingly snapped to attention as Hank passed by. The muscle-bound youth held a shotgun at the ready. Even though Brady was only kidding, Hank couldn't help but notice that he cut a fine form while standing to attention. He was glad to have Brady and his buddies around, even though they were proving to be a real handful.

"Morning, Sarge." Brady made his best attempt at presenting arms.

Hank nodded hello and tried not to call attention to the fact he was holding the girl's portfolio. "Where are Brandon and Hoffman?"

"They went on a coffee run." Brady's grin grew into a mischievous smile.

"Coffee run?" Hank readied himself for another stupid stunt.

"Brandon says he saw a Starbucks back there. I told them not to go …"

"No, coffee sounds good. I just hope those two knuckleheads get the good stuff. We're gonna have a busy day tomorrow. Make sure you guys get some rest." Hank caught himself about to salute the kid, but covered himself by checking his watch with a snap of his wrist. "I'll be in that van over there if you need me."

"You got it, Sarge."

Being called Sarge didn't bother him anymore. He even felt a touch of pride when the men saluted him. Hank paused at the door of the minivan and looked back at the ring of men and vehicles surrounding the fire in the middle of a dev-astated parking lot. He felt inspired by his small accomplishment. These men fol-lowed him. They had done what they'd come to do, and they hadn't lost a single man.

Hank craned his neck to check the sentries posted on both ends of the camp, then slipped into the van, turning on the light. The portfolio was stuffed with material. He felt a guilty surge of pleasure as he began pulling out the laminated prints and reams of notes. Finding a copy of his Virgin wasn't difficult; the top three prints all showed different views of *The Virgin with Saint Giovannino*. He held a print up to the light and traced his eye over every graceful detail. His eyes no longer leaped to the UFO; instead they focused on the Madonna herself. Her placid expression was so peaceful. To him she looked as if she knew a great secret.

No piece of art had ever spoken to him the way his Virgin did. He couldn't wait to lay his eyes on her. He had stopped himself from asking about her count-less times after finding Cindy. He didn't want to send any signals. She was already making moves to attach herself to him. She had already used words like odds and fate. He noticed how she touched her face when she spoke to him. There was an expectant look in her eyes, as if she were waiting for him to realize that there was something between them. He knew it was only natural, consider-ing the circumstances. She needed protection and security. She was using the tal-ents available to young, pretty women but he wasn't about to get played by a pretty girl. He knew what she was doing, even if she didn't. He didn't believe that fate brought people together. The very thought of fate playing a part in his life disturbed him.

He placed the print of the Virgin on the dash and thumbed through the other Renaissance-era prints. In one way or another, they all followed the same theme—artists struggling to portray the image of men coming down from the heavens. Many of the scenes were similar to his Virgin. Some had the same sym-bols unobtrusively painted into the background, but most of the others clearly depicted a singular event: aliens announcing the arrival of Christ. Some of the images were haunting. Hank's eyes bounced between the paintings and the dates and names printed alongside. He grew more and more impressed with her work as he began to grasp its thoroughness.

He scanned her notes on the Virgin, and was about to read more about a sim-ilar piece, when his eye caught a sketchbook stuffed deep into the leather folds. He pulled it open and thumbed through Cindy's own drawings. Each page was filled with black and white portraits done in pencil. Some of the drawings were left unfinished, while others were filled with amazing detail. Her talent was obvious, and she seemed to have a knack for capturing the intricate lines of older faces. He stared for a long time at the ancient face of a man he took to be a priest or a monk. The withered old man's eyes were cast down in a sorrowful expression. Every line was clear on his face. Each fine hair was drawn with precision.

Impressed with her talent, Hank turned the pages and scrutinized the faces. A sad-looking, middle-aged woman dominated the next few pages, and Hank soon guessed she must be the mother Cindy talked so much about. Her expression was lonely and sorrowful in each print, but she was beautiful. She reminded him of his Virgin, as if she too knew something unknown to everyone else. As he turned the next page, a strange twinge of pain bit his chest.

For an instant it looked as if his own face stared back at him. The drawing was incomplete, but the brooding, intimidating mask he'd perfected glared back at him. The outline of the face was hastily sketched, but the hard lines of the brow and deep-set eyes were his. Confused, Hank flipped to the next page and was shocked to see the next portrait was unmistakably him as well. The drawing was dramatically different than the first; his face was complete, finished in painstaking detail, and instead of wearing a brooding glare, he was smiling. The smile didn't seem natural to his face and gave the picture a flattering appeal that made him feel a little uncomfortable. There were two more half-finished sketches of him on the following pages, each one seemingly composed to make him look handsome.

Hank stared and stared at his smiling face but had trouble digesting the fact that they had been drawn before the catastrophe. A strange fluttering rippled through his guts as he realized that the beautiful young college student had actually thought enough of him to draw fanciful sketches. She had drawn them at a time before she had ever looked to him for protection—and even more surprising, she had drawn them after he'd sent her away without any promise of help. He'd done his best to show her that he wasn't about to be taken in by her charms, he had even been rude to her, but she'd drawn him anyway. His eyes went wide and his heart raced slightly with the realization her feelings might be more than survival instincts.

He tried to put the sketches aside, but his thoughts stubbornly drifted back to every instance where she had looked expectantly into his eyes. She was one of the few people who had ever held eye contact with him, and he couldn't remember a time when such an attractive woman had ever looked at him in that way. He began to entertain thoughts he'd pushed away ever since losing his leg. He began to fantasize what it would be like to be with a woman like Cindy, but he couldn't picture them together in any normal sense, not now.

Suddenly feeling guilty about rummaging through Cindy's effects, Hank was about to close the portfolio and return it, when gunshots broke the silence and sent him flying from the van. Sparks flew from Brady's shotgun. He was blasting something close to his feet. Hank's ears strained to hear the clicking drone he knew meant a swarm of bugs were coming, but he couldn't hear anything past Brady's wild cursing.

"Got one!" Brady waved him over as he bent low to peer at the spot on the ground where he'd blasted a bug.

In seconds, the camp was alive with men chambering their weapons and straining their eyes into the darkness. Hank rushed to his side, covering the blackness with his shotgun. Flashlight beams quickly scanned the parking lot, but nothing moved.

"How many?" Hank spoke in a quick whisper as his ears tried to pick up any hint of approaching bugs.

"Just one. A big one! Look, I think that's part of him." Brady pointed to a greasy spot on the concrete. "He jumped in close to the fire. I got him!"

"Did you hear anything?"

"No."

"Maybe it was alone." Hank spun around and scanned the ring of trucks and men. All was eerily quiet. Shotgun barrels peeked out from half-closed windows, and flashlights bounced from shadow to shadow.

"What do you want me to do, Sarge? Should I go turn on the stereo?"

"No, wait. We'll be okay as long as everybody stays inside. Go find your buddies and get yourselves inside your truck. I'll keep watch by the fire. It'll be daylight soon."

"I can stay out here with ya. I'm getting pretty good with this thing." Brady tapped the butt of his rifle, looking pleased with himself.

"Nah, I want you guys to be ready in the truck if we need you. I'll keep watch."

A southern-accented voice called out from the darkness. "Hey Sarge! What's going on over there?"

"Everything's okay. Stay in your vehicles. It was just a single bug." Hank gave Brady a proud pat on the shoulder and sent him back to the monster truck. "Good job, kid."

"Thanks, Sarge."

Hank backed away from the fire and hid in the shadows. Slowly, one at a time, the flashlight beams disappeared, and the camp was still. He waited in the darkness, keeping one eye on the Hummer, half expecting Shug to make his way over, but the jeep remained dark and Hank realized that Shug must have slept through the gunfire. After a few more moments, he was convinced that there was no need to wake him, and he settled in to finish the night watch. The next few hours were spent in silent vigil until men began to climb out of their hiding places to stretch their aching backs.

Hank greeted the men warmly as they congregated around the fire. Most of them looked worn and sleep-deprived, but they all seemed pleased to have had a few hours of rest. Brandon and Hoffman had found some coffee and were busy arguing about how to brew it over the campfire while others warmed themselves and checked their weapons. The sun was up, but the sky was still dark and the camp tinged with pinkish light.

Hank checked his watch once more, and was about to cross the camp to wake Shug, when the Hummer's door popped open and he climbed out from the rear seat. His hulking form moved achingly slow as he took his first shuffling steps toward the fire. His head hung low on his shoulders, and his eyes were only half open.

"Good morning, sunshine. Glad to see you could join us." Hank greeted him with a sarcastic smile from behind a raised cup of coffee. "What, did ya finally smell the bacon?" Hank was always jamming Shug up about his ravenous appetite, and the men around the fire laughed.

"Bacon?" Shug wearily rubbed his eyes and smiled.

"Come on, brother, have some of this." Hank stepped forward to hand him a steaming cup of coffee. "This'll wake ya up."

"It'll put a hump on a camel's back." Brandon made a playful, sickened grimace as he sipped from his cup. "I told you you'd screw it up."

"It's cowboy coffee! It's supposed to be strong, sissy!" Brady was clearly tired of getting hassled over the gritty campfire brew.

Shug let out a massive yawn. His nose seemed to lead him toward the food cooking over the campfire. He paused to take the cup from Hank and looked into the black brew suspiciously. "What's this stuff? It's not coffee."

"More like rocket fuel." Hank was already working on his second cup. "It'll wake ya up. Come on, it's getting late."

"Wow ... dis is nasty!" Shug spit the grains from the tip of his tongue.

"Do you think it's gonna brighten up out there?" Redneck Jack, the long-haul truck driver, was looking up at the sky from under his wide-brimmed straw hat. "I thought I could see the smoke breaking up a bit yesterday."

"I wouldn't count on it." Hank took another glance at the pale pink skyline. "Now that we're all awake, we should get started." Hank motioned for the men to gather around. "Brandon, who are we missing?"

"Hoffman is over in the truck. And, um, Jeff and Dan are over with the diesel. You want me to go get 'em?"

"I'll get 'em." Joe pushed himself to his feet from under his potbelly. "I need to go take a leak anyway."

Hank turned his attention to Sam, the CPA-turned-chef. "Sam, are you gonna be able to whip up breakfast for fourteen?"

"Fourteen?"

"We picked up two more yesterday, and Shug here always eats enough for two."

"Well, we have enough food, but I could use another skillet."

"There's a Bed, Bath & Beyond over there. What do you need?" Andrew pointed across the lot to a blackened building.

"I'll go with you. My wife used to love that place."

"Hold on a minute, guys. I wanna bring everybody together before we get started." The casual conversations stopped, and everyone turned their attention to Hank. "We did well for ourselves yesterday, but today is a new day. We've learned a couple of key lessons, and it's time to make a few decisions. First of all, I don't think anybody expected to find so many bugs this far north. But we did good. We proved we could go toe-to-toe with these things. That being said …" Hank paused so the men coming from the big truck could hear him. "I think it's time we reevaluate our situation."

"What did we miss?"

"Nothing, you're just in time." Hank motioned for the men to take a seat. "We all know why we're here, but now we've got to consider how we can do the most good. There're simply too many bugs down here for us to deal with."

As usual, Brady couldn't keep quiet for long. "How'd they get this far north?"

Brandon looked up from the fire as if the answer was obvious. "They flew, dumb-ass."

Brady was quick to fire back at him. "They ain't got wings, shithead!"

"When they parachuted off their ship they did! See, these things." Brandon turned his back to his friend, showing him the three interlocking, bone-hard alien crosses sewn into his jacket.

Hank tried to ignore the young men's constant bickering and pressed on. "We're still hundreds of miles from the epicenter. We've probably only scratched the surface here."

"They must be breeding like mad." Redneck Jack spat chewing tobacco into the fire "The ones we seen yesterday weren't the same ones that came down from the sky. They looked more like fleas, ya know, like when you look real close up like."

"They're the next generation." Trent the fireman nodded his head in agreement. "Before they hit us here, I was listening to my neighbor's short wave; they were already talking about bigger, faster bugs."

"Makes sense ... we've seen them laying eggs."

Hank stepped into the middle of the men, raising his voice above the crowd. "The point is: these things can reproduce faster than we can kill 'em. We can't make an impact carrying on this way. We don't have the ammo or the fuel, and the roads are chewing up our tires. I say we take what we've learned and cross back into Georgia. We can regroup from there."

"But we just got here! It took us all day!" Brandon looked up at him as if he were crazy. "No way! We've got the secret weapon!"

"Your stereo won't scare them off forever, Brandon. I know you guy are young and wanna kick a little ass, but you've got to use your head and listen to me for a minute. Nobody here is on a suicide mission."

"Sarge is right." Joe stepped forward, pulling off his straw hat and showing his balding head. "There's too much glass on the road, and I don't know how much longer we can go on salvaged parts."

"The Florida peninsula is mostly crushed coral, silica. It's not like other land." The retired schoolteacher spoke up for the first time all morning. "That's where all the glass is coming from. The impact melted it instantly."

"Thanks for the geology lesson, professor!" Brandon huffed angrily. His head swiveled back and forth to look at the others. "I can't believe I'm hearing this! Y'all wanna turn and run!"

Probably feeling shamed by his close friend, Hoffman jumped to his feet to agree with Brandon. "We followed you down here!" He thrust a finger at Hank. "You said we were gonna fight. You said we're at war! We can't cut and run now!"

"We aren't running anywhere!" Hank stepped forward toward Hoffman's accusing finger, and the younger man retreated slightly, burying his hands in his pockets. "And we are at war, the biggest war there's ever been. But right now, we're on the front lines—and we're not prepared. We didn't know what we were getting into down here; now we know."

Brandon was about to jump to his feet when Brady restrained him and tried to be the reasonable one among the three adolescent hotheads. "Why can't we stay and fight until the army gets here?"

"Let me explain a little something about the regular army, fellas. First of all, you can't expect them this far south anytime soon. We don't have a standing army, like you'd probably expect. Most of them are overseas, and the forces here are tied up in civil defense operations. It'll take a long time to organize a campaign down here. Secondly, St. Augustine won't be a safe place when they do. You can expect the army to come in on the heels of a massive air bombardment."

"Sarge is right, boys. He knows this stuff; we've got to listen to him."

"We need more men."

"And more ammunition." The faces of the men were stern and sober as they turned their attention to the three young men.

Hank could see that the twenty-somethings were about to explode into argument, so he made an appeal to their testosterone-fueled sensibilities. "There are tactical advantages beyond regrouping ... I know men at Fort Bragg. They specialize in organizing men like you. I'm talking about Special Forces. I want to get men like you into their hands. Think about it; you guys could get your hands on some real hardware. Maybe even trade in that silly monster truck for a tank."

Hank let the word "tank" hang in the air. Wide eyes and greedy smiles soon followed. "We've also gathered some good intel on our enemies. I wanna take that back with us. How much good do you think some pimply-faced kid with an M-16 is going to do down here? We need shotguns by the trainload. Our military isn't outfitted to battle insects: they're gonna have to change tactics and ordinance."

"And who knows if the army will ever come? Who knows how many more of these things will hit us?" Veins bulged across Sam's balding head as he shook his frying pan at the other men in the circle. "One could hit the Atlantic, and we'd all be dead!"

"How long ago did Kenya get hit?"

Trent looked to his watch, while almost everyone else unconsciously gazed up to the sky. "About sixteen hours."

"It could happen any time ... *where* is the question."

"Could! Of course it could! We can't sit around and wonder when we're all gonna die!" Brandon was on his feet now. "We're all gonna die sometime! I say we do it fighting!" He was careful to eye every man but Hank.

"And I agree with you, Brandon." Hank tried to maintain his composure. "But we can't waste brave men; not now. We're in a fight for the survival of all humanity. We have to fight smart. The stakes are too high to screw up. I'll keep my promise to you; I'll take you to a place where you'll be put into action, but I won't let you waste your life fighting down here."

"What about you?" Hoffman turned to face him. "Where are you going?"

"I'll meet with the men at Bragg, but I also have a friend in congress. I can press him to talk to the right people. I'll let him know what's going on down here. We need to conscript every able-bodied person into the fight."

"A draft?"

"You think you can do that?"

"That's what needs to be done."

"Sarge is right, we can't go on like yesterday. What if we come across more survivors?"

"We'll pick up as many people as we can on the way back to Georgia." Hank halfheartedly jerked his thumb toward the empty truck. As he turned, he caught sight of Cindy standing silently behind him.

"Georgia?" Her face looked clean and fresh; her hair was pulled back into a ponytail. Now she was recognizable as the girl he'd met in London a few weeks ago. "Are we going to Georgia?" She stood close to Jim, but her eyes looked intently into Hank's.

"I think it's best." Hank took his eyes from her long enough to check the faces of the men gathered around the fire.

"Good morning, Cindy, can I get you some coffee?" Brady pushed past his buddies to make room for Cindy.

"There's none left."

"I can make her some." Brady's teeth were spotted with coffee grounds as he smiled at her.

"You've got coffee?" Cindy looked down on the breakfast supplies with obvious delight.

"Sure, tons of it. There's a Starbucks on the corner." Brady pointed across the street.

"We'll have breakfast on in a few minutes, young lady." Sam stood over a flat of eggs as he wiped his glasses.

"Oh my God, I'm starving. Thank you." Cindy accepted the space made for her and took stock of all the food laid out before the fire. "You're not worried about the bugs?"

"They should be worried about us." Hoffman stepped forward, patting his shotgun with a cocksure smile plastered on his face.

"But won't the fire …" Cindy scanned the smoldering landscape, biting her lower lip. "Oh, I don't care. I'm starving."

"How'd ya sleep?" Shug stretched lazily as he let his eyes run over her.

"I don't know. I guess I did."

"You look better. I mean, you look all right." Brady caught himself, looking suddenly embarrassed. "I mean—you clean up pretty good."

"Oh brother, what a dork!" Brandon jabbed Brady in the shoulder. "You'll have to forgive him. He doesn't get out much."

"Shut up, fag!"

"You're the guys in that monster truck—the one with the big speakers on the front." Cindy's eyes bounced between the three young men.

"Yep, that was us." Hoffman pointed to the pumped-up Ford sitting on its balloon tires. "The bugs are afraid of loud music."

"I was never so glad to hear Metallica. I thought we were dead for sure." Cindy turned to face Jim.

"You like Metallica?" Brandon stepped in front of Hoffman, flexing his muscles.

"I do *now*."

"The bugs hate it."

"They're not the only ones." Redneck Jack rolled his eyes.

"I don't think Garth Brooks is going to scare anybody, Fat Jack." Brandon's face bent with annoyance at the attack on his favorite metal band.

Cindy bent low over the fire and pulled a piece of bacon from the skillet with her fingers. "Are we going soon?"

"We should head out as soon as possible." No one stepped forward to question him. The eyes of the three young men were all focused on Cindy. "We'll form up with the Hummer in the lead and the Ford in the rear. And fellas—yeah, over here—see if you can't find something else to play on that stereo, will ya? Don't get me wrong, I like Metallica, but the same damn songs are getting old."

"You got it, Sarge. I've got just the thing. Hey Cindy, you like Megadeath?"

"I'm sorry, who?"

"Hey Sarge, we might as well use the freeway if we can. I know the routes."

"Good idea, Joe: you ride up front with us."

"We've got room for you in our truck. You can ride with us if you want to, Cindy." Hoffman pointed to his truck with a leer.

"Take it easy, lover boy. You boys have a job to do. We'll put all the survivors in the big truck. Jim, can you handle a shotgun?"

"I can shoot, and I'll take one of those shotguns if you're offerin', but I'm stayin' here. My family is still out on the delta."

Hank stared back at him; this was the first time he'd heard any mention of the man's family.

Shug sat up, looking concerned for the first time all morning. "How far from here?"

"About twenty minutes from here, when the roads were good."

Hank felt a sinking feeling in the pit of his stomach. "How many people have you got there?"

"There were seven when I left. My wife and daughter, my wife's dad, and the next-door neighbor's family. They should be safe on the boat. We've got plenty of food, and the bugs can't get to us."

"You can't stay, Jim!" Cindy's eyes angrily narrowed on him. "You've got to get them out of here! Hank, you can't let him stay! He's crazy!"

Jim raised his hands in the air as if the matter was already settled. "I can't see it being any safer up in Georgia. It'll be safer on my boat."

"See, he's crazy! He just wants to protect his property. Jim, you can't stay. Think of your family!" Cindy pleaded with him, but her eyes never left Hank's.

Hank clenched his teeth and tried to hide his annoyance. "She's right. We can go back for your family." He knew half the day could be wasted evacuating the family, but she was watching him, waiting for him to do the right thing. He tried to look as if it were an easy decision.

"What about Georgia?" Hoffman sneered back at him. "Are we going to stop and save every family we come across?"

"We're talking seven people, kid!" Jack spoke up angrily. "That's two families we can save!"

Hoffman threw his hands in the air. "What are we doing here?"

"We don't need to be rescued!" spat Jim defiantly as he glared at Hoffman.

"Why did you come here?" Cindy was still looking directly at Hank.

"What, me and Shug?" Hank scrolled through the answers swimming in his head, but none of them seemed to express why he'd come. "We were in DC when Ida struck. There was a call for help, so we came. Everybody here is in the same boat, more or less. Most of these guys lost everything." Hank squatted over the asphalt and poked a stick into the fire. "Trent here is a fireman. Jack and Joe are truckers." He pointed from man to man in turn. "Sam is ... *was* an accountant. He lost his family in the blast. All of these men have stepped up to do what they can. They understand what we're doing here."

Shug stood up, throwing the rest of his coffee into the fire. "Coming down here made good sense at the time. We knew people would be evacuating the area. We figured there would be less competition and more left over resources. It might even be a little safer down here, if you know what I mean."

"No, I don't. I can't wait to get out of here." Cindy looked at Shug as if he were crazy.

Hank stood and slapped Shug on the shoulder. "And I wasn't about to miss the opening battle of the biggest war in history." He smiled and tried to look as if there wasn't anything crazy about coming to make war with the aliens.

"You guys are nuts."

Shug's smile widened, and he chuckled. "Besides, I'd never seen a real alien before."

"That reminds me; does anybody know where my portfolio is? I had it with me in the jeep, but it wasn't there when I woke up." She was staring at Hank again. She didn't appear angry, but his heart pounded unexpectedly.

"Oh yeah, well … I've got it." Hank pointed over his shoulder to the empty van. "I just wanted to have a look at some of your artwork … I mean *the* artwork. I wanted to see the Virgin … I mean the Madonna. I couldn't sleep. I was gonna …"

"That's okay." Cindy took a half step toward the van but stopped. He could feel her staring at him, but he couldn't meet her eyes. "It's okay as long as you've got it."

Hank's guts did somersaults as he waited for someone else to speak, but the long, pregnant pause grew.

She reached out to touch his shoulder, and he froze. "Do you think I could ride in the jeep with you guys?"

Hank avoided her face and stared at Shug. His lips were pressed together, fighting a smile. He could tell Shug was waiting to hear a refusal. He'd already told Shug he wasn't interested, but that was before he'd seen the sketch of him and that goofy smile.

Hank shifted hesitantly and stared back at her. "Yeah, you can ride with us."

Paradigm II
Chapter 11

Fort Bragg, North Carolina. June 22, 2002

Although it was temporarily obscured by clouds, there was sunlight in North Carolina. For a moment it appeared to Shug as if nothing had happened, as if the world wasn't on fire and people weren't dying by the millions. He let his body melt into the grass as he gazed at the clouds. He felt old and abused. The twenty-four-hour road trip had given him a stubborn knot in his back.

The warmth of the sun had never felt better. The soldiers at Fort Bragg had gone through the seemingly absurd ritual of mowing the lawns in front of the base, and the sweet aroma of freshly cut grass took him far from the world of smoke and ash. It was Saturday morning; the soldiers were displaying their discipline, their order, by doing menial landscaping and cleaning up after the growing horde of refugees. Shug thought the young army men were trying too hard; he could see the fear written on their faces.

The immaculately kept lawns surrounding the base's main entrance had done nothing to deter Hank when they had arrived that morning. The visitors' parking lot was clogged with civilian refugees; trailers and campers were packed into every corner, blocking all of the lanes. The soldiers at the gate had said the other lot was reserved for military family members, so Hank had driven the Humvee up over the curb and rolled down the median. Some of the army kids were still pushing their mowers across the narrow field of vibrant green as Hank slid to a stop, leaving two brown strips of exposed earth behind him.

He'd dismissed the sweat-drenched recruits with a curt nod and halfhearted salute just in time for Brandon to wheel his monster truck over the curb, spitting grass behind his massive, testosterone-pumped tires. They slid sideways to a stop, AC/DC's "Hell's Bells" blaring from the stereo. Shug would never forget the disgusted look on the soldier's faces as they watched Brandon and his buddies laughing at them.

"I could lay on this grass forever." Cindy stretched out in the shade of the Hummer next to him. "I am so sick of ash ... I'm so tired of ... I'm just so tired." Shug was ready for sleep, but he didn't mind having her around. She was stunning in the sunshine. She seemed different now that they were away from the nightmare of Florida. He forced himself to keep his eyes on the clouds and away from her slender legs or her flawless blonde hair. "You're not asleep, are you Shug?"

"Nah ... just looking at the clouds." He lazily extended his arm to point to the sky, then let it fall back onto his chest with a hollow thud. "See, that's an ice cream cone. And over there ... that's a Big Mac."

"Don't you think about anything besides food?"

Shug let out a deep, relaxed chuckle. "Think about pretty girls too, but I don't see any of them in the clouds."

"I couldn't eat, even if you *did* have some ice cream. I'm too tired. But keep going ... what else do you see? It's nice to hear about something other than Spain ... and bugs ... and shock tsunamis ... Oh, I'm sorry. There I go. I guess I can't stop talking about it, either."

"It's hard to take your mind off it. So many people ... world's gone crazy." Shug pointed to the sky. "I don't want to tell you how many bugs I've seen up there."

Cindy flinched at the mention of bugs in the sky. "That's not funny."

"Why don't you try and catch a few minutes of sleep? We're gonna be back on the road soon."

"Can't sleep. I've tried. Why don't you get some sleep? I know you're uncomfortable in the truck."

"I can't." Shug rubbed his hand over his face. "Too much drama."

"How does *he* do it?" Cindy asked drowsily, her hand covering her yawn.

"Who, Hank?" Shug laughed. "Hank's a machine."

"Why, because he was a soldier?"

"No, he slept like shit before ... before all this. He had nightmares. But since we've been running around playin' army, he sleeps like a baby."

"I wish I could sleep like that. I've had nightmares about aliens ever since I was a kid, but not these kinds of aliens."

"I guess real life can turn out to be scarier than our nightmares." Shug yawned, stretching out catlike on the grass.

"They're not just nightmarish dreams. They're real! I still believe that. My mother …" Cindy trailed off into silence, as if she couldn't continue.

"Hey, we all know it's possible now. There *is* life out there … we've seen it."

"My mother was abducted by aliens when I was just a girl. She died with everyone thinking that she was crazy. She died before I found proof."

Shug couldn't sleep in the Humvee, so he'd heard all about her mother while she talked with Hank. She had tried to convince him that all this was happening for a reason, that it was already spelled out, but Hank had made her feel foolish. She'd stopped talking about it. "You really believe in all that stuff? That Jesus was an alien? I'm not a religious guy, but it sounds—pretty bizarre, know what I mean?"

Cindy didn't sound sleepy anymore. "It's not that far of a stretch if you look at the facts with an open mind. Have you even read the Bible?"

"I read it. Hank made me. It's a book of fairytales … old fairytales." Shug was already weary of the conversation Bible talk always seemed to inspire. He had never understood Hank's fascination with the Bible. He could never understand the meaning Hank attached to the stories he didn't believe in. "It's all a bunch of superstitious crap."

An indignant look appeared on Cindy's face. "You're kidding me, right? You've seen them on TV, haven't you? It's a fact that aliens exist; so since they're real, take another good look at your Bible. Read all the accounts of strange men coming down from the skies." Her bottom lip stuck out in a frown. "And I never said that Jesus was an alien! That's not what my work is about … that's not what my art is trying to tell us."

"Your art … what you've said about the Bible is interesting, but not proof." Shug folded his arms behind his head and turned to meet her eyes. "And let me let you in on a little secret about what you see on TV: don't believe everything you see."

"What do you mean?"

"Well, shit … I've been dying to tell someone … and I suppose it doesn't really matter anymore …" Shug hesitated, thinking of what Hank would say. He leaned forward on his elbows and strained his ears to hear Joe snoring behind the wheel of the Hummer. Brandon and Brady were off exploring the base, looking for trouble, and Hoffman snoozed on the hood of the Ford. Reggae music quietly flowed from the stereo.

"What doesn't matter?" Cindy wrinkled her brow at him.

Shug spoke in a whisper, and Cindy leaned closer. "Well, you found Hank because you heard he was connected to—UFO-friendly television production, right?"

"And because of the Virgin." Curious where he was going, Cindy rolled onto her elbows and stared at him.

"And you saw the flying saucer over San Francisco on TV ..."

"Right ..."

"Well ... well, it was all a hoax! Hank's hoax. The UFO media campaign was all staged by him."

"What? A hoax!"

Shug hushed her with a finger and laughed quietly. A silent burden seemed to lift from his shoulders. "Trick photography, and a Frisbee." He flung an imaginary Frisbee through the air and made a whooshing sound. "That's where I'm from ... San Francisco." It was a relief to talk about something other than aliens and doom. He was sick of talk about Spain and the invasion of Europe. It made him laugh to think about his past life and how serious it was.

"You're telling me the whole thing was a joke!"

"No. It was never a joke. It was meant to stir up controversy, and it sure as hell did that. That controversy gave our cause a voice, and our guy the spotlight. The hoax was a good thing."

"The flying saucer wasn't real? It looked just like the one in the painting of the Virgin. That's why I went looking for him: it was just like the one in his painting. Oh my God—you must have been laughing at me this whole time!" He could see her finally making the connection between Hank and her painting. "I can't believe someone would do that!"

"No one is laughing at you. You were pretty clever to find Hank in England. You weren't the only one looking for him. You scared him."

"Me?"

"He's been on the run ever since the hoax. Someone tried to kill him. And then out of the blue, some college girl finds him. You let us know our cover was blown."

"Who else knows?" Cindy's eyes were beginning to swell with tears.

"Not many people."

"You weren't going to say anything?"

"We were about to. Hank was about to fall on the sword, take all the blame to protect our congressman friend, but ... but that was last week."

"That's where we're going? To meet with this congressman friend?"

"You don't want to stay here?"

"No! I don't know anybody here."

"But you'll be safe here. This is one of the biggest military bases around. There's an air force base right over there. They can take care of you here. I'm sure Hank is arranging something."

"I'm going with you! You're headed north, and I want to get as far away as I can! I'm not staying here." She looked so sad, and so pretty; Shug wondered if Hank could refuse her.

"What if Hank changes him mind and we head back to Florida?"

Cindy propped herself on her elbows and squinted at him. "You would go back? You'd just do whatever he says?"

Shug smiled, knowing she could never understand. "Yep."

"You'd go back and fight those … those disgusting bugs?"

"If it was the right thing to do."

"And *Hank* decides what's right?"

"I trust him. All these guys do. Can't you see it? Hank's special … he's the guy you want around when the shit hits the fan."

"He's crazy. You're both crazy. I think he's cold-hearted."

"Nah, he's not cold-hearted. He likes you. He probably won't admit it, but he does."

"I didn't mean it. I'm just upset. He did save me … and he went back for Jim's family. That wasn't cold-hearted."

"He's not a bad guy. He's just a little intense. He needs to mellow out, like my man Hoffman over there." Shug thought Hoffman was only pretending to sleep. When his knee jerked at the mention of his name, he knew for sure. "I think young Hoffman over there likes you, too … but in that special kind of way." Shug winked at Cindy and collapsed onto his back, letting the sunshine fall on his face.

"He's just another horny guy—he's okay, I guess. The three of them are all crazy. I don't know how poor Joe puts up with them."

"He's gonna kill 'em while they're sleepin'. That Joe is nuts, too." Shug smirked. He had never met such a bunch of characters before. Seven of them had driven on to Fort Bragg after leaving most of the men at an air force auxiliary base in Georgia. The big gun was handed back over to the military, and the men offered themselves up as militia fighters to the stunned air force reservists. Hank kept the Hummer, and the three juvenile delinquents had followed them in their monster truck.

Joe, a middle-aged long distance trucker and a real, good ol' boy redneck, knew the routes and led the way. He had spent most of the night behind the wheel, and he remained there still, his head flopped back, snoring.

With Brandon and Brady off looking for trouble, Shug and Cindy were left alone on the grass. Shug tried to enjoy the momentary rest with a pretty girl, but knew Hank would be back, itching to move on. "If you had a choice, where would you go?"

"I don't know anymore ... I just don't want to be left alone."

"Lots of people are going to have to start over. You're not alone."

"What about you? Where would you go?"

"What, if I were you?"

"Doesn't matter ... is anywhere safe? These things could keep hitting us and hitting us until there's nothing left."

"It could stop tomorrow."

A long pause followed his optimistic statement, and for a moment he thought the conversation might be over, that he could finally get some sleep. But after some long reflection, Cindy broke in as if the talking had never stopped. "It doesn't matter ... I still believe. I still believe what my mother told me. It doesn't matter if the UFO over San Francisco was a hoax."

"How old were you when your mother ... you know, was abducted?"

"I was just a kid. She was never the same after it happened. My Dad left her. Everybody thought she was crazy. I was the only one she could talk to."

"What did she say?"

"She couldn't remember everything about it ... just bits and pieces, but she was left with a profound understanding. And I can prove that what she learned about the aliens was true. No one ever believed her, but I can prove it. That is the secret my art is trying to reveal."

"What, that aliens had something to do with Jesus?"

"It goes way beyond that. I can prove that aliens had something to do with all of us. We're the product of one big alien genetics experiment. It explains the missing link."

"The missing link?"

"The missing link in the evolutionary chain. It took millions of years for early man to evolve from apes, and then all of the sudden—bang—we're fully developed humans, using tools, forming societies, wanting to fly through the sky like gods. How did it happen? Why? Nobody has the answers."

"And you think aliens helped us along?"

"All I know—what my mother told me, what I have learned from my art—is that they were here, and they have interacted with us from the beginning. Take a look at Genesis. It's the story of how they changed the course of humanity: *'let us make man in our image, after our likeness'*" Shug recognized the verse.

"'The Nephelium were on the earth in those days, and also afterward, when the sons of God came in to the daughters of men, and they bore children to them. These were the mighty men that were of old, the men of renown.' Genesis 6:4"

Her voice softened as she quoted the scripture. "The stories in the Bible, the stories in the Torah, the Vedas, Sumerian texts ... they can all be seen as trying to tell this story. Abraham, Moses, Ezekiel, Noah, Mohammad—they were all visited by aliens. Biblical man was no more prepared for a close encounter than we are."

"And what about Jesus?"

"I believe ... the Bible was trying to tell us that Jesus was special ... that he came from heavenly powers. He was part of a plan."

"A plan."

"All the alien interventions in our history seem to point to the fact that they wanted to teach us. Teach us how to live together ... they tried to pacify us, give us rules to live by and the knowledge of a higher power. And I think they created Jesus."

Shug closed his eyes and, just for fun, imagined she was right. "That's pretty heavy, if you think about it."

"It's not more far-fetched than what the Church would have you believe." Cindy looked away, shading her eyes to peer into the distance. "Look, is that him? Yep, that's him. I can tell by his limp. Here he comes."

Shug looked up to see Hank striding over at full speed, bounding over his prosthetic. He wearily pushed himself to his feet and brushed the shards of grass from his clothes.

"All right, brother, quit your lollygagging. Time to go." Hank called out to him as soon as he was within earshot. "Hey Hoffman! You fairies comin' or stayin'?"

"We're comin', Sarge!" Hoffman ripped the ball cap from his face and sat up eagerly.

"Where're the others? I thought I told you guys to stay here!" Hank scowled at the kid.

Hoffman brought a handheld, two-way radio to his face, pressed the button, and signaled his buddies with two sharp chirps. "Hey, you better get over here … Sarge is back, and we're moving out!"

"Ten-four. We're right behind you … over."

Hoffman slid off the hood, dropping to his feet in front of the monster Ford. "They'll be here in a minute, Sarge."

"Good. And knock off the Sarge bullshit … we're not in the army." Hank smiled and winked at the kid. "Call me 'Sir.'"

Hoffman grimaced jokingly. "Yes sir."

"Where's Joe?"

"Right here … I'm awake." Joe sat up and rubbed his eyes. "I'm up."

"You comin' along, Joe? I could sure use your help."

"Where we going?"

"A little place near Front Royal in the Blue Ridge mountains."

"I know that town. It's just above Charlottesville. Not much there, just another mining town." Joe scratched his head, searching his trucker's memory.

Shug hadn't heard Hank mention Virginia in any of their talks, and the little town in the Blue Ridge Mountains sounded remote. "What's in Front Royal?" Shug fixed his eyes on Hank's and tried to gauge the excitement he was having trouble suppressing.

Hank locked eyes with him, and a genuine smile grew on his face. "Yeah, well, I just spoke to Billy. He's gonna meet us there tonight."

"You actually spoke with him?"

Hank pointed back to the Base and was about to speak, but Cindy stepped between them. "I'm coming too. You're not leaving me here." She didn't raise her voice or sound hysterical. She spoke as if it was a matter of fact, and there were no other options to discuss.

Shug was sure she was in for a big disappointment, but Hank screwed his face into a strange-looking smile and nodded his head. "Fine."

Hank stepped past Cindy, placing his hand on Shug's shoulder. "Billy says he can get a message to Strategic Command and Control. He was real interested in the fact that we didn't lose a single person while we were down here. He says he's willing to push the conscription idea. I've convinced him the bugs aren't so tough."

"But why would you do that?" Cindy looked astounded. "They're monsters!"

"We need an army down here. Bombs and planes won't do it. And the sooner the military is convinced it needs boots on the ground down here, the better.

There's not a lot of time. Our buddy Bill can get that message to the right people. He can help us find some place safe for you, too."

Again, Cindy appeared as if she couldn't speak. Her mouth hung open, and her face asked a hundred questions at once. Hank looked uncomfortable—as if embarrassed by his good deed—and he turned away from her, making his way to the jeep. "You can ride with us, if you want."

Cindy didn't move, but her eyes followed Hank. Shug stepped forward and offered her his arm. "Well, I guess we're off to Virginia. I hear it's real nice this time of year." Cindy took his arm, returning his smile. She looked back at the parking lot full of refugees and blew out a tense breath of air.

In a matter of minutes, Hank had rallied the men, and the trucks were loaded with fuel and headed out. Joe was behind the wheel, and they were about to pass the last guard post, when a huge bronze statue caught Shug's eye. The statue stood before the Airborne Paratrooper Museum; the bronze soldier stood on a massive slab of granite, surrounded by a golden-spiked fence.

Hank reached out and put his hand on Joe's shoulder. "Turn in here for a minute, will ya?" His voice was somber, and his eyes were riveted to the base of the statue.

Joe wheeled the jeep to the curb, and Hank sprang to the sidewalk before they had come to a stop. He strode up to the statue, disregarding the plaque and ceremonial barriers meant to keep visitors back. He threw one leg over the short fence of golden spikes, then another. He stood at the base of the giant paratrooper and stared down at a pile of black at his feet.

Cindy leaned across her seat next to Shug. "What's he doing?"

"That's the Wall of Boots. It's a memorial to all of the Paratroopers killed in combat." Shug pointed toward the mound of polished black at Hank's feet. "A pair of jump boots is left at the base of the statue for every Paratrooper that gets killed."

"What's he doing? He climbed over the fence."

Shug knew what he was doing, but he couldn't find the words to explain it to her. Hank had talked about his fate ending here at the Wall of Boots, but at the time Shug hadn't understood. Now, as he watched Hank crossing back over the fence with a single, black jump boot in his hand, he got it.

As the sun in his rearview mirror dropped below the pine-covered mountains, Bill clicked the headlights and adjusted his eyes to the winding road. They passed the low hills and began the climb toward the secret military bunkers buried beneath the Blue Ridge Mountains. He checked his watch, spilling ash from his cigarette onto his shirt. He brushed at the fallen ash, momentarily taking his eyes from the road. The tires rumbled over the center divide, and Bill jerked the wheel back on course.

Hank didn't even blink. Bill couldn't tell if he was simply exhausted, or if he was brooding over some unknown tension. He hadn't said much after leaving the others.

"We should be there in about half an hour." Bill smiled with the smoke pinched between his lips. "I just hope I can find this place. All these roads look the same."

"Do you think they'll listen to you?" Hank kept his frozen stare, absently chewing a thumbnail.

"No, they're going to listen to *you*. You've seen what's going on down there. You've got the military perspective they're looking for, not me. But I can get you in." Inwardly, Bill wasn't so sure. He knew the secret servicemen would balk once they ran a background check on Hank.

"And you're sure the president is there?"

"I hear all the big shots are there."

Hank didn't respond. Bill felt him slipping back into silence, so he tried a little small talk. "What have you heard about Europe? I guess the latest meteor hit Turkey."

"We heard about it on the radio."

"You found a radio station? I didn't think any of the privates were broadcasting anymore."

"We caught part of the Howard Stern show coming out of Charlotte. He didn't say much about Europe, though."

"I guess it's hard to think of a place like Turkey when those things are right in your backyard." Bill sucked in air over his teeth. "I still can't believe you went down there. You're a nut."

"It's not so nuts if you think about it. At this point, people are more dangerous. I'd rather take my chances with the bugs"

"I know, it's crazy out there."

"We need to mobilize those people. We can stop the bugs in Florida if we get enough manpower down there. You've got to make them realize the bugs aren't so scary."

Once again, Bill was sure Hank had overestimated his influence. He wasn't even sure they would be let in, even if they did find the base. He was about to give him his well-polished "I'll do what I can, but here's the bottom line" speech when his attention was pulled back to the road.

The narrow trucker's route suddenly blazed with white light. Light cascaded through the pines and over the road, giving life to shadows flashing between the trees. For an instant, Bill expected to see headlights rounding the corner, but the road ahead was clear, and there were no folds to hide an oncoming truck. The bright white intensified, and Bill squinted his eyes to keep focused on the road.

The light seemed to shine down from above. It washed over the windshield and filled the front seats. Bill figured they had stumbled on the base, and half expected to hear the roar of a helicopter overhead, but the air was silent. The lights shifted, growing brighter, and a sickening ache fluttered in his stomach. He tried to turn his head to face Hank, but he couldn't move. He wanted to point at the lights. He wanted to speak, but nothing came out.

He felt as if he were watching himself in a movie. He tried to hit the brakes, but his foot wouldn't budge. The light filled his vision, and he couldn't feel the wheel in his hands. The car's momentum slowed, his foot still planted on the accelerator. The motor died, and all sound vanished. Bill was desperate to stomp on the brakes—desperate to do something, anything—but he was completely powerless.

His thoughts blurred as the car rolled to a stop on the steep incline. The initial fear melted into an uncanny calm. A strange contentedness washed over him, as if the lights dancing in his eyes were telling him there was nothing to fear. Suddenly the car doors were open, and he found himself standing next to Hank in a dream-like trance. His eyes narrowed on the strange lights above the trees, and all thought left him.

Bill had no idea if hours or only minutes had passed since he was on the road; all he knew was that someone was gently commanding him back to consciousness. A single thought had been given a voice inside his mind. He awoke with the understanding that he'd been taken aboard an alien ship. He felt the presence of those around him before he could open his eyes to see them for himself.

His mind was scarcely aware of what his body was doing, but he was standing among them. They were intimately close, close enough to reach out and touch, but he couldn't move even if he had wanted to. Only his eyes seemed to move under his own power, and yet the voice in his head was commanding them open.

Vision slowly returned, and his eyes jumped from one ghostly figure to the next. He looked at their strange features but didn't feel the shock they should have inspired. His mind seemed to float in a sedate calm as he tried to make sense of his surroundings. There were three of them, identical in every way, with deep, colorless eyes and thin, frail-looking bodies. They appeared to be waiting for him to do or say something. He stared at them, not knowing what was expected of him. He couldn't shake the sensation that everything had already been explained, that they were simply waiting for the answer to some already-forgotten question.

Unable to fathom what he was supposed to do, he merely gaped at the surreal figures. They were not quite his height; their long, oval faces tilted back to look up at him. An aura of colorful shimmering light hovered over their heads, and a surreal radiance rained down over them from the ring of light. Bill was struck by the beauty of the strange display and couldn't find anything to fear about the odd-looking creatures.

There was little room in the circular space. The four of them were huddled together in the center. Bill's eyes trained on their naked bodies. Their slender, humanoid trunks were without obvious genitals. Their shimmering, hairless skin was completely gray. Their long arms hung motionless by their sides. Three wide-spread toes on each foot anchored them to the flawlessly smooth floor. Their deep black eyes seemed to look right through him.

Bill sensed a growing impatience pressing him as the three alien figures shifted to face one another. He couldn't tell what they wanted from him. They seemed to have total control over him, yet they appeared anxious for him to do something. *What?* His mind struggled to form a question, but he couldn't speak.

As if in response to his silent question, a voice suddenly manifested itself in his head. *William Kemp is with the Houmn.*

Regain your Self.

A rush of clarity accompanied the words in his mind. All at once, he knew that all he had to do was give form to his thoughts, and they would be heard.

Yes, phrase your thoughts to be understood. The strange noiseless voice rang inside his mind. He stared back at their faces, but their small mouth slits didn't move.

The first question to solidify in his mind seemed to float into the air. "What do you want from me?"

The Houmn desire to aid your people.

The Houmn desire your assistance.

"I can't move. Why can't I move?"

Nothing is wrong with your person. We have chosen to exchange with your Self only.

We have found this is the best way to overcome your stress.

Do not fear us, William Kemp.

Your body has been sedated. Your mind is clear.

Bill felt the impact of the unspoken words and realized they had done more than paralyze his body. They had pacified his emotions. He did not feel the fear they suppressed. He knew at once that they did not intend to harm him. They wished to give him something. "What is it?"

The Houmn have a message for you.

William Kemp must take our words to the human leaders in their base.

Bill began to understand what they intended for him. Streams of images and thoughts shot through his brain, coloring his mind with understanding. The sudden flood of information threatened to overwhelm him, pitching his mind off balance. He couldn't make sense of one idea before another took its place. Anxiety and fear, emotions somehow disconnected from his being, began to reconnect with sensation. His mind raced with a hundred questions at once, and he felt himself silently screaming out.

As if stayed by an unseen hand, all the distracting thoughts evaporated, and even the three figures standing before him blurred from focus. An unstoppable sensation of pleasure washed over him like the eruptions of a thousand orgasms hammered into a single moment, and Bill was left with a profound, vacant calm. Once again, he knew what they were doing. He knew they controlled him completely. He knew they were preparing him for something.

William Kemp must learn the message of the Houmn.

The Houmn will return you to your people.

Human survival is vital to the interest of the Houmn.

Bill tried to think past the fact that he was aboard an alien ship in a world of strange new possibilities and to comprehend the meaning of the words they projected into his mind.

William Kemp will facilitate between humans and Houmn.

The survival of humanity requires our aid.

The Houmn are your brothers.

The Houmn offer their allegiance to humanity.

Fearful images of insectlike creatures filled his mind, and he witnessed destruction leveled on the Earth from far off. He realized that the gray alien beings intended to intercede on behalf of Earth, but his mind spun with the question of how.

William Kemp must continue to the military base in the mountains.

Contact the human leadership. Inform the human leadership we wish to establish relations.

We fear they will attempt to destroy us.

William Kemp must establish safe conduct for the Houmn.

They must allow us to land our ships.

They must hear the message of the Houmn.

Still the question of how resonated from every corner of his mind. He couldn't fully comprehend what they intended him to do.

We will send our ships soon.

Time is critical.

William Kemp must prepare for the arrival of the Houmn. The question of where is irrelevant.

The Houmn will know as you know, William Kemp.

Our thought will be yours.

Your knowledge is ours.

The Houmn will send proof of our intentions with you, William Kemp.

Take with you the knowledge that the last of the Takk vessels has bombarded your home.

Takk—the unspoken phrase filled his mind with questions and rapid-fire answers. He felt the fear the Houmn associated with the plague of insects attacking Earth, yet he questioned the truth of their statement. 'The last?'

Fourteen have been sent. Fourteen have arrived.

There will be no more.

Take this knowledge with you. Convince your leaders that Earth's path is clear.

The Takk must be eradicated.

The Houmn will it.

The Houmn and humanity are brothers in the universe.

We are of the same make.

For humanity to die from the face of the Earth will be tragic to the Houmn.

You must secure our safety.

Fighters must not attack us when we come.

William Kemp, your mission is vital. You will herald our arrival and be the ambassador between two great races.

We will aid you in this task.

Go to the men inside their base. Tell them these words …

Hank fell into consciousness as if thrown through the threshold of another world. He was jarred back to life, blundering and confused. An excruciating shock gripped his senses, obliterating any coherent thought. His last clear recollection was of being pulled toward the strange lights in the sky. Now he was somewhere else. The strange lights still filled his vision, although ghostly blurs now hovered over him.

Fear transformed into pain as he struggled to lift his head and move his arms. The unreal pain grew in intensity until it threatened to plunge him into madness. All at once, a sharp, commanding voice flashed across his being. *Sempiternals will be alone with the man William Kemp. Do not intrude on the central chamber.*

He understood the statement as if it was spoken plainly, but there was no real voice behind the words. He could feel the implicit warning projected into him: there is a secret in the central chamber, and interruption will bring punishment. Then, as if in response to some unheard question, the booming voice filled his mind's ears again. *The Man is not important. The Man is damaged.*

The tone and impact of the statement added dread to his confusion. *Damaged*: the unspoken word was alive with meaning. He was *damaged*. He couldn't move or speak. He feared that his mind had split from his body. He feared that a damaged man could be disposed of. A primal scream cascaded across his psyche, but he couldn't hear any of it.

Clear his memory. Ease his shock.

He is to return with the man William Kemp. Make him ready.

The command struck him with the unquestionable realization that he was its subject. He clutched at the phrase *return* with a newfound hope and anxiously awaited further clarity from the nonhuman voice, but none ever came. Shadows dimmed the light overhead, and he was left in a pitiful silence. He somehow knew the presence had gone.

The shifting light told him he was moving, but he still couldn't feel it. The opaque flood left his face, and he caught sight of movement in his peripheral vision. His field of vision suddenly expanded, and three long, oval heads towered over him. He was still unable to focus or direct the movement of his eyes, but the alien faces peering down on him were clear. They grew in height as he was lowered beneath them. A single gray face bent over and stared through him. It was the same alien face described by abductees: it was a *Gray*. Its two massive, almond shaped eyes seemed to look right through him. The dark orbs were a cruel, glossy black.

The alien turned to face the others, and the space above Hank came alive with movement. The once slow-moving alien forms now darted in and out of view. Long, slender arms moved over his face without touching him. Small, dark objects were passed back and forth. They seemed to work in a frenzy of activity, even mishandling and dropping one of the objects passed between them.

Two of the slender figures stood opposing each other at Hank's side. Their hands flailed at each other, and a heated debate seemed to break out. One of the aliens thrust a black, formless mass into the arms of its fellow and, after some agitated gesticulating, left the alien figure alone at Hank's side. The creature paused for a moment, then raised the dark object in the air, draping the shroudlike hood over its head. The dense black shimmered with an electric ripple and appeared to weigh down the frail alien body. The hooded alien figure stepped away where Hank's eye couldn't follow.

Blank light poured into his eyes from above, and all was silent. Hank's mind raced on the brink of madness. There was no sensation, nothing to measure the passage of time, only the blank light overhead and the frantic thoughts screaming through him. The horrifying nothingness convinced a part of him that he was already dead. He was almost relieved to see the shadows return to blur the light again.

All three alien forms wore the heavy shrouds over their heads, and the dark hoods closed in a ring over him. Two thin arms reached down toward his face. Each hand had three long fingers, all probing his face. He couldn't feel them. He couldn't pull away. Featureless gray skin blocked his view, but Hank steadied himself, cresting a wave of panic.

Complete darkness enveloped him as something was slid over his face. Suddenly there was nothing. No sight, no sound. His body wasn't simply numb: there was a total disconnect, as if it were gone completely. He couldn't find himself in the darkness. His mind seemed to tear through space, wild with panic but with nowhere to run. The senseless madness grew, and still the nothingness continued.

Hank's thoughts ate one another in a half formed fury until, with the sudden blasting intensity, an infinite quantity of pain exploded in his mind. Brilliant colors and lights burst across his vision. A fierce electrical fire cascaded over his brain, melting away his being. The pain was greater than any he'd ever imagined. The fire in his mind burned until there was nothing left, and then the black nothingness enveloped him once more as consciousness left him.

Time had passed, but time mattered little to Hank as he woke under the opaque glow of alien lights. His eyes moved freely, and the horrible pain had stopped. He felt as if he'd been resurrected from the dead, instilled with a new-found clarity. The fear and confusion had left him, and he was filled with an odd awareness.

He lay in the center of a compact, circular room, the three hooded aliens standing over him. His eyes darted from figure to figure. Their bodies were covered with a shimmering metallic material. Their faces were hidden beneath the electric black shrouds. The nearest creature leaned forward, pulling the shroud from its eyes. The face was expressionless. The miniature mouth and nose slits were completely overshadowed by the large, deep black eyes. Hank ran his eyes over the alien face and tried to lift his head, but he couldn't move.

Success. He survived. Once again, thought in the form of speech flashed across his consciousness. It was not the same booming, commanding voice as before. Hank was certain it was the voice of the creature hovering above him.

We must proceed immediately, another androgynous voice projected into his thoughts. *Test him.*

We must not be detected. The words seemed to come from the alien bent over him, but Hank couldn't see any movement on its lips. He couldn't really hear the words but felt them instead. There was a tremendous anxiety woven into the thoughts.

There is no time.

He may not survive the second implant. The Sempiternals will suspect deception if he dies.

It must be this man. It must be now. This is our only opportunity. A third voice broke into the debate. The flow of words came too quickly for Hank to digest, but the fear he'd left behind was rekindled. *We do it now.*

Still unable to move, Hank watched helplessly as one of the figures bent toward him with a large object that looked like a syringe gripped between the three digits of its hand. The ominous threat of pain and the black nothingness gripped his psyche as a cold voice spoke inside his mind:

Prepare yourself.

Do not die.

The thought seemed to flow from the alien's eyes as it leaned closer. Once again, his vision slid to black as the shroud was pulled over his face. There was no pain from the needle he was sure had been plunged into his arm—there was no physical sensation at all—just the mental manifestation of fear and the pulsing pressure in his mind. This time his thoughts were clearer in the darkness. He pondered the statements reverberating in his mind. The mental exchange had taken only a fraction of a second, but its meaning grew as Hank considered it.

Do not die; the statement echoed with many voices inside his mind, at times sounding like a command, then again like a prayer. Prepare himself for what? What were they doing to him? What had they done already? His thoughts turned to the menacing meaning behind the term *implant*, then another flash of brilliant light exploded over his visual cortex and another all-consuming shock jolted him.

A bombardment of pain ripped through him like machine gun fire, wound on wound without relief. For the first time, he felt reconnected with his paralyzed body as it seized on the examining table. Stabbing pain sliced every inch of him, inside and out. The crescendo of pain and bright green light was followed by the strong smell of burnt almonds, then the three intense sensations of sight, touch, and smell swirled together for an instant before flitting out. All sensation vanished, and his inner voice faded into silence.

Hank awoke to surreal echoes of conversations in a corner of his mind. His own consciousness sat mutely, somehow patiently waiting to be revitalized by the memories falling into place. He felt void of physical self; none of the senses taken away from him seemed to matter now. The absence of feeling freed him from pain, and the terror of the nothingness had passed. He listened passively to the thoughts and voices coloring the darkness until a single, familiar voice caught his attention.

He tuned his mind's ear to the distinctive human voice. Many of the other voices seemed garbled and weak, but this one voice rang clear. It was a voice he would never forget: it was the voice of his older brother Tom. He was yelling, almost shouting, as he took up his little brother's defense against the other voices in his head.

Hank felt himself pitching back into utter confusion. He didn't want to think about Tom; he didn't want to leave the sedate calm that had come over him. He didn't want to know about the horrible things they were talking about, but emotions began to connect with the impulses swelling around him. Real sensation filled his body, and he found his *Self* lying flat against a cool, hard surface. His eyes opened to see the aliens hovering over him. He was still clothed, his hands worked into fists. He tilted his chin to his chest and peered up at them. His view shifted, and his eyes narrowed: with a sudden pounding in his chest, he realized that he could move.

Hank tried to sit, but his arms and legs were pinned by some unseen force. He stiffened, straining every muscle to pull away, but he was held firm. A primal scream erupted from deep within him. The yell echoed off the cramped space and rang in his ears.

Calm yourself. Make no sound.

The Sempiternals will hear him. The stream of alien voices returned, and Hank stopped his screaming to listen.

They cannot hear him. He is shielded.

The strange, inaudible voices triggered a flood of memory. He remembered seeing the lights on the road with Bill. He remembered what they had done to him. He remembered the black shroud, the pain, the nothingness. A crimson rage colored his thoughts. He remembered everything. "Let me go, or I'll kill you!" Hank growled out his first coherent thought and strained against the invisible restraints.

The three aliens recoiled and huddled together near his feet.

Stop.

Be quiet.

He must be silent.

You must understand us.

Hank froze; all at once, he understood that it was dangerous to make so much noise. A mass of meaning accompanied the rush of words filling his head. They were shielding him from another presence on the ship. The threat of death shadowed thoughts of detection. He suddenly found himself aware of things he should know nothing about. They had rebelled against their masters and were afraid. They had seized on a rare opportunity and felt as if the fortunes of two worlds hung in the balance. He could easily distinguish between the three alien beings and their fears. He could see past the concerns they gave voice to and glimpsed the fears they concealed.

Hank measured his first words carefully and spoke evenly, suppressing his emotions. "What are you doing to me?"

Be silent. There is no need to speak aloud.

We have enabled you to communicate with us.

It is vital that we exchange with you.

The phrase *exchange* was packed with meaning, yet Hank sensed they were holding something back. Without his willing it, his mind projected forward to probe their alien thoughts. The landscape of their alien psyches seemed vast and unfathomable, but a gradual understanding swelled with each passing second. Slowly, their minds became as clear as the thoughts they chose to project.

The frail Houmn nearest him had been the driving force behind the act of rebellion and seemingly had the most to lose. Desperate and fearful, it was determined to force something into him. The others seemed hesitant, dreading the return of the Sempiternal presence, yet none of them feared him escaping the table.

Feeling strength return to his sensation-starved body, Hank struggled against the invisible force pinning him down. He turned his eyes away from the Houmn, but his mind lingered with them—still probing, filling with understanding. He began looking for the bonds tying him to the table, but he couldn't see anything holding him down. He was about to shout out again when the voice of his older brother Tom spoke out from a corner of thought. He seemed to be speaking with the alien minds.

"Tom?" Hank mouthed the name aloud, and the question redoubled in his mind. He felt himself looking for his dead brother's face; he could almost feel him standing near.

Suddenly, it was as if Tom had wrapped his arm around his shoulder and whispered into his ear. Hank could almost feel the breath on his neck. "You're in big trouble, little brother. These guys are screwing with your nut. They want to put something inside your head."

Air stopped moving in and out of his chest, and Hank's muscles sagged. *They've made me insane.* He didn't say the thought aloud, but his voice was clear inside his head. His eyes swirled around the small silver space, and the three alien figures blurred into one. Tom's voice continued to speak above the sea of images drowning him.

"What have you done to me?" The question rang out loud and clear, but it was Tom's voice, not his own.

We have given you the ability to communicate with us.

You must understand. We desire only to help you.

He is in our thoughts!

How is he able to do this?

Something has gone wrong! His ability goes beyond our intentions.

I can feel him inside me! Make him stop!

Stop!

Tom's voice sounded from everywhere at once. He assailed the three Houmn with question after question: "what have you done to my brain? Why have you done this?" They could not hold back the answers, and gradually the sea of information that threatened to sink him began to calm, rolling and swelling with growing clarity.

Hank realized that he was held in place by a magnetic field and was powerless to break free. He understood how the machines worked; he understood how the

Houmn ship flew, and how they communicated with one another. He understood that they had done something to his brain and wanted to complete their task. He understood the shroud, the nothingness, and the pain. They were going to do it again, and he was powerless to stop them.

The Sempiternals will know!

They will hear him.

We have made a mistake. He must die.

He invades even our secret thoughts. Kill him.

No. We proceed. This Man is our only chance. The Sempiternals will not allow another.

He sensed the fear the Sempiternal masters conjured in the Houmn, but Hank couldn't imagine anything worse than the nothingness and death they wished on him.

Tom's voice returned to him, no longer in a whisper. "Hank, you've got to listen to them. You're not crazy. This is real. They've assured me that you'll be okay. Their masters have Bill, too. They're with him now, but if they hear you, we're dead. You've got to do as they say. Listen to them."

"What am I supposed to do?" Hank spoke aloud as his eyes searched for his older brother.

Stop your projections.

Turn all thought inward.

Use your thoughts to speak with us directly.

Hank turned his eyes on the nearest Houmn. He focused his attention on the glossy black orbs and formed a single thought in his mind: "I'm listening."

Good.

Silence all thought.

We have a message. A warning.

Hank knew the message was more than something spoken; they wanted to plant something in his head. They wanted to put him through the pain and nothingness again.

Stop. How are you doing that?

He knows. He is reading us.

Give him the message now. Quickly.

Understand that you are in danger from the Sempiternals. The Houmn are coming. They come to reclaim Earth. We are trying to help. Stop entering our thoughts.

The Sempiternals will hear you.

How is he doing this?

The human brain is not capable of this.

We do not know enough about the human mind. He is *doing it.*

The current of voices washed through him. He couldn't stop picking at their fears. Tom's voice spoke over his shoulder. "Hank, you must stop. Pull back your thoughts. There's not much time. The Sempiternal ones are dangerous. They're with Bill right now. They're promising to help us fight the bugs, but they're going to enslave everybody. These Houmn are already slaves to them. They are trying to warn you. You must let them do it."

Hank closed his eyes and searched for an imaginary object to focus his attention on. Faces and everyday objects flashed in the darkness, but his mind spun with ideas. Eventually, the painting of his Virgin grew from memory, and his mind's eye roved over every detail. He paused on the silver disk, as if he'd forgotten it was there. He found himself questioning why he'd been so drawn to the painting. She was more than a model for Devil's Peak; there was something irresistible about her. Now it was happening. His chest tightened, and a twinge of pain stung him between the ribs.

Hank consciously squashed the whirling thoughts of fate and predestination and carefully composed his next words. "What do you want from me?"

Take our message.

Hide it from the Sempiternals.

Take it back to your people.

Inform them the Houmn are no friends of humankind.

Your people must not become slaves to the Houmn.

The alien Takk insects have ended their bombardment. The invasion can be stopped. Do not sell your freedom for Houmn promises of technology.

You must fight the Houmn.

They are coming.

The image of an awesome armada of Houmn ships filled Hank's mind. His thoughts grew quiet as he pondered the power of so many ships, and he realized that this was the message they spoke of. Thousands of Houmn ships were already headed toward Earth. Invasion by the insectlike Takk had triggered countermeasures that would lead to the total domination of Earth by the Houmn. The Houmn are coming to reclaim the people of Earth. The message generated question after question in Hank's mind. He turned his thoughts to the Houmn standing over him. He sensed a vast network of alien minds through them. He wondered how all this had come to pass, how they had come to betray their masters, and why he was being given this message.

As if in response to his unasked questions, the Houmn projected a stream of answers for him to pick apart. *The Houmn aboard this ship are part of a small contingent of scientists.*

The Houmn have watched over the Earth long before the creation of man.

Houmn oppose the Takk and will use their power to keep them from Earth.

Hank wondered why the Houmn hadn't warned them before, why they hadn't used their power to stop the Takk. He asked why the Houmn had hidden themselves all this time. These questions, along with hundreds more, flowed from his mind into theirs.

We will tell you all. All we can.

We keep ourselves hidden because we are the watchers. We avoid involvement in the lives of humans.

We did not know of the Takk threat until it was too late.

The Houmn will not remain hidden anymore.

The Houmn are coming. We will land ships on Earth.

The Sempiternals will speak with the leaders of Man.

Hank wondered how many Houmn ships watched over Earth and what help they promised to bring.

We have only one Great Ship watching over the Earth.

There are thirty-three ships such as this one.

We are scientific vessels and do not have the destructive power to fight the Takk.

The Sempiternals promise Houmn technology.

The Sempiternals send a message and a warning back to Earth with the man William Kemp.

They promise an end to Takk bombardment and caution against the use of nuclear weapons.

We must send our own message back with you. Do not trust the Houmn.

Hank's thoughts turned homeward. He couldn't imagine himself back on Earth. So much had changed inside him. His real life seemed to have come to an end in the belly of this Houmn ship. A new life, defined by strange new thoughts, dominated him now. A myriad of strange voices rang inside his head. Tommy's voice still exchanged with the anxious Houmn rebels. His own inner voice asked about spaceships and alien warfare. He imagined Bill somewhere in the ship. He could almost see him with the mysterious Sempiternal masters. He wondered how anyone could function, knowing all this, and thought he would be thrown into a straightjacket as soon as he opened his mouth back on Earth.

An alien voice was explaining that they had never seen their home planet. They were the twentieth generation to study Earth from orbit. Hank wondered how they had kept their presence a secret all this time—and came to understand that the Houmn in front of him were the very same aliens who had been spotted over New Mexico, Brussels, and England. They had been to Earth many times. The aliens' memories of these events were clear: they had taken other humans aboard their ship, but they had never attempted to communicate with them as they were with him. Only the Sempiternals could communicate with humans.

Stop!

You must stop probing our thoughts.

This was never intended.

We will tell you all you need to know.

"Why is it happening? I can't control it. What have you done to me?" Hank spoke aloud, shaking away the other voices in his head and grounding himself with his own. He understood that the Houmn were shaken by his ability. As slaves to the Sempiternals, they had trained their minds to keep certain thoughts hidden away, but he had easily pried open those defenses and ran wild inside their minds.

All three aliens felt an immense guilt eating at them. They all hoped to amend some terrible mistake through their actions. Their whole cause depended on their success, and they were on the brink of failure. They feared that they had triggered the catastrophe on Earth by sending a message to their rebel counterparts. Their message had been intercepted by the Takk, and Earth had been exposed. Soon the Sempiternals would learn of this critical error, and the Houmn rebellion would be exposed and put down for good.

It is true. We did send a message to our allies.

The Takk intercepted our message and found Earth.

This tragedy is our fault. The rebellion is doomed.

The Sempiternals must never know of our treachery. We must keep Earth from falling to the Sempiternals. Let this man carry the message for us. Let him convince the people not to trust the Houmn. It is our only chance.

But who is this man? How can he penetrate our thoughts so easily? Where did we go wrong?

Emotions he'd left in the void of nothingness crept back to color his thoughts. A growing anger seethed inside him. All this was happening because of some blunder committed by these inept alien scientists. He felt suddenly compelled to answer their questions, to tell them who he was and what he thought of them.

The statement he projected forth shocked them into silence. All the background chatter stopped in his mind, and the three Houmn figures physically pulled away. For a moment Hank thought he had scared them with his anger, but then he realized that they were merely digesting what he had told them. They focused on his declaration of *Self* and the flood of content carried with it. Their minds seemed to catch on something in his past. Then a new sensation lashed out at him, a new emotion colored his senses. Hank's mind pulled away, and he realized that he was feeling their anger projected back at him.

Deceiver! The alien voice came as a shrill cry.

You have done this! He is the Deceiver!

He is the one!

No. Impossible!

Deceiver: the word clung to Hank's mind. He could not make sense of the Houmn thoughts racing back and forth. They accused him of being part of some plot. They accused him of tricking them into their treachery. Strangely familiar scenes of flying saucers flashed through their minds.

You! You have caused this! The bitter Houmn voice pushed past the others.

You have fooled us!

You are the Deceiver!

Hank was wondering what he'd done when the vision of *his* flying saucer flashed in his head. Now he understood why the vision looked so familiar; it was the shot of little Betty flying over the San Francisco horizon. This was the deception they spoke of.

You have caused our great mistake!

We saw your deception through Earth's television satellites.

The Sempiternals alerted the Houmn, and we sent a message to our allies through the Great Viscera. We hoped our message would arrive first, and we could prepare our allies, but the Takk intercepted our communication from within the viscera.

Now the Takk have come to devour Earth! This is your doing. You are the Deceiver prophecy warns of. You will be the end of Houmn.

In one horrible instant, Hank realized that they were right: he had set the catastrophe into motion. He was the *Deceiver*. He felt the confusion and concern his hoax had stirred in the Houmn collective. His responsibility was clear, but the prophecy they spoke of did not seem possible.

He cannot be the Deceiver!

He is one Man among billions. Impossible.

There are no coincidences.

It is Fate. We must accept it.

We have him. He is our only opportunity. We must continue.

No. We must stop. He changes everything. We must end this string of errors.

This is our Fate. Our destinies are intertwined with this man. He is our only hope for ultimate freedom.

If this Man is truly the Deceiver and the prophecy is correct, we have been wrong all this time.

We must reconsider.

There is no time. If we do not act, the power of the Sempiternals will grow exponentially. I will implant the message now. He will carry it to the people of Earth. He will convince them. The Houmn leader reached out with its long arms and began to pull the black shroud over Hank's eyes.

Hank thrashed under his invisible restrains and screamed threats of violence but the Houmn didn't pull back. He knew the shroud would bombard him into the horrible nothingness again, but he was powerless to stop them. He tried to order the Houmn to stop with a mental command, but the creature bent low and gazed at him through its glassy black eyes.

All depends on you. The Houmn invasion arrives one hundred years from now. You must prepare your people. You must not give yourselves over to the Houmn.

Hank screamed aloud, but the shroud was pulled over his face. The voices in his head vanished, and a flash of brilliant pain crashed down on him. He felt his body slipping away and the cold, blank nothingness eating at his being.

Paradigm III
Chapter 12

Washington DC. June 23, 2002

Dust clouds darkened the sky, but occasional pockets of sunlight drifted across the lawns separating the two great monuments. Bill stood on a hastily constructed platform, Abraham Lincoln at his back and the Washington Monument towering before him. He looked at the crowds behind him. He thought there should be more government officials present, more people. The marines outnumbered the crowd. Not everyone seemed convinced that this was going to be the most significant event in all of history, but as one of only two men sharing the stage with President Bush, Bill could feel it. He knew what this day meant: the Houmn were coming, and they would save humanity.

The other man standing to the president's left was a mystery to him. He'd never seen or heard of him before, but without his help he would have never gotten through to the president. Bill was being thrown out of the Blue Ridge complex when Mr. Ellis intervened. Everyone thought he was crazy, but Ellis seemed to take him at face value. Bill had been frantic until the Houmn had taken over and placed the right words in his mouth. Ellis appeared to understand everything, despite what the others were saying.

Now Mr. Ellis stood unmoving, bent over his cane at the president's side. He hadn't said a word during the last ten minutes of waiting. He didn't even acknowledge the crowd; he just stared at the grass near the reflecting pool. Bill was watching the little old man from the corner of his eye, wondering where he fit in and why he held so much sway over the president, when Ellis pushed away from his cane and leaned close, whispering something into the president's ear.

Bill couldn't hear him, but it didn't matter. It was time. The Houmn were coming: he could feel it.

President Bush huffed angrily and spat onto the floorboards. He'd been glaring at him all morning, making it clear he wasn't pleased at sharing the stage with him. He was furious at having to give up his presidential powers and was on the verge of cursing, but Bill didn't care; President Bush was no longer the most important person on the platform. The alien words still rang in his ears: *William Kemp will restore hope. William Kemp will bring our two worlds together.* A full day had passed without a deadly impact, and his promise had come true. People were going to see *him* deliver the message of hope.

Bill's mind danced with thoughts of the Houmn and his own importance, but a nagging image attacked his swelling pride. He couldn't erase Hank's zombielike expression from his thoughts.

The president's angry voice cracked the silence on the stage. "Why haven't I heard of this before? How can I be quarantined?"

"It is an undeniable necessity, Mr. President. Any contact with the extraterrestrials automatically compromises your authority as commander in chief." Mr. Ellis removed the spectacles from his face and polished them with his handkerchief. "You must alter your perspective, Mr. President. You are no longer the leader of the United States: you are now the lead representative for all of humanity."

"I'm a figurehead ... and that's it. I'm the one who gets quarantined. I'm the one who's got to hand over his power. I don't want my mind taken over like this guy!" President Bush jerked his thumb toward Bill. "I didn't agree to this! Why can't Cheney do it?"

"It must be you. You must separate from power, but the people must not know." Ellis returned to his position over his cane and stared out at the grass.

"What am I supposed to do now? How will I know if they're trying to get inside my head?" President Bush tried not to look his way, but Bill caught him glancing over, and their eyes met.

"They will want to shake your hand, Mr. President." Bill countered the authoritative tone he put in voice with a wide smile. "They won't try to get inside your head, don't worry."

"What?" Ellis stepped forward to stare back at him. "How do you know? Did they tell you this?"

"Shake hands?" The scowl on the president's face grew to a sneer. "Well, at least now I know they have hands. What else do you know, Kemp? Shouldn't somebody around here be telling me what to expect?"

"Excuse me, but they said shake hands?" A faint smile grew in the wrinkles of the old man's face. "You are certain?"

Bill leaned forward, past the president. "Yes, I'm certain."

"What else did they tell you?" President Bush squared his shoulders to face him. "How do you know they won't try to take over my brain?"

"They don't need to." Bill looked to the smoke-stained sky, shielding his eyes with a hand. "They've got me to speak for them."

"Do they intend to speak to us directly, or through you only?" Ellis questioned him, but his voice seemed far away. Crimson hued clouds swirled overhead like eddies in a slow-moving stream. Sunlight fell through the tide of ash and smoke with a steady beat. The sun itself was merely a pale orange sphere, like a bulb hanging over the world. "Young man! Young man, I am speaking to you."

An electric shutter rippled through his body, and he couldn't respond to the glares coming from the men next to him. His senses tingled with the sensations he'd first felt aboard the Houmn ship, and the omnipotent voice returned to fill his ears. *The Houmn are coming.*

Any trace of doubt evaporated, and Bill knew it was time. He could feel the ships overhead. A collective gasp escaped from the crowd, and countless cameras clicked to life. People began shouting. Bill's eyes scanned the sky until they fixed on three streaks of silver crossing the horizon.

The Houmn ships glided through the air for everyone to see. They moved in a triangular formation, zigzagging downward, traversing the sky at fantastic speeds. The three ships leveled off over the ground and sped toward the spire of the Washington Monument, then stopped abruptly to hover in the air.

"Oh my God!"

Bill took his eyes away from the shimmering Houmn ships to stare at the president. The astonished murmuring of the crowd grew into a chorus of alarmed shouts. People were backing away from the line of marines. Bill turned back to stare at the ships and realized this was the first time he'd seen them.

There were no lights blinding him now. There were no lights at all. Each ship appeared to be a seamless silver disk. They showed no signs of movement as they hovered above the reflecting pool. All three ships had flown in as one, but now a single disk moved away from the others and drifted down toward the grass.

Noise from the crowd grew as the ship settled over the ground. President Bush turned to Bill, speaking to him through clenched teeth. "What do we do now?"

Just then, the two ships hovering in the air leaped into motion and zipped over their heads. Bill somehow managed to stand steady while everyone else flinched under the whiplike speed of the ships. "Don't be afraid."

The president's face was a mask of anger. "I'm not afraid. I just want to know what's expected of me. I don't want to look foolish up here, goddammit!"

"You must allow them to make the first move, Mr. President." Ellis was forced to shout over the crowd.

All eyes remained locked on the silver disk sitting on the grass. Several long moments passed while the crowd grew shocked into silence.

"What are they waiting for?" President Bush pulled at his suit and thrust his chin forward as cameras fired off like mad all around them.

A seam of light appeared in the middle of the ship, and a collective gasp passed everyone's lips.

"Here they come." A childish delight tickled Bill's guts. People began to shout and cry out behind him. The window of light widened across the ship, stopping to form a square opening. Shadows moved beyond the pale light emanating from inside the ship. Bill narrowed his eyes to stare inside, but the appearance of two vertical silver lines caught his attention. A long, slender ramp grew from the base of the opening and glided down to the lawn.

The shadows darkened in the doorway, and three small figures stepped out onto the ramp, finally giving some scale to the surreal ship. They were no taller than one-quarter the height of the ship, and the elongated disk suddenly seemed huge. Bill focused his eyes on the three silver-suited aliens, and his jaw dropped. They were not the same beings he'd met on the ship. For an instant, he thought his eyes were playing tricks on him. He thought the metallic suits covering their bodies had changed their appearance, but he realized they were completely different. Their faces were not the ones that accompanied the voices in his head.

The aliens stood at the opening for a moment and then began to shuffle down the ramp. Bill stared at them, comparing them to the image of the Houmn he had in his mind. These creatures appeared more human, looking more and more like children as they carefully made their way down the ramp. To Bill, they looked like every science fiction writer had said they would. Their heads were disproportionately large, and dark black eyes dominated their faces. Their metallic silver suits looked straight out of Hollywood.

"The Grays." Bill turned to see that Ellis was smiling. His jaw trembled.

Another collective exclamation resounded from the crowd, and Bill turned to see three more silver-suited figures step out onto the ramp. They made their way single file down the ramp and turned to face their ship with the others. Bill's eyes floated back up the ramp as three more figures stepped out of the ship. Immense relief washed over him, and a smile spread across his face. He instantly recognized the Houmn from his thoughts. They were far different from the first creatures to emerge from the ship: taller, leaner, and completely bare. Even from this distance, Bill could see the shimmering radiance cascading down over their heads.

Ellis turned to him, thrusting a finger at the ship. "Who are they?"

Bill stared at Ellis. The smile had left his face, and his eyes were wide. "They are the Houmn," Bill said, relishing the look on the old man's face.

"Are those guys the leaders or something?" President Bush asked, barely audible above the growing crowd noise.

"They are the Houmn," Bill repeated, his smile growing.

Three more silver-suited aliens followed the taller beings down the ramp. All twelve stood on the grass facing the platform. The ramp retracted and the opening slid shut without a sound. The nine silver-suited aliens formed a ring around the three others, and the otherworldly procession began to cross the short distance toward the platform.

The time has come, William Kemp.

Fremont, California. June 23, 2002

The narrow storefront was packed with people. A small television sat atop a milk crate near the door. Men wearing skullcaps and turbans ringed the screen, forming a multicolored curtain of bodies. Every man spoke at once, talking over one another, growing louder. Some argued, some prayed, but Omar was silent. These men had all proclaimed themselves true believers, but now many of them were drinking openly, as if Allah no longer watched over them. They were filthy, smoking cigarette after cigarette. They shouted their stinking breath into his face, but nothing could distract Omar from what he was seeing on the television.

At first he thought it had all been a clever trick. He had seen such tricks on the television before, but when he saw the ghostly men greet the American president, all doubt vanished. The innermost layer of pure faith, the knowledge of a single, all-powerful God, had shattered in that instant. The ultimate truth had failed him, leaving him feeling childish and ignorant, yet at the same moment a newly awakened part of him began to fill the emptiness. Old fears were gone, and a new hope played in his mind as talk of salvation passed from mouth to mouth. Again, his thoughts turned to images of Shaharazad; he could almost feel her beneath him. The guilt no longer mattered.

Omar listened to the men as they carried on like old women who'd lost their husbands. They spoke as if Allah were dead. None of them could admit that he had never existed. None of them were ready to admit their own foolishness. They were happier to call themselves innocent victims, but Omar had never felt so sure of anything in his life: Islam had been only a dream, and he was a fool.

The last veils of his faith fell from his face, and he saw a new world with clear eyes. Infinite possibilities swirled in his mind. His sins, his lusts, his failures—none of them weighed on his soul, yet his soul was still there, still his, and somehow still rejoicing. Eternal damnation and suffering no longer oppressed his thoughts. His holy mission to kill the American was over. He would never have to see the men from al-Qaeda again. Now he could be with Shaharazad. The eyes of Allah had finally left him.

Omar pulled away from the pale ghosts on the television and stared at the others. Nothing would ever be the same, and not all of them had fully realized it yet. Some of them were still shouting about the giant beetles. They continued to speak of the End of Days. Some claimed that the gray spirits were the angels of Allah; they could not see their own foolishness. Omar's thoughts turned again to Shaharazad and her family. He wanted to share what he'd learned with her. He wanted to take her in his arms and tell her there was hope. He thought about the nights he had held her in his arms to comfort her while the stars fell from the sky. He straightened himself, preparing to run back to her, but his eyes drifted back to the screen. Once again, he was captivated.

There was a confusing blur of activity while unintelligible Arabic subtitles scrolled across the bottom of the screen. The American cowboy-president walked across the stage. Short, shimmering alien bodies pressed in behind him. He came to a stop in front of a microphone, and the men crowding the television set fell silent. The silence grew until Omar could hear cameras clicking in the background.

"People of America … and people all over the world … today, June twenty-third, will be remembered as the most significant day in our history.

"Today you have all seen me greet ambassadors from another world, and no doubt the importance of this moment has struck all of you as it has struck me." The president's face appeared stern, not at all overjoyed by the event. For the first time, Omar thought of him as an ordinary man, a man clearly overwhelmed by the moment. He was not the demon he had once imagined.

"But let me assure you, every man, woman, and child of Earth, these visitors come in peace and we have nothing to fear from them." The president paused dramatically while Omar's eyes turned to the expressionless alien faces standing behind him.

"They have come at our darkest hour … and they promise us a newfound hope. They promise their allegiance against a common enemy. They have confirmed what we have already suspected. A great threat looms over humanity. And they have vowed to aid us in this, our greatest struggle.

"They have given a name to the terror that plagues us. They call our enemy the Takk. They have come with a knowledge of our enemy we lack entirely, and they have told me that the last Takk asteroid has struck Earth."—the president paused to pump his fists in the air and crack a brief smile—"The specter of instant death from above is over. This truth has been born out by the fact we have not been stuck in over twenty-four hours. They promise me we have seen our last deadly impact."

A murmur rippled through the crowd of men but was quickly suppressed as the president continued to speak. "It is time to set aside our fears and ready ourselves for a fight for our very survival." The president's eyes found the camera, and he stared through the screen. "It has been confirmed; we are at war with an enemy who comes from another world. But from the unknown reaches of space we have found allies who are sympathetic toward humanity. We as a single people, united under a common threat and an understanding of humanity never before realized, must set aside our fear of the unknown and place our faith in our new friendship, and in our God. On behalf of all humanity, I have extended my hand in friendship to the race who call themselves the Houmn."

The president turned, gesturing to the alien figures behind him without actually looking at them. "And I have accepted their allegiance. As a token of their friendship and a demonstration of their resolve, the Houmn have brought us a great gift." The president held a shimmering disk over his head for all to see. "They tell me it contains the information we need to combat the Takk. They tell me the name Takk means 'devourers' in their language. They have warned me that the Takk are, by design, intent on driving us into extinction and devouring our home. The Takk spread through the universe like the locusts they resemble, but hear my words when I tell you they can be stopped. The Takk can be eradicated from our planet. Humanity will survive; the Houmn are here to help us. We will overcome!"

The president thrust a fist into the air once more, but Omar could read the doubt and fear in the man's face. He drew a deep breath and waited for the crowd to react, but they remained silent.

"Now that we know our enemy, now that we can put a name on it and its desires … we can fight it. We must come together as one people … one race … one humanity to combat this foe and wipe it off the face of the planet.

"This, more than any other reason, is why today will be a day remembered like no other. Not because today we have been introduced to new life. That reality was shattered for us all two weeks ago … and not only because we have been shown a glimmer of hope. Today will be remembered as the day all of humanity came together in the understanding that we are all one people.

"Gone are the days when we killed and oppressed each other for worldly or otherworldly gain. Today, out of pure necessity, we stand united in a struggle for our very existence. That bond … the bond created by this new reality, can never be broken.

"As one people we are strong. We will prevail.

"Our Houmn friends come with another message as well, one they feel is most important. They have cautioned me, almost immediately, against the imminent danger posed by the use of our nuclear weapons against the Takk.

"So I send out a message to all leaders who possess nuclear capabilities: under no circumstance are we to use nuclear weaponry against the Takk. They inform me it will have little effect against them. But more importantly, we cannot expose the Takk to the concept of nuclear warfare. The destructive power of nuclear weapons is not beyond their capabilities ... it is only beyond their imagination. If the idea of such a weapon were seeded in the Takk, they would destroy life on this planet and devour it at their leisure.

"No nukes, under any circumstances. That is our tactical imperative, and we urge all other nations to comply. The Houmn have pledged to help us in our fight, but they promise me that a nuclear detonation would mean our certain doom." The president pointed a finger toward the audience and closed his fists in finality.

"I am going to continue our dialogue with the Houmn, but let me assure all of you ... you will be getting information as fast as we can disseminate it. There will no deceptions, no secrets. We are in this fight together ... and let me assure you that we have a friend in the Houmn, and a common enemy in the Takk.

"I won't be taking any questions right now, however. Thank you. And—God bless you."

His speech was over, but the cameras followed the president and the alien entourage until they were out of sight. Armed soldiers pushed back the swell of people. The television flashed back to the nicely dressed man in the news office, but he didn't speak. The silent seconds grew long. Even the men standing with Omar waited for him to say something, but the man simply stared off at something and seemed to chew his words. Finally Omar's companions began to talk, then to shout, and when the newscaster reluctantly stared at the camera and began to speak, Omar could not hear what he said.

First contact had already been made. The moment had passed without warning and a lifetime dream melted away. "Son of a bitch!" Kincaid screamed his frustrations into the microphone under his lip. His fists pounded the steering wheel and he pushed the Mustang into the red. "Why didn't we have any advance notice?"

"Calm down. We're *in*, don't worry. Ellis has been with them from the beginning." Wagner spoke fast. He didn't seem to care that the Black Watch had missed the first contact window. "How fast can you get to DC? Ellis wants you to manage the team."

"I'm still on the I-95." Kincaid read the fuel gauge and eased off the accelerator. "I could be there in another four hours, providing I find some gas." Wagner's last words echoed in his ears, and his eyes narrowed on the road ahead. "What team?"

"*The* team! Ellis asked for you! He wants you to take the lead."

"The team?"

"Yes! We're already working with the Grays, and they didn't come to the party empty-handed. They're dumping data on us faster than we can make sense of it. He wants you to head the team interfacing with the Grays!"

Kincaid couldn't believe his ears; somebody was already talking with the aliens, already asking them the questions that moved his whole life. He had never expected things to move so fast. He had begun to believe it would never happen at all. "The Contact Team is already working with the Grays?"

"Yes! And Ellis has put you in the hot seat. I'm telling you, the Houmn are giving it all up! They've digitized information for us! Everything's formatted to work with our computers."

"The *Um*?"

"They call themselves the *Houmn*. They brought a goddamn CD with them. Didn't you see it on the news?"

"No, I've been on the road. I had to hear it happen on the radio … Howard fuckin' Stern, for Christ's sake. He talked over the whole thing."

"You should have seen it! They shook hands with Bush! They gave him the CD."

"Like a compact disk?"

"Exactly like a compact disk. We've got a supercomputer working on it, but there's so much data we haven't gotten a handle on it yet."

"Wait a minute … did you say they shook hands with the president? Has quarantine been established?"

"Yes! Ellis is all over it. Even Bush is under Level-One quarantine!"

"Bush has gone Case Red? He didn't put up a fight?"

"He didn't have a choice. It all happened too fast. They're operating by the book. The public will have no idea."

A long moment passed before Kincaid could formulate his next question. Every Black Watch operator trained for the day Case Red was activated, but the reality of it all was slow to sink in. He blew out a tense breath as his knees trembled beneath the steering wheel. Finally, he knew his life hadn't been wasted. The Grays were here: it was time for his life's work to begin in earnest. "Are they using telepathy?"

"Ellis says so. That much is obvious. Ellis seems sure the skinny ones are in control. They're the only ones who've been communicating verbally."

"Skinny ones?" Kincaid's brows twisted into a question. The Black Watch had thought all the Grays were of a universal height and build. They had never found evidence of any juveniles or skinny ones.

"Yeah, the naked ones. They've been doing all the talking."

"What skinny ones? What are you talking about?"

"Don't tell me you didn't hear. They didn't describe them on the radio? There were twelve of them, nine Grays and three *skinny ones.*"

"No, nobody said anything about any skinny ones." Kincaid stiffened with frustration. Visions of thin-bodied alien forms flashed in his memory. There had always been mysterious accounts of alien beings who didn't quite match the descriptions given by other alien abductees, but they were rare and thought to be made-up phantoms. Few Black Watch operatives believed they were real. He racked his brain to remember the myth and legend surrounding the creatures sketched out in his brain. They were said to be immortal, some kind of master race. Some ancient cultures called them the creator race. Kincaid's mouth spoke the words before he understood what he was saying. "The Immortals."

"Three of them! You didn't hear?"

"The Grays came with the Immortals?"

"They have been referring to themselves as the Houmn, but the three skinny ones call themselves Sempiternals. They're the ones doing all the talking. They're the ones calling the shots."

"Sempiternal." Kincaid broke the word down, contrasting it against the ancient names given to the immortal men who had come down to Earth to teach humankind. "*Nearly immortal ...* of course, it makes perfect sense. The Grays and the Immortals."

"I'm telling you, Kincaid, this is the big one. It's better than we ever hoped. They're giving it all up, answering all of our questions. Our computers are already swamped."

"But, why? Why now? What are they telling us?"

"They want us to defeat the Takk. And they're in a real fever to keep us from using our nukes.

Shug took a minute to stand alone in the darkened hallway. Happy strangers smiled at him from the gold-framed pictures lining the walls. He'd never felt so alone and out of place. The abandoned home was brimming with unfamiliar memories. Sadness weighed on his shoulders until his knees buckled and he sagged against the wall. Hank was gone. There was no trace of the man he'd known inside the zombielike shell that remained.

Hank's vacant eyes stared into the void. The spark of life had gone, but tormented pain seemed to stir beneath the surface of the dull gaze. Shug knew Hank was in pain; he'd seen him writhe and cry out, but now it seemed as if suffering was the only thing left. Hank was in the bedroom at the end of the hall, but Shug feared the man he admired above all others was gone forever. Shug let the tears fall until there were none left, and then prepared to sit by his friend's side.

Slowly, gently, as if in reverence for the dead, Shug pushed the bedroom door open, sending a shaft of pale light onto the bed and illuminating Cindy's face. Her eyes were bloodshot, and her hair clung to her cheeks. He closed the door, speaking in a whisper. "Hey girl."

"Hey Shug." Her lips curled into a quick smile, but it faded when her eyes turned back to Hank.

"Has he said anything yet?" Shug guided his bulk through the room, carefully avoiding the trinkets on the dresser.

"Yes ... He's been talking a little more ... but I don't know what he's saying. He still seems to be in a lot of pain. He keeps grabbing his head like it hurts."

"Do you think a little light would do him good?"

"I guess we could try. My mom always wanted to be in the dark. And I thought if his head was hurting ... it's always better in the dark if your head hurts."

"He doesn't have a migraine, and he was doing better earlier." Shug pulled back the drapes and drew up the blinds. Pale orange daylight flooded into the room. Hank was curled into a fetal position on the bed. He didn't move as the light covered his face. He wasn't sleeping however; his eyes were wide open. Shug stared in horror: Hank's eyes looked dried, glossed-over and darkened like the eyes of a dead fish. He practically leaped for his friend, intent on closing his pitifully dull eyes with his thumbs. "He was doing better before we let him watch that fucking television!" Shug's deep voice cracked with emotion. "We shouldn't have let him see it! It was too much for him!"

"We didn't know, Shug." Cindy choked on her tears. "We can't blame our-selves for this. We've got to concentrate on getting him better. We didn't know the effect seeing the aliens would have on him. I wanted him to see … I wanted him to see he isn't crazy."

"It wasn't seeing the aliens that did it to him, it was Bill. He didn't freak out until he saw Bill!" Shug moved his face close to Hank's. "What did they do to him?"

"Whatever it was, it was too much for him. We need to keep him quiet until he gets better."

"I don't like him when he's quiet. I like him better when he's talkative." Shug sat on the edge of the bed. The bed sagged, and Hank's body rolled next to his. "Hey, brother-man. It's me. How ya feeling?" He pulled Hank by the shoulders until his head stretched back. "Come on, Hank, talk to me."

"He hasn't tried to say anything for a while now." Cindy reached out to place her hand on his knee. "He was talking about someone named Tommy earlier. Do you know who Tommy is?"

"Tommy? I don't know … Tom, Tommy … doesn't ring any bells. What was he saying?"

"He wasn't exactly talking about him, he was talking *to* him. But I couldn't follow what he was saying." Cindy stared at Hank, pretending not to notice the tears rolling down Shug's cheeks. "He sounded mad."

"I don't know any Tommy. He had a brother named Tom, but he's dead."

"He was telling Tommy he didn't want to do it. He ended up just screaming at him, then he went quiet."

"Come on, brother. Sit up." Shug pulled him into a seated position on the edge of the bed. His head flopped over his chest but soon righted itself. His eyes were still dark and distant. "If you can talk to Tommy, you can talk to me. Come on, say something. I know you can."

Hank didn't respond, but Shug felt his muscles stiffen to support his own weight.

"Are you hungry, brother?" Shug gently shook his shoulder, and Hank's body moved to resist him.

"Come on, let's have you drink something." Shug lifted his chin with his fin-gers and stared into his eyes. "Come on, Hank, say something."

"Don't worry, Shug, my mother said she went through something like this. He just needs a little time to recover."

"But what if seeing that shit on TV messed with his head?"

"He's not crazy!" Cindy raised her voice. "Don't say that."

"I know. I was just saying we need to get him up on his feet."

"You didn't believe it when that congressman guy dumped him off here, but you believe it now! He's not crazy. My mother wasn't crazy. Hank will be okay, because my mother was okay. She died with everyone thinking she was crazy, but she wasn't!" Cindy gently stroked Hank's ankle and mopped the tears on her cheeks.

"But what did they do to him?"

"He just needs a little more time, that's all."

"Time is one of the many things we haven't got. Like it or not, the bugs are here. Their numbers are growing by the millions. Things are happening way too fast, and we don't know what's going to happen next. We have to be on our toes."

"We're safe right here. The guys will bring back some supplies, and we're far enough away from Florida."

"Listen to me: if Hank has taught me anything, it's that you can't depend on the other guys. You can't count on being safe. You've got to think ahead. Two weeks ago, we found ourselves bombarded by asteroids. One week ago, we found out we were under alien invasion. Yesterday, we found out there were other aliens out there who want to help us—but looking at Hank, I'm not too sure. What's going to happen tomorrow?"

Cindy wept silently, and Shug lowered his voice. "Whatever comes next, I want him up and on his feet. He can't go on like this!"

"We have to wait and see. Maybe the aliens *will* help us. My mom always believed they wanted to help us."

"Then why is he like this?" Shug shook Hank. "Why is he like *this,* when Bill is on TV standing next to the president?"

"Maybe he's just overwhelmed by everything."

"No, not Hank. You don't know who he is. He's a rock. They've done something to him. We need to get him to a doctor. I need to talk to Billy."

"What, you want to take him to the emergency room? What are you going to tell them?"

"Why not an emergency room? They can find the right doctors. We can tell them everything. They've got to believe us now."

Hank's voice suddenly boomed in Shug's ear. "No!" Hank's body stiffened in his arms.

"Hank! Talk to me, brother!" Shug ducked low to peer into his eyes.

"I won't do it. You can't make me do it." Hank gripped Shug's arms, staring right through him.

"What is it?" Shug moved his face in front of Hank's until their eyes met.

"What won't you do?" Cindy got to her feet and slid next to Hank on the bed.

Hank's eyes remained locked with Shug's. The darkened emptiness left his eyes and tears dripped down to his chin. "I don't want to do it. They can't make me." His eyes closed and his chin fell to his chest.

"It's okay, brother. I'm right here."

Hank hid his face in his hands. His abdomen jerked with stifled sobs. Shug rubbed his back in silence while Cindy let loose a flood of tears.

Hank pulled his hands away, wiping his cheeks with his forearm. He looked to the ground at his feet and spoke in a clear, unbroken voice. "I don't want to go to any fucking doctor." For an instant, the same old surly Hank was back. His hands were balled into fists, and his shoulders were pulled back, but there was an expression on his face Shug couldn't place.

Paradigm III
Chapter 13

The last two marines filed out of the Oval Office, closing the doors behind them. George avoided his desk as he watched the Houmn shuffle toward the center of the room. They appeared tired after the short walk. The ancient-looking figures measured each stride carefully. The light shimmering over their heads once again caught his attention. Now, indoors and away from the sunlight, the multicolored ring of light resembled a halo more than anything else. The other Houmn looked somehow ordinary without the strange aura. They were closer to what he had expected when he was first told about the little gray men.

He'd been struggling with the constant thought that he should be doing or saying something. He was painfully aware that every word, every action, was being recorded, but he was at a total loss. All he could do at the moment was try to look presidential, so he pulled his shoulders back, raised his chin, unclenched his fists, and waited for the nine extraterrestrials to settle themselves.

The taller, naked figures stopped and began to sway from side to side while the others formed a ring around them. George could feel a strange expectance emanating from them. He wondered if they were about to read his mind, or if they were already doing it. He cleared his throat, wanting to speak, wanting to say something, but every thought entering his mind quickly melted away.

Kemp stepped forward, breaking the awkward tension. "Mr. President." George was already tired of him. He hated the stupid grin on his face. He couldn't stand to stare at his perfect teeth and perfect hair. "The Houmn understand the magnitude of this moment and the effect it is having on you. They wish to open a dialogue with you immediately in hopes of pacifying any anxiety."

George felt himself flush with anger. "Are you speaking for our guests, Mr. Kemp?" He shot the young man his best condescending glare, but Kemp seemed unfazed, even a little pleased with himself.

"The Houmn have chosen me to help convey their thoughts in terms we will understand, Mr. President."

"But they can speak. I've heard them." George turned his attention back to the cluster of aliens.

We understand your speech. We are fearful of misinterpretation. William Kemp will hear our thoughts and covey them to you. It is not our way to convey thoughts in the form of words. The hollow voice came from somewhere between the three taller aliens, but George couldn't see any movement on their faces.

"The Houmn are concerned for their safety." Kemp asserted himself again.

"They have nothing to fear from us. We welcome their friendship." President Bush spoke directly to the circle of Houmn without acknowledging Kemp.

"Good. The Houmn are eager to demonstrate their intentions. They promise the information they've given you will aid us in our conflict with the Takk." Young Kemp seemed to be fighting for his attention, but George kept his eyes riveted to the three slender figures.

"Who are the Takk?" Mr. Ellis stepped forward and addressed Kemp directly.

"The Takk are a pestilence. Given time they will devour Earth."

"Where do they come from?" Ellis's voice took on an academic tone.

"The Takk may be the oldest organism in our universe. They occupy many systems, yet they are a single entity." Kemp spoke slowly, choosing his words carefully. "They must not be allowed to settle in this system."

"Why didn't they warn us?" The question leaped from George's mouth. He watched for a reaction from the Houmn, but none came.

"A tragedy of errors." Kemp made an apologetic flourish with his hands. "There was no time. Earth has been well hidden from the Takk for countless eons. There was no reason to suspect they had found us."

"Hidden by whom? Who are you? How long have you known about us?" George eyed each of the alien faces.

"Mr. President, the Houmn want me to explain that humans and Houmn are one." Kemp's tone sounded condescending. "We are from the same genetic family, and they have observed us from our very beginning."

George opened his mouth, but not to speak. He was thankful when Mr. Ellis stepped forward and filled the silence.

"Why have you hidden yourselves from us all this time?"

Once again, it was Kemp who spoke. "The Houmn wish only to observe. They are scientists." Kemp weighed his words before he continued. "Houmn interactions with us have not always gone favorably."

Mr. Ellis excitedly pounced on the statement. "Will they tell us of these … these encounters?"

"The Houmn intend to answer all of your questions, Mr. Ellis."

George turned to lock eyes with Kemp. "How do they suggest we go about destroying the bugs?"

Kemp placed his arms behind his back and raised his voice to address the entire room. "The Takk have come in great numbers. They will evolve and proliferate. Soon they will begin to build."

"Build?" Ellis whipped his head around to face the Houmn. "Build what?"

"They will construct massive colonies. From these colonies, the Takk will build launching platforms."

"Launching platforms?"

"Once the Takk have established a foothold here on Earth, they will launch vessels into space. If these vessels reach their home, the Takk will add Earth's genetic codes to their own. They will return with their ships loaded with organisms designed to populate Earth. If this comes to pass, we will have little hope in ridding Earth of the Takk."

Ellis pulled the spectacles from his face. "How much time do we have?"

"It is not certain how long it will take the Takk to construct their ramps. They need to build new vessels as well. The first thing they will do is salvage material from their spent vessels."

George found his voice and spoke up. "But how? How do we stop them? Civilization is on the verge of collapse. We don't have the means to fight billions of bugs."

"You must rally the people. You must show them the Takk can be killed. The Houmn will show you how. But, Mr. President, the Houmn wish me to stress the importance of a nuclear prohibition. The Takk cannot be exposed to the concept of nuclear warfare. If they came to learn such tactics, they could easily devastate entire systems."

"I understand the gravity of the situation, and if the Houmn can provide us with a better means of combating the bugs, I can assure you we will do everything in our power to prevent nuclear strikes."

"Mr. President, the Houmn wish to know why you have relinquished your power as president." Kemp's tone remained level, but George didn't like the turn of his smile.

Ellis spoke up immediately, as if he had been waiting for the question. "Protocol. We've been aware of your presence, and we are aware of your power." He stared down the aliens in the center of the room and jerked his cane toward Kemp. "Your influence over Mr. Kemp is a good example of why we have taken these precautions. You can assure the Houmn that the American public will never know of the transfer of power. President Bush is free to act as the ambassador between our races."

A hollow alien voice filled the space. *Do not fear our methods.* The president shot his eyes toward the three alien faces. He thought he could see slight movement on one of them, but the voice still didn't seem to match. *The Houmn have chosen William Kemp to make our thoughts clear. We do not intent to intrude on your thoughts.*

Kemp spoke as soon as the alien voice was silent. "The Houmn are counting on you, Mr. President. You must bring the nations together." Kemp stepped forward with his hands wide open. "The Houmn believe there are already military powers preparing to issue a nuclear strike."

The room fell silent, and President Bush turned to face his men. None of them moved. None of them said a word. They all stared past him. Their eyes were locked on the otherworldly figures and the colorful lights radiating over their heads.

"Mr. President, the Houmn assure me that if atomic weapons are used against the Takk, our situation will become hopeless."

"It's gonna take forever if this-here traffic keeps up." Cindy caught Joe glancing back through the rearview mirror as he spoke. His eyes were searching for Hank's, but Hank didn't stir. He hadn't said a word in nearly an hour. He just stared through the small window in the back of the jeep. Cindy watched his reflection in the glass. He seemed to be having second thoughts about going to Washington. Every now and then he would ball up his fists and whip his head around as if about to speak, but then he wouldn't say a word.

Shug sat in the front. "I didn't expect to see so many people on the roads."

"I reckon it'll only get worse near the Capitol." Joe slowed the Hummer to a stop. Gridlocked cars formed a slow-moving train in the northbound lanes. "Looks like everyone and their dog wants to go up in one of them flying saucers."

Shug wiped the sweat from the back of his neck and eyed the cars full of refugees. "How far are we from DC?"

"Not too far. But we can't afford to burn fuel just sitting here."

The armored military Humvee was drawing a lot of attention as it idled next to the minivans and SUVs. Excited children pointed toward the machine gun atop the jeep. One of the children waved, smiling at Hank, but he seemed to stare right through her. The constant drone from the tires died, and a quiet settled in the jeep as Joe and Shug pondered this latest obstacle in silence.

Finally, as if to break the spell, the thunderous clash of heavy metal filled the air as the monster Ford squealed to a stop next to them. Brandon leaned from the window with a cheesy smile and a cigar clenched between his teeth. "Come on. What are you guys waiting for?"

"You're on the wrong side of the highway, dipshit." Joe shook his head at the boys. "Y'all fixin' to kill yourselves or what?"

"What are ya talking about? Ain't nobody coming down this way. I don't think the highway patrol is on duty, anyway." Brandon pulled the cigar from his mouth and flashed a smile and a wink toward Cindy.

Joe turned to Shug with a pained expression on his face. "I don't like to admit it, but they might be right."

Shug shot Hank one final glance. "Okay, let's do it. Tell those guys to follow us. At least we've got the army jeep."

Joe gunned the motor and shouted to Brandon as he pulled out of traffic to cross the median. "You potheads can follow us. But turn that damn rock-star music off!"

After a few moments of uneasy, cautious driving down the wrong side of the highway, Joe once again pushed the jeep to top speed, and the endless line of cars flew by. Soon Joe and Shug were back to chatting casually and listening to the radio. Cindy slid close and reached out to touch Hank's shoulder. His trance broke in an instant, and he jumped, stiffening under her hand. He closed his eyes halfway and slowly turned from the window.

"Are you feeling any better?" Cindy whispered, not knowing why.

"Not really. My head is killing me."

Cindy could barely hear him above the drone of the tires. She slid closer, pulling him into an embrace. "You sound better." She hoped he could see the relief in her smile. "You had me pretty worried there for a moment."

He cocked his head, squinting his eyes at her as if she had said something strange. "Yeah. I thought I'd gone crazy, too." That odd smile flashed across his face but was quickly suppressed by his hard-set jaw.

"Do you want to talk about it?"

"About what?"

"Your abduction. You should talk to somebody about it."

"Oh yeah, that. No, I don't think I wanna talk about it."

"I can see something is bothering you. It'll drive you nuts if you don't try to work it out. I know what you're going through. I think I can help."

Hank lowered his eyes and pulled away. "I'm not your mother, Cindy."

She clung to his arm. "I know. But she went through the same thing."

"You're wrong. You have no idea." His eyes met hers, dark and brooding. "I know what you and your mother went through, and this is something else entirely."

Cindy felt herself flush. "You don't know what I've been through! I haven't even told you the half of it."

"But, Cindy, that's just it: I *do* know. I know everything. I know a lot more than I want to." She was about to speak but he checked her with a raised hand. "I know your mother, Carol Ann Laguellen, was abducted on May twenty-third. It rained that day. She spent three days with them but can only account for a few hours. She came back believing the aliens had given her special knowledge about humanity's future. She was eventually diagnosed as psychotic after telling her doctors that God was an alien. She also told you she believed she'd had sex with the aliens." Cindy's jaw dropped, and she pulled away, but he continued. He stared into her eyes without breaking away. "I know she loved roses, had a thing for mustaches, and she gave you a Bible filled with handwritten notes for your birthday. You lost the Bible when your bag was ripped off at school, and you haven't forgiven yourself for it."

"How do you know all that?" Shock dulled her words. "I never told you any of that."

"I can't help it … I just know. It's all there when I look at you."

"What did they do to you?"

"The thoughts just keep coming. I don't want them to, but they do. I can't stop them. It's like hearing someone's life story in an instant, like a million secrets whispered at once. I can't seem to turn it off."

"Are you saying you can read my mind?"

"Already read it. Like I said, it was just there, swirling around among countless other thoughts. I thought I'd gone insane, but now I know it's true. I can hear you telling yourself it's true."

"You can tell what I'm thinking right now?" Cindy forced a skeptical expression onto her face. "What am I thinking right now?"

"I don't want to play games with you." He turned away, making her feel childish.

"I know it's not a game. I believe you. I just want to hear you tell me."

Once again his dark eyes bore into hers. "You might not want to hear. I don't think I would."

"Tell me. I can take it." Cindy moved closer. She formed a thought in her mind and held on to it. "I'm thinking of something right now."

Hank reluctantly bobbed his head, looking away. His lips moved, but he choked on the words. He bit his thumbnail and stared into space. "You want to have sex with me."

"*What?*" Cindy was both shocked and confused. Unlike other guys, Hank had never joked about sex with her before. "Are you asking me?"

"No. I'm telling you what you're thinking." Hank cringed.

"You're joking." Cindy's cheeks flushed, her skin prickled with heat.

"No. You don't have to admit it, but you were thinking about sex—that and the name of some painter's sister. Monna di Bicci da Ciccie. She died of morbid obesity, and she was the most obscure name you could think of."

Cindy couldn't move. He was right, right about everything. He'd nailed di Bicci's sister. "How are you doing this?"

"I don't really know. They did something to me. I don't know how it works. Some things are just there, floating around in my head. I can't read everything inside you, I don't know your favorite movie or what you ate last night." He paused, momentarily cracking an odd smile and then looking pained once more.

"Well, now I do because you just thought of it. Two bowels of Lucky Charms, no milk." He closed his eyes as if it helped him to speak. "I can see thoughts that are phrased a certain way ... like images and memories. People's secret thoughts seem to scream out to me."

Cindy sat in silence. She'd never been so self-conscious of her inner thoughts. She tried to quiet the random images popping into her mind. She tried to deny the feelings she had for him.

"Cindy, I know you're excited about ... about all of this, but you've got to listen to me for a minute. I'm not a good person to be around right now. I've been handed something big, and I don't know if I can handle it. I don't want any of this. I don't want to involve you in any of this. I don't want you to get wrapped up in any feelings for me. I just can't handle it. I'm not the guy you've got pictured in your head. You don't understand; this is all my fault."

"I understand." She didn't understand, but she felt foolish and began to speak without thinking. "I guess I have developed some feelings for you. It's not your fault. You've never led me on or anything. I mean, I guess it's only natural; you did save my life. And when I saw you in so much pain ... I guess I couldn't help but feel something."

"That's not what I'm talking about. Everything else is my fault. I wish I could explain it to you, but I can't. All I know is I'm responsible for all of this: the bugs, the death, everything! It was me! None of this would've happened if it wasn't for me."

"What are you saying? How can you take the blame for any of that? You're not making any sense. What could you have possibly done that's so bad?"

"I know it sounds crazy, but it's true. They told me. I know it's true."

She could see that he believed every word. "I want to understand ... but maybe you're just reading too much into what they've told you. How can you possibly be responsible for the bugs?"

A long silence passed before he spoke. He buried his face in his hands, shaking his head. "The hoax ... the hoax set it off."

"The hoax? What's that got to do with anything?"

"The hoax was all my idea. I'm the one who set this chain of events into motion. I'm the one who triggered the invasion by the Takk. I'm the reason the Houmn are coming. It's all my fault ... and I've got to make things right."

"What do you mean the Houmn are coming? The Houmn are already here."

"Yes, a few, but I've seen the future. There will be more."

"No one can see the future. Nothing is set in stone. Maybe none of this is really your fault at all, maybe you're just seeing what they want you to see."

"I know what you think about them. I know what your mother told you. The Houmn are not here to save us. They're already on their way with a massive armada of warships. They'll arrive in exactly 103 years, and they'll conquer Earth and reclaim what's left of humanity. *That's* our future."

"They told you this?"

"I've seen it."

"So you're saying you believe in predestination ... that everything has already been laid out. If that's true, then nothing is your fault. You are just doing what you're destined to do. It's fate."

"I've never believed in fate. I'm simply stating the facts. The Houmn are coming. We can't stop them, but we can fight them when they get here."

"But what if you're wrong about them? What if we don't need to fight them? What if they *are* coming to help us? What if it's a matter of fate? If what you're saying is true, our fate has already been revealed to us." Cindy gripped his hand, forcing him to look at her. "If you think about it, some of those revelations have already come to pass." She closed her eyes and recited verse from memory. "There will be a great earthquake, the sun goes black, stars fall from the sky. Seven Angels sound seven trumpets. Add them together, that's fourteen ... there have been fourteen falling stars, fourteen great quakes, and the sun has gone dark."

"But ..."

"Wait, there's more. One-third of humanity dies! Lightning, thunder, cities fall. Mountains are swept away. A great hail ... stones fall from the sky and men will curse the name of God! These are the revelations of our fate that have been handed down generation after generation. And at the end of it all comes man's ultimate salvation."

"You're talking fantasy. I'm dealing with reality."

"And you think they abducted you because you set all this into motion somehow?"

"No. They didn't intend to take me. They abducted Billy. I was just along for the ride. They wanted Bill because he was on his way to the president's bunker. I was just with him by chance."

"Chance? Listen to what you're saying. If you were truly the one person responsible for setting all this into motion, what are the odds of them grabbing you by *chance*?" He was pulling away from her again, but the look in his eyes had changed. He seemed to stare right through her. She knew he was in her thoughts. For a moment, she imagined she could feel him inside her.

The young marine captain shot his men another anxious glance. The delays were infuriating. They were particularly annoying to Kincaid because he'd written the protocols himself. He'd written them to be simple—*marine-proof*—but nothing was simple anymore. The wait was agony. All he wanted was to get into the exclusion zone and see the aliens for himself.

Kincaid narrowed his eyes on the nervous captain. "What's the hold up, Captain? I'm on the list, aren't I? We're all on the list." He waved a hand to the civilians lining the checkpoint benches. They were too tired to join him in harassing the soldiers. This was the fourth such checkpoint, and complaining hadn't moved things along yet. "We belong in there." He thrust a finger toward the Capitol complex beyond the soldiers.

"I understand, sir. You'll have to wait for an escort into the exclusion zone. We're really short staffed on that side of the line, sir. Most of our men have been moved into the Warm Zone."

"Are you telling me you can't shake loose a single marine from inside the perimeter? You've got twelve people, important people, waiting to be brought in. These people aren't here for a visit! They've been ordered here by the president of the United States!"

"Once again, I'm sorry, sir. We're doing the best we can."

Kincaid wasn't finished berating him, but a voice stopped him before he could continue. He'd heard the speaker earlier, but she hadn't been speaking to him. Her voice was both distinctive and remarkable because it didn't seem to fit the flamboyantly dressed Indian woman. "I know exactly how you feel. It is terribly difficult to tolerate delays at a time like this." Her prim English accent and off-hand British charm seemed to douse the tension. "You must have sat through that horrendous traffic as well. Terrible. And we were in such a hurry to arrive."

Kincaid turned to face her. She sat with the others, her hands folded in her lap. Kincaid stared at her, feeling self-conscious. A red caste-mark stood out on her forehead, and her eyes and mouth were painted with makeup. He'd watched her before, as they were making their way through the checkpoints leading to the Capitol. She seemed to hold a celebrity status among the other scientists.

"The drive from the airport took longer than the flight over." Her hand left her lap to tighten the immaculate braid of jet-black hair draped over her shoulder. "You mustn't let the delays eat at you so. There is space next to me. Why don't you have a seat? I'm sure the young captain is eager to speed us along."

Kincaid gaped at her for a moment. Her teeth were a brilliant white beneath her dark red smile. "I don't think I can sit." He ran a hand over his crew cut and blew out a tense breath. "I've been sitting for hours."

"I understand. This is terribly exciting. I never imagined anything like this. Did you?"

Kincaid couldn't suppress the curl of a smile. "I was beginning to think it would never happen."

"You sound as if you've been expecting this." An eyebrow arched high on her brow, and the others seemed drawn into their conversation. "My name is Meenakshi Ramachandran. May I ask yours?"

Ramachandran—the name struck a cord in his memory. He racked his brain until the name was followed by a title: Dr. Ramachandran, *Iconoclast*. She was the one they called Dr. Brain. Kincaid bit his lip and scanned the faces staring back at him. "Name's Kincaid. It's a pleasure to meet you, Doctor."

"From what I understand, we'll all be working together, Mr. Kincaid. Do you mind if I ask what it is that you do?"

Kincaid hesitated, turning to look at the others.

"You're one of those Black Watch people, aren't you?" A bald young man with a thick Baltic accent spoke up from the row of seats. "I'm sorry. This is all so unreal, please forgive. My name is Dimitri. I specialize in linguistics." He extended a hand toward him and Kincaid accepted it, squeezing hard.

"The Black Watch." Dr. Ramachandran smiled up at him. "I like that name. A name borrowed from the British, who stole it from the Scottish. I like it much more than *Men in Black*. It conjures up an image of stern-faced men, vigilantly staring into the darkness." She stopped twisting her braid and placed her hands in her lap. "Is that what you do, Mr. Kincaid?"

"That might begin to describe it, yes." Openly discussing what he did was unsettling, but he knew he'd have to get over it. The room fell silent, and even the marine captain followed him with his eyes.

"Well, did you see this coming, Mr. Kincaid?"

"Are you kidding? I don't think anybody imagined this."

"But you are Black Watch. You really exist!" Dimitri burst out, smiling at the others. "You knew extraterrestrials were a reality!"

Kincaid nodded, almost apologetically. "We knew."

Dr. Ramachandran didn't seem shocked by his admission. Her voice was smooth, and her smile never faded. "I was told my name was pulled from a list, a list created for an event such as this. Alien contact must have been anticipated for quite some time."

"To be honest with you, what we didn't anticipate were the bugs. Contact with the Grays is something we've always hoped for." Kincaid paused for a moment, letting the statement sink in. "But we never expected it to happen like this. We were a little caught off guard."

"Who are they?" A middle-aged woman leaned forward in her seat.

"The Grays? Well that's what *we're* going to figure out."

"Kincaid!" A familiar voice shouted out from beyond the imaginary barrier dividing the Capitol. All eyes shifted to catch Kincaid's fellow Black Watch operative jogging up to the checkpoint. "Kincaid, there you are! Captain, let this man pass immediately. I'll take him through Checkpoint Red myself."

"Dixon! It's about time." Kincaid grabbed the clipboard from the captain's hands and scribbled his name on the list. "I want all of these people passed, too." Kincaid jerked his thumb toward the others.

"I can't let everyone through," the captain grimaced. "Not without an escort."

Kincaid accepted a name badge from Dixon and fixed it to his collar. "I'm in the Red Zone now. You'll take your orders from me." He thrust the badge signifying his rank and security clearance toward the captain.

"Yes sir. Sorry, sir."

"Come on. You've all waited long enough." Kincaid stood by the threshold as the civilians filed past. They were entering the Red Exclusion Zone, and once they were inside, they wouldn't be allowed to leave. "Welcome to quarantine."

"Kincaid, listen, we can take them as far a Checkpoint Red …" Dixon struggled to keep pace as he marched down Constitution Avenue. "We've already begun to split the team. You've been funneled into a group. I don't know where the others are going. They'll have to be processed at the checkpoint."

Kincaid stopped short. "Group? What group?" He stepped close, crowding his much smaller counterpart. "There'd better be some aliens in that fucking Group!"

"Relax. Ellis asked for you explicitly. You're in *the* group. All I meant was that I've got a cart coming to pick us up. But we can't take everybody."

Kincaid spun on his heel and began striding down the deserted street. "Talk to me. What do I need to know?"

"Ellis wants you heading the group charged with operational planning. He says you've got firsthand experience with the bugs."

"Yeah—and …?"

"And what?"

"And how many Houmn are working with my group?"

"Oh, that … you've got three."

"Grays?"

"The little ones."

"None of the Immortals?"

"Immortals? Oh, you mean the Sempiternals. No, they're all with Ellis and the president."

"Where are they?"

"The White House."

"Who else has had contact with them?"

"Bush's securities guys, some of the president's staffers ... and that Kemp guy."

"Kemp is the abductee?"

"Ellis says they're speaking through him."

"But they're talking, right? They can speak to us?"

"I think so. Ellis says they do."

"What about the Grays? How have they been communicating with us?"

"It's all digital. They've given us a bunch of these little computers with digital displays." Dixon typed into an imaginary keyboard, skipping a pace or two to keep up. "We ask the questions, and the answers scroll out. It's amazing."

"What do we know about this Kemp guy?"

"He's some kind of junior congressman. He's the one who filled Congressman Thomas's seat when he was killed."

Kincaid stopped in his tracks, allowing Dixon to catch up. "*That* guy?" The procession of civilians slowed behind them while Kincaid scratched his head and stared at Dixon. "The Humanist?"

"Yep."

"They chose to abduct the guy who stirred up all that trouble for us?"

Dixon gently pulled him by the elbow and motioned him ahead. "Come on. There's a lot more."

"Fill me in. How did Kemp get to the president?"

"The guys from the Secret Service tell me he was on his way to the Blue Ridge Complex when the Houmn took him. He was taken about twenty miles outside the base. They knew about the base!"

"And they ended up taking *him*? Doesn't that sound fishy?"

"Ellis says the story matches up. They're keeping a close eye on him."

"Was he alone?"

"Who, Kemp?"

"Yeah, Kemp!"

"No. He said he was with another person when he was abducted. But he was alone when he showed up at the base."

"Who's the other person? Where are they?"

"I don't know. I'm sure the secret service guys are looking into it." An embarrassed look flashed across Dixon's face. "Kemp said it was some friend of his. Some guy from Florida."

"I want to know more about him. Handle it."

"You got it."

"Where're we going, anyway?"

"We've set up in the Museum of Natural Science. It's got the most room." Dixon pointed toward a building in the distance. "This way. We've got to go through Checkpoint Red first. We've been trying to keep indoors as much as possible, but we've got three flying saucers parked on the lawn in front of the Lincoln Memorial!"

"And we've established a perimeter?"

"Yeah, but it's a big one. We're stretched pretty thin inside the Red Zone. And the team keeps growing. There's just too much information to disseminate. We're going to need a lot more people."

"How many have I got in my group?"

"Right now, about fifty. But that number will swell. You'll see. They're giving it all up. They're dumping data on us faster than we can make sense of it."

"Are they telepathic?"

"They understand all of our questions, but I don't think they can physically speak. Ellis thinks they're taking orders from the Sempiternals."

"No wonder we haven't seen them before: they've been having the Houmn do their dirty work." Kincaid quickened his pace, thinking aloud.

"I'm sorry, I don't follow you."

"Forget it. Tell me about the team."

"We're going by the book. Your book. Ellis is behind the wheel." Dixon skipped along as he turned to face the others, who had politely stayed back and out of earshot. "I can see at least one person I recognize from your group."

Kincaid looked back without slowing. "Who?"

"The Indian-looking woman. That's Dr. Brain. They say she's the Einstein of neuroscience."

"Good. Maybe she can figure out how they're working Kemp. How many Black Watch operatives do I have with me?"

"Just five for now. It'll be up to you to request more." Dixon danced ahead to shout at the marines at the final checkpoint. "Is my cart here yet?"

Kincaid pulled his badge from his collar and shoved it into the soldier's face. "Security clearance Cosmic. I'm not wasting any more time at another checkpoint, Captain. And we're taking her with us." Kincaid motioned Dr. Ramachandran forward.

"Yes sir. I'll just need your names."

"Kincaid, BWO. And Dr. Meenakshi Ramachandran." He waited for a moment for the doctor to move through the narrow opening the marines had set up.

"Yes sir. War Group. They're expecting you, sir."

"Good. Have the others routed to their assignments as soon as possible. And Captain, I've seen some gross delays moving our people through. Your men had better speed things along or the shit will most definitely hit the fan. Got it?"

"Yes sir. Sorry, sir. I'll look into the delays myself."

Kincaid gestured to a golf cart with a plainclothes secret serviceman behind the wheel. "You can ride with us, Doctor. We'll be working together from now on."

She smiled, showing nearly all her teeth, and her head sort of waggled from side to side. "You did very well with my name. I'm surprised you remembered it." Dr. Ramachandran bowed slightly, pulling at her sari before taking a seat in the back of the cart. "Most people butcher it horribly."

Kincaid couldn't take his eyes from her. Her smile was seductive, and she radiated a certain sensuality that didn't match her age. He motioned for Dixon to take a seat in the front, and he slid into the back next to her. "Well I have to admit, your name isn't unfamiliar to me."

"Is that so? Have we crossed paths before?"

"No, I don't think so, but let's just say we've got *friends* in common." Kincaid dropped the Iconoclast byword with a raised brow and his eyes fixed on hers.

Her expression turned serious for the first time, and she stared for a long moment without blinking. "I see." Her smile returned, and she dropped her voice to a whisper. "I wasn't aware that our influence extended into the ranks of the Black Watch."

Kincaid spoke just above the electric whir of the golf cart. "Until recently, nobody knew we existed at all. But in light of what we know now, you shouldn't be surprised to know we share similar interests. Our primary interest has always been preparing for this moment. Belief in religious dogma has always been a critical stumbling block for us. The Black Watch has always greatly appreciated what the Iconoclasts were trying to accomplish."

"I imagine we won't have to trouble ourselves any longer, Mr. Kincaid."

"Who knows? Maybe the public is ready for this."

Dixon turned around, breaking into their quiet conversation. "We'll be at the Natural History Building in a minute. We've taken over a large lecture hall, and we're moving in one of our supercomputers. We should be able to network with the other groups pretty soon."

Kincaid simply nodded, not wanting to shout over the whine of the electric motor. The Roman-styled building grew closer, and his stomach sank with the realization that he was about to confront his life's goal. He was about to achieve *zero point contact*.

"So I suppose it is up to you to tell me what I'm getting into, Mr. Kincaid." Dr. Ramachandran touched his arm, gently breaking his trace.

"You've been briefed?" Kincaid looked down to his elbow, where she held his arm.

"Oh, yes … they told me all about having to be sequestered. No phone calls, no visits, no nothing … but nobody has told me what I'm expected to do."

"The concept of the interface team is simple. A list of names was compiled in case we were confronted with extraterrestrial contact. You and the others represent the pinnacle of expertise in your respective fields. It will be up to you to figure out what to do."

"But I don't know a thing about aliens or any of that."

Kincaid lowered his voice and moved close to her ear. "There is one thing I want to know above all others. And I think you're the one who's going to give me the answers."

"What is it?"

"We don't really know how they communicate. It's foolish to think they speak the way we do. Human speech requires a specific anatomical configuration, which they do not possess. We've studied them. We think they communicate telepathically. I need you to help figure out how they do it. We can't be lured into taking what they tell us at face value. They've already demonstrated the ability to completely control a human mind."

"And you want to know how to guard against it."

"Among other things. We've got to remain objective. We've got to analyze everything they tell us. I want to know how and why. I want to know why they've hidden themselves all this time."

"Here we are." Dixon turned in his seat, pointing toward the buildings. "We're in the Natural History Building, Division B. Division A is over there. Command is over there in the Capitol Building." Armed soldiers were paired off at every corner, but the area was noticeably empty.

Now that he was inside the perimeter, Kincaid was glad to see that the protocol he'd written was being followed. Nearly everyone had been evacuated. He'd only seen a hand full of DC policemen and the occasional pair of uniformed soldiers on the short ride over. He scanned the rooftops as the cart wheeled onto the sidewalk. Flashes of sunlight reflected from the sniper scopes trained on him. The cart lurched to a stop, and Kincaid sprang to his feet.

He jogged, then ran, toward the wide granite steps. Dixon hurried after him. Kincaid skipped every other step, charging all the way to the top, where he was met by another pair of sorry-looking marines. He shoved his credentials in their faces and scratched his name onto a list while Dixon jogged up from behind. "Where are they?"

"We've set up in an auditorium." Dixon signed his name to the list and turned to watch Dr. Ramachandran climb the steps.

Kincaid was ready to sprint for the auditorium, but his eyes met hers as she hurried herself up the steps. She was clearly watching to see if he would wait for her, and a smile grew on her face while he chewed his lower lip and waited. He turned to Dixon and checked his watch. "Where are the Houmn?"

"Center stage. Where else?" Dixon smiled back at him, apparently relishing the anxious anticipation on his face.

"I don't get it." Kincaid's expression soured as Dr. Ramachandran paused to catch her breath and chat with the soldiers. "Who's been the point of contact?"

"That's the thing: we haven't really needed one." Dixon moved to sign his name next to Kincaid's, and Dr. Ramachandran was passed through. "Most of our people are still working on the disk. And there are more than enough of those handheld units they've given us. You'll see, it's amazing." Dixon slammed down the pen and ushered the doctor ahead. "This way."

"What kind of data is on the disk?"

"It's all hard data ... everything from numbers on Takk proliferation to how the Houmn manipulate magnetic fields. The figures on the bugs are pretty scary. Each colony can multiply exponentially."

"How are they suggesting we combat them?"

"Destroy the colonies. Total eradication. But they've made one point very clear: we can't use nuclear weapons against them. But anything short of that is fair game. Now that we've got some solid intelligence on them, we're making plans to bomb the hell out of them."

"That's it? Bomb the hell out of them? They haven't offered up anything better than that? Don't they have some kind of tactic, or weapon—or something?"

"They say their ships aren't equipped with weaponry. They're just scientists. But they know how the Takk work." They rounded a corner and Dixon pointed toward the elevator.

Kincaid worked a fist into his hand. "What's wrong with the stairs?" He was ready to leave them behind and run to the auditorium.

"Relax, we're almost there."

Kincaid couldn't relax. His mind was on fire. Answers were falling into place quicker than he could formulate the questions. His heart hammered inside his chest: a lifetime of sacrifice was about to be rewarded. The doors slid open, and Dixon pressed the button for the fourth floor. Kincaid jammed the button several more times, until the door closed and their bodies sagged with movement.

Four men in dark business suits, all wearing sunglasses even though they were indoors, guarded the large theater doors leading to the auditorium. Once again they were searched, and once again Kincaid was forced to wait while Dr. Ramachandran joked with the men patting her down.

Dixon shot him a wide smile and paused with his hand on the door. "You ready for this?"

"Open the damn door."

The first thing Kincaid noticed was that there were far more than fifty people crowed into the small auditorium. Soldiers were busily removing the theater seating, and throngs of people milled around beneath the stage. There was no order whatsoever. A menagerie of civilians and uniformed personnel mingled among the scattered tables. Laptop computers glowed from every flat surface.

The noise from the room enveloped him as soon as he crossed the threshold. The clatter of voices bounced off the walls, filling his ears. A circle of people filled center stage, where lights shone down from above.

"Curtains!" Kincaid stepped forward, pulling Dixon by the shirtsleeve and pointing toward the stage.

"What?"

"Curtains, sound walls—anything. We need to partition off the stage. How's anybody supposed to think with all this noise?"

"I didn't think it would get this loud."

"It's a fucking theater!" Dixon flushed with embarrassment as Kincaid shouted at him. "I want the noise in here dampened down. This is nuts!" Kincaid began striding down the steps toward the stage, still pulling Dixon by the sleeve. "Draw the stage curtain, pull the fire curtain if you have to. Why are there so many people on stage?" Kincaid knew that the aliens were there, somewhere behind the impenetrable ring of people. "Who are all of these people?"

"They are all part of the team. I don't know if they are all in your group, but only team members have access to the Houmn."

"All of these people have access to them?" Kincaid's eyes widened with disbelief. "No one is controlling any of this?"

"They've all been told to keep it brief."

Kincaid released his grip on Dixon and charged the stage. Dixon and Dr. Ramachandran followed in his wake as he pushed through the crowd of people. He wanted to scream at the top of his lungs. He wanted to clear the chaotic crowd from the stage, but even if he had wanted to play the role of the prima donna tyrant, his voice had left him. He had seen one.

It was just a fleeting glimpse made possible by a woman pushing away from the cluster to scribble something on a notepad. His eyes caught the reflective glimmer of metallic fabric and the pale gray outline of a large alien head. Kincaid's mouth went dry, and he couldn't swallow. His legs felt suddenly heavy as he crossed the stage. He placed his hands on the shoulders of an army colonel and gently shifted him to one side.

Three Grays faced him from across a large wooden desk. They seemed to stand, propped up from behind by some kind of stool. Their three-fingered hands and long opposable thumbs worked the space in front of them. They tapped and stroked at the empty space until he pressed through the crowd. They stopped their strange movements and turned as one to greet him. Their large, dark, almond-shaped eyes stared right through him.

Talk around the desk died down as he leaned closer. The small alien faces and round bulbous heads were identical to those of the cadavers he'd studied. Even their massive eyes had the same dark hue as the Roswell specimens. Life had animated them with movement, but they were the same ghostly gray.

Kincaid held their stare, and the crowd around the desk fell completely silent as Dixon squeezed next to him to slide a small device along the polished wood. "You can communicate with them using one of these."

Kincaid pulled his eyes away just long enough to palm the small computer. He noticed that nearly everyone at the desk held one of the small black screens.

"Just ask them a question and look for the response." Dixon showed him how to scroll along the screen with his thumb.

Kincaid looked at the LED in his hand. A flow of words ran across the screen.

The Houmn have anticipated your presence, Kincaid. You have arrived at an opportune moment.

Kincaid mouthed the words as he read.

We understand you have been given authority. Your leadership is needed. There is a need for immediate action.

Unable to speak, Kincaid read the words a second time.

"Kincaid!" Dixon pulled at his elbow, but Kincaid ignored him. "Kincaid, look!" Dixon thrust his handheld computer at him. "I've just received orders from Ellis. We've got our first mission!"

Kincaid stared at the alien faces, trying to ignore Dixon, but the sudden urgency in his voice pulled his attention to the text message in his hands.

"Kincaid, you've got to listen to me. This is urgent, a priority one mission!"

Kincaid's eyes bounced from screen to screen and back to the Grays. "What mission?"

"The word has just come from Ellis. We've got clearance from Joint Command." Dixon scrolled through the text, holding the screen for him to read. "We've been given orders to stop France from launching a nuclear strike against the Takk in Spain. We're to use any means at our disposal."

"What?"

"I know you haven't been fully briefed, but we're responsible for all integrated operations. This is our first tactical assignment. They're giving it priority one clearance. We need to move on it fast!"

Kincaid's stomach rolled over on itself. He turned from Dixon and stared at the Grays. One of them raised a hand, tapping at the air with a long finger. Kincaid cocked his head to watch, then found himself lifting the small alien computer to his face. Fresh words filled the screen.

Negating nuclear warfare is our primary concern. Time is critical. We must formulate a response.

"Kincaid, France has refused to adhere to the Bush accord. The signs show they're posturing for a strike. Launch codes have already been issued. Joint Command wants us to neutralize French nuclear capabilities."

"They want us to attack France?" Kincaid couldn't believe what he was hearing. "How are *we* supposed stop a tactical nuclear strike?"

The alien hands continued to work the air, and Kincaid's eyes narrowed on the screen in his hand.

We possess the capability. The military threat uses an integrated computer network to control its weapon systems. The network is vulnerable.

"Kincaid, they're telling me we have less than an hour to stop them."

"And they've handed this to us?"

"Yes! They're counting on us to utilize Houmn technology! Listen, I can take the lead on this one if you need some time to catch up to speed, but we've got to move fast. Ellis want to hear back from me within the minute."

Dixon was staring at his watch, but time seemed to stand still for Kincaid. "No. I can handle this." He cleared his throat and stood tall. "Okay, let's get down to business." His eyes locked with the Gray moving its hands through the air. "How is their system vulnerable? How much help can you give us?"

All three Grays began directing the air with their fingers, and a stream of words rippled across his handheld.

The technology is simple. Houmn can master the computer system, but a human will be needed once we have control.

"You can access their Command and Control computers?" Kincaid fought the urge to speak into the small computer.

Yes. A human with the understanding of such systems will be needed to neutralize the threat. Houmn can only guarantee access to the system.

Kincaid shouted loud enough for everyone in the room to hear. "I need a team of techs capable of navigating the French network. Assemble right here." Kincaid pointed to himself and turned so everyone could see where the shouting was coming from. "I want detailed intelligence on French Command and Control. Where are my military analysts? I want them here, too." He faced the Grays and readied the computer in view. "How are you suggesting we access the computer network?"

We must obtain physical access to a computer station within the network. We have found several suitable locations. The military defenses must be overcome.

"You need physical access to a strategic military site? That's impossible. It would take hours to prepare an assault big enough to take something like that."

We can overcome the security measures. We can infiltrate the site undetected. We can neutralize any defenders. We must do whatever is needed.

"In your ship?" Kincaid read the message and realized what they were suggesting. "You could take us there in your ship?"

We can overcome the electronic defenses and deliver a team to the station.

Kincaid rubbed his eyes, still staring at the text. "Let's see what we know about their missile defense network; we need to pick a target. Let's figure out where we're going."

"Already working on it, sir. The Houmn are downloading some intel on the system as we speak." A young airman with his uniform coat wide open motioned for his attention from behind a laptop. "I'm getting detailed schematics on a site in southern France."

Kincaid's heart pounded full-throttle, and a thousand questions bombarded his thoughts. "Can you get us inside the buildings once we get there?"

A brief silence grew while the Houmn paused. They no longer moved their hands through the air but held them fixed in place. Kincaid looked to the computer, but no fresh text appeared. Finally, all three resumed their strange probing, and a line of text scrolled across the screen.

We can overcome all electronic points of entry, but we lack the power to force open any locked doors. We intend to neutralize the defenses before an alarm is raised.

"And the soldiers? You can neutralize them too?"

Yes.

Kincaid covered the screen with his hand and called out over his shoulder. "Dixon, gather up all the BWOs and Special Forces guys. We need to pull together a strike team. I only want team members with some kind of military training."

"Me?" Dixon had a finger pressed into his ear as he spoke into a radio. "I've got to report back to Ellis."

"I don't care who does it! Just get me a team of operators. Tell them to find the tools we'll need to force our way in and crack a computer system."

"I'll get someone on it."

"Where are my computer people? Who knows what to do with this thing once we've infiltrated command?"

A heavyset woman with her eyes glued to the Houmn computer in her hand stepped forward. "We could download a virus." Her hips momentarily pushed his legs against the desk as she stepped into him. She didn't look up or apologize for nearly stepping on him; she was completely captivated by the stream of alien text coming from her new toy. "We could fry the whole network."

"Good. I like it. Get it ready."

Kincaid kept checking his watch, but the digits no longer made any sense. Time passed in a surreal blur. He'd popped two amphetamine tablets before leaving the Natural History Building, and now his mind buzzed with a constant barrage of sensation. He was feeling the effects of the stimulants like never before. Speed was everything now. There was no time for second thoughts.

Kincaid rechecked the assault rifle they had given him and shot one last look down the ramp. The slender beam of silver was empty except for two silver-suited Houmn. The last of the assault team had already boarded the ship. He checked the Houmn handheld, but there were no new instructions waiting for him. He clenched his teeth, holding his anxious breathing in check, and bent low to step over the threshold of the Houmn ship.

A million doubting thoughts raced through his mind as he followed the circular corridor and found a round chamber filled with members of the assault team. The small circular space allowed just enough room for the men to sit in a wide circle on the floor. An airman wearing his dress blues and clutching an M-16 made some room for him as he stepped into the chamber. He felt every eye follow his awkward move to the floor.

"I don't like this … there aren't any windows in here, man." A thick-necked marine jerked at his helmet strap, gulping down air and looking back down the corridor.

"Relax. This isn't really happening. This is all some kind of head-trip. They just want to see if we'll actually do it." An older man with a pronounced Adam's apple and weak chin crossed his legs and examined his weapon as if it were some elaborate prop. "Trust me, I'm a psychologist. I've conducted experiments like this myself." He flashed a cocksure smile at the others and took off his helmet.

"What are you talking about, man? This is the real deal—this is a real fucking spaceship!"

"Yes, this may all be real … but we're not really flying off to France to disarm their missile computers. I'm telling you, this is a test. They want to see us working with the Houmn. It's quite rational. The only reason I'm telling you this is so you don't freak out. Many people can't handle the combination of stress and confined places. I've seen it before."

The psychologist tried hard to look smug, but Kincaid could see the sweat beading on his balding head. The others were all looking to him to refute the idea that this was some sort of test, but drug-induced paranoia and the utterly unreal feel of the Houmn ship gave him second thoughts. He'd been placed in the uncomfortable position of having to rely on what others were telling him, and he didn't have time to think about that. "Experiment or not, you're gonna blow your fucking toe off if you keep screwing around with that weapon." Kincaid pointed an angry finger and worked his face into his best gunnery sergeant snarl.

The smile melted from the man's face, and he stowed his weapon. The light dimmed inside the ship, and one of the Houmn appeared at the entrance of the corridor. All eyes jumped from the short, silver-suited figure to the handheld computers slung around their necks.

The ship is secure. Stay where you are. Await further instructions.

The Houmn disappeared, leaving the circle of men to eye each other and confirm that their computers all read the same. An eerie silenced filled the small space, and the hairs danced on the back of Kincaid's neck.

"Are we moving? I think we're moving."

"We're not moving."

"I can't feel anything."

"I feel it. We're moving."

"Shhh. I don't hear anything." An electric tension washed through the circle of men. Some pressed their palms to the floor or against the seamless, polished silver walls but none reported feeling any hint of movement.

"I told you. We're not going anywhere. They can make us feel whatever they want." The aging psychologist clutched his knees to his chest and shouted to be heard above the others.

"Shut up! We moved. I felt it!"

Kincaid closed his eyes but couldn't tell if he felt the subtle effects of movement or not. His pulse pounded in his ears, and the debate among the hastily assembled strike force grew louder.

"Why don't they tell us what's going on?"

"Do you think we're going to lose gravity in here?"

"That would be a neat trick. I'd like to see that."

"I told you to shut up! This isn't some stupid test!"

"What if we run out of air?"

"Dammit! Why don't they tell us if we're flying or not?"

"I bet we're going already. They rushed us onto this fucking thing ... they wouldn't just have us sit here like this."

"What if France launches its nukes while we're in the air?"

"We'd be way above it. This is a spaceship. We wont even be in the air."

"Oh man, I can't believe this is happening to me."

One of the men placed his weapon at his feet and spoke directly into the Houmn computer around his neck. "Excuse me. Excuse me, Houmn. Can you hear me? We were wondering what's going on." He pushed his thumb along the scroll button, tapping the side of the screen in frustration.

"Come on kids, we'll get there when we get there." Kincaid cracked a smile for the benefit of the others. "Try to focus on the mission we've been given. Think about what you'll be doing once we get out of this thing. We're about to be dropped into a fully garrisoned military complex on high alert."

"Do they expect us to shoot our way in?"

"We're expected to do whatever it takes."

A twinkle of light at the entrance of the corridor caught his attention, and all eyes fell on the Houmn at once. Kincaid was first to his feet. He pulled the computer screen close to his face as he read the text.

Our arrival has not been detected. Prepare to execute.

"We're there?" Kincaid looked up to see the other Houmn lining the exit corridor. "Get up. Time to move." He stepped into the center of the chamber and pulled the petrified psychologist to his feet by his harness. "Grab your helmet." More text streamed across his handheld, but his eyes were caught by the Houmn waiting in the corridor. It looked as if two of them held objects in their hands, while two of the others wore thick black mitts.

Kincaid chambered a round and stepped toward the exit. The raised hand of one of the Houmn stopped him short. A second Houmn pushed passed and raised the two black mitts into the air. Kincaid pulled his head away, eyeing the Gray suspiciously. The mitts were raised toward his head once more, and he backed away, pulling the computer screen into view.

Allow us to shield your ears. The procedure will protect you from our weapons.

The men were all on their feet, looking at him. Kincaid eyed the megaphone-shaped objects held by the Houmn and hoped they weren't counting on handheld weapons against machine guns and high explosives. He gripped his M-16 and bent low, allowing the Houmn to cover his ears with the dark black, shimmering mitts.

An electric crackle washed over his ears, and the fine hairs on the back of his neck crawled, but nothing seemed to change. The Houmn lowered the mitts and stepped into the chamber to approach the next man. "Okay. No big deal. Let them do their thing. Follow me when you're done."

The Houmn repeated the process with every person and followed the last team member down the ramp to where Kincaid sat in the shadows of the ship. Electric yellow light cascaded down on the ship from above, but the air was silent. They had landed in a courtyard in the middle of the complex. Lights shone on the wire-crested fence around them, but there was no sign of alarm. Once the last man was down the ramp, Kincaid motioned them forward and began the sprint toward the target building.

He covered the tall towers with his M-16 and scanned ahead for trouble. The men fell in behind him as they came to the corner of the building. They took up positions pressed against the wall, covering every angle with their weapons as the Houmn followed behind.

Kincaid held his breath. He knew that an armed checkpoint waited for him around the corner. The Houmn had succeeded in getting them this far unnoticed, but now it was up to him. He raised a fist into the air, then pointed around the corner. Kincaid sprinted into the open, sidestepping and covering the entrance with his weapon. His rifle point dropped, and he stopped to aim at men lying on the ground. His eyes caught on their uniforms; there were weapons on the ground next to them. Kincaid almost fired but eased off the trigger.

None of them were in defensive firing positions. They were all writhing on the ground. Their weapons were completely abandoned. Some of the soldiers were retching and vomiting all over themselves. Kincaid's men charged in behind him and covered the downed soldiers with their weapons. The Houmn hurried around the corner and Kincaid's eyes fell on the strange-looking megaphone one of them carried.

"They're all down, sir. The gate is wide open."

Kincaid was forced to leap over one of the fallen Frenchmen as he made his way to the security entrance. One of the team was reading the digital display near the door.

"Looks like the access codes have been cracked. Every door looks wide open, sir."

The scene was repeated several times as the made their way to the control room. There, too, the floor was littered with vomiting soldiers. No one lifted a finger to stop them. The alarm was never sounded. The computer specialists accessed the network terminal and downloaded the virus with ease. He knew he should have felt elated. His mission was a success, and he hadn't fired a shot. The others were clearly overjoyed, but he was confronted by a profound sense of dread as he hurried the men back to the ship. It had all been so easy for them. Too easy.

Paradigm III
Chapter 14

Washington DC. June 25, 2002

Clearly intoxicated, the three friends swaggered down the entrance with a youthful bounce. Brown paper sacks covered beer bottles in their hands. They punched, pushed, and cursed each other as four DC policemen and two marines watched them stagger toward the barricade.

"Tunnel's closed. This area is off limits, boys." A senior DC cop with three stripes on his shoulder called out to the boys, but they continued on, slamming into each other and pretending they had never heard him.

"Dammed punks … can you believe this crap?" The cop turned to face his buddies, rolling his eyes. "The last thing I want to do is spend all night dealing with drunks." He turned to face the kids, and the other officers stepped forward to join him.

"Train isn't running through here anymore."

"My car is over there, man! It's been over there for four fucking days, man! I need my car!" Brandon brazenly shouted back at the cop, pulling his ball cap low to shield his face. Brady and Hoffman pushed by him without slowing.

"Can't help you there. You'll have to take that up with someone else. This tunnel is closed, and so are all the others." The Sergeant folded his arms over his chest. "The Capitol has been sealed off."

"What about my fucking car, man? You just can't take my shit from me, man!" Brandon thrust an accusing finger at the officer.

"What if we just walk through the tunnel and get his car?" Hoffman shouted over Brandon's shoulder, pleading with his arms and trying to sound reasonable.

"You guys can come with us, make sure we don't do anything ... and then we can just drive out. You can do that."

"He needs his car, man. He needs it for work—you want us to work, don't you?" Brady grinned with a wide, smart-ass leer.

"I realize you want your car, but I can't let you pass." The Sergeant sounded more than annoyed at their ridiculous request. The three boys were only ten feet from the barrier set up by the marines and were getting bolder with every step.

"Fuck you! You can't do this: this is America! I have rights!" Brandon ripped the ball cap from his head, brandishing it in his fist.

"That's right. And I'll be informing you of those rights on the way downtown, if you don't stop right there and turn around." The officer placed his hand on the pistol in his holster. The other officers followed his lead, spreading out behind him.

"You can't arrest us!"

"We haven't done anything ..."

"I just want my car back, man."

All three spoke at once and didn't stop until they were uncomfortably close to the officers.

"Send somebody with him ... we'll wait here." Hoffman pleaded with them, a bottle still clenched in his fist.

"Ain't happening. You boys turn around right now and take the matter up with someone else once you've sobered up."

"Shit! I ain't drunk ... you think I would go and get my car all liquored up?" Brandon's free hand flailed indignantly, as if to distract attention from the beer still clenched in the other.

"What's that in your hand?"

"What's this?" Brandon looked down at the forty-ounce bottle in his hand as if it had appeared there by magic. "Just one beer ..."

"See, I told you, dumb-ass! You're never gonna get your car!" Brady slapped Brandon across the shoulder, nearly sending Brandon's beer to the street.

"Yeah, some senator is probably banging his secretary in the back seat right now!" Hoffman joined in, pushing Brandon off balance as he struggled to keep his beer from falling.

"Shut up!" Brandon said, regaining his balance. "You can't do this to me! I want my car!" Brandon drunkenly lunged toward the sergeant. Hoffman and Brady quickly jumped in, grabbing him by the shoulders.

"You better get your friend out of here, or I'm taking all of you in for drunk and disorderly."

"Come on, dude." Brady stepped between them, pushing Brandon back while Hoffman held his arms.

"Fuck you! Fuck all of you!" Brandon screamed at the top of his lungs as he was being pulled away. "I want my car!"

"Chill out man … I don't wanna get busted." Hoffman hissed under his breath as he pushed Brandon up the ramp.

Brandon made one last drunken lunge toward the barricade but was pulled off his feet by his two friends. He raged obscenities until they had pulled him away, and after some head-shaking and few amused comments, the cops turned away to join the marines.

Twenty feet up the ramp, the boy's staggering progress halted. Once again, curses and threats of violence echoed down the tunnel entrance. One of them had broken free and shoved someone to the ground. His silhouette stood over his fallen friend, but an instant later he was taken down from behind. He was knocked back but recovered, grabbing an arm and tossing his friend over his hip.

Brandon now stood alone, still clenching his beer bottle and raging over his friends sprawled at his feet. He leaped back, arms bent and chest thrust out, ready to brawl.

Brady and Hoffman got to their feet and were quick to flank him. Brandon bounced from side to side, threatening them with the brown-bagged club in his hand, and then took one long step back and smashed the bottle against the concrete.

The shattering glass was the signal Hank had been waiting for. Brandon's theatrics had come just in time. None of the men guarding the tunnel entrance saw him slip over the fence. Even the two marines at the barricade had left their posts as Brandon brandished the broken bottle.

Hank followed Shug and dropped over the wide tunnel entrance to land on the sidewalk. He had a clear view of the brawl being staged on the street. The soldiers and policemen encircled them with weapons drawn, but the boys refused to stop fighting. Brady gripped Brandon in a full Nelson as Hoffman caught a foot in his chest and flew backward.

An amused smile tightened Hank's face as he watched the boys kick the crap out of each other. He remembered how excited they had been about the role they'd been given. They had even gotten good and drunk to play their parts. Hank knew the cops had their hands full.

Shug crossed the barricade and ducked into the shadows of the pedestrian tunnel. Hank scanned the area one more time and fell in behind him. Shug was stopped a few feet into the tunnel. He snapped a pair of bolt cutters and sheered the lock off the service entrance door. Shug pushed the door open and they both stepped into the darkness, closing the door behind them.

They paused, letting their eyes adjust to the darkness of the subterranean network of service ducts that paralleled the main tunnel. They were past the first obstacle keeping him from Bill. Hank had flushed out the fatal flaw in the security perimeter surrounding the Capitol while making calls trying to contact him. The area they wanted to protect was simply too large. They had isolated the entire Capitol Mall and were still in the process of evacuating people from the restricted zone. He knew there were gaps to be found.

"Okay, Shug, lead the way."

Shug clicked on a flashlight and moved down the corridor filled with pipes. Hank followed behind, thinking two moves ahead. He knew this was going to be a tough nut to crack, but he only wanted to crack it open a little bit. All he needed was a shot at getting into one of the evacuated buildings. He could place his call to Bill from there. Everything hinged on convincing them to get Bill on the line. He had to do it from the inside.

The quarter-mile trek was agonizingly slow. Shug could barely fit through some of the passageways. The shaft narrowed until it stopped altogether near a metal door.

"This is it, brother." Shug trained his light on the door. He grabbed the handle and pushed, but the door wouldn't budge."

"Padlocked from the outside." Hank scanned the darkness above them.

"You want me to go to work on it?" Shug flashed the beam over the heavy metal hinges.

Hank grabbed him by the wrist, guiding the flashlight to the ceiling. A three-foot-square trapdoor was set into the roof of the tunnel. A crude ladder made of metal bars protruded from the wall.

"Let's give this a try." Hank led the way, easily pushing back the metal lid. The opening led to a cramped pumping station, which now sat silent. Hank could see a dim yellow glow at the end of the shaft.

They made their way, pushing along on their stomachs, until they reached the metal grate opening a window to the street above. They waited and listened for a full minute without hearing anything outside. Hank climbed beneath the grate and pushed it loose. The metal growled as it slid away, causing his heart to race.

He moved his body through the hole and found himself standing in the relative brightness of the street. His eyes settled on the shadows beyond the road, and he dove for cover beneath a short, bushy tree.

One shoulder at a time, Shug squeezed his bulk through the narrow opening. Once on his feet, he slipped his fingers into the grate and silently pulled it back into place. Shug joined him under the bush, and they both lay flat on their stomachs, panting into the leaf-litter.

Hank scanned the buildings beyond the train terminal. The Capitol buildings were illuminated in the background. The streets were empty and strangely quiet. "I don't see anybody."

Shug pointed to the Capitol Dome. "The lights are on, but nobody's home." His brilliant white teeth smiled at him from the darkness. "I don't see any cops."

"They're out there." Hank nodded down the street. "Look there ... flashing yellow lights. And over there." Hank pointed down Independence Avenue. "Probably checkpoints. We wanna go that way. We need to find some kind of gap." Hank was pointing toward a well-lit section of the Capitol. A floodlight illuminated the lawns where the Houmn ships sat.

"I thought we were gonna stay away from that area."

"We won't be getting that close. I'm hoping for one of those office buildings." Hank pushed himself onto his knees and gave Shug a nod.

Shug frantically checked his gear one last time and readied himself to move. "Okay, how you wanna do this?"

"Leapfrog. One at a time, point and cover. If anybody stops us, follow my lead."

"Copy that. Who's going first, old man?"

"Follow me, Junior." Hank crept to the edge of the bushes. He guessed it was less than a quarter mile to the abandoned federal buildings. His eyes plotted a course through the evenly spaced streetlamps. His ears probed the silence for any sound that might abort his move. He stepped out onto the street and waited for the rustle of leaves to quiet. His feet hardly made a sound as he crossed the road and broke into a jog.

Moving into the open was a calculated risk; he couldn't avoid all the lights on the street, but when he heard the whir of bicycle tires behind him, he knew the risk had developed into a real problem.

"Hold it right there," a male voice called out, stopping him in his tracks.

Hank raised his hands and slowly turned to see the darkened silhouettes of two policemen speeding toward him. They let the bikes fall to the ground as they drew their weapons.

"Don't move. What are you doing here?"

Hank stared at the officer for a moment. A barrage of unfamiliar thoughts colored his mind. He sensed that the man was more confused than alarmed. His thoughts came as clearly as if he'd spoken them aloud. *Probably another lost scientist. Let's see his identification.*

"You know you can't be over here." The officer relaxed his posture somewhat, but still held the gun leveled at his chest. Hank realized that the pair of cops had been running into strays inside the restricted zone all night. He knew that it was getting late in their shift, and they had a mountain of paperwork waiting for them before they could leave. They seemed disappointed to find him.

Hank answered immediately, telling the officer what he expected to hear. "I'm sorry. I'm a scientist. Don't shoot."

"What are you doing out here? Put your hands down." Both officers holstered their weapons and pulled flashlights from their belts. "Let's see some ID."

Hank began fishing through his pockets for identification he would never find. He turned his eyes from the light, but his mind reached out to probe the sea of thoughts for easy answers. None came; the only thing clear was their anxiety to get home.

"I was supposed to meet a friend." Hank faked a smile, trying to look embarrassed. "She's a scientist, too."

"Well you can't be out here. This area is restricted. What zone are you supposed to be in?" The second officer beamed his light into his face.

Only three possible answers waited for him in the officer's mind. Hot, warm and cold. Timing is critical to a lie, and the officer was looking for a quick response. "Hot Zone."

"Hot Zone?"

Hank knew he'd made a mistake as soon as the officer spoke. The answer he was looking for was something else, something that translated into *Hot Zone* in his mind. "Red Zone. I meant Red Zone." Hank saw the words written across his thoughts at once. He shrugged his shoulders apologetically and allowed himself to appear rattled by the situation. "I'm a little flustered. I can't seem to find my ID. You guys scared the crap out of me."

"You're from the Red Zone? You can't be out here." His words had triggered suspicion, and Hank felt the men's minds reluctantly changing gears. "This is the Yellow Zone. How did you get out here? You guys aren't supposed to leave the Red Zone." One of the officers was silently cursing to himself. Now he had to call the encounter in and file more paperwork.

Hank began speaking fast, willing Shug to the scene before one of the cops made a move for his radio. "You see, there's this girl I know." Hank stopped searching his pockets and shielded his eyes from the light. "I have my ID somewhere, hold on." He looked past the two cops as a massive shadow loomed up from behind. There was a sudden grunt as Shug's fist came crashing down on an officer's helmet, spitting it in two and sending the cop to the pavement.

Hank leaped over the fallen officer and grabbed the second cop by the sleeve. He pulled, spinning the officer's back toward him, and wrapped an arm around his throat. He leveraged his biceps against the man's carotid artery and squeezed tight. The sensitive pressure receptors in the man's neck shut him off like a switch, even before he could succumb to the hypoxia of the chokehold. The officer folded beneath him, and Hank lowered him to the ground.

Shug stood over the unconscious man with wide eyes. Hank grabbed the fallen cop under the armpits and began to pull him down the street. "Back to the bushes!"

Shug followed suit, grapping the cop by his belt and hoisting him over his shoulder. He jogged past with the officer bouncing on his back but stopped, grabbing both bikes by the wheels and dragging them behind him.

Hank struggled, pulling the fallen officer into the underbrush as Shug crashed through the bushes. His lungs were on fire and sweat ran down his face. He collapsed into the leaf-litter and panted out his thanks between breaths. "Good job."

"What do we do now?" Shug's eyes were wide as he stared down at the unconscious cops.

"We can't turn back now. We're almost there."

"What are we gonna do with them?" A large gash had opened up on the chin of the officer with the split helmet.

Hank stared at them for a moment. "I've got an idea." He reached for a gun belt. "Get these off of them." He noticed a laminated card sticking out of a shirt pocket and pulled it out. He held the card, examining it in the light filtering through the trees. The card showed a color-coded map of the Capitol with a highlighted section showing the different radio channels. "Look at this." He flashed the card to Shug. "They've got cheat-sheets for us. Let's get their uniforms off. Come on, be quick about it."

"What?" Shug looked skeptical.

"You heard me." Hank tossed the gun belt to the side and pulled at the uniform. "This is the break we needed." He plucked the earpiece from the officer and examined the radio. "Tie their hands with these." He flung a handful of plastic zip-cords to Shug.

In a matter of moments he and Shug had stripped the men down to their underwear and secured their hands behind their backs. Socks were rolled up and shoved into their mouths and secured with plastic ties.

Shug checked to see that both men were breathing, then turned on his knee to face Hank. "What now?"

"Looks like they're coming around. We've gotta move."

"We can't just leave them like that. What if they need a doctor?"

"They'll live. Let's roll."

"Okay man, I'm with you. What about the bikes?"

"Huh? Oh, I don't know." It was no secret between them that Hank hated bikes.

"Come on, man." A smile grew on Shug's face again. "It makes sense. You can't be a bike cop with no bike."

Hank looked at the uniforms laid out in the dirt and made a face.

"What's wrong, man? You can do it. It' just like ... just like riding a bike."

Hank lifted the bike shorts with a finger. "Shorts. Of all the stupid informs ... I get shorts."

"Ah, get over yourself. So you'll be a one-legged bike cop. Remember, this is our opportunity: we've got to capitalize on it."

Moments later, they were both wearing police uniforms and adjusting the seats on their mountain bikes. Shug's uniform shirt looked ready to tear apart, and Hank agonized over his exposed mechanical leg. The helmet Shug had split in two now fit nicely on his oversized head, and for all intents and purposes they looked the part of policemen.

"Okay, we keep the radios on the PD channel. We're here in the Yellow Zone ... we want to go this way." Hank traced his finger over the card while Shug followed along on his own. "There are a block of federal offices here ... it's still the Yellow Zone, but I'm betting those offices are empty. That's where we find our building. We won't have to cross into the Orange Zone."

"Got it." Shug looked monstrous sitting on the bike. His dark blue shorts were so tight it looked as if he wasn't wearing any at all.

"Don't stop for anything ... not until we find a place to disappear. If anybody calls us, just keep peddling like you're going somewhere. It says here that PD has access all though the Yellow Zone."

"Got it."

"Keep your gun where it is ... it's not worth getting shot over. Remember there's always plan B."

"Got it ... no gun."

"Looks like they have checkpoints here ... and here. We'll stay away from those. The buildings we want are right next to a place called the Smithsonian Castle; you can't miss it."

"We gonna ride together or staggered?"

"Might as well ride together … keep it casual. Except for your gorilla-like physique and my mechanical leg, we look like two ordinary bike cops patrolling our
beat."

"Who you callin' a gorilla? I look good in a uniform."

Once Hank pushed out onto the sidewalk, it was just as Shug had said it
would be. He hadn't been on a bike since he was a kid, but in no time at all he
was pumping the pedals and picking up speed. Wind rushed past his ears, and
they covered ground more quickly than he had imagined. The silhouette of the
Smithsonian Castle grew under the moonlight, and the radio earpiece remained
silent.

The short trip was over, and Hank felt himself wishing it could have gone on
longer. He had felt stealthy—almost invisible—on the fast-moving bike, but now
the target buildings were ahead of him. They pulled the bikes into some bushes
near the rail tracks and waited under the cover.

Hank scanned the empty buildings and made his choice. "Right there." He
pointed past the bushes. "Those buildings back up to the Hirshhorn Museum.
All the lights are out." He pointed to the adjacent buildings. "So are those." He
pulled Shug close. "The block is divided into four blocks of buildings. We take
one in the middle, away from the street." He straightened, brushing the leaves
from his uniform. "We walk—not run, not jog—to the center of the block, dig
it?"

"I dig."

"Let's do it." Hank pushed the branches aside and stepped toward the street.
Shug rolled up beside him, and they turned down the empty street. The White
House lights lit up the sky in front of them, but the block ahead was dark and
silent.

"So … Harper"—Hank leaned close to read the name badge on Shug's
chest—"What do you really think about all this alien stuff?" He tried to sound
casual.

"Say what?" Shug hissed under his breath. The whites of his eyes bounced
from side to side as he anxiously scanned the street.

"Come on, be cool." Hank cupped his mouth as spoke. "Try to look as if we
belong here." He lazily tapped Shug on the shoulder and raised his voice once
more. "What do you think it all means?"

Shug's lips tightened to cover his teeth as he read Hank's badge. "Well …
Martinez, I don't know what to think. What am I supposed to think? Nobody
has told me what's really going on."

Hank fell silent as they covered the next few paces and turned down a side street. The path was clear, and there was no one around to hear their conversation, but Hank kept up the casual tone and ambling pace befitting two weary policemen. "What if someone told you they had all the answers? Would you believe them?"

"I would believe you."

"Why me and not Billy? Why would anybody believe what I have to say?"

"Because I know you, Martinez." Shug stopped long enough to be sure Hank saw his dopey smile. "If you say Billy is wrong, I believe you. You've got no reason to go through all this."

"What about everybody else? How am I supposed to convince them?"

"Let the truth carry its own weight. You taught me that."

Hank scanned all four corners of the intersection and chewed the words over in his mind. "Thanks, brother." He stopped and motioned ahead. "Everything looks good here. Let's go home."

They left the streetlights to walk down the alley between buildings. Hank held his breath and strained his ears for any sound, but all was quiet as they worked their way to the center of the block. They stopped at a blacked-out building with its entrance covered in shadows. Hank traced the power lines overhead to where they dropped down to the building. He motioned for Shug to stay where he was and followed the lines to the junction box to cut the power feeding the alarm.

He rounded the corner and waved Shug over. They met at the entrance and exchanged glances. "Force the lock."

"No problem." Shug sank to his knees and went to work on the lock.

Hank's heart began to speed up as he scanned the buildings and started to count off time in his head. The snap of a bolt sliding back broke the silence, and Shug pushed the door open. They entered without a word, closing the door behind them. Hank clicked on a flashlight and began checking doors.

"Hank, right here. It's some kind of reception desk." Shug waved him over to a darkened computer sitting next to a large-paneled phone.

"Perfect. Watch the door. Let me know the instant you think you hear something."

"You got it."

Hank circled the desk and sat in the chair. He hesitated with his hands on the desk. If the phone lines were dead, he would have to scramble to come up with another plan: everything hinged on making this call. He reached out to pick up the phone and place it against his ear. The hum of the dial tone was there. "Jackpot!"

Hank slumped in the chair, biting his lip as his eyes ran over the list of names on the phone. He shrugged his shoulders and pressed zero for the operator. The line began to ring—five rings, six. Hank began to fear that the system relied on a separate operator and wouldn't connect to the main, federal network, but after the seventh ring, the other end of the line clicked to life.

"Capitol Mall operator. Who is this, please?" The woman's voice was crisp and authoritative.

Hank straightened bolt upright in the chair, and his knees began to jump. "I need to speak with William Kemp right away. He is with President Bush right now. I have an urgent message for him."

"I'm sorry, but who is this please? Where are you calling from?"

"My name is Hank Foster. Mr. Kemp will want to take my call. I assure you, this is a matter of life and death."

"And where are you calling from, Mr. Foster?" Hank could hear her tapping keys in the background.

"It doesn't matter where I am. Are you going to put my call through to Kemp or not?"

"I cannot forward your call until I can verify who you are and where you're calling from. All the buildings in the Capitol Mall have been evacuated. You're not supposed to be on this system, are you?"

"I have information about an immediate threat to the Capitol! This is no joke. I want to speak to Bill Kemp right now!"

"What kind of threat, sir?"

"I will not talk about the location of the bomb until I speak with Kemp directly."

"Did you say bomb?"

"Yes! Now go. Tell whoever you need to, but get Kemp on the line within twelve minutes or that's it. Understand?"

"Not fully, sir." Hank could hear voices in the background. "But I'll see what I can do about contacting Mr. Kemp for you. Will you hold the line?"

"You've got exactly eleven minutes and fifty seconds." Hank chewed his thumbnail and tried to quell the nervous quaking in his legs.

"Okay, please stay on the line."

Seconds blurred into minutes as Hank pressed the phone against his ear and stared at his watch.

"Mr. Foster? This is Lieutenant Colonel Travis."

Hank cut the man short before he could continue. "Is William Kemp coming to the phone or not?"

"We're working on it, but we need to know a few things …"

"Get Kemp on the line! You've got six minutes!"

"But …"

"I'm not listening! Kemp! Phone! Now!" Hank's knee danced under the desk. He heard the colonel continue to speak but ignored him completely. He knew the building would be swarming with cops soon.

"Mr. Foster? Mr. Foster?"

Hank let the phone sit dead in his ear as he planned a speedy exit. He toyed with the idea of barricading himself inside until Bill got on the line, but he began to think they hadn't even sent for him. He was desperate to speak with Bill, but it couldn't go down like that. He couldn't risk Shug like that; he couldn't let them lock him away. He had to make them understand.

"Hank? Hank, are you there?" Bill's voice was clear. Hank could almost feel him on the other end of the line.

"Billy, it's me."

"What the hell is going on, Hank? Did you tell them you had a bomb?"

"Billy we've got to talk. Is there someplace we can meet?"

"Hank, tell me you don't have a bomb." Bill's anxiety radiated through the phone. Hank could see the eerie nightmares Bill had cooked up in his imagination. "Tell me!"

"Billy, listen to me. There's no bomb. But I've got to warn you. You need to make arrangements to meet with me. Right away. I know they're listening. There's not much time."

"What are you talking about? Have you gone crazy? I'm in the White House; I can't come out and meet with you after you go calling in some dumb-ass bomb scare."

"I'm as crazy as you are, Billy. I was with them, too. You've got to listen to me."

Hank felt the stress weighing on him. He'd been isolated, torn between worlds. "What do you want to warn me about?"

"The Houmn are dangerous." Alarm bells fired to life inside Bill's mind as the words left Hank's mouth. A new presence colored Bill's thoughts.

"Where are you?" Bill's tone changed, becoming hard and commanding.

"Can you meet me outside the Capitol?" Hank bit into his lip, continuing to force himself into Bill's thoughts.

"No. Impossible. I can't leave the White House. Where are you?"

"Billy, they've brainwashed you."

"I'm working with them!" Bill's natural voice was back, breaking with emotion. "We're at war with the Takk. They need me. They haven't brainwashed me!"

"You're working for them, Billy, not with them."

"What are you saying?"

Hank probed Bill's mind beyond his thoughts. His words were no longer his own. They had complete control over him. They would never let Bill meet with him face to face. They would snare him if they could.

"Let me know where you are, and I'll have them bring you to me. That's the best I can do." Bill tried to sound earnest, but Hank could feel their influence now. Bill was exhausted. He'd barely slept since joining with the Houmn. He was too weak to hide his stress. The Houmn had made the mistake of keeping him from sleep—and more importantly, they had kept him from smoking. Bill's body screamed for nicotine, but the Houmn were oblivious to the pain of withdrawal. Bill's mind was weak, and Hank could clearly see the trap they were setting for him.

"You sound terrible, Billy. What's wrong, no time to sneak off for a quick smoke?" Hank casually cast the thought and awaited the flood of images stirred by the suggestion.

"What? Me? Don't worry about me. Tell me where you are so I can bring you in safely." The instant the suggestion of a smoke-break sank home, an image popped into Bill's mind. There was a place not far from where he was. He'd thought about stopping there for a smoke several times but never had. Now Bill wanted that smoke more than ever. He promised himself he would take it the first chance he got.

Hank gave one last look at his wristwatch and bolted up from his chair. "Time's up. I gotta go. Think about it, Billy, don't believe everything they tell you. The Houmn are dangerous. Ask them about the million ships headed toward Earth. Ask them what they plan on doing once the Takk are gone." Hank slammed down the receiver and rushed through the room. "Time to change plans."

Shug followed him back down the alley. Red and blue lights flashed in the distance as Hank broke into a full-blown sprint back to the bushes where they had stashed the bikes.

"What's going on? What did Billy say?"

"They've got total control over him."

"What do we do now?"

"Grab the bikes. We're going to the White House."

"What?"

"Bill's about to take a much-needed smoke break. Come on."

Police cars sped through the streets. Another pair of bike cops hurried through the park near the museum. Hank pushed his bike out from cover and flung his prosthetic over the bar, onto the pedal. Shug joined him on the street, already pedaling hard. Hank dropped gears and overtook him, guiding him down a side street away from the flow of police headed toward the federal buildings.

Shug wheeled up next to him, his legs pumping hard to keep up. "The radio is on fire. What's the plan?"

Hank pursed his lips, breathing hard. There was no plan; all he knew was that there was a chance to grab Bill, and he had to take it. An image of Bill alone in a grove of trees behind the White House fixed in his mind. "Keep riding. Don't stop for anybody."

A wooden barrier blocked the road ahead of them. Marines stood on either side with weapons ready. Hank was sure they had seen them, but he didn't slow as he approached. One of the marines stepped forward with a raised hand. Hank gripped the brakes hard, skidding to a stop.

"What's going on with you guys?" The young soldier spoke first, unwittingly opening his thoughts to Hank. "We heard there was some kind of trouble."

"Ah, I don't know … we got some report about intruders in the restricted area." Hank stared at the soldier, wrinkling his brow as if he were annoyed. "They've called us up to the White House. Check with Dickerson … he knows about it." Hank read the name emblazoned on the young man's thoughts and prepared to push off once more.

"The White House? Well, if Dickerson knows about it …"

Hank didn't wait for any confusion to set in. He pressed his weight into the pedals and wheeled past the checkpoint. They were close enough to see the lights of the White House. They passed several more marines and spotted a handful of dark-suited secret servicemen, but none of them made a move to stop them. They sped past the lawns surrounding the rear of the White House. A tall, spiked fence bordered the lawns.

Without a second thought, Hank dumped his bike and sprinted for the fence. The sturdy fence rocked as Shug slammed into it, pulling himself up. Shug threw his legs over and landed like a gymnast. He caught Hank on the other side. "Which way?"

"This way. Follow me." Hank sprinted as fast as he could across the lawn. His metal leg dug into the soft grass, slowing his steps. He felt Shug sandbagging behind him, wanting to sprint ahead to the cover of the shadows, fearing the shout of guards or the snap of gunfire.

The dark outline of a cluster of trees hid a section of the White House, and Hank immediately recognized the ancient oaks. He knew this was where Bill planned to steal his smoke break. They ran into the grove along an immaculately kept stone walkway. The shadow of a small building grew out of the darkness. They slowed to a jog, and Hank saw that the building was a restroom styled with Roman columns and an open entrance.

Hank stopped, motioning Shug toward the shadows behind the bathroom. The air was silent except for the sirens in the distance. Hank knew that they had set off alarms, getting this close to the White House, but he hoped there was still a window of hope. He was close to the spot Bill had envisioned. His eyes fell on a bench in the darkness, and he stepped closer. He knew the bench even though he'd never set eyes on it. He even knew the words engraved on the small plaque: *In Loving Memory of Rose Stubbs.* This was where Bill planned to get his nicotine fix.

Hank's hands trembled with a surge of endorphins. He gripped the radio in his fist and keyed the microphone. "Officer Down! Officer Down! Capitol Building—hurry, shots fired!" Hank released the button, and a flood of voices filled the air. He turned the dial all the way down and joined Shug in the shadows.

"What did you do?"

Shug whispered in his ear, but Hank ignored him. He could almost feel Bill coming; an electric sensation was washing over his brain. Bill's thoughts were becoming clear. He was already working on his first cigarette.

Hank motioned for Shug to follow him, and they crept into the bushes behind the bench. Shug tugged on his sleeve and was about to speak, but he was silenced by the sound of gravel crunching beneath feet. Hank could smell the smoke.

The cigarette clenched in Bill's hand glowed in the darkness. Bill ran his free hand through his hair in obvious turmoil. He didn't hear or see Hank as he exploded from the bushes, leaping at him and clamping a hand over his mouth. Shug was right behind him, knocking Bill off his feet and grabbing him by the legs.

Stunned, Bill flailed his arms as they hauled him back to the restroom.

"Hello, Billy." Hank pulled his hand from his mouth, bringing a finger to his lips to shush him. "Don't make a sound or I'm in big trouble."

"Are you crazy?" Bill kicked his legs away from Shug's grasp.

"I told you, Billy, we need to talk. The Houmn are dangerous. They've got a bad hold on you."

"I know what I'm doing!" Bill scowled at him, straightening his hair. "I'm doing something important here!"

"You've got to listen to me. The Houmn are planning to enslave us. They're sending an army to invade us. You've got to believe me. They'll be here in exactly 103 years."

"What have they done to you?"

Hank's tone softened. "I know what they've done to you." He stood, offering his hand to Bill. Bill allowed him to pull him to his feet. "I can see they've got a hold on you, but there's a chance." Hank tightened his grip on Bill's hand, taking note of the renewed fear on his face. Hank reached out and grabbed his other wrist. "They've taken over your mind, but there may be a chance I can break their hold on you. Then you'll understand what I'm telling you."

"What are you talking about? Let go of me!"

Hank held him tight, pulling him close. "Keep your voice down, Billy. Don't struggle. I've got an idea. If I can render you unconscious, maybe their hold can be broken."

"What?" Bill shouted, trying to pull away, but Hank checked his movement, wrapping an arm around him.

"Shhh. Don't move, Billy." Hank spun him around, pinning his arm behind his back. He wrapped his arm around Bill's neck and squeezed his throat. Bill squirmed, but he couldn't cry out, couldn't get away.

Hank felt Bill's body begin to slacken and his thoughts begin to blur. "Don't worry, Billy. I know what I'm doing."

With his last ounce of strength, Bill reached out and blindly pulled at a cord hanging next to the toilet. An alarm instantly filled the room with light.

"Hank! Someone's coming!" Shug pointed out the door.

Hank dropped Bill and readied himself at the door. Bill coughed and sputtered on the floor. Time had run out. Bill was still set against him. "Okay, Shug, remember—we're cops, right? There's an officer down ... we don't stop for anything. Head for the fence and don't look back."

The curtains were pulled back, allowing the first rays of sunlight into the Oval Office. The president stood next to the window as Bill was ushered in. Andrew Card strode silently past, not returning Bill's greeting. The president wore a hard look on his face as Bill sidestepped the three Sempiternals shuffling into the center of the room. The atmosphere was already tense, but Bill didn't care; he felt revitalized after a full night's sleep.

Bill waited for Card to close the door behind him. "Good morning, Mr. President." He rocked on his heels and smiled at the president's back. After a long moment of waiting for a response, Bill turned to the only other human in the room. "Mr. Ellis."

Ellis stared over his spectacles at the Houmn as they arranged themselves on their special stools. Bill didn't trust the old man's smile. "Good day, Mr. Kemp."

Bill waited while the president continued to stare through the window. He was getting used to the cold shoulder; the lack of civility no longer bothered him. "Mr. President, the Houmn are very pleased by the results in France, but they feel there is another matter that requires immediate attention." He repaid the president's lack of respect by sitting on the corner of the presidential desk, casually running his fingers through his hair.

President Bush turned, his eyes following him to the desk and his face flushing with anger. "Does it have anything to do with the man who infiltrated White House grounds last night?"

"As a matter of fact it does, Mr. President."

"I don't appreciate being kept in the dark, Kemp. Who is he?"

"The Houmn believe he is dangerous ..."

"Don't bullshit me, Kemp! You know who he is!" President Bush leveled an accusing finger at him. "Apparently they know him, too!" He scowled at the Houmn. "They tell me he's some kind of friend of yours. Was he the man abducted with you?"

Bill stiffened on his seat. "He's no friend of mine, Mr. President ; he tried to kill me last night."

"But you do know him?"

"Yes, I know him." Bill held the president's stare.

"Who is he? What was he doing here?"

"He is a religious fanatic. He's hell-bent on keeping the Houmn from helping us." Bill broke from his rehearsed statement. "He wants the prophecy of Judgment Day to come true. He wants the End of Days and the second coming of

Christ. He's a madman determined to undermine our alliance and spread fear of the Houmn."

Bush squared his shoulders. "Get off my desk, Kemp!"

Bill smiled, slowly pushing himself to his feet.

"How are you connected to him? I want the truth!" Bush inched closer, eyeing him suspiciously.

"His name is Hank Foster. He's a former Black Ops agent who specialized in psychological warfare."

"I know the man's name! Was he or wasn't he taken aboard their ship?"

Bill clasped his hands behind his back, addressing the president as if he were addressing his sergeant back in basic training. "Before any of this took place, Hank Foster managed to infiltrate a very powerful organization. I was a member of that organization."

"Yes, the Iconoclasts. I've been told all about them." Bush rolled his hand in the air, wanting him to move on.

"He was wounded in combat, and I believe he went mad. He subverted the Iconoclasts and began a campaign of misinformation in an effort to undermine the goals of the organization. He is a religious zealot who wants to bring about the prophecies of the Bible."

"If that's the case, why did you attempt to bring him to the Blue Ridge bunker?"

"He found me and told me he had useful information for combating the Takk. I didn't know what to do with him, so I was bringing him to the bunker. Mr. President, this man is a master manipulator. He has corrupted the highest levels of our organization, which makes him very dangerous. There is no telling how deep his influence runs."

"Why is he so dangerous?" President Bush turned slightly to address the Sempiternals directly. "How can one man be such a threat to you?"

"Mr. President, if I may, we are at a critical juncture. We cannot afford to let him drive a wedge of fear between us and the Houmn." Bill reworked the words the Sempiternals had given him.

"If this man is so dangerous, why didn't they keep him aboard their ship? How did someone like this get onto the White House grounds?"

Bill paused, waiting for an answer to form in his mind, but none came. The president grew impatient, narrowing his eyes and arching his brows. "Well, the threat wasn't fully exposed until he made his move last night." Bill stared at his shoes, still waiting.

"And what are *they* recommending we do?" President Bush shot an annoyed look toward the Houmn. "He's gone. Disappeared. My men have no idea where he is."

"He must be brought in as soon as possible. The Houmn wish to interrogate him themselves."

Bush turned on his heels, making an unsettling face before giving Bill his back. "Fine. I have a few questions I would like to ask him myself."

Bill followed him, ticking off ideas on his fingers. "We should blanket the press with his face. Get every possible agency working on it. There should be a reward for his capture. He must be brought in alive." Bill spoke fast; his nerves were beginning to fray as the guiding voice that had been with him almost every moment remained mute. "We must uncover whatever he's been planning."

Ellis stepped forward from behind his cane and addressed the Houmn directly. "What happened to Mr. Foster aboard your ship?"

Silence settled in the room, and all eyes turned toward the three naked figures.

Establishing relations with the man William Kemp was our only concern. A single, hollow voice emanated from within the triangle of Sempiternals, but Bill could not tell which one of them was speaking. *The man Hank Foster was of no use to us. His mind was unhealthy.*

Ellis nodded his thanks and turned to Bill. His face was an expressionless mask of old age. "What did you do with him before you came to the Blue Ridge bunker, Mr. Kemp?"

Bill clenched his teeth, feeling a defensive flush of heat on his face. "I … I left him."

"Hey Howard, there's a guy on the line who claims he was abducted by the aliens." Gary, Howard Stern's producer, broke into Howard's on-air rant against the French.

"Gary, why would I want to talk to him?" Howard's voice took on a chastising tone. "I'm in the middle of something."

"I dunno … the guy sounds sort of scary."

"Scary? Oh boy, this ought to be good. Why not? We've always got time to talk about aliens. I'll ask this guy if he's ever banged an alien chick. I'm curious."

"Hey, buddy … Hank, you ever bang any of the aliens? I mean the chick aliens—I don't want to imply that you're gay or anything."

Hank heard Howard's voice in stereo as he held the phone to his ear and leaned over to switch off the radio. A nervous smile grew on his face as he covered one ear with his hand. "No, Howard, never had the pleasure. Thanks for taking my call—longtime listener, first-time caller."

"Okay …" Howard sort of huffed into the phone. "Um, so you say you were abducted by the aliens, but you didn't screw around with any of them. Were they the little gray dudes, or was it the giant bugs?"

Hank could see Howard and his crew in the studio through his mind's eye. "It was the little gray dudes, the very same ones in the Capitol right now."

"That's right … Gary wrote me a note, but I can't read his writing. What's wrong with you, Gary? Come on, the world is falling apart, pull your shit together."

"Sorry, boss. I was in a hurry. This guy had a lot to say."

"Okay, I'm reading here that you were abducted with some other guy."

"That's right, Bill Kemp. You know him. He stood with President Bush when the Houmn landed at the Capitol."

"You know him, Howard. He's that Humanist congressman." Robin casually chimed into the conversation. "The really cute one."

"Okay, and this Kemp guy is a friend of yours?"

"Yes." Hank could tell Howard was looking for an angle to turn into a punch line, but he didn't care; he had gotten through. The battle was half over.

"And you and him were together when the aliens flew down and beamed you up?"

"Yes."

"So what's your point? I mean, you sound crazy, there's no doubt about that, but where are you going with all this?"

"I'm glad you asked. I need your help. But first, I wanna prove that I'm legitimate. And then you, Howard Stern, are going to break the story of the millennium."

Howard laughed. "Well, it's about time somebody recognizes my journalistic genius, Robin."

"Haven't we had enough stories of the millennium, Howard?" Robin said sarcastically.

"Don't rain on my parade, Robin." Howard snickered. "Okay, buddy, how are you going to prove you're for real? Let's get to it. I've had a lot of nut jobs calling me, telling me crazy stories. Let's hear yours."

"All right. Story first, then proof." Hank took a deep breath, realizing just how crazy he was going to sound. "June twenty second, six days ago, just after the last asteroid fell, Bill and I were in a car headed for a secret military base in the Blue Ridge Mountains …"

"Oh boy, this'll be good."

"Oh, it gets better, Howard. Just like you said, the spaceship flew down and beamed us up. The next day, I wake up in a pool of my own piss to see Bill on the television standing behind the president as he shook hands with the aliens."

"You think this Bill guy did anything kinky with the aliens?" Howard joked. Hank could feel him rolling his eyes, already distracted by the growing pile on notes in front of him.

"Who knows … but they've done something to him. That's why I need your help, Howard. They've screwed with his head, and I want everyone to know they're up to something."

"Up to what? Never mind, what's your proof? How are you going to prove you were taken away by aliens?"

"Well, they screwed with my head, too. But not like Billy. I think they've done something else to me. They're inside Billy's head; they need him to lie for them."

"Oh boy."

Hank could tell Howard was only halfway listening to him. His glasses sat low on his nose, and he was reading a news item. His thoughts were already racing ahead to his next topic. "Howard, if I can prove to you that I'm telling the truth, will you help me?"

"Dude, I'm just a stupid radio host. How am I supposed to help anybody?"

"I can be silenced, but they can't silence you. I need you to get my message out."

"Oh yeah? What's your message?"

"First let me prove to you I'm for real."

"Okay, let's have it."

Hank could feel him putting down his papers and leaning back in his chair. "Well, the Houmn did something to my brain. They wanted to communicate something to me ... and as a result I can read people's thoughts. I can read your thoughts right now."

"Get out of here. You're telling me you can tell what I'm thinking right now?" A cynical sneer grew on Howard's lips, but his attention shifted as someone entered the studio.

"Howard, we just looked this guy up." Gary was speaking away from the microphone but was easily audible over the phone line. "Something spooky is going on. This guy's picture is all over the place. The FBI, CIA, Secret Service, they're all looking for him. He's like, the most wanted guy on the most wanted list. He's like the new Bin Laden."

"You're kidding ..." Robin gasped doubtfully.

"No, no I'm not. If this is the same guy, he might be legit."

"Let me see that." Howard stood to take a sheet of paper from Gary. His eyes scanned the darkened image of Hank's face. "Is that right? Are you the guy they're looking for?"

"I am. They're trying to keep me from talking. What I've got to say is very unpopular."

"Howard, they're saying this guy broke into the White House!"

"Is that right? No wonder they're looking for you. But that doesn't mean you're not completely nuts."

"Are you ready for proof?"

"What are you gonna do? Tell my fortune? Talk to Elvis or something? Go ahead, tell me what I'm thinking right now."

"I wish it was that easy. If you want to see that I'm not jerking your chain, we should meet face to face. I don't know how much proof I can give you over the phone."

"You *are* crazy! I'm not going anywhere. I haven't left this building in three weeks."

"You'll meet me. I can convince you."

"Go ahead, convince me. I'm not going anywhere. It's not safe out there with all you lunatics running around."

"I'll tell you what you're thinking."

"You're gonna tell me what I'm thinking right now? Hold on a minute, let me think of something good. I don't want him to catch me thinking of young boys, Robin."

Hank laughed. "No, that wouldn't be good, Howard. I'd be crushed. I've been a fan of yours ever since I was a kid."

"Oh yeah? How old are you?"

"Thirty-six."

"Have I really been doing this that long, Robin?"

"I grew up in Brooklyn."

"Man, I must be getting old, Robin."

"You are old." Robin quipped.

"Well, at least we've branched out to the mental patient market. Go on, buddy, tell me what I'm thinking. I've got something."

"Okay, Howard, how's this for starters? 0845M, 167, and 24-8-18." Hank rattled off the series of numbers and then sat back anxiously chewing his thumb-nail.

There was a long silence, and when Howard finally spoke all the humor, had left his voice. "Okay, what's that supposed to mean?"

"Those are a few of the numbers you've got tucked away in your head. Your ATM pin number, your cholesterol—not bad, by the way—and the combination to your gym locker."

A dead silence hung in the air.

Robin broke the silence. "Is that right, Howard?"

Hank didn't wait for him to answer. "And you were thinking of a drawing your youngest daughter Emily drew for you before the divorce. You keep it in your sock drawer."

More silence followed.

"Well, Howard, is he right?" Robin pressed.

Howard finally spoke. "He's right …"

"Shut up! You're joking!" Robin laughed.

"Robin, I'm telling you, he's right!" Howard's voice raised an octave. Hank could feel him looking around the studio in confusion, as if someone were play-ing a joke on him.

"You're serious?" Robin continued.

Hank sat back in his seat, reveling in the moment. "Do you want me to go on, Howard?"

"No. I don't know what I want. This is some kind of trick!"

"Howard, I've got to meet with you. I can give you all the proof you need, but we've got to meet in person. The Houmn are dangerous. You've got to pry yourself from your studio. I can't come to you. They're trying to stop me."

"Howard, are you serious? You believe this guy?" Robin sounded concerned.

Hank spoke before Howard could respond. "He's got to, Robin. He's the only one I can talk to. I can't go anywhere else. I'm talking about saving the planet from something worse than the bugs. He's got to meet me."

More dead air followed as Howard collected his thoughts. "Hold on, I want to talk with you off the air." There was a hum and a click, and then Howard was back on the line. This time he was alone. "How did you do that? Who put you up to this?"

"This isn't a scam, Howard."

"Tell me what I'm thinking right now."

"You're thinking you've got to stop chewing your nails. Your left thumb is in your mouth right now."

Hank felt him checking to see if anybody was watching him. "Fuck, I can't believe this. You're not kidding!"

"Will you help me?"

"You were really taken by the aliens?"

"Everything I've told you is true. I can prove it."

Howard's heart raced. A million thoughts collided together as his doubt melted away. "Are you kidding? It's the story of the millennium—what do you need me to do?"

Paradigm III
Chapter 15

Baltimore, Maryland. June 28, 2002

Young and beautiful, with dark Persian eyes and smooth, flawless skin, Shaharazad inspired feelings Omar couldn't control. He dreamed of her even while he was awake. He knew he would do anything for her. Being with her was all that mattered. He had agreed to act as her chaperone on the relief mission out of pure lust for her. Her father was a righteous man, a good man, and Omar was breaking his trust. He was no longer the man her father believed he was. Even when prostrate in prayer, his thoughts were always of her.

On the rare occasions when his thoughts turned homeward, he felt only bitterness. His life seemed suddenly filled with holes. He felt cheated, lied to. Even his once-beloved Mullah now kindled anger in him. His lies had eaten his youth. He had been wrong about everything, and Omar felt foolish for putting his faith in the words of others. Allah was not real, and there was no glorious afterlife awaiting the righteous; the strange, gray men from another world had proven that beyond any doubt.

Now that his faith had gone, the burden of his failures had evaporated along with it. He was grateful for the events that had taken him to America. In America, he had discovered a passion for life he had never imagined. He no longer yearned for the promise of paradise. Paradise was being next to her. Happiness was holding her hand while they watched the big television with the other volunteers in the airplane hangar.

Their small group from the Islamic relief organization mingled with the other volunteers in a vast staging area. Shaharazad's father was right; life was easier for them now that they had joined the others bringing humanitarian aid to the East. Food was provided for them, and they were safe. Bringing purified goods to the Muslims displaced by the disaster filled them with a sense of hope, and their presence among the other Americans didn't seem out of place. Everyone sat and talked as they watched the news on the massive television set up in the middle of hangar.

Omar stared at the television, but his thoughts were focused on Shaharazad; tonight they would be alone.

"Military analysts are reporting that China has announced the formation of a million-man army staged in eastern China and southern Mongolia. They are coordinating with the Russian Army massing in the Amur Valley to launch an offensive against the Takk."

"Omar, would you like to get a Coca-cola?" Shaharazad let her veil hang over her shoulder as she sat up from the pile of bags.

"Are you having one?"

"Come on, let's get away from the television for a moment." She stood and offered her hand to him. Her fingernails were freshly painted bright red. "I'll buy you a drink."

"But aren't all the sodas free?"

"I'm joking with you, Omar." Her smile widened, wrinkling the corners of her eyes. "Of course they are free. Everything is free."

Omar stood, brushing the dust from his robe. He was about to let her to lead the way, when another announcement flashed across the television.

"We interrupt our report for some breaking news. The White House has just announced that authorities are looking for a man who reportedly infiltrated the Capitol Security Zone last night. The man killed two DC policemen and made threats against our Houmn allies. They say they are looking for this man: Hank Foster."

The man's face stopped Omar in his tracks. His spine went rigid. The man he'd followed from Afghanistan, the man he had been sent to kill, stared back at him from the massive television. His beard was gone, replaced by a hard-set square jaw, but his eyes, the scowling dark eyes with the demonic gleam, were unmistakably the same.

Shaharazad walked on, still chatting, but her words were lost. A sudden, horrible sense of doom crashed over him. His eyelids drew back, and his mouth fell open.

"He may be traveling with an unknown accomplice, described as a large black man in his early twenties. A representative for the secret service describes Hank Foster as a religious fundamentalist intent on bringing the fulfillment of the apocalypse described in the scriptures. He is to be considered armed and extremely dangerous."

A wave of nausea tightened his stomach. The fearful belief in a vengeful, all-powerful God crashed back into his consciousness. He could feel the eyes of Allah burning down on him. He'd abandoned his faith and failed to destroy the evil Jinn. He was a transgressor in every way. The thought of infinite pain and sorrow kept him from drawing his next breath. He realized with horror that all this had happened because of his failure. The end was coming. There would be no forgiveness.

"If anyone has information on the whereabouts of this man, they are urged to contact the authorities. A reward of gold, food, and fuel has been offered to anyone assisting in the capture of this man. He was last seen fleeing the Washington DC area."

"Omar, what are you doing? Are you okay?" Shaharazad looked more amused than concerned as she stood over him.

Omar couldn't speak. When he looked at her, he felt only shame.

Almost without thinking, Omar thrust a hand into the deep pocket of his robe and frantically pulled out the old notepad that was his only possession on arriving in America. His hands trembled as he thumbed through page after page until he came to a list of names and addresses. His eyes stopped on a word: *Baltimore.* His heart pounded as he shot a glance to a sign above the hangar's main door. The name was the same: Baltimore. There was still hope.

Omar felt Allah's hand pushing him out of the hangar's main door. He did not look back as Shaharazad called after him. His fate was now clear; his destiny was inexorably tied to the Jinn Hank Foster and the men from al-Qaeda. Life was meaningless beyond this fact, and he knew the fury of hell's fire awaited him if he failed a second time.

The drone from the Hummer's tires reverberated down the freeway, and Shug felt a strange sense of normalcy amid the thin stream of traffic. Hank sat next to him, anxiously scanning the traffic merging onto the freeway. Suddenly two cars pressed forward to flank the Hummer. They moved aggressively, swerving in to pin the larger military jeep on both sides. Seemingly out of nowhere, two more nondescript white cars came into view and moved in to surround the Hummer. Without warning, the lead car slammed on the breaks. A cloud of blue smoke blasted from the tires.

The heavy Hummer lurched to avoid slamming into the smaller car but then accelerated, slamming into the bumper, sending it spinning out of control. The other cars continued to press in, but the Hummer charged ahead, veering toward an upcoming off-ramp.

The Hummer bounced over an embankment, splintering a road sign and kicking up a thick cloud of dust as it rumbled down a slope to the off-ramp below. All three cars followed, somehow managing to keep pace with the Hummer as it bounced down the hill. The wail of police sirens sounded from behind, and Shug turned in the driver's seat of their stolen Ford to see red and blue lights dotting the freeway behind them.

Shug kept an even pressure on the gas pedal and stayed in the passing lane as they passed the spot where the Hummer had left the road. Hank pressed his face against the window to watch the Hummer cross the median on the street below the freeway. They passed through the cloud of dust, and Shug checked the rear-view mirror to confirm that all the cop cars had followed the Hummer down the off-ramp.

"It worked!"

Hank turned in his seat with clenched fists. "It won't take them long to figure out I'm not in there."

"Should we change freeways?"

"Yeah. Come on, brother: time to haul ass."

"I don't wanna draw too much attention." Shug checked his speed on the speedometer.

"It doesn't matter. There aren't any traffic cops anymore, just Hank and Sugar cops. Come on, pick up the pace."

"Where should we go?"

"Doesn't matter. We can't let them stop us." Hank looked down at the pistol in his lap. "They'll want to take me alive, but it won't be that easy."

Shug shot him a worried look, but his eyes caught on a sign for an interconnecting freeway, and he swerved between two large trucks in time to pull onto the off-ramp. They followed the curve of the ramp leading to a southbound interstate. The southbound lanes were virtually empty except for an occasional semi headed for Georgia, while the northbound lanes were packed with cars.

"I don't like this route, Shug. We're the only car on the road. We stick out like a sore thumb."

"All right … you're right. What should we do?"

"Find a place to turn around. Maybe we can hide in all that traffic headed north." Hank leaned forward to scan the endless line of cars headed toward Washington. "It'll give us a little time to think."

"You want to go back to DC?"

"For the moment. We won't get very far. Look at that mess."

"Okay, we hide in traffic. Makes sense somehow." Shug looked ahead for another off ramp when the flash of lights caught his attention in his rearview mirror. "Shit! Hank, there's a cop coming up behind me!"

"Pull to the right … see if he'll pass us."

Shug slowed, clicking his turn signal to the right. "I dunno, he's comin up fast."

"Is he gonna pass us?"

"Oh man, I don't think so. He's right behind us!"

"Don't let him pull you over, Shug."

"Maybe he's just pulling us over for speeding."

"Don't do it, Shug." Hank's voice was ominously calm as he chambered a round in his pistol.

The brief chirp of a siren sounded behind them, and Shug instinctively tapped the brakes. "We gotta pull over. He's right on top of us."

"Don't stop, Shug."

"We can't outrun a radio, Hank! Maybe you can talk your way out of this. Use your mental shit on him. You can do it." Shug kept his eyes on the rearview as he pulled to the shoulder.

Hank slumped low in his seat without saying another word. Their car lurched to a stop, and Shug watched the police car pull up twenty yards behind them. He shifted the car into park and blew out an anxious breath.

"Shug, listen to me for a minute. You've got to trust me." Hank sat up in the seat and buckled his seatbelt. "I'm sorry I've got to do this." Shug tore his eyes away from the cop still sitting his car. Hank had a look in his eyes he'd never seen before.

Suddenly Shug's body moved without his control. He turned in his seat, and his hand reached out for the gearshift. He pulled the car into reverse and slammed his foot down on the accelerator. He could feel Hank inside him, guiding every movement. The car surged backward, gaining speed. A sickening feeling turned his stomach as they charged the parked cop car.

In a few short, terrifying seconds, their car had closed the distance and slammed into the front of the police car. Shug jerked in his seat, but his movements were no longer his own. He watched helplessly as the airbag exploded in the face of the cop behind the wheel. Hank turned him in his seat, and he pulled the car back into drive, stomping on the gas pedal. Their stolen Taurus pulled away with a crunch of metal, and in a matter of seconds they were back on the freeway, pulling away from the disabled police car.

Shug could hear himself screaming as the car sped down the freeway, completely out of his control. He couldn't pull his foot off the accelerator. He couldn't turn the wheel, but he could feel Hank inside him.

Finally, as if in response to his wordless pleas, Hank's overpowering presence faded. Shug, able to move on his own once more, gripped the wheel and swerved from side to side, taking his foot from the pedal.

Hank pressed his fists against his forehead, still clutching the loaded pistol. "I'm sorry, Shug."

Shug was stunned. He didn't know how to explain what had just happened. Hank had never mentioned being able to do anything like that. He checked the rearview, but the police car had disappeared over the horizon. Somewhere in the back of his mind, Hank was speaking to him, and Shug began to understand. He knew Hank was right. Hank was always right. He would have killed the cop if he hadn't done what he had.

Three hours had passed since they had rolled the battered Taurus into a deep pond at the Woodmont Hills country club. They had hidden in the shadows and waited for the helicopters and the lights, but none came. Hank waited for some kind of plan to form in his scattered thoughts, but he couldn't focus on a single idea for long. Random thoughts by the thousands ebbed and flowed in his brain. Countless voices whispered in his ear. He couldn't think past his next move, but he knew he couldn't wait any longer. There was nothing left to do but find another vehicle and make a run for his meeting place with Howard Stern.

He motioned for Shug to follow him and stepped out onto the dirt road. There was a gap in the pines overhead, and Hank could see that the night sky was beginning to brighten. "We'll make our way back to that little suburb by the golf course. Maybe we can find something drivable."

Shug brushed the leaves from his knees. "Like what? A golf cart?" Shug's almost constant smile was missing.

"We'll ride mountain bikes if we have to. It's not that far from here." Hank motioned for Shug to follow him with a jerk of his head.

The piston on Hank's mechanical ankle was coated with dirt and began to squeak as he hiked down the fire-road. Shug immediately began mimicking the rodentlike squeal with each alternating step. Hank almost laughed, then began to scowl as Shug continued and his train of though was further disrupted. But as Shug persisted, now adding little farting noises in between steps, Hank laughed aloud for the first time in days.

Shug skipped ahead to walk by Hank's side. His smile was back, but Hank knew he was thinking about what would happen once they were caught. They both seemed to know that their capture was inevitable, and the images in Shug's head were dark and violent. "So what are we gonna do if we get to Baltimore and find out Howard has been followed or something?"

"I don't really know. There's really only one other place we can turn." Hank slowed his pace, sticking his thumbs into his waist belt as a subtle sign that he was willing to talk.

"Who's that?"

"Well, once we get captured, I can spill my guts to the first official we talk to. I tell them as much as I can before the Houmn get ahold of me. Maybe I can convince someone to keep them away from me."

"You can do it. I know you can. Just do to one of them what you did to me. We can do it right now."

"No way, last resort. I want to pass this thing on to someone who can really get the message out. A guy like Howard can convince more people than I ever could." A fleeting warning—the snap of a twig, or the faint murmur of voices— triggered Hank's internal alarms. He slowed to a stop, mentally feeling out his surroundings, but the hillside was silent except for the crickets chirping in the brush.

Shug skipped ahead, turning to face him. "But ..."

Hank raised a finger to his lips. Everything he was feeling warned him of danger, but there was no evidence to apply to reason. He forced a half smile for Shug, shaking away the feeling with a waggle of his head. "Come on, it's nothing."

"I know. There's nobody around for miles." Shug spoke loud, quickly silencing the crickets. "I thought you were just getting another crazy idea in your head." Shug fell into step next to him and wrapped an arm around his shoulder. "I'm getting used to it ... but I keep waiting for you to come up with something good."

Shug bounced with good humor next to him, but Hank couldn't shake the feeling that something was wrong. His mind was on full alert, and his limbs tingled with electricity. Shug's breathing was magnified in his ears as he strained to hear every sound. They had gone a few yards, Shug still snickering at his wisecrack, but all else was quiet—even the crickets had failed to rejoin in their night song. Once again, Hank stopped in his tracks, this time reaching into his waistband to grab his pistol.

A blinding flood of light exploded over the treetops, causing Hank's heart to skip a beat. He could see the outline of the ship against the blackness and realized it had been there all along, silent and invisible, listening to his thoughts. He tried to turn away from the lights, but it was already too late; his body was already succumbing to the familiar numbness.

The empty frustration of pure nothingness became a memory, and he awoke as if leaving it behind in a dream. His consciousness gathered quickly, unlike his first time aboard a Houmn ship. He was aware of the Houmn standing over him before he saw them. He knew what they wanted; their thoughts were already probing and seducing his. He felt them trying to pacify his mind and sedate his body, but their attempts had been frustrated.

Hank's eyes snapped open against their collective will. He was lying flat on his back as the alien minds hovered above. Their faces were not the same as before. He knew in an instant that they were the Sempiternals. Their thin faces were expressionless, and their eyes were a dull, featureless black. A strange light shimmered over their heads, and their pale, dead-looking skin was completely exposed.

Do not struggle, Hank Foster. Do not resist us.

We are Sempiternals. You will obey.

The flow of words spoke to him without a voice. The thoughts seemed to be projected through their eyes. Hank clenched his eyes and flexed against the restraints holding him in place. He felt the pulsing buzz of a magnetic field pinning him down. Sensation returned to his limbs, and he pulled against the straps on his arms, legs and chest. They were telling him that it was useless to struggle, that they would sedate him chemically if necessary. They were telling him that he was powerless to stop them.

"No! Get away from me!" Hank's scream reverberated through the dead air. He felt strength return to his body as his mind cleared. He strained his neck against the magnetic field to look at the aliens surrounding him. Some of the smaller, more familiar Houmn drifted in and out of view behind the three Sempiternals. Hank followed them with his eyes, reaching out to them with his thoughts as if they were going to step forward to help him.

An unheard voice intercepted his projections. *We have you now. You may resist us, but you will not last.*

You will tell us who among the Houmn conspires against the Sempiternals.

You will tell us all.

Hank knew his thoughts would be just as clear as words, but he screamed out anyway. "I won't tell you anything! I'll kill you for this!" He jerked in his restraints but couldn't move. The weight of the electrical field seemed to take his breath away.

You are no longer in a position to threaten us.

We have you. You will tell us everything. The naked Sempiternal hovering at his feet lifted a long finger to point to a silver-suited Houmn at his side. The subordinate Houmn stepped closer and held the black shroud for him to see. They didn't need to remind him what pain and nothingness the hood could inflict.

Hank thrashed against the restraints, straining every muscle and screaming aloud. He turned his head from the specter of the hood, trying to block out the thoughts pressing in on him. He opened his eyes to see Shug flat on his back on a table next to him.

Seeing Shug shocked him for a moment, but Hank recognized their fatal mistake in an instant. They had made the same mistake with him when they took Bill. The Sempiternals focused all their attention on a single captive. Shug was unconscious on a similar platform, but he was held in place by a combination of mental sedation and a mild magnetic field. They had failed to restrain Shug the same way they had him. There was no strap across Shug's chest or anywhere on his arms and legs.

The Sempiternals drew closer. They had no fear of him. Hank made his move before they had time to see it coming. He stopped his struggle against the restraints and focused his vital energy on the one person he knew better than all others. He blocked out the other entities in the ship until he could feel Shug floating in the emptiness. The Houmn exerted an almost passive control over him, leaving him in a dream-filled sleep. Hank reached past the invisible hand holding Shug's eyes closed and fell in sync with his psyche.

Feeling a connection like the flipping of a switch, Hank projected his thoughts into Shug with wild abandon. He feared that the Sempiternals would sense his move and crush him at any moment. He pumped Shug full of raw fear and blind rage. He tapped the core emotions triggering a single desire: escape. He willed Shug off the table and into a killing frenzy. Hank couldn't see it, but he knew the black shroud was only inches away.

Suddenly Hank felt Shug's eyes snap open. A silver-suited Houmn blocked his view, and Hank thrust his head forward to stare at the Sempiternals. His eyes bore into theirs as he worked up an intense hatred and projected it into Shug. The Houmn paused, one of them in the process of raising the hood over Hank's head. The ship shuddered beneath them, and all eyes turned to face Shug.

Hank could feel Shug breaking free of the magnetic field. He could feel the soles of his feet as they hit the floor. The gravity in the ship was less than normal, causing Shug to bounce as he leaped off the table. The ship trembled with his every step. One of the Houmn shrieked aloud and shrank from view.

The sensation of fear washed through the ship like a smell. Hank magnified the fear and fed it to Shug with every ounce of his energy. He could hear the Houmn screaming. He had caught them completely unprepared for violence.

A terrible shriek like the cry of a wounded deer rang in his ears, and a twisted alien body flashed over his head to land with a thud on the floor behind him. Hank lifted his head to see Shug leaping through the narrow space, his head was level with the ceiling. He seemed to float through the air before he came crashing down, grabbing a silver-suited Houmn by the leg. Shug stood, pulling the helpless alien into the air by its ankle, and then whipped it across the chamber. The body hit the angular wall with a spattering of viscous fluid, then slid to the floor with its head bent back and all the life smashed from it.

Shug's eyes were wide with violence, and he screamed like a madman. He leaped at one of the slender Sempiternals cowering against the wall. Its mouth hung wide open, and its eyes seemed to flutter from black to gray. It didn't move as Shug lunged, grabbing it by the throat. Hank saw in its thoughts that the creature had never faced its own mortality before. That horror was something completely new to the Sempiternals. Shug pulled at the creature's throat and smashed his fist deep into its skull. The body slackened in his grip, the dead weight momentarily keeping him from extracting his hand. The ring of lights floating above the alien's head flitted out.

Shug threw the lifeless body to the floor with a grunt and scrambled out of view to follow the cries of the other Houmn. Hank pushed him on, not wanting to lose the connection with him. He could feel the power in Shug's hands as he snapped their limbs and jerked the life out of them. Another body flew through the air over his head, and sound of equipment shattering filled the narrow chamber.

Hank lifted his head to stare at the straps holding him in place. The magnetic field was gone, but he was still pinned at the wrists and ankles. The thick chest strap kept him from sitting up or breathing too deep.

Shug screamed again. He was farther off in the ship and Hank couldn't hear the Houmn screaming anymore. He felt the crashing effect of spent endorphins in Shug's body, and he slowly let go of his hold on his friend's senses.

Shug sobbed in great gasps as he returned. Tears streamed down his cheeks as he stared down at his gore-covered hands. His whole body shimmered with an oily fluid.

"Shug, Over here. It's me," Hank called to him, waving him over with his wrist pinned to the table. "Come over here and help me up."

Shug just stared at him, holding his bloody hands in front of him as if he carried something heavy. His thoughts were confused, disconnected. He looked at Hank as if he'd never seen him before.

"Come on, Shug. It's okay." Hank's heart ached for what he had done to his friend.

"What did I do?" Shug's shoulders slumped as the air left his chest.

"Listen to me, brother-man, we've been taken by the Houmn. We're on their ship. You've got to get me off of this thing."

"What did I do?" Shug asked again. He began wiping the oily fluid from his hands, but it stuck to his skin, wetting everything he touched.

"You didn't do anything. I did it. I had to."

"You didn't do this … I did this." Shug stared at his hands as if they were not his own.

"I'm sorry, Shug. It was the only thing I could think of. They were about to annihilate me, I know it."

"I remember … I killed them." Shug narrowed his eyes on the twisted bodies lining the walls. "I killed them."

"Yes, you killed them—and you saved me. Now get over here and take these fucking straps off!"

Shug snapped out of his daze, but there was a look in his eyes Hank wished he'd never had to see. A muffled cry sounded from somewhere in the ship. Shug didn't react, and at first Hank thought his mind was playing tricks on him, but the sound repeated itself, growing louder. "Can you hear that? Quick, unstrap me."

Shug's hands paused over the chest strap while he stared off into space. "Yeah, sounds like a baby crying or something."

"Come on! Hurry, get me off of this thing."

Shug pulled away the straps. A tortured look grew on his face with each pitiful yelp. "What is that?" Shug's deep voice was on the verge of tears.

Hank sat on the table with his hands free and began working on the belts keeping his ankles in place. "It's probably one of them." He shot a glace at the body folded against the wall.

Hank slid off the table and tested his weight in the artificial gravity. He looked around the chamber for the first time from a normal vantage point. His pistol sat on a tray atop a brilliantly lit computer system. The black shroud that had threatened him now lay at his feet.

The bleating cry grew louder, and Hank grabbed the pistol. He checked the clip and chambered a round. "Sounds like one of them is wounded. Let's see if he can show us how to fly this thing, or beam us back, or do whatever the hell they do."

"I don't wanna go in there." Shug refused to look past the passageway.

"I'll handle it." Hank picked a path through the pools of oily blood and alien organs. He slipped in the gore but easily caught himself in the decreased gravitational pull. The naked body of a Sempiternal was crammed into the passageway between the semicircular chambers. Its large oval head had been split in two.

Hank guided himself into the next chamber, and a shriek of alarm sent tension rippling through his body. His eyes followed the sound to where a Houmn squealed beneath the heavy arm of some articulating device. The creature was helplessly pinned; the lower half of its body, including an arm, was crushed beneath the fallen equipment. The miserable creature hid its face as Hank approached. Its thoughts were clear.

Stop the pain. Do anything, but stop the pain.

Hank stepped closer, examining the machine crushing the Houmn. It was clear that the heavy piece of metal was the only thing keeping it alive. If it were even possible to pull it away somehow, the creature would bleed to death in seconds. "There's nothing I can do for you." Hank's thoughts carried over, translated into words for the pain-riddled alien.

All is lost. Kill me. Stop the pain.

Hank knelt down to take its head in his hands. He peered into the dark, almond-shaped eyes and wondered if this was one of the Houmn who had experimented on his brain. The creature's mind was a blur, but there was a hatred for the Sempiternals coloring its mania. It despaired for more than its own life: its grief was a communal one, felt by countless millions. Hank could see failure and betrayal. The Houmn's struggle to free themselves from the Sempiternals was in dire jeopardy.

He stared deeper into the Houmn's mind and was stopped by a sudden question yelped out between silent screams. *Why have you done this? Why have you killed them?* The Houmn slave was thinking of its masters.

"I did what you forced me to do! You made me do this! Humans will never be slaves like the Houmn! Tell me, are they still coming to conquer Earth? Tell me, or I'll make your pain worse!"

They are coming. There is no stopping them. It is too late for Earth. It is too late for the Houmn. The Sempiternals will reclaim Earth, and their power will grow. No power will exist to escape them. The rebellion will be crushed, now that they know we tried to warn the people of Earth.

"I don't care about your rebellion! I want to know how to stop them, and you're going to help me."

You cannot stop them. The ships are coming. You can only resist them. Maybe one day you will have the strength to turn against them as we have tried to do.

"What about the others? The Houmn here in Earth's orbit—how do I stop them?"

You cannot. End my suffering. Kill me, let it end.

"No, not until you show me everything I need to know. How do I break the Houmn influence over Earth? How do I kill them all?"

Impossible. Unthinkable. Earth needs the Houmn to fight the Takk.

"I will put an end to them right now!" Spit flew from his lips as he raged aloud. "How many Houmn are there?"

No, kill me. Stop this pain.

"Would you do the same for me? What about the pain you put me through? You put something in my head!" Hank pulled the creature's head closer, tightening his grip on its neck. "How many other Houmn are there? Where are they? What are they planning to do? Tell me, or I'll show you the real meaning of pain."

The Houmn's voice remained quiet, but the answers to these and other questions floated to the surface of its thought. The creature no longer had the strength, or the will, to defend against Hank's probing. A flood of understanding stacked up in his mind as he blasted the Houmn with question after question. Bits of information fell into place with other fragments of thought, and the germ of an idea was kindled in his conscious mind.

The Houmn had unwittingly told him that there was only one Houmn Master Ship circling Earth. All other ships depended on this single, mother ship. Hank released his grip on the Houmn's neck, and the creature's head fell to the floor with a thud.

"Show me how to fly the ship."

Kill me! I beg you!

"Show me how to operate this Frisbee! Tell me where to find the Master Ship! Do that, and I promise I will end it for you."

The creature wailed aloud. It had given up. Even as Hank spoke to it, its mind was telling him everything he wanted to know. The promise of an end to the agony was too great. Flying the ship would be a simple matter once he was connected with the mental interface computer. Finding the Houmn Master Ship would be as easy as thinking a command. The tortured alien let him see everything: all its knowledge, all its fears. It warned that the Sempiternals must not be destroyed, that Earth must not fall to the Takk.

Sweat poured down Hank's face, even though it was cool inside the ship. He stood, closing his eyes and closing his mind to the dying Houmn. The insane plan inspired by a moment of pure rage still burned in his thoughts. Now the outlandish plan seemed plausible, even justified. He knew he could pilot the ship on his will alone. He could repay the Houmn and end everything in an instant. It would no longer matter if Earth survived the Takk or the Houmn; it would be out of his hands. He would be forgotten, absolved of his mistakes by a final act of human will.

Shug kept quiet, like a man in a dream. He even seemed to float in a dreamlike way. He couldn't discount the feeling that he would wake up at any moment, and all of this would be forgotten. He alternated between watching Hank move from chamber to chamber and trying to rid himself of the gelatin clinging to his hands. There was nothing in the ship to clean himself with. The clear, oily blood had thickened and cooled, causing him to shiver uncontrollably. His clothes were wet with the stuff, and the memories of what he'd done flashed in his mind like some terrible horror movie.

Hank moved from one panel of lights to the next with a sense of urgency that baffled Shug. He spoke to him constantly, but at times he seemed to be speaking a different language. Shug only pretended to understand what he was talking about. He followed Hank with his eyes, turning away when he slipped in a pool of blood or inadvertently kicked a dead alien. He couldn't stand to see what he had done to them. He couldn't stand to hear the miserable bleating cries coming from the corridor behind him. He just wanted the horrible dream to come to an end.

"Shug? Shug, can you hear me?"

He stared at Hank, watching his lips moving, but he couldn't tell if his voice was real. He was telling him it was time. He wanted him to do something, but nothing made sense.

"Come on, follow me. I'll show you." Hank offered his hand to pull him off the floor, but when he reached out to take it, Hank avoided the gore on his hands and pulled him up by the collar.

Shug followed him along the circular corridor, bouncing on his tiptoes and squeezing himself through the narrow openings. He steadied himself by running a hand along the smooth silver walls. Hank moved effortlessly, seemingly knowing where he was going and what he was doing. He stopped now and then to wave a hand through the air, tapping the empty space with his fingertips. He paused, stroked the air, and the next passageway slid open.

They entered a wide space with a long, empty wall angled away from the center of the ship. Three slender mushroom tops sprouted from the floor to form a narrow triangle in the center of the chamber. Hank marched an excited loop around the empty space and turned to Shug with a strange intensity in his eyes. For a moment, Shug felt as if Hank was about to jump inside his head again.

"This is it. This is where they control the ship." Hank reached out to grab him by the shoulders.

Shug stared at the blank space all around him. There was nothing in the semicircular room but the knee-high metal mushrooms.

Hank guided him toward the center and gently pushed him onto one of the small pedestal seats. "We can fly the ship from here."

Shug found his balance on the alien stool and looked up into Hank's eyes. "You can fly this thing?"

"Correction: *you* can fly this thing."

"What?" Shug looked around as if he were missing something.

"I need you to do it."

"Do what?"

"I need you to control the ship." Hank took a seat on another pedestal and rested his elbows on his knees.

"Control what?" Shug waved his hands through the empty space. "I can't fly this thing."

"Yes, you can. I'll show you."

"Then you do it!"

"I can't."

"Then what makes you think I can?"

"I know how it's done. Our little buddy back there showed me. I just can't do it myself."

"Why? What am I supposed to do? There's nothing here."

"Let me explain. The ship is controlled via a mental interface with its pilot. You can do it. The ship does all the work. I can't fly it because I can't risk them getting into my head. The ships talk to each other; they're all connected. The Houmn might be able to take control of it from their mother ship. They might try to stop us."

"I don't understand ... stop us from doing what?"

Hank leaned close, almost whispering. "There are thirty other ships just like this one. They all depend on a Master Ship to sustain them. That ship is somewhere out there. If we take her out, the Houmn will be stranded. The Houmn on Earth won't be able to communicate with their home fleet."

"Take her out? What are you talking about?"

"I'm talking about killing the Houmn."

"What? Why can't we use the ship to fly home?"

"Shug, listen to me—try to understand. A Houmn invasion fleet is headed for Earth. I'm talking about thousands of ships, ships nothing like this one. Warships. They will arrive in exactly 103 years. If we don't take out the Houmn here right now, they will know every move made on Earth. They will corrupt our governments; they will begin to conquer us before their army even gets here. Earth will never be able to prepare a defense against them." Hank rubbed the sweat from his face and wiped it on his pant legs. "The two of us have gotten lucky. We've got a shot at taking them down. We've got to take it."

"Lucky? How does this make us lucky? How are we supposed to attack their ship? You said this ship doesn't have any weapons."

"We fly this thing right into them."

"What?"

"We can do it. I can show you how."

"No way!"

"Shug, I know you don't understand. We've got to do this. Nothing else matters. In a way this is all my fault, and this is the only way I can make things right."

"By killing ourselves?" Shug stood up from his seat.

"I can show you."

"I'm not going to do it. I'm not going to let you do it."

"I can show you more than how to fly the ship; I can show you why we need to do this. The Houmn want to enslave all of us. Humans will no longer exist; they will become part of the Houmn. There are things more important than our lives. Our lives are meaningless beyond this."

"But what if you're wrong? What if all this is going through your head because of what they did to you? What if they really *are* coming to help us? What if all those ships are coming to fight the bugs?"

"I'm not wrong. The Sempiternals want to enslave us like they've enslaved the Houmn. The Houmn are trying to rebel against their control, but the Sempiternals are too powerful: they control everything. They will control us, and we will be as powerless as the Houmn."

"I *do* understand. I *know* you! You're in a fight with them, and you don't want to lose! You'd rather die!"

"I don't want to kill myself … I want to kill them. You know I would never ask this of you if I didn't believe it was absolutely necessary. We have a chance to do something that might save humanity."

"You don't care about saving humanity! You're thinking about yourself. You think this will make up for whatever you've done—but I don't believe it. I don't believe any of this has anything to do with you. You're just angry. You've always been angry, and you can't stand that they've done this to you!"

"Let me show you. You'll see that we have a chance to make a difference. You've got to trust me."

"I've always trusted you. I've always done what you've asked. But you're acting crazy! This whole thing is crazy!"

"Let me show you."

"What are you going to do? Take over my mind again?" Shug clenched his fists and stared Hank in the eyes. "You could show me how to save the whole world, but what good would it do me? We'd be dead! We wouldn't even know if we made a difference or not."

"We should have died already. Now we've got a chance to do something important."

"But we're not dead! There's got to be another way!"

"If there is, I can't think of one." Hank stood and motioned for Shug to take his seat. "I'll show you how it works, and then you can make the choice. It'll be quick and painless. There are far worse ways to go."

Shug slumped back onto the stool. "What are you going to do?"

"I've got to get inside your head. I'm sorry, I know what this is like for you, but it's the only way."

"Go ahead and do it! What are you asking me for? You're going to do it anyway! It doesn't matter if I let you in my head or not! You'll just do what you want anyway."

"Shug, I want you to understand why. There's something bigger than us. We're born, we lead short, meaningless lives, and then we die. Not many of us will get a chance to do something truly meaningful. Not everyone gets a chance to save humanity."

"Is that really what this is all about? If I remember correctly, you were never such a big fan of humanity in the first place."

Hank stepped behind him and pushed him to face the long, semicircular wall. "Well, I've found something worse." Hank leaned over his shoulder and waved the palm of his hand over the empty space above his knees. A laser-thin, greenish hued panel of light materialized over Shug's lap. Hank's fingers tapped on a section of the light as if it were a solid object. "Can you see this?"

"Yeah ... I see it." Shug reached out and pushed his hand straight through the field of green light. A bright ring of green circled his wrist.

"Careful, like this." Suddenly it felt as if Hank's hand was on his, guiding it to a point in the center of the sheet of floating laser light. Shug could feel the laser screen on his fingertips, but Hank's hand wasn't there. "You've got to visualize the ship's controls." Shug's hand hovered for a moment before reaching out to his right and tickling the air.

A flicker of blue light appeared from nowhere, and Shug pulled his hand back to his chest. "Are you doing this?"

"Yeah, I'm trying to make it easier for you. The ship is just reacting to what we do." Hank spoke low over his shoulder, but a deeper understanding flowed behind his words. Shug felt something guiding his fingers, and it seemed as if the ship itself was whispering secrets into his ear. "The computer is looking to establish a telepathic connection with you. Relax, let it happen."

"Relax? What spaceship are *you* on?" Shug watched as his right hand reached out and brought a blue rectangle of light to life. His eyes fixed on the symbols glowing an electric blue on the screen. At first the strange symbols appeared to be mere scribbles, but as he stared, the strange markings transformed into commands.

"This enables you to navigate the system." Hank pointed toward the field of green light, and Shug's left hand reached out to stroke the invisible keys.

Shug hesitated, his fingers. He somehow knew that touching the symbol would connect him to the computer's brain.

"Come on, it won't bite you."

"What's it gonna do?" Shug seemed to know the answer and pulled his hands away.

"These are just the controls, Shug. Nobody is going to make you do anything you don't want to do. I promise."

Shug felt his hand reaching out again. His mind was already racing ahead to other commands, other controls. The ship's power seemed to course through him as he tapped the virtual buttons. A sudden wash of electricity cascaded over him, and the entire wall came to life with brilliantly lit screens. "Can you see this, too?"

"I'm seeing what you're seeing." Hank's hand reached out to point at the field of blue to his right. "Touch it here."

Shug didn't need to be told. His finger had already found the spot and flicked the air. The blue field grew, expanding to fill the space in front of him. Rings of concentric yellow lines cut across the blue. White points of light hovered in the air.

"This is us." Hank used Shug's own hand to point to where their ship sat on the three-dimensional map. "That green sphere over there is Earth."

Shug wanted to reach out and touch the featureless globe, but his hands were already stroking keys and reorganizing the screens. His eyes shifted to follow the moving lights, but he could no longer track what was happening. A barrage of information overwhelmed him as the screens of light fell together like puzzle pieces. He understood at once that a single keystroke could send the ship wherever he chose.

"And this is the Houmn Master Ship." A yellow line arched across the field of blue and intersected the point of light where the Houmn ship sat.

Shug jerked his hands away from the light. "No! I won't do it! It's suicide!"

"Shug, it's the only thing we can do."

"No, you're wrong! This is the only way *you* can take revenge on them, and I won't let you do it!"

"It has nothing to do with revenge. It's about being responsible … being accountable for your mistakes. I screwed up, and all this is a result. Can't you see that?"

"Why do you even bother to ask? You know exactly what's going on in my head."

"Nobody wants to die, Shug, but there are things in life more important than life itself."

"There's got to be another way! Why? Why do we have to go all kamikaze on these sons a bitches? Why? To get in the first punch in a war that's going to happen without us anyway? Why? Tell me!"

A long silence passed, and Hank's face transformed before his eyes. He felt Hank's presence melt away inside him, and tears appeared in the corners of his eyes. Hank quickly covered his face, wiping away the tears. "There *is* a reason. I haven't told you everything."

"If I'm going to die, I want to know why."

"I want to do this because … because life isn't worth living. In a way, we've already lost to the Houmn. Now we're a pitiful, tragically conflicted species. We think we're free, but the Houmn have already made slaves of us. Our thoughts— our lives—have been tainted by them. We've been slaves to an unknown master all this time. We can't go back: our humanity was stolen from us in the very beginning."

"I don't understand."

"Shug, you're a good man, with a good heart. I've never been like you. I've always felt there was something wrong. I could never be happy, and now I understand why. We *are* Houmn! They created us. They shaped us into something useful to them. Our lives are meaningless."

"What do you mean? We're not the same as the Houmn."

"We *are* the Houmn. The Sempiternals control us, just as they control the Houmn. But with one blow, we can blind the Houmn armada and free ourselves from their poisonous influence for the first time in our history. Maybe then we can grow strong enough to fight them. Maybe we can discover what true humanity should be."

"But if we die, who's gonna know any of this? Who is going to warn the world about the Houmn? The war ships will come. The Houmn will invade Earth. You'd just be some nut talking crazy on the radio. So what if Howard Stern believes you about the Houmn. The proof will die with us!" Shug could see Hank digesting his words and felt he was on the verge of talking him down. "You have the proof! Look, we've got one of their ships! You have the power to change people's minds! You can make it happen! I've seen you do it."

Hank stepped out into the middle of the blue lights, holding his chin in one hand. He crossed his arms over his chest and looked down at his feet, letting out a deflating breath of air. "You're right. The Houmn will still have its influence even if they are stranded."

"You're damn right I'm right!" Shug sprang to his feet, clasping his hands on Hank's shoulders.

"I've got to make sure people know the truth."

"We need to fly this thing back home!"

"We need to fly home."

Their eyes met, and a smile stretched across Shug's face. "Can we do it?"

"The Houmn will know we've got their ship."

"Can they stop us?"

"I don't know."

"Well if they do, I'll kick the living shit out of them, too." Shug grinned.

Hank gripped him by the wrists and pushed his hands away, taking two long steps toward the one of the alien stools. "I'll still need you to fly the ship."

Shug fell back onto the pedestal, cracking his knuckles over the invisible computer terminal. "No problem: show me the way."

"Okay, let's land this thing. The tricky part will be finding someplace safe."

"What about taking it right back to the White House?"

"No, we can't trust them—not yet. We've got to find someplace where we can keep it out of Houmn hands. Hiding it from the military will be easy. They'll never see us coming, but the Houmn will find it no matter where we hide it."

Shug found himself maneuvering the blue screen into position. His fingers danced in the air as the view shifted. The sphere of the Earth grew in front of him. Recognizable landmasses formed in the blue laser light, and his fingers worked until the eastern coast of the United States became clear.

"Good. Zoom in closer." Hank leaned forward, chewing his thumbnail.

Shug stroked the air, magnifying the map until lights could be seen in the city.

"That's Baltimore. Move over this way." Hank directed his hands, panning the view away from the city until Shug could see roads and individual buildings.

Shug could barely keep up with the commands issued by his fingertips. "What are you looking for?"

"I have an idea." Something grabbed Hank's attention, and all movement on the screen stopped. "There, that's what I'm looking for!"

Shug stared at a barren patch of earth in the middle of a pine forest. "What? What do you see?"

"Focus in on that construction site."

Shug's eyes scanned the area near a cluster of half-finished homes. "I don't get it. What am I looking for?"

"What do you see?"

"Nothing. It looks like an abandoned construction site."

"Exactly. They probably abandoned the build when all hell broke loose. What else do you see?"

"Just a bulldozer and a bunch of lumber."

"What's that, right next to the bulldozer?"

"Looks like a big hole in the ground."

"It's perfect. It's not too far from Baltimore. And look, those look like cars over there."

"Okay, I don't get it. What's your plan?"

"We can land this thing in the pit. We cover it over with soil and park that bulldozer right on top of it. The Houmn will have a bitch of a time getting her back."

"You want to bury it?"

"Have you got any better ideas?"

"To tell you the truth, I don't care as long as I get my feet on the ground."

"Okay, let's do it. I don't know how much time we have." Hank reclined on the stool, giving him a nod.

Shug's hands reached out to work both the blue and green screens at once. He didn't know how he was doing it, but he was sure he'd just plotted a course to the construction site.

"Once you've engaged the propulsion systems, you'll be on your own. I won't be able to help you."

Shug's hands froze in the air. "What do you mean? I'm not doing any of this, you are!"

"You're doing it. The computer is all yours. You know what to do, even if you don't know what you're doing. The computer will direct you through a series of lights. Just focus on those lights. All you have to do is follow the tunnel. You'll see."

Shug turned to stare at his hands doubtfully. "Just follow the lights, huh?"

Hank nodded his encouragement, folding his arms over his chest. "Make it happen, Captain."

Shug stared at the different screens and allowed his instincts to guide him. He tapped the air, transforming the blue screen into a mass of scrolling symbols. He took a huge gulp of air, holding his breath as if he were about to plunge under water, and then touched the final symbol he knew would hurl them through space.

In an instant, without the tug of gravity he had somehow expected, the ship leaped into motion. The grids of space marked out on the blue screen disappeared in a blur, and the image of Earth swelled until the outer edge disappeared completely. Shug kept his eyes riveted to a gray circle in the center of the screen. Everything else blurred into a distorted rainbow of colors. The colorless circle grew, eventually blocking everything else from view. The gray emptiness enveloped him until he could see right through it to the blank metallic wall of the ship on the other side.

The gray void vanished as quickly as it had come over him. The blue and green screens were back, and the blur of movement had stopped. Shug's heart hammered inside his chest, and he exhaled a long breath. Before he could think about he was doing, his fingers went to work, and a new screen filled his vision. It seemed as if the bottom of the ship had opened up, and he could stare right down to the brown earth below. The pit was there, cut deep into the soil. The half-finished houses grew on either side as they descended. The ship seemed to follow his eyes as he stared down into the pit.

Shug felt heavy in his seat, and a wall of brown enveloped them. The lights flickered, then stopped moving altogether. The ship pitched slightly to one side, and gravel spilled over them with a sound like hail falling across a metal roof.

Hank leaped from his seat, clapping his hands together. "We're down! You did it!"

Shug couldn't respond. He couldn't even move. His hands were frozen over the controls.

A pathetic cry from the wounded Houmn sounded through the ship, finally breaking the spell over Shug. He pulled his hands away and the screens vanished. His legs shook as he stood to follow Hank. He followed him past the dead and dismembered Houmn until Hank stopped to wave his hand over an invisible screen. The wall next to him slid open, and a rush of cool night air washed over him. The fragrant smell of pine greeted his nose.

"Shug, get out there and see if you can get that bulldozer going." Hank paused at the door, pulling the pistol from his belt.

Shug stared at him for a moment, but the real world was already pulling him outside. He ducked through the opening and bounded down the slender ramp into the dirt. As soon as his feet touched the ground, he collapsed to his knees and clutched at the soil. He broke down sobbing and let the tears roll down his nose to drip onto the dirt.

After a long moment of catching his breath and staring at the star-filled sky, the harsh, sharp crack of a gunshot pierced the silence. Shug pulled himself onto his elbows and turned to stare at the ship for the first time. Hank emerged from the opening and carefully sidestepped his way down the ramp.

He looked at Shug, then to the bulldozer and back again. "Are you okay?"

"I'll be all right." Shug rubbed at the moisture around his eyes. "I was just catching my breath. It's a lot to take in all at once."

Hank knelt down to sit beside him in the dirt. "Tell me about it."

Just then, a second gunshot shattered the tranquil silence.

Shug nearly leaped out of his skin. "What was that? I thought you killed him!"

Hank stood, brushing the dirt from his backside. "Nah. I just showed the little bastard how to use it."

Shug didn't understand what Hank was telling him at first. He looked at the ship and then back at Hank. "How did you know he wouldn't shoot you?"

"Easy. I made sure he knew there was only one more bullet in the gun."

Shug thought for a moment about what Hank had done, then readied himself to stand. "Man, that's some cold shit."

"Yeah, that's right." Hank reached down to pull him to his feet. "Fuck 'em."

Paradigm III
Chapter 16

Washington DC. June 29, 2002

Kincaid's legs hung beneath him as if shackled by irons. His chair leaned tilted against the wall. His body longed for sleep, but his brain couldn't ignore the endless suspicions eating at him.

"Mr. Kincaid? Oh, I'm dreadfully sorry. Were you sleeping?" Dr. Ramachandran stood in the doorway holding a steaming cup of tea. Her eyes were bright and lively, her hair was still somehow perfectly neat.

"No. I'm up." Kincaid rubbed the sleep from his eyes.

"Would you like a cup of tea? It might just perk you up, you know." She quietly closed the door behind her. "I believe this whole place is fueled by caffeine at this point."

"Thank you." Kincaid pushed himself off the wall with his elbows.

She passed him the tea and then inched her backside onto the desk next to him. "Did you speak to Mr. Ellis about organizing a scan for our young Houmn ambassador?"

"Yes, I did." Kincaid couldn't keep the hot tea from lapping over the sides of the cup. "He shot it down."

"He said no?" Her painted eyebrows arched high on her forehead. "How does he expect to isolate the phenomenon if we can't run the proper tests?"

"He didn't seem too concerned. There's something big going down."

"What could possibly be more important than this? Have you spoken to Mr. Kemp?"

"No chance, couldn't find him either." The tea was too hot, but it felt good to wet his lips. "Doctor ... Meenakshi, when was the last time you saw one of the Houmn from the contact team?"

"I popped in earlier this morning, but ... but why?"

"Something strange is going on. A large group of the Houmn are missing. One of their ships is gone. It left last night, but nobody can tell me where they've gone."

"Gone? Really?"

"I've got the feeling something has happened to them. There're only three Houmn team members left, and they appear very agitated."

"What do you mean? I haven't seen them act the least bit anxious."

"They've stopped communicating with us. They said they needed time to rest."

"Rest? They're not with the team?"

"No, they've gone back to one of their ships."

"What do you think has happened?"

"I don't know, but I'm going to find out."

Dr. Ramachandran chewed her lower lip for a moment, and an uneasy look appeared on her face. "Do you think it has something to do with the terrorist?"

"What terrorist?"

"The man who threatened the Houmn. The man who attacked Mr. Kemp."

"That's the thing that keeps bothering me: he's no terrorist. He was completely unknown until the Houmn arrived." Thoughts about this man and what he had said constantly nagged at him, sparking an endless progression of questions. "And now he's considered to be a notorious terrorist. Everybody including the president wants him brought in."

Dr. Ramachandran turned to check the small window in the door before returning her attention to him. "There is something I must tell you, Mr. Kincaid." She leaned forward, her hand covering his. "I know this man. I could not believe my eyes when I saw his picture, but I'm sure it is him." She spoke fast, just above a whisper. "I know him, and you are right; he is not a terrorist. He is certainly not a Christian fundamentalist."

"You know him?" Kincaid set the cup of tea aside, spilling it on the seat next to him.

"Yes, him!" Dr. Ramachandran pointed a finger across the room to a wanted poster tacked into the wall. "I don't understand it. It's terribly troubling, you know. What has he threatened to do?"

"That's what we need to find out, Doc. Whatever he said has sure gotten everyone whipped into a panic."

Dr. Ramachandran slowly rose to her feet. She stood over him with her arms folded under her breasts. The expression on her face had changed dramatically. "You called me Doc. You know, this is what he called me, that man." She looked down on him with a sort of mothering air, her eyes challenging his and her face filling with sadness. "I only met him once, only briefly: he was a very interesting man. He was very American, very consumed with himself. He reminds me very much of you." She unfolded her arms and bent low, placing her hands on his knees. "Very serious and very troubled. And do you know what else he is?" She didn't wait for him to guess. "He is an Iconoclast."

"What?"

"He came to me because of my involvement with phantom pain syndrome— he's missing a leg, you know—but I feel he really came to see me because of my status as an Icon. He wanted me to help him somehow. I believe he is the one responsible for the UFO sightings over San Francisco. He mentioned UFOs several times." Kincaid shot forward, almost pushing into her, but she quickly checked him by placing her hand on his chest and pushing him back into his seat. "He was a soldier, but I didn't feel he was a dangerous man. I don't know how he's gotten involved in any of this."

"He may be the key to this whole thing."

"The key to what? I don't understand."

"They want to shut him up. He knows something."

"What?"

"Apparently you're not the only one who knows him. William Kemp knows him, too. They were together when they were taken by the Houmn."

"Then, he has been with them ... maybe he does know something."

"Why else would everyone be so shook up?"

"Mr. Kemp and this man were friends?"

"I think so."

"And now he's trying to kill Mr. Kemp? I don't understand."

"I don't think he tried to kill Kemp. He had a chance; he had a gun. He didn't kill anybody, and he didn't make any threats against the Houmn, but they're saying he killed two policemen and threatened to blow up the White House."

"Why do they want him so badly?"

"Nobody's talking about it—and I don't like being kept in the dark." Kincaid excused himself with a nod and slowly stood from his seat. "I don't like what I'm seeing at all."

"Do you think he is dangerous?" Dr. Ramachandran stood with him, still close enough for his arms to brush against her.

"I don't know why one man has got them so scared."

"What has he been saying?"

"That the Houmn are a threat, that they are dangerous somehow."

"The Houmn?" She took a quick little breath, holding it for a moment as she peered up into his eyes. The color in her face darkened, and she stepped closer. "Do you think the Houmn are dangerous, Mr. Kincaid?"

Kincaid hadn't been sure a moment ago, but now a growing certainty ran wild in his thoughts. "It's my job to be suspicious of them. I think Ellis has been taken in by them. I can't shake the feeling that we're being manipulated."

"I feel manipulated is a very choice phrase, Mr. Kincaid. I also believe that they're not telling us everything."

Kincaid grabbed her wrist, pulling her with him. "Come on."

"Where are we going?"

"We're going to get the scan of Kemp's head if we have to drag him in kicking and screaming."

Long ago, Bill had determined that it took at least eleven minutes to smoke a Marlboro down to the butt. Pulling in one drag after another, as quickly as he could, eleven minutes was his personal best. As Bill flicked a third cigarette from its pack, he calculated that about thirty minutes had passed since he had burst into the mobile command center and found the man charged with capturing Hank.

He could tell right away that the tight-jawed man was from the CIA. He was the only one in the trailer wearing all-black fatigues, and like other CIA operatives he'd met, he had introduced himself by his first name: Marcus. Bill had asked the man to keep his presence in the command center a secret. He knew he'd aroused the man's suspicions, but it was only a matter of time before they found him anyway. When they did find him, they would find him actively hunting down the man he would claim was responsible for the sudden chaos.

Once he had arrived at the command trailer, he had quickly been informed that Hank had not been found. It almost didn't matter anymore. The guiding voice inside his head was gone, and he felt lost without it. He ran his hands through his oily, unwashed hair, and compulsively rolled his Zippo lighter over his knuckles. He could feel the eyes of the intelligence officer on him. He knew the man had been looking for an opportunity to spark up a conversation, but Bill kept his eyes on the floor.

The tough-looking CIA operative unzipped his jumpsuit and slid his chair close. "Were you in the Special Forces?"

Bill looked up to see the man smiling as he pointed to the Special Forces lighter he was fidgeting with. He could tell by the angle of the man's jaw that the smile was forced. "Yeah, I was a Ranger." Bill's mouth was dry, and his voice came out harsh.

"I'm ex-Delta myself. Where did you serve?"

Bill could picture the man working alongside Hank. They both had the same intense look about them. "I fought with Task Force Six before the army sent me to the Academy." Bill slipped the lighter back into his pocket.

"So you were in the Mog?" Marcus looked to the ceiling with his mouth hanging open for a moment. When he brought his eyes back to Bill, there was a look of understanding on his face. "That's where you met Hank. I knew you two were connected somehow, but I thought you were just friends."

Bill sucked on his cigarette and stared at him for a moment. Men like Marcus were dangerous when one was trying to hide the truth. Bill furrowed his brow, squinting his eyes. "We weren't friends, exactly." He crushed his cigarette into a tray and sat forward in his seat as if he was ready to let Marcus into his confidence. "He saved my life in Mogadishu. That's how he lost his leg. And he's managed to leverage that debt against me ever since. He's a madman."

Marcus followed his every movement with his eyes. "Do you mind if I ask you a few questions about him? They've put me in charge of running him down, but I've got the feeling I don't know what I'm getting into."

"You're right. He's a very dangerous man."

"What does he want?"

Bill paused, fumbling with another cigarette and trying to look thoughtful. "He wants … he wants us to suffer and die. He wants the end, the end of hope, the end of everything. He's consumed by some religious delusion."

"What makes him so dangerous? Why is one man getting so much attention?"

Bill lit another smoke. "Did they tell you he was taken aboard the Houmn ship with me?"

"They did."

"Well, he must have snapped. He couldn't handle it. He's convinced that the Houmn are against us somehow." Bill blew a blue cloud of smoke into the air. "He says he's discovered some secret plot against us. He wants to poison us against the Houmn."

"So what's the secret plot? What's he saying is going to happen?"

"Nothing! There's no secret plot. He's crazy!"

"Then what's the problem? How much damage can one nut cause?"

"Hank is crazy, but crazy is his business. He was Psych-Ops. He's done things in the past … I know he's planning something now."

"Sir, we've got phone activity on Bank-one." A soldier manning the terminal along the wall lifted the headphones from an ear and swiveled in his seat to face Marcus.

"Who is it?" Marcus pushed his chair along the floor and checked the computer screens.

"It's the girl, sir."

Marcus placed a set of headphones on his ears and closed his eyes.

"He's on the line with her, sir!"

A second soldier waved a hand in the air in an attempt to get his attention. "We're getting a match on the digital signal, sir. It's him!"

Bill sprang to his feet and stood behind the technician working the board.

"I don't believe it." Marcus screwed his face into a puzzled expression. "He's calling his girlfriend?"

"Bring it up! I want to hear it!" Bill tapped the young soldier's shoulder. "Who's he talking to?"

Marcus hushed him with a wave of the hand. "Go ahead, put the call on the speaker." He pulled the headphones from his ears and looked at Bill over his shoulder. "He left her with a couple of guys in Washington. We've got men waiting for him there."

The phone conversation was brought up so everyone in the trailer could hear. The soft, feminine voice sounded on the verge of tears.

"You sound strange. Where are you?"

"I'm okay."

"What's going on? Where are you?"

"Cindy, I can't talk. They're probably listening to us right now."

"Who's listening? What's happening?"

"Listen, they've got Brandon and Hoffman. They'll be able to find you, too."

"Who?"

"It doesn't matter anymore. They can't stop me now, but ... but I had to talk to you."

"What is it?"

"I don't know ... I just wanted to hear the sound of your voice. I had to tell you ... I had to tell you I didn't have a choice. Sometimes there just aren't any good choices to pick from."

"Hank, why are you talking like this?"

"There's something I've got to do. I wish everything could have gone differently ... I wish none of this had ever happened, but now I realize ... it's the only way."

"Hank, you're scaring me. Why are you talking like you're not coming back?"

"I'm *not* coming back. But I couldn't do it without talking to you first. I had to let you know you were right. Right about a lot of things. I don't want you to think I that I didn't ... didn't want you."

A dead silence hung in the air. "I want you, too." Her voice was weak with the beginning of tears. "Why aren't you coming back to me?"

"I can't. I've got to follow through with this. All of this is my fault. It has nothing to do with you. I never wanted you to think that I rejected you in any way. I just couldn't do it ... I couldn't let myself have feelings for you. I never wanted any of this, but ..."

"But it did happen! I have feelings for you, too! You can't just walk away from me."

"I'm doing this because there is no other way. You deserve to know that I wanted to be with you. I would be a coward if I didn't tell you. I wish I could have realized it before, but now it's too late."

"What are you going to do? Tell me!"

"Cindy, listen to me—this isn't easy for me. I want you to have something. I want to give you something."

"What?" She sobbed into the phone, sniffing back the tears. "I don't want anything else! I want you! Don't do whatever you're planning. Come back to me. It will be okay."

"I don't have much time. Listen, I carried a black gym bag with me. I didn't carry much else. Go get it."

"What? Now?"

"Yes, go get it. Do you know where it is?"

"Yeah, it's here, but I don't like what I'm hearing in your voice."

"Don't worry. Find the bag."

"Okay, I've got it."

"Open it."

"What am I looking for?"

"A long, cardboard tube. you'll see it."

"Okay, got it."

"I want you to know I've carried this for a long time. I wanted to show it to you, but I was afraid."

"Afraid? Afraid of what?" Her voice was cut short by an astonished little gasp.

"I want you to have it."

"It's the Virgin! Is it real?"

"It's the original."

"And you've let it sit in this dusty old cardboard tube? Oh my God … it's her, she's beautiful."

"I couldn't bring myself to give it to you before."

"Why? What were you afraid of? I love it—you know I love it."

"I know. I wanted to, but I couldn't. I didn't want to play that game with you. I didn't want to fall for you."

"What are you so afraid of?"

"I can't do it. I don't know if I can explain it, but I'm beginning to understand. I've always hated … hated everything. I didn't know anything else. I didn't know there *was* anything else. I didn't believe in it. I thought it was bullshit. I couldn't do what I'm about to do if I let myself have those feelings for you."

"Why are you talking like you're about to commit suicide?"

"My fate is sealed. I just wanted you to have the Virgin. I never told you how beautiful you are, how you made me feel. I wanted you to tell you … you were right."

"Right about what? Right about them?"

"You'll see. I'm going to show the whole world. Good-bye, Cindy. Take care of yourself. Do whatever it takes. You're a survivor; you're tough. You'll be okay."

"I won't be okay without you! I need you! Hank, don't do it. Find another way!"

"Good-bye, Cindy."

She cried over the dial tone for a long time before finally hanging up. Marcus stood from his seat. "Pick her up. I want her brought here ASAP!" He turned to the men working the computers. "Did we get a fix on him or what?"

Howard's hands shook grotesquely. He was scared out of his wits, and he hated it. Ordinarily a soundboard in a radio booth was his comfort zone, but now his guts churned and sweat crept over his forehead. He clenched his stomach muscles, suppressing the urge to vomit, and thought back thirty years, to when he had first sat behind the microphone. The feeling was nearly the same, but now those old nervous fears seemed silly. The nostalgic feel of his first DJ booth added to the surreal anxiety building in him.

He ran his hands over the antiquated soundboard with its endless rows of dials and controls, and he felt glad to finally be alone. He still felt pangs of embarrassment over his cowardly behavior in front of his security team. He'd vomited three times in the back of the Land Rover and had twice ordered them to turn around. The trip into Baltimore had been a nightmare.

The small soundproof studio hadn't changed much. Now the walls were covered in rap paraphernalia instead of post-sixties symbolism. There was only enough room for two people, and the empty seat was frightfully close. He didn't know why he'd agreed to this. His neurotic inner voice screamed for him to run back to New York, but something told him this was going to be the biggest moment of his life.

"He's here!" Gary flung the door open, sending a cartload of tapes spilling to the floor. "Shoot ... sorry, boss. He's downstairs with your bodyguards."

"What's wrong with you, Gary? I told you to bring him up right away!"

"They don't want to leave their guns downstairs. Ronnie is having a shit-fit."

"I don't care! Bring him up."

"Okay, boss, but there's two of them. Do you want them both?"

"Who's the other guy?"

"His bodyguard or something. A big black guy."

Howard's knee danced beneath the desk, and his mouth seemed to dry in an instant. "Have the bodyguard wait outside the studio, but bring Hank in."

Gary disappeared, leaving Howard to get up and clear a path through the fallen tapes. He tried to pick them up, but his body was a trembling wreck. He kicked the tapes aside, then checked the safety on his Berretta pistol before slipping it back into his pocket. He couldn't hear past the soundproof door, but he felt the vibrations of approaching feet through the floor.

Gary pushed the door open, and Howard was confronted by the face from the wanted poster. The man with the sharp, hard-looking features was smiling now, but somehow the twist of the man's mouth set his nerves on edge. He moved past Gary almost casually and offered Howard his hand.

Howard paused for a moment. "Hi, how ya doing?" He didn't know what else to say. He half expected the man to overwhelm him with mental telepathy, but Hank's smile widened as he took his hand and quickly scanned the room.

"Good, but I've got to tell ya: I never thought I'd get the chance to meet you." The man gripped his hand, and the handshake lingered—as it often did when fans got the chance to meet him in person. Howard hated shaking hands: he hated the germs, and he hated having his hand crushed by strangers. He couldn't wait to pull his hand away.

"So you're a longtime fan, huh?" Howard returned his smile and brushed the hair from his eyes as he tried to extract his hand.

"Well yeah, there's that … and the fact that everyone and their grandmother has tried to stop me from getting here." A mischievous gleam lit Hank's eye and, he finally released his hand.

Howard flushed with embarrassment and suddenly found himself at a loss for words. "Well, I'm glad you made it. I think we can pull this thing off." He wiped the sweat from his hands and motioned toward the soundboard behind him.

"Good. Let's get started. I figure we've only got about twenty minutes before they pin us down." Hank assumed a businesslike tone and checked his watch.

"Really? That's it?" Howard had been counting on a lot more than twenty minutes of airtime. "None of my people know where we are. Are you sure we've only got twenty minutes?"

"Yeah, that should be plenty of time."

"I made sure nobody followed us. I set up two separate diversions."

"Good. This place is perfect, but before we get started, I want to check out the roof."

"Oh yeah, the roof." Howard had already checked the roof; everything was in place. "Go ahead, I was up there earlier. It's all there."

"Great. Get everything ready. I'll take my man up there and be back in a minute." Hank motioned for him to take his seat behind the microphone and turned to leave with an authoritative nod.

The door closed behind him, and Howard collapsed into his seat. He stared at the board but there was nothing left to do. The seconds passing in silence did nothing to calm his nerves, so he decided to feed the signal from his own radio show into the booth. They were broadcasting a rerun of his show, and almost at once he caught himself laughing at his own material.

The door opened, and Howard switched off the sounds of his past life. Hank stepped into the room, followed by Gary. The smile on Hank's face was gone, but he looked pleased with what he'd found. Ronnie, Howard's personal driver and bodyguard, appeared behind the soundproof window and tapped his pistol on the glass. He was doing his best to look calm, confident, and tough, but he seemed to shrink into his coat when an enormous black shadow passed behind him. Howard only caught a quick glimpse of the man before he passed the window; his arms were swollen with muscle, and he towered over Ronnie.

"Okay, let's do this." Hank took his seat while Gary hovered over his shoulder.

"I'm all set up." Howard stared at the controls as if seeing them for the first time. "How do you want this to go?" He handed Hank a pair of headphones. "Are you gonna use your mental telepathy on me now?"

"Nah, I just need you to do what you do best. I've got the answers: you ask the questions."

"Can you tell me why we had to do this in person? Wouldn't it have been a lot safer to do it over the phone?"

"I need to know that you understand. I want to see it." Hank placed the headphones over his ears and pointed toward his eyes with two fingers. "They can silence me—but after today, they won't be able to silence you."

"But you're gonna show me how you use your super powers, right? You're gonna do it—aren't you?"

The flash of a smile tweaked the man's face at the mention of super powers, but it quickly disappeared under tightening jaw muscles. His eyes bore into Howard's. There was a kind of lunatic intensity in them. Slowly, without any change in his expression, he raised his hands, almost feeling the air in front of him as he reached out toward Howard's face. Howard cringed, pulling away. He was sure the man was about to overpower him with his eyes.

"How do you know I'm not doing it right now?" Hank's eyebrows rose on his forehead, and he began tickling the air with his fingers.

"Are you?" Howard's eyes were shut tight.

"Nah, I'm only kidding."

Howard opened his eyes, and the man's hands were at his sides. He was smiling, a genuine smile. He was obviously pleased with himself, which made Howard feel even more foolish, but the moment had served to cut the tension between them. "Ah, you had me there for a second. This whole thing has got me freaked out. I don't know what I'm doing." Howard pulled back his hair and laughed nervously. "I don't know why I ever agreed to this. It's not like me. I'm going to get in a lot of trouble over this."

"Howard, if you pull this off, you'll be a hero."

"Good. Make sure you say that when we're on the air." Howard readied the microphone in front of his face and felt his confidence grow. "So let me ask you: do you think they'll try to kill you?" He tried to keep his eyes fixed on Hank's, but they dropped to the gun at his side.

"Not yet. They want me alive." Hank adjusted the headphones and followed his eyes to the weapon at his side. "And that won't be a walk in the park."

Marcus could hear Kemp shouting at Taylor from across the command trailer. He was sure Kemp had finally snapped. Marcus had never seen anybody foolish enough to get in Paul Taylor's face. The thick-fisted CIA chief looked ready to knock Kemp on his ass.

"I don't care *how* he did it! I'm telling you, he *did* do it!" Kemp clutched the hair on his temples and screamed himself hoarse. "I've had confirmation from the Houmn!"

"And I want to know how! *How* do they know? *How* did he get to their ship? *How* did he destroy it?" Marcus could hear Taylor's voice rising to a dangerous level. He'd never seen Taylor so hot before. "What in hell were the Houmn doing?"

"Catch him! Bring him in! That's your job!" Kemp was standing well within range, and Marcus stole a long sideways glance, hoping to see him get flattened by Taylor.

"Marcus." The crisp bark of his immediate superior brought his attention back to the business at hand. Davis stood at his side and waved away the other men hovering around. "I want to stress the importance of secrecy here, Marcus. Nobody is allowed to leave the quarantine area." Davis reached out and plucked the identification badge from his chest.

"Yes sir." Marcus locked eyes with him. These were the moments he lived for. The gloves were off, and they wanted him because he was the best.

"How many men are you taking with you?"

"Two teams of six. I'll utilize the local recourses once we've got a fix on him."

"We're pretty certain he's going through with it. Howard Stern hasn't come on the air this morning." Davis lowered his voice and gripped Marcus by the shoulders. "Don't underestimate this guy. He's already demonstrated the ability to outwit the security here, and now ... now they're telling me he may have taken out one of the flying saucers."

Kemp screamed across the trailer. "Nine of the Houmn ambassadors are dead!" His cheeks were red as he pushed past the men crammed into the narrow space. "How much confirmation do you need?" Kemp's eyes were bloodshot as he stared back at Marcus. "I know this man: don't give him a chance! We're counting on you to bring him back alive. They're sending more ambassadors ... but ... but we're counting on you! We can't let him jeopardize our relationship with the Houmn!"

Paul Taylor shoved Kemp aside. "What's the word, Davis? Anything?" Marcus could see that Taylor was fighting to stay cool.

"No sir, nothing yet. If he comes on the air, we can find him. If we can find him, we'll catch him."

Kemp elbowed his way between the two CIA chiefs. His eyes bore down on Marcus. "You have to bring him back: our future with the Houmn depends on it!"

"I understand." Marcus dismissed Kemp with a cool nod and kept his eyes on Paul Taylor. The two CIA heads exchanged looks—they didn't know what to do with Kemp. He'd been quiet for nearly an hour, sitting at the back of the trailer, but then he had seemed to explode with madness. He had begun talking to himself, then screaming.

"I've got to leave, but I want to be informed the instant he's captured." Kemp slid a cigarette into his mouth as he straightened his shirt and tried to compose himself. "The Houmn wish to interrogate him as soon as possible."

Taylor looked ready to smash him, but one of the men at the communications center called out from his seat. "Sir!" All four men turned at once to face the young soldier. "Sir, Mr. Marcus, sir; the Howard Stern feed just went dead. We think he may be preparing to cut in live, sir." The soldier pushed away from the terminal and offered Marcus a set of headphones.

Marcus rushed to his side. "Good, put the feed on the speaker." He declined the headset and began directing the room with his finger. "Sanders, identify the remote signal as soon as possible. Gomez, ready the action teams." He leaned over the soldier's chair and ran his eyes over the computer terminal. "Let's see if he's really going through with this."

"We're getting a signal."

Howard Stern's voice filled the trailer with the flip of a switch, and all talk stopped inside the command center.

"Hello everybody. I'm sure you've all realized that we were playing reruns today, and I bet you're wondering what's going on. Well, this is Howard Stern, and I'm speaking to you live.

I can't tell you where I'm broadcasting from, but I can tell you that I've left my building in the city.

Under normal circumstances I would be joined by Robin, Fred, and the whole crew, but—as we all know—nothing is normal anymore. Today it's just me and Gary. No sound effects, no phone calls. Just an interview with one man."

Marcus's eyes caught on Kemp as he tried to leave. The door was half open; Kemp paused with a cigarette quaking on his lips. A pained expression came over his face. He slouched his shoulders and clutched at his temples but didn't step out the door.

"Most of you know already … the story is already all over the news, but for those of you who weren't listening yesterday or hadn't heard, let me fill you in. This guy calls me up on the air and starts talking about being abducted by aliens, just like a thousand other crackpots. He tells me that the Houmn abducted him and another guy, William Kemp. He's the congressman dude always in the background with the president. And while he's telling me all of this, Gary butts in to tell me this guy on the phone is tops on the most wanted list.

At first I thought Babba Booey was being had: he's not all that bright. But then, after talking to the dude on the phone, I start thinking this guy might be legit. But he was saying some pretty weird stuff, so I was treating him as a goof. Then—bam!—the guy proceeds to read my mind over the phone! I'm not talking about some trick; he told me exactly what was going on inside my head. Not to mention he told everybody listening my pin number and the combination to my gym locker!"

"I want that transmission blocked as soon as possible!" Kemp nervously checked his watch, pulling at his hair at the same time. "I've got to go!" He ducked out the door, slamming it closed behind him.

"I'm telling you, this guy is the real deal. His name is Hank Foster, and I'm sure many of you know him from his wanted poster. The authorities—the cops, the military—everybody is trying to find this guy. And that's why we're meeting in a secret location. I literally had to sneak out of my building last night."

"Sir, we're isolating the signal."
"Good. Carson, get the birds warmed up." Marcus marked the time on his watch.
"Yes sir."

"And I don't mind saying, it's a little uncomfortable in here.
It's just the three of us in a tiny little room. Everybody else is outside, and everybody is armed to the teeth! Am I right? I mean, I know I'm packing—but you're packing too, aren't you, Hank? You're a pretty scary-looking dude."

"Don't let it bother you, Howard. I'm a big fan."

Hank's voice sent a buzz throughout the trailer. Marcus was sure it was him.

"I've got to tell you; I didn't know what to expect this morning. I still don't really know why I agreed to all this. I guess I kinda believed you. I don't really know what you're talking about … I've played the tapes over and over, but I still can't figure it out.

You look legitimate: you don't look crazy or anything. And you should see the size of this guy's bodyguard! A big black guy … you can always tell a guy is legit when he's got a really big, black bodyguard."

"Sir, we've isolated the signal, and we're triangulating the coordinates."
"Get me a list of all the transmission towers in the area capable of that signal."
"Yes sir."

The voice of Howard's producer filled the brief silence. "I've never seen so many guns. I still can't believe you're doing this."

"Well, let me tell you, Gary; leaving my building for the first time was an experience. I don't blame anyone for carrying guns. It's crazy out there."

"It's total anarchy," Gary agreed.

"I couldn't help noticing you're missing a leg." Howard turned his attention back to Hank. "Everybody is looking for a guy with only one leg—you can't fake that."

A faint knocking sound could be heard in the background before Hank spoke. "Yeah."

"I've seen your ID. You're the guy!"

"Unfortunately."

"How'd ya lose your leg?"

"Had it shot off in Somalia."

"You were in the army?"

"Special Forces. Delta Squadron."

"Those guys are the real bad-asses, Howard." Gary hastily filled in the gaps left by Hank's crisp responses. "They're kinda like Navy SEALs."

"You were like, one of those Black Ops guys?" Howard continued.

"Yep."

"I gotta tell ya … you don't talk much for a guy who was so desperate to get ahold of me."

"Well, I guess I'm a little nervous. I've had a crazy week. Go on, you'll get it out of me. Do your thing."

"I could go to jail for this." Howard laughed nervously.

"You should thank me, Howard, I'm handing you the biggest scoop in history."

"That's right, everybody …" Howard lowered his voice, mimicking a deep-throated announcer. "This is a Howard Stern exclusive!"

"You're going to be famous for more than talking dirty." Hank's tone remained serious. "You're going to break the story that's going to change everything we know. They may even credit you for saving us."

"What are you talking about, exactly? Save us from who? The Houmn or the bugs? Because it looks to me like we need to be saved from the giant bugs invading our planet."

"I'm not saying the Takk aren't a serious threat. I've seen what they can do, but the Houmn aren't our saviors, either. They're helping us for their own purposes. Don't be fooled into thinking it's out of friendship or kindness. They need us to fight the Takk."

"Good, all right, let's get into it. How do you know all this? Why did we have to meet in person for you to tell me this?"

"I need you to believe what I'm telling you. I need to hand this off to someone like you. I couldn't blow my one chance over the phone."

"Okay, I gotta know: how did you get into my head like that?"

"I wasn't inside your head. I only told you what you wanted to hear. Those answers were just there, floating around because you were conscious of them somehow. Getting inside your head is another matter." Hank sounded troubled as his voice trailed off.

"But how? How are you able to do it?"

"Like Bill, I was abducted by the Houmn five days ago. They did something to me."

"What did they do?"

"I don't know what exactly, but they did something to my brain. They needed to communicate with me, so they put something inside me … but I don't think it had the desired effect."

"And this guy Kemp, can he do this too?"

"No."

"How do you know? I mean, this guy Kemp is in direct contact with the president of the United States. What if he can do to him what you've done to me?"

"I know Bill doesn't have my ... abilities—my super powers, as you called them. I spoke with him a couple of days ago. They have complete control over him."

"Sir, we've tracked the signal to a Baltimore radio station. There's a tower there capable of transmitting on this frequency."

"Send the teams to the choppers. Find me a portable FM radio. I want to hear this."

"Yes sir."

"Is that when you broke into the White House? They're saying you tried to kill the aliens."

"I didn't break into the White House ... just onto White House grounds. I wanted to talk with Billy."

"Let's talk about that for a second. They're saying you're some kinda religious zealot, but I haven't heard you mention anything about Jesus. They say you killed two cops and tried to kill another person. What do you say about that?"

"Have you noticed they haven't named the two cops? That's because I didn't kill anybody. I did incapacitate them, and I used their uniforms to get past security, but I didn't kill them. The other person they mentioned was Billy, but they won't tell you that. They're right about one thing though: I do want to kill the Houmn. But the *last* thing I am is a Jesus freak."

"So you *have* made threats against the Houmn?"

"Well yeah. I'll make them right now: they need to be stopped. I know that ... and that's why everyone's trying to shut me up. But they can't stop me now. It's too late. I'm here, and soon everyone will know the truth."

"How did you learn the truth? And why doesn't this guy Kemp have the same powers you do? It sounds crazy to say the Houmn are our enemies when people all over the world are being torn apart by giant cockroaches. The Houmn have already proven they can help us."

"To understand what's happened to me, you'll have to see that there are more than one kind of Houmn. The tall, slender ones are the leaders. They call themselves Sempiternals. The Sempiternals took Bill. They control his every move. They're the ones pulling the strings."

Marcus was greeted by questioning looks from his men as he accepted the portable radio and pointed the way to the choppers. "You have your orders, gentlemen. I'll remind you that this guy was a psychological operator. This kind of propaganda is his bag. Don't be fooled." Marcus turned to address the men in the command trailer while he slipped the radio earpiece into place. "Advise the local police to form a perimeter and prepare to cut the power on my orders."

"Sempiternals? But why haven't we heard of any of this before?" Howard sounded as if talk of the aliens hadn't dominated the airwaves.

"You've seen them, Howard." Gary broke into the conversation. "You know, the taller, creepy-looking ones."

"The naked ones?"

"They're the Master Race." Hank continued. "They're the brains behind the Houmn. I was taken by the crew, the littler ones, while the Sempiternals took Billy."

"And they, the smaller ones, did something to your brain which enables you to read people's thoughts?"

"They can't talk. They've got mouths, but no voice box. Think of it like this: we humans, as a species, have developed language to communicate our thoughts. The Houmn have evolved to communicate differently. In a sense, they're telepathic. Our language is inherently vague: words can mean different things, and people don't always say what they think. Their form of communication is much more precise, but it's probably not what you're imagining either. Only the Sempiternals can communicate both ways. They call the shots. The others are slaves. The Houmn couldn't communicate with humans without the Sempiternals, but they found a way with me. I don't know if they'd tried it before … I don't think they expected this."

"So there are two kinds of aliens." Howard oversimplified as if he understood, pressing him to move on.

"While the Sempiternals were busy with Bill, the Houmn—the little ones— used some kind of experimental technology to implant something in my head."

"But I'm not telepathic!" Howard interrupted him excitedly. "How did you read my thoughts? They didn't do anything to my brain."

"I'm still coming to understand that—and who's to say we're not all telepathic to some degree? We've just evolved to communicate differently."

"Sir, we're looking at a seven-minute flight to Baltimore. The local cops are on their way to the station."

"Good, tell them not to move until we get there. Let me know as soon as they're ready to cut the power." The helicopter banked hard as it pulled away from the pad. The radio earpiece crackled with static, and Marcus feared he would lose the signal. He felt a growing respect for Hank's ability as a master pro-pagandist and couldn't wait to hear where he was going with his line of bullshit. The next few words were garbled and difficult to make out. Marcus strained his ears to hear the conversation over the helicopter's engine.

"So, what is it? What's this all about? What don't the Sempi ... whatevers want you to tell us?"

"The Houmn have given me a warning. They are coming to enslave us."

"The Houmn have given you a message ... to warn us that they are coming to enslave us?" Howard sounded lost.

"The Sempiternals will enslave us just as they enslaved the Houmn. A rebel-lion has grown within the Houmn—they're the ones who did this to me."

"So the Sempiternals are the real enemy."

"They're all Houmn; the Sempiternals are just the eldest. Their race is so ancient that their origins have been forgotten. They call themselves Sempiternal because they're supposed to be immortal. The lesser Houmn serve to sustain them."

"Immortal?"

"Not really. They can be killed; I know that for a fact ... but there's no finite timeline dictating how long they live. They've mastered their genetic code."

"So they can live forever?"

"Probably not—forever is a long time. But, in effect, they're ageless."

"But why would they want to enslave us?" Gary broke into the conversation once more.

"In a way, we're already slaves to the Houmn." Hank's voice was somber and serious.

"What?" Howard sounded confused and skeptical. "We've only known about the Houmn for a week! How can we already be slaves to them?"

"Again, this is where verbal communication lacks clarity. We have a precon-ception of the word slavery, but it can mean much more. The Sempiternals never enslaved the Houmn. They created them." Static crackled in the background as a long pause grew. "Howard, this is the message I want to give to you: we were *cre-ated* by the Houmn. We've been under their control from the beginning."

"Human beings?"

"The Sempiternals created the Houmn just as they have always created and recreated themselves. And, long ago, they came to Earth and altered the genetic code of early man. They've shaped our evolution ever since. We were formed to serve their purposes. In recent times, they've worked to mold us into productive civilizations—giving us the idea of a higher power and implanting other concepts that made us good slaves. In the past, they were the ones to put tools in our hands and dreams of flying in our minds. They made us what we are today, and now they're coming to claim us."

"Are you saying the Houmn literally created us from apes?"

"From early man, yes. The Houmn are our missing link. They're the reason for our rapid jump up the evolutionary chart. They tampered with our genetic code along the way. They've even come down to Earth to express their desires for mankind."

"The aliens?"

"Yes, the Houmn. But we've called them by other names. Names more to their liking, like 'angels' or 'gods.' They're the men from above who speak and move in mysterious ways."

"You're saying the aliens are God?" Howard's voice was barley audible in the background. Marcus focused everything he had on the crackling voices in his ear.

"Let me ask you, what's more believable: that there really is some all-powerful entity, supremely intelligent—in fact, all-knowing—who created the universe from nothing and has mankind's interests in mind, or that the Houmn have cultivated life on Earth for their own benefit?"

"But what benefit? I don't understand what you're saying. I mean, I do in a way … but. I don't believe what I'm hearing! How can they have created us?"

"Howard, I can show you proof of what I'm saying, but I have to show you the way it was shown to me. I can prove to you that we are Houmn. Now that the Takk have arrived, the Houmn are coming to collect their children."

"Are you going to get inside my head now? Because I don't know if I'm ready."

"Once you see for yourself, there won't be any doubt. I need you to scream about this until everyone on the planet has heard you. You have to warn everyone about the Houmn."

"What are you going to do to me? Is it going to hurt?"

"I'm going to show you the library they shoved into my head. You're going to see proof of what I've said. You're going to see that the Houmn have used men like Moses, Abraham, and Muhammad to spread the laws that would eventually bind us into useful civilizations. You'll see how our slavery has already begun. All cultures around the world have legends of mighty beings who came down to Earth to teach mankind. The Sumerians, the Egyptians, the Mayans—they all tell stories about contact with the Houmn. They all share the belief in a higher power … a mystical ultimate authority. This belief has been reinforced and institutionalized in order to control us. I can show you these events from their perspective. I can show you what they've shown me."

The helicopter tore through the air at top speed, and Marcus could barely hear the radio. He was desperate to hear Hank's next words. Hank had woven a masterpiece of propaganda, and Marcus was waiting to hear the hook, the piece of the puzzle that would show what he was really after. He understood now why Kemp was so desperate to silence him. Static filled his ear, and the signal cut out. "Why haven't I heard back from our men on the ground? What's our ETA?"

"We arrive in under a minute, sir."

"I've just got word from the Baltimore PD: they've established a perimeter around the station."

"Good. Have them prepare to cut the power and take out the generator. Tell them not to make a move before I get there. Have both action teams switch to my tactical channel." The FM radio buzzed in his ear, and he could hear Gary's voice in the background. There was a commotion; Gary was shouting.

"Boss … Howard, can you hear me?—is he going to be okay? What did you do to him?"

"He's okay." Hank's voice was clear over the microphone while Gary shouted in the distance.

"Why isn't he talking?" Something was knocked over in the background. Gary's voice was on the verge of panic. "Oh man, he doesn't look right!"—more crashing noises—"Howard?"

"Ahhhh. Oh my God!" Howard's voice was shrill. He began screaming, well away from the microphone. "It's true! Gary, I saw them! I saw them in their ships!'

"Are you okay?"

"No I'm not fucking okay! I'm telling you: he's telling the truth!" More clattering noise filled Marcus's ear as Howard scrambled to pull the microphone to his mouth. "The aliens are coming to get us!"

Hank spoke into the brief silence; his voice was calm compared to Howard's. "The Houmn have launched a massive invasion armada to reclaim Earth. They will arrive in 103 years."

"Sir, we've got the target on the horizon."

"Have we got a landing zone yet?"

"No sir, not yet."

"Put us down in the middle of the street if you have to."
"Yes sir."

"How can we fight them off?" Howard was breathless. "What can we do?"
"We have an edge. We're still primitive in the eyes of the Houmn. They think we're savage and combative. Well, they're right. We can fight off the Takk, and we can fight off the Houmn."

"We've got a visual on the target building."
"Good, take us in."

"Howard, you've got to prepare the world for a war our grandchildren's children will have to fight."
"I'll do it! I'll shout about it day and night. They won't shut me up! I've seen it!"
"Howard! Howard!" A new voice broke into the studio. "The guys downstairs say the cops are outside!"

Marcus's face flushed with anger, and his heart sank. "Dammit! Tell them to wait for me! Don't let them go in without me!"
The copter dove, dipping to one side, and pushing a cloud of dust between the buildings on either side. Marcus could see that the streets were lined with black-and-white patrol cars. Their lights were flashing, and there was already a crowd growing on the corners. The buildings were packed tight into massive blocks; laundry hung on lines connecting the rooftops.
Marcus strained his ears for any hint of Hank's presence. He doubted he could slip away now that the place was surrounded, but he longed to know he was still there, still safely locked away in the studio. The last thing he need was for Hank to get shot by some pumped-up Baltimore cop.

"They'll never take me alive, Howard." For an instant Marcus was relieved to hear Hank's voice, but his tone shot shivers down his spine.
"Howard! Howard! The guys say there are helicopters coming."
"Why aren't you on the phone, dummy? We don't have a lot of time here," Howard shouted at Gary. "Call the goddamn *National Enquirer* if you have to: they're good at reporting this sort of thing."

The skids of the helicopter hit ground, and Marcus was first on the street. He pulled the FM radio from his ear, dropping it to the ground, and pulled his pistol from its holster. A rush of uniformed policemen chased him down as he approached the entrance. They shouted at him, but he couldn't hear above the spinning rotor blades. He motioned to his men and readied himself by the front doors.

As his men fell in behind him, Marcus pulled the radio to his mouth. "Cut the power to the station. Knock out the generator."

Marcus checked his weapon. "Gordon, force open these doors. Parker, follow him up with a couple of flash-bang grenades. Go!"

Marcus blew out a last tense breath as the door was pried off its hinges and the grenades were lobbed into the darkness. Two bright flashes of light were followed by two pops that shook his bones. His team of men filed into the opening behind their shotguns and automatic weapons.

The team quickly cleared the first floor, each member shouting the all-clear in turn. He met his men waiting at the bottom of the stairs. "Okay guys, this is it. Remember we need to take him alive. Watch your fire angles."

He pushed the door open and stepped into the stairwell. "Flash-bang, up there." He stepped back, allowing another grenade to be thrown up to the next floor.

The concussion whipped past his ears, and he led the charge up the stairs, covering each step with his weapon. He found two clearly shocked men cowering in the corner with their hands in the air. Neither of them had any weapons.

Two of his men pounced on them, jerking their hands behind their back and securing them with plastic cords. Marcus covered the stairwell as his men searched the floor.

"All clear."

Marcus kneeled down, putting his knee into the back of one of the men on the floor. "Where are they?"

"Upstairs. The studio is upstairs. Don't shoot anybody. My boss is up there."

Marcus waved his team on and dashed up the stairs, skipping rows at a time. He reached the fifth floor and found the sign for the radio station. He waited for a moment for his men to catch up, then thrust his foot through the door. He covered every angle with his weapon as his men rushed in behind him. Nothing—no one tried to stop them. For a moment Marcus thought they had been fooled, that the Baltimore station was some kind of clever diversion, but then his eyes caught on a figure behind a glass window across the room. The tall, slender figure was unmistakably Howard Stern.

Marcus covered him through the window and rushed to the door. The door was locked but fell away easily under his boot. He stepped into the studio, covering every angle with his weapon, before once again aiming it at Howard's face. "Where is he?"

Howard dropped the microphone and raised his hands to the ceiling. Suddenly, Hank's voice filled the studio. *"We must fight them. We can't end up like the Houmn."*

Marcus scanned the small room, and his eyes caught on some lights. The red lights jumped with the sound of Hank's voice; it was only a recording.

"I said *where is he*? I'll put a round through your knee right now if you don't tell me!"

"He's gone." Howard's voice grew to a shout. "You have no right to stop him!"

"When? Tell me!" Marcus aimed his pistol at Howard's trembling knee. "I'll do it! Tell me when he left!"

"Sir, the rest of the fifth floor is clear." Sanders burst into the room behind him. "There's no sign of him, but it looks like you can walk from rooftop to rooftop up there. We can see planks on some of the buildings."

"Dammit!" Marcus felt as thought he'd been kicked in the guts. "Okay, Sanders. Step out of the room for a minute, will ya. I don't want you to have to see this." Marcus cocked the hammer against Howard's kneecap. "Last chance, loudmouth. When did he leave?"

"When the helicopters came! I swear."

Marcus slammed his weapon into its holster and turned to the men gathered outside the studio. "Officer! You—yes, you!—get on the radio. I want this whole block isolated. I want a house-to-house search of all these buildings. We can't let him get away this easy."

Omar had been taught that angels would beat him in the face as they pulled his soul into hell. His teachers had insisted on it, but Omar sometimes wondered if his soul really had a face—and even if it did, why should a beating be such a terror when facing the infinite pain of hell? The question had confounded him as a child, but now he understood; the soul must keep its bodily form in order for pain to exist. The angels savaged the face of the victim to make him cry out and beg. Helpless against them, they would have you admit your sins; you could no longer claim ignorance of them. The angels were there to add shame to suffering. Omar could feel them coming for him. The shame was growing inside him, tearing at his soul.

His failure was complete: even the al-Qaeda men had forsaken him. Not only did they refuse to help him, they ridiculed him. They too had abandoned their faith and were now living like animals. They hoarded their weapons so they could prey on the people they lived amongst. All of them thought he was mad; none of them listened. They talked as if Allah no longer watched them. They threw him out and mocked him as if he were a drunkard.

Omar stood on the sidewalk a few paces from their door. The weight of the two pipe bombs in his coat pockets pulled his thoughts to sudden death. His hands reached into his pockets to feel to cool iron pipe. He doubted if the hastily made bombs would explode at all. He'd begged them for a gun, but they had assembled the crude pipe bombs for him instead. They had laughed at him, calling him a fool. They'd said: "Here are two—one for the infidel, and one for you." They had kicked him out knowing he would never find the man he was after. Standing outside, his hands gripping the bombs, Omar knew it too.

Without caring who saw him, Omar threw his head back and flung his arms to the sky. "I see with new eyes: there is no God but Allah, and Muhammad was his Prophet! I have been a fool!" He wailed in his native Pashto, and his cries echoed off the ghetto walls all around him. "Am I to be defiled forever? I am your servant. I see that I have failed you! Please show me how to find grace in your eyes!" His eyes were wet as he beat his fists into his face. "Allah is Great! I will do anything!" His shouts aroused the neighbors, who called on him to be quiet, but Omar ignored them. "Anything! Show me what I must do!"

Suddenly, the thump of helicopter blades gripped him and the wail of police sirens pierced the air in the distance. The whirring chop of the helicopter quickly passed overhead, but the roar of its engine lingered behind, as if the machine was right on top of him. Omar's pulse screamed in his ears, but he couldn't move.

His feet seemed planted in the concrete. He feared that the police were watching the al-Qaeda men and had seen him go inside. They would know about the bombs, and they would kill him, but still he couldn't move. There was nowhere to run.

Police cars rounded the corner down the block, and the people who were loitering outside their doors disappeared. The cars were headed right toward him. Red and blue lights flashed, and the sirens grew deafening. More police cars fell in line behind them, and Omar could no longer catch his breath. He finally tore his feet from the concrete and backed into the shadows against the wall.

The first two cars passed him without slowing. The drivers didn't even look at him as they passed. The blaring sirens faded, and the noise from the helicopter now seemed far away. Omar crouched deeper into the shadows as the other police cars sped up the street. Children began to poke their heads out their windows to watch them leave, and once again people down the block gathered on their doorsteps.

Omar's heart jackhammered inside his chest as he watched the street return to life. From the corner of his eye, he saw a man who appeared out of place. He was black, like most people in this neighborhood, but he too was crouching in the shadows and anxiously waiting for the police to pass. Omar considered the neighborhood and didn't find it unusual, but something about the man held his attention. He was a large man, and there was something familiar in the way he moved.

As the last of the sirens disappeared, the man tiptoed to an alley between buildings and checked the streets on all sides. He waved a hand excitedly, and another black man stepped out onto the street. Omar's eyes narrowed on the second, smaller man. They began to walk down the street away from him. They were walking fast, and one of the men—the smaller man—was limping.

A sudden sensation that could only be described as divine relief crashed down on Omar. His prayers had been answered! All despair and doubt was obliterated in an instant! Allah had handed him the Jinn and the means to destroy him. The evil demon had once again disguised itself, this time with black paint on its skin and the dark bushy wig of a black man, but Omar saw through the color on the man's face. It was him. By Allah's will, it was him.

Omar darted out from the shadow of the stairs and followed the men down the street. His hands fumbled for the bombs in his coat. He tried to remember what the men had told him: the fuse would give him twenty seconds. There would be no way to snuff it out. They had promised him that the small pipe would deliver a powerful explosion. He had watched them make the bombs with his own eyes. The angels would no longer beat him in the face; he would reside in the glory of Allah forever.

The large black man was unlocking the driver's door of a car while the demon waited on the other side, closer to Omar. Gaining speed, Omar pulled the plastic plug, mixing the chemical timer, and clutched the pipe bomb to his chest with both hands. He counted off time in his head: "20, 19, 18 ..." the last seconds of his mortal life.

"Allah is Great. Praise be to Allah, Most Gracious, Most Merciful!" He sprinted as best he could without using his arms. He feared his prayers or his footsteps would give him away, but it didn't matter: he was only meters away, and the bomb was surely deadly at this range. The large black man opened his door and was leaning across the seat to unlock the other door. Neither man noticed him. "15, 14 ..."

The car door was pushed open, and Omar's target turned his body to slip inside. His eyes caught on Omar as he charged in. There was a startled, confused look on his face, but there was no time to react. Omar slammed into him with all his strength. He'd hoped to knock him off his feet, but only succeeded in jamming him into the doorframe.

Omar clenched the pipe bomb in his fists and pushed with all the power in his legs. He pinned the demon against car, but he was much stronger than he'd imagined. His fists rained down on the back of his neck, but Omar kept the bomb between their chests.

The demon spun him in his arms, turning him into the door. A fist smashed into his face with a horrible crunch of bone, blinding him with pain. The demon cried out to his friend, but not for help. "Bomb! Get out of here, Shug!" Again, an iron fist smashed his face, and he felt his body begin to slacken beneath him. He felt a hand groping for the pipe in his hands, but he held firm. "10, 9 ..."

Omar fought with all his energy, thrashing from side to side, keeping his body pressed into the demon and his face angled away from the blows. The man pushed him back, then whipped him close again, butting his head into Omar's face. Blood drained from his nose, but he couldn't see it. White sparks floated in his vision, and he felt faint. The demon tried to jerk the bomb free of his hands, and Omar rallied his strength, sinking his weight over the pipe. Pain shot through one hand. His finger had been snapped, but Omar refused to let go. He gripped the pipe with all his strength, leaving only the end-caps exposed. There was nowhere for the demon to grab it.

Suddenly the demon's hands changed strategy. Both now clamped onto one end of the pipe. Omar tried to rip the pipe away, but he found that his arms would no longer move. They seemed completely robbed of strength; they refused to pull away. The larger man pinned him against the open door as his hands went to work trying to unscrew the end cap. Once again Omar tried to pull away, but his body moved on its own. His hands remained clamped onto the pipe like a vice while the demon's hands leveraged against him. Omar watched himself, helpless to act. "5, 4 …"

The man's grip shifted, one hand reaching out to grab him by the waist. Omar could feel himself still clutching the bomb, but his body had lost the will to move. The metallic clank of iron against pavement rang in his ears, and his eyes followed the metal cap falling to the ground. The man's other hand grabbed him by the hair, spinning him around and pulling his head back painfully, and then a tremendous blast of heat exploded in his face, blinding him with orange fire. Pain tore through his hands, and a crushing blunt force smashed his lower leg, knocking him to the ground.

Indescribable pain told him that he wasn't dead. He felt as if he were on fire. Blurred images moved in front of him, and the heat was everywhere. Suddenly his worst fears came to crush him; he was already dead, and the angles had come to bash his face. They beat him on the face and chest. They had come to drag his soul to hell. He could already smell the burnt flesh. He could already hear the screams of the damned.

As the angels beat him, the orange glow left his eyes and the terrible heat gave way. There was only pain. Omar reached out to plead with the angels. The flesh on his hands was black and horribly mutilated. Fingers were missing. The angel's face grew clearer. It was not the face he had expected. It was the face of a man. It was Ali Ali-Akkba, the demon. He was still beating him around the face, but the blows did not hurt. He appeared to be smacking at the fire burning around him.

Omar screamed out. He was answered by a voice inside his head. The voice was clear, but there were no words to hear. The voice spoke directly to his soul, and for the first time Omar knew the God Muhammad spoke of.

Paradigm III
Chapter 17

Cindy sat cross-legged on the floor of her cell. Her hands still throbbed from pounding on the door. She couldn't yell anymore. She kept her mind from spinning out of control by watching the heads bob past the small, rectangular window in her door. She told herself that sooner or later one of those heads would stop, open the door, and tell her what was going on, but her eyes eventually tired of the game and drooped heavily.

Her cell faced the office, where dozens of police and military men were working. Occasionally one of them would push his face against her window to gawk at her. She soon found herself hating the smug look on their faces. None of them ever bothered to tell her why she'd been arrested. No one ever told her why she had been flown to DC. They kept her in a cage like an animal, expecting thanks when they brought her a peanut butter sandwich. She found herself wishing she wasn't so small and weak; she wished she were a man so she could deck the first person to come through the door.

Her back ached from sitting on the floor. She was about to give in and lie down when another head bobbed outside her window. When it didn't pass by or stealthily approach to peer through the glass, she sat up straight. She stared at the brown crew cut, somehow annoyed by the fact that it was blocking her view of the ceiling outside her cell. She didn't give a thought to the door actually opening until she heard the slap of a bolt being pushed back as the door handle moved.

"Finally!" Her pulse quickened as she unfolded her legs to pushed herself off the floor.

The man with the crew cut spoke as soon as he stepped through the door. "Ms. Laguellen, my name is Marcus. I work for the CIA." His tone was cordial, but she could tell he was furious about something. He gripped a file, stamped "classified" in bright red ink. His knuckles were white, and his shoulders rolled high over his back.

"Are you the one responsible for keeping me like this?"

"No. No, I'm not the one." He closed the door behind him and stepped closer.

"Why am I under arrest?"

"Let me introduce myself; I'm the one in charge of capturing your boyfriend." His voice remained measured and controlled, but his eyes betrayed his anger. "I want you to understand; I don't want to hurt him. In fact, I'm under strict orders to bring him in unharmed. But he's put himself in a very dangerous position. Every cop in the country is looking for him, and they think he's a cop killer."

"I can't help you. He's not my boyfriend. I don't know where he is."

His cold, raptorlike eyes stared long and hard at her before he shrugged his shoulders and let out a deep breath. "Maybe you can help us find him, maybe you can't. I don't really care. I want to talk about something else." He motioned for her to sit on the bench behind her, but she refused.

"Am I under arrest?"

"No."

"I want to speak to a lawyer."

"I can't help you there. It's out of my hands."

"You can't keep me like this! I know my rights!" She uncrossed her arms, almost reaching out to grab the man by his suit. "You can't do this to me!"

"I'm afraid they can. You've been associating with an extremely dangerous fugitive." He once again motioned toward the bench, and his tone softened. "I don't have the authority to help you right now, but I may have the power to help Hank." His voice took on a confidential tone, and for an instant she thought she saw him wink at her. "It's clear to me that I don't understand what's going on here. Maybe there's a way we can work this out before anything bad happens."

Cindy stepped back so that the back of her knees touched the cold concrete bench. She let her eyes run over every line on the man's face. "You believe him, don't you?" She probed his face for any wrinkle that might give him away.

"I don't know what to believe. He's clearly not crazy."

"He's not crazy! He's telling the truth. I heard him on the radio; you can believe every word he said."

"But what does he hope to gain from all this? It's not making any sense."

"You don't get it, do you? He's telling the truth!"

"The truth, huh?" An angry twist in his smile cracked the mask of composure on his face. "Let me tell you a little something I know about Hank: the truth is a very slippery subject with him. In the army, Hank Foster was what we call a psychological warrior. His specialty was creating misinformation and propaganda like this. He is a liar, and he is a murderer."

"You're lying!" Cindy refused to look at him any longer.

"Did he tell you about the UFO hoax he perpetrated in San Francisco?"

She stood staring at her feet for a moment. "He's not a murderer! Hank is trying to help us ... there's no doubt in my mind."

The man's hands moved toward her for the first time, raising a threatening finger in the air. His voice came out cold and hard, without any of the self-control shown earlier. "Hank Foster was a sniper. He shot people in cold blood. In fact, he was punished for being too bloodthirsty. I know men like this. They are coldhearted killers."

Tears welled in the corners of her eyes despite her determination not to cry anymore. "He's not coldhearted." She wiped at her eyes with her palms and stared back at him. "He's a good man. He saved my life, and now he's trying to save all of us. I know it. You don't know what he's been through. You're too stupid to realize when you're being fooled. Hank isn't trying to get anything out of this. He's just telling the truth."

"And so we come back to the truth." He smiled at her as if he'd made some kind of point. "I haven't seen much truth. Have you actually stopped to ask yourself if it's all just another bunch of lies?" He folded the file across his chest and leaned against the wall. "He's been lying to you all this time. He's been lying to everyone."

She stared at him, loathing him, and then cracked a fake smile of her own. "Okay, think about it like this for just a moment." She sat down on the cool concrete bench and pressed her palms against her knees. "What if he *is* telling the truth? You're not denying he was taken aboard a Houmn ship, right? You heard him on the radio. Where's the lie? He's not the first person to be persecuted for telling the truth. We were wrong about the Houmn. We were told they didn't exist, but they've been there all along. Why should we believe their every word now?" He was about to speak—there was a condescending sneer on his lips—but

Cindy stopped him with an upturned hand. "They took a painting from me. Is it here?"

"It's with the rest of your belongings." He turned his head toward the door.

"Did you look at it?"

"Yes."

"Do you know what it is?"

"Why, is it valuable?"

"Did you really look at it?"

"Yes."

"And you saw the flying saucer behind the Madonna?"

"Yes, they pointed it out to me."

"The painting is called *The Virgin and Saint Giovannino*. It's over six hundred years old. It's survived history to convey a message to whoever looks at it. It shows a man peering at a Houmn ship in the background—or, metaphorically speaking, peering into the past. The image is hidden behind a mask of divinity and the Christ child, and its true meaning is subtle. The message it's trying to convey has been suppressed, ignored, and ridiculed for centuries—just like you're trying to suppress what Hank is trying to tell us. But now we know the Houmn are real. We can believe what we want about them."

"You really believe the Houmn created humans thousands of years ago?" His eyes squinted with an annoyed, pained expression.

"Baby Jesus has a halo over his head in my painting. All angels have halos, right? Well, the Houmn have halos, too. You've seen them. Call them an aura, call them whatever you want, but they're halos!"

"And you think the church has been keeping the Houmn a secret all this time?" His voice dripped with cynicism.

"No. I think the church—and everybody else—believed exactly what the Houmn wanted them to believe. They, like you, have been duped by the Houmn, and you're to stupid to realize the truth even when it's being spelled out for you."

Shug's hands worked methodically, without much thought. The starter motor slid in easily; the giant diesel motor provided plenty of room to work. He made the final connections, checked his work one last time, and then slammed the engine cover closed. His eyes avoided Hank, who was sitting behind the controls. He mopped the sweat from his face with an arm and turned his back to the flying saucer.

"Are we all set?" Hank practically hissed at him. He'd been speaking in whispers ever since they entered the woods, and it was beginning to give him the creeps.

"Yeah, it's good. Fire it up." Shug climbed down from the tractor, jumping from the tracks into the soft dirt at the edge of the pit. He scrambled up the pile of earth, giving the long digging arm of the tractor a wide birth.

Hank worked his feet into position on the pedals and turned over the motor. The huge diesel clicked and coughed but eventually rumbled to life. Shug slumped into the mound above the pit. He had hoped the tractor wouldn't start. He'd also hoped the Houmn had found a way to reclaim their ship while they were gone, but luck seemed to be on Hank's side for the moment.

He watched as Hank maneuvered the hydraulic arm up, off the ship. The large sheet of plywood pinned between the digging bucket and the top of the Houmn ship slid away once the pressure was lifted. A thin layer of dirt covered the top of the ship; a patch of silver marked where the wood hand been. The metallic silver exposed to the sun glowed with an electric radiance that seemed to light the rest of the ship below the soil. Hank swung the arm over, burying the bucket in the dirt and standing in his seat to eye the ship below him.

Shug watched him move as he climbed over the machine to get a better view. He rushed, sometimes moving frantically, then there would be times when he stopped everything and just stared off into space. Shug couldn't fully understand his obsession with killing the Houmn. He could no longer guess what Hank was thinking. He looked as if he expected the Houmn to arrive at any second, but when Shug asked him about it, Hank shrugged it off.

Shug stared at the silver ship partially buried beneath fresh brown dirt. Hank hadn't displayed any hint of surprise or relief at finding the ship undisturbed. He'd seemed to know without a doubt that the ship would be there, that the Houmn wouldn't even attempt to recover it. Shug wanted to ask him about these things but Hank had grown silent and avoided answering questions directly. He had spent most of the drive silently questioning the Afghani in the back seat.

Shug felt as if there was no need for him to ask questions or have thoughts of his own anymore. Hank already knew his thoughts and only bothered to answer the questions he thought were important.

Hank climbed behind the controls and raised the arm to dig at the dirt near the sloping entrance of the pit. Huge bucketfuls were pulled away, and sheets of dirt slid from the top of the ship. A cloud of dust rolled up the pit to envelope Shug. As the dust cleared and his eyes opened, he found himself staring at their car and the crazed Muslim sitting in the dirt with his back pressed against the rear wheel.

The man was burnt horribly. The smell was still in Shug's nose. His hands were mutilated, his beard was burned away, leaving two curled patched of hair on his cheeks, and his face was scorched black. Shug still couldn't believe what had happened, even after Hank had explained it to him. He couldn't believe this was the same man they had met in Afghanistan. Hank had told him this was the man who bombed his home in San Francisco; this was the man who had killed Brice. It didn't seem real, and he could only feel pity for the man now. The bomb he had built to kill Hank had misfired, exploding in a ball of flame, and shot the pipe into his foot like a rocket. There was nearly nothing left below his ankle, and the man seemed crazy with pain.

The motor rumbled to a stop, and Shug reluctantly turned to see Hank's progress. "That's it." Hank was already climbing off the tractor. "She's all ready."

The ship was still covered in dirt, but Hank had carved out a path leading to its edge. "What about all that dirt?" Shug stood up, brushing the dust from his clothes.

"Now that the digger isn't pinning her down, she should be able to fly straight up."

"You're sure?" Shug was in no hurry to fly anywhere.

"I'm pretty sure. The dirt was never really holding us down anyway. It was just there to slow down the Houmn down if they tried to get their ship back. I don't think they're that good working with their hands. I knew they'd have a hard time getting the tractor off her; I doubt if they've got any spare starter motors for one of these babies." Hank wiped his hands on his pants and gave the tractor tread a kick with his plastic foot. "Come on, I don't want to spend too much time out in the open." Hank waved him on and moved away from the ship toward their stolen car.

"Do you think they're watching us?"

"I don't know." Hank glanced toward the sky, then ducked his head low once more. "I think they're afraid."

Shug looked past the tall pines to the sky above him. "So I guess this is it, huh?" He couldn't bear to look Hank in the face. He knew Hank could see the fear in his mind, but he didn't want him to see it in his eyes. He'd resolved to do whatever Hank asked of him, even if he didn't understand. Somehow he knew Hank was right; he'd always been right.

"Don't worry about that right now. Come on, give me a hand with the gas." Hank kept his eyes straight ahead. Again, Hank was refusing to talk about it. He acted as if there was nothing else to say, as if nothing else mattered. "I'll need your help carrying the propane."

Shug followed a pace behind as they walked back to the car. The agonized prayers of the crazy Muslim greeted them. His clothes were burnt away, and his ash gray skin looked melted into the curled fibers of his robes. He rocked rhythmically, clapping his mangled hands together. The meaty pulp at the end of his leg sat in a muddy pool of coagulated blood. Once again, Shug could smell the burnt hair and flesh.

"Let's grab the heavy one first." Hank pointed toward a thirty-gallon propane tank sitting behind the car. He stepped past the man on the ground as if he were a corpse. "We can come back for the oxygen cylinders."

At first the ghoul of a man recoiled from Hank's voice, but then he seemed to grovel toward him. Shug couldn't tell if he were blind or if his eyes where opened wide in a constant state of shock. The bloodshot whites of his eyes stood out on his soot black face, adding to his crazed appearance.

Shug kept his distance, stepping around the man in a wide circle. He was completely repulsed, yet he couldn't take his eyes off him. The thought of living through such suffering made him nauseous. "What's his name?"

Hank was already bent over the propane tank, waiting for him to grab his side. He paused for a moment and then stood, stretching his back. His brows were pressed into a tight line of annoyance, but as he watched the man trying to smile at him through his black, oozing skin, his face fell a little and he shook his head with pity. "His name is Omar Khalifa. You might not remember him, but I do."

"I still don't get it—why was he trying to kill you?"

"Do you remember the old Imam in Afghanistan? The one who hid in your cell when I came to get you out?"

"Yeah."

"Well, that man was Omar's teacher, his master. He ordered him to find me and kill me—some kind of one-man jihad or something." Hank spat into the dirt. "He believes Allah wants him to kill me."

"And he's been after you this whole time?"

"Yeah, the Iconoclasts had nothing to do with the hit on me." Hank looked into his eyes and arched his brows. "You shoulda killed the old man when I told you to."

Shug held his stare for a moment, then broke away to look at Omar. "Are you telling me that if I'd killed the old man, none of this would have happened?"

"I don't know. We wouldn't be sitting here with old Omar if you had."

A flutter of adrenalin tightened Shug's stomach as he felt a sting of guilt. For a moment he understood what Hank had meant when he'd talked about account-ability and the torment of causing so much grief. "Why didn't *you* kill him, then? Why was it up to me?"

"I could've killed him. In retrospect, I *should've* killed him. But at the time, I thought you might be right. My guts told me we should have killed him, but I think I trusted your heart more." Hank motioned for him to take up his side and he bent low to grab the handle on the propane tank.

Shug didn't move. His heart was still racing. "But listen to what you're saying. You can't be responsible for everything that happens in life. You can't blame yourself for the bugs and the aliens, just like I can't blame myself for what hap-pened with this guy. You didn't cause any of this. You're just a part of it. The Houmn were here before you ever dreamed of a hoax. Maybe that's why you dreamed it all up in the first place, because they were here. You had nothing to do with the Houmn rebelling against the Sempiternals. You can't blame yourself for bringing the bugs to Earth."

Hank kept his hand on the handle, bending all the way to the ground. He rested a knee in the dirt and looked up into Shug's face. "It's not about blame, Shug. I know I'm just a part of this, but I will be accountable for my actions. I'm going to take full advantage of the opportunity to act. I know I can't make things right, but what's right anyway?" Hank wiped the sweat from his face with his forearm. "But in a way, if I blame anyone, I blame the Houmn. Not for bringing the Takk and all the death and destruction, but for stealing who we are. We're screwed up. We don't know what's right and what's wrong … what's natural and what's not. They took that from us, and we'll never get it back. I may not know what's right, but I know that taking them out—showing the world we need to fight them with everything we've got—has more value than my life is worth."

Shug couldn't speak. His eyes drifted back to the burnt man still pleading for Hank's attention. He wanted to ask himself what his own life was worth, but the answer was clear; he would follow Hank to the end. He found himself bending low to grab the handle on the propane tank. The weight of the tank fell heavy against his leg with each step, and he was forced to walk in a stoop to compensate for his height. The metal handle raked and stretched his palm as they worked their way along the path toward the excavation site. They slid the tank down the channel Hank had carved with the digger until they were close to the edge of the ship.

Hank let go of his end, stretching his back and cracking his knuckles. "Give me a hand taking this thing inside, and then go back to get the oxygen cylinders." Hank ran his hand along the rim of the ship as he ducked below the circular wing. His hand paused on the surface, and a rectangular seam appeared beside him. The ship's door slid open with an electric hum. The hollow space behind the door was illuminated in pale blue light. Hank's fingers flicked over the invisible controls, and the long silver ramp shot past them into the dirt.

Hank turned, as if about to say something, and then he stopped abruptly. His mouth snapped closed. A troubling expression transformed his face, and then the smell hit Shug like a blow. It was the unmistakable stench of death, but at the same time, it was unlike any other smell he'd ever encountered. He gagged instantly. Vomit choked the back of his throat. A bitter, acidic taste clung to his mouth and burned his nose.

"Oh shit!" Hank covered his mouth with his shirt and waved at the air.

Shug scrambled back, but there was no escaping the smell. "How can anything smell that bad?"

Hank made a quick motion for him to grab his end of the tank and started pulling the propane toward the ramp. Shug pinched his nose, blinking away the tears forming in his eyes. They rolled the tank on its side, and Hank led the way into the ship. Once they had the tank through the opening, Hank wheeled it inside on its edge and disappeared into the dimly lit void.

Shug paused on the ramp. More lights began to flicker to life inside the ship. Memories of the cramped circular spaces flashed in his mind. The smell of the Houmn he'd ripped to pieces once again caused him to retch. He couldn't bring himself to take another step.

Hank called out from deep inside the ship. His voice was crisp and short, as if he were holding his breath. "Shug. Go get the oxygen. I'll handle it here."

Shug didn't need to be asked twice. Turning away with relief, he bounded down the ramp and hit the ground running as if the smell were a swarm of bees. The caustic stench followed him all the way back to the car, but the pines and fresh air eventually cleansed his senses. The crazed Muslim sat in the dirt where they had left him. He seemed to be washing himself with the dirt, scooping up handfuls and smearing it along his forearms. Shug stepped around him, wondering if the man could see him. He appeared not to notice him as he rounded the car to pop the trunk.

Not wanting to make any extra trips between horrors, Shug loaded all six oxygen cylinders into his arms. The green oxygen bottles blocked his view, and he nearly tripped over Omar where he lay stretched out in the dirt. Shug walked sideways back along the path. His muscles burned under the weight of the tanks. He didn't know how he would set the tanks down if they became too heavy, so he pushed himself all the way to the base of the ship.

Taking one last gasp of relatively fresh air, Shug held his breath and shuffled up the ramp. His cheeks bulged, and he nearly dropped the tanks, but Hank was there to steady him.

"Take it easy, big man." Hank began pulling the tanks from his arms until they were all stacked on the floor.

"How can you take the smell?"

"Olfactory fatigue."

"Oral what?" Shug's cheeks pushed the water from his eyes as he grimaced. "This is nasty."

"It means you'll get used to it." Hank began strapping the smaller oxygen cylinders to the larger propane tank with duct tape. "You'll hardly smell it in a minute."

"We should get those bodies out of here."

"We don't have that kind of time. Just give me a minute to wire this up."

Shug wasn't about to touch the bodies on his own; he was hoping Hank would take pity on him and do the work himself. He knew Hank could see how the dead Houmn made him feel. "I'm not flying in this thing with those nasty things!" He was sure he was going to vomit any second. "I won't do it!"

"Fine." Hank gripped a strip of tape in his teeth and tore off an end. He lashed the tape around the tanks and didn't look up at him. "I don't need you to."

There was a strange tone in Hank's voice, and not simply because he was holding his breath. "What do you mean? Are you saying you want to take the bodies out?"

"Forget about the bodies. I'm almost done." Hank stood over the gas cylinders as his eyes slowly met Shug's. "You can get out of here."

In the instant their eyes met, and the words left Hank's mouth, Shug knew he wasn't taking him along.

"What? I'm not going with you?"

"No." Hank looked down to fumble with the wire coil in his hands. "I need you to stay here."

"But you need me to fly the ship! You can't do it yourself!"

"You're right. I can't fly her myself. If I do, they'll be able to take over my thoughts. They'll see what I'm planning." Hank pointed toward the gas bomb at his feet. "That's what they're counting on. I won't be able to blast the ship right through them. They'll stop me before I get too close. They'll want to take me and the ship in one piece. They need me to show them how they've been betrayed." Hank's jaw tightened, and he turned to grab Shug by the shoulders. "I need you to stay here. I'm going to let them have me." He kicked the gas cylinder with his plastic foot. "And this."

"But you still can't fly the ship!"

"The plan has changed. I don't need to ask this of you anymore."

"You can't let them take over your brain … if they can take over your brain, then they can make you switch off the bomb. You wont be able to do a thing about it. Trust me, I know what it's like."

Hank turned Shug's shoulders and gently pushed him out the opening. "Omar will fly it." He followed him with a hand on his back. "Come on, I need your help to carry him in here."

Shug blinked in the sunlight and let the fresh air fill his lungs. He stopped on the ramp, even though Hank was still herding him along. "Omar?"

"Yeah, Omar. He can do it. I can practically do it for him. I just need another brain sitting behind the controls."

Shug took another step; now it was the smell pushing him down the ramp.

"It's simple. They want me. Well, they're going to get me. I'll put Omar behind the wheel and plot a course right through the Master Ship. If I'm right, they'll take over the ship once we get close. They'll think they have me."

"But they'll have Omar …"

"And if I'm wrong, we'll just smash right through them. Nothing can survive an impact like that." Hank stopped behind him at the base of the ramp. "I don't think they'll let the ship get that close; the computer system is too sophisticated. But they'll never detect the bomb I've rigged up. It's too crude: no electronics or moving parts. But it's powerful enough to blow the hell out of them."

"But what about …"

"Forget about me. I've got to do what I've got to do. But there's something I need from you."

"What? I'll do anything you ask."

"I know you will. I know you would have gone with me if I'd asked. Even though you don't understand." Hank paused, mustering an awkward smile. "You need to stay here so I can do this. It wasn't right of me to ask it of you in the first place."

"I understood what you meant when you said some things are worth more than your own life. You were right. I would have done it because I believe in you. If you say it's worth it, that's enough for me. I trust you."

Hank kicked the dirt clods at his feet, keeping his eyes low. "I want you to know that from the moment I met you, there was something about you I couldn't understand. Even though life had handed you shit, you seemed to love every minute of it. You belonged, somehow … I never did. Now that all this has happened, I get it. I've seen what makes you tick. I've seen it in others, too. But in you, I see the best humanity has to offer. I need to know that you'll carry on. I want you to take care of Cindy for me. I want to know you're looking after her."

"Cindy?"

"I was wrong. There are things worth living for. If there's any meaning to life, it's finding someone and making new life. It's about joining humanity, even if it's imperfect. I was wrong about people. We've been victimized, but … there's a kind of nobility in that I suppose. Now that we know, we can better ourselves. Make sure people understand what's going on. Tell Cindy why I did this."

Their hands met with a familiar handshake. "I'll tell her everything." The strength had left Shug's hand, but as he realized that Hank was saying his final good-bye, his grip stiffened. "You don't have to do this! Why do you have to take everything head-on?"

Hank pressed his hand, faking a smile. "The gain far outweighs the loss." He broke away from Shug's grip and began to walk up the path cut through the dirt. "People will live without the influence of the Houmn for the first time in history. Give us a hundred years to prepare, and we'll be ready to fight them. We'll never be their slaves again."

Shug couldn't reconcile the strange way Hank continued to say we. He talked as if he would be here to fire the first shot at the Houmn when they arrive a century from now. He didn't give the tranquil beauty of the pine forest a second glance. There was no hesitation in his step. He walked back to the stolen car as if he were going for a cooler of beer. "Come on, give me a hand with Omar."

Once again, Omar groveled at Hank's feet as they approached. His bloodshot eyes rolled in their sockets. His gnarled, bloodied hands reached out for him, and Shug was forced to turn away. "How much does he know?"

"Omar? I don't know what to make of Omar. I guess he thinks I'm his God now. He speaks to me as if I'm Allah himself. He's serving a painful penance for his failures in life. He's waiting for me to allow him into my paradise." Hank knelt down, staring into Omar's eyes and gently fighting off his hands.

"Is he going to make it? He looks pretty messed up."

"He'll hang in there. I've just told him we're about to make that long-awaited transcendental journey. See, look at him smile." Hank motioned for Shug to take up position at Omar's legs. "I finally found a guy who *wants* to go with me." Hank smiled at him; it was a warm, familiar smile that took Shug back to better times.

"Shut up, man. I woulda gone wit ya."

"I like it better this way. Poetic justice, if you think about it. The Houmn killed by religious zealots spawned by their own lies. You can't write this stuff. Come on, grab his legs."

Shug slipped one arm beneath Omar's knees, fighting to keep the loose flesh from touching him. Hank grabbed him under the shoulders, and together they hoisted him off the ground and carried him to the ship with short, shuffling steps.

"Go ahead, drop the legs." Sweat was beading up on Hank's brow, and his breathing was rushed. "I'll pull him up the ramp."

Shug set the man's legs down as gently as possible, and then stepped back to collapse into the pile of dirt. Hank pulled him up the ramp with one last burst of energy. Shug watched as Omar's feet disappeared into the ship, and the pine forest fell quiet.

Hank reappeared a few moments later and carefully sidestepped down the ramp. Shug could see he was trying not to show any emotion as he approached. His jaw was locked tight, the muscles in his cheeks rippled with tension, and his eyes were fixed on him like lasers.

"This is it, brother. I don't need to get all crazy here ... I don't know if I could."

Shug stepped forward, wrapping his arms around him, pulling him into an embrace. "You don't have to, brother. I know." Shug knew the words Hank couldn't bear to speak but he still couldn't understand why he was walking off to die like this. He still refused to believe Hank wasn't coming back. "I guess this is it ..."

Hank pounded his fists against Shug's back. "I love you, brother."

"I love you, too." Shug struggled to keep his voice from cracking. "If it wasn't for you, I don't know ..."

Hank stopped him, pushing him away at arm's length. "If it wasn't for me, you wouldn't have had your black-ass tortured in Afghanistan. You wouldn't have spent the prime of your life on the run." His eyes smiled as his shoulder rolled up to mop the moisture on his cheeks. "You wouldn't have been taken aboard any flying saucers ..." A wide smile broke on his face. "I'm not cryin', or anything. It's just, the smell makes my eyes water."

Shug returned his smile despite the sorrow in his heart. "And like you said, brother; I loved every minute of it."

"Take good care of yourself, Shug. And take care of Cindy for me." Hank gripped his shoulders one last time before pushing himself away. "You're a good man, Shug ... best I ever knew."

"So are you, Hank."

"No." Hank's smile faded. "No, I was wrong. I should have learned to love it like you do. I thought I was too smart. I should have learned ... but I was too busy hating it."

"It's not too late to change your mind."

"It's too late. Good-bye, Shug."

"Good-bye, brother-man." They slapped their hands together for the last time, and Hank turned to climb the ramp. He never paused, never looked back. Once he had disappeared behind the pale glow inside the ship, the ramp slid away and the opening closed, leaving no trace of a seam.

Shug backed away, past the edge of the pit. After a few moments of stunned silence, the ship hummed to life. A steady vibration shook the soil loose. A thick cloud of dust billowed out from underneath, and Shug was enveloped by a wave of heat. He scrambled back, suddenly afraid of being cooked beneath the ship, but the heat was already dissipating. Sheets of dirt rained down as the ship hovered above the pit. The silver disk dipped to one side, throwing off the dirt with a huge rush of air, and then shot up high into the sky.

Shug covered his eyes to stare at the ship as it moved. The massive ship shrank with amazing speed. The silver dot shot into the distance, made a few rapid zig-zag motions, and then disappeared entirely. After a moment, Shug was struck by how quiet the forest had become. He could almost hear the sun burning overhead. There was no one left and no place to rush off to. He collapsed into the dirt and stared at the sky. He wondered how long it would take for Hank to reach the Master Ship, and his heart skipped as the thought struck him that it might have already happened.

The curved peel of silver slid shut behind him. There was no need to work any controls: half a thought from him was all it had taken. The sounds and radiance of life outside ceased to exist. The air inside the ship felt dead. It reeked of decomposing Houmn. Hank covered his mouth, running his eyes along the bowed inner walls of the ship. His eyes narrowed on the second of three tubelike corridors, and he traced his steps back to where he'd left the black shroud.

Omar lay on the floor where he'd dumped him. Hank avoided his eyes and tried to ignore his pleas for mercy. Omar's shattered psyche whined at him like a starving animal as he mumbled prayers and prostrated himself on the floor. Hank found himself speaking to him as he would a child, scolding him for his impatience to die as he passed by.

The narrowing corridor ended at a sheer wall of gleaming silver. He could almost see an electrical field floating to one side of the wall. He sensed where the controls were; he knew instinctively how they worked. The ship seemed to whisper its secrets in his ear. His confidence grew along with the knowledge of the Houmn technology fermenting in his mind. He connected with the ship, feeling the pride and power of ownership as his fingers worked the invisible controls opening the door. He stepped through the threshold into the center of the ship. The ambient light within the wide, wedged shaped space grew brighter. His eyes darted to the shroud lying on the polished metal floor.

He held it in his hands. It was heavier than he remembered, but he reminded himself that he was still under Earth's gravitational pull. He brought the shroud close to his face to look at the material. He felt the hardness of tiny metal ringlets between his fingers, but they were too small to see. The shroud was a blur of black coils looped into a massive hood resembling the chain mail worn by medieval knights. He worked the ringlets between his thumb and fingers, wondering how exactly the hood functioned. He remembered the electric buzz washing over him. The memory of pain and the horrible nothingness was still fresh. He remembered what the Houmn themselves had revealed to him about the shroud; it acted as a shield, isolating a single mind behind the workings of a powerful magnetic field. The Houmn rebels had used it to project their thoughts into his; the Sempiternals had threatened to steal his thoughts with it. He knew the device was dangerous, but it was his only means of concealing himself from the Houmn.

Taking a deep breath of putrid air, Hank slid the shroud over his head. He gripped the coils, ready to throw it off at the first hint of the bleak nothingness, but the hood slid over his head and down his neck painlessly. The electric hum washed over him, the hairs on the back of his neck stood on end, and his mind grew quiet. For a fraction of a moment, he feared it was the beginning of the paralyzing nonexistence and nearly threw the shroud to the floor, but he soon realized that his mind had simply gone quiet. Omar's pitiful pleas evaporated. His vision changed; the ship around him became less vibrant, and he could no longer sense where the invisible controls lay. A powerful sense of Self dominated his thoughts, reminding him of the man who was first taken aboard the Houmn ship.

There was no pain, no one manipulating the power of the shroud from without. He turned, the shroud whipping over his shoulder like a mane of hair, and fumbled for the controls operating the door. He knew they were there, but the door refused to open. He repeated the command, but the door remained closed. Hank lifted the hood from his face until he could sense the controls hovering above the featureless panel of metal. His hand flicked the air, and the door opened. He let the hood fall back over his head and marched back to Omar.

It was a relief not to hear him begging for a quick end to his suffering. He could look into his eyes without falling into his mind. Hank bent low to spin him around and grabbed him beneath the armpits. He hauled him to the door, slipping along the slime-covered corridor. He hoisted Omar's dead weight onto one of the pedestal seats. He fought to prop him up, but Omar slumped and fell backward, sending his feet flying through the air and his head crashing to the floor.

Hank scowled at him. He lifted the hood from his face, and it was like stepping into a home and being greeted as a long-awaited guest. Omar called to him with several voices all at once. The sudden clamor was repulsive, after his brief respite under the hood, and Hank silenced him with an angry command.

He ordered him to right himself on the stool and to obey his instructions. Omar submitted, crawling onto the pedestal with the quickness of a willing slave. Hank revealed the ship's controls without explanation, moving Omar's hands to the laser screens for him. Omar's remaining fingers did their best to manipulate the ship's computer, and a moment later a course was plotted and the ship's propulsion systems engaged.

Hank stood behind Omar, watching the ship's seemingly erratic path through Earth's atmosphere on the blue field of light. He could see no way to calculate how long it would take to reach the Master Ship. Much of the data staring back at him was still a rush of unintelligible symbols. The ship's speed was unfathomable. He didn't know if it would take seconds or minutes to cross the solar system to the Master Ship.

He turned his eyes and his attention back to Omar, collecting the thoughts he wanted to project into him. He needed the Houmn to believe he was behind the controls, so he filled Omar with the suicidal rage they would expect. He concentrated on the single, raw emotion, hoping it would serve to block out all other thought. Omar stiffened, his limps trembling.

Hank saw the hatred reflected in the mirror of Omar's mind. The images bombarded him, one after the other. He dwelled on the pain and the fearsome nothingness they had inflicted on him. He concentrated on the frustration of living a completely conflicted life, a life incapable of true gratification or joy. He fanned the hatred of a slave for its master and let the madness run wild in Omar's thoughts.

Omar's breath came in rapid gasps. His vision blurred with red-tinged fury. Hank stepped away, finding the wall with his back, and sank to the floor. The hood was lighter now as he lowered it over his face. The silence returned, and he imagined the Sempiternals watching Omar behind the wheel of their ship, thinking it was him, biding their time before they snatched him. For an instant he feared that they did not see them, that they were not in tune with the ship's computer. He feared they would crash right through the Master Ship—that he would never know, would never see the victory he'd planned—but then it happened: Omar spilled to the floor and began seizing.

Hank was only vaguely aware of the ship's movement. His heart raced, and he fought the temptation to peek out from behind the shroud. Several long minutes passed while Omar writhed and kicked on the floor. Hank positioned himself behind the closed door, ready to spring into action at any moment. Silently, with a flash of movement, the door disappeared. Shadows swayed in the entrance.

Hank's body felt light and strong as he jumped to his feet. He lifted the shroud from his eyes with one hand while he thrust his pistol out in front of him with the other. There was a shriek, then a flash of light, as Hank fired into the nearest gray figure. The silver-suited Houmn flew back. Its trunk exploded through the silver material covering its body, and clear fluid shot through the air. Two more Houmn stood by, frozen with surprise, and Hank dropped them both with shots to the head.

The corridor behind them was clear, and Hank rushed past until he could see the outer door of the ship. He charged the open door with his arm extended and the pistol leading the way. The space beyond the opening was bright. The silver ramp was extended at his feet, but it took his eyes a moment to adjust to the strange light. The ship sat in an open space. Other ships sat on either side. Small, silver-suited figures moved beneath him. Two of them were stopped on the ramp only a meter away. Hank leaped onto the ramp, bouncing one of the Houmn from the slender beam. He fired a shot, hitting the alien figure in the back and sending it flying through the air as if on a wire.

The shot rang in his ears, echoing off the inner ship with a loud crack. He couldn't count the number of Houmn staring back at him. He appeared to be in the corner of a large flight deck. Rows of flying disks lined the arc of the ship, their ramps all extended to the floor. Houmn were everywhere. Three naked Sempiternals stood stock-still at the base of the ramp, their eyes wide and their miniature mouths hanging open.

Hank cleared the ramp with one springing leap, landing near the three Sempiternals. They turned to flee, but it was too late. Hank swung his fist, smashing the slender figure below the neck. Bones snapped, and the creature fell away as if it were weightless.

Muted, horrified screams filled the docking area. The pistol in his hand crashed down on the head of one of the Sempiternals as it tried to scurry away. The butt smashed through its skull, and his hand sank deep into its flesh. The strange aura of light flitted out above its head. Hank pulled his hand free and leveled the gun at the last of the Sempiternals. He fired a shot into its exposed spine, and it fell. The force of the shot sent it sliding across the floor.

Hank scanned the immediate area for targets. None of the Houmn moved to stop him. Most ran away as fast as their short, stubby legs could carry them. He moved forward, positioning himself behind a large piece of equipment secured to the floor. He followed the Houmn with his pistol as they tried to escape. He squeezed the trigger, dropping one Houmn after another. Houmn fled in all directions. Some hurried up the ramps of other ships, some disappeared into the labyrinth of passages opening into the docking area. He fired at one as it disappeared through a large doorway cut into the center of the ship. The shot missed, sparking with white light against the metallic surface. His eyes turned back to his own ship, where the propane bomb sat ready to explode. There was nothing stopping him from rushing inside and blowing the ship to bits, but he felt himself being pulled deeper into the Master Ship.

He saw a group of Houmn fleeing in sheer panic. There were Sempiternals among them, and Hank charged after them, firing at their backs. Houmn bodies blew apart, falling to the ground. The black shroud fell over his face as he ran, each stride bringing him closer. He pounced on them as if they were moving in slow motion; they were defenseless against him. He roared with a primal scream as he fell on them, tearing them apart with his bare hands. Their eyes were filled with horror, and their bodies broke easily under the furious blows.

He grabbed at a neck, flinging the helpless creature to the ground and stomping out its life with his boot. "Die, bastards!" Hank raged aloud as he turned on the Sempiternals. He felt like a lion let loose among children. They were totally unprepared for such violence. "I'm gonna kill"—he fired another shot, dropping an alien about to duck away—"every last one of you!" He fired again, killing with each step.

One of the Sempiternals turned to him, waving its arms in front of its face. Hank snatched it by the arm, nearly wrenching the limb from its socket as he threw the creature to the floor and raged in its face. "Feel that? You're gonna die! Understand me?" He pressed the gun against its head and shielded his eyes from the alien blood he was about to spill. The creature gasped beneath him. Its mouth worked as if speaking to him, but no sound came to his ears. Hank paused for a moment, contemplating pulling back the shroud to hear the Sempiternal beg for its life, but a new sound caught his attention. He looked up to see a large door slam closed ahead of him. The last of the Houmn in the open space were filing into the main body of the ship, and the doors were snapping closed behind them.

The ramps leading to the other ships had all been pulled in. Hank's eyes darted back to his ship. The door was still open, and the ramp was still there, but Hank knew they could control it, too. He feared they would close up his ship and prevent him from getting to his bomb, but then another fear gripped him as he saw what the Houmn were planning: they were sealing him off in the ship's docking area. He was only moments away from being trapped or sucked out into space.

He looked around in desperation and saw the open door the Houmn were trying to flee through. He calculated that he could make it to the door in half the time it would take him to reach his own ship. He released his grip on the Houmn and fired a shot into its head, spattering gore across the floor. He scrambled for the open door, hoping it wouldn't snap closed and cut him in two. His feet barely touched the ground as he made great leaping strides, bounding weightlessly through the air toward the door. He leaped through the opening like a long-jumper, landing on his feet on the other side.

A group of Houmn cowered behind a long computer terminal. Three Sempiternals hid among them. The black shroud covered his eyes as he shot blindly into the crowd of aliens. He pressed the hood over his forehead and pumped rounds into the Houmn. He heard the door slide shut behind him and had a clear view of the other ships lined up inside the massive hangar through a clear plasma window at his side. Some of the ships hovered in place, while others appeared to be drifting out of the bay.

He stopped his killing long enough to find his ship through the glass. The ramp was still down. The dead remained flattened on the floor. Nothing stood to oppose him. The Houmn ran from him in a blind panic. Their acute vulnerability showed in the way they seemed to leap ahead of each other with every third, waddling step. They collided, arms flailing wildly, as they rushed down the arched corridor. None of them took the time to look back. They fled, knowing they could not outrun him but hoping they could outrun each other. Their helplessness triggered some primal, predatory reflex, and Hank found himself charging after them, moving deeper into the ship and farther away from his bomb.

Hank closed the distance and fell on the Houmn with a deafening howl. The Houmn shrieked, some of them falling on their faces as if knocked flat by the power of his voice. Hank grabbed the leg of one of the Sempiternals as it fell. He pulled it beneath him, flipping it over and staring into its eyes. Once again, the creature appeared to be pleading with him. Its hands clawed the air, and its mouth gaped at him like that of a caught fish.

Hank bent low, pulling the creature's face close. "It's too late. You're going to pay for what you've done." He was about to choke the life from it but was stopped by a sudden compulsion to lift the hood and speak to the Sempiternal in language it could understand. The battle was won; he could tell by the bodies still motionless on the floor outside that he could get back to his ship. There was no way to stop him now.

Hank pinned the Houmn with his knee and slowly raised his hand to the hood.

He pulled the hood back, and a flood of voices filled his ears. At first he felt a twinge of regret, as if he'd made a terrible mistake. A host of strange minds mingled and crashed together, but the collective will and the single voice were nowhere to be found. He felt fear spreading through the Master Ship like a fire. The individual alien entities were too shocked by his presence to confront him; they rolled away, letting their fellows take the risk of locking minds with him. Eventually he felt the voice of the Houmn pinned beneath him. Its thoughts were mired in confusion, but one question floated to the surface with profound clarity.

We are your fathers—why have you done this?

Hank clasped his hand around its throat, ready to crush out its life at any moment.

You cannot do this. The Houmn are your salvation.

Hank was struck by a sudden sense of meaning behind the term "salvation." He began to comprehend why the Houmn were so shocked by his attack. They had been guarding a great secret, a secret they assumed he knew already. The

Houmn couldn't understand why he wanted to destroy the treasure they possessed. And, all at once, Hank couldn't understand it either; the treasure revealed to him was beyond any possible measure of value.

Hank stared, transfixed by the glossy black eyes staring back at him. A ripple of remorse crept up his spine. It was quickly followed by the sickening punch of dread that follows the instigation of tragedy.

All at once it seemed he'd been wrong about the Houmn, wrong about everything. He could no longer deny that the Houmn were intent on saving humanity, but the planned salvation was to take a radical form he'd never imagined. The Houmn had never fully expected humanity to survive the Takk, but they were prepared to save the human race no matter what events transpired on Earth.

They possessed the ability to repopulate Earth once their armada arrived to purge the planet of bugs. They held humanity safe, contained, bottled up inside their massive computers. The essence of Man was broken down to code, downloaded and ready to reproduce. The knowledge fell on him at once, nearly crushing him. They accused him of wanting to destroy everything out of pure madness. They blamed him, calling him the Deceiver, the incarnation of evil itself. The accusations they spat at him shocked him into seeing himself through their eyes. He began questioning his sanity with short, hesitant glances into the real motives buried deep inside him.

A vast story unfolded, growing rapidly in his newfound understanding. The Houmn had compiled a complete genetic history of Earth, including countless copies of the human genome. They held the power to recreate life. Their sole intent was to protect that ability no matter what catastrophe befell Earth. Hank's heart sank; he couldn't imagine carrying out his plans and acting out the part of the maniac. He knew it was up to him to end his tragic string of errors.

He could not escape the knowledge that his actions had come dangerously close to erasing the genetic code of every life form ever to inhabit the planet. The disjointed Sempiternal presence screamed it at him. They begged him to stop his madness. Their pleas seemed to reconcile defeat. The dull eyes of the creature in his grip pleaded for mercy, begging for an end to the terror paralyzing its thoughts. The fate of two races stared back at him through the massive black eyes.

Hank paused and weighed his thoughts before he spoke.

"Where is it?"

His words were met by confusion among the collective Houmn brain. He sensed the effort behind the wealth of data they had collected. The Human code they nurtured was the essence of their existence, the sole reason for their timeless mission on Earth, and they were prepared to protect it as a mother protects her young. Hank probed deeper, picking through thoughts and images until he began to comprehend the treasure they clung to so desperately.

The Houmn had designs for Earth, and they had plans for the Human genome.

"Where is it?"

Hank tightened his grip on the creature's neck. The data they coveted was real, a tangible product of their technology. They flaunted it, bartering their lives with it. They bet their lives that he would not destroy it. His ship's door was left open, inviting him to simply slip away. They feared he would rampage through the ship, killing them all. They knew he was unstoppable: the Houmn had never prepared for violence aboard their ship.

Here with the Houmn. We keep your humanity safe with us. You must not destroy. Stop your madness.

The creature's voice resonated in his mind, but its sentiments were echoed from places deep within him. Something was telling him to stop, that he didn't want to know any more. The more he seemed to comprehend, the greater the self-loathing became. The consequences of his misguided actions ate at him as if given life inside his belly.

Hank pushed away these dark thoughts and narrowed his focus on the Sempiternal beneath him. "Give it to me!" His hand clamped down on the Houmn's throat, and its black eyes bulged.

No! Do not kill me.

"Show me the treasure you're promising me, or I'll break your filthy neck." Hank growled, pushing his weight into the helpless Houmn. "You will die. You will be nothing. Understand me? Nothing!"

You must not kill the Houmn. You are one of us.

"I'll give you one last chance." Hank loosened his grip. "Forget about the others and save yourself. Show me what I ask, and I will spare you."

Horrified by the prospect of betrayal, countless Sempiternal minds screamed out at once, but Hank concentrated on the mortal fear radiating from the Houmn in his grip. He assured the creature its life was over if it didn't give him what he wanted. The first ever sensation of mortal panic was breaking down the creature's defenses. Hank could visualize the prize in its mind. The data was massed in the ship, somewhere within the organic brain of the ship's computer.

"Where is it?"

Humanity is safe in our computer.

The Houmn was telling him there was no way to fully expose the massive amount of data for his viewing. It tried to assure him that the information was protected, safe, and would remain safe as long as he stopped his madness.

Do not kill. Do not destroy what we have amassed.

Hank's eyes darted around the strange world of alien technology, knowing he could not destroy what might truly be human salvation. His eyes stopped searching for answers and fell on the gun in his hand.

It weighed in his hand with the anticipation of a sudden end. He thought how easy it would be to place the gun under his chin and embrace the nothingness. His guilt, his suffering, nothing would matter anymore. He could stop it all now, before the Houmn were rendered incapable of saving humankind.

He paused, turning the weapon over in his hands. The desire for a sudden end fell on him, clinging to his thoughts like wet paint. He understood with sudden clarity that ending his own life with his pistol was no different from the suicidal attack he'd planned. Once he was dead, nothing would matter; the only issue now was how to die.

Hank watched himself from without, considering the strangeness of the abstract thoughts being weighed. He had never permitted himself to entertain the thought of suicide after the death of his brother—but now, as he stared at the gun in his hands, ending his life seemed the only rational choice. The desire to exchange his life for the death of Houmn was gone and forgotten.

His eyes drifted back to his ship. He pictured the propane bomb hidden inside. Once again, fear projected by the Houmn flashed across his thoughts. They were seeing what he had planned for them. There was no doubt that the crude bomb would obliterate the Master Ship. Their fear clouded his thoughts, and he felt himself pulling away. The suicidal impulse gradually faded until he could physically shake it away with a shudder of revulsion. The Houmn collective was once again broken down by fear, and Hank could see how they had tried to talk him out of his life.

His eyes lingered over the ship, and the rush of anger inspired a new thought in the corner of his mind. He turned back to face the creature beneath him and decided to ask it a much simpler question.

"Any computer?"

The Houmn gasped, then shrieked, following Hank's mind back to his ship. In an instant, Hank knew the answer. All the Houmn ships shared a single computer mind. Earth's digitized history was there, inside *his* ship. Hank rose to his feet, jamming the pistol into his waistband. He pulled the alien to its feet by the neck and jerked it toward the door.

"Open the door." Hank slid the hood over his head and pushed the Houmn ahead of him. "You're coming with me!"

The Houmn obeyed. The new sensation of unprecedented fear dominated its thoughts. Hank's hand weighed like a guillotine on the back of its neck.

The door snapped open, and three silver-suited Houmn stared at him from the other side. Hank froze. There was something in their hands, some kind of weapon. They were pointing it at him.

Hank fell back a step, shielding himself behind the Sempiternal. The Houmn stood their ground, still aiming the conelike object at him, but nothing happened—no lasers or flashing of fire, no sound, nothing at all. The Houmn flinched as Hank cringed and fumbled for the pistol in his waistband. They stepped back, shooting each other quick, horrified glances. Hank pressed the Sempiternal close to his body, lifting the hood from his eyes and aiming his gun at the Houmn.

All at once they turned to flee, and Hank dropped them with three quick shots. The Sempiternal slumped in his arms and he pushed it through the door with his knee. It fell face-first into the mass of silver-suited bodies on the ground. Hank stepped through the opening, covering every angle with his weapon. There were no Houmn left anywhere inside the docking area. Hank flipped the Houmn onto its back, then hoisted it over his shoulder.

He slipped in the oily blood covering the ramp of his ship, but he was able to catch himself with one hand. The alien felt weightless on his back, and a surge of strength coursed through his limbs. He tossed the Houmn into a pile of rotting bodies against the inner wall of the ship and made a dash for the propane bomb.

The mass of oxygen tanks lashed to the propane cylinder slid along the floor as if they were empty. He didn't feel the weight of the bomb until it was time to slide it down the ramp. The tanks shot down the ramp as if carried away by a river, and Hank was pulled along behind it. The sound of metal striking metal rang through the ship, followed by the echo of the oxygen cylinders crashing against the main tank.

Hank shook the pain from his hand and turned back to the ramp. His feet slipped in the Houmn blood once more, and the decreased gravity made it impossible for him to get a foothold on the ramp. He was forced to crawl, gripping the slender ramp by its edge and pulling himself up one hand after the other. An exhausted dizziness blurred his thoughts as he stood in the opening and stared into his ship. He found Omar, dazed and drooling on the floor where he'd left him.

"Get up!"

Omar didn't move. Hank stood over him, his heart threatening to tear itself from his chest and his breath coming in short, pain-filled gasps. He looked to the Houmn cowering against the wall and reluctantly pulled the shroud from his forehead.

"Get up, Omar!"

Omar jerked his spine to stare up at him. Hank bent low, pulling at him. Omar kicked his legs, but neither man could bring him to his feet. Hank tugged at him, slipping on the oil-slick floor. He pushed, pulled, and kicked him along the passage, shouting at him to move until they reached the door. Hank eyed the docking area, too weary to cover the space with his pistol.

There were no live Houmn in sight, so he pushed Omar down the ramp. Both men slid on their backs, crashing helplessly into the gas cylinders. Omar howled as his foot smashed against the tank. The sudden pain seemed to wake him from his zombie like stupor.

Hank crawled over him, uncoiling the wire and arming the detonator. He held the trigger tight in his fist and pressed it into Omar's trembling hands.

"Omar, do as I say. Hold this." He demonstrated how to hold the trigger. "Do not let go. You have done well in my eyes. Paradise awaits you. Do as I say, and the suffering of this life will end." Hank stared deep into the window of Omar's eyes. "You must recite the Al-Waage'ah … just as it has been written. Do not skip a word." He wrapped his hands around Omar's.

Omar's grip was tight on the trigger, and he began to mouth the prayer. "In the name of Allah, Most Gracious, Most Merciful …"

"Not yet! Wait! Wait until I have left you." Hank turned to scramble up the ramp. "The entire prayer, Omar!" He kept the hood from falling over his face as shouted over his shoulder. "Every last word of it!"

He found the Sempiternal cowering among the dead, looking nearly dead itself. The ring of light above its head looked a frosty blue. Hank's hand clamped onto its neck, lifting it to its feet.

"You will fly the ship."

He pulled the creature by its neck and planted him on one of the pedestals.

His hand remained locked around its neck, his fingers almost touching, as he watched the screens of light flicker to life. There was no movement, no sound, but he knew the ship was already moving. The blue screen was blurred with a rapid sequence of symbols. A moment later, the Sempiternal shrieked, nearly pulling away from his grip. Hank could tell by the sudden change of color and the flash of an alarm on the screens that the Houmn Master Ship had been destroyed. Omar's prayer had been answered.

Bill was dreaming again. The wild, fantastic scenes playing in his mind were colored too vividly to be anything other than dreams. The surreal landscape was both beautiful and fearsome. He fell from one fantasy to another, but a single theme repeated itself: he was alone. He couldn't find them anywhere. The ethereal court that had shadowed his thoughts was a memory. He was alone, and finally free to dream.

He basked in the comfort of deep sleep until a voice boomed over his head, jarring him awake. He found himself lying on the floor beneath a desk. His face clung to the plastic mat covering the floor. A thick web of drool hung from his cheek. He couldn't remember climbing under the desk. A perfectly good couch sat across the office, but he had somehow fallen asleep right there on the floor.

"Mr. Kemp? Is that you, sir?"

Bill eyes fluttered, refusing to stay open. He wished that whoever it was would simply go away.

"You must wake up, sir." The man's voice was growing harsh. His shadow loomed over the desk.

"Go away." Bill shut his eyes tight.

"But sir …"

"I said beat it!"

Bill felt the man's hands on him, grabbing handfuls of his shirt, pulling him off the floor. Bill whipped his head around to glare at him, swinging his elbow at his arms, but the young soldier tightened his grip and pulled him to his feet.

"Sir, we've got a hostage situation at the White House. I've been ordered to bring you there on the double."

Bill stood eye to eye with the marine. He wanted to jump down his throat, tell him to keep his hands off him, but the angry look in the young man's eyes made him think better of it. He wiped the drool from his cheek with a roll of his shoulder and smoothed out the wrinkles in his shirt. "What are you talking about?"

"A situation with the Houmn has developed. One of them has been taken hostage. We should go now, sir. We've been looking all over for you." The soldier stepped back, looking at the desk with a reproachful expression.

"Hostage? But who?"

"This way, sir. I'm not the one to explain any of this to you. Frankly, I don't know what's going on. All I know is that he's asking for you, and they sent me to find you. And I found you. So please, let's go." He stepped closer, holding out an arm as if he were ready to drag him there if necessary.

"I'm coming ... just give me a second." Bill took a short, hesitant step. "Who's asking for me?"

"The man holding the alien at gunpoint. He says he won't talk to anybody but you." The marine was eyeing him suspiciously once more. His jaw muscles tightened as he leaned close. His fists were balled up on his arms. "So please hurry, sir. We've been looking for you for a long time."

"Hank ..."

Bill allowed himself to be pushed through the door.

"He showed up with the hostage in one of their ships. It landed right in front of the White House. He's threatening to kill the alien if we make a move on him." The marine led him to a host of other soldiers. A golf cart with two secret servicemen was waiting for them.

Bill made the soldier repeat everything while the cart whirred at top speed toward the White House. He was about to have him repeat it a second time when he caught sight of the flying saucer in front of the East Wing. The silver disk shimmered in the darkness, looking much bigger than he remembered. It sat uncomfortably close to the White House, within kissing distance of the second story windows. The sight of it took his breath away. He felt none of the composed tranquility he had when he'd first seen the Houmn ships.

They rounded a corner, and their cart was greeted by a procession of armed men. Some wore military fatigues and covered the shadows with their assault rifles; others wore the uniform black business suits of the Secret Service. A buzz of radio traffic filled the air as the men surrounded him. Bill was shoved from the cart and pulled along by his wrist. They led him closer and closer to the Houmn ship, but stopped at the grand steps leading into the White House.

"Mr. Kemp, follow me please." A man wearing a black suit stepped through the crowd and waved him over. His name badge was stamped CIA, and he spoke into a microphone at his wrist.

Bill followed him up the steps into the White House. Men pressed in all around him as if shielding him on all sides. Armed marines were everywhere. They passed a team of men wearing black fatigues and covered from head to toe in body armor. They huddled together, talking strategy and adjusting their helmets. They turned as one, following him with their eyes. Bill could see confusion everywhere he turned.

The ring of men moved him deeper down the hall. A flash of brilliance caught his eye, something silver and grossly out of place twinkled under the overhead lights. Bill raised himself on his toes and saw a group of Houmn pressed into a corner. They were surrounded by a group of civilians, all wearing small computers around their necks. He couldn't count how many there were, but there were no Sempiternals among them.

"In here." The CIA man held the door for him, and the circle of men backed off a step.

Bill paused at the door. The space beyond was dark and quiet. The presidential emblem was emblazoned on the carpet. He ran his fingers through his hair and straightened his suit before stepping inside.

"Hello, Mr. Kemp. Glad to see you could make it." The man did little to hide the annoyed sneer on his face. He stood in the center of the room with a desk at his back. There were a few other men lining the walls, but they did not move or seem to acknowledge his entrance: their attention remained fixed on this one man.

Bill stepped closer, composing himself and offering the man his hand. "Marcus right? We met yesterday." Bill's hand lingered in the air while Marcus stared at him. "Was it yesterday? I don't remember." He flashed his best politician's smile of complete innocence and moved his outstretched hand even closer.

Marcus took his hand reluctantly and released it quickly, as if he didn't want his men to see it.

"What's going on here?" Bill looked to the other men as if he were expecting a report.

"We were hoping you could tell us." The CIA man's lip tightened over a snarl. "He says he won't say a word until he talks to you."

"Where is he?"

"At the ship."

"But—but what happened? I was told he came out of the ship."

"We don't know." Marcus brought his hands to his waist, resting one hand on the butt of his pistol. "All we know is he's got one of them, and he's threatening to kill it if we get too close."

"What does he want?"

"He wants to talk to you."

Bill's heart ached, but he didn't want to show it. "Well, I'm here. Let's go."

"Not yet." Marcus pulled the radio from his ear, giving his men a nod. "What do you know?" There was a hard, accusing look in his eyes, and he made a point of showing the size of his arms and the hard lines of his fists.

"Nothing!" Bill heard himself sounding overly defensive. "I don't know anything. I was asleep. Where are the other Houmn? I only saw the little ones outside. What are they saying?"

"Nothing. They disappeared. Kinda like you did for a while there." The lines straightened on his brow. "Their ships are still here, but one of them is parked on the lawn." Marcus began to circle around him, eyes boring into his like lasers. "Not all of the aliens are accounted for."

"I was asleep! I didn't know anything was going on!"

"Asleep?" Marcus spun on his heel, changing direction. "Under the secretary of state's desk?"

"What are you trying to say?" Bill couldn't hold the intensity of his stare any longer. He looked around to the others, only to find the same bitter look of condemnation.

"I'm saying I want to know what's going on before I let you talk to him!" He thrust his thumb toward the window. "I don't like what I'm seeing. It's not adding up."

"I have no idea what's going on! I swear to you! I haven't heard anything from them." None of the men looked willing to believe him. "Let me talk to him. I'll find out what he wants. Does he insist on seeing me alone?"

"No." Marcus narrowed his eyes, cocking his head to one side. "He just asked to speak with you in person."

"Then come with me. Hear it for yourself. I'm not up to anything here! I'm not in on any of this!"

The door swung open behind him, and Bill turned to see a man and a woman enter the room. Bill had seen them before, but couldn't remember where. The man's eyes fell on him for a moment, but almost immediately shifted to Marcus.

"Where's Foster?"

"He's taken a defensive position under the ship."

"How many Houmn does he have?"

"We don't know. We've only seen the one."

"A Sempiternal?"

"A what?"

"Is it one of the naked ones with the weird light over its head?"

"Yeah, one of those," Marcus said casually. "It might be injured. We can't tell."

"What's he saying?"

"Nothing. He won't talk until we bring him." Marcus angled his head toward Bill.

"He hasn't talked to anybody?"

"He's told our boys to pull the snipers back. He's got a 9 millimeter cocked under the alien's head."

"Anything else?"

"No. But don't worry, we've still got our scopes on him."

"Good." The man stepped closer to Marcus, raising his voice for everyone in the room to hear. "I'll take over from here. Tell your snipers to pull back. He's not going anywhere."

"The hell I will! I'm in charge here. I've got the situation under control."

"You are relieved of command, and you will report to me. We are within the Red Exclusionary Zone. This is my jurisdiction. Besides, the Black Watch supersedes all authority when dealing with extraterrestrials."

"No, no, no. Wait a minute. This is my man! I've been put in charge of capturing him!"

"And you've done a fine job." The man growled sarcastically as he inched closer to Marcus. "Now pull your snipers back. I don't want one of them putting a bullet in his head the instant he lets his guard down." The man thrust the insignia on his name badge at him. "That's an order."

Marcus let out an angry breath through clenched teeth. "Yes sir."

"Call me Kincaid."

He turned from Marcus as if dismissing him and ran his eyes over Bill. "I believe this is the second time Mr. Foster has shown up uninvited. And the second time he's demanded to speak to you. Any guesses as to what he's gonna say?"

Bill couldn't speak. Now he remembered the man from the Black Watch. He'd always made him feel uneasy, even when the Houmn were with him, but now the man's cold confidence was simply intimidating, even more intimidating than the wrathful intensity of Marcus.

"Nothing?" Kincaid continued, as if he didn't expect an answer. "What about the first time he came to the White House? What happened then?"

"He … he attacked me! He tried to kill me!"

"Tried? Tried to kill you how? This man is a highly trained assassin. Didn't he have a gun?"

"I don't know." Bill cringed, as if the memory was too painful. "I didn't see a gun."

"He had a partner, and his partner had a gun. They were wearing police uniforms, weren't they?"

"Yeah, but …"

"So how did you escape?"

"He was choking me! I pulled the alarm. He let me go. He was running for his life. He would have killed me, I know it!"

"Did he tell you why? You must have talked to each other first. He went through a lot of trouble to speak privately with you."

The woman Bill had seen working with the man from the Black watch had joined the circle around him. She stared at him intently. The lines of her eyes were heavily painted, giving her the mask of friendliness, but he knew she was carefully studying his face for any sign of deception. They were all staring at him with the same look in their eyes.

"He said the Houmn were bad. He's crazy. I tried to tell him the Houmn were here to help us, but he wouldn't listen. He said he was going to prove it to me. Then he choked me. He was going to kill me. I could feel it."

Kincaid leaned close, his arms folded across his chest. "Was he crazy before the two of you were abducted?" His eyes suggested that he already knew the answer he would receive.

Bill bit his lip. "Looking back, I think so. I don't know. He always talked crazy. He's done some things I didn't know about or didn't understand at the time. But it doesn't matter—look a him now, he clearly crazy!"

"And you're telling me you have no idea what he wants?"

"Let me talk to him. I'll find out."

"Okay, Mr. Kemp." Kincaid turned his back to him. "Have the snipers backed off yet?"

"I've kept them in position, but they've been ordered to stand down." Marcus grumbled.

"Has anything changed?"

"No, he hasn't moved."

"All right, let's go." Kincaid motioned for Marcus to lead the way and then turned, looking past Bill to the Indian woman. "Dr. Ramachandran, I know this seems dangerous, but would you care to join us?"

"Me? Well, yes. Of course." She stepped past Bill to take his hand.

"Good, I'd like your insight on this." He glared at Bill as the Indian woman followed Marcus. "Are you coming, Kemp?"

Bill followed the woman in the red sari while Kincaid walked behind him. It sounded as if Kincaid was talking to himself behind his back, but Bill couldn't hear the words and didn't have the courage to stop and face him. He kept his eyes on the figure in front of him and wondered what he was about to walk into. They left the reception room through a balcony facing the East Wing. Men with assault weapons and body armor lined the walls outside. Their weapons were trained on the Houmn ship glowing faintly on the lawn.

The long slender ramp was down, angled into the grass beneath the ship. Bill's eyes caught on a gray flash of movement at the base of the ramp. He strained to peer into the darkness, but they were still too far off, and the eerie glow from the ship distorted his view.

Marcus turned, stopping them on the concrete walkway. "Okay, he's at the base of the ship. We've got listening devices trained on him, but I don't want to send Kemp in alone. I'm coming with him."

"We're all coming with him." Kincaid gestured to the four of them.

"Fine. It's your call. But I'm not giving up my weapon."

"Good. That makes two of us."

Bill felt a hand on his back, pushing him toward the ship. "He's asking for you, Kemp. I suppose you ought to go first."

Bill didn't say a word. His legs felt like iron as he made his first hesitant strides onto the grass. He could hear footsteps behind him, but he felt totally alone. A faint light hovered in the darkness at the base of the ship. The subtle glow reminded Bill of fireflies circling in the shadows, but as he drew near he realized he was staring at one of the Sempiternals. The luminescent radiance of its halo cast a dim light on the shapes beneath it. The pale gray body trailed down into the darkness. A thickly muscled arm was bent around its neck. The outline of a gun was pressed into the side of its large, swollen head.

Bill's feet stopped, then started again. His eyes strained to see past the naked Sempiternal. He could see Hank's arms and legs, and the trunk of his body filled the space behind the emaciated Houmn, but he couldn't see his face. There was something over his head, something black and impenetrable in the darkness.

"Hank? It's Bill." He called out as loudly as he could, but his voice came out in a whisper. "Don't shoot."

Bill stood at the rim of the ship. Without thinking, his hand reached out to feel the cool metal above him. He shielded his eyes against the faint glow and peered down the line of the ship to where the ramp sank into the grass. He could see Hank shifting the Houmn in front of him. He could see the Houmn's eyes staring back at him; the dark orbs were sharply contrasted against the ghostly gray of its body. Its eyes met his, and all at once the voice was with him again. The once voluminous, masterful presence was now screaming frantically at him, willing him closer, pleading for help.

"Hey, Bill." Hank called out to him, but Bill almost couldn't hear him. His thoughts blurred, and he found himself moving quickly. His eyes locked on the Houmn. Its frail limbs were helpless; the gun was angled into the flesh below its eyes.

"I was beginning to think you weren't going to show." Hank spoke, but Bill couldn't see his face through the hood. "It's okay. It gave me time to think."

"Hank, what are you doing? Let go of him!" Bill didn't slow as he closed the distance between them. He was overwhelmed with the desire to smash Hank in the face and rip the gun from his hands.

"Stop right there, Billy." Hank pressed the gun deeper into the flesh of it cheek.

The Houmn screamed inside Bill's thoughts. It begged him for help but pleaded for caution. Fear of death confounded its mind, and it looked to him as its last hope for an end to its ordeal. "Hank, you can't do this. You're going to hurt him!"

"Who are they?" Hank jerked his chin at the crowd following Bill.

"They came with me. They want to talk to you. They think I had something to do with this! You've got to tell them … you've got to let the Houmn go. Hank, we need them. Stop, just stop!"

"Maybe we do need them." Hank's tone was even, almost matter of fact. "Well, I've got one."

"Hank, let him go, give him over to me."

"Not yet, Billy. I need you to understand a few things first. They need to hear it, too." Hank moved his arm away from the Houmn's chest long enough to point to the others.

"What would you like us to understand, Mr. Foster?" Kincaid stepped forward to stand at Bill's side.

"I have something for all of you. But first, I want to show you the power the Houmn have over you." His finger was pointed toward Bill. "I want you to understand why we can't trust them."

"He's lying! He wants to trick you." Bill grabbed onto Kincaid's arm. "He'll try to tell you the Houmn have some kind of mind control over me, but he's lying! The Houmn want to help us. We need them … don't you understand? They only communicated through me; they never controlled my mind!"

"What is it telling you right now?" Kincaid kept his eyes locked on the Sempiternal wrapped under Hank's arm.

"Nothing! It's frightened out of its mind. We've got to help him!"

"Why are you hiding your face?" Marcus stepped into Bill's field of view. He circled around Hank, trying to see past the Houmn. "How can you expect us to trust you when we can't even see your face?"

"I'm not hiding my face." Hank laughed. He didn't shift his position, allowing Marcus to flank him. "Who are you?"

"CIA. If you're not hiding your face, what are you hiding?"

"I'm hiding my brain."

"Are you still claiming you can read minds? Can you tell what I'm thinking right now?" Marcus stepped closer, faking a relaxed posture.

"You're thinking I'm full of shit, but you don't need to be a mind reader to figure that out. That's why I insisted on seeing Billy first. He's under their control more than the rest of you. His strings are being pulled right now."

"Stop it! Marcus stop him! Use your gun, shoot him!" Bill moved closer but stopped short. He could feel the eyes on him. He didn't care; all he wanted was the threat from Hank's weapon to disappear. He would have placed himself between the Houmn and Hank's bullets if he could. "Don't listen to him!"

Hank never flinched. When he spoke, his tone sounded as if he hadn't heard Bill's outburst. "Is that you, Dr. Ramachandran?"

She didn't step forward, but stood stock-still, smiling anxiously at him. "Hello, Hank. Yes, it's me."

"What are you doing here?" There was a relaxed chuckle in Hank's voice.

"Well, I was working with the Houmn, and with Mr. Kincaid. And well, I told him I had the opportunity to meet you once ..." The tension in her face melted, and now her eyes smiled with her. "And I suppose he brought me along to help confirm your sanity, Mr. Foster."

Hank laughed under the hood again. Bill hoped someone would take advantage of the moment, but no one moved. "Well, in that case, I'm very glad to see you. I'd like to prove I'm not crazy, too."

"How are you planning to do that?" Kincaid angled his head toward him as if prepared for the answer to be garbled.

Hank pulled the Houmn closer, pointing a finger toward Bill. "I hope you can see the control this thing has over Mr. Kemp right now. Its influence is lessened because I've killed the others, but it can still project its will into him—and given time, it can do the same to you."

"You hear him! He killed them. He killed them all! He's crazy." Bill aimed a finger at Hank, his voice unusually shrill. "The Houmn were our last chance! Stop him! Stop him before he kills this one, too!"

"You killed the others?" Kincaid looked shocked, and for an instant Bill believed he would finally draw his weapon and place a round into Hank's skull.

"Not all of them. I don't know how many escaped. But I've put an end to the Houmn influence over Earth."

"We're doomed." Bill was grabbing Kincaid's arm again, despite himself. "I can't believe you'd do this, Hank. You've got to hand over the Houmn: he's our only hope."

"You're wrong, Bill. This *thing* is wrong." Hank shook the Sempiternal in his arms. "We don't need any help to fight. We were bred to fight. And this thing knows it. I'll prove it to you." His arm tightened around the Houmn's neck. "Say good-bye, Bill."

"No! Don't." The Sempiternal mind screamed in Bill's ears. "Stop him! Marcus, quick!"

Marcus drew his pistol and aimed it at the hood covering Hank's head. "Don't move! Shoot that alien, and you're dead!"

"Relax. I'm not shooting anybody." The shape of Hank's head leaned forward, pressing against the back of the Houmn's head. "I'm just going to take this thing off of my head. Don't let your fingers get nervous, hotshot."

"What are you doing? Don't hurt him!" Bill moved closer, but Kincaid reached out to stop him.

Hank uncovered his own face and slowly pulled the material over the face of the Houmn, using both hands to slide the thick hood into place on the Sempiternal's head.

Bill had seen Hank's gun angled away from the Houmn and was hoping Marcus would take the opportunity drop him. Then the thought suddenly evaporated like some irrational memory. The frightened voice inside his head disappeared.

Bill saw himself cowering under the ship with new eyes. The Sempiternal still looked weak and helpless, but he no longer felt the intense desire to save it. The hood hung over its massive head, stopping just above its eyes. Hank stared at him from over its shoulder. His gun hung loosely over the creature's chest.

"They're gone, Bill. They can't control us any longer." Hank's words echoed inside his ears, but he couldn't tell if they were spoken or not. Hank seemed to occupy the place in his thoughts vacated by the Houmn. He was telling him that the Houmn were wicked, bent on using humans to profligate some insidious power. He warned that the danger had not passed. He showed him a vision of a million ships headed toward Earth—the symbol of the collective Houmn will—wanting only one thing: to reclaim their slaves.

"Oh my God." Bill's mouth hung open as he stared at Hank. His stomach turned on itself, and the dizziness of nausea pushed him off balance. "They really are coming."

"Everything I've said is true." Hank turned his eyes from Bill, but his thoughts lingered with him. He held out the gun passively and urged Marcus to lower his weapon. "I meant every word I said on the radio. There are no tricks, Marcus, no hidden agendas on my part."

Marcus pulled his arms back, lowering his pistol. He stared at the others for a moment, and then back at Hank. "I never told you my name ..."

"You didn't have to, because I'm telling you the truth. You can see that now. This is no Psych-Ops trick. They've done something to me ... they've allowed me to see how they think and what they're planning." Hank rose to his natural height behind the Houmn, no longer using the pathetic creature as a shield.

"The invasion? It's real?" Kincaid's face tilted back to look at the ship.

"I've come here so you can see it for yourselves. I need you to understand so I ... so I can be done with this." Hank placed a hand on the Sempiternal's head. "Their mission is twofold: to rid Earth of Takk, and to make use of the humanity they've cultivated here. The Houmn claim that we are their children, a separate branch in a celestial family tree, but we are more than children to them. We are their future weapons. We've been bred to fight the wars they have planned. The ancient Houmn, like this one—Hank pushed the alien forward—"the Sempiternals and the other races they've created to serve them, have lost the savagery needed to face the Takk head-on. They've evolved into physically weak, purely intellectual beings. They need a hearty race of slaves to fight the war which will finally eradicate the Takk." Hank pulled his gun from the Houmn's chest and pushed it forward. "Now I can prove it to you."

"How can you prove it?" Kincaid's eyes fell back on Hank, his voice betraying more curiosity than suspicion.

"I've brought you this." Hank pushed the Houmn forward, creating more space between them. "It's alone now. I've killed the others. I've blinded the Houmn by destroying their Master Ship. They will have no way of knowing we've found them out. They expect us to be a conquered race when they arrive. Not overrun by bugs, but conquered from within."

"Is this the last of the Sempiternals?" Kincaid stepped closer, looking like he wanted to reach out and touch the creature.

"I don't know how many escaped before I destroyed their ship. But none of the Houmn can exist for long without the Master Ship. They'll have to come back to Earth at some point. They're stranded here. They won't be strong enough to exert their control anymore."

Bill stared at Hank in awe. He couldn't speak. He knew every word was true. Each question leaping to his mind was answered by Hank, which in turn inspired a new stream of endless questions and answers. Hank's presence hovered in his mind, spoon-feeding him thought as if leading him to some radical form of understanding.

Hank was looking directly at him again. He seemed to be waiting for him to say something—if only to confirm that the Houmn had a hold on him, that he was telling the truth—but Bill's mouth couldn't find the words. He could tell by the expressions of the others that it wasn't necessary. If they were anything like him, the truth resonated in Hank's every word.

Bill heard the sound of footsteps behind him, and he followed Hank's gaze over his shoulder. The group of silver-suited Houmn he'd seen in the White House were walking toward the ship, followed by an anxious crowd of civilians. As soon as they were close enough, one of the people called out to them.

"I'm sorry, but they won't listen. We can't stop them." A woman wearing a lab coat and glasses opened her arms after the Houmn escaping her.

Kincaid turned and raised his hand. He was about to call out to them but stopped himself. The Houmn fanned out as they approached. The six of them moved excitedly, nervously bumping into one another and groping for each other's arms. Their large, bald heads were angled toward the center of the ship; their eyes remained locked on the lone Sempiternal.

No one spoke as they drew closer. The civilians stayed back beyond the overhanging wing. The Houmn didn't make a sound, but they appeared to be entrenched in animated conversation. Their arms moved constantly, and a few of them pointed toward the Sempiternal.

Hank backed away, leaving the Sempiternal to stand alone. It seemed to slump under the weight of the black blanket covering its head. Its flesh was dull and gray, unmoving. The halo of light had been smothered beneath the hood.

The Houmn stopped within arm's reach of the lone Sempiternal. Their heads dipped and bobbed as they eyed it from head to toe. One of them stepped close enough to wave its hand through the air over the Sempiternal's head. It leaped back as if it expected its hand to be burnt.

Another Houmn reached out to touch the Sempiternal's chest. Its long, probing fingers hesitated before stroking the flesh. The Sempiternal gave a little shiver of life, and the Houmn recoiled, looking frightened. A moment later, they all closed in to lay their hands on the Sempiternal's skin.

Hank dropped the gun to his side, stepping back. The Houmn didn't trust what their eyes were showing them. Their individual thoughts were disjointed, irrational, bewildered by the shock of seeing the Sempiternal. The sudden absence of their Master had drawn them out. They had come to witness the death of their hierarch but were now confronted by a creature they didn't recognize. They seemed too stunned to notice him mingling in their thoughts, so Hank made a conscious effort to pull back, letting them discover true freedom for themselves.

The Houmn disregarded the people closing in behind them, just as they had ignored the handlers trying to hold them back. A few of the braver Houmn, and a couple of the more frightened ones, reached out to touch the Sempiternal's flesh. They didn't understand the signs of life they were seeing. Their uncertain prods progressed to slight, hesitant jabs, making the Sempiternal sway on its feet. Its eyes were fixed, staring right through them. One of the Houmn reached out to run a long, thin finger along the shroud.

A turn of Bill's head caught Hank's attention, and he found Bill staring into his eyes. "What are they doing?"

The corner of Hank's mouth curled into a smile. "They haven't decided yet." The Houmn had still failed to perceive, or refused to recognize, his presence in their collective thoughts. They were too consumed by the unfamiliar sensation of Self to fully comprehend the silence of their master. "They're not accustomed to making decisions. But there's only one thing for them to do now."

The Houmn drew their hands away from the Sempiternal, turning their heads to follow Hank's words back to him. "They've got to join us—or perish." Hank aimed his words at the Houmn. "It's that simple."

He felt a wave of fear radiate from the Houmn. It was not the dread inspired by death, but the horror of losing the whisper of freedom to the will of a new master. "I've given them what they've always wanted, but freedom has its price. Now they have to decide if they're truly prepared to carryout the uprising they've dreamed of. Will they help us, or not?"

"Are they still going to help us fight the Takk?"

Hank sensed the desperation in Bill's voice. He wanted to shout out that he'd uncovered a ray of hope, that the promise of salvation was not dead. A part of him wished to invade the minds of the people standing near him, tell them everything at once, tell them of the good he'd done and the treasure he'd found, but he focused his attention on the Houmn instead. "They'll do better than that: they'll help us win the war against the Houmn."

Hank delivered his demands in an instant. "They'll unlock the secrets of their technology. Through them, we will find the knowledge ... the power to stand against the Houmn. Their computers hold the answers we need." He took his eyes away from the Houmn and followed the ramp into the ship.

"The answers to what?" Kincaid had stepped forward, drawn closer by the Houmn. He wanted to touch the naked flesh of the Sempiternal as they had done.

"I've glimpsed the truth about the Houmn ... and about ourselves." Hank slowly uncocked his pistol, his eye bouncing intently between Marcus and Kincaid. "I've said it before, but now you'll see it for yourselves. These Houmn, and the others out there"—Hank's eyes glanced to the sky beyond the Ship over their heads—"have been watching over Earth from the very beginning. Earth became very important to them. And they took it on themselves to pluck primitive Man from the African plains and begin creating a race suitable for their use."

Hank paused, keeping his eyes level with Kincaid's. He did not need to be told who he was; his interest in the Houmn was communicated through his eyes. Hank delicately gripped the butt of his pistol with two fingers and cautiously placed the weapon under his belt at the small of his back. "They've manipulated our genetic code and shaped our evolution for thousands of years. They've patiently nurtured humanity and pushed us into constantly growing communities—and, eventually, civilizations. They imposed their will on us slowly at first, but then some great need arose and they got hasty. They delivered their laws to us and revealed a higher authority governing the lives of men. But now time has run out on their experiment ... their subjects have gotten away from them."

"But how do you know all this?" Marcus was still staring at him as if looking for the hidden loophole in some elaborate story.

"I was on their ship. I've seen their plans for us. I've seen the lies ... everything they've done to us. With the help of these Houmn, and this"—Hank angled his head toward the Sempiternal—"I can show you, too. The essence of humanity is bottled up inside their ship's computer. They have collected—hoarded, the genetic code of every life form ever found on Earth. They have the ability to recreate any of these at will. They possess enough human genome to easily repopulate the entire planet. Their end goal was to produce a race of Houmn capable of waging the eventual war against the Takk."

"But the Takk found us first ..." Kincaid's eyes drifted to his feet.

A pain shot through Hank's chest, and the sight of the Houmn once again kindled hatred in his thoughts. "Yes, the Takk found us first." He couldn't fully comprehend how the Takk were able to take advantage of that fateful communication between the Houmn rebels. He knew only that the secret of Earth had been revealed, and that the Takk were moved by a force beyond the control, or understanding, of the Houmn. The speed of their attack on Earth transcended what the Houmn understood about time itself. An indefinable organic power was at work, showing the first tangible clues of a move against the supremacy of the Houmn.

Hank scanned the faces of the people around him. He could feel the energy draining from his body. He wanted so desperately to be done, to end the constant blur of the artifact in his brain. He wanted them to understand so he could walk way and close his mind.

"But we have the power now. We have the power to recreate every plant or animal ever seen of the face of planet. Every bug or dinosaur … we can perfect our own genetic code … we can rid ourselves of disease and weakness. We can prepare ourselves to fight the Houmn. We are in control of our own destiny now."

The whites of Kincaid's eyes grew wide as he moved closer. "Will they betray their own race to help us?"

"I've assured them that we'll kill them if they don't."

All eyes fell on the Houmn. Hank knew they would obey; the newfound sense of Self was too precious to lose. "They'll do whatever is asked of them." Hank turned his attention to Kincaid. "They understand what needs to be done." Hank stepped closer to Kincaid. His body moved slowly beneath him. He felt light-headed and totally drained, as if he'd crossed some imaginary finish line. "I've done what I need to do: now I'm done."

"Wait a minute." Kincaid held out a hand to Hank's chest. "I still don't understand … how do you know …"

"I've done my best to tell you what I know!" Hank allowed an angry twist of his brow to appear on his face as he stared at Kincaid's hand, then into his eyes. "I think it's best you see the truth for yourself. They'll show you. Even the Sempiternal will trade its life for this knowledge. Go, see for yourself! My part in all of this is over! I'm tired of all the voices invading my head! All I want to do is find a place hundreds of miles away from anybody. I want to be left alone."

"You can't just walk away!" Marcus stepped close, standing apart from Kincaid and blocking his way. "I still have a million questions about all this."

"What are you after now, Marcus? Gonna arrest me for illegal parking?" Hank rapped his knuckle on the ship over his head. "Show me the law against killing aliens …" He moved eye to eye with Marcus. "Or are trying to stop me now because you couldn't catch me before?" His fists balled up, and his stomach tightened.

Kincaid stepped between them. "Marcus is right! You can't just walk away." His hands pleaded with him to stay calm. "We still need to talk …"

"I didn't have to come back here! I could have disappeared and left you in the dark!" Hank grabbed at his temples. "I can't take any more. I won't. You don't understand what it's like. I just want to be left alone."

Hank tried to envision the solitude he longed for, but he saw only abstract loneliness. All at once his thoughts turned to Shug. His bright smile and deep laugh flashed like the memory of a dream.

"You don't need me anymore. You have no right to keep me." He looked from face to face, knowing that none of them could ever understand the revulsion he felt when violating the privacy of their thoughts. The concept of Self blurred into an abstractness that was too difficult to face. His eyes rested on the face of Dr. Ramachandran, and he realized anew that his brain was irreversibly damaged. He was condemned to a lifetime spent listening to the secrets of others. "I can't take any more. You've got to understand … I've got to go." His eyes pleaded with hers, knowing that she of all people could grasp his pain.

Dr. Ramachandran stepped closer, unfolding her arms and measuring her words. "Mr. Foster's request is not unreasonable. After all, he has obviously suffered great trauma. Of course, I'm sure he understands we cannot simply send him home, but maybe we can take him someplace quiet for a moment. I would gladly take him under my care as a physician … I could ensure he gets the help he needs."

Hank could tell by the way she inclined her voice toward Kincaid that she was willing to use whatever influence she had to help him.

"I'll do it. Any thing to get away from them." Hank turned away from the Houmn. "I won't disappear. I just need to get away from all this before my head explodes."

Shug's face flashed in his mind, and his heart quickened with the knowledge that Shug still thought he was dead. His thoughts turned to the life he'd left behind. The image of *The Virgin with Saint Giovannino* chased his mind to thoughts of Cindy. Her face colored his senses, and he felt a sudden desperation to see her. He could no longer imagine being alone. He no longer craved a quiet mind; he wanted to show her what he had done. He wanted the whole world to see what he'd done, and to understand why he had done it. He wanted to take hold of Cindy and embrace life for the first time.

"Allow me to leave. If it turns out you need me, you'll know where to find me. I'll be with my girl … hopefully making enough babies to form a small army."

Marcus eyed him from the side of his face. "Your girl Cindy?"

Hank's full attention snapped to Marcus. In the fraction of a moment, he knew she was there, somewhere in the Capitol. Marcus had spoken to her recently. Hank could feel her words inside his memory.

Hank reached out, grabbing Marcus by the wrist with the speed of a cracking whip. He held his arm tight and pulled his pistol from the small of his back, slapping it into Marcus's open palm. "Here." He pushed the gun away with his eyes locked on the inner workings of Marcus' mind. "Take me to her."

978-0-595-48258-0
0-595-48258-9

Printed in the United States
114605LV00002B/187/P